IAN IRVINE

A TALE OF THE THREE WORLDS

Chimaera

Volume Four of THE WELL OF ECHOES

ORBIT

First published in Great Britain in December 2004 by Orbit
This paperback edition published in June 2005 by Orbit
Reprinted 2006 (twice), 2008, 2009, 2012, 2014

A CIP catalogue record for this book
is available from the British Library.

ISBN 978-1-84149-325-1

Printed and bound in Great Britain by
Clays Ltd, St Ives plc

Papers used by Orbit are from well-managed forests
and other responsible sources.

Orbit
An imprint of
Little, Brown Book Group
100 Victoria Embankment
London EC4Y 0DY

An Hachette UK Company
www.hachette.co.uk

www.orbitbooks.net

CONTENTS

PART OF THE SOUTHERN HEMISPHERE OF SANTHENAR

LEGEND

- Mountains
- Hills
- Desert
- Salt Lake
- Marsh, Swamp
- Conifer Forest
- Broadleaf Forest
- Tropical Forest
- Grassland
- Reef
- Main Road

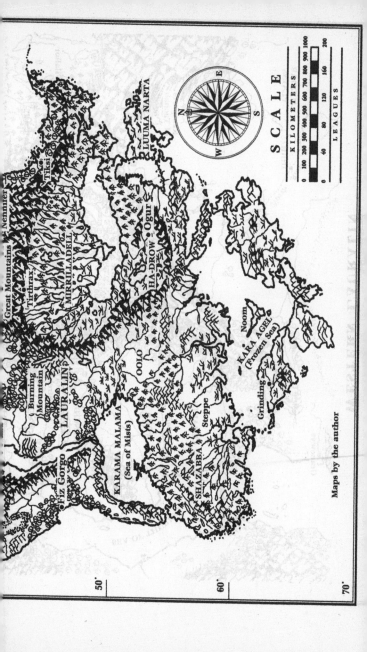

Maps by the author

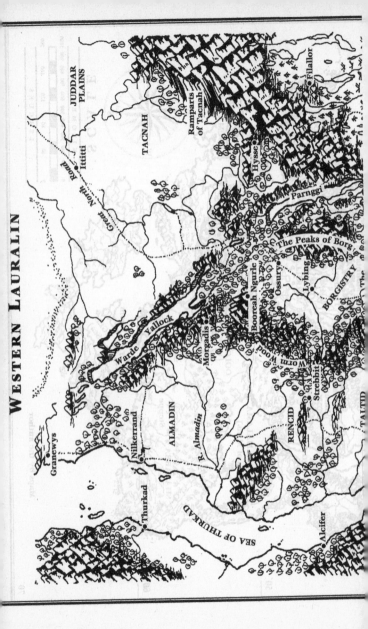

WESTERN LAURALIN

JUDDAR PLAINS

Filaillor

Great North Road

Ittiti

TACNAH

Ramparts of Tacnah

Hysse

Parnggi

The Peaks of Borg

Booreah Ngurle

Ossury

Lybing

BORGISTRY

Warde   Yallock

Morgadis

Worm Wood

Granewys

Nilkerrand

ALMADIN

Strebbit

RENCID

R. Almadin

Thurkad

TAILTID

SEA OF THURKAD

Alcifer

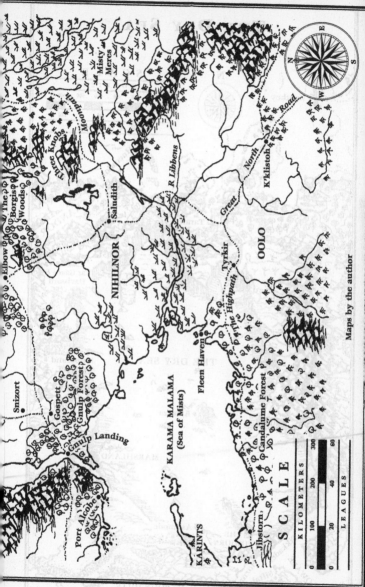

Maps by the author

ACKNOWLEDGMENT

I would like to thank my editors,
Kay Ronai and Nan McNab, for their
hard work and patience over the five
years it's taken to write this series. Thanks
also to my agent, Selwa Anthony, for her support,
and to Janet Raunjak and Laura Harris at
Penguin Books, and to Tim Holman at Orbit Books.
And, not least, to everyone at Penguin Books
and Orbit Books who has worked so hard to
make this series such a success.

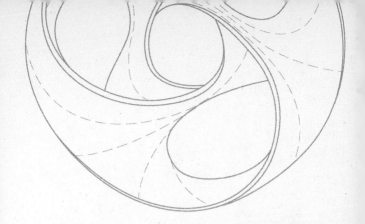

PART ONE

AMPHITHEATRE

ONE

L ittle Ullii, the mildest and meekest person in the world,
tested the blade of the pilfered dagger concealed in her coat.
She was going to revenge herself on the man who had been her
first friend and only lover, and the father of her dead baby. She
was hunting Nish, and when she found him she planned to cut
out his heart, for that was just what he'd done to her.

'Seeker? *To me!*'

Ullii started and looked around guiltily. She loathed Chief
Scrutator Ghorr almost as much as she hated Nish, but she
feared Ghorr as only the truly helpless could. He was a brute, a
monster, and she was in his thrall. She scurried to his side to
betray the rest of her friends.

The Council of Scrutators had attacked the ancient fortress of
Fiz Gorgo before dawn with overwhelming force and complete
surprise, taking most of their victims in their beds. With Ullii to
pinpoint them, mancers as powerful as Yggur and as subtle as
Malien had been captured within minutes, along with dozens of
lesser victims. Now only a few remained, but among them were
the two that Ghorr wanted most desperately.

His victory was almost complete and Ghorr was going to
finish the rebellion here and now. The trials would be swift, the
executions swifter. By the end of the day no one, from the least
scullery maid at Fiz Gorgo to Lord Yggur himself, would be left

3

alive. And every detail of the trial and the bloody executions was to be recorded devotedly by the war artists, recorders and tale-tellers. The whole world had to know that there was no escape for traitors, not even those hiding in distant territories under enemy occupation. Every citizen of Santhenar, down to the smallest child, must hear the tale of the rebels' brutal end, and take the lesson.

But Ullii plotted a different fate for Nish; Nish who had slain Myllii, the beloved twin brother for whom she'd searched since she was four. He had claimed it was an accident but Ullii knew better. She had to take retribution with her own hands. Without it, neither Myllii nor her son Yllii could ever find peace in their graves. She was going to carve out Nish's treacherous heart and feed it to the carrion birds that were already circling above the walls of Fiz Gorgo in expectation of the feast.

Ullii crept down the corridor beside the chief scrutator. Her eyes were masked against the torches of his troops, for Ullii was so sensitive that bright light burned her eyes. Fortunately she did not need to see. Her mental lattice, her unique and, to others, incomprehensible way of viewing the world, told her where she was even in darkness.

Her ears were covered to keep out the clangour of battle and bloodshed, the roars of the soldiers, the screams of their victims, the thud of weapons against armour, flesh and bone. Ullii could not see Nish in her lattice because, lacking any talent for the Secret Art, he did not appear there. But her most sensitive sense was not veiled in any way. She was tracking Nish by his scent. Nowhere he could go, nothing he could do could prevent her from finding him among the myriad of other smells and stenches that threaded the frigid air of Fiz Gorgo.

Fortunately Ghorr was not aware of that talent and, in the afterglow of a victory more complete than he had ever dared hope for, he seemed to have forgotten about Nish. He was not in the same league as the great mancers Gilhaelith, Malien and Yggur. Nish was insignificant compared to the unexpected discovery of Tiaan and the priceless flying construct, not to mention the powerful and enigmatic amplimet, a crystal that drew power

4

from the field without human intervention. Ghorr's personal guard had already secured all of them and the chief scrutator could not help gloating over it.

He heaved her back by the arm. 'Stay behind, Seeker. Don't endanger yourself. We've yet to find the arch-fiend, Xervish Flydd, and he could slay you with a single glance.'

Ullii knew that wasn't true, and moreover Flydd had treated her far more kindly than the chief scrutator ever did. However, she stopped at once; Ghorr took pleasure in inflicting pain, particularly on the weak and powerless.

'Well?' he said, pulling off her earmuffs to roar in her ear, though she could hear him clearly through them, and he knew it. 'Where is the renegade, Seeker?'

Before she could answer, a soldier came running. 'Two people have barricaded themselves in a chamber down to your left, Chief Scrutator, surr. Mancer Squilp says the place has a strong tang of the Art.'

'Is it Xervish Flydd, Ullii?' said Ghorr, crushing the bones in her gracile arm.

She closed her eyes behind the mask, the better to visualise her lattice. The noise hurt and the violence frightened her, making it difficult to concentrate. The lattice was faint again today. It had been fading for weeks now, and that filled her with dread. What if she lost it completely? Ullii had created her lattice as a lost and lonely little girl and, in the desperate years since, it had been the only thing keeping her sane. Her solitary achievement had given her pride in herself. It was now the only crutch she had left.

'Hurry up!' hissed Scrutator Fusshte, thrusting his pock-marked reptilian face at her behind Ghorr's back.

Ullii recoiled. Fusshte was a creeping monstrosity whose nearness brought her out in goosepimples.

Ghorr urged him out of the way. 'She can't be forced, Scrutator,' he said acidly. 'Won't you ever learn?'

Fusshte backed off, but Ullii saw his malevolence as a corrosive knot in her lattice. Even Ghorr was preferable to the slithering horror that was Scrutator Fusshte.

'Well, Seeker?' said Ghorr.

'It's Xervish,' she conceded. Ullii had once regarded Flydd as a friend and knew she was betraying him to his doom, but she wasn't strong enough to resist. Even if she had been, Ghorr would happily break her to find his enemy. 'And Crafter Irisis.'

'Splendid,' said Ghorr. 'What are they doing, Ullii? Surely they know that locking themselves in is useless?'

'Breaking the floor,' said Ullii with lowered head.

'Reinforce the mancers just outside the door,' snapped Ghorr to a messenger, who hurried away. 'Captain,' he turned to a hulking officer, each of whose intricately tooled military boots could have accommodated Ullii's head and neck, 'lead us to the room below Flydd's. Bring two squads. Fusshte, take a third squad down the far stairs and cut off the other exit.'

Ghorr allowed his troops to take the lead, then caught Ullii's arm and hauled her down the stone staircase. As they crossed a landing, a muffled roar shook the building.

'Quick, Captain!' said Ghorr. 'Flydd's broken through. Take him and Irisis alive and there'll be a bonus for you.'

The soldiers hurtled down the steps, swords raised. Ghorr kept well back. The chief scrutator guarded his life like a miser his hoard.

They reached the bottom step, rounded the corner and there, in the flickering light of the soldiers' torches, stood the fugitives. Irisis had stopped dead when she saw the soldiers, then raised her sword. Flydd glanced over his shoulder at the cluster of dancing torches and his skinny shoulders sagged. Scrutator Fusshte and his heavily armed troops blocked the only way out.

Ullii lifted her mask for a moment. Xervish Flydd, a small man of some sixty years, looked more scarred and emaciated than ever. Though it was bitterly cold, he wore just a bedsheet, hastily knotted about his hips. Beautiful Irisis Stirm was dressed in brown woollen pantaloons and a loose shirt which could not conceal her luxurious figure. Her yellow hair was unbound. They were both covered in grey dust.

Ullii pulled the mask down, as if to hide from her former friends, but Flydd had already seen her. He shook his head,

6

a moment of desolation, and Ullii knew she had done a terrible wrong. But what else could I do? she thought plaintively, slipping into the shadow behind Ghorr before Irisis could see her.

'Xervish Flydd,' said Ghorr in a treacly voice. 'Irisis Stirm. I'm so pleased to see you both again.'

Irisis shifted her weight, holding the sword two-handed, but Flydd drew her back. 'There's no point, Irisis. Put it down.'

After a long hesitation, she let the sword fall. The soldiers took hold of the pair and swiftly bound their hands.

'These are the last,' said Fusshte. 'Let's get the trials underway, Chief Scrutator. The executioners grow impatient.'

'The executioners wait upon my pleasure,' Ghorr said icily. 'Take the prisoners out to the yard, Captain.'

Ullii pressed back into a niche in the wall, hiding from herself. Flydd had let her down, certainly, but he'd been kind to her too, and always looked after her. And she'd betrayed him to a monster.

Taking off the mask, she rubbed her eyes, trying to work out where it had all gone wrong. As Flydd was dragged past, his eyes met hers for a second. He knew Ullii had betrayed them; he was looking right into her heart and, worst of all, he understood.

The guard jerked on the rope; Flydd stumbled away. Ullii crouched down in her niche, shivering violently. Cold rarely bothered her but now she felt like a statue carved of ice. She was just as bad as Ghorr.

Irisis was dragged past. Hastily pulling down the mask, Ullii turned her face to the wall until the crafter had gone by. Irisis would neither understand nor forgive.

The troops led their prisoners upstairs, gloating and calculating their shares of the reward, and getting in vicious blows when Ghorr wasn't looking. Ullii remained where she was. Ghorr took little notice of her at the best of times and, now that he had his enemies at his mercy, would not give her a moment's thought. It was easy to conceal herself in the darkness, for no one was more skilled at hiding than she.

She slipped into a room that had already been checked while Fiz Gorgo was searched one more time. Finally, the soldiers tramped out into the yard. The scrutators had gone. Ullii tracked the knots they made in the eye of her lattice. They went out through the broken front doors of Fiz Gorgo and up onto the outer wall, from whence they were hauled up in rope chairs to the comfort of the hovering air-dreadnoughts, doubtless to indulge themselves in an orgy of congratulations. The prisoners and their guards were left to shiver in the ice-crusted yard until the preparations for the trial were complete.

Fiz Gorgo was silent now. Ullii put her head out the door. The darkness was comforting and she felt the lattice strengthen a little, but she had lost her purpose. Seeing Flydd that way had thrown her. Then a familiar tang raised bumps on her arms. *Nish!*

She tasted the air, nose up like a mouse. To Ullii, Nish *was* his smell, and she could have identified him anywhere. She'd picked him out from sixty thousand soldiers and slaves when he'd been sentenced to haul bogged clankers out of the sodden battlefield at Snizort last summer.

There was a trace of his spoor down here, though the scent was old. On the ground floor it had been stronger. Ullii took off the mask and earmuffs. Her sensitive eyes could see well enough in the dark, not that she needed to. She eased up the farther stair, the one Fusshte had come down. The stench of *him* drowned out all other smells: stagnant water in the flooded labyrinth below, mould growing on the walls, the faint odour of woodworm and rotting timber, and even the unwashed, sweaty reek of the soldiers. Fusshte had a sour, festering stink that made her nostrils pucker and her toes curl.

It was brighter on the ground floor. A gloomy daylight seeped in through the broken front doors, though it cast little light around the corner to this narrow hall. The breeze was blowing away from the doors and she could not tell if Nish was out there. Dare she look? Easing to the shattered remnants of the great doors, Ullii covered her eyes with her fingers and peered out.

She didn't see Nish. The prisoners were kept apart, save for Flydd and Irisis, and each was surrounded by burly guards. All the men of Ghorr's guard were tall and Nish, a small man, would not be visible behind them.

8

Ullii went back and forth, testing the air for every tendril of odour, and, around the corner, picked up an old scent. She could even tell that Nish had been weary when he'd come this way. He'd plodded down the corridor before stopping for a moment. Why? Ullii smelt Irisis's fresh, creamy tang and her fists clenched involuntarily. Nish and Irisis had been lovers once, before Ullii had met him. She sniffed the air. He'd gone into *her* room!

She tracked him to the bed and he'd been in it. He'd lain with Irisis just hours ago. How dare he? Ullii didn't operate on logic – as far as she was concerned, Nish had been hers ever since they'd made love in the balloon in the treetops near Tirthrax, at the end of last winter. He'd made her pregnant there, and even though he'd killed her brother since then, she would share him with no one.

It firmed her faltering resolve. She tracked Nish to his little room. The bed was cold but a fresher scent led around the corner, into the main hall and up in the direction of the front door. There she lost it.

Ullii crept along the hall on her toes, keeping to the left-hand wall, ready to dart away should someone approach. She could hear the guards talking in the yard, gravel crunching under their boots and an occasional mutter or plea from the bound prisoners, always answered with a jeer or slap.

She headed for the stairs to one of the tower balconies she'd seen from Ghorr's air-dreadnoughts, so she could look down into the yard. A few steps up, she detected Nish's spoor once more, and it was fresher. He'd gone this way in the last few hours.

Unfortunately he'd come down again; she smelt him on the other side of the staircase as well. Nonetheless, she continued up to a landing on the second floor, where she went down on her belly and crawled to the edge. The scent was stronger here. He'd spent some time with the tall mancer she now knew to be Yggur.

Ullii looked down into the mist-wreathed yard and made out Yggur easily, as well as the even taller mancer with the frothy hair whose attempt to escape had enabled her to find Fiz Gorgo

9

in the first place. They were bound hand and foot, and tightly gagged to prevent them speaking any spell or word of power. Flydd and Irisis stood together, not gagged but surrounded by a double halo of guards. The old Aachim mancer, Malien, was by the wall, also bound and gagged, and watched by a pair of Council mancers. The other rings of guards enclosed people she could not identify, but Nish was not among them.

So how had he, alone of all the clever people here, managed to escape? Not knowing the answer, Ullii crawled back to the steps and allowed her senses to guide her.

A faint odour led up, though only to chaos that was also her doing. Using her lattice, Ullii had pinpointed the locations of several uncanny devices designed to protect Fiz Gorgo. The top of this horned tower had housed one of them, but it and the other devices had been blasted by amplified sunbeams from the air-dreadnoughts at the beginning of the dawn attack, melting the very stone and destroying everything inside. Nish could hardly be up there now, though she could detect no track coming down.

Nonetheless, the lingering scent trail went up, so Ullii followed. By the next turn of the stair the stone had grown perceptibly warm and she smelled the peculiar dry odour of overheated rock. On the turn after that the steps were sprinkled with ash, charcoal and gritty granules of slag.

It was hard to move silently here for the grit squeaked underfoot, a high-pitched abrasive sound that irritated her sensitive ears. She trod as softly as she could but by the next turn of the stairs the ash and grit were ankle-deep. At the landing after that the stairs were blocked by a crusted flow of melted stone, black on the outside but deeply cracked and glowing within. The crust, resembling dirty glass and slag, was embedded with pieces of charcoal and half-burnt wood. A sagging pewter mug protruded from one edge.

The flow was so hot that it dried out her eyes. Ullii could not find any way through the smoke and heat haze so she went down to the main hall, crisscrossing the building like a mouse hunting for food. None of Nish's scent traces led out of Fiz

Gorgo. The most recent was the one that had gone up the steps to the destroyed tower. Perhaps he'd gone up twice and only come down once.

Climbing an adjacent tower, one that hadn't been attacked, she peered through an embrasure. The mist was growing thicker and turning to light rain that drifted on the breeze. It was miserably cold and dank but Ullii preferred cold to heat.

From here she had a good view of the ruined tower. She'd led Ghorr's forces to it, had pinpointed exactly where the defensive devices were, and where to aim their incandescent, rock-melting beams of crystal-boosted sunlight. The horned tower was now bent like a banana, a couple of floors below the top. The beam had burned in through an embrasure, liquefying everything inside that chamber. The thick outside wall had bent like toffee then set again, though the stone was sadly cracked and fretted. Pieces of stone fell as she watched, and the wall steamed gently in the rain.

If Nish had been in that chamber, he could not have survived. Even had he been in the rooms above, the heat must have burned him alive. Not a pleasant death, nor what she'd intended for him. Before Ullii cut out his heart, she'd wanted him to know *why*.

Two

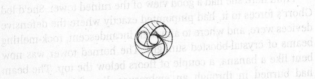

After leaving Irisis in the early hours of the morning, Nish had gone back to his cold bed, but had not managed to get to sleep. He couldn't stop thinking about the morrow. They were due to leave in Malien's thapter to attack the Council of Scrutators' secret bastion, Nennifer, and attempt to overthrow them, for the Council was never going to win the war. Indeed, it no longer seemed that it wanted to, for the war kept the scrutators in power. But Nennifer was defended by a thousand crack troops, hundreds of mancers and all manner of uncanny devices, so how could a handful of people, even including Flydd, Yggur and Malien, hope to breach it? It seemed, at the least, suicidal. And why were he and Irisis suddenly being kept in the dark? It hurt, after all they'd done over the past months.

Despairing of ever getting to sleep, Nish dressed in his discarded clothes, which had already taken on the frigid dankness of the room. Pulling on icy boots, he laced them up and stamped his feet, trying vainly to maintain the warmth he'd had from the bed. At the noise, someone muttered angrily from the next room.

Nish shrugged into his coat, pulled a floppy hat down over his neck and ears, and went to the door. With his hand on the latch he thought about going back for his sword, but Fiz Gorgo was the safest place on Santhenar. He left it leaning against the wall.

He had planned to go out the front doors and pace around the outer wall, but as he cracked the door open, such an icy wind coiled in that Nish closed it and headed for the tower instead. This time he did not stop at Yggur's balcony, but felt his way up the snake-coiled stone stair to the very top. It was pitch black outside – he could see nothing through the embrasures.

On the fourth- and fifth-floor landings, open doors led to black rooms. Nish didn't look inside; he hadn't brought a lantern. The rooms on the sixth and seventh floors were locked and, he suspected, sealed with the Art. They held some kind of defensive artefact – Nish had once overheard Yggur telling Flydd about it. He trudged up to the eighth level, a lookout tower that had not been manned during Nish's time in Fiz Gorgo. Not even the lyrinx, who owned the rest of Meldorin, came near Fiz Gorgo.

At the top he peered out the western embrasure towards the town of Old Hripton, several leagues away around the bay, but the icy breeze made his eyes water and he couldn't see any lights. Pulling his coat around him, he sat on the stone bench that ran around the circumference of the room. As soon as he sat down, Nish felt drowsy, so he folded up the hood of his coat for a pillow, lay on his back and closed his eyes.

Despair chased the drowsiness away. The world lay in ruins. The Council had failed, the war was in its last desperate stage and the enemy was going to win it. Whole nations had been wiped out, vast regions depopulated as if a great plague had crept across them. Few people had any hope now. They were just going through the motions of fighting and dying. From the lowest peasant to the rulers themselves, hopelessness was all-pervading.

The scrutators attacked despair as they attacked every other crime – with violence – but violence no longer had any effect. A people without hope were glad to die. Human civilisation was going to fall and even its precious Histories would disappear as though they had never been. Nish felt like weeping but his eyes were gritty dry.

And so, Flydd's mad plan to attack Nennifer. If the corrupt Council could just be overthrown, men and women of stout

13

heart might still be able to hold back the horde and set the world to rights. If anyone could do it, it would be Flydd, who had made the protection of humanity his life's work. But Nish knew it was folly; no attack could succeed against such defences. They were all going to die, yet somehow it seemed worth it to go out in such a noble, reckless endeavour. Humanity was going to disappear anyway, and falling in battle against the scrutators was better than being eaten by the lyrinx. There wasn't a person on Santhenar who did not shudder at that thought. It didn't seem right that all humanity's greatness should be extinguished in such a lowly, savage way.

Nish was drifting in and out of sleep when he heard a curious squelchy *plock*, like a hammer being whacked into wet dough some distance away. He thought about getting up to see, but weariness overcame him. Surely it was just a frog jumping onto the stone floor.

Plock, plock. His subconscious must have continued to puzzle away at the sounds, for Nish woke with a jerk. It wasn't a frog – it was the sound made by a crossbow bolt embedding itself into a human body.

He shot up, heart pounding, and stumbled to the nearest embrasure. It was growing light outside, the sun's first rays illuminating a layer of mist that blanketed everything below the treetops. Nish looked out and the blood froze in his veins.

There were air-floaters everywhere – no, air-dreadnoughts – gigantic vessels each supported by five airbags, and three or four times the length of Flydd's air-floater. The sides of each vessel were lined with soldiers and at the prows fluttered the silver pennant of the Council of Scrutators. Nish counted nine air-dreadnoughts, then six more from the other side of the chamber. No, seven – a sixteenth hung high above, on watch. Fiz Gorgo was surrounded.

Nish opened his mouth to roar out a warning, but snapped it closed. They'd already shot the sentries and would do the same to him. Besides, no one in Fiz Gorgo would hear him from here. As he ran for the stairs, eye-searing beams lanced out from cartwheel-sized mirrors on the air-dreadnoughts, converging on the secret chambers of the tower below him.

The floor swelled beneath his feet, grew burning hot and the world exploded in his face. The last thing he saw was a nebulous, shield-like bubble rise through the stone like some phantom created by a master of the Art. A corner of it enveloped him just as his head thudded into the wall.

Nish roused to the odours of burning cloth and smouldering leather. He lifted his head but it hurt. He was lying on what had been the floor of the lookout, but was now a jumble of cracked and broken slabs collapsed onto the domed ceiling of the secret chamber below. An edge of rough stone dug into his ribs. Nish slid off it onto a flat slab, which proved to be uncomfortably warm. He rolled onto a cooler one and looked straight through the wall. A triangle of stone had fallen out leaving a hole he could have put his head through. He moved and the walls appeared to shift before his eyes. No, the top section of the tower was tilted and was surely going to collapse.

The slab under him was growing hotter. Nish rolled off onto the next without checking it first, and pain seared through his back and buttocks. He pulled himself to his feet and picked his way across the rubble, his boot soles smoking. The floor in the centre was burning hot. The blast had made an inferno of Yggur's secret chambers and the floor could collapse through the dome at any moment. He could feel the stone quivering.

He sprang across to the nearest embrasure, where the floor seemed a little more solid, and began beating at the smoking cuffs of his trousers. A section of cloth the size of a saucer fell out and the skin underneath began to blister. He pressed it against the damp stone, then did the same with his boots until the fumes disappeared.

His calf was really stinging now. Scrambling from slab to slab around the perimeter of the chamber to what looked like a marginally safer position, Nish discovered that seepage had frozen on the inner lip of one embrasure to form grey ice. He broke off a piece and held it to the blistered flesh until the burning eased, though as soon as he took the ice away the pain came back, worse than before.

There was nothing he could do about it. Edging to an embrasure that looked over the yard, Nish peered out, careful to make no sudden movement that would betray him. The sky was full of descending ropes, each bearing a squad of armoured troopers clinging to hand- and foot-loops. Several ropes had already touched down on the outer wall and troopers were running along it, taking charge of the defences and picking off Yggur's guards as they ran from their barracks.

Another squad, already in the yard, was preparing to storm the front doors. Across the far side of the yard a group of twenty or more soldiers, dressed in the distinctive uniforms of Chief Scrutator Ghorr's personal guard, were breaking into the shed in which the thapter was stored. How could they have known it was inside?

It was the Council! Fiz Gorgo had been betrayed. Nish slid out of sight as an officer glanced up at the smoking tower. Had he been seen? He couldn't tell. He heard the thunder of boots as a host of troopers surged through the broken front doors.

They'll get a shock inside, he thought. Yggur, Flydd and Malien would together be the match of a small army. He looked down again and saw a group of warrior mancers follow the advance guard, staves at the ready, and after them squad after squad of heavily armed men. No, there was little hope; the scrutators were too well prepared.

Smoke began to seep up through cracks in the dome. Tossing away the fragment of ice, Nish snapped off another and pressed it to his burning calf. The stone he was standing on was growing hotter and he couldn't see any way out. The stair was completely blocked by hot rubble. He couldn't possibly climb down the wet stone on the outside of the tower. His only means of escape was by jumping out one of the embrasures, though below him the drop was eight floors to the paved yard – certain death. In the other directions, the fall was five floors onto the sloping roofs of Fiz Gorgo, which were tiled with thick slabs of lichen-covered

16

rock. He'd either crash straight through, tearing himself to shreds on the broken slabs, or, more likely, break all his leg bones as he landed.

The yard offered a quick death; the roof, lingering agony. If he stayed here, he'd be either cooked or smoked to death. The stone groaned and the tower lurched, as if a lower layer had become plastic. Falling into the inferno was his other doom. Nish hopped from foot to foot. The soles of his boots were smoking again. There was nowhere to go. Or was there?

The horned roof above him was framed with metal rods that had to be cooler than what he was standing on, and if the tower collapsed, there was a faint chance that the roof might hold together. If the tower stayed up, he might, just possibly, survive up there until the inferno went out. It didn't seem likely but he had no alternative.

Nish eased a smouldering beam out of the rubble, with much burning of fingers and the soles of his feet, and propped it against the wall. He dragged himself up it, caught hold of an iron rod and pulled himself up onto the roof framing.

It was worse than uncomfortable, for the rods cut into his flesh wherever he perched, but it was safer than where he'd been. Before long a curving crack appeared in the top of the dome. The chamber below had turned the orange-red of molten rock. If the conflagration inside was hot enough to melt stone, his end could not be long in coming.

And why delay it, he thought bitterly, since everyone I care about is going to die. Nish had no illusions about his friends' fate once they fell into the hands of the scrutators. There were no prisons on Santhenar. Minor miscreants were punished by servitude in the front lines, for men, or the breeding factories for women, or by other forms of slavery appropriate to the needs of the unending war. All other criminals were executed as an example to all, the only variation being in the ironically appropriate manner of their deaths.

Tears pricked his eyes when he thought about Irisis, his dearest friend, being tormented by the scrutators. No – he had to cling to hope, no matter how slender. Surely Yggur and Malien,

17

two of the truly great figures from the Histories, were still at large? Yggur was a mancer of overwhelming power and cunning, a legend who had struggled against Rulke himself, back in the time of the Mirror, and even before that. Yggur was more than twelve hundred years old; had seen everything and survived everything. How could the scrutators beat him?

And yet ... the Council had known where Yggur's secret defences lay, and had destroyed them from afar without being detected. What if Yggur had been targeted the same way, as he slept? If he was dead, all hope was lost.

The tower gave another of those plastic shudders that made his stomach lurch. Nish clutched the rod with both hands. Waves of colour like inverted rainbows shimmered in the air and, suddenly, he saw right through the stone dome, as he had that ghastly night last summer after his father, Jal-Nish, had forced Nish's hands into those uncanny quicksilver tears distilled from the destroyed node at Snizort.

He was looking into a seething hell – a cauldron of molten stone seemingly suspended in mid-air where the floor of the lower chamber had once been. What could be holding it up? The roiling globe drifted toward the side wall, only to be repelled back towards the centre. It rotated one way and then the other, emitting little bursts of glowing plasma that licked the soot-coated walls clean wherever they touched.

Nish could only imagine that the ferocity of the blast had been contained by some unknown aspect of Yggur's secret defences. He prayed that it stayed contained, for the radiating fury looked potent enough to consume the walls of the tower.

The fiery globe swelled, contracted, swelled again and burst open, sending an incandescent jet straight up. Burning through the top of the stone dome, it sucked back then blew an orange spurt of molten rock-glass up through the hole. It arched high across the room, solidifying into a glass lance that split down its length as it cooled, forming a pair of curving blades as sharp as a giant's scimitars.

The strange-sight that had allowed Nish to see the globe vanished so suddenly that he cried out. An attack of vertigo had

18

him clinging desperately to the rods, his sweating hands slipping on the warm metal.

There came another molten squirt, splitting to form another pair of glass scimitars, and then another and another until the chamber was webbed with them. Nish hung suspended above a hundred razor-sharp blades. It had to be a residue of Yggur's Art – such perfect, deadly blades could not have formed by accident – but it had trapped him as effectively as any weapon of the enemy's. If he tried to get down, he'd be sliced like a slab of buffalo on a butcher's block.

Heat billowed up through the hole, streaming directly over him. His eyelids began to rasp when he blinked. After ten or fifteen minutes Nish could feel his skin drying and cracking in the heat. He was desperate for something to drink.

From his refuge he could see part of the yard. A bound and gagged prisoner was led out to its centre, surrounded by soldiers. The prisoner was an elderly woman, one of Yggur's kitchen servants. Other servants followed, each with an escort of the scrutators' finest, then several of Yggur's guard. After them came Malien, heavily bound, Gilhaelith and, to Nish's despair, a stumbling, bloody Yggur.

Each new prisoner was a further blow to his hopes. Nish counted them down, and when Flydd and Irisis were dragged into the yard, he gave a groan of despair. The scrutators had them all, from the least to the greatest. He was the only one still free. Ghorr had out-thought them. All the time that Yggur and Flydd had been planning their secret assault on Nennifer, Ghorr had been readying his own vastly superior forces. By the time Tiaan and Malien had reached Fiz Gorgo in the thapter, five days ago, Ghorr's fleet of dreadnoughts had already been on its way. The irony was bitter.

Down in the courtyard the prisoners were still, all but one. Irisis was struggling, ignoring the cuffs and kicks of the guards. She would do so to the end. Irisis was a rebel and could never be anything else, and Nish loved her for it. The realisation shocked him. He did love her and that made it so much worse.

Nish had expected the search of Fiz Gorgo to take some time,

19

but shortly the scrutators emerged, along with the remainder of the soldiers, and were lifted up to the air-dreadnoughts in suspended baskets. The prisoners and their guards remained in the yard, shivering and stamping their feet.

The inferno below him had begun to cool, but the broken beams on the floor were smouldering, coating him with soot and catching at his lungs. Nish shifted on the rods, trying to find a way down without cutting himself to shreds. He could see none. He might have broken one or two glass blades with his boots, but the ones below were out of reach and dropping onto them was out of the question.

He climbed up under the roof, trying to see if any of the rods could be unfastened. They were fixed solidly, but while he was there Nish happened to glance up through a cracked roof slab and saw that the scrutators' mechanicians were building a vast ropework construction, like a horizontal spiderweb, above Fiz Gorgo.

They had begun by anchoring the air-dreadnoughts to the outer walls with vertical cables as thick as a big man's biceps. Now, working a good fifty spans above the ground, suspended ropers were hauling across horizontal ropes, stretching them drum-taut and lashing them into a network.

The instant the great rolls of canvas were lowered, Nish understood what they were doing. They were building a suspended amphitheatre, and it could only be to try the prisoners here. Ghorr wasn't going to give such a collection of great mancers the least opportunity for escape, but he'd not miss the chance to consolidate his power either. The Council of Scrutators loved its spectacles, and the tale of such a trial would spread like wildfire throughout the known world, to bolster its dread reputation.

Nish tried to calculate how long the construction was going to take. Though the ropers worked with such dexterity that they must have practised the operation many times, it would take hours more to adapt their general design to the specific configuration of Fiz Gorgo. He didn't know what time it was, for a thick overcast had rolled in from the west and not a glimmer of

20

sun came through it. Nish thought it must have been around ten in the morning. The scrutators would want to complete their grisly business well before dark, which was around five at this time of year, so he didn't have long at all.

Didn't have long for what? He was trapped in a half-molten tower likely to collapse at any moment, being cured like a ham in a smokehouse, and his arms could barely hold him up. Half dead from dehydration, he had been reduced to licking the sooty condensation off the underside of the roof slabs. He was unarmed, opposed by hundreds of the toughest fighters in the world and dozens of mancers aching to impress their masters. Furthermore, the scrutators, collectively, represented the most powerful force ever assembled on Santhenar. The very idea of trying to rescue his friends was absurd.

But it would not go away.

THREE

The western side of the horned tower had stopped steaming. Ullii hoped it had cooled enough to climb, for there was no other way of getting to the top. Unfortunately it was also the side that faced the yard.

She went up the stair as far as she could go, eyeing the hot rubble in case a way past it had opened up. She could now discern a gap below the under-spiral of the stair, but everything radiated such heat that she could not get near it. Here and there, ribbons of molten metal, shiny as quicksilver where their coatings of grit had cracked, congealed in puddles on the treads.

It had to be the outside. Ullii squeezed through an embrasure that did not face the yard and found herself just above one of the roofs of Fiz Gorgo. She lowered herself to a roofing slab, adjusted her mask so it allowed in just a slit of light, and looked up.

The tower had been built of rough stone and the joins offered many hand- and foot-holds. Ullii was naturally dextrous, so the climb would not have been beyond her, had the tower been dry. Besides, her lattice revealed its secret strengths and flaws in a way that no one else could see. She looked up, closed her eyes and its network of cracks, crevices and stress-points opened up to her.

She pulled herself as far as the next floor, the fifth, but above that the stone was too hot to hold on to. Ullii edged sideways around the tower, one eye on the yard. If anyone looked up she would be seen, for her pale clothing and skin would stand out against the dark stone.

Fortunately the rain had become heavier, and colder, and the soldiers in the yard had their hoods down. Curling her toes around a projection no thicker than her finger, Ullii eased around the curve of the tower until she was directly above the yard. If she fell, she would die.

Above her, at the lower point of the bend, the wall was networked with horizontal cracks. If she could cross above them the worst would be over. She went up, stretched sideways to reach a convenient crack shaped like a lyrinx's smile, and up again, sliding the fingers of her left hand deep into a crevice. She jerked them out and thrust them into her mouth – the inside was hot. She turned her head from side to side, eyes closed, sensing the heat on her cheek. There, to her left and above, where the rock was cracked like a mosaic, it felt cooler. It didn't look very stable, though.

Ullii edged left as far as she could go, made sure her footing was sound and reached up. The first piece of the mosaic grated under her fingers and she had to hastily press it back before it dropped on her face. She fingered another, which also moved. The whole area was loose. She would have to go further and hope she could find a way around it.

It proved to be hard, slow work, for Ullii had never regained the wiry strength she'd had before she lost the baby. She edged along a tiny crack, just wide enough to get the tips of her toes inside. A span to her left and a span up she saw an easy path, though she wasn't sure she could get to it. She felt very tired.

Suddenly her head spun and the lattice vanished. Ullii let out a cry of anguish, lost her grip with her left hand and nearly fell. She clung on with her toes and her right hand, scratching at the rock with her left and breaking her fingernails.

Ullii recovered quickly, though her heart was thundering and her calf muscles screaming. Her toes slipped. She worked them back into the crack but couldn't find a comfortable position. Her left foot had begun to cramp and panic was eating away her

23

confidence. The lattice was her life, her being, and compensation for all her other frailties. It made her unique and allowed her to survive in this cruel and hostile world. What if it didn't come back?

She'd lost it before, briefly, after times of extreme stress, but never when her life had depended on it. At such moments it was normally at its strongest. Since Nish had killed Myllii, and Ullii had lost her baby, the lattice had slowly weakened. She lived in dread that it would disappear completely.

Concentrating on her breathing, Ullii let go with one hand and massaged her calf until the cramp was gone. The panic faded but the lattice did not come back. She would have to do without it.

Opening her eyes, she worked out a path upwards and closed them again. Her supersensitive fingers and toes would tell her all she needed to know. Vision would just be a distraction.

After much trial and error she found a way around the cracked area and up onto the bend in the tower, here clotted with glassy dribbles of melted rock that had oozed through cracks in the walls and congealed on the outside. Some knobs were too hot to hold, and others would not have borne her weight, but she found a pair rooted deep in the wall that were as solid as a staircase, allowing her to rest for a while.

Ullii wasn't thinking about retribution now, for the climb had taken too much out of her. She no longer knew why she was climbing, only that Nish had come up and not gone down again. She didn't see how he could have lived but she wouldn't believe he was dead until she saw his body.

The other urge that kept her going was the need to hide from Chief Scrutator Ghorr. Ullii did not know how she was going to survive on her own, but she was never going back to Nennifer.

She was clinging on with her toes and the fingers of one hand, while she wiped the trickling moisture off her forehead, when she heard a glassy *crack* from inside the open watch-house at the top of the tower. It was followed by a muffled groan or curse.

It could have been the tormented rocks contracting as they cooled, but Ullii did not think so. It had sounded human, and *very* familiar. She sniffed but could smell only hot rock. If Nish was up there, the breeze was blowing his scent away. She scrabbled up to the seventh level. Her fingers were aching and she'd broken most of her toenails. Ullii needed to rest but drove herself on; she had to know. The wall and the embrasure above her were steaming, and a trickle of smoke issued from a deep fissure to one side of it.

Ullii peered over the lip of the embrasure and was confronted by a network of hundreds of spears and blades of rock glass, arching up like scimitars from a hole in the centre of the floor. The room was full of them. A hole in the jumbled floor was blocked by congealed glass, still cracking as it cooled.

Now she smelt Nish, though it was a strange, baked odour, the arid smell of desiccated skin. Ullii felt for the knife in her pack but did not pull it out. It was enough to know it was there. A trail of smoke drifted across her face, burning the membranes in her nose. She breathed through her mouth, her eyes watering as she scanned the floor. There was no sign of him. She looked up through the network of glassy blades and there he was, his arms and legs wrapped desperately around the iron rods that supported the roof. He looked as if he could barely hang on.

Instinctively she bared her teeth, but the gesture faded as her eyes adjusted to the gloom. He was coated, no, *crusted* with smoke and soot. His hair and skin were black and the individual hairs of his beard stood out like bristles. Skin was flaking off his nose and lips, the whites of his eyes were like chips of marble on black velvet, and he was shaking so hard that his teeth clattered.

Nish licked cracked lips and Ullii saw blood on his tongue. She pulled herself up onto the sill of the embrasure, staring at him, overcome. Rage warred with a most desperate longing for him to put his strong arms around her and make everything all right.

Nish saw her and let go with one hand, reaching out. 'Help me, Ullii.'

His agony showed in the crevices around his mouth, the shuddering of his arms, the staring eyes, but that was nothing to

25

her own pain. He'd lost nothing; she had nothing left. He'd torn it all away.

'Water,' he croaked, tongue rasping over his lips. 'Please.'

The begging made her think less of him. Nish had always been strong. Now he was weaker than her and she felt nothing but contempt. 'Come down.'

'The blades will cut me to ribbons.'

She hoped so. Ullii wanted to see his blood run free. 'Jump!'

Nish considered all possible ways down, biting his sooty lip. 'I can't.'

Ullii had always resisted using her initiative. In the long years when the only thing she'd wanted had been her brother back, it had been easier to drift. Now the desire for retribution was so strong that it seared her.

She moved around to the next embrasure, out of sight from below. Taking her boots out of her pack, Ullii put them on then climbed onto the sill and hurled her pack up into the middle of the chamber. The fragile glass sang as it smashed and, with a tinkling roar, the central part of the network fell to the floor. She wove between the remaining spears, glass crunching under her soles, and eased her head over the sill on the yard side. Several guards had looked up at the sound, but only briefly. Pieces were falling off the tower all the time.

Nish was staring down at the gap. The pack had carved an elongated scar through the glass spears, though it wasn't much wider than a human body.

'Can you throw the pack again?' he said.

It lay under a network of quivering spears, so precariously perched that a breath could have dislodged them. She shook her head.

Nish pulled himself along the supporting rods, choosing the spot carefully. He couldn't drop – he had to throw himself through at just the right angle and, even had he been fit and strong, that would not have been easy. His hands were shaking. He rubbed his palms down his trousers, coating them with greasy soot. He tried to rub it off again but only smeared it

26

everywhere. Nish gripped a rod, lowered himself until he was hanging full stretch, and began to sway back and forth.

Ullii could see the fear on his face but it no longer gave her any pleasure. Nothing gave her pleasure any more. She pulled out the knife, just to be ready.

'What are you doing?' he said, hanging motionless.

'You killed Myllii.'

'Myllii?' he whispered dazedly.

Surely he hadn't forgotten? He truly was a monster. 'I'm going to kill you for that, Nish.'

He closed his eyes, which turned his face into an ebony mask, then opened them with a flash of white. 'I'm sorry. It was an accident. He just reared back –'

'It's too late to say you're sorry *now*,' she whispered, overcome by memories still vivid and clear.

'Ullii,' he begged. 'Please.'

'Too late. Too late.' She turned away, the blade hanging down. Ullii couldn't look at him. Why was he saying it now? Why not back then, when it had mattered?

'What about our baby?' croaked Nish. Sooty flakes of skin broke from his lips and drifted upwards in the rising air. 'Would you kill our little baby's father?'

'There is no baby!' she said in a thin scream. 'Yllii is dead and that's your fault too!'

FOUR

Nish's hand slipped and he flailed about wildly before getting another grip. 'Yllii?' he rasped.

'Your *son!*' It was an accusation – how could you not know his name? And an attack – it's *your* fault.

'My son?' That threw him. His lower lip trembled. 'Dead? How?'

How could he not know? Having lived Yllii's death every possible way over the past four and a half months, she found Nish's ignorance incomprehensible. It didn't occur to her that he had no way of knowing these things. 'You killed him!' Ullii shrieked, half-mad with rage and grief.

Nish clung desperately to his perch. 'You ran away, Ullii, and I couldn't find you. I don't know what happened from that day to this. But whatever happened to our son, I wasn't there.'

'You weren't there,' she whispered. 'You were *never* there when I needed you, Nish. You didn't care.'

'I wept tears of blood for what I'd done to Myllii but I couldn't undo it. Please, Ullii. What happened to our son?'

She swept the blade through the air. 'Come down.'

'Put the knife away first.'

She gave a half-hearted slash, screwed her eyes up, then laid the knife on the floor among the shattered glass, within easy reach. Nish would come down. He had to know what had

28

happened to his son and it gave her the upper hand. At least he cares about Yllii, she thought, even if he hates me.

'Come down, Nish.'

She studied him from under her eyelids. He seemed to be weighing her intentions. Now he began to swing his legs, trying to line himself up with the gap. Ullii could have done it with her eyes closed but he lacked her natural dexterity, and that pleased her selfish little soul. It wasn't often that she felt superior.

Nish sucked in a breath, swung, and threw himself at the gap.

Before he let go, Ullii knew he'd miss. He'd swung out a little too far, a fraction too hard. His legs went through the gap but his body wasn't lined up properly and he was heading straight for a pair of razor-sharp blades.

Nish jerked backwards and twisted sideways at the last instant, and his torso passed through safely. He whipped his head back, the blade shaved a clump of hair off the left side, nicking his ear, then he was through, all but his flailing left arm. It went side-on into a blade, cutting a deep gouge in his forearm before the glass broke. Blood spurted up as he slammed into a sloping slab of stone that was mercifully free of glass.

He didn't move for a second or two. Blood pumped straight up from his forearm, coating one of the blades above him before dripping all over his face. Moving painfully, he got a thumb to the artery and the flow stopped. He looked up at her, the blood still dripping on his face, and across at the knife. She did too.

Ullii still planned to kill him. She took up the knife but Nish didn't move. Blood welled out under his thumb and he pressed harder. She hated him for all that had happened to her since she'd been taken to the manufactory a year ago. Because of him she was alone in the world. She had no brother, no son, no friends, and now the lattice, her last resort and only comfort, had gone away. She didn't know how to get it back.

'I didn't know Myllii was your brother,' Nish said quietly, his voice barely audible over the singing of the blades in the wind. 'I thought he was attacking you. Or holding you so the soldiers could carry you off to the air-floater.'

He looked ghastly, with his face and arm drenched in blood,

and the rest of him covered in soot and flaking skin. She wavered.

Nish went on. 'I told Myllii to stop but he reared backwards and the knife went straight into him. I'm so very sorry.'

Ullii closed her eyes. She was back at the campsite, holding Myllii and feeling his shock as the knife slid into his back. Tears welled out through her eyelids like drops of blood from a wound. *Had* Nish said that? She couldn't remember – she'd been too overcome with joy at finding her twin after so many years of searching.

Nish could be lying. He'd used her before and he was, after all, the son of his father, Jal-Nish, the worst man Ullii had ever come across. She'd been a good judge of people once, but Ullii couldn't tell about Nish any more.

'What happened to Yllii?' he said softly.

You killed him too, she wanted to scream while stabbing Nish to the heart. Ghorr had told her so, many times, and so had Scrutator T'Lisp, the wicked old woman who had trapped Ullii with Myllii's binding bracelet. They'd told her that Nish was evil incarnate and had to be destroyed. Ullii had believed them at the time, and for a long time after, but looking back on her months in Nennifer she began to doubt. Chief Scrutator Ghorr was a monster whose handiwork she'd seen many times in Nennifer, and on the long journey here. He'd ruined Fiz Gorgo, killed dozens of innocent people and planned to torture the rest of them to death. And she had helped him, and betrayed every one of her former friends, so what did that make her?

'Tell me everything, Ullii,' he said softly. 'From the moment Myllii first appeared in the clearing, until now. I have to know.'

She began haltingly, fingering the bracelet that still clung to her wrist, immovable. Just reliving that night of Myllii's death was torment, and the time after was worse. She could still feel Yllii's sharp fingernails scrabbling at her insides.

'She did it,' Nish said when Ullii had finished that part of the tale. She turned her face up to him blankly, lost in another time, another place.

'Scrutator T'Lisp killed our baby,' he went on. He reached out

30

to her, thumb still pressed against his arm, but she pulled away. 'I did you wrong, Ullii, and I'm sorry, but I'm not the real villain. Ghorr ordered Yllii's death so you would be free to track down Xervish Flydd for him. No one else could have found him.'

'No,' she said softly. 'No one could but me.'

'T'Lisp worked her Art so that you'd take Myllii's bracelet, and the instant you put it on you came under her control. But then you let slip that you were pregnant, and T'Lisp knew that while you carried our baby you'd be no use to her. She directed her scrutator magic against Yllii, through the bracelet. She lied to you and she killed Yllii. And now Ghorr –' Nish broke off, as if he'd thought better of it.

Ullii sank down among the shards of green glass, not noticing as they dug into her calves. She didn't want to believe Nish. If what he said was true, in serving Ghorr she'd been using Yllii's death for an even greater evil.

She thought it through ponderously, for her mind was sluggish and reluctant to face the truth. It had been easier to blame Nish; to think that the agony of Myllii's death and the grief at his loss had caused the death of her baby. But how could that be? She clutched at her belly, and the knife which she still held in her left hand, pricked her; the memories that T'Lisp had wiped from her mind came cascading back.

Yllii had been all right until the following night, when she'd touched the bracelet – still immovably fixed to her wrist by scrutator magic – and seen that vision of Ghorr and T'Lisp again.

Myllii, she gasped, *clasping the bracelet in panic, but again came that flash of the scrutators.*

Come to us, little seeker, *mouthed Ghorr.* We've work for you.

'Leave me alone,' she said aloud. *'My little baby needs me.'*

Baby? *Ghorr said to the others.* She can't have a baby – it'll ruin her precious talent.

She must have dreamed that, for the next instant they were gone as completely as if she'd only imagined it; then gone completely, her memories of the moment wiped clean.

Myllii wasn't there either, but that awful screaming rang in her ears again. She reached out to the baby's knot, for the screaming

31

seemed to be coming from there. An agonising pain, far worse than the baby's kicks, sheared through her belly. She wrapped her arms around her stomach, trying to protect the baby, but the pain grew until it was like barbed hooks tearing through her.

Ullii made a supreme effort to reach beyond the pain but the barbs ripped through her flesh and she felt a great convulsion inside her, a bursting agony, as if the baby's sharp fingernails were tearing desperately at the walls of her womb. Something burst inside her, then water gushed out between her legs, carrying the baby with it.

'No!' Ullii screamed, falling to her knees and clawing at the ground, but it was too late.

The baby, a little boy no longer than her hand, lay in a puddle, kicking feebly. She picked him up, staring at him in wonder. He was pink and healthy, and so beautiful that she felt a flush of love, but as she nursed him in her hands, the cord stopped pulsing and her stomach contracted again and again to expel the afterbirth. Ullii lifted the baby to her breast.

'Yllii. Your name is Yllii,' she said, as if that could protect him.

She desperately wanted him to live, for it was the only happy link left between her and Nish, the only good memory of their time together, and she loved him so.

Yllii gave one feeble suck, a little sigh, but his head fell away from the nipple and blood from his mouth trickled down her breast. Ullii tried to blow the breath back into the infant but the pink colour faded steadily from his face. The baby breathed no more.

Ullii looked up at Nish, not bothering to brush the tears away. 'T'Lisp did kill our baby,' she said at last, her voice as brittle as the glass underfoot. 'She did it to please Ghorr, using this bracelet.' She rose, letting the knife fall. Ullii did not look at Nish. Her fingers tore at the bracelet on her wrist, but it didn't move. She took a deep, shuddering breath. 'And all this while I've been serving and helping them. I brought them here so they could kill the only people who have ever been good to me.'

'You couldn't have known.' Nish's eyes were fixed on the bracelet.

'I knew what they were doing,' Ullii said, wrenching at it until it cut into the skin. She didn't care. It burned her now; it made her Ghorr's creature. Ullii would cut off her hand if there was no other way to be rid of it. 'And I knew I was doing wrong, serving them. I was afraid of Ghorr; that's why I did it.'

'Is that all?' said Nish, who knew of old how obsessional Ullii could be.

'I wanted retribution for Myllii and Yllii. No!' she said savagely, 'I called it retribution but it was just revenge. I wanted you to suffer. And Flydd too, because he didn't save Myllii.'

'What about Irisis?'

'I didn't want to harm her,' said Ullii uncomfortably.

'But you have, Ullii. You've condemned her to die like everyone else. And Tiaan too, who never did anything to you. Not to mention Malien and Yggur, whom you've never met, and Inouye, the pilot of the air-floater. She's such a quiet little woman, not much older than you, Ullii. And she's so afraid.'

'Why?' said Ullii.

'Inouye is terrified that her man and her little children will be punished because she obeyed Fyn-Mah and helped to save Flydd's life and mine. She's afraid that wicked Scrutator Ghorr would even torture her innocent children.'

'He wouldn't . . .' Ullii said, uncertainly. 'How old are her children?'

'Sann, the boy, is nearly four. Inouye's daughter, Mya, would be two and a half, I suppose.'

'So young,' she whispered. 'Have you met them?'

'No, but Inouye often mentioned their names. No mother ever loved her children more,' he said deliberately.

'I loved Yllii more than anyone else could ever love their baby!' she wailed, jerking the bracelet up and down her wrist until it scraped off the skin in crumpled strips.

'I know you did,' he said, very quietly. 'But would you let Ghorr kill Inouye . . . if you could save her?'

'I don't know her,' Ullii said sullenly.

'Would you allow Scrutator T'Lisp, who murdered our baby, to torment innocent little Sann and Mya?'

33

Ullii shuddered and pulled the mask over her face, then scuttled between the glassy blades into the darkest cranny of the chamber.

'Ullii?'

She put her hands over her ears. She had to block him out. She knew what Nish wanted of her, but it was too hard. It was much safer to drift, to hide.

He kept calling. She couldn't block him out completely, and of course Nish knew that. Eventually she took her hands away from her ears.

'Yes?' she said quietly.

'I need your help, Ullii,' said.

'What's the matter?'

'The gash in my arm is still bleeding. If you can't fix it I'm going to die.'

'Good!' she said mulishly, though Ullii had a shrinking feeling inside. Already she'd taken a little comfort from his presence. She didn't feel quite so alone. 'I can't do anything about it.'

'Of course you can. You always carry a needle and thread in your pack, to sew up your spider-silk underclothes.'

'Can't reach it,' she muttered.

'See that long spear of glass, there? Reach under and hook it through the strap of the pack and drag it out.'

'It'll cut me.'

'Wrap your shirt around your hand or something. Don't you have any initiative?'

It was the wrong thing to say. Ullii simply closed her eyes and scrunched herself up in the corner.

'Ullii?'

She blocked him out.

He was quiet for a while, and then he said, 'If I die, you'll be all alone up here.'

'I can climb out.'

'Down to Ghorr and the scrutators?'

She scrunched herself up into a tighter ball. 'You can't help me, Nish.'

'I wasn't planning to. Ullii, I've been a fool. I treated you

34

badly, and hurt you terribly. I've done stupid things and I'm sorry for them . . .'

'Yes?' she said when he did not go on. She liked hearing him talk like that.

'I have to do something good to make up for it . . .'

She didn't reply at once. Ullii was no fool – he was trying to lead her somewhere and she didn't want to follow. But neither did she want to be alone again.

'What, Nish?'

'You've done wrong too, Ullii. You betrayed your friends. You've condemned Flydd and Irisis, and everyone else in Fiz Gorgo.'

'It wasn't my fault. Ghorr made me do it.'

'No, Ullii. You chose to help Ghorr.'

'He forced me.'

'You didn't have to find this place. You could have told him that you couldn't see anyone in your lattice.'

'He was too strong. He was going to hurt me!'

'You could have resisted.'

'He threatened me with Scrutator Fusshte. He's the most evil scrutator of all, Nish.'

'You could have resisted even Fusshte,' Nish said inexorably. 'You could have pretended that you'd lost the lattice. They wouldn't have known any different.'

'It was as if Fusshte was looking at me though my clothes; even through my skin.'

'I'm sure that was horrible, but you betrayed your friends and now they're all going to be put to death in the most awful way. Once the scrutators have killed them, the last hope of the world will be gone. We'll lose the war and the lyrinx will eat us all, even you, Ullii. And it'll all be your fault.'

'No,' she said in an almost inaudible squeak. 'No, no, no!'

'Yes,' Nish said.

Ullii couldn't make herself any smaller or any more insignificant. She couldn't close down her senses to keep him at bay and she couldn't escape. She had no choice but to take in what he was saying, though she knew he was manipulating her.

She *had* betrayed her friends and, for the first time, Ullii had to face up to it. She'd known it all along, but had put it out of mind – even those awful sounds as the guards on the wall had been slain without warning.

And how many people were yet to die? Dozens stood in the yard, waiting in the freezing cold for their doom. She looked out the embrasure. The vast rope-and-canvas platform would soon be finished. Two prisoners were being hauled up in a rope net, their arms and legs dangling out through the mesh.

She heard a faint, mournful wail – a young woman's cry of soul-rending anguish. It wasn't Irisis, for she would never have given way like that. Was it little Inouye? Was she wailing because she would never see her babies again, or because she knew that even they would suffer for the crime she'd been accused of?

Nish stood up, still holding his thumb over the gash, and looked over her shoulder. 'It's nearly midday. The trials will begin as soon as the last prisoners are lifted up to the amphitheatre, and Ghorr will want it well over before dark. He won't dare stay here after the sun goes down. Air-dreadnoughts are too vulnerable to flying lyrinx.'

His nearness made her uncomfortable, though the scent of him had always calmed her. Ullii tried to rouse her previous fury by thinking about all the things Nish had done to her, but at the look in his eyes, so familiar, so guilty, so vulnerable, she could not. Violence was simply not in her nature. What would be the point, anyway? Myllii and Yllii couldn't be brought back and the sooner she joined them the better. 'What do you want from me, Nish?'

'I want you to help me. We've got to try and save them.'

'They have hundreds of guards,' she said dully. 'And dozens of mancers watching over them. I can't do anything and neither can you.'

'We have to try.'

'I'm too scared.'

'I'm scared too. But look – we've both done wrong, Ullii, and this is the only way we can make up for it. We have to atone for what we've done.'

FIVE

The operation on his forearm was more painful than it should have been, because Ullii couldn't bear to look at the gash and insisted on sewing him up with her eyes closed. Each time the bloody needle, trailing its red threads, came at him he flinched and Ullii jumped, then forced it through his skin and flesh as if to cause the maximum of discomfort. Nish gritted his teeth and restrained himself from crying out, though it wasn't possible to remain silent when she roughly pulled the sides of the gash together and tied the threads.

'Thank you,' he said once it had been done and bound with the tail of a spare shirt from her pack. 'Now we'd better find a way out of here.'

Nish knew it was hopeless. Ullii was too timid; if he'd had his choice of all the co-conspirators in the world, he couldn't have found someone with less initiative.

He looked out the window and blanched. How had she climbed the tower without ropes or irons? It was beyond him and that wasn't cowardice. Nish simply didn't have the skills to climb down that sheer face. If he tried, he'd certainly fall to his death.

The rubble blocking the stair was still too hot to approach. The rods that supported and tensioned the roof were immovable; he'd tried them earlier.

'Ullii, you'll have to climb down and find some rope. I can't get out any other way.'

'Rope?' she said, as if she'd never heard of such a thing. 'I don't know where there's any rope.'

He thought for a moment. 'Do you know where the front door of Fiz Gorgo is?'

'Yes. I went through it with Ghorr.'

'If you can climb down –'

'Of course I can climb down,' she said, tossing her head.

'Then go out into the yard. It's empty now, but be careful. Ghorr might have guards posted. Around to the left, near the wall, there's a little stone shed that Inouye uses – she's the air-floater pilot. The innocent one whose little children are going to be murdered,' he said deliberately. 'The door won't be locked, and you'll find coils of rope in there. Can you bring one back? And make sure it's long enough . . .' He gauged the distance down to the roof. 'You'll need about eight or nine spans. Do you know how much a span is?'

She gave him one of her famous looks and climbed out the embrasure on the side away from the yard. Nish watched her go down, amazed at how easy she made it look, and even more amazed that such a timid person could do it at all. But then, Ullii could be surprisingly competent when she had no choice in the matter.

He glanced up. The amphitheatre looked almost complete now. The ropers, who earlier had been swarming like sailors in the rigging of a merchant vessel, were gone apart from a few above a tower on the other side of Fiz Gorgo, who were tensioning lines with a complicated array of pulleys. He couldn't see what was going on above the deck.

Nish looked further up, to the nearest of the air-dreadnoughts, but immediately jerked his head below the sill of the embrasure. For a moment he'd thought the grey robed mancer had been staring straight at him. He took another peep. The brass spyglass was not pointed his way at all, but at the horned tower to his left. It had also been struck by that initial blast, but whatever the strange energies or magics inside, they had not been completely liberated. The tower was sagging more than this one and glowing redly three floors below the roof. Bladder-like extrusions of molten material were being forced out of the slit embrasures. One burst, filling the air with shards of brown glass which set instantly, glittering in a momentary ray of sunlight, before tinkling to the paving stones of the yard.

The tower slowly tilted as if the stone were made of toffee. One of the horns fell off and plunged through the roof, smashing its thick slabs to fragments. For a few seconds it looked as though the tower would go the same way but it subsided suddenly, twisting like a length of barley sugar, and landed in the yard with a crash that shook the whole of Fiz Gorgo. Residual magics fumed and flickered, then went out.

Nish's tower shuddered and leaned a little further from the vertical. Ants swarmed in the pit of his stomach, but the tower stabilised. Cries came from the amphitheatre and a wave churned across the canvas, snapping several of the guy ropes. A roper, caught by a lashing end, fell backwards from his perch, plunging head down and arms spread, to his death. Nish lost sight of the man as he passed behind the roof on the other side of the building.

His tower gave another, smaller shudder and rock spalled off the walls. It couldn't last long. Nish scanned the air-dreadnought, keeping his head below the embrasure. The mancer was watching the drama on the amphitheatre. Nish prayed that he hadn't seen Ullii climbing down, or she'd have walked into a trap. He couldn't see her in the yard.

Nish's thoughts went to his friends. The trials would soon be getting underway and they wouldn't take over-long. Long enough for the theatre and the lavish spectacle, and long enough for the artists, recorders and tale-tellers to get each victim's story down, but not long enough for anyone to receive a fair trial. The scrutators did not believe in fair trials.

Come on, Ullii. What's keeping you? Ghorr might have tried Irisis first, for she'd once discovered a secret that threatened every mancer, and the chief scrutator didn't want it to get out. If the punishment was carried out after each trial they might be readying her now. Before she was tortured and slain, Irisis would be stripped naked and exposed to the icy wind and the leers of the witnesses. The artists and tale-tellers would be ordered to capture every detail of her magnificent body before the punishment, and afterwards. In this prudish world the human form was rarely depicted unclothed, but where criminals were concerned nothing was left to the prurient imagination. If such a beauty could be brought low, it could happen to anyone, and few people would fail to take the lesson.

And then, the flaying knives . . . Nish ground his fists into his eyes but couldn't keep the hideous images at bay. How could they do that to anyone, much less to Irisis?

There was still no sign of Ullii. He paced back and forth in the narrow space between the glass spears. It was as confining as any dungeon cell, though at least the floor was cooling down.

Nish stepped onto a chunk of stone, which ground underfoot. He picked it up and, without thinking, hurled it into the network of glass blades, bringing down a good half of them. It made a colossal racket but he felt better for it. It was good to smash something, and it gave him more space to move in.

The drizzle began to turn to cold rain which would make Ullii's climb even slower. But it might speed up the trial; the scrutators liked their comforts.

Across he went, and back, having to tread carefully on the tilted slabs, then around the glass-clotted hole in the centre that was still too hot to approach. Nish kept going until, suddenly, his knees gave out. He'd been too anxious to eat dinner last night, and there had been nothing since. He was ravenous, and so very tired. He found a relatively cool perch by the cracked embrasure and squatted down with his back against the wall. Resting his cheek on his arms, he tried to think of a way out.

Nish was continuing to run outlandish schemes through his mind, like a schoolboy daydreaming about being a hero, when a shrill cry rang out. He got up and twisted his head out the embrasure. He saw nothing but the sixteen air-dreadnoughts hanging in the air above the canvas amphitheatre.

He looked down. No sign of Ullii either. She must have been taken, in which case his hopes were gone. He was trapped until the tower eventually collapsed and took him with it.

There was no point waiting tamely for his death. Weaving across to the other side, he climbed into the narrow embrasure and crouched there, looking down. Was there a chance, if he jumped? He didn't think so. The roof had only a gentle slope below him and, though the slabs were thick, they were also old. Even from here he could see that they were cracked and pieces had flaked off. He wouldn't slide – the slab would crumble under the impact and he'd go right through.

Nish crouched, then stood up straight. He chose his point, bent his knees and prepared to spring. He straightened up again.

'What are you doing, Nish?'

He turned hastily, slipped and had to clutch at the edge. Nish's knees were shaking as he stepped down. He felt a fool. Ullii had a coil of rope looped over her shoulder.

'What took you so long?' Nish snapped. He couldn't help it, but he regretted the outburst at once.

In the olden days Ullii would have curled up and gone into one of her states, and he would have got nothing out of her for hours. Something had changed. She simply said, 'The shed was locked. I had to search Fiz Gorgo.'

'I'm sorry. I thought they'd caught you.'

'Ghorr will never touch me again,' she said with such intensity that Nish shivered. It was hard to believe that she was the same person as the cringing Ullii he remembered.

'What do we do now?' he said.

'I don't know.'

Nish hadn't expected a positive response; he had only spoken aloud because it gave him the illusion of not being so desperately alone.

'Is there anything *you* can do?'

She stared at him blankly.

'With your talent, Ullii?'

'No,' she said.

Nish couldn't, wouldn't give up his friends. He had to believe

41

there was a way out. 'Ullii,' he said carefully. He moved closer, but not so close that she would feel he was using her, though of course he planned to. 'Do you remember how you got Irisis out of Nennifer?'

She leaned away, almost touching one of the remaining glass blades. 'How did you know that?'

'Xervish Flydd told me. And I've talked to Irisis about it, too.'

'What of it?' she said mulishly.

'I just thought you might be able to use that talent again . . .'

'Can't!'

'Why not?'

'Lost my lattice.'

'When did that happen?'

Ullii turned away, looking down at the floor.

'If you don't tell me, Ullii, how can I help you?'

'No one can help me.'

She said it with a remote edge of despair that tore at his heart. It was almost as if it didn't matter any more. He couldn't imagine what was going on in her mind.

'Then please, please help *me*, Ullii. No one else can. Do you want all the good people up there to die at the hands of Ghorr?'

'No one can save them.'

'And Scrutator T'Lisp, who murdered Yllii?'

'Our son,' she said dreamily. '*Our* son, Nish. How could anyone do such a wicked thing?'

He couldn't think of anything to say, but he put his good arm around her and held her close. It didn't help him but it might help her.

Ullii shuddered, a wrenching spasm that shook her from head to foot, then turned his way, staring at Nish with wide, colourless eyes, shiny with tears. The light was hurting her but she would not put on her mask.

'And she'll murder other little babies if *you* don't stop her,' he said brutally.

Nish was acting on a hunch that Ullii hadn't lost the lattice permanently. In the past her talent had come and gone, but it had always been available when she'd really needed it. Could he draw it out of her now? Or if not, could he get her into a situation where she had to use it to survive?

Nish was aware that he was manipulating her again, but there was little he wouldn't do to save his friends. Time was running out and he'd worry about the consequences later.

The tower shook and pieces of heat-scarred rock crumbled off the walls. 'Try your talent again, Ullii. Can you see anything in your lattice now?'

She strained, rather obviously. 'No.' The word was just a breath. 'Can't see past it.'

'Past what?'

She looked down at the floor. 'Blocking me.'

Nish scratched his head. 'Do you mean there's something down there below us that's stopping you seeing the lattice?'

'Don't know where it is. Could be anywhere.'

He sighed. 'Perhaps you'd better give me the rope.'

After much trouble – for he had to swing back and forth along the rough stone of the tower and was worried that it would rasp through the rope – Nish caught the edge of an embrasure below the bend in the tower. The stone was warm to the touch. He pulled himself onto the ledge and peered in. He could see the ash-littered stairs and, if he craned his neck up to the left, the point where they were blocked with a glassy slag of melted rock.

They climbed in. Ullii cut off the remainder of the rope and coiled it over her shoulder.

'We have to get up onto the outer wall without anyone seeing us,' he said. 'Though I don't see how –'

Ullii pushed past him and trotted down to the ground floor, where she crept through the empty halls of Fiz Gorgo.

'Are you sure you know where you're going?' he said after they'd been wandering for a good ten minutes, apparently aimlessly.

Ullii didn't deign to answer. Nish followed, more despairing with every step. Irisis's time could already have run out. Now they were going up again, along a dark and narrow stair that Nish hadn't known existed. Yggur hadn't encouraged exploration of Fiz Gorgo. After several turns they entered an open chamber topped with a cupola made of copper crusted with verdigris. Ullii peered out and up. Nish joined her.

They were not far from the outer wall of Fiz Gorgo, a section bordered by swamp forest. Some ten spans to his right, one of the huge rope cables, thicker than Nish's upper arm, anchored the amphitheatre to the wall. Forty or fifty spans to his left was another, and so they went all the way around the fortress. The cables ran vertically up to the floor of the amphitheatre, a good thirty spans above his head here, then continued to the circle of air-dreadnoughts even further above that.

'Can you see anyone?' he said.

Ullii shook her head. Nish stood edgewise at the opening and searched the walls. He couldn't see a solitary guard, though that wasn't surprising. Ghorr believed Fiz Gorgo to be empty, and the air-dreadnought guards would see anyone coming from Old Hripton a league before they could get here. There were no lyrinx in this part of Meldorin and, given their fear of water, no risk of an attack on foot through twenty leagues of swamp forest. The only risk was from the air, and the sixteenth air-dreadnought had been placed on high to keep watch.

'I meant with your talent,' said Nish. 'Has it come back at all?'

She didn't answer. Whatever Ullii was thinking, she didn't want to share it with him. She hugged her little triumphs to herself, while problems simply made her close down. She was the most frustrating human being on the planet.

He moved away a couple of steps then glanced at her, covertly. The haggard, haunted look was gone. She *did* have the lattice back, he was sure of it. She just wasn't going to tell him until it suited her.

'What can you see, Ullii?' he said ever so softly, trying to be no more than a whisper in her ear. It took all the self-control he had. He wanted to scream at her – *my friends are being tortured up there. Your friends, too. Do something!*

Again she pretended to strain, screwing up her eyes, clenching her jaw until the sinews of her neck stood out, knotting her little fists.

He wanted to slap her. Was she mocking him? But it was fruitless to go down that path, and it reminded Nish that he was as much to blame for her state of mind as anyone.

SIX

'Tell me what's wrong,' Nish said, taking her in his arms.

'No,' she said, her voice muffled. She went rigid but made no attempt to pull away.

'Where did the lattice come from, Ullii? It really is the most marvellous thing . . .'

'I made it!' she snapped. 'It's mine.' Then, plaintively, 'No one else can understand.'

'Of course they can't. There isn't anyone like you in the world, Ullii. You're unique.' He wasn't just cajoling or flattering her. She *was* unique.

She rubbed her cheek against his chest, not in any suggestive way, but as if it comforted her. In times past she wouldn't have been able to bear the coarse cloth against her skin. Was she losing her sensitivity as well?

'When did you make the lattice?' he murmured to the top of her head.

'When I was five. To look for Myllii.'

'And now that he's gone, you don't need it any longer.' Nish could have kicked himself as soon as the words left his mouth, but it was too late to take them back.

'I don't need it,' she said wonderingly, then with resolve: 'I don't need the lattice any more. I know where Myllii and Yllii are.' She pulled away and sat down, her back against the stone

46

wall, staring into some inner space as if Nish didn't matter either.

Nish knew she meant it. He'd been clinging to the hope that Ullii could somehow perform a miracle, as she'd done to break Irisis out of Nennifer, but it wasn't going to happen.

He couldn't take on hundreds of alert soldiers, all those watching mancers and the scrutators themselves, except by dying with his friends in a symbolic act of defiance. And that would only make the scrutators' victory complete. If they didn't get him, it would be one tiny flaw in their control of the world, he rationalised. He would devote his life to finishing the job Flydd had started – bringing the Council down.

But it wasn't any comfort, and the thought of his friends' approaching torment brought to mind those dying soldiers at Gumby Marth, begging Nish to put them out of their misery. He hadn't been able to; he simply hadn't had the courage, if you could call it that, to put a knife to their throats and end their suffering. Just so had his father begged for death after he'd been maimed by the lyrinx, and Nish had failed him too. He couldn't bear to let his father go, monster though Jal-Nish had become – and look at the misery *that* failure had produced.

Nish couldn't save his friends, but he might be able to give them a quick and merciful death, and spoil the scrutators' victory. Would that be good for the morale of the common people, or a fatal blow in the endless war against the lyrinx? There was no way to tell. He could only try to make the best decision, and leave the world to fate.

Either way, it was something else he'd have to atone for, but it wouldn't be another reckless folly. Recklessness had been burned out of him. He would coolly plan the deaths of his friends and weep for them afterwards. He *would* find the courage this time. But how was he to do it, and how much time did he have? He had to know what was going on in the amphitheatre.

Leaving Ullii to her inner contemplation, Nish fastened her rope to the opening, climbed down to the roof and scuttled across to the outer wall. Clots of mist drifted in the air but he could still be seen if an alert guard chanced to look down. *Or if they realised he was missing.*

47

Sooner or later, someone must discover that Nish was not among the prisoners, and Ghorr would send a squad into Fiz Gorgo to hunt for him. Nish knew he was, relatively speaking, a minor criminal. Nonetheless, his execution would serve as another lesson to all – not even the son of a scrutator was immune from the justice of the Council.

Nish raised his head. There was no one in sight. Voices echoed down from the amphitheatre, though he couldn't tell what was being said. Slight depressions in the taut canvas marked points where groups of people were standing to witness the trials. Unfortunately, he couldn't establish the positions of individuals.

Nish crept to the nearest vertical cable, reached up as far as he could and heaved. He managed to pull himself up a couple of body lengths before his fingers slipped and he slid down again, burning his hands. The cable was thick, taut and smooth, and damp as well; he couldn't grip it tightly enough to hold his weight. He'd never climb it this way.

He went down the inner stairs of the wall to the yard, thence to one of the equipment sheds for an axe. The edge hadn't been sharpened for a while but he couldn't hone it on the wheel without making a racket. It would have to do.

Up on the wall again Nish judged his mark, drew the axe back over his shoulder and swung it with all his strength. The blade bounced off – the cable was as taut as stretched wire. Besides, he realised belatedly, chopping one cable wouldn't make any difference, since the amphitheatre was held up by fifteen of them, each solidly braced with cross-stays.

If he could collapse one side of the amphitheatre, his friends would fall to a merciful death, though that would require the simultaneous failure of at least three adjacent vertical cables. Once that happened the highly tensioned ropes would spring back, tearing the canvas deck apart or forming a slope too steep to stand on. Quick-thinking people near the edges might survive if they caught hold of the remaining ropes, but all those in the centre would fall to the ground or the roofs of the fortress. Not a pleasant way to die, and it wouldn't just be the prisoners, either. Hundreds of soldiers and witnesses might be killed as well.

Nish couldn't dwell on that or he'd never be able to do it. This was war, and there were always casualties. It was the only way to save his friends from their barbaric fate, and at least it would be quick. Neither could he worry about the scrutators being wiped out, leaving the world leaderless at this critical stage of the war. Ghorr left nothing to chance; he'd always have a way out.

How to put his plan into effect? He couldn't do it from the wall – the instant he hacked through the first cable, the soldiers would shoot him down. In any case, cutting the cables down here wouldn't collapse this side of the amphitheatre. Since the cables ran up from the deck to the air-dreadnoughts, they would float up, lifting this side of the deck.

It had to be done just below the deck. If he could climb up, soak three or four cables and their accompanying cross-stays with oil, then set fire to them simultaneously, it could work. If the blazes were big enough, the cables might burn through before the guards could put out the fires.

If, if, *if*. The plan was outlandish and couldn't succeed. It also left unanswered one vital question – how was he to get away afterwards? Nish gave no further thought to that either. After such a crime, it seemed fitting that he'd given himself no way out.

There was a great roar from above and the amphitheatre deck shook as though hundreds of people were stamping their feet. Were the trials over? Were they torturing Flydd already – or flaying Irisis alive?

Nish forced himself to stay calm, to ignore what was happening up there. All that mattered was what he did down here, and only cool thinking could deliver his friends now.

He ran down to Yggur's great coolrooms and larders, where the provisions for Fiz Gorgo were kept. In the second pantry, he discovered what he was looking for: a set of meat hooks hanging from a rail. He selected two that looked suitable, then hacked a slab off a ham and tore at it like a savage while he headed for his room. There he strapped a knife to his belt, his crossbow to his back and filled a deep pocket with quarrels. A flint and steel went in as well.

Tearing a bedsheet into strips he thrust them into another pocket, a pair of leather straps in after, then went down to the lower storerooms where the barrels of whale oil and naphtha were stacked. Though Yggur was capable of making glowing globes powered by the Art, the lamps in Fiz Gorgo generally burned oil. Nish filled a silver wine flagon with distilled naphtha which had probably come all the way from the tar pits of Snizort. After stoppering it carefully, he slipped it into a basket made of woven leather and threw it over his shoulder. Lastly he rummaged in the tool room until he found a clamp shaped like a thumbscrew for a giant. Nish spun the screw out and gauged the space. It was just large enough to fit over one of the vertical cables. He tied it to his belt with a length of cord.

Feeling like a wandering tinker with his load, Nish returned to the wall, laid out his meat hooks and straps and considered how best to bind them on.

'What are you doing, Nish?'

Nish jumped. He'd thought Ullii was still up in the cupola, but her voice came from right behind him. He explained.

Ullii's eyes, which were still unmasked, grew large. She put her hand over her mouth. 'You'll be killed.'

'I expect so,' he said more calmly than he felt. 'But all my friends, save you, are up there. Even if it costs me my life, I won't let Ghorr torture them to death.'

She looked up at the amphitheatre and the colourless hair stirred on her head, as if she could see right through the deck to what the scrutators were doing there. Nish imagined that she could feel the anguish of the prisoners – Ullii had always been sensitive to that kind of thing.

'I'll help you,' she said.

'Thank you,' he said, astounded by the offer, so uncharacteristic of her. 'Though I don't see how you can.'

'I can climb the cable without hooks.'

Since Ullii never exaggerated, he believed her. 'Could you give me a hand with these?'

She strapped the hooks to his wrists more securely than he

could have done himself. He took a deep breath and turned to the cable.

Reaching up as high as he could, Nish dug the hook on his right wrist into the strands of the cable. He had to force it in. He put all his weight on the hook and it held. He pulled himself up, which made his gashed arms throb, and stabbed the other hook at the cable, half an arm's length higher. It skated off the taut fibres. He tried again, carefully judging the angle, and this time the hook dug in. Already his muscles were aching and he'd only gone half a span. Twenty-nine and a half to go.

He would never do it. Just hanging by the arms was exhausting and willpower was not going to be enough. He simply didn't have the strength to climb all that way. Yet, how could he not go on?

With his free hand Nish fumbled at the clamp, tried to get it over the cable, and dropped it. He hauled it up again, wound the screw out as far as it would go and forced it over. One-handed, he tightened the screw and climbed onto the shank, relieving the strain on his wrist at last. Sweat was dripping into his eyes.

Ullii came up the other side of the cable until she was level with him, moving easily. Her eyes met his.

'I can't do it,' he said, fighting back tears of frustration. 'I simply can't do it, Ullii.'

Ullii was holding the cable between her thighs and feet, and pulling herself up with her hands. She didn't seem to be under any strain. She was so slight that he could carry her with one arm, but Ullii was remarkably dextrous.

'I said I'd help you, Nish.'

He couldn't have climbed halfway without her but, with Ullii's help to embed his hooks into the ropes while he rested on the clamp, and then to slide the clamp up and hold it while he screwed it tight, Nish managed to inch his way up the cable, span by span. Even then, when they had but five spans to go and twenty-five extended below them, Nish didn't think he would ever make it. He made the mistake of looking down, whereupon

51

his head spun and his stomach heaved. He wasn't particularly afraid of heights but this was different. He lost his grip and hung by the grace of the right hook while he vomited all down the cable.

Ullii kept her eyes politely averted until his aching belly was empty, then wiped his face on one of his strips of rag and dropped it, fluttering in the damp breeze, into the yard.

'It's not far now,' she said in an overly encouraging voice, like a teacher to a lagging child.

Nish didn't have the strength to reply. Besides, this close to the deck, they might be overheard. He wasn't encouraged. There must come a point where, no matter how strong the will, his muscles would simply not be able to respond. He was almost at that point now. Each time he hauled himself up another arm's length, he had to rest, and the bandage on his left arm was red and soaked.

They went up another laborious span, followed by another. Ullii clung above him, pulling his left hook up as far as it would go and working it into the strands of the cable. Once it was well in, he tried to heave himself up. His muscles refused to move.

'I'm sorry, Ullii,' he said. 'I'm done.'

She looked exhausted too. Her pale face had a grey tinge and her colourless eyes were rimmed with red and yellow. 'I –'

The shout came straight through the canvas: a man's voice, nasal, whiny, and not comfortable with the authority he'd been delegated. 'Quiet, if you please. The executions will now begin.'

Nish's heart hammered at his ribs. Who would it be? Please, let it be anyone but Irisis or Flydd.

A brief pause before the man continued, 'We will take them in order of the trial. The first will be Pilot Inouye.'

Nish caught his breath, then let it out in a rush. To his shame he almost smiled with relief. He caught Ullii's eye, and she looked shocked. She'd identified with the little pilot, of course. How could she not, after Nish's tragic tale?

'Come!' Ullii hissed through her teeth. 'Quickly.' Going hand over hand up the cable, more like a monkey than a human being, she hung on with one hand and began to pull at Nish's arm.

With the last of his strength, his screaming muscles managed to move him up another half-span, more or less.

Someone began shouting up above, a creepy, sibilant voice that had to be the vile Scrutator Fusshte. Nish couldn't make out what he'd said but shortly he heard the whiny voice again, calling, 'No, bring her back, lads.'

After a pause he went on, barely audible over the sighing of the wind through the cables, 'The scrutators bid me execute the greatest criminal and traitor first, in case the enemy should attack. Ex-Scrutator Xervish Flydd,' he said in tones that were almost respectful, 'if you would be so kind as to step into the flensing trough.'

'I'm just in time,' Nish said to himself. 'I will get there. I *must*.' He hauled himself up another half-span and hung on, panting so loudly that he couldn't believe the people above wouldn't hear him.

Ullii fixed his hooks, went down and slid the clamp up the cable. Nish rested on it, trying to still his breathing so he could hear what was going on. Someone was talking in a deep rumble, though Nish couldn't make out what he was saying.

There came a muffled wail, cut off abruptly as if by a hand clapped over a mouth, or a fist thrust into it. The prisoners were cracking up and he still had to climb two spans – the equivalent of four paces on the ground.

And then Irisis spoke and the sound of her voice, defiant to the last, brought tears to his eyes. 'Take heart, Xervish. It'll be over more quickly than you think.'

Flydd laughed, though there was no humour in it. 'Somehow, that's not nearly as comforting as when I said it to you.'

'Begin, Master Flenser!' Chief Scrutator Ghorr roared like an actor on a stage. 'I'll double your fee if you can take this scoundrel's skin off in one piece – I've a special use for it.'

This galvanised Nish's trembling muscles and he went up half a span, then three-quarters before grinding to a halt. Another man spoke, inaudibly. Perhaps he was talking to himself as he prepared to peel the skin off the living flesh.

Nish kept moving. Only one span to go. His muscles felt as

though they were melting and oozing down his arms. He laid his head against the cable, despair washing over him. He was going to be too late to save Flydd.

'Hold just a moment!' cried Scrutator Fusshte. 'There's something wrong.'

Nish only caught part of what the other man, the whiny one, said. 'I've done everything . . . in the rituals.'

Nish's skin crawled, and every hair on his body stood up. He knew what Fusshte was going to say.

Fusshte snarled, 'I'm not talking to you!' Nish heard his feet pound across the canvas. 'One of the greatest villains of all is missing. Where the devil is the arch-traitor, Artificer Cryl-Nish Hlar?'

SEVEN

Above them there was shouting, yelling and the sound of running feet. Ghorr said in low and deadly tones, 'You bloody fool, Fusshte, why didn't you check? You begged to be put in charge of the minors.'

'It's not my fault. I told Voine to go through the list . . .'

'Don't give me excuses!' Ghorr hissed. 'What's the good of my creating this great spectacle if your incompetence is going to ruin it? Morale is a fragile plant, scrutator. Get your men down there and find him instantly. I won't have a single blot on this victorious day. Not a smear. Fail and you'll join the prisoners, scrutator or no!'

Ullii's mouth opened and she almost lost her grip. Nish reached out to steady her. She wiped her face and climbed higher. Looping her arm around the cable, she dragged up his left hook, slammed it into the strands, and then moved the right.

Above them, orders were roared. Feet pounded across the canvas. 'What do we do?' Nish whispered. His mind had gone blank.

'Up!' she mouthed. 'Under!'

He reached up with his weak left arm and forced its hook into the rope. He twisted out the other hook and tried to go again but the left hook pulled out. Nish slipped, clutched at the cable but his sweaty hands couldn't get a grip. Ullii shinned down to him, grabbed his swinging arm and expertly slid the hook in between the strands of the cable. After doing the same with the other hand she went down and tightened the clamp.

Nish clung there, shaking. 'I thought I was gone,' he whispered. 'I thought everything was lost.'

She touched her cheek to his, repaying him in kind, and it made all the difference. She pointed up underneath the canvas and began to climb to the knots where the horizontal stay ropes were fastened to the vertical cable. He followed carefully, the near-death experience bringing him a little strength. He slid his clamp around a stay rope that ran towards the centre of the deck and tightened it so it could slide along but not pull off. Nish went wearily, hook over hook, along the stay until he was five or six spans in from the edge and not so readily visible in the gloom.

'You'd better tie on, Ullii, just in case.'

Ullii fashioned a rope harness around her chest, tied it to the stay rope and hung from it while Nish caught his breath.

Shortly, some thirty or forty spans to their left, a series of rope baskets were lowered over the edge, each containing about a dozen soldiers. The baskets were lowered swiftly to the yard. Nish counted them. Nine – more than a hundred soldiers, just for him, and any one of them could take him. It was enough to make him smile and, thinking about what Fusshte had said, he gave a wry chuckle. So they considered him a great villain. He'd better not disappoint them.

'Don't move,' Nish mouthed. 'If they look this way . . .'

Ullii scowled. She didn't need to be told. It was dark under the canvas, but not so dark that an alert eye couldn't pick them out. And the scrutators' guards were very alert.

They waited until the grounded baskets had emptied and most of the soldiers had disappeared inside Fiz Gorgo. The remainder spread out through the yard and began to search the sheds and barracks.

'Now,' Nish whispered. 'We don't have much time.'

He reached back and lifted the flagon of naphtha over his shoulder. With it banging against his chest, he hooked his way towards the edge of the deck, where the horizontal ropes were tied to the cable in a series of complicated knots the size of melons, and carefully poured a measured dose of the clear, pungent liquid over the knots. The fumes made his eyes water. The liquid was quickly absorbed into the fibres, wetting the cable below for a span and wicking up for half that distance.

'We have to do this to the next three cable knots.' Nish pointed to each of them so she'd not be in any doubt. 'Then I'll set fire to them with flaming crossbow bolts.' He drew a handful of rags from his pocket, poked them in through the mouth of the flagon until they were soaked, squeezed the excess naphtha back into the flagon then put the rags back in his pocket. 'As soon as that's done we go down the ropes as fast as we can, if we get the chance.'

'What if we don't?'

'We die with everyone else.' He expected Ullii to shrivel, for she'd always had the keenest sense of self-preservation, but she didn't react.

'I'm ready to die,' she said. 'Give me the flagon.'

Nish saw the sense in that. He couldn't swing from rope to rope without her help, while she didn't need his.

'If there's any left, reach up and pour it onto the rope that runs around the outside of the deck.'

Ullii nodded, stoppered the flagon, put it over her shoulder and then she was off, swinging hand over hand along the rope, her safety rope dangling below her, unfastened. Nish could hardly bear to watch. One slip, one oily piece of rope or even a place where she couldn't reach far enough up under the tight canvas to get a grip, and she would fall to her death. He moved along his stay rope towards the centre of the deck, so he'd have a good angle for each shot.

Not far away, Ghorr roared, 'Continue with the executions. Master Flenser, get the hide off the old villain without delay. If the lot aren't finished within two hours you'll be joining them.'

Nish heard a rebellious mutter among the master torturers. Evidently it wasn't done to threaten their kind. Trying vainly to put Flydd's torment out of mind, Nish lifted the crossbow off his back and tied it around his waist, in case he needed it in a hurry.

He wrapped a naphtha-soaked rag around one of his bolts, tying it on tightly with threads stripped from the side but leaving a tail of cloth to stream out behind. When satisfied that it would fly true, he slipped it into his pocket and did the same to another handful of bolts. He'd need three to light the three distant knots after he'd set the first one afire, plus a few extras in case he missed or dropped one.

A scream rang out above him – a cry of sheerest anguish – that made Nish's hair stand up. To wring any kind of reaction out of Flydd he must have been in agony – the man had practically invented stoicism.

Ullii, who had already soaked the second knot and was halfway to the third, went still, rotating on her wrists until she was staring at Nish. He waved her on. Until she'd done the fourth knot and turned back, there wasn't a thing he could do.

Before she'd got there, Flydd's screams had become continuous. Nish fitted a bolt into the crossbow, only to discover that he'd lost the flint and steel. It must have fallen out of his pocket when he'd slipped earlier, and without it he had no way to set the naphtha-soaked rag alight.

He felt an urge to throw himself down into the yard for his stupidity. Why hadn't he secured it more carefully? Ullii waved, telling him that he could fire any time. He beckoned her back.

Was there anything he could make a spark with? The amphitheatre was just rope and canvas with an occasional brass fitting – no help there. His pockets contained nothing except dirty lint. The stock of the crossbow was wood and the fittings brass, though the bow itself was steel. Nish wrapped a spare length of soaked rag around the bow then struck across it with the tip of his knife. It made an audible click but didn't result in a spark.

He tried again and again, torn between the need for a spark, now desperate judging by the hideous shrieks coming from above, and the need to avoid detection.

Ullii was halfway back now, flying hand over hand along the rope. She stopped to signal him. He held out his hands. She grimaced – or was it a sneer of contempt? Not securing the flint and steel was an inexcusable blunder.

He kept striking, hoping the sound would be muffled by Flydd's screams, but they stopped suddenly and someone called from the centre of the amphitheatre. 'What was that?'

Nish froze. The shrieks resumed only to break off in mid-cry, as if Flydd had been struck down.

Ullii had stopped, hanging from one hand, but now she resumed, swinging towards him faster than before. He held his breath. One slip and she was gone.

'It's him!' cried Ghorr. 'It's that bloody little bastard Cryl-Nish Hlar. He's down there somewhere. *Find him and bring him to me, alive!*'

There was a stampede across the canvas. Nish struck furiously at the metal, but could not produce a spark. An uproar broke out, a horde of people roaring out his name, laughing, cheering and clapping. The prisoners were cheering him on and Nish felt such a surge of encouragement that for a moment he knew he *could* save them.

Reality crashed down on him as Ghorr roared, 'Shut them up. The snivelling little coward can't do anything.'

'What if he has the seeker with him?' came Fusshte's slithering voice.

Ullii had passed the last knot but now stopped in mid-swing. No man terrified her more than Fusshte did. Nish held out his arms to her and she came on, more slowly, her mouth working.

'Where is the seeker?' said Ghorr.

'I haven't seen her since we took Flydd.'

'And you didn't think to check?' Ghorr's voice became shrill.

'She was in *your* custody, Chief Scrutator,' Fusshte snarled. 'She's your little pet. She must be with him.'

'Of course she is, but we know how to deal with Ullii,' Ghorr said. 'Where's Scrutator T'Lisp?'

'Up on her air-dreadnought.'

'Get her down here right away.'

Nish abandoned his spark-making as hopeless and began sawing at a cross-stay, not that it would make any difference.

No difference at all. His blunt knife made barely any impression on the tough fibres. It would take minutes to cut through, and minutes he didn't have. As soon as one of the soldiers thought to look underneath the deck, they'd be seen. Sharp-shooters could pick them off with crossbows from the ground or through holes cut in the deck, or the mancers destroy them in any number of hideous ways.

Ullii was still about ten spans away when the canvas creaked above Nish, as if someone was creeping across it. He readied the crossbow, knowing that it could make no difference if he shot one soldier, or even ten.

'There's a funny smell over here,' yelled a soldier from near one of the knots Ullii had soaked. 'Like lamp spirit.'

Nish couldn't breathe. A hand appeared over the edge, clutch-ing at the melon-sized knot. It was a long time before the other hand appeared beside it. Perhaps the soldier was afraid of heights.

The soldier's head appeared, bald patch first, looking the other way. Nish readied the bow then froze, hoping vainly that he might not be seen in the gloom, or that the soldier might be careless.

The head turned towards Nish, upside down and red-faced. He did not appear to see him. Nish breathed out, but unfortu-nately Ullii moved.

Nish fired, but not in time to prevent the soldier's triumphant cry.

'He's down here, surr, underneath the deck. And the seek –'

EIGHT

The bolt struck him in the throat, the soldier lost his grip and fell, head-first, as dead as a stone, the naphtha-soaked tail fluttering at his throat like a necktie. But the alarm had already been raised.

An exultant Ghorr shouted, 'Captain, call your men back. T'Lisp?'

There came a mutter that Nish could not decipher, just as Ullii reached him. Then came the scratchy, old woman's voice that sent Ullii crawling into his arms. Nish hooked his way further from the edge and began to reload the crossbow.

'What is your will, Chief Scrutator?' the old woman said breathlessly.

'The seeker is underneath the canvas and I want her, *unharmed*. Use the bracelet and compel her to you, Scrutator T'Lisp. If you can bring the artificer as well, all the better.'

'At once, Chief Scrutator.'

'What are we going to do?' whispered Nish.

Ullii scrunched herself tighter in his arms, whimpering.

'Come on, we've got to get further from the edge!'

They crept in. Nish clamped on securely, eased himself out of Ullii's grip and tied her trailing safety line to the stay rope. He had just gone back to striking sparks when Ullii's eyes rolled up.

'No,' she said in a choked whisper. 'I won't!'

'It's T'Lisp, Ullii, and she murdered our son. Don't give in to her.'

He took her hand but it just lay limply in his. Ullii didn't seem to be there at all. Then all at once her grip grew tight and she jerked him towards her, her eyes now focussed and feral.

'You've got to fight her, Ullii.'

She went for Nish as if it was he who was trying to possess her, clawing, scratching and biting. He fought her off, then slapped her across the cheek.

She put up one hand, staring at him. 'Nish, I'm sorry . . .' Her eyes crossed and she went for him again.

He pushed her away, harder this time. Ullii lost her grip and fell until she reached the limit of her safety line. The harness pulled tight around her chest and the shock broke her free of T'Lisp's compulsion. She hung on the line, slowly revolving, staring into space.

Nish retreated along the rope as quickly as he dared, realised that his hooks were also steel, and swiped at the nearest with his knife, across and back. Not a spark.

A soldier was lowered over the side of the amphitheatre on a line, thirty or forty spans away to his left, followed by a second, a few spans nearer. Nish rotated on his hooks. More soldiers appeared to the right.

Nish struck furiously at the steel. His plan had failed – should he take the easy way out and let go? Suicide wasn't in his nature, but allowing himself to be caught was also suicide, the only difference being in the excruciations Ghorr would put him through first.

Still trying to make a spark, he didn't notice the change that had come over Ullii, the sudden calm and resolve. He didn't see her edging towards him until she was almost within arm's reach. Her face was a mask that showed nothing at all, though her eyes were fixed on him and her free hand clenched and unclenched. She reached up and unfastened her safety rope.

'Ullii,' he hissed, holding the knife out crossways as a barrier. 'What are you doing?'

Her fingers flexed but she did not reply.

'Ullii, Scrutator T'Lisp is controlling you. She's telling you to come after me, isn't she? Is that what you really want to do?'

She hung there for a moment, one-handed, like an acrobat.

'T'Lisp is evil, Ullii,' he went on quickly. 'As evil as Ghorr or Scrutator Fusshte. You've got to resist her.'

'I can't,' Ullii gasped. 'She's too strong.'

'Try with your very heart.'

'I can't do it, Nish.'

'*She killed Yllii!* Try for our son's sake, as you've never tried before. Look for your lattice and use it against her, or the whole world is dead.'

'She said that before,' Ullii whispered. 'She told me I had to help her or you would destroy everything.'

'I may be a fool, Ullii, and I may have done some stupid things in my time, but I don't hold the fate of the world in my hands. The scrutators do.'

'I . . . don't know.' She had to force it out.

'Who do you believe, Ullii? Think of all you know about me, the good and the bad. And then think about the scrutators, and decide whom you can trust.'

Ullii really did try, and the struggle was reflected on her face, then she broke and launched herself through the air at him. Her arms went around his chest and her hands locked in the middle of his back, binding his arms to his sides. She bared her sharp little teeth and went for his throat.

'No, Ullii,' he cried, ducking his head out of the way. The impact had sent him swinging wildly and Nish was afraid his hooks would pull out. He couldn't get his hands up to fix them, and if he managed to break free of Ullii she would fall.

She went for his throat again.

'Ullii, it's Scrutator T'Lisp controlling you. You've got to stop her.' Out of the corner of his eye Nish could see the soldiers fastening their climbing ropes to the horizontal stay cables, preparing to come after them.

'Ullii,' he said, forcing himself to be as measured as possible. 'Would Myllii want you to do this?'

It was the wrong thing to say. 'You killed him,' she screamed, trying to bite his nose. Nish jerked his head sideways and her teeth fastened onto his cheek and sank in through the skin. The pain made him lose control.

'And you're killing me, for the scrutators who killed our son! Can't you get that through your thick skull, you stupid little bitch! You're killing *me*.'

Ullii reacted as if she'd been struck across the face. She threw her head back and her eyes focussed on Nish's bleeding cheek.

He'd broken through, if just for a second. 'Please, Ullii, if there's anything left in the lattice, *use it*.'

Ullii strained, squeezing him so hard that his ribs creaked. A red mist passed before his eyes, Nish came over all faint and her face began to fade, replaced by the oddest vision.

A black, barbed knot, like a spinning ball covered in hooks, was whirling towards him. Other knots near and far were out of focus. He had to be seeing Ullii's lattice. So it wasn't lost after all.

'If I lose it,' Ullii said plaintively, 'I'll have nothing left.'

It took an effort to reply, for he couldn't draw breath. 'You're not going to lose it.'

'It's been fading for weeks. It's nearly gone. To use it will take everything I have left.'

Nish managed to raise his head and open his eyes. 'If you give me up to them, how would you explain that to little Yllii?'

Tears welled in her eyes, as pink as if they'd flowed across caked blood. 'You don't know what you're asking.'

'When Ghorr takes us, he'll torture me to death and give you to Fusshte to play with.'

She drew a deep breath and in his vision the spinning knot slowed then stopped. Glowing filaments extended out in all directions, while the centre went from black to orange to blue-white.

Nish's brain felt as though it had revolved in his head. 'Ullii?' he gasped.

The soldiers jerked on their ropes, one man spinning like a spider dangling from a web, another freezing into a rigid spread-eagle. A third lost his grip and fell.

The clamour from above ceased abruptly. Nish felt a swelling

64

pressure and caught a whiff of charred hair. People cried out in horror or disgust; he could hear them running. Someone retched, right above his head. Then, *boom-splat*, and something heavy thudded onto the deck.

The canvas began to char in the shape of a head and neck. As Nish stared at the blackening fabric, it pinholed and clear fluid began to drip through, followed by a loop of yellow slime that grew ever longer. Droplets of watery blood ran down the dangling thread.

Plop. An eyeball slid through the slowly enlarging hole, dangling from its optic nerve. A red-raw tongue slithered through another hole as the charring spread across the canvas.

Then, to Nish's disgust and horror, a smoking face, bare of skin, flopped down on its skinless, wattled neck. The canvas parted to reveal the other eye, staring at them, *still alive*. It was Scrutator T'Lisp, all that was left of her.

Ullii cried out in horror and tried to throw herself out of the way. Nish crushed her to him with his free arm as the blue-lipped mouth opened, the yellow, angled teeth parted in a smile that was mostly rictus. For a moment Nish thought T'Lisp was going to scream a death spell at him, but a revolting sucking gurgle cut off what she had been going to say. Her jaws were forced open, she heaved once, twice, three times, then her intestines oozed out of her mouth, popping and squelching as they came.

Nish's stomach heaved, though all he brought up was a thin green trickle of bitter bile that burned his throat and mouth. He spat the residue carefully to one side of a now limp Ullii and wiped his mouth with the back of his hand.

By the time he'd finished, the other eyeball had popped out, but the charred canvas gave way under the ruined creature's torso and, thankfully, it fell through.

Framed by the hole, not two spans away, was the horrified face of Chief Scrutator Ghorr, spattered with the indescribable remnants of his former colleague. Red-brown fumes wisped from the sable collar of his coat and, to his left, Scrutator Fusshte was doubled over, choking. Behind him a pair of soldiers reeled in circles as if drunk. Whatever Ullii had done, it hadn't just affected T'Lisp.

'There – are,' slurred Ghorr, sluggishly raising his arm at them.

Acting purely on instinct, Nish swung the crossbow up and fired through the smoking hole. The bolt struck Ghorr in the left shoulder, driving him backwards out of sight.

'Ullii,' Nish gasped. 'Get a grip. You've given us our chance!'

With eyes screwed shut, she reached up for the rope. Nish fumbled a rag-wrapped bolt out of his pocket, slipped it into the groove of the crossbow and wound furiously. He touched the tails of the rag to the smouldering canvas and the rag flared. Taking careful aim at the nearest of the naphtha-soaked knots, he fired.

The bolt went true, embedding itself in the knot, and blue flame flickered there. Nish fired three more flaming bolts; each hit their target. Fire licked up and down the vertical cables and ran around the circumferential ropes between them. It was done.

The people on the amphitheatre began shouting, screaming and stampeding away from the fire, whose flames were already nibbling at the edges of the canvas. The cables were thick and it would take a good while for fire to weaken their tightly woven cores, though the canvas would burn through in a minute. Flame ran up one cable like a wick, causing cries of panic from the scrutators, rightly terrified of an explosion of floater-gas that would threaten all their craft. Two of the soldiers hanging over the side fell, ropes blazing. The others swiftly pulled back out of sight.

'Put it out!' someone screamed.

Across at the nearest knot, cloaks were flapped as the soldiers tried to smother the flames, though after each thump the fire sprang out again.

Someone shouted, 'Water, quickly!'

Nish didn't dare stick his head up through the hole, but he put his ear to the canvas and their voices came clearly to him.

'You can't put out naphtha with water, fool,' came Ghorr's halting voice. Though in much pain, he was still in control. 'Cut up sheets of canvas . . . roll it round the ropes . . . smother it.

Guards – carry me to my lifting chair. What's it doing way up there? Lower it at once. Healer? Where's my healer, dammit?'

'Are we to abandon the executions, then?' said Fusshte. He spoke thickly, as if his tongue had swollen to fill his mouth.

'Of course not,' Ghorr snapped, regaining control of himself. 'The spectacle must go on. The Council has to show that it's in control. We can't be driven away by a renegade traitor and a squeaking mouse.'

'If a spark rises up to one of the airbags and sets off the floater gas –'

'It won't if you take control of the fires. Get on with it! Get a squad of soldiers to each fire and check the rest of the cables. And shut that rabble up.' The prisoners were shouting, cheering and urging Nish on. 'Where's my captain?'

'He's trying to put out the cable fires.'

'Take charge here and calm the witnesses. Order must be restored at once.'

Fusshte ran and gave the commands, then came back. 'And if we can't put out the fires?'

'Have the baskets lowered halfway, just in case,' said Ghorr. 'Separate out the most important witnesses to go in the first lift. Where's my healer? My shoulder . . .'

'He's coming down now. What about the others?' said Fusshte. 'It'll look bad if you sneak off and abandon them.'

'How dare you speak that way!' cried Ghorr. There was a heavy thump, as if he'd slumped to the canvas, and a gasp of pain. 'If the cables burn through, the rest of the witnesses will be sacrificed. They'll be doing their duty. I'll allow no risk to the air-dreadnoughts.'

'What about the prisoners?'

'Let them fall to their doom, all but Xervish Flydd. Without him they're nothing, and I'll see the rest of his blood run before the day is out. Bring Irisis Stirm too.'

'And Cryl-Nish Hlar?'

Nish reached over and lifted the naphtha flagon off Ullii's back. It gurgled satisfyingly. He whipped out the stopper, folded over a twist of soaked rag and screwed it in so that it was tight.

'Take him alive, if you can,' Ghorr said. 'And if you can't, I want him dead with a thousand crossbow bolts in him. I'll not be made a laughing stock by that treacherous little cur.'

'It's a bit late for that,' said Fusshte softly.

'What did you say?' Ghorr hissed.

'You wanted all the credit for this victory for yourself,' said Fusshte in a low and deadly voice. 'So you must take the blame for the scrutators' humiliation and failure.'

'There is no failure,' snarled Ghorr. 'We've got all we came for, and more.'

'But you've lost more, and that's what's going to be remembered. The amphitheatre can't last ten minutes.'

'I've strengthened the cables with our Secret Art.'

'Against *fire*? When it falls, the whole world will know that the chief scrutator has had his nose pulled by a renegade traitor and a squeaking mouse. And won't they laugh.'

'Anyone who so much as smiles will be executed on the spot.'

'Which will only prove that you've lost it. You're finished, Ghorr.'

'Then why aren't you doing anything about it?'

'I'm waiting for you to abdicate.'

'Be damned! Lower my chair, fools,' Ghorr roared.

'Leave it where it is,' Fusshte ordered.

Nish was astounded. Revolt among the scrutators was unheard of. How could he make use of it?

'Yesterday you might have destroyed me with a snap of your fingers,' Fusshte went on. 'After today you won't have the authority. The chief scrutator survives only so long as he proves worthy of the office, Ghorr, and you've failed in front of your fellows. Without my support you'll suffer the same fate as Ex-Scrutator Flydd. Scrutators leave office only one way, as you should know. You made the rule, after all.'

'Where's my chair?' said Ghorr. 'Why isn't it coming?'

'I signalled the operator to pull it back up. The chief scrutator can't flee like a rat from a burning hold. It wouldn't be good for the dignity of the Council.'

'Damn you, Fusshte,' Ghorr ground out. 'I'll see you flayed alive for this.'

'I doubt it,' Fusshte chuckled. 'Look! They've obeyed my orders, not yours. You're finished, Ghorr.'

'We'll see about that.'

'Oh, indeed we will, Chief Scrutator.' Fusshte raised his voice. 'Soldiers, Cryl-Nish Hlar still lurks below. Take him if you can, but if you can't capture him before the amphitheatre collapses, *kill him.*'

NINE

Five soldiers were lowered over the far sides of the amphi-theatre, well away from the flames. They fixed their harnesses to the horizontal ropes and began to inch their way across.

Nish slipped the crossbow onto his back and tied the prepared flagon to his belt. A fierce glee spurred him on. Whatever happened now, he and Ullii had given the Council a slap in the face and his friends a chance to die with dignity. Now what? Fall to his death, or see if he could do a bit more? Fight on, and if the soldiers looked like taking him, he'd jump.

'Ullii!' he whispered. 'We can't stay here.'

She didn't move and her eyes had rolled into her head. She'd hardly budged since she'd killed T'Lisp. Had the horror of what she'd done driven Ullii mad? He shook her gently by the shoulder. She didn't react. He shook her harder.

She slowly turned his way and her eyes rolled down. 'It's too late, Nish. The lattice is gone this time.'

'You can worry about that later,' he said. *If you're telling the truth.* She'd said that before so he doubted her. 'Come on. Up through the hole.'

To his surprise she acted at once, swinging herself up onto the smouldering deck and crouching there. 'Keep a sharp look-out,' he said.

'There's no one looking.' Ullii reached down to him.

'What are they doing?'

She turned her head each way, like a cat. 'Running around like ants.'

Nish adjusted his hooks and managed to stretch a leg up onto the deck. Ullii caught his arm, the injured one, and pulled him through. 'Down!'

He lay on his belly beside her, expecting to see soldiers advancing on them from all directions, but no one was looking towards the small hole burned by T'Lisp's body. He saw only chaos. The vast amphitheatre deck, some hundred and fifty spans across, was wreathed in smoke and drifting mist that concealed swathes of the surface. Fumes trailed up from the canvas in a dozen places. People, or bodies, lay here and there, some twitching and thrashing, others still. Nish assumed that Ullii's lattice-working had brought them down.

Squads of soldiers had gathered around two of the burning cables and were trying to smother the flames by wrapping lengths of canvas about them. It didn't seem to be working. At the other two fires the deck had burned through, leaving nowhere safe to stand. Several soldiers were perched precariously on the ropes, beating at the cables, while the others milled around and an overseer shouted orders from a safe distance.

The rest of the witnesses, numbering some hundreds, had crowded onto a crescent at the far edge of the amphitheatre, as far as they could get from the fires. Squads of anxious-looking soldiers roamed back and forth, trying to keep them in order. The prisoners remained in the centre, in a pen walled with barbed ropes. A squad of Ghorr's personal guard had their crossbows trained on them.

Nish had wondered why the soldiers hadn't attacked in greater strength. Now he realised that there weren't enough. Fusshte had sent more than a hundred down to Fiz Gorgo to hunt for him, and just as many must have been lifted up to the airdreadnoughts after the trials finished. He could see fewer than a hundred on the deck, most of whom were occupied in trying to control the fires, the prisoners or the terrified witnesses.

One of the fires flared up, someone screamed and soon there

was wholesale panic among the witnesses. A small group broke off from the mob and ran. The rest stampeded after them, making waves across the canvas. A group of soldiers tried to restrain them but were trampled. The squad behind them began firing into the crowd, which wheeled and stampeded the other way. Fusshte ran out in front of the stampede, holding up his arms. The leaders stopped dead, only to be trampled by those behind, before the mob finally came to a gasping, groaning halt.

The panic spread to the robed mancers, and then to the other scrutators, who were fruitlessly trying to reach their chairs, which had been left hanging from their air-dreadnoughts as a ready means of escape. Unfortunately the once taut deck had sagged under the weight of hundreds of people, the chairs were now beyond reach, and no one on the air-dreadnoughts seemed to be doing anything about it. Thirty spans off, Ghorr was standing on tiptoe with his back to Nish and Ullii, staring up at his chair, which had been lifted even further and now hung a good ten spans above his upstretched arm. The other arm dangled limply, drenched in blood.

'Lower it!' he screeched, turning round and round.

'He's afraid,' Ullii said wonderingly. And then she laughed. 'The chief scrutator is afraid he's going to die.'

'I never thought I'd see the day,' said Nish, who was beginning to think there might be the faintest chance to rescue the prisoners.

Their side of the deck, which was pitted with holes and smoking patches of canvas, was empty apart from the soldiers desperately trying to smother the cable fires. Belching black smoke kept driving them away and at once the fires sprang out anew. Officers ordered them back but the soldiers were becoming more reluctant every second.

The prisoners were crowded together in their pen, some shouting, some jeering, others watchfully silent. Their fate was all too clear once the cables burned through. Nish counted their guards – eleven. Far too many for him to deal with. His greatest fear was that the soldiers would be ordered to slay the prisoners before the amphitheatre was abandoned.

On the far edge, opposite the fires, a large ropework basket was being lowered to the deck. A group of witnesses rushed it and began fighting to get inside. A meagre, snake-like scrutator, probably Fusshte though it was difficult to be sure through the wreathing mist, roared at them to stay back. No one took any notice. Beyond it a lowered net had been commandeered by a group of robed mancers, who might have been able to control the crowd had they not been so intent on saving their own skins.

The mancers' net rose jerkily into the air, pulling those inside into a compressed jumble of bodies with arms, legs and heads protruding through the meshes. At least Nish no longer had to worry about them. A scrutator was lifted, in a series of jerks, up into the smoky mist in her suspended chair. Nish didn't recognise her.

The utter confusion gave Nish an idea. He didn't think he could reproduce Fusshte's sibilant tones, but he could probably do a passable imitation of Ghorr's deeper voice and it might make a difference.

Crouching down so that he couldn't be seen clearly, Nish put his hands around his mouth and roared. 'Guard! To me. *To me!*'

The men guarding the prisoners' pen spun around, searching for their master. Ghorr had his good arm in the air and was still shouting for his chair, though from a distance it might well have seemed that he was crying for them to come and restore order.

'To me, damn you,' Nish yelled.

The guards conferred. Eight of them formed into lines, four by two, and marched in the direction of the chief scrutator. Off to Nish's left, blue flames flared then ran up a cable for several spans. A horizontal stay rope gave with a ping; canvas snapped like a sail in a high wind. A woman shrieked, high and shrill.

Someone sang out, 'It's going!'

The beaters at the burning cable abandoned their posts and fled to the safe side of the deck. One man ran across a hole burned in the canvas and disappeared.

There was pandemonium among the witnesses. One of their guards dropped his weapons, ran to the nearest cable, kicked off

73

his boots and went up it like a sailor up a mast. Others moved to join him.

'Stop!' shouted Ghorr.

The soldier kept climbing towards the air-dreadnought.

'Captain,' raged Ghorr, 'take him down.'

The mist was thickening all the time and Nish couldn't see who Ghorr was giving orders to, though he could see the soldier, who was still climbing desperately. The man looked down in terror, tried to pull himself out of the way of the bolt then threw up his arms and fell. Streaming mist cut off the scene, though Nish could well imagine what was going on. Ghorr was still shrilling orders but Nish could no longer make them out.

'Now!' Nish said urgently. 'Ullii, could you –?' He looked around. Ullii had vanished.

He cursed her under his breath, in a rueful sort of way, though he should have been used to it by now. Fitting a bolt to his crossbow, Nish flitted from mist patch to mist patch, towards the prisoners' pen.

Three guards remained, still covering the prisoners with their crossbows. They looked nervous and it wouldn't take much for them to go on the rampage. How could he overcome them, all alone? He still had the naphtha flagon over his shoulder but didn't dare use it. Like as not, such a blaze would kill everyone.

A soldier came running through the murk, calling out to the guards. He gasped out an order then turned back. The first guard nodded and returned to the pen, hefting his crossbow as if to shoot.

Nish aimed at the centre of the soldier's back and fired. The soldier grunted and fell. The others whirled, raising their weapons. Nish lay still, carefully fitting a bolt to his bow but not daring to wind back the cranks, for the sound would give him away instantly.

They were looking in his direction and must know roughly where the shot had come from. The leading soldier saw him, aimed and fired in one smooth, well-trained movement.

Nish threw himself to one side and the bolt carved a painful streak down the outside of his thigh. He came to his knees, frantically winding his cranks as the second soldier brought up his weapon. Nish squeezed the lock but the bolt, which hadn't been seated properly, shot out sideways and landed on the deck beyond his reach.

Nish looked up despairingly. The prisoners pressed up against the barbed ropes, staring at him. He could sense them willing him on but there was nothing he could do.

'It's the artificer,' said the first soldier. 'Take his weapon, Ragge. Chief Scrutator Ghorr will pay a fortune for him alive.'

'But not necessarily whole,' grinned Ragge.

'Ghorr didn't say anything about whole.'

Ragge drew his knife, a long, curving blade that would have been ideal for gutting a buffalo. 'He won't mind if I take a little trophy. It'll go for a pretty price in the markets when we get back.'

Nish slid one hand into his pocket for another bolt.

'Move your hand again and my friend here will take it off at the wrist,' said Ragge. 'He's the best shot in the Guard.'

Nish palmed the bolt but kept his hand where it was. The soldier could shoot him before he got it out of his pocket. Ragge's eyes were red-veined, his mouth twisted in a sick kind of malice. Such were the people that Ghorr gathered around him. No man could serve such a monster without having his own hefty dose of evil.

'Get up,' said Ragge.

Nish came to his knees and tried to rise.

'Stay just like that,' grinned the guard.

'You like them on their knees, don't you,' said the other. 'Come on – this place could collapse any minute.'

'It'll be a while yet. Its strength comes from the cross-stays, not the canvas.' Ragge came towards Nish, the knife held low. He would strike upwards to maim, and it would be a difficult blow to evade.

Then, from the corner of his eye, Nish saw the most astonishing sight – a tall figure flying over the fence of the prisoners' pen as if fired from a catapult. Yellow hair streaming out behind her, Irisis came down, hands still bound, and kicked with both feet at the guard with the crossbow.

The blow would have been perfect except that she hadn't been thrown quite far enough. She didn't strike the soldier in the back of the neck, as she'd intended, but between the shoulders.

The impact drove him to the deck, where he landed so hard that the crossbow went skidding across the canvas. Unfortunately it didn't go off.

'Look out!' Nish cried, rolling out of the way of the knife.

Irisis landed awkwardly, bounced on her feet and went for the fallen crossbow. Ragge had spun around at the melee. He ran towards his comrade, then turned to Irisis when it became evident she would reach the crossbow first, though it was moot whether she could use it effectively with bound hands.

Nish slipped his bolt into the slot and back-pedalled, winding his cranks. Ragge spun on one foot, looking from him to Irisis. Nish's crank was half wound, enough to fire though not to do much damage.

Irisis reached the fallen crossbow and snatched at it, but could not pick it up cleanly. She was just raising it when the other guard threw himself at her and tore it out of her hands.

Irisis went down hard. The guard stood up and aimed the crossbow at her face. Nish froze. His weapon was fully wound now but he couldn't decide what to do. If he shot at Ragge, the other man would surely kill Irisis. But if he fired at Irisis's attacker and didn't kill him instantly he and Irisis would both die, for Ragge would gut him before he could reload.

Nish swung the bow from Ragge to Irisis's attacker.

The man deliberately gave his crank another wind. 'Put it down,' he grated, 'or I'll shoot her in the face.'

Disfigurement was the thing Irisis feared most. She'd always been vain about her looks. Ragge wore a loutish grin and Nish knew he had no choice. He'd sooner lose his own life than see Irisis suffer so.

He fired without warning, not for her attacker but for the man's crossbow. It was not an impossible shot for an accomplished archer, as he was, but it was a difficult one, the soldier being a good ten spans away. If he missed, or the soldier managed to fire first, at least Nish wouldn't have long to regret his folly and Irisis's ruin.

The bolt struck the soldier's right hand, then the lock of the crossbow, knocking the bow sideways. The soldier shrieked, jerked it back towards Irisis's face and squeezed the lock.

At least he tried to, but nothing happened. He looked down stupidly to discover that the bolt had taken off his fingers. That was all Nish had time for. Ragge, taking in the situation at a glance, lunged at Nish with the knife. Nish hurled the useless crossbow at the soldier's head but he ducked out of the way.

Nish went backwards, fumbling for his small, blunt knife. Ragge laughed when he drew it and slashed the air in front of Nish's face. Nish went the other way, straight into a left hook that lifted his feet off the canvas. As he hit the deck, Nish realised that he hadn't even seen it coming.

He landed on his back and the knife went flying. Nish's head was ringing. He looked up dazedly as Ragge put a large foot squarely in the middle of his chest and reached lower down with the knife.

'Trophy time, traitor.'

Without further word, or even a change in expression, he fell forward on his face, the huge knife puncturing the canvas beside Nish's arm. The thick legs knocked the wind out of him.

Nish rolled over and dragged himself out. The bolt had struck Ragge in the back of the neck, severing the spine and killing him instantly. Irisis was on her feet ten spans away, holding the other crossbow in her bound hands. The soldier who'd attacked her was backing away, staring at the bloody stubs of his fingers. She brandished the bow at him and he stumbled off into the mist.

Irisis came across, holding out her hands, and he cut her bonds with the big knife. She set down the crossbow, and Nish saw that the lock lever was bent to the left. It was a wonder she'd been able to fire it at all. Irisis embraced him.

'You look grotesque. What on earth have you been up to?'

Nish rubbed his sweaty, sooty, flaking cheeks. 'It'd take too long to tell.'

'That was a brave thing you did, Nish.'

'It might have failed. I could easily have missed and then you –'

A shadow crossed her beautiful face. 'But you didn't. You trusted your judgment and your skill and they didn't let you down. Come on, your cables can't have much left in them. Whose mad idea was it to set fire to them?'

'Mine. I . . .' He hesitated, not knowing how she would react. 'I thought it better to kill the lot of you than leave you to Ghorr's brutal mercies.'

'Quite right. I would have done the same for you.'

'How did you get out?' he said as they hurried across to the pen.

'I stood on Yggur's clasped hands and he catapulted me over the wall, as if he had the strength of ten men.'

'Really?' said Nish. The bound and mostly gagged prisoners were trying to crawl out of the pen. He hacked through the barbed ropes.

Inouye, the little pilot, was on her knees on the deck. He tore off the gag, cut her hands free and she fell on her face. He left her there, for there wasn't time to look after her.

'Where's Flydd?' Nish was terrified that he'd find him a bloody, flayed corpse, and he wouldn't be able to deal with it. He couldn't see him anywhere.

'He's over at the flensing trough.' Irisis jerked her thumb into the throng. 'But first we take care of the able-bodied.'

She was right. The strongest and the most powerful must be freed first. And the most powerful were Yggur, Malien and the strange mathemancer, Gilhaelith. Nish couldn't see Malien and didn't know what to make of tall, woolly-headed Gilhaelith. He found Yggur on the other side of the pen, struggling furiously with his bonds, and surrounded by a halo of uncanny mist that made him difficult to pick out in the hazy gloom. The gag had been pulled down to reveal a corner of his mouth, and that had been enough for him to use his Art.

Nish came up behind and caught his bound wrists, intending to free him. Yggur whirled and Nish gasped 'Friend!' as the knee went for his throat, a blow that could well have killed him.

Yggur pulled the blow, which merely thumped Nish hard in the shoulder. Nish ducked behind him and hacked through the wrist ropes, taking off a good bit of skin in the process. Yggur didn't flinch. Nish slid the knife under the gag, cutting the cloth.

Yggur staggered. He'd been beaten, evidently, and was not at his best, but he flashed Nish a savage grin. 'Let's get to them. Free Fyn-Mah and Flydd, if he's still alive, then the others. But not Gilhaelith. He's more trouble than he's worth.'

'But surely any help is better than none?' Nish glanced at the tall mancer, whose look of black rage boded ill once Gilhaelith was free.

'If it hadn't been for him we wouldn't be here now,' Yggur said.

Nish didn't understand, but there was no time to ask what Yggur meant. 'What about Malien and Tiaan?'

'Ghorr has already sent them up to the air-dreadnoughts.' Yggur was shaking his hands to restore the circulation. Now he raised his fists high, as if calling power to himself, then snapped them down. Mist condensed in a series of crescent-shaped clouds around the pen and Yggur spun it into a smoky brown doughnut around them.

'There's not much time,' said Nish, cutting the bonds of the prisoners one by one. They had formed a line in front of him, and another before Irisis. Yggur's retainers were nothing if not disciplined. 'The cables must burn through any time now and, once they go, this side of the amphitheatre will collapse.'

'I don't think it'll collapse from the loss of four cables,' said Yggur. 'It should just sag. But once the scrutators have saved their necks, and those retainers they can't do without, they'll cut the deck free from above, no matter how many of their loyal servants remain on it.'

Once all the prisoners other than Gilhaelith had been released, which took only a minute or two, Nish handed his crossbow and bolts to one of Yggur's surviving soldiers and went looking for Irisis.

'Where's Flydd?' he said to Yggur as their paths crossed.

'He was at the flensing trough.' Yggur grimaced as he pointed into the mist.

'I'll go after him. Have you got a plan?'

'Fight for our bloody lives!'

'With two crossbows and a couple of knives?'

'It's a whole lot better than we had five minutes ago.'

Yggur began to form the smoky mist into spectres and walking corpses bearing the faces of the witnesses, which he sent drifting across the deck. Someone screamed in horror or despair, others joined in and shortly the witnesses stampeded again.

Putting his hands up to his mouth, Yggur made a series of barking sounds that reverberated across the amphitheatre and back. After a short silence there came, from the slough that surrounded Fiz Gorgo on three sides, the hair-raising cry of a lyrinx. At least, it sounded like a lyrinx. The mist broke, only to re-form more tightly. The soldiers called to one another in voices tinged with fear. The air-dreadnoughts might not fear the lyrinx when high in the sky on a clear day, but they were perilously vulnerable tethered here in poor visibility.

Other lyrinx cries came from all around and suddenly there was uproar. Nish heard the snapping twang of dozens of crossbows as the soldiers fired madly into the mist-shrouded swamps, thinking that the enemy were attacking. Nish wasn't entirely sure that they weren't. The scrutators and mancers, no doubt clinging to their escape chairs, were screaming to be lifted to safety.

'They're calling the enemy against us,' came Ghorr's outraged voice. 'Kill them! Kill them all. A thousand gold tells for the heads of *each* of the chief villains, including Crafter Irisis and Artificer Cryl-Nish. A hundred tells for each of the others, dead or alive.'

Nish squinted into the mist. Oh for a crossbow and a glimpse of his enemy. He would have sent a bolt through the chief scrutator with no more thought than stepping on a cockroach.

Dead or alive. He stopped, one foot in the air, then cast a look over his shoulder. A thousand tells was a colossal fortune, more than an officer could earn in ten lifetimes. And all anyone had to do to earn it was kill him.

'There must be a hundred soldiers out there,' he said to Yggur.

'I dare say,' said Yggur, 'though most are keeping order among the witnesses or protecting their masters while they scramble to safety. Go across to the edge of the mist, Nish, and – *wait!*'

Nothing happened for a tense moment; then a soldier, in the uniform of Ghorr's personal guard, put head and right shoulder through the mist, sighted on the nearest person, Yggur's elderly cook, and fired. The bolt took her in the ribs beside the heart and she dropped without a sound. The soldier ducked back into the mist before anyone could return fire.

Yggur let out a roar of fury and, thrusting out his fist, he spun in an arc, flailing shards of ice into the mist.

Nish heard a grunt of pain and the thump of a body hitting the canvas. Yggur ran into the mist and came back, dragging the offending soldier by the throat. In a colossal feat of rage, Yggur lifted the man high with one hand.

'Is this the quality of the chief scrutator's guard, that you only dare make war on unarmed old women? No wonder the Council is losing the war.'

'Condemned – criminal,' gasped the soldier. 'Price – on head – hundred tells.'

'You won't be collecting it, my friend.' Yggur spun the soldier in the air, caught him as he turned upside down and drove him, head-first, straight through the canvas deck to the hips, where he wedged, caught by his belt, his thick legs kicking.

Avoiding the thrashing boots, Yggur stripped the soldier of knife, sword and bolt bag, and tossed them to two of his men. He kicked the fallen crossbow to another.

Two more soldiers hurtled out of the mist, but at that moment, with an enormous *twang*, one of the vertical cables snapped. The amphitheatre shook as if it had been hit by an earthquake and a hip-high wave passed across the canvas, tossing everyone off their feet. Before the soldiers could get up, the prisoners had swarmed over them. Red pooled on the canvas.

A smaller wave reflected back from the other side. Nish glanced up at the tethered air-dreadnoughts, which were just outlines in the mist. The one whose cable had snapped shot upwards and disappeared. Ghorr roared imprecations at the sky. Nish could not make out the words but Ghorr's tone conveyed his alarm. The air-dreadnoughts had been moored so close together that uncontrolled flight was a danger to them all.

'Any minute now they'll rush us,' said Yggur. 'Nish, take your knife and cut out the canvas on three sides of a long rectangle, like this, but leave a strip at each corner.' He made a shape in the air. 'Round there and there.' He gestured to his left. 'Flangers, take one of the swords and do the same to the right, around to there. And remember where you've cut. Don't fall through on the way back.'

'What about behind us?' said Flangers.

'We'll keep watch. Though, with the fires over there, I doubt they'll attack that way.'

'I'm sure they want us to think that,' Flangers muttered.

Nish cut the canvas where Yggur had indicated, so the deck looked more or less whole. The cuts looked obvious to him, but might well trap a soldier charging through the mist, intent on gold and glory.

In the meantime, Yggur set out his other guards on either side of the holes, with barbed lengths of rope stretched on the deck between them. He had dispersed the remaining prisoners behind the pen and wherever else they could find any cover. And then they waited.

'What if we were to try and climb down one of the cables?' said Nish, acutely aware that time was running out.

'We'd fall,' said Yggur. 'Climbing down ropes is harder than it looks.'

Nish unfastened the naphtha flask and handed it to Yggur. 'You may be able to do something with this.' He had no patience for waiting. Judging by those earlier screams, Flydd could be dying now, or dead.

Nish slid into the swirling mist, keeping low and moving slowly. He wondered where Ullii had got to. Well, she could take care of herself. A pity he hadn't got a better glimpse of the amphitheatre before Yggur brought the mist down – Nish wasn't sure he was going the right way. A big man-shape loomed up to one side and Nish flattened himself to the deck. It was another of Ghorr's guard, sword held out in front of him. The soldier didn't look Nish's way and disappeared again.

A sudden whiff of smoke caught in the back of his throat. Surely the remaining cables, tough and tightly woven though they were, must go soon. He moved on, looking around fearfully, only to crash his knee into an elongated object like a metal bathtub with a wide platform around the edges – the flensing trough. The mist was now so thick that he couldn't see all of the trough at once, though he could see blood spattered on the bottom and stains running down to the plughole.

Behind him there were roars and the clash of sword on sword. The soldiers had attacked. Should he run back? No point – he was unarmed. If Yggur couldn't stave off the attack, there was nothing Nish could do.

He heard a cry, trailing off. Someone had broken through one of the canvas flaps. Nish rubbed his throbbing kneecap as he edged around the bathtub.

He scanned the deck. He could hear fighting not far away, but couldn't see a soul. He turned the other way and his eye fell on someone huddled under the flensing trough, wrapped in a bloodstained cloth. The face was so wracked that for a moment Nish didn't recognise it. And when he did, Nish wished he hadn't.

'Xervish!' he whispered.

The dark eyes turned slowly to him, though there was no recognition in them. 'I am unmanned,' he said and closed his eyes again.

Nish put his hands under Flydd's arms and hauled him out. Flydd couldn't stand up so Nish hefted the scrutator in his arms. He didn't weigh much at all. He headed back to where he thought the punishment pen must be, but hadn't gone far before he was thrown off his feet by another deck-shaking *twang*. The second cable had gone. If the fire was steadily eating its way around the edges of the canvas, it couldn't be long before the whole structure collapsed.

The deck wasn't nearly as taut as before; Nish now found himself walking down a perceptible slope. He carried Flydd back towards the pen, but as he loomed up out of the wreathing smoke, someone leapt for him.

'Xervish?' It was the small figure of Perquisitor Fyn-Mah, who looked almost as haggard as Flydd. 'Is he all right?'

'I don't know,' said Nish. 'Would you look after him?'

Fyn-Mah took Flydd from Nish's arms. There were tears in her eyes. 'No man should have to suffer so, no matter what the crime. What has happened to our humanity?'

'The scrutators devoured it to keep themselves in power,' said Nish, and walked away before he wept with her.

T EN

Nish crept back through the brown miasma, moving carefully. He encountered several bodies – two soldiers and one of the prisoners – and then the barbed rope. 'Don't shoot,' he yelled, keeping well down. 'It's me, Nish.'

Irisis was out in front of a small band of prisoners, swinging a length of barbed rope. Several more prisoners were armed but there were no attackers to be seen.

'We've got to find a way down, and quick,' said Nish, running towards them.

'What if we made canvas slings and used them to slide down a cable?' said Irisis.

'Too dangerous,' said Yggur.

Another cable went with a whip crack; a sinuous heave of the canvas threw bodies in the air and everyone off their feet. He felt as if the deck had smacked him under the chin. Screams from the far side of the amphitheatre trailed away to nothing.

'They shouldn't have been so close to the edge,' said Yggur, shaking his head as the deck stilled; then it sagged beneath them to form a broad valley a couple of spans deep at the bottom. There were shouts of 'Look out!' from above, followed by the sound of breaking timbers. Two air-dreadnoughts had collided.

'What if we cut a couple more cables?' said Nish. 'The deck might sag enough for us to slide down it onto the roof.'

'It'd throw us off.'

'We could cut holes through the canvas and tie onto the stay ropes. When the deck drops low enough we slide to safety.'

'If we tie on, we'll be helpless when they attack.'

'If the deck's that steep they won't be able to come after us,' Nish retorted. 'Anyway, they'll be too busy trying to save themselves.'

'It doesn't pay to underestimate the scrutators!' snapped Yggur. 'Nonetheless, it's the best plan we have. Nish, take one of the soldiers' swords and hack the cable away over to your right, past the last burning one. Flangers, do the same on the other side. If the deck still stays up, sever the one after that, but be quick about it. If the air-dreadnoughts cut us loose first, we're dead.'

'Surely they won't do that while they still have hundreds of soldiers and servants down here.'

'And still you underestimate Ghorr,' growled Yggur. 'Once the Council have been winched to safety, they'll happily abandon everyone else before they risk their own lives. Tie on securely – and watch for backlash when the cables go.'

'I'll give you a hand,' said Irisis, turning to walk with Nish. She slipped her left hand into his, swinging the barbed rope in her right.

They crept through the uncanny mist, which was thicker than ever near the deck, though it did not extend far up. Nish caught occasional glimpses of the air-dreadnoughts through it. The soldiers and crew were hanging over the sides, calling down, and men stood at windlasses to wind the scrutators and important witnesses up, though no one had yet been raised more than a few spans. 'They seem to be having trouble with the winches,' said Nish. 'Is that also Yggur's doing?'

'I expect so. He's an extraordinary man, Nish.'

'It makes all the difference having you with me,' Nish said. 'I don't feel frightened any more.'

'Nor should you, with me looking after you.' She grinned.

'I didn't mean it that way.'

'Anyway, you've got nothing to worry about, Nish. I know *you're* going to survive the war.'

'We're both going to survive it, Irisis, and live to a grand old age, and be greatly honoured.'

'I may well be honoured but I won't be around to see it.'

Irisis was prone to making gloomy statements like that. She had a strong belief in her own mortality, and since Nish didn't know what to say, he just squeezed her hand.

They were close to the edge now. 'Careful here,' she went on. 'If that last cable burns through you'll be over the side before you can pick your nose.'

'I don't pick –' he began.

She gave a snort of laughter. 'Oh, Nish, you're so predictable.'

'Did you predict I'd climb the ropes and set fire to the amphitheatre, just to save your wicked and worthless life?' he said, nettled.

'I knew you'd do something. I just didn't see how it could work.'

'It hasn't yet,' he reminded her.

'It's infinitely better than it was twenty minutes ago. I'll happily die with you beside me.'

'You might have put that better.'

Nish felt with his boot for one of the stay cables, cut a strip out of the canvas and used it to tie on. Irisis did the same.

'Better hurry,' she said, glancing up. 'Once that lot reach the air-dreadnoughts they'll cut us loose and go.'

He followed her gaze. Three nets and a basket jammed with people were being hauled up, jerk by jerk. Many other ropes dangled down through the mist. It was well into the afternoon now; surely no more than two hours to sunset. Ghorr must be getting worried.

Though there was just the gentlest of breezes here, higher up the wind was whistling through the rigging of the air-dreadnoughts, shaking them from side to side. Every jerk pulled on the cables, which groaned as they stretched and contracted. Somewhere, not far off, a man was moaning, the same shivery sound over and over.

Nish caught a sudden whiff of blood. 'Let's get on with it.' He put his sword to the cable and began to saw back and forth.

The blade was sharp, but the tough fibres parted reluctantly. 'It's as if some other force is holding them against me,' said Nish.

'What twaddle,' Irisis said good-naturedly. 'You're just making excuses. Give me a go.'

She took the blade and drew it back and forth a couple of times. One or two strands severed but the rest held. 'Maybe you're right; the air does have the tang of scrutator magic. Perhaps they've cast a glamour to strengthen the cables.' She handed the sword back. 'Go harder.'

He hacked away. A strand parted with a ping, curling out of the weave and running up the cable for half a span.

'Pull me up, damn you!' Ghorr's cry came echoing down in a sudden silence.

'His struggle with Fusshte goes on,' said Nish. 'Without it, I wouldn't have had a chance.'

'I suspect Yggur had a hand in that too,' said Irisis.

'What do you mean?'

'He couldn't do anything, bound and gagged as he was. But once we realised you were free I managed to rub the gag down from the corner of Yggur's mouth with my shoulder, when the guards weren't looking. He used his Art to strengthen the mist and create illusions that heightened Ghorr and Fusshte's distrust of each other. It wasn't much but it made a difference.'

Nish paused to wipe the sweat out of his eyes, and as he did, something moved in the mist to his left, further around the circumference of the deck.

'What was that?' he said out of the corner of his mouth.

Irisis glanced casually to her right, fingering the coil of barbed rope, her only weapon. 'I can't see anything. Keep going. You've hardly made an impression at all.'

'I'm doing my best,' he grunted.

'Put the sword down and step away from the cable.'

The voice, which was vaguely familiar, came out of the mist. Nish was trying to work out who it could be when a very short man appeared, a handsome dwarf with a leonine mane of dark hair. His short cloak dragged on the deck and he walked with the lurching gait of a drunken sailor, for his left leg was supported by metal calipers. The dwarf's hand was held out before him, the fist partly concealing a small brass object.

'Scrutator Klarm,' said Nish, giving a last hack before allowing the sword to fall to his side.

'I have a knoblaggie in my hand,' said Klarm. 'I'd prefer not to waste it, but I will if you force me to. You'd never cut it anyway. Come with me, please. You too, Irisis Stirm,' he said as she backed into the mist. 'If you run, I'll make Nish suffer for it.'

'Run anyway,' said Nish, casting a frantic glance at her. Irisis stayed put, as he'd known she would.

'You know what they'll do to us, Scrutator Klarm,' said Nish. The dwarf scrutator was reputed to be a fair man.

'The law is the law and you are traitors,' said Klarm, 'tried and convicted under the code of the scrutators. We can't afford to be merciful, no matter how much we might wish it. And I do – you're a brave man, Nish; a legend in the making. As for you, Irisis Stirm –' he bowed in her direction and Klarm had such presence that it didn't seem a ridiculous gesture '– I acknowledge both your courage and your loyalty. And I've always admired Xervish, but division at such a time must be fatal.'

'Flydd cleaved to his oath even after the Council had cast him out and condemned him to slavery,' said Nish. 'Do you know what finally caused him to rebel?'

'There's no time – very well, be quick.'

'It happened at Snizort, after my colossal stupidity put Tiaan into the hands of Vithis the Aachim. Ghorr demanded that my father prove his worthiness to be a scrutator by passing sentence on me for my folly. Or, as Ghorr saw it, my treachery. And father did. Jal-Nish condemned me to a brutal, shameful death, not to mention the knowledge that I would be expunged from our family Histories. Scrutator Ghorr was so pleased that he made my father a full scrutator on the spot.'

Nish met the dwarf's eyes and went on. 'When Flydd heard what he had done – and I remember his very words, for I've never seen him so shocked and disillusioned – Flydd said, *For the chief of scrutators to encourage such a deed, to demand it as proof of worth to become scrutator, shows that the Council is corrupt to the core.* At that very moment, Flydd repudiated his oath and swore that Ghorr had to be brought down, and the Council with him. And that he, Xervish Flydd, would devote the rest of his life to doing so. It was a moment I will never forget.'

It shook Klarm too. Nish saw it in his face. 'Surely you knew that, surr?' he went on.

'I wasn't there,' said Klarm. 'I knew only what I was told. I'm not a member of the Council, and the Council does not publicise its doings.'

'But you do believe me?'

Klarm let out an age-weary sigh. 'I can read men, Cryl-Nish. I know truth when I hear it. Nonetheless, this is the only council we have and the world can't survive without it. Put down your blade, untether yourselves and come with me.'

Nish could no longer see the knoblaggie concealed in Klarm's hand, and didn't want to find out what it could do to them. Klarm might well be an honest man but he was as hard as any of the scrutators, and they didn't bluff.

'Pull me up *now!* You'll pay for this, you fools!' Ghorr's voice was perfectly clear this time.

They all looked up but Yggur's mist had come in again and Nish could only see the cables disappearing into brown.

'That's Ghorr!' said Irisis. 'I'll never forget that voice if I live to be a hundred. It echoes in my nightmares.'

'What congress have you had with the chief scrutator?' said Klarm.

'Not the kind you're thinking of,' she snapped. 'He beat me black and bloody in Nennifer, a dozen times at least.'

'Ghorr *beat* you?' Klarm said incredulously.

'He was too clever to let it show, but after each visit I couldn't stand up for a day, or sit down. He inflicted all manner of excruciations on me and enjoyed every moment of them.'

Klarm frowned. 'I –'

The mist parted up above as if Yggur had blown it away and Nish saw the remaining air-dreadnoughts straining at their cables like party balloons in a gale. They were swinging back and forth in the wind, their multiple airbags bouncing against each other and the rigging in mortal danger of tangling. Their motions jerked the cables and rippled the deck, and sent the ropes of the hanging chairs and baskets swinging in wild arcs.

'There's Ghorr,' said Irisis. 'They're finally pulling him up.' The chief scrutator was swaying in the air halfway between his air-dreadnought and the deck.

'I wonder what the matter is?' said Nish. 'They started hauling him up ages ago.'

'Get on with it, you fools!' screamed Ghorr, his face purple with rage.

'The windlass has jammed,' said Irisis, who had exceptionally keen eyes. 'Or broken. Looks as if they're trying to move his rope to a hand winch.'

'Surely they'd have to lower him first,' said Nish, whose artificer training had taught him that much. He tried to see across to where Flangers was cutting the other cable but mist still clung to the deck.

'You'd think so,' said Klarm. The rope dropped sharply, whereupon Ghorr screamed at the operators. 'But . . . he's *afraid*!'

'Afraid?' Nish glanced down at the dwarf scrutator. There was a strange light in his eye. Revelation? Could they sway Klarm in so little time?

'The chief scrutator has failed in front of the witnesses he was trying to impress.' Klarm shook his head in disgust. 'This whole spectacle – the attack on Fiz Gorgo, this marvellous amphitheatre, the trial and punishment – was designed for one purpose. To impress the artists, recorders, tale-tellers and witnesses with Ghorr's power, reach and implacable resolve to extinguish all opposition. But he overreached himself and the failure only reveals his folly.'

'The air-dreadnoughts had to be close together to hold up the amphitheatre,' said Nish.

'Which shows what a vainglorious notion it was. The Council advised him against the scheme,' Klarm said quietly. 'I suggested a less extravagant trial, but Ghorr had spent too long planning this spectacle and would not be dissuaded.'

'Why didn't he take us back to Nennifer or Lybing, for public trial?'

'I cannot say. I –' Klarm broke off as something else occurred to him. 'Can Ghorr have been *afraid* of Flydd?'

'Perhaps he was,' said Irisis.

'And now he's failed in front of his own witnesses,' Nish added. 'And he knows the penalty for failing the Council.'

'Not to mention losing his carefully constructed place in the Histories,' said Irisis.

'There's nothing he can do about that,' said Klarm.

'Unless . . .' Nish looked Klarm in the eye and knew that he'd reached the same conclusion. 'Unless Ghorr should be the only one of the Council to return.'

'He wouldn't go that far,' Klarm said unconvincingly. 'Ghorr is a man who knows his duty.'

'All the witnesses would have to die as well,' said Nish.

'Just the artists and recorders,' said Irisis. 'His own people from Nennifer won't dare talk.'

High above, Ghorr's rope had been looped over the side of the air-dreadnought while the artificers unwound it from the partly dismantled windlass. They fed the slack onto a hand windlass, which spun under the load, tearing the handles out of the attendants' grasp. Ghorr dropped a couple of spans before being brought up with a tooth-snapping jerk. He squealed in fright, then roared at his officers to take personal charge. A pair of burly captains hurled the attendants out of the way, took hold of the winch and began to wind furiously. Ghorr rose into the windy zone, where a gust sent him swinging through a long arc. He yelled at his officers, who wound harder, but he swung the other way into the path of three witnesses who were being lifted in a rope basket from the other end of the air-dreadnought.

'Get out of the way!' he shouted, but they could do nothing to avoid him. Ghorr smashed into the basket, his chair began to spin, came back the other way, and the basket and chair whirled around and around each other as their ropes spun together.

The chief scrutator tried to rotate his rope chair the other way but it wouldn't go. The amphitheatre gave a convulsive heave that snapped the cables as taut as wires and pulled Ghorr's air-dreadnought down by a good span and a half. Nish, Irisis and Klarm were thrown to the canvas.

'It's going,' Ghorr cried. 'Pull me up, then cut the cable.'

Nish picked himself up. Ghorr's captains were trying to heave the twisted ropes apart but they wouldn't budge.

'Cut them loose!' said Ghorr.

A shiver went through everyone on the air-dreadnought, as well as the witnesses crowded on the amphitheatre. The officer in charge of Ghorr's air-dreadnought drew himself up. 'Those are the *recorders*, Chief Scrutator,' he called frostily.

'And doing their duty to the end,' Irisis said softly. 'Look, the blonde one is writing her record even now.'

Ghorr's reply could not be heard, though his stance said it all. There would be a penalty for that defiance. He threw his cloak off, followed by the securing rope harness, and climbed onto the sides of his rope chair, which swayed dangerously back and forth.

'What's he doing?' said Nish.

'He's trying to untangle it himself,' said Scrutator Klarm. 'It can't be done one-handed. He'll fall.'

Ghorr stood up, hooking his injured arm around the rope with a gasp of pain, and reached up.

'He'll never get enough leverage,' said Klarm. 'Not on a moving chair.'

The wind was whistling through the rigging of the air-dreadnoughts, whose sides were crowded with staring people. The witnesses on the amphitheatre deck were equally silent and still.

The twisted ropes, with their human cargo, began to swing like a pendulum. It had grown very cold. Ghorr reached up, again and again, and his hand went back and forth. He wasn't trying to free the ropes – he was sawing at the rope holding up the recorder's basket.

The recorders realised it at the same moment but none of

the women screamed or pleaded. They stood up, holding their scrolls with simple dignity, and kept writing.

'There's an image that will live in the Histories after we're gone,' said Irisis soberly.

Their end wasn't long in coming. The ends sprang out of their rope, which began to untwist under the weight, before pulling free.

'If they hit the deck they may still survive,' said Irisis hopefully.

Nobody contradicted her, though Nish knew that such a fall, a good thirty spans, must kill them. The basket fell, the three women still standing and recording all the way down. It plunged through the mist, hit hard near the edge of the amphitheatre, the women crumpled into a mess; then basket, rope and contents went over the side.

'Up!' said Ghorr in a hollow voice, sliding back into his chair and fastening the ropes about him.

The crew of his air-dreadnought did not move.

'Up, damn you, or you'll all taste a scrutator's quisitory.'

They remained as silent and still as the figures on a painted jug. The crew must have been as shocked as those on the deck.

'He crossed the line,' said Irisis. 'He's finished.'

'Not if he reaches his craft before the other scrutators do theirs.'

Klarm turned a strained face to them. 'I've served Ghorr for many years, and he would not go against the best interests of the Council. It's all that's kept us alive, the past dark decade.' He didn't sound as though he believed it any longer.

'His actions give the lie to that argument,' said Nish.

'The chief scrutator knows much that we do not. He always has the interests of the world at heart. He must have had a reason. He *must* . . .' Klarm closed his eyes as if in pain.

The mist on the amphitheatre was almost gone now, revealing five suspended baskets and another eight nets bursting with people, crammed together like fish in a trawl net. All hung in mid-air while the shocked winch-hands waited to see what was going to happen.

Nish noticed a hanging chair moving slowly, almost furtively, up behind one of the nets.

'Is that Scrutator Fusshte?' Nish squinted at the meagre, dark-clad figure in the chair.

'It is.' Irisis shuddered. 'Hello?'

Ghorr was jerked down, then up. He stood up in his chair, cloak trailing in the strengthening wind, and began shouting up to his air-dreadnought. He pointed at Fusshte.

'What's he saying?' said Nish.

'I can't make it out,' Irisis replied.

'He's called Fusshte a traitor,' said Klarm. Then, as if he could not believe what he was hearing, 'Ghorr has ordered his men to shoot him.' He knuckled his eyes with his big hands and stared up at the drama, disbelievingly. 'Oh, oh, oh!'

'Ghorr knows what will happen to him if Fusshte takes over,' said Irisis. 'And surely Fusshte must take over, now.'

'It doesn't do to predict the will or the ways of the Council,' Klarm rasped.

Fusshte signalled to his people to stop lifting. He stood up in his hanging chair and bared his meagre chest, offering himself as a target to any soldier who dared shoot down a member of the Council. Looking up to the soldiers in his air-dreadnought, Fusshte held out his arms, as though addressing them in the speech of his life.

'He looks so calm; so measured,' said Irisis. 'The loathsome little worm.'

'But not a coward,' said Klarm. 'The prize is within his reach and he's risen above himself to grasp it. Any one of Ghorr's loyal guard might well shoot him down, and Fusshte knows it. Yet he dares to defy his chief. He risks all to gain all.'

'To be chief scrutator when Ghorr falls,' said Nish.

'Aye. Fusshte has always wanted that. He's served as a loyal deputy for a decade, and even now he won't cut down his chief, or repudiate him. He simply offers the contrast to the Council and the witnesses, and allows them to make their own choice. Sometimes a champion will fail at the highest hurdle while the underdog rises to it. Fusshte, it seems, is such a man.'

'Yet a worm nonetheless,' said Irisis, 'and no more worthy of the honour than Ghorr, for all Fusshte's courage. What's going to happen now?'

No one fired. Ghorr's men began hauling him up, furiously. Fusshte closed his shirt and sat down while his attendants did the same, as if it were a race and whichever of them reached their craft first would win the Council as well as the day. Nets fell from the air-dreadnoughts and the remaining soldiers and witnesses fought to get into them.

'You'd better get to your work, if you have a plan to save yourselves,' said Klarm. 'The instant those nets lift off, they'll cut the cables from above.'

Nish slashed his blade across the cable, again and again. A few more strands gave but that was all. The fibres were so resistant they must have been ensorcelled.

'And risk taking half the baskets with them?' said Irisis.

'If the amphitheatre collapses while the air-dreadnoughts are still cabled to it, there'll be a conflagration not seen since the enemy burnt the naphtha stores of Runcimad,' said Klarm.

'You'd better run, Scrutator Klarm,' said Irisis. 'If you're going . . .'

Klarm turned to her, his handsome face troubled. 'You cannot imagine how hard it was for one like me to rise to scrutator. When you're only the height of a child, your peers cannot take you seriously. I strove harder than anyone to become scrutator, and now I wonder why. Flydd was right. The Council is corrupt; I can serve it no longer.'

'What will you do?' panted Nish, hacking furiously but fruitlessly.

'I don't know. Give me that.'

Nish handed him the sword at once. Despite his words, Klarm did have a natural authority that was hard to resist.

'The cables were strengthened with scrutator magic at the beginning,' said Klarm. 'That's why they resisted the fire for so long. Check your straps.'

They did so. He drew the blade back over his shoulder, sighted on Nish's meagre gash and swung the blade with all his strength, muttering words under his breath as he did.

The blade went a third of the way into the cable. He wrenched it out and swung it again. It passed the halfway point this time, the cut strands unravelling and spiralling up the cable for at least a span, and with a groan the remaining strands stretched and snapped.

The cable lashed up; the deck whipped away from beneath their feet. Nish was thrown down, crashing hard into Irisis. Klarm went up in the air and Nish thought he was going to go over the side, for the scrutator wasn't tethered.

Klarm fell near the edge. Nish caught him by the hand and the dwarf's grip crushed his fingers. The deck snapped back, the precipice beneath them reverting to a gentle slope.

'One more cable should do it,' said Klarm. 'Run! They're getting ready to cut us free.'

The slack on the baskets and nets was slowly being taken up, for the weight of people in them was immense, but the air-dreadnoughts weren't planning to wait for them to be lifted all the way. Already burly men stood by the cable capstans, each with a great two-bladed axe over his shoulder, just waiting for the word.

Most of the mancers, officers of the guard, and the most important artisans and artificers had been saved. Many more were now being lifted to their craft. Almost two hundred witnesses remained on the deck, however, and for them there was no way of escape. The nets and baskets would not be lowered again. The air-dreadnoughts had to be cut free before the amphitheatre collapsed, and those remaining would be sacrificed to save the rest.

Flame licked spans up another cable – Yggur must have used the last of the naphtha on it. Half a dozen witnesses attempted to climb the life ropes, but all fell to their deaths as the ropes were plucked like gigantic strings, or were cut loose by those on the air-dreadnoughts. A gaggle of witnesses, knowing they were going to die, ran back and forth, screaming or wailing. The remainder simply stood where they were, staring up, out or down.

'Kill the prisoners!' Ghorr yelled as he was lifted into his air-dreadnought, but the last soldiers on the deck, knowing they had been abandoned, were concerned only for their own survival.

Nish and Irisis raced to the next cable, Klarm close behind. They fastened their safety ropes. Klarm buried the blade deep into the cable.

'Again,' cried Irisis. 'They're cutting.'

Klarm laid a hand on the cable, spoke words of scrutator magic to unbind the spell and gave the cable three mighty blows. It was now under such tension that the blade made little impression. He hacked again then tossed the blade to Nish.

'Have a go. I'm spent.'

Someone was shouting at them. It sounded like Yggur but Nish, chopping furiously, had neither the time nor breath to work out what he was saying.

Hack, hack, hack. 'It's nearly through!' Nish said.

'If this works,' said Irisis, 'the deck will fold in that way.' She pointed. 'We won't have much time.'

Nish hacked again. The cable seemed as tough as ever.

'Come on, *come on*!' said Irisis.

Nish gave up his chopping, which didn't seem to be doing much good, and sawed the blade back and forth, the fibres pinging apart as he worked.

'It's going,' said Irisis. 'Get ready!'

Nish gave a final hack and the cable tore apart. The deck pulled inwards, Irisis yelled, 'Jump!' but the deck went from under Nish, who found himself flying over the edge on the end of his safety line.

He was hurtling through the air on the wrong side of the deck. Up above, the soldiers were chopping furiously, coordinating their strokes so as to sever each of the cables at the same time. Nish jerked to a stop in mid-air, then tried to pull himself up the swinging strip of canvas, but it was hard to hold on. He would never get there before they cut loose the amphitheatre.

Klarm came over the side, hanging onto the rim of the canvas with one immensely strong hand. Reaching down with the other he gathered in Nish's safety line, jerked it up, up, up until Nish was within reach, then dragged him over the edge.

'Go!' he grunted as he slashed Nish's tether.

Nish threw himself into the U-shaped canvas valley that now ran down towards the slab-covered roofs of Fiz Gorgo. He couldn't tell if Klarm had followed, though Nish did see the soldiers hack through the last supporting cables, one, two, three, four, five, and then six. Only two to go.

And as he gathered speed and the cables fell towards him, Nish saw something else. A tarpaulin covering a net hanging below the keel of Ghorr's air-dreadnought had slipped, exposing a curve of dark metal. It was the thapter.

Ghorr had it and Tiaan, as well as Malien and, presumably, the amplimet.

He'd won after all.

ELEVEN

The lucky ones who had made it to the hanging chairs, baskets and nets were being drawn up towards the air-dreadnoughts, swinging back and forth, crashing into one another and, where they could, fending each other off to avoid their ropes tangling. They were not always successful. A pair of nets became hopelessly tangled and, despite the screams of the occupants, the smaller was cut loose. It had to be, for the nets were attached to different air-dreadnoughts and threatened them both. Incredibly, the small net did not pull free but hung upside down from the larger net as the air-dreadnought rose to safety.

Terror made the occupants of the chairs and baskets irrational. A brief duel flared between a mancer and a lesser scrutator, sending bolts of fire across the sky and ending with the mancer blackening in his chair. The scrutator, alive but lacking clothes or hair, was jerked up to safety.

Irisis jumped the instant the cable went, expecting Nish to do the same. She fell into the canvas valley and felt it deepening under her. Across the valley the other prisoners were also jumping. Yggur was standing by Gilhaelith, as if uncertain what to do about him, then with a swift movement he slashed the mathe-mancer's bonds. Gilhaelith jumped. Irisis wondered why Yggur had such a set against the geomancer. For a moment it had looked as though Yggur would leave Gilhaelith to his fate.

Her feet caught in a fold in the canvas and Irisis went tumbling head over heels down the deepening valley, now sliding on her chest, now her left side, friction burning through her clothes. She felt the skin go from her hip and tried to throw herself the other way. She was moving too fast. The deck seemed to be falling as quickly as she was, and she was going to hit the roof hard.

The canvas stopped with a jerk that tore a great rent along one side. Irisis kept sliding, on her back now, and she could smell her hair smouldering. She lifted her head and pressed her heels against the fabric to break her fall.

Now her backside was burning but there wasn't far to go. The canvas valley had looped down to within a couple of spans of the roof, forming a dip at the bottom. She shot down it, slowed rapidly at the dip then toppled over the edge onto the sloping roof slabs, landing hard enough to wind herself. She slid into one of the roof gullies, rolled over and came to her knees.

Something flashed towards her. Reacting instinctively, Irisis threw herself to one side as the flensing trough hurtled past and smashed through the roof. She didn't have time to think about her narrow escape; the valley above her was full of falling, sliding and toppling people, though she couldn't see Nish among them. Someone small came flying down ahead of the rest, rolling and cartwheeling and emitting a thin, moaning cry. It was Inouye.

Hitting the dip faster than Irisis had, the little pilot shot into the air and came flying out. Irisis dived, caught Inouye and fell with her, wrenching her shoulder as they landed in the gully. Before she could get up, a clot of witnesses came sliding down, locked together, and hurtled over the dip.

Irisis scrambled up to them on hands and knees, heaving them out of the way before they were crushed by the next bundle of humanity. Most seemed to have suffered no more than bruising or minor broken bones, though one unfortunate lad had landed on his head with a dozen others on top of him and died instantly of a broken neck. Irisis let his body slide away down the slope. There wasn't time to think about it, for the next group of people were already on her. Where was Nish?

'I need help,' she gasped, dragging men and women out of the tangle and flinging them left and right. It was exhausting work, and several times she was knocked off her feet as people rushed down more quickly than she could clear them out of the way. All the other debris came down as well, including dead bodies, abandoned weapons, torturing tools and lengths of barbed rope.

Flangers shot off the end, landed on his feet and immediately set to. A pair of Yggur's guards arrived and did the same, though not even four of them could deal with the deluge of human jetsam that now filled the lower section of the canvas valley.

Irisis rolled under the end of the slide as about thirty people tumbled down together, landing so hard that their combined impact cracked the roofing slabs. There would be broken backs and necks among that lot.

She still couldn't see Nish but didn't have time to worry about him – people were pouring down faster than they could be moved out of the way. The dead and injured formed a fleshy mat which at least broke the falls of the later arrivals, though the groans as they took the impacts were bloodcurdling.

'Help us!' she shouted at the able-bodied witnesses, who stood in dazed, silent clots around the end of the slide. One or two came forward; the rest remained where they were, too shocked to move.

Two more of Yggur's guard landed, followed by a body, the elderly cook who'd been shot early in the fracas. Flangers heaved it to one side without ceremony. Then came Yggur's seneschal, his under-chef and maid-of-all-work. The seneschal had broken both legs but the others started dragging the injured out of the way with disciplined efficiency.

Yggur slid down on his backside, though he managed to stand up just before the end, sprang right over the fallen and landed on his feet. One of the last to jump, he'd come down in a grey streak, passing some of the other prisoners on the way.

'You've done well,' he said, surveying the scene in a single glance before taking his turn with the injured.

The amphitheatre didn't completely collapse, for the air-dreadnought crews had not been able to cut the last two cables. Part of the deck was now draped over the roofs and towers of Fiz Gorgo, while the rest stood up at an angle as the two remaining craft were pushed away on the wind. The canvas was jerking and snapping under the strain.

They worked for several minutes without speaking, until the bulk of the sliders had been moved to safety further down the roof. When they were only coming down in ones and twos, Yggur drew Flangers and Irisis aside.

'Arm yourselves. We're not out of danger yet. The air-dread-noughts haven't gone far, and the hundred-odd soldiers who were sent down to look for Nish are still here somewhere. They may not stay loyal once they realise that the scrutators are going to abandon them. But then again, they may.'

They armed themselves with swords and crossbows that had collected in the roof gully.

'I don't see anyone out in the yard,' said Irisis. 'They may not realise that we've survived.'

'Someone will signal them. Look out!'

It was Fyn-Mah, cutting a curving path down the slide, still holding a bloody Flydd as tightly as before. Irisis and Yggur stood together and caught the pair as they came over the edge.

'How is he?' Irisis said.

Flydd's eyes were closed, his fleshless lips blue and he sagged in Fyn-Mah's arms. He looked as if he'd been dead for a day.

'He may survive,' Fyn-Mah said, 'if he can regain the will to live.'

Yggur jerked his head and Fyn-Mah carried Flydd down to the bottom of the roof gully, refusing all offers of help.

'Where's Nish?' said Irisis, looking up anxiously. 'That seems to be everyone.'

'I thought he was with you.'

'I jumped first. I haven't see him since.'

103

Yggur frowned. 'I don't see anyone coming – ah, there he is.'

Nish came skidding down, shot off the end of the dip and Yggur plucked him neatly out of the air. The seat of Nish's pants was smoking and he'd lost skin off his left arm, but he was beaming.

'We did it!' he cried, though his euphoria faded when he saw the pile of dead, and dozens more with broken bones.

'A lot of those were dead before they came down,' said Irisis. 'We didn't lose many from the collapse.'

Nish stood up, beating out his backside as he looked back up the slide. One last figure came rolling down the now gentle slope as the amphitheatre collapsed, draping itself over the towers. The burly little man hit the dip, bounced high, tumbled in the air like an acrobat and landed on his feet.

Yggur lunged at him but Nish cried hastily, 'He's a friend! Klarm – Scrutator Klarm – cut the cables and saved my life.'

'Did he now?' Yggur said dubiously. He scrutinised the dwarf, then nodded. 'You're with us, then?'

Klarm bowed low. 'After seeing Ghorr's craven display, how could I do otherwise?'

Yggur thrust out his hand and Klarm took it. 'I'm glad to have you.' Yggur called his soldiers and household to him. 'The struggle is far from over. The scrutators have more than a hundred soldiers below, not to mention the soldiers and witnesses here, and we can't count on them aiding us. We must watch our backs and be prepared for anything.' He called out in a commanding voice. 'Come this way, everyone. We can get in through the roof down here.' Yggur lowered his voice. 'Though after that we must prepare to do battle – what is it, Nish?'

'See that?' A canvas-shrouded net was slowly being winched up to Ghorr's air-dreadnought. 'It's the thapter.'

'Are you sure?' said Yggur.

'Yes. The tarps slipped just before I came down. And they've got Tiaan, too.'

'And Malien,' said Yggur. 'So we have no choice. We must go after the thapter. The air-floater is still sound, is it not?'

'It was, the last I saw of it,' said Irisis. 'But if they get the chance I'm sure they'll destroy it.'

'Then we'd better get to it first. Fyn-Mah, you're in charge here.' He deputed a number of his household staff to assist her. 'Nish, Irisis, Flangers and Klarm, come with me. Vance, Mayl, Bowyer and Menny,' he said to his surviving soldiers, 'you too. As soon as we're inside, go to the armoury and get your light armour, crossbows and weapons for close-in fighting, then meet me at the west door. Inouye, I need you too.'

'Has anyone seen Ullii?' said Nish.

'She didn't come down the slide,' said Irisis. 'I'd say Ghorr has taken her back.'

They broke in through the roof and ran all the way down the steps. Yggur's troops headed for the armoury. Everyone else followed Yggur into his workshop where, after some deliberation, he took a glassy spiral and a rock-crystal orb out of locked cases and thrust them into pockets in his cloak. They met the soldiers by a side door that led into the yard.

'We'll run into Ghorr's troops before too long,' said Yggur. 'Leave the initial confrontation to me – we can't afford to be tied down in a battle against such odds. We can't survive it.'

'What's your plan?' said Flangers.

'Any resistance to be met by obliterating force, after which we offer the rest a chance to make an honourable surrender.'

'And if they don't?'

'Ask me then.'

As they went around the corner they encountered a pair of Ghorr's guard. Yggur kept walking, and shortly he was confronted by eighty or more soldiers.

Yggur put up his hand and looked the leaders in the eye. 'You have all seen what we saw,' he said, not loudly but in a carrying voice. 'Chief Scrutator Ghorr, a craven cur if ever I saw one, criminally slew three innocent recorders – women of child-bearing age – and has run like the dog he is. After this day he will no longer be scrutator. Ghorr will be replaced by Scrutator

Fusshte, who cannot compel the loyalty of his fellow scrutators. By the end of the week the members of this Council, who abandoned two hundred witnesses to their deaths, and will soon abandon you, will be at war with each other.

'And so I ask you: do you cleave to your oath to these contemptibles, or will you put down your weapons, make an honourable surrender, then follow me? Surrender or death: those are your choices. Choose swiftly. I'm in no mood for delay.'

The soldiers looked uncertain. One of their captains spoke to another, they nodded then cried, 'Attack: we outnumber them ten to one.'

They raised their swords and surged forward. Yggur didn't hesitate: he drew the glassy spiral from his pocket and tossed it to the ground at the feet of the two captains. It burst like a miniature sun and the incandescence swelled to envelop them both, before shrinking just as quickly. The light winked out and the captains were not men any more.

Yggur allowed the soldiers to stare at the smouldering remains for a good minute, then said, 'Well?'

They laid down their arms. 'Raise your right hands and take my oath,' said Yggur and, to a man, they did.

Yggur ordered them to go up to the roof, assist the injured, then recover the bodies.

He waited until they had passed through the doors before letting out his breath in a groan. 'Ugh!' he said. Yggur staggered for a few steps but kept on, limping. He scowled, as if it wasn't the pain that troubled him so much as being affected by it.

'What's the matter with him?' Nish said quietly to Irisis.

'Aftersickness. Using power comes at a cost and he's drawn an awful lot from himself today.' She ran to catch up to Yggur. 'Can we count on them, surr, or will they attack us once our backs are turned?'

'Should the scrutators flee, I expect they'll serve faithfully enough. But if the fleet comes to ground after us, as it may, I dare say they'll turn again.'

They reached the air-floater, which was tethered in a corner of the yard, without further incident. It had not been touched.

'It's a wonder Ghorr didn't order it destroyed,' said Nish.

'He probably planned to take it with him.'

After checking that they weren't visible from above, they climbed into the air-floater. Yggur, now limping badly, had to be helped over the side. He leaned against the ropes for a moment before heading into the cabin. At the door he turned. 'If you would come with me, Scrutator Klarm? To your positions, everyone. Inouye, stand by your controller but don't draw power until I give the word.'

Nish scanned the sky. The air-dreadnoughts were all over the place. Four maintained their station, high above. Two, one of them being Ghorr's, were still trying to cut their cables. Three others had been driven downwind over the swamp forest. Another three had become hopelessly tangled and were drifting sideways with the wind, spiralling around each other. The remainder were out of sight.

Klarm followed Yggur inside and the canvas door slapped closed. After a series of rumbles, a rather tenuous mist formed in the yard, enveloping the air-floater.

The door opened. Yggur was panting. 'That's the best I can do. Inouye, rise up over the wall, then head south for Ghorr's craft. Take it slowly or you may pull out of my concealment.'

'I can't see Ghorr's machine,' she said.

'The lookouts will tell you which way to go.'

Flangers went to the bow, while Nish and Irisis hung over the rail on either side, staring into the mist.

'I can't say I like this plan,' Nish said quietly.

'What plan?' said Irisis.

'Precisely.'

They rose slowly. Nish couldn't see anything but mist, swirling and coiling at the lower levels, streaming across the deck as they rose into the stronger winds at altitude. A little way above the towers, the mist parted below them and he looked back to where the amphitheatre had been.

It had completely collapsed, apart from a triangle of canvas sticking up, like the fin of a shark, where it had draped over one of the towers. Two cables ran into the sky at an angle of thirty

107

degrees, taut as wires. They were still attached to the two air-dreadnoughts, which had been driven out over the forest.

'Run in the direction of that cable,' said Yggur, pointing to the nearer. 'But stay at this height.'

'How come they didn't cut those cables?' said Nish.

'I used the Art on them,' said Yggur with a grim smile. 'No blade can cut them, no fire burn them for as long as the spell holds. To untether themselves they'll have to take apart the winch drums. It took quite a bit out of me, but it was worth it.'

The taut cable angled up into streaming mist. Yggur had a minute-glass in one hand and was watching the sands run as he estimated how far they'd gone. 'We should be past Ghorr's craft now,' he said to Inouye. 'Go up and turn to face the other way.'

She did so and he extended his arm, chanting under his breath. The mist spun into a narrow, dark funnel in front of him, like water swirling down a plughole. The funnel extended horizontally, stretching, thinning and wavering back and forth as if searching for something.

Yggur strained, and through the opening Nish caught a glimpse of a section of rigging, then part of an airbag.

'Too high,' grumbled Yggur, who seemed to be having trouble holding his arm up. He directed the funnel, whose opening wasn't much bigger than Nish's head, down and across and back, then tracked up the port side of the vessel. 'Is it the right one?'

'It's Ghorr's,' said Nish. 'I just saw the top of the thapter hanging below it.'

The funnel was directed up and towards the stern, and there Ghorr stood, issuing orders. A pair of soldiers were hacking fruitlessly at the cable holding his air-dreadnought to the collapsed amphitheatre. The craft was shaking in the wind.

A gust caught the air-floater, heeling it over. Inouye spun the rotor up to full power and slipped the craft expertly up into the lee of the airbags of Ghorr's much bigger machine. The mist funnel closed over.

'I can't hold the concealment much longer,' said Yggur, clinging to the door. 'Nish, see if you can see what they're doing.'

Nish got down on his belly on the deck and put his head over the side. Another wavering tube opened up through the mist below him, though his view was so restricted that it took a while to work out what he was looking at.

'Ghorr has just whacked the mirror operator over the head. He's shouting!'

'He's been doing a lot of that lately,' said Irisis, hanging onto his legs as the air-floater lurched one way and then the other.

'He's dragged the big crystal-powered mirror around. That must be what they blasted the defences with at dawn.'

'I dare say,' said Yggur. 'Has anyone seen us?'

'They're not looking this way,' said Irisis.

'He's pointed the mirror at the cable winch,' said Nish.

'It won't do him any good unless he gets some sun on it,' said Irisis.

'If I can make mist, he can break it. He's getting ready to flee,' said Yggur. 'Inouye, take us down.'

'What's the plan?' said Irisis.

'We board the air-dreadnought from the bow and take it while they're distracted down at the stern. Flangers, what's the matter?'

'He's got at least ten soldiers against our five,' said Flangers. 'Plus a mancer or two. Not to mention the other air-dreadnoughts.'

'Then we'll just have to fight all the harder,' said Yggur. 'The other machines won't trouble us. They won't dare come close enough to board, in case the airbags tangle.'

'They're close enough to fire their javelards.'

Yggur waved his hand and the mist obscured everything. 'Take us down, Inouye. Once Ghorr blasts that cable he'll be off and this little craft won't catch him. If we lose the thapter we've lost our only chance!'

TWELVE

'Drop us down to the bow, Inouye,' said Yggur. 'Can you do that in the mist, or should I –?'

'I can do it,' she said.

'Klarm and I will attack from behind,' Yggur went on, 'and then we rush them. Soldiers, follow me. Flangers, stay back with your crossbow and keep watch. Irisis, get into the cabin and free Malien and Tiaan. Once we've secured the air-dreadnought, escort them down into the thapter. Nish, go down the ropes, cut through the canvas and open the hatch of the thapter. Don't fall off.'

'Very funny,' said Nish, who was beginning to sweat. The odds were too great, the plan foolhardy in the extreme. It relied too much on Yggur, who was already exhausted, while Klarm, despite what he'd done earlier, was an unknown quantity. When confronted by Ghorr, might Klarm decide that his oath to the scrutators still bound him? A turncoat might turn again.

'What if Malien and Tiaan aren't here?' said Irisis. 'We won't have anyone to fly the thapter.'

'I'm sure Ghorr would have kept them close by.'

The air-floater dropped so suddenly that Nish's stomach was left behind. He clutched the rail with one hand and eased his short sword in its sheath. His palms were damp. All that had been saved with such agony could be lost even more quickly.

How could Inouye tell where to go anyway? He couldn't see a thing.

She brought her craft out of the mist and up against the bow with the barest bump. Yggur clambered through the rope rails, limping more than before. Klarm put his hand on one of the stanchions and leapt the ropes, landing lightly on the deck.

'Let me go first,' whispered Klarm. 'He may wonder how I got here, but he won't think of me as an enemy. It'll get me a span or two closer. Stay back, around the curve of the deck out of sight. When you hear me use my Art, rush them down the other side.'

Yggur frowned, as if he too had his doubts, then nodded. 'Go.'

Klarm headed down the port side, moving sure-footedly on the lurching deck despite his caliper. Yggur remained where he was, gnawing at his lower lip, before waving an arm at his soldiers. They followed him, hugging the curved canvas wall of the main cabin.

Irisis caught Nish's eye and mouthed, 'Good luck!'

He nodded stiffly. She put her head around the corner to look down the starboard deck. 'It's clear, Flangers.' Weapons at the ready, they went forward into the mist, which had begun to thin just when they didn't want it to.

Nish turned to his own task. The thapter hung in its nets some five or six spans below the central keel of the air-dreadnought. He could just make it out. It was a long way to go down a rope, though not far enough below the keel for the air-floater to approach it directly. He fingered the coil of rope over his shoulder. He'd already lashed it into a harness at his waist, so it was just a matter of tying it to the side rail and going down.

Once he had done that, Nish checked his knots carefully, slipped through and hung on with hands and feet while he judged his approach. It wasn't going to be easy; the thapter wasn't directly below him, but in under the vessel by several spans. He'd have to lower himself a bit further than that, then swing in, catch hold of the net ropes and go down them.

Suddenly the mist parted, the sun shone through and a torrent of white light was followed by the ear-piercing screech of metal being torn. Ghorr must have blasted the winch apart. The deck was thrust upwards so hard that Nish lost his grip and fell. High above, he could hear the airbags thrashing as the big craft was torn free from the cable. The ragged cable end, attached to the torn remnants of the winch drum, lashed past below him.

Reaching the limit of the rope, Nish was brought up with a jerk that made him bite his tongue. The harness pulled so tight that it felt like a noose cutting him in half, and he could only draw in half a breath.

The freed air-dreadnought began to drift over the walls of Fiz Gorgo towards the swamp forest. Nish was trying to loosen his harness when a thudding boom made him look up. Someone was blown over the side, trailing blood and smoke. It was one of Yggur's soldiers, the stocky man called Bowyer. Wide eyes met Nish's momentarily as he fell.

Swords clashed on the deck; there were grunts and cries of pain. Nish put it out of mind and began to swing his legs. He'd need quite an arc to reach the top of the thapter from here.

He swung back and forth, slowly building up momentum, until the air-dreadnought lurched sideways, sending him headlong towards the top of the thapter, which was exposed where the tarpaulins had been folded back to allow entry. He threw out a hand and managed to catch hold of the hatch handle but was moving too fast to hang on. He kept going, now spinning on the end of the rope, swung around the other side and collided with a black, crunchy object suspended from another rope.

The ropes tangled and began to orbit around each other. Nish and the black object spun in together and he came face to face with a charred corpse, fumes still rising from its empty eye-sockets. With a strangled gasp, Nish tried to push it out of the way. Ribs cracked and the mouth fell open, revealing startlingly white teeth surrounded by charcoaled lips.

Close to panic, Nish fought down his terror. It was just a dead man in a hanging chair, the mancer who'd lost that airborne duel earlier. All he had to do was spin the body the other way, the ropes would untangle and he'd swing back towards the thapter.

Nish was about to do so when something made him glance up. Ghorr was standing at the rail, watching him.

Nish should have gone for the thapter but his presence of mind had deserted him. He hung there, staring at his enemy.

Ghorr drew a knife and with a single slash cut through Nish's rope.

Irisis waited until Klarm had passed round the curve of the cabin, then slid along the starboard wall, pressing hard against it. Flangers followed, his crossbow at the ready. Reaching the forward door, a lath frame covered in canvas on leather hinges, she pulled gently on the latch. The door opened inwards and she slipped into a gloomy, cramped room about four spans by three. It was the crew's cabin, their gear and sleeping hammocks neatly stowed, canvas trestles strapped against the walls. There was no one inside.

'Must be the next one,' she said, easing out again.

The next room turned out to be the galley and larder; the one after that, the officers' quarters. 'There isn't an upper floor, is there?' she said over her shoulder to Flangers.

'I wouldn't think so.'

She edged round the curve. Ahead, some ten spans away, just visible through the rapidly thinning mist, stood a group of uniformed soldiers in the colours of Ghorr's personal guard. They had their backs to her, watching something being done at the stern.

'Then it'll have to be this door. It's the last.'

She pulled on the latch but it did not move. 'It's held fast, though I can't see a lock.'

'Must be Ghorr's quarters,' said Flangers. 'Cut the hinges.'

She slit the bottom hinge with her knife and pulled the door out enough to slip through. Flangers followed.

'Guard the –' she began, but Flangers had already taken up position.

This chamber was as large as the first, though darker, and only served two or three people. Broad hammocks were still slung in position. The floor was covered in silk carpets, and the walls in tapestries and hangings. She turned her head this way and that, trying to pierce the darkness, and suddenly the faintest pattern of the field appeared in her inner eye.

Her eyes pricked with tears. Her artisan's pliance, which enabled her to see the field, had been taken from Irisis soon after she'd been captured. She hadn't seen the field since, and for her to visualise it at all now, her pliance had to be almost to hand.

Irisis closed her eyes momentarily, the better to *see*.

Something rustled in the darkness. 'Tiaan?' she whispered, opening her eyes.

'Mmpfh!'

As her eyes adjusted, Irisis made out a bowed figure tied to a strap attached to the wall. It wasn't Tiaan but a much older woman with grey in her hair.

'Malien!' Irisis ran to her, cut the gag off and freed her wrists and ankles. 'How are you?'

'Parched. It's been a long day,' Malien said in a dry croak. She shook her numb hands. White marks were scored into her wrists.

Irisis lifted a wine skin from a hook, jerked out the stopper and passed it across. Malien couldn't hold the wine skin, so Irisis supported it while the older woman took a couple of hefty swigs. 'That'll do. We're going to need our wits –'

A blast followed by the shriek of tearing metal jerked the floor so hard that Malien's knees buckled. Irisis was thrown against the lath-and-canvas wall. The flimsy structure of the air-dreadnought creaked and groaned. The craft jerked twice more, not so hard this time.

'Yggur laid a spell of durability on the mooring cable,' said Irisis, hanging onto a swaying tapestry. 'Ghorr must have blasted the winch apart.'

'And your plan?' said Malien, on her knees and unable to rise.

What am I going to do with her, Irisis thought. 'Nish is opening the hatch of the thapter, which is hanging below us. Yggur and Klarm – he's on our side now, at least I hope he is – were going to take on Ghorr and his mancer.'

114

'Just Nish?' said Malien. 'Does he realise there are guards inside?'

A deadly chill spread through Irisis's innards. 'This attack was planned in some haste.'

'I can well imagine,' said Malien dryly. 'We'd better get after him.'

'My artisan's pliance is here somewhere. I sensed it as I came in.'

Malien turned her head back and forth, three times, then pointed. 'Try that cupboard.'

It was locked so Irisis levered the lacquered wood apart with her blade. A number of objects fell out, gems and jewellery. She felt among them and as soon as her fingers touched her pliance the field condensed around her. Again that prickling of tears in her eyes – an artisan who'd lost her pliance could go mad with longing for it. Irisis wasn't emotional, as artisans went, but as she put the chain over her head she felt the tension smooth away.

Swords clashed; men grunted and groaned outside the door on the far side of the room. A bloody blade speared through the canvas wall and was withdrawn again. A man screamed in agony.

Malien cast a glance that way, before turning back to Irisis. 'I assume you plan to escape in the thapter?'

'That's right.' Irisis had her own sword out and her head cocked, listening to the swordplay and footwork outside. 'Is something the matter?'

'Ghorr has my controller crystal. I can't operate the thapter without it.'

Irisis cursed under her breath. 'Any idea where he might keep it?'

Malien closed her eyes and put her hands over them. This time she didn't turn her head. After some seconds she said, 'Is there a metal box under that cupboard?'

Irisis tilted it and looked beneath. The brass box was locked and chained to the floor, though it was just an ordinary lock and she was expert at picking them. She had it open in a moment and held out the blue-green crystal. 'This it?'

Malien nodded and tried to stand up but her legs still wouldn't support her. She grabbed for the cupboard, her wrist gave and she collapsed again.

'Do you know where Tiaan is?' said Irisis. 'Or the amplimet?'

'They were taken to one of the other air-dreadnoughts. I don't know which one.'

Outside, the sounds of battle grew louder. Something burst with a loud pop and, momentarily, a brilliant green light illuminated the weave of the canvas. Objects fizzed in all directions, leaving fuming trails that Irisis could see in her mind's eye. The canvas walls flapped in and out like the skin of a drum. Someone cried out; it sounded alarmingly like Yggur. If he had fallen . . .

The port door burst open and a pair of soldiers pushed in. Irisis struck at the first, whose eyes hadn't yet adjusted to the gloom. Her sword point crunched into his wrist bones, the weapon fell from his useless hand and he stumbled backwards. Tearing down one of the silk carpets one-handed, Irisis tossed it over the head of the second soldier.

As it obscured his vision she leapt for the starboard door, but before she got there it was forced open. Flangers kicked the door shut but a long sword came through it, touching the fabric of his trousers. With one hand he wrenched the door sideways, trapping the sword for a moment, while with the other he thrust through the gap.

The point of the long sword flipped up, as if its owner had dropped it. Flangers wrenched the door off its remaining hinge, hurled it at the soldier outside and sprang at him, sword flailing.

The first soldier stumbled and was shouldered out of the way by a giant of a man carrying a long sword in one hand and a curved scimitar in the other. He feinted at Flangers with the scimitar, then pinked him in the shoulder with the point of the sword, though Flangers had leapt backwards so quickly that the blow did little damage. He turned towards the far door but more soldiers appeared behind the first. They were trapped.

Irisis tried to come to Flangers's aid but there wasn't room to get past him. Leather squeaked and she looked over her shoulder. Another soldier was pushing through the far door.

He flexed his arms and came at them. Now soldiers advanced from both sides, slowly driving them into a corner. There was nowhere to go. Irisis glanced at Malien, who was still flexing her numb hands, but she shook her head as if to say, 'I can't do anything yet'.

Irisis moved in beside Flangers and prepared to die. 'I had a feeling it was going to end this way,' she murmured.

'I'm sorry, Irisis – you deserve better. But for myself, I'll be glad to go.'

Flangers had never got over the time when, fleeing from Snizort in the stolen air-floater, Fyn-Mah had ordered him to attack Klarm's machine. Its gasbag had exploded, killing everyone except Klarm, and maiming him. Flangers still regarded that as a treasonous act for which, honourable soldier that he was, he could only atone with his life.

'Hold!' The order came over-loud, as if the man who gave it was no longer sure of his authority. The voice was hoarse, cracked but still recognisable – Ghorr.

He pushed through the doorway and the soldiers gave way. Ghorr's costly garments were torn and spotted with burn marks, his left arm hung limply and his shoulder and side were stained with brown blood. His hair was greasy, face soot-stained, eyes red, and his formerly dark complexion had gone the green colour of bile. Clots of yellow material in his beard could have come from mouth or nose.

'Cut their hamstrings so they can't move,' said Ghorr. 'Then bind them and bring them to the bow. This is going to end right now.'

THIRTEEN

'Well, well, well,' came a throaty, amused voice from the doorway. 'What have we here?'

Ghorr turned. It was Scrutator Klarm, limping so ostentatiously that he had to lift his calipered leg with both hands. He looked up at the chief scrutator, who stood more than twice his height, grinning broadly. 'How did you catch these wretches? I saw them escape the collapse.'

Irisis looked from Ghorr to Klarm. Had he been pretending all along, so as to bring them here and ingratiate himself with the chief scrutator? If not, and he was still on their side, his acting was worthy of the Master Chroniclers' Medal.

'They'd have to be mighty clever to escape my vengeance,' said Ghorr. 'Where did you spring from? I thought you were dead.'

'No man climbs ropes as well as I do,' Klarm lied in turn. 'I trust you're going to dispatch them right away?'

'The instant all the air-dreadnoughts are free, I'll order my shooting squad onto the front deck. Once they've taken a dozen bolts each, I'll personally sever their heads from their bodies and toss them into the bogs of Orist like the vermin they are. Take care of these two, would you, Klarm? I must attend to Yggur.'

'It'll be a pleasure,' Klarm said with a savage grin, but Ghorr was already on the way out.

The troops advanced on Irisis and Flangers. Irisis was readying herself to attack the leading soldier, the giant, when Klarm spoke.

'What are you doing, fellow?' said Klarm.

'Chief Scrutator ordered us to hamstring them, Scrutator Klarm, surr,' replied the giant, reaching for Irisis. 'So they can't escape.'

'Not in here, you damn fool,' said Klarm. 'The blood will ruin the carpets. I'll take care of them. They can't escape.' Sounds of fighting came from outside and above. 'Go! The chief scrutator needs you.'

They went at a run, though not without a backward glance. Irisis eyed Klarm warily. Was he for them or against them? 'What's going on?'

'The battle went against us,' said Klarm. 'Ghorr had *three* mancers and they proved too strong for Yggur –'

'I thought you were supposed to be helping him?'

'A change of plan,' Klarm said blandly. 'He kept me back, just in case, and it was lucky he did. My skills wouldn't have shifted the balance.'

'Is Yggur –'

'His men only took out five of the guard before they were cut down. He felled two of the mancers and injured the third, but Ghorr forced him up into the rigging.'

'Is he all right?' said Irisis.

'I don't think so. It took a lot out of him.'

'Well?' she said.

'What?'

'Are you for us or against us?'

Klarm looked disconcerted. 'I've given my oath.'

'Precisely,' she said savagely. 'Which oath do you hold to – the one to Ghorr or the one to us?'

'If I'd been against you, you'd be hamstrung by now. Come on.'

Irisis gave Malien her arm. 'How are you feeling?'

'My age, doubled and redoubled,' said Malien, pulling herself up, 'but the circulation is coming back. What's the plan?'

'I'll see what I can do for Yggur,' said Klarm. 'You'd better go down to the thapter. Flangers, guard the rail while they do.'

Ghorr slashed the rope and turned away. Nish fell hard until he was brought up, swinging wildly, by the other end of his rope, which was still twisted around the dead mancer's. He rotated below the charred feet of the corpse as the windings began to unravel.

Nish whirled around, swinging his legs to increase momentum, and shot past the side of the thapter, not close enough to grab hold of anything. He went around again, one eye on the nets, the other on his rope, which had only a couple of windings to go before it pulled free. There was no chance of making the top of the thapter. All he could do was try for the side of the nearest net.

As he swung by, Nish threw his arms out as far as he could reach. Three fingers of his right hand slid between the meshes and the lower curve of the thapter. He closed his fingers on the net, knowing he wasn't strong enough to hold his swinging weight with such a meagre grip. He flailed with his weak left arm just as his rope pulled free, but missed.

The jerk almost tore his shoulder out of its socket and Nish felt a stretching, burning pain there. The net began to rip through his fingers. He flailed again, got his left hand and arm through the meshes, and locked his wrist around the net. It eased the strain, just enough, though fresh blood began to seep through the stained bandage.

Taking a better grip, he pulled himself through a mesh, resting between it and the tarp while he kneaded his throbbing shoulder. He untied the dangling rope and climbed up the net underneath the tarpaulins, which had come loose and were flapping in the wind of the air-dreadnought's passage.

At the top, the tarpaulins had shifted again, partly covering the hatch, and he had to feel for it, then hack through the canvas. He looked up to see if he'd been observed, but saw no one at the rails.

Nish lifted the hatch carefully and, seeing nothing to trouble him, crawled inside. He was just going down the ladder when he was seized from below.

'That's one,' said a rough voice, binding him and whipping a dirty gag over his mouth. 'Now for the others.'

Irisis put her head around the remains of the door, where a hot tarry odour reminded her unpleasantly of Snizort. Something was burning off the bow, yellow flames and flashes lighting up the remnants of smoky mist. The deck was empty. She flattened herself against the outside wall and motioned to Flangers and Malien to follow.

Stealthy creaks came from above the cabins – people creeping across the roof framing, hunting Yggur. She couldn't do anything for him. Their first priority was to recapture the thapter, no matter who or what had to be sacrificed to get it. Irisis hadn't been able to see that before, but it was clear to her now.

She tiptoed to the rail and saw a world in chaos. A long way behind, smoke trailed up from the canvas-draped towers of Fiz Gorgo. To her left the ghostly outlines of three air-dreadnoughts, locked together by their airbag cables, spiralled slowly around each other. As she watched, the cabin of the lowest craft rolled onto its side, spilling people over the rails. A few clung desperately to the ropes but a sudden lurch of the doomed craft shook them free.

She dismissed everything from her mind but what she had to do. The thapter hung below the keel of Ghorr's air-dreadnought in its slings of nets, and the canvas no longer covered the hatch, which suggested that Nish had made it inside.

'Are you ready, Malien?'

Malien lurched along the rail, her knees wobbling. 'I can't get down by myself.'

'I'll do what I can. But once we're inside, how do we disable the guards?'

'I don't know,' Malien said limply.

Irisis had never seen her so listless. 'Do you know how many there were?'

'Two, maybe three.'

121

'Can you fly the thapter?'

'In the direst extremity, I can draw on a deeper strength for a minute or two.'

'You might have to, to take care of the soldiers.'

'If I do, I'll collapse before I can fly the thapter.'

Irisis hadn't realised Malien was in such bad shape. 'Can you climb down the rope?'

'Not in ten lifetimes,' Malien said.

Irisis thought for a moment, then rigged up a line to the nearest stanchion, ran a couple of turns around it and tied the other end carefully around Malien's waist. 'This is the best I can do. Can you manage?'

Malien had gone white. 'You'd better be quick.'

Irisis helped her over the side, holding the rope taut. Malien leaned out, her feet on one of the ribs of the keel. 'Ready?'

Malien nodded stiffly.

Taking a firm grip on the rope, Irisis checked that the thapter was below them. It was swinging gently in its nets. 'All right. Step off.'

Malien pushed off with both feet and the rope jerked as her weight came on it and slipped around the stanchion. She was heavier than she looked. Bracing herself, Irisis allowed the rope to run and Malien dropped sharply. One arm shot into the air but she regained control and it fell to her side. Irisis couldn't see her face – Malien was looking down.

A scuffle broke out behind Irisis. She glanced over her shoulder. Flangers, his back to the rail, was fighting two of Ghorr's guards. The line jerked again and Irisis turned away. She had to rely on Flangers to hold them off long enough to get Malien down. And herself.

A brilliant flash lit up the rigging, followed by a hollow, echoing boom – an air-dreadnought exploding not far away. The airbags wobbled back and forth and the vessel followed more sluggishly, its cables creaking and groaning. The heavy thapter barely moved and, consequently, appeared to stand out from the vessel at right-angles before swinging back.

Malien went whirling around on her rope. Another explosion

sent the airbags dancing the other way. The ropes thrummed, pulling so tight that Irisis felt sure the craft was going to tear apart. Malien's head came up and her mouth was wide open – she thought she was going to fall.

Irisis gauged the swing of the vessel relative to the thapter, paying out Malien's rope as fast as she dared. Malien was going to pass over the top of the thapter before swinging far out the other way. The vessel began to move again. There were only seconds to act.

Irisis recalculated the trajectories and, just before Malien's swing passed over the hatch, let go the rope. For one ghastly moment she thought she'd got it wrong and dropped Malien to her death. The thapter moved precisely as she'd thought it would and Malien landed hard on the top of the thapter, next to the hatch.

Her knees collapsed but Malien caught the handle of the hatch with one hand while she looped a bight of her line around it with the other. She raised her hand to Irisis, lifted the hatch and slipped through.

A youth fell past, his mouth open in a silent scream, so close that Irisis could see the spots on his chin. One second he was there; the next, gone to oblivion. She looked up instinctively. A length of smouldering rope came by, spinning end over end. It had just missed the gasbag above her. Should another burning fragment land on a gasbag, exploding floater-gas would blow the craft apart.

Pieces of wood rained down, shreds of canvas and other unidentifiable debris that had once been a majestic air-dreadnought. It began to snow, though the flakes were black as soot. A little whirlwind spun through the air, split into two, rejoined and disappeared.

Shadows moved up in the rigging; beams flashed and flickered. Yggur must still be alive, though how long could he last under such an attack? He'd been exhausted before they began it. Flangers had disappeared. He'd probably been killed and heaved over the side while her back had been turned.

The thapter's hatch had fallen closed so she couldn't tell

what was going on inside. Better get down to Malien's aid. Irisis had one foot over the rail when the outline of another air-dreadnought appeared, straight ahead. It was hanging in the air in their path, buffeted by the breeze but not moving. Why not? Its dangling cable appeared to have tangled in one of the forest trees and the crew were struggling to cut it free.

Ghorr's air-dreadnought was drifting straight towards it. Why didn't the pilot turn or climb? If she didn't act soon they were going to collide. Irisis ran down to the stern, where she discovered the pilot's chair empty. A woman in a pilot's uniform lay unconscious against the wall – she must have been knocked down in the fighting.

Irisis raced through her options. If she didn't go to Yggur's aid he was probably going to die, though if Malien was in trouble Yggur would expect Irisis to help her first. But at the rate the air-dreadnought was drifting, it would crash into the other craft before she could reach the thapter.

There was no help for it. She'd have to try and take the controller, though Irisis wasn't sure she even knew how it worked.

FOURTEEN

Before he'd realised what was happening, Nish had been grabbed and held fast. A second guard took his weapons, bound his hands, and pushed him down through the lower hatch of the thapter. He bounced off the metal ladder and landed hard on his backside on the floor below.

Stifling a groan, Nish looked up. The lower hatch remained open, suggesting that they expected to be dropping other people through it. Ghorr must have assumed that Yggur would try to recover the thapter. Perhaps he'd hung around Fiz Gorgo to lure the escaped prisoners back.

He rolled over, looking around. The egg-shaped interior was empty and the guards would have removed anything that could be used as a weapon. However, they didn't know the machine the way Nish did. During his time in the service of Minis the Aachim, and since then with Yggur, Nish had spent many weeks learning about the workings of constructs and thapters, honing his artificer's skills on them. He could have taken this machine apart blindfolded, so surely he could create some opportunity to escape.

Nish levered himself to his feet, which was awkward with his hands bound. He eased out one of the drawers, careful not to make a noise. It was empty. The thapter rolled like a ship in huge seas. He hung onto the handle until the motion eased, then opened one drawer after another. All had been emptied. The cup-boards and other storage spaces were likewise bare. The guards had been thorough.

Sitting down with his back to the wall, Nish tried to think of any concealed compartments that the guards might not have discovered. None came to mind. The thapter rolled so far to the right that he was dropped onto the side wall. He braced himself as it went back the other way. Above, the soldiers were swearing, uneasy. Well they might be, in such an uncanny and alien craft so precariously suspended in mid-air.

Thump. It sounded like someone landing on the top of the thapter. Irisis? He crawled across to the ladder and looked up as Malien slid through the hatch, one hand raised as if to cast some kind of charm against the occupants. She did not get the chance, for one of the guards whipped a bag over her head before she could speak. They bound and gagged her too, but laid her on the floor out of the way, partly closed the upper hatch and waited.

When Irisis came they would take her just as easily. Ghorr would have his public executions after all and, with the thapter, the victory might be enough for him to keep the chief scrutator-ship. Yggur's half-baked plan had turned a kind of victory into ruinous defeat.

Not if I can help it. Nish grasped at a desperate idea. Edging into the far corner of the egg-shaped space, he crouched down and twisted the concealed, recessed knob above the thapter's driving mechanism. Its hatch sighed open. Nish couldn't make the mechanism work to drive the thapter, of course. No one could but specially trained Aachim, and Tiaan, wherever she was.

And no one but Malien or Tiaan could make the thapter fly, for Malien had modified this one in a way that employed her own unique talent for the Secret Art, and she'd taught that to no one but Tiaan.

But he did know enough to carry out the series of tests that Aachim artificers employed when maintaining and repairing constructs, and perhaps one of those might be used to good effect. Nish considered the tests in turn. One caused the ceramic thyrimode to rotate in an orbital fashion, producing eerie squeaks and squeals that might alarm the guards and bring them down to investigate. No; it wouldn't be enough. He had to shock and terrify them.

Another test heated the muncial gyrolapp, a series of thick-walled glass tubes connected in a spiral like a string of stubby sausages, until its metal case glowed red hot. What if he smeared grease all over the case, then ran the test? The grease would produce a lot of smoke and a horrible smell, and the guards might flee, thinking the thapter was on fire. It wasn't much of a plan, and yet, the soldiers didn't sound at ease. It might create an opportunity, though he would have to be ready to act the moment one occurred.

He wriggled to the opening and reached in with his bound hands. He closed his eyes, the better to sense his way in through the maze of tubes, coils, globes, wires and crystals mounted above the reciprocating mechanisms. Had he been sitting in the dark with it in front of him, Nish could have identified any part by feel. Here it proved difficult to get his arms into the tightly packed space, and when he tried his gashed arm hurt abominably.

Nish went back to the centre and peered up the ladder. The soldiers were watching the upper hatch. Returning to the opening, he identified the case of the muncial gyrolapp, which was at the very furthest point he could reach. Scooping grease from a receptacle just inside the hatch, he smeared it all over the case, then set the gyrolapp to heat. Nish wiped his hands on the floor and, just as he was about to close the cover, noticed a prise-bar in its bracket on the wall of the compartment.

Snapping it out of its mounting, he slid it under his coat. On a whim, Nish set the ceramic thyrimode to rotate as well. The eerie noises couldn't hurt. He quickly closed the hatch, though he didn't fasten it, and rolled to the other side of the cabin.

The thyrimode gave a gentle whirr then began to run, almost silently at first. The thapter wallowed like a round-bottomed tub in a heavy swell, whereupon the mechanism emitted a brief, mournful squeak. Nish came to his knees, staring in the direction the sound had come from, waiting for a response from upstairs.

'What was that?' said one of the soldiers.

'Just the prisoner whining,' said the other. 'He'll do better than that when the master disemboweller gets his hooks into him.' He snorted with laughter.

The thyrimode emitted another squeak, longer and more shrill.

'Didn't sound like a man,' said the first. 'Go and have a look.'

The squeaks rose and fell, died away and began again until they swelled into an eerie, continuous moan. The soldier came running down the ladder, took in Nish on the far side of the room, his mouth open and eyes wide, and turned towards the source of the sound. It took him some time to find the hatch.

'Larg? Come down here. The Aachim bitch must have made it go.'

'Not allowed to leave my post,' said the other. 'You know that, Aln. The prisoner might have done it.'

'Him?' Aln's voice was a sneer. 'Remember what Ghorr said? Only Aachim can operate the cursed thing. And Tiaan the artisan.'

'See what the matter is,' said Larg, 'and get a move on. There could be others coming.'

Aln fiddled with the latch, trying to discover how it worked. The moaning from the thyrimode grew louder, as if it were grinding itself to pieces. He glanced over his shoulder at Nish, who hadn't moved.

'I can smell something burning,' Aln called.

Larg did not answer. Aln lifted the hatch of the mechanism, releasing thick clouds of brown, acrid smoke. The shrilling grew so loud that it made Nish's ears ache.

'Larg, Larg, we're afire!' Aln was on his knees, staring into the hole, but made no attempt to lower the hatch. He had no idea what to do.

Larg came thumping down the ladder and ran across the chamber. He took one look into the cavity, which was still belching fumes, then banged the hatch down.

'What are we supposed to do now?' said Aln. 'If it's destroyed, Ghorr will blame us. We're dead men, Larg.'

Larg paled. He stared around the chamber, his larynx working. 'We'll have to put it out. See if you can find some water –'

The room was thick with smoke. Nish slowly rose to his feet, trying to appear frightened. Neither of the soldiers took any notice.

'Water's no good,' said Aln. 'We'll need to smother it with sand or something.' He began to pull out the drawers, feverishly.

'Sand will ruin the mechanism,' said Larg, heading towards the ladder. 'See if you can find a rug or a blanket.'

Aln stared at the fuming hatch despairingly, then followed, evidently unwilling to remain below on his own. Nish tensed. This might be the only chance he got. When Aln came by, Nish rotated on the ball of one foot, swinging the heavy prise-bar hard and low with his bound hands.

It struck the soldier on the kneecap with a nauseating crack, he went down and Nish fell on him from behind, driving his knees into the fellow's back. As Aln hit the floor, Nish managed to fumble the knife from his belt.

He went backwards, trying to manipulate the blade with his bound hands so as to cut his bonds. It was an awkward operation, almost impossible.

'Larg!' cried Aln. 'Help.'

Nish slipped the knife through his fingers until he could touch his wrist ropes with the tip of the blade, though he couldn't exert much force. He pushed the tip across his ropes, pulled it back then pushed it again.

Larg appeared, feet first. He drew his own blade and began to come down, one step at a time. Nish pushed again and again. The ropes did not give. He forced harder and the point of the blade dug into his wrist, drawing blood.

'Drop it!' said Larg, reaching the bottom of the ladder.

Nish pushed too hard and the knife slipped from his fingers and skidded across the floor. He looked up at the soldier in desperation. He didn't bother to go after the blade – Larg could cut his throat before he reached it and, with bound hands, he couldn't possibly attack an able-bodied soldier armed with a knife.

Larg smiled evilly, sprang onto the floor and kept going down. What was the matter with him? A thread of blood began to ooze from the side of the soldier's neck, where a tiny knife had been embedded to the hilt.

Nish went to the ladder. Malien stood at the top, the gag around her throat, swaying.

'Thank you,' he said. 'How did you do that?'

'I used the control levers to tear off the gag, then employed my Art to loosen my bonds. Take his knife and come up.'

Nish did so. She freed his wrists and he carefully fastened the lower hatch. Cracking the upper hatch, he peered out through the gap.

'I can't see anyone on the air-dreadnought.'

'That's bad. They must all be dead.'

Nish blanched.

'Or round the other side,' she added hastily.

He opened the hatch a fraction more. 'No, I can see Irisis, at the controller. It looks as though she's trying to pilot the air-dreadnought. Trying to turn it.'

'Find out why,' said Malien, polishing a blue-green striated crystal on her sleeve and inserting it into its socket. 'She was supposed to follow me.' Gripping the controller levers with both hands, she strained until her face went red. Nothing happened.

Nish climbed up through the hatch and let out a yelp. 'Malien, we're heading directly for another air-dreadnought. Its rope is tangled in the trees.'

'The thapter doesn't want to go,' she said calmly.

'Do you think it could be because I put the mechanism into test mode?' said Nish.

'You did what?'

He explained. 'It was all I could think of to distract the soldiers.'

'Run down and stop it, quick as you can!'

He hurtled down the ladder and leapt the body at the bottom, not even thinking about the second soldier.

Nish lifted the cover, reached in through the fumes and shut off the thyrimode and the gyrolapp. The shrilling groans stopped at once. He was rubbing his stinging eyes when Aln fell on him, beating him about the head and shoulders with his fists.

Had the soldier been armed, Nish would have died. He went down but managed to roll out of the way. The soldier lurched after him on his battered knee, his face contorted in agony. Nish couldn't feel sorry for him – Aln had been happy to joke about Nish's fate. He kicked out, caught the soldier in the side of the knee and he collapsed next to the dead man, crying in pain. Nish scrambled to his feet.

'It's done, Malien!'

'I heard. Come up, quickly!'

He pulled himself up the ladder and fastened the hatch again. The mechanism groaned then roared to life.

'Put your head out of the hatch,' Malien snapped, taking a firm grip on the levers. 'Get ready to cut the ropes holding us in the nets. *But not till I say so.*'

Larg's keen blade in hand, Nish cracked the hatch open and looked forward. The other air-dreadnought loomed up, directly ahead.

'We're getting very close,' he cried.

'I know. Ready?'

He caught hold of one of the main ropes. 'Yes. Go, quickly!'

Malien jerked the levers. The thapter didn't move. She began muttering to herself.

'What's the matter?' Nish said, watching the air-dreadnought come ever closer. He could hardly bear to look.

'Ghorr must have locked the controls. Now, how would he have done that?'

'They use scrutator magic, a special form of the Art . . .' he began.

Malien knew that, of course. She had closed her eyes and was passing her hands across the controls, moving them in circular sweeping motions. Shaking her head, she began checking the glass plates, on which patterns moved in coloured lines and swirls.

Cocking her head to one side, she said 'Ah!' Her long Aachim fingers danced on the glass, then she jerked out an agate knob, banged in several others with a sweep of her hand and spun an insignificant thumb wheel below the binnacle.

'We're going to hit!' Nish cried. 'Do I cut?'

She didn't answer. Malien was too engrossed. Her other hand caressed the knob that made the thapter fly but she still didn't move it.

The two air-dreadnoughts merged with stately inevitability. The leading airbags touched, flattened against each other and slid past with silky hisses. The port and starboard airbags of Ghorr's craft struck their counterparts full on, pushed by, and their support cables tangled. The cables thrummed as they snapped taut, stopping the airbags within a few spans. The suspended vessel of Ghorr's air-dreadnought kept moving, curving in an arc towards the side of the other machine.

'Malien, can't you do anything?'

People on the other craft were screaming and running from the point of impact, though the pilot stood at her controls, her face frozen into a mask of horror. Her precious air-dreadnought, the mainstay of her existence, was going to be destroyed.

Malien's eyes remained closed though her fingers were still dancing. Now her eyes snapped open. 'I have it,' she said softly. 'Cut the ropes.'

She pulled up on the flight knob and the thapter jerked. Nish had just put his knife to the first rope when the bow of Ghorr's air-dreadnought drove right through the side of the other vessel amidships, snapping its keel and breaking it in two. One of the rope slings broke above his head and before he could cut the other the thapter rolled in the remaining net until it was tilted on its side.

It began to slide down.

FIFTEEN

After a desperate couple of minutes during which the two air-dreadnoughts came ever closer, Irisis was forced to abandon the controller, which was too different from the kind she'd spent her life crafting. She had no doubt that, given time, she could make it work, but time had run out.

With only twenty or thirty seconds to impact, she ran along the port deck, looking down at the thapter. It still hung in the nets but she was relieved to hear the sound of its flight mechanism, and to see Nish reaching out of the top hatch. He had a knife in his hand and looked set to cut the ropes. They'd done it.

He had his back to her. Irisis didn't call out, not wanting to distract him in those last vital seconds. She took a firm hold of the ropes and held her breath – why didn't they go? What was the matter? She braced herself for the impact, which was not as bad as she'd expected – at least, not to Ghorr's craft. The other vessel was smashed in two, hurling its crew everywhere.

Irisis hung onto the side ropes while Ghorr's craft came to a shuddering halt, the airbags lashing about wildly. She expected them to tear open, or even one to explode in a cataclysm that would spread to all the airbags and send the flaming wreckage into the swamp forest. It didn't happen. The airbags held and so did the ropes. The cable of the wrecked vessel, still tangled in one of the swamp forest trees, anchored them in place.

The thapter was gone, though Irisis didn't remember hearing the song of its mechanism. Had Malien got it moving in time, or had it fallen into the mist-wreathed swamp? Irisis couldn't tell.

Malien and Nish were beyond her helping, one way or the other, which reduced her options to one. She headed back the way she had come, looking up for Flangers, Klarm or Yggur. It occurred to her that they might all be dead and she'd be more usefully employed saving her own life. Irisis didn't give that any further consideration, for it wasn't in her nature, though she didn't see what she could do where the mighty had failed.

She circumnavigated the outer deck without seeing a soul, apart from a few battered survivors clinging desperately to the dangling wreckage of the other air-dreadnought. One, a woman Irisis could not see, called out piteously, 'Help me.'

Irisis turned away. She was still seeing an occasional flash from above, which meant that either Yggur or Klarm must have survived. She clutched at her pliance, a momentary comfort, then tucked it back inside her shirt. Best if no one knew she'd recovered it.

'Help me, please help me.'

She climbed onto the roof of the cabin, tied a length of rope to the rigging and swung across the gap onto the stern section of the other air-dreadnought, which now hung vertically from a single airbag.

The pilot, a little woman who rather resembled Ullii in her pale hair and blanched skin, had her arms and legs wrapped around the steering arm of the vessel and was crooning softly to herself. She didn't look up as Irisis landed catlike just above her. The cry must have come from further down.

Irisis fastened her line to the rail so she could get back to Ghorr's vessel, and went down the vertical side, using the meshed rails like a rope ladder. The woman who had cried out was lying on what had been the rear wall of one of the cabins, and she had two broken legs. She was middle-aged, thin, with lank dark hair and a cast in her left eye.

'I'm sorry,' said Irisis, making her as comfortable as she could. 'The best thing is for you to stay here until it's all over.'

'Don't leave me,' the woman screamed, throwing her arms around Irisis's neck in a crushing grip.

'I can't get you to the other craft by myself. You'll be safe here.' As safe as anyone else, she added silently.

The woman began to wail. Irisis disengaged herself as gently as she could and went out the now horizontal door, closing it behind her. The cries followed her all the way back up the rail. Coming across had been the wrong thing to do. She should have kept on with her own work.

The pilot was now standing up on the stern, wild-eyed. She'd removed her precious controller from the steering arm and hung it around her neck.

'It'll be over soon,' Irisis said, trying to sound reassuring as she unfastened her rope from the rail.

'It's over,' said the pilot, and stepped out into space.

Irisis was so shocked that she had to hang on to the rail for a moment. She looked down and wished she hadn't.

Get on with it, she told herself. Yggur and Klarm may need your help. Ignoring the cries from the wreckage, she swung back onto the roof of Ghorr's cabin.

Down the other end a series of ladders and knotted ropes led up to the four main airbags, which were distributed at the points of a diamond, and to the smaller central airbag high above them. They were held in place by a vast network of ropes, and it was no wonder the craft needed a crew as big as a sailing ship. The airbags and ropes became blurry outlines halfway up – Yggur must have carried his mist up with him. Irisis touched her pliance and could see power being drained from the field up there. Yggur and Ghorr were still at it.

She unfastened her line and looped it around her waist, then rested her foot on the forward cabin roof while she caught her breath. The roof, which was about fourteen spans by four, was stacked with rolls of canvas and airbag silk, barrels of tar, coils of rope, and boxes, chests and barrels of supplies, all tightly roped down. The supplies were covered in tarpaulins but spaces between them made ideal hiding places for guards who could shoot her in the back as she climbed.

Don't be paranoid, she told herself. The guards are dead or up attacking Yggur. But where were the crew? It was like a ghost ship. No doubt some hadn't been lifted from the amphitheatre, and others had been killed in the fighting, but she couldn't see a soul. Irisis eased into the first alley, probing ahead of her with the tip of the weapon, lifting the tarpaulins and feeling between the crates and barrels.

She didn't discover anyone, but as she went aft Irisis realised that what she'd thought was another crate was in fact a square cage. She could see the bars through the stretched canvas. She tapped on the canvas and heard a faint, mewling cry, a very familiar sound.

'Ullii?' she said, carefully cutting across and down, then peeling the canvas away.

The little seeker lay on the floor of the cage, though not scrunched up into a ball, as was her wont when distressed. She lay stretched out with her hands gripping the bars in front of her and her toes clenched onto the bars on the far side of the cage. Her colourless hair was a wild tangle, her eyes red and staring.

Crouching down, Irisis reached through the bars. Ullii did not like to be touched, as a rule, but she didn't react when Irisis's hand met her bare shoulder.

'Ullii, what has Ghorr done to you?'

Ullii made no reply.

'Why didn't you free yourself?' said Irisis. 'The way you freed me that time in Nennifer.'

Ullii turned those tragic eyes on her. 'Lattice gone.'

'It'll come back,' Irisis said lightly. 'Now, let's get you out of here.'

'Gone forever,' said Ullii. 'Nothing left. Want to die.'

'Nonsense,' Irisis said briskly. She couldn't deal with that after the pilot's shocking suicide. She smashed the lock off with the butt of her sword and wrenched the door open. 'Come on.'

Ullii followed lethargically, evincing no curiosity, though

Irisis was used to that. She turned to the rope ladder that led up into the rigging. An occasional flash still came from the nebulosity above, though weaker than before.

She climbed up into the mist, which thickened until she could only see a few of the rungs of the ladder above her, and just the top of Ullii's head below. There was *something* up here, more than mist and smoke. She touched her pliance. Power was being drawn in dozens of places, though Irisis could not tell what it was being used for.

She began to sense a structure to the mist. It was like a series of scalloped platforms connected by stairs and ladders, though that could hardly be a part of the air-dreadnought. It was a creation of the Art, but Irisis couldn't tell whether it was Yggur's strange Art or Ghorr's scrutator magic.

As they reached the level of the four main airbags, the airbags appeared transparently in the distance, as if this place were only partly of the real world. Rigging ran between them, holding them in place, though here it appeared like strands drawn out of cloud or webs spangled with dewdrops. Tenuous paths led down and up, into nebulous cloud chambers. Between them, staircases ran to airy pavilions, arches and gates that had no part in an air-dreadnought's rigging.

The flashes, now blue and red, came from higher up. Irisis put one foot out towards the first of the staircases.

Ullii snatched at her arm. 'Not there!'

Irisis stepped back onto firmness then probed ahead with her sword. It went straight through what had appeared to be solid matter. The staircase was a deceit. Were any of the stairs and pavilions real, or was it a snare as cunningly designed as a spider's web?

'How did you know?' she said, shaken.

Ullii let go of her arm. 'I can still *see*,' she said with that all too familiar hint of scorn that made Irisis smile. Ullii wasn't as deep in despair as she made out.

'Perhaps you'd better lead the way.'

Ullii went up, across and up again, stepping sure-footedly,

always seeing the true paths among the traps and deceits Yggur and Ghorr had set for each other, which Irisis could not detect even with her fingers wrapped tightly around her pliance and the field streaming through her inner eye.

Up here she encountered deck upon deck, terrace upon terrace, pavilion upon pavilion, all linked like a misty maze, but one step off the unseeable path and they would fall fifty spans into the swamp forest.

'Dwarf!' said Ullii as they rounded a mist bank surrounded by a shimmering rainbow in shades of green and yellow.

A span or two off the path, trapped in a cell shaped somewhat like a pumpkin, the little man clutched at the bars. Klarm looked at Irisis, she at him.

'Should I set you free or leave you here where you're safe?' said Irisis.

'If you don't free me the right way, the cell will simply dissolve into bottomless air,' said Klarm.

'And if I leave you here?'

'If Ghorr is defeated, or victorious and so chooses, the cell will simply dissolve into bottomless air.'

'Then I'm not taking much of a risk. But just in case, tie on to this.' She passed one end of her line through the bars, tied the other around her hips, took Klarm's hand and braced herself.

'Ullii?' said Irisis, acting on a hunch.

Ullii cursed Irisis under her breath, but put her hand to the lock and the cage melted into empty air, giving the lie to her earlier words about losing her lattice. Irisis, with some effort, swung Klarm up onto a solid footing.

'Where's Yggur?' she said.

'He was up there, earlier,' said Klarm, pointing between the topmost airbag and the starboard one, where a gauzy path branched into three. The middle path passed through a triumphal arch, though nothing could be seen beyond it but blue-black emptiness. The right path terminated at what appeared to be a stone garden seat, while the left one wound off into mist. 'But this labyrinth changes all the time. I don't know where he is now. Ghorr may have him already!'

'How did it get here?' Irisis said as they mounted a stair like airy crystal.

'Ghorr hunted Yggur up here and Yggur created this place as he went – it was the only defence he had the strength for. Even here, at the seat of Yggur's power, it was the one shelter he could make without the aid of crystals or artefacts.'

'But it didn't work.'

'It saved his life but he can't escape it. Ghorr is the father of scrutator magic and he's got a whole air-dreadnought full of crystals and devices to store and channel his power. Every deception Yggur creates, Ghorr sees through it. And now Ghorr is starting to take control of the labyrinth, and turn its traps and deceptions back on its maker.' A dull red flash carved slices off the sky above them. 'See how weak he is. In a few minutes it'll be over.'

Ullii led them to another cell, this one a cube of glassy nothingness not unlike the steps they were standing on. A bloodstained Flangers, with minor wounds in a dozen places, had been imprisoned inside it, spread-eagled. Ullii freed him as she had Klarm and he hobbled after them.

They mounted a bifurcating ramp to a higher level, a sheer white plane on which rolled two enormous spheres. The nearer one was three or four spans across and made of smoky glass with a metallic lustre. A smaller sphere moved inside the larger, though Irisis could not see what it contained. The distant sphere was even bigger, completely transparent, and contained innumerable smaller spheres, all rolling about inside the larger one.

'That's Yggur,' said Ullii.

A feeble red flash lit up one of the small spheres and they saw a tiny figure inside, staggering from one rolling, tumbling sphere to another like a rat trapped in a maze. The red light silhouetted the occupant of the nearer sphere and it was unmistakably Ghorr.

White light jagged out from Ghorr's hand, illuminating Yggur's outer sphere and licking around the outside until it found a way in. One of the inner spheres glowed green, went dark and disappeared. Shortly Irisis heard a faint tinkle, like glass smashing. Looking more closely, she saw that a number of the small spheres had already imploded, leaving just transparencies as tenuous as soap bubbles.

'If Ghorr catches Yggur inside one . . .' said Irisis.

'With a thousand shards of glass driven through his body, it'll be the end of him,' said Klarm.

'He's doomed anyway, surely?'

'As long as there were lots of spheres he could outguess Ghorr. Once there are only a few, sooner or later Ghorr will pick his destination at the same time as Yggur jumps.'

'It's not Yggur's way to be trapped like that. He'll come out first and attack head-on.'

'He's too weak. Ghorr would annihilate him.'

'Then we've got to stop Ghorr.'

'What if I were to attack his sphere from behind?' said Flangers. 'I could take Irisis's sword.'

'The sphere was created with the Art,' said Klarm. 'You couldn't break it with a sword, and as soon as you tried he'd roll right over you.'

'It might give Yggur the chance he needs,' said Flangers.

'And you might be throwing away your life for nothing,' said Irisis. 'No, Flangers – sword against sword but the Art against the Art. What can we do, Klarm?'

'Ghorr still holds the keys to the chief scrutator's chest and, despite his earlier setbacks, he's still the strongest of all the Council. If he can overpower Yggur, or take him alive, the other scrutators will support him. They worship power – it's the very meaning of the Council's existence. Although Ghorr stands revealed as a coward and a vicious thug, if he has the power he holds the Council in his hand.'

Ghorr's sphere rolled the other way, emitting a double flash that burst two of the glassy bubbles inside Yggur's sphere. It spun crazily and wheeled off, wobbling across the floor, the figure inside staggering like a drunk.

His options were shrinking to nothing, and Irisis couldn't let that happen. 'Ghorr has to be overcome. He must fall.'

'He stripped me of my scrutator magic before he put me in

that cell,' said Klarm. 'I can't stop him and I don't think anyone can.'

They were above the mist here. Irisis looked back at the survivors of the air-dreadnought fleet, which had gathered over Fiz Gorgo and were turning towards them. 'What about Fusshte?' His craft was heading in their direction and she could see him at the bow.

'By the time he arrives, Yggur will be dead.'

Irisis felt an overwhelming urge to attack blindly, in the hope that something would happen that she could use to her advantage. She was at her best when she acted instinctively. 'Then it's up to me.'

She ran towards the middle of the white plane. 'Ghorr!' she cried, waving her arms. 'Chief Scrutator Ghorr.'

A triple flash imploded three globes. 'Ghorr!' Irisis waved her sword over her head, but as soon as his sphere turned in her direction she tossed the weapon onto the floor and put her hands in the air.

'Ghorr!' she screamed. 'I'll tell you my secret. I'll tell you everything.'

He sent another flash towards his opponent, who reeled off, then spun in her direction. The sphere came right up close, looming four times her height above her. It carved circles around her, though Ghorr never took his eyes off his wounded opponent.

'You'll tell me how you, a mere artisan with no talent for the Secret Art, killed Jal-Nish's mancer on the aqueduct at the manufactory?'

'Yes,' she said.

'And how you *really* escaped from your locked cell in Nennifer.'

Good. He didn't believe that Ullii had done it.

'Yes, yes,' she said. 'That too. I'll tell you everything if you'll just spare Yggur.'

'Why do you care? Is he your lover too?'

Yggur was not, but Irisis lowered her eyes and said nothing. Let him think what he liked. All she knew was that, with Flydd

141

so brutalised, perhaps beyond recovery, Yggur was their last hope.

'Disgusting!' he said, for that was not *his* vice. 'Well, spill it.'

She looked over her shoulder. 'Do you want them to know too?'

Ghorr spun the sphere, directing a spear of light at Yggur's bubble, then another and another. All three hit their target. Yggur was still moving from one of the remaining globes to another, but very slowly.

The front of Ghorr's sphere shimmered to transparency. 'Step through!'

Irisis had been hoping to entice him out but, clearly, with Yggur still at large, that was a vain hope. She stepped reluctantly towards the transparency.

She felt no resistance, though the instant she was through, the wall began to harden behind her. Irisis panicked and tried to throw herself out again, but it was too late. She put her hands against the wall of the inner sphere. It was just as impenetrable. She was trapped and Ghorr was safe.

Irisis beat on the glass. He simply sneered and turned away. 'Did you really think I'd be taken in that easily? I'll crush him like the roach he is. I'm not going to give him any chances.'

'What about my secrets?' she said plaintively.

'I'll have all the time in the world to devote to you, Crafter Irisis, once I'm back in Nennifer at the head of the Council and you're hanging upside down on my dungeon wall.'

SIXTEEN

Nish hung on desperately as the thapter rolled. The note of the mechanism rose a little, then fell again. The machine slipped through the nets before stopping with a jerk that threw him halfway out of the angled hatch.

'What's the matter?' he yelled.

Malien took a while to answer. 'Ghorr has a lock put on it that I'm having trouble breaking. I can get the thapter to lift, though not enough to make it fly.'

'Better work fast. We're slipping through the nets.'

'I can feel it!' she snapped over her shoulder. 'I'm doing all I can, Nish. If that doesn't work, then falling to our deaths is our fate.'

'I don't believe in fate,' he muttered.

She gave him one of those looks that implied he was speaking above his station. Even Malien, the gentlest and most broadminded Aachim he'd ever met, was not entirely free of the legendary Aachim arrogance.

The thapter slipped further, the mechanism roared and the machine lifted against the meshes before falling back.

'Still locked?' said Nish.

Malien didn't look up. 'No, but I'm having trouble drawing power.'

'Ghorr must be using it,' he said.

'Of course,' she said. 'I see it now, and he's using colossal amounts of power.' She stood up straight and gently lifted the flight lever; the thapter rose and, with a delicate wriggle and a shake, slipped free of the meshes.

It immediately dropped sharply and she struggled to hold it as she clutched the flight controller with both hands. The mechanism roared and faded. She directed the thapter towards a mud island in the swamp, landing with a thump that splattered mud and reeds everywhere.

'Are you all right?' said Nish.

She leaned against the side for a moment, then slid down to the floor. 'I'm weaker than I thought. Should be able to do this in my sleep.'

Nish stared up at the air-dreadnought. The mist had dissipated everywhere except among the tangled airbags, where it was thicker than ever. A flash made it glow milkily. Something was going on up there.

Malien sat with her head on her knees. Nish tried to curb his impatience as her breathing slowly returned to normal. Ghorr was close to victory, Nish knew it.

'Malien, we've got to help Yggur.'

'What can I do, Nish?' she said softly. 'I can't force strength where there is none.'

'Ghorr has Yggur trapped. And Irisis. He's got them all.'

'How can you be sure?'

'I don't know, but I am sure.'

'Where are they? I can't tell.'

'Up!' Nish said urgently. 'They're up among the airbags. You'll have to –' He broke off, expecting another flash of arrogance.

Malien got up, lifted the thapter and turned towards Fiz Gorgo, shaking her head. The mechanism faltered; the thapter dipped and her fingers worked furiously to bring it back up again. She put the nose down, travelling slowly between the trees. 'I can't take him on. I can barely keep this thing in the air.'

'But . . !'

'I know,' she said gently. 'I'm sorry, Nish, but I simply can't

144

do anything about it. We have to retreat while we can, and hope to take him on later. There's a right time for every battle and this isn't it.' She turned the thapter away.

'There won't be a later,' he said bitterly. 'They'll be dead!'

'Just give me an hour . . . or two.'

'We don't have that long. Ghorr won't dare linger once it starts to get dark. He'll kill them straight away, or take them with him to torture them to death at his leisure.'

The thapter dipped again. Malien swerved in through the branches of a swamp forest giant. Nish ducked instinctively.

'I must rest, Nish. Just give me an hour.'

'What if you were to let me try?'

'Try *what*?' she said forbiddingly.

'Just take me up there. I've got to do *something*, Malien.'

'He'll crucify you, Nish, then flay you alive. If you could have heard the things Ghorr said about you earlier, you wouldn't go within a thousand leagues of him. He blames you for everything that has gone wrong today, and rightly so.'

'I know, and I'm terrified of him, but I still have to go. He hates Irisis even more than he loathes me, Malien, and if he keeps her alive it would only be to wring such torments out of her that the very ethyr will echo with her agony. I have to go to her aid, no matter what the cost. I can do nothing else.'

She took one hand off the controller to grip his shoulder. 'You're a true stalwart Nish. I was quite wrong about you when we first met, back in Tirthrax.'

'I was such a callow, selfish fool then that I can't bear to remember it.'

'I'll drop you up top but after that it's up to you. I won't risk the thapter.'

'If he wins, he'll be back for it in the night.'

'And we've precious little strength to resist him. But we all must do what we can.'

By the time the thapter hovered just above the white deck, Malien was close to collapse. Nish stepped out onto the surface, whose foundations seemed tenuous in the extreme. Should it

145

fail, or the Art that supported it be withdrawn, none of them would have to worry about the future.

The surviving air-dreadnoughts now began to draw in around Ghorr's, cutting off any escape, though they made no effort to intervene. They would see the conflict through to the end, and only then would they strike. Or bow to the victor.

Klarm duck-walked Nish's way, Flangers limping beside him, carrying Irisis's sword but so worn out that he could barely hold the tip up. Ullii came two steps behind, peering around at Nish as if expecting him to be angry with her. He didn't have the energy.

'Where's Irisis?' said Nish.

'Ghorr has her.' Klarm indicated the closer sphere, presently rolling towards another whose seething inner globes were mostly shattered-glass grey, though a few were transparent. 'Yggur is in that one, but he's failing rapidly and I'm powerless to help him.'

Behind them the thapter lifted, almost soundlessly, side-slipped into the mist lower down, and was gone. Ghorr's great globe rolled around them, rotating slowly, though the inner globe remained in the same orientation no matter what the motion of the outer. Irisis was trapped between the two. The globe stopped, leaving her spread-eagled upside down, staring despairingly at Nish. She waved her hands as if to push him away.

The globe stopped while Ghorr inspected the new arrival, then whirled away to orbit Yggur's limping, failing sphere. White light forked out, once, twice, and two more inner globes exploded. Ghorr raised his good arm and a treacly brown fan of light touched Yggur's outer sphere, which dissolved from the base like sugar in the rain. The last surviving globe, with Yggur still inside, fell to the milky floor where it stuck fast in the gooey remnants of the sphere.

Nish ran towards it, pulling out his sword as if he could break the sphere and free Yggur from his magical confinement. As he came close Yggur sagged against the wall, then stood up straight and forced out his arm, sending a final blast at his nemesis.

Had it been a ruse to lure the chief scrutator close? Nish

allowed himself to hope so. Surely Yggur had been playing with Ghorr, just waiting for this moment, and was now going to destroy him.

Red lightning forked out from Yggur's fingers but a counter-blast turned the surface of his globe into a mirror, outside and in, that reflected the blast back on him. Nish didn't see what happened inside, though he could imagine the effect on human flesh of so much power expending itself in such a tiny space. The mirrored sphere turned black, then white and silver again, only to burst around its equator, emitting a circumferential blast of steam.

It fell in two halves, which spun like tops across the floor. The empty half went whizzing by Nish. The other spiralled directly towards Ghorr's sphere, stopping just a few spans away.

Ghorr stepped through his inner sphere, then the outer, though the opening closed behind him at once, leaving Irisis trapped inside. He walked up to the slowly rotating hemisphere, which was still steaming.

Nish ran, though he knew it was all over. Even had Yggur survived that terrible back-blast he would be helpless against Ghorr, who seemed to be growing stronger as the battle went on. He would reassert control over the Council, attack Fiz Gorgo a second time and regain the thapter as well as all the prisoners. Victory was within his grasp.

Nish skidded to a stop beside the hemisphere. Yggur lay inside, his long frame clenched into a ball, his hair a frizzy mass of black. His clothes had been turned to char while his exposed skin was coated with soot. He lay unmoving.

Ghorr prodded Yggur with the platinum-shod tip of his staff. Yggur did not move. Ghorr jabbed it hard into his ribs. Nothing.

'A pity,' Ghorr said dispassionately. 'A great man and a great mancer – probably the greatest of all, before *me*. I could have learned much from him. But, like many a great mancer down the aeons, hubris was his downfall. He fought me all the way but neglected to protect himself against his own power.'

He turned to Nish. 'My guards let me down last night, in

failing to ensure that you were taken. They will pay for it.' He raised his hand.

Nish's sword grew too hot to hold. He dropped it and it fell straight through the white floor. Nish rubbed his burning palm.

'But not nearly as much as you, Cryl-Nish. Oh, how you're going to suffer.'

Irisis had watched despairingly as Yggur's defences were broken, globe by globe, but she plunged to the depths of the abyss when Nish suddenly appeared on the edge of the platform. Why had she been so reckless? How could she have imagined she could overcome Ghorr? She'd assumed, because he'd previously fled like a craven cur, that he was a broken man. A cur he undoubtedly was, but he was still the strongest and best-equipped mancer on Santhenar.

Yggur was beaten, broken and probably dead. The burning sword fell from Nish's fingers and disappeared through the floor. Ghorr had everything except the thapter and soon he would have that as well. Oh Nish, why didn't you stay away? She couldn't bear to think of Ghorr torturing him. She'd sooner take the pain on herself.

She felt all hot and congested; her face was bloated from hanging upside down. Irisis pushed against the wall and found that she could move a little. She heaved and thrust until she got herself right way up, but could go no further.

Irisis couldn't hear what Ghorr was saying, though she'd spent enough time in his hands to imagine it. He would be treating Nish to a picturesque description of the excruciations to come. Ghorr would torture Nish on the spot to discover the whereabouts of Malien, the thapter, and his last remaining enemy, Xervish Flydd.

And Nish couldn't hold out, for he felt pain keenly. Then, as Ghorr gestured over his shoulder in her direction, Irisis realised that Nish's torture would only be the first act. He'd soon switch to torturing her in front of Nish, and Nish would snap. He'd tell Ghorr everything rather than be the cause of a friend's agony.

There had to be a way out. If Ullii had been stronger-minded, she might have saved them, but even at the best of times Ullii could only perform her wonders to save herself. She'd rescued Irisis back in Nennifer purely because Ullii had felt so threatened. Unfortunately, Ullii wasn't directly threatened now.

And then a possibility popped into her head. What if she, Irisis, were to attack Ghorr the way she'd killed Jal-Nish's mancer on the aqueduct a year ago?

Under the most desperate duress, Irisis had constructed a concealed packet of pure force and manipulated it to the place from which Jal-Nish's mancer had been drawing power from the field. The power had been too much for the mancer to bear. It had blown her to pieces and Ghorr had been so threatened by what Irisis had stumbled upon, all unwittingly, that he'd tortured her in fruitless attempts to uncover the secret. Fortunately Ullii had spirited her away from Nennifer first.

Yet Jal-Nish's mancer, strong though she had been, could be no more than a novice compared to Ghorr. Moreover, Ghorr could have gleaned enough from Irisis's tormented ramblings to fashion a protection for himself. If he had, attacking him this way was tantamount to suicide. But she had to try.

Taking her pliance from around her neck, Irisis clasped her hands around it, careful not to let Ghorr see that she'd recovered it. Hands in front of her as if begging, or praying, she sought for the field. It was all around her, and very strong here, swirling in threads and streaks of red and blue, plunging into fringed sinkholes, and arching out again. The sinkholes were the draw points that supported this whole phantom architecture in the sky.

Nish cried out. Irisis couldn't hear it through the wall of the sphere, though she saw his face contorting in agony. The field vanished and she couldn't find it again. She closed her eyes. She couldn't look upon his torment and do what she had to do. Wrenching the field back into her inner eye, Irisis scanned it for the place from which Ghorr was drawing power.

Ah, he was clever. Yggur had created this phantom labyrinth, but Ghorr maintained it by drawing from five or six parts of the field at once. That would make it difficult to do what she had done before – perhaps impossible. Moreover, he did not draw power through a simple object like a crystal or pliance, as all mancers she knew did. Ghorr used a myriad of such devices linked together on a belt studded with crystals and linked by threads of wire. It spread the load throughout his body and protected him from overloading – though, in truth, he was such a powerful mancer that it might not be possible to overload him.

Defeating him was as far beyond her as reaching to the moon. Irisis unclenched her fists, opened her eyes and Nish doubled up in such agony that she could *feel* it. How could that be?

Nish fell forward and Irisis saw Ullii contorted behind him. Nish's pain was hurting her and she was broadcasting it throughout her lattice. So Ullii *hadn't* completely lost it.

It gave Irisis heart. Reaching into the field, she began to weave its tiny threads into a lozenge shape, representing one of the crystals on Ghorr's belt. Following the patterns of the power he was drawing, she linked the lozenge to another, then another, continuing until she had made a crude representation of the nine crystals on his belt. Irisis then shuttled back and forth, weaving linkages between the lozenges and checking to make sure that they were as close as possible to the linkages of his belt. It was just like making her jewellery, really, and she'd been doing that since she was little.

A multicoloured fan flashed into her mind, then vanished. Though Irisis hadn't seen it before, she knew what it was – it was the way Ullii saw her lattice. Ullii's despairing broadcast must be sending it to her. The fan was clustered with knots, near and far, representing the surviving scrutators and mancers on the air-dreadnoughts, as well as Malien, Gilhaelith, Flydd and any other person who could use the Art. Other shapes denoted every crystal and artefact within leagues of Fiz Gorgo.

But the lattice was dominated by one gigantic knot, a globe clad with poisoned flails. It was the way Ullii saw Ghorr.

Another silent scream from Nish, though this time Irisis managed to divert it so as to protect her ethereal weaving. When it was as precise a representation as she could manage, she passed a spindle through each of the lozenge-crystals and spun the field around it until it was tightly concentrated there. Lastly, she wove a concealment around each lozenge. Unless Ghorr was scanning the field constantly, he wouldn't realise what she had done.

Now! she thought, as Nish arched up again. Irisis moved the ethyric belt so that the positions of its lozenges of pure force matched the places Ghorr was drawing power from, via the crystals on his belt. She withdrew from the field carefully, lest he become suspicious.

She opened her eyes to see Nish doubled over again and Ghorr raising his arms to strike. But Ghorr did not strike. He froze and her heart began to hammer. Ghorr looked around uneasily. Irisis did not meet his eye, afraid that he would be able to read what she had been up to.

A movement in the distance caught her eye. Scrutator Fusshte stood at the bow of his air-dreadnought, a spyglass to his eye, waiting like a jackal for his chief to fall. Or like a sycophant, should Ghorr succeed, to pledge allegiance anew. Either way, success or failure, Fusshte would emerge the stronger.

She looked back to Ghorr, who squeezed one fist. Nish cried out, arching his back and forming his fingers into hooks. Come on, Ghorr, she thought. Take the power, *now.*

Ghorr did so, then suddenly doubled over, gasping and clutching at his chest. Flecks of red sprayed across the white floor. He retched, coughing something red out onto the floor that looked for all the world like a piece of lung.

Yes! You stinking swine, take that. Irisis rose to her feet, brandishing one fist. You're not as clever as you think.

He snapped upright and she realised that it had been a ruse to identify who was secretly attacking him. Whirling on one foot, Ghorr flung out his arm, his thick middle finger pointing at her throat.

The outer sphere split like the segments of an orange, frigid air buffeted her, then the inner sphere crashed into her back, knocking Irisis off her feet. Before she could move it rolled up her spread legs, over her buttocks and settled in the hollow of her back, where its base seemed to flow and mould itself to her contours. It was so heavy that she could not budge it, and her chest was pressed against the floor so tightly that she could hardly draw breath.

The base of the sphere flowed up her back, spread around both sides of her neck and began to draw tight. She threw out her arms before it trapped them too, and forced her fingers up in front of her throat, trying to hold back the invisible straps that were close to joining into a noose.

Ghorr had known what she was doing all along, yet felt so confident that he'd allowed her to continue. Perhaps he'd been hoping to discover her deadly secret. And now he had it.

The straps joined to form a belt, an analogue of the one she'd woven and powered by the same spindles of force. He had a keen sense of irony. The belt pulled tight, cutting off her breath in mid-gasp, and Irisis was not strong enough to hold it back. Her fingers were trapped, the knuckles digging into her throat and crushing her windpipe. In two or three minutes she would be unconscious, and two minutes after that, dead.

A choking minute went by. Ullii's fan-shaped lattice appeared and suddenly, instantly, Irisis knew what she had to do. She focussed on that flail-covered sphere, the seeker's unique rendering of Ghorr, and remade it.

She turned the flails to drooping, overripe bananas, the black sphere into a rotting pumpkin covered in blowflies, with fat white grubs crawling out of oozing holes in the skin. It was all she could think of to do. Not enough, surely, though Ullii's sense of humour was rustic in the extreme.

The belt snapped tighter and she felt the bones of her neck shift. She wondered if she'd die of a broken neck before she suffocated. Time slowed right down and the last thing Irisis saw, before all went opaque, was Ullii suddenly convulse with laughter.

For an unknown time, seconds or hours, the field swirled in stately patterns more beautiful than any she'd ever seen. Dying wasn't so bad after all.

152

The patterns vanished, the pressure eased and cold air rushed down her throat, and then the world went insane. Her eyes flicked open, though what she saw could not be happening. The ticking rotors of the surrounding air-dreadnoughts emitted tortured groans as they spun up beyond their maxima. There were cries as the great craft lurched in all directions, colliding and tangling with each other. Two exploded in a colossal fireball that seared her exposed cheek.

The phantom labyrinth sagged underfoot before going hard as crystal, flinging Nish and Klarm in the air. The deformed sphere on Irisis's back crumbled like week-old bread. Pieces of the floor broke away and once again black snowflakes drifted down, while red wisps of acrid vapour, like the fumings from an alchymist's cauldron, condensed in mid-air.

Ullii's lattice fan was stretched like a rubber sheet, as if she'd taken it in her hands and pulled it. The knots on it were drawn out to black streaks, all but one. Ullii let go of the lattice and Ghorr's rotting sphere went flubbing up above the fan as if she'd fired it from a catapult. It came down again and splatted against the lattice, which snapped back and wrapped itself tightly around Ghorr's knot, squeezing it into a tighter and tighter ball until, finally, with a burst of light, both knot and lattice vanished.

Ghorr shrieked as he fell halfway through the floor. His clothes exploded into rags, revealing a wattled, sack-like belly bulging between a pair of tightly laced corsets, fat-marbled upper arms, the left one stained with old blood, and wobbling fish-belly thighs. The illusions he'd maintained for decades evaporated. His lips shrank, displaying yellow, corroded teeth and retreating gums, and jowls saggy enough to contain a handful of marbles each. The mane of hair vanished apart from a few dingy straps dangling over his ears.

The tightness around her throat was gone. Irisis sucked in a breath, rubbing her bruised throat as she tried to work out what Ullii had done. She'd destroyed Ghorr's knot, an analogue of his mancer's self, and her lattice in the process. She'd damaged Ghorr, stripped him of much of his mancer's power, but had she destroyed it utterly? Surely not, or this phantom world would have vanished and they would all have fallen into the forest. So something still remained. What would he do with it?

She got up and limped across to join her friends.

SEVENTEEN

'You haven't finished me yet,' said Ghorr. 'But I can finish you.'

'Your power is broken, Ghorr,' said Klarm, making no secret of his derision. 'You'll never get it back.'

'There's more than one kind of power,' Ghorr choked, trying to pull the rags over his sagging, repulsive frame.

'You needn't bother,' said Irisis. 'It'd take a sail to cover that up.'

Ghorr shot her a venomous glance, took three steps to the collapsed remains of his sphere and from inside lifted an unusual multiple crossbow. Irisis hadn't seen one like it for ages. A massive device that only a strong man could use, it fired five bolts at once. Jal-Nish had designed the bow as a lyrinx killer long ago, though it had proved too unwieldy in the battlefield. Before anyone could move, he had its five bolts trained on them.

'Come out, Yggur,' he said.

Nails scratched on glass, then a blackened hand flopped over the nearer side of the hemisphere. A frizzy head and ebony face rose up above the side, frost-grey eyes brilliant against the soot.

'Out!' Ghorr jerked the crossbow at him.

Yggur climbed out and staggered across to the others, charred pieces of clothing flaking off him like the black snow of a few minutes ago. He could barely stand, but at least he was alive.

'Five with one blow,' Ghorr said. 'It'll have to do. Any last words, my friends? A simple acknowledgment of my mastery will do.'

Klarm began to speak but Ullii, who was standing beside Nish and Irisis, said quietly, 'Do you love me, Nish?'

After a long pause he replied, 'Ah, Ullii, I'm sorry. I thought I did, once and . . . I'll always care for you. But no, I don't love you. I can't.'

'Thank you,' she said quietly. Turning to Nish, she took his hand in her little hands.

'What for?' he said numbly.

'You've set me free. My lattice is truly gone this time and it will never come back. There's nothing to keep me now.'

'I don't understand.'

She let go of his hand. Klarm was still speaking.

'Enough!' snapped Ghorr. 'You never did know when to stop, Klarm. That's why you were never admitted to the Council.'

'For which I'm mightily glad, as it's turned out,' said Klarm.

Ullii took a small step forward. She looked little and frail, her skin was practically transparent, but her back was straight and her head held high.

'What pathetic last words,' said Ghorr to Klarm. 'Anyone else have anything to say?' He took no notice of Ullii. Ghorr had always held her in contempt. *Run away, little mouse*, he'd sneered in Nennifer. 'Cryl-Nish?'

Ullii kept moving, and all at once Irisis did understand. 'No!' She reached out for the seeker.

Ghorr swung the crossbow at Irisis, struggling to keep it steady, and Ullii sprang.

He fired just as she reached him, knocking the crossbow to one side. Four of its bolts tore through the snowy floor but the fifth struck Ullii in the chest, felling her instantly.

Ghorr let the useless bow fall. As Flangers and Irisis threw themselves at him, he tore one of the crystals from his belt, formed a circular section of the floor into a slide, leapt into it and disappeared.

Nish fell to his knees and lifted Ullii's head into his lap.

156

There was a neat hole in the centre of her chest, hardly bleeding at all. 'Why did you do that?' he wept. He kissed her on the forehead and then on the mouth. 'Dear Ullii, you didn't –'

He felt a hand on his shoulder. Yggur stood there, looking down sombrely.

'I didn't want to be here any longer. I'm going to Myllii and Yllii,' she said with a joyous smile. Ullii squeezed Nish's hand, closed her eyes and died.

'Come on,' said Klarm. 'As soon as Ghorr gets to the bottom he'll dissolve this place, and then we're done. I've got a little power back but not enough to maintain all this.'

Nish picked up Ullii's body, cradling it in his arms. There was no point to it, for she was gone, but Irisis would have done the same. Ullii had, despite all her frailties, been one of them for a long time now. The spirit might be gone but the mortal flesh demanded a dignified completion.

'We'll never get down in time,' said Flangers. 'He must be nearly there now.'

'Look!' cried Irisis, pointing to a rope ladder that ran up to the high central balloon. 'That's real.'

They ran, and Irisis could feel the floor becoming more insubstantial with every step. Pieces fell out, leaving ragged holes that she had to dart around, or try to leap, and hope that what lay beyond was solid. She reached the ladder just ahead of Klarm, whose dwarfish scuttle could be surprisingly fast, considering the caliper.

'Up!' he snapped. 'Give them room.'

Irisis went up a span. Klarm remained where he was. Flangers laboured across, his feet sinking into the floor and clouds of its failing material pulling up every time he lifted his feet. Yggur lurched a few steps behind. Patches of red skin were exposed where his charred clothing had flaked away.

The phantom world shook; chunks of floor fell away on all sides. Flangers came up the ladder. Klarm helped Yggur to the rope. 'Go down!'

Yggur began to do so, mechanically and painfully.

Nish was still several spans away, making slow progress, but would not lay Ullii's body down. In the circumstances, Irisis began to think he was being excessively noble. 'Come on!' she snapped.

Klarm stepped onto the floor, thrust out an arm and jerked him to the rope ladder. Nish clung to it with one hand.

'She's gone, Nish,' Irisis said. 'She doesn't care.'

'But I do,' said Nish. 'She loved me and I couldn't repay her by loving her in return.'

'Love doesn't work that way,' she said waspishly. 'I should know.'

He went on as though she hadn't spoken. 'And, despite everything I did to her, she gave her life for me.'

'Ullii was glad to go,' said Klarm. 'There was no longer anything to keep her here. We need not weep for her, Nish – only for ourselves.'

'I intend to bury her with my own hands, and then to honour her,' said Nish. 'I let her down – that's why she's gone.'

Irisis gritted her teeth but said nothing.

The ladder shook and slowly began to move through the mist.

'Well spoken, lad,' said Klarm, 'but first we must get out of here. We're still on Ghorr's air-dreadnought, do you realise, and judging by its motion the pilot has come to.'

'Ghorr will start shooting at us soon,' Irisis muttered.

'He won't want to, for fear of hitting the airbags,' said Klarm.

'What's left of his crew will come out of hiding, and he can recruit others from the survivors of the other craft,' said Irisis. 'If he hasn't already cut it free.'

'Is there any way we can signal Malien?'

'She's probably too *weak* to come for us,' said Nish, unable to conceal his resentment at her earlier abandonment, as he persisted in seeing it. 'She couldn't help before. She could barely fly the thapter when she left me here.'

'She may have recovered by now. I'll do what I can.' Klarm scuttled up the rope ladder as far as he could climb, and a green light flashed and flickered there. As he was making his way down again, a crossbow bolt whistled through the rigging, not far away.

'Already they attack,' said Flangers. 'And we're weaponless. We must go higher.'

'What's the point?' said Nish, hefting Ullii's body on his arm. 'We can't defend ourselves.'

Irisis moved up. Flangers climbed around Nish and followed. Even Yggur, beaten though he seemed, ascended half a dozen rungs. 'Are you coming, Nish?'

Nish clung to the rope with one hand. His shirt was smeared with Ullii's blood. 'I can't climb and carry her too.'

'Pass her to me,' said Flangers.

'She's my burden,' Nish replied, looking down at her face. Ullii was at peace. 'I'll take my chances.'

Another bolt whipped through the rigging, clipping a rope in half and sending the severed ends dancing. The air-dreadnought lurched suddenly and jerked upwards. Irisis looked down. Someone had cut free the broken bow section of the other air-dreadnought, though its airbags were still tangled in the rigging of Ghorr's machine, giving it extra lift at the expense of control. Two men were now sawing at the ropes from which the stern section was suspended.

'No!' she yelled, remembering the woman in the cabin with the two broken legs. *You'll be safe here*, Irisis had told her.

The last ropes were severed and the stern section, still hanging vertically, fell towards the swamp. Irisis tried to console herself. Perhaps Ghorr had taken the injured off first, unlikely as that seemed. The stern section struck a tree, tearing off branches and smashing to pieces. Objects that looked like people fell out. Ghorr's craft gave another lurch and lifted out of the mist into the light of the setting sun.

'The bastard has managed it,' said Nish. 'After all he's done, Ghorr is going to get away.'

'I don't think so,' said Klarm. 'Here come the jackals.'

Irisis looked the way he was pointing. The surviving air-dreadnoughts, led by Fusshte's brown-nosed craft, were heading in an arrowhead formation directly for them.

'Faster, pilot!' Ghorr cried in a cracked voice.

The sound of the rotors became more shrill, though the

159

air-dreadnought went no faster. The drag from the tangled airbags meant that he could never outrun his pursuers.

'Cut those airbags free,' he shouted at his crew. 'Then bring down the prisoners.'

Three men began to run up the rigging. The first airbag was released, then two more. The air-dreadnought leapt forward. One man headed for the fourth airbag, while the second and third angled across to where Nish and the others clung to the rope ladder.

Irisis was preparing to fight them bare-handed when, with a swoop and a whoosh, the thapter rose out of the swamp forest, wove expertly through the rigging and hovered next to the ladder. Two strong-armed guards lifted Nish, Ullii's body and all, in through the hatch. They took Yggur next, the others followed and the thapter darted away. Nish went below. Yggur did too, aided by the guards.

Irisis stayed up top with Klarm and Flangers. 'Perfect timing, Malien.'

'It was sheer good luck,' said Malien, 'and it's about time we had some of it. I came as soon as I could summon the strength. Twenty minutes ago I couldn't even stand up.'

'You arrived in time and that's all that matters.'

'It's been an endless day; a day of continual reversals. But now I think we're going to see the end of it.'

'I hope so,' said Klarm. 'Though I wouldn't put it past Ghorr to have one last ace up his sleeve.'

'He no longer has a sleeve,' said Flangers prosaically.

Malien circled out of range of the scrutators' javelards, keeping a wary eye out for signs of activity at the crystal-powered mirrors, though so far there had been none. With spyglasses they watched the drama unfold. Ghorr's air-dreadnought had risen slightly above the fleet, fleeing as quickly as its rattling rotors could take it, but Fusshte's was steadily overhauling it.

'He's failed in front of all the scrutators,' said Irisis. 'Surely not even Ghorr can overcome such a reversal.'

'Let's just watch and see.'

Scrutator Fusshte's crew manoeuvred his craft up beside Ghorr's. His soldiers were arranged along the side, their crossbows and javelards pointing at the other vessel.

'Would they shoot him down?' said Flangers. 'A chief scrutator?'

No one answered. Fusshte was seen to shout orders to Ghorr's craft. Ghorr's depleted crew were also spread along the sides, holding their weapons, though they did not point them in the direction of Fusshte's air-dreadnought.

Ghorr's craft jerked forward, making one last desperate attempt to get away. Smoke rose from the rotor mechanisms. Fusshte's air-dreadnought matched his pace. More orders were shouted and, as far as Irisis could tell, ignored.

Fusshte called his captains to a brief conference, after which they hastened back to their troops. Fusshte's pilot manoeuvred the vessel a fraction closer, and the men at the javelards pointed their weapons upwards and fired. Floater gas rushed out of one of Ghorr's airbags, it collapsed, and the craft dropped sharply.

Ghorr's operators worked the floater-gas generators but the vessel continued to lose altitude. Other air-dreadnoughts moved in to the sides and one shadowed him from below.

'That's it. It's got to be the end,' said Irisis.

Malien moved the thapter a little closer, the better to see.

Ghorr raised his arm and directed a fiery blast at his tormentor, but it fizzled out long before it reached him. Fusshte was laughing as he moved in for the kill.

'He's finished,' said Irisis. 'He's lost his power.'

'Ghorr's a hyena,' Klarm replied. 'He could be trying to lure his enemy into range.'

Fusshte didn't deign to reply to the attack, but his javelard operators shot out another of Ghorr's airbags. Fusshte's craft moved closer.

'Is he planning to board Ghorr's vessel in mid-air?' said Flangers.

'I don't think that's possible,' said Malien. 'I can't tell what he's up to.'

161

Ghorr, his hideousness now enveloped in a black cape, climbed onto the ladder above the rotors, as if to get a better shot at his enemy.

Yggur came up from below, wincing with every step. He'd cleaned himself up, washed the soot off and was wrapped in a blanket. His skin was swollen and blistered, both eyebrows had been singed off and the frizzy hair at his right temple was already beginning to crumble.

'Ah, the endgame,' Yggur said thickly, as if even his tongue was blistered.

'What's Ghorr holding?' said Malien sharply.

'Looks like his scrutator-magic belt,' said Irisis. 'Surely he can't be planning to –' She'd once seen an operator call power directly into his crystal, and the result had not been pretty. She couldn't imagine the cataclysm if a master mancer did it with all his crystals at once.

'I'd better move out of range, just in case,' said Malien, and the thapter veered off sharply.

Fusshte must have recognised the danger, too, for his vessel also turned away, though slowly. Such huge craft were not capable of rapid manoeuvring. The other craft followed his lead. The one below Ghorr's vessel went hard to port but Ghorr's pilot matched the movement, dropping towards it.

'Is Ghorr deliberately trying to crash into it?' said Irisis.

No one answered. Fusshte shouted an order and one of his javelard operators fired a warning shot above Ghorr's head.

At first it appeared as though Ghorr had tried to duck out of the way, but slipped and fell. Irisis clenched her fists as he plunged towards the swamp, thinking it was over. However, as soon as he was clear of his own craft, Ghorr flung out his cape, which formed a scalloped curve like a great batwing. He swooped one way, then the other, curved around in a circle and landed gently on top of the port airbag of the air-dreadnought below his own.

'He's got the luck of a thousand men,' said Klarm. 'I couldn't have done that if I'd practised it all my life.'

'What's he planning?' said Malien.

'To climb down the rigging and seize control of the air-dreadnought before the other scrutators can manoeuvre back into range.'

'And he'll do it,' said Flangers. 'He's going to get away after all.'

Ghorr was struggling across the top, having difficulty moving across the spongy surface in the wind, though he was steadily making his way towards the rope rigging that ran down the side.

'I'll be blowed,' said Klarm. 'The man's unstoppable. I think he might do it after all.'

Irisis thought so too, for the other vessels, having turned away with the wind, were having trouble forcing their way back against it. They wouldn't get within firing distance in time. Her heart was hammering in her chest, her fists tight with rage at the thought of him getting away. Fall, you swine, *fall*.

Ghorr was just reaching for the ropes, while the paralysed crew watched from below, when a gust of wind caught his wing and lifted him into the air. He wrenched at the wing, which collapsed, and landed so hard that one of his boots tore through the fabric of the airbag. His leg went in, all the way to the hip. Ghorr thrashed madly, trying to extricate himself, but only succeeded in tearing a larger hole.

He raised his arms as if trying to use his Art to stop his fall, but disappeared inside.

'He'll hold his breath while he tears a hole through the bottom,' Irisis said. 'He's indestructible. He'll come out, slide down the rigging and be off –'

She was cut off by a gigantic explosion of floater gas that sent tongues of flame fifty spans into the sky. It was followed within seconds by other explosions as the remaining airbags went off. What was left of the air-dreadnought plunged into the swamp, making an enormous muddy splash.

No one spoke. The remaining air-dreadnoughts circled the spot twice, but as Malien moved in their direction they turned away and headed for the eastern horizon at high speed.

Irisis let out her breath and unclenched her fists. Her nails had dug white crescents in her palms.

'Well,' said Malien after a considered pause, 'I very much believe that it's over. We won't be seeing them in Fiz Gorgo again.' She turned the thapter down towards the crash scene, in case there were any survivors.

They found none, but as they were lifting off again, Klarm said, 'What's that?'

'What?' said Flangers.

'That horrible red rag hanging in that tree.' As they came alongside the bloody, gruesome object, Klarm began to laugh. 'Trust Ghorr to go out in his own unique way. This is truly an end for the Histories, though not one he'd want to be remembered for.'

It looked like some kind of elongated membrane, waxy on the outside but red within, with strands of hair on one end and a grey thicket in the middle. Irisis recoiled. 'It's his skin,' she said, disgusted. 'The explosion blew Ghorr right out of his skin.'

'An entirely appropriate ending,' said Klarm, 'considering the number of victims he ordered to be flayed alive. I'm sure Flydd will appreciate it even more than I do.' He frowned at that thought, rubbed his chin and cast a glance down at the swamp. 'I wonder if Ghorr could be down there now, his heart still beating?'

'Not even Ghorr could have survived the fall, even if he did live through the explosion and the skinning,' said Malien. 'A great mancer can do a lot with the Art, but he can't protect himself from a fall of fifty spans.'

'We'd better make sure,' said Klarm. 'If he landed in a thick bed of reeds it might have saved him, and he could then use his Art to fashion some kind of substitute for his skin.'

'I don't see how,' said Malien. 'Oh, very well. I'd like to make sure of him too.'

After some searching they found the body, which had landed on the upraised branch of a fallen tree and burst open. There was no doubt that it had once been the chief scrutator, and none that he was now dead. They left the corpse where it lay for the scavengers to feed on, and headed back to do what they could at Fiz Gorgo.

'Swing by the skin again, Malien,' said Klarm. 'I'll have it tanned and stuffed and keep it in the corner of my workroom. And in the difficult days to come, whenever someone tells me that things were better in the time of the scrutators, I'll bring Ghorr's skin out to illustrate the tale I plan to write, of his life and death, and his evil regime.'

'Don't be disgusting,' said Irisis. She had never hated anyone, not even Jal-Nish, the way she'd hated Ghorr, but she could not countenance that.

'It's not worthy of you, Klarm,' said Malien. 'Let's get back and see to the living.'

'If you plan to overthrow the Council, and prevent them from ever rising again,' Klarm said carefully, 'first you must destroy them in the eyes of the people. Ridicule is the best way to do that, and there's no better symbol than this.'

'Oh very well,' said Malien, and brought the thapter close while the gruesome object was retrieved. 'Can we go now?'

'Yes, thank you,' said Klarm, still chuckling as he rolled the skin up carefully and packed it away.

Malien turned the thapter back to Fiz Gorgo.

'Does anyone know what happened to Tiaan?' Irisis wondered.

'She was taken up at the same time as I was,' said Malien. 'But to a different craft.'

'Do you know which one?'

'No.'

'I hope it was Fusshte's,' said Irisis.

'Why?'

'The Council came here with sixteen air-dreadnoughts and they've left with seven. The others exploded or crashed and I doubt if anyone would have survived.'

'Where's Gilhaelith?' Yggur asked his captain in charge the moment they trudged through the broken doors of Fiz Gorgo.

Everyone looked at everyone else. No one had seen him since they'd come down the slide, hours ago.

'Search Fiz Gorgo,' Yggur said grimly. 'He must be found and safely secured.'

'But surely . . .' Malien began.

'Ghorr didn't find this place by accident,' said Yggur. 'I had a protection around the entirety of Fiz Gorgo and I don't see how the Council could have seen through it, even using Ullii's talents. Gilhaelith definitely had a hand in it. I've just been to his cell and found the proof.' He displayed a handful of rock-salt crystals. 'They've got the print of the Art all over them. Gilhaelith made a working, down in his cell, which allowed Ullii to look through my protection.'

'That doesn't mean he deliberately betrayed us,' said Nish.

Yggur gave him a cold glare from beneath frizzled, soot-stained brows. 'But it does reinforce my initial opinion of the man, that he's unreliable, untrustworthy and completely lacking in judgment. Find him!'

They hastened to do his bidding, all except Irisis, who fell in beside Yggur as they went down the corridor.

'He's gone, hasn't he?'

'I'm afraid he has,' Yggur said grimly. 'And he's going to cause us no end of trouble unless we find him quickly.'

He organised his remaining soldiers into search parties and sent messages to the nearby towns and villages, to hold Gilhaelith at all costs. They did not find him, though his trail was not difficult to discover. He'd taken advantage of the chaos when everyone had come down the slide to slip away into Fiz Gorgo. There he'd gathered weapons, a sackful of provisions and as much gold as he could carry. Avoiding the guards, he had slipped out through the gates into the mist and headed up the track for Old Hripton. He'd chartered a boat, making no secret of his destination. Then he'd set sail around the northern end of the island of Meldorin, thence heading down the Sea of Thurkad.

Yggur put his head in his hands when his messengers came back with the news. 'I can only assume that he is heading back to Alcifer.'

'To do what?' said Nish.

'Betray us to the lyrinx?'

'Well, it's out of our hands. What happens now? There was a plan . . .'

'To attack Nennifer and overthrow the scrutators?' said Yggur.

'Yes,' said Nish. 'Has Gilhaelith betrayed that as well?'

'Ghorr gave no sign that he knew, and it would have been included in the charges against us had Ghorr known of it. But . . .'

'The longer we delay, the more likely it is that the Council will learn of it,' said Irisis.

'Flydd was the key to the attack,' said Yggur. 'It's going to take time for him to recover . . . if, indeed, he does.'

'Do you mean . . .' Irisis began.

'Oh, I'm sure he'll live, but the damage goes deeper than that. I hardly dare mount the attack without him, though I'm equally reluctant to wait until he recovers.'

'Either way it's going to be a bigger gamble than the one we've just been through, and less likely to succeed,' said Irisis. 'But let's worry about that tomorrow. I'm going to cook a victory dinner.'

'Better to call it a survival dinner,' said Yggur. 'I'm not yet sure that we've had a victory.'

'Coming, Nish?' said Irisis, taking him by the arm.

'I'm not really in the mood just now,' he said. 'I think I'll go for a walk.'

She stared at him for a moment, then suddenly she understood and gave him a quick hug. 'All right then. I'll see you later.'

Nish watched her go, not sure whether to pray for Flydd's quick recovery or to hope that his convalescence would be a lengthy one. Then he went outside to walk along the track that ran around the edge of the swamp forest. He had to think through the loss of Ullii, not to mention the son he'd never known, and never would. And then, find a suitable place to lay Ullii to rest. A quiet, pretty spot, as far from grim Fiz Gorgo as he could carry her.

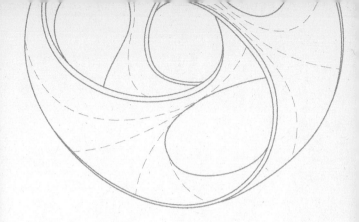

PART TWO

EIDOSCOPE

EIGHTEEN

Gilhaelith shaded his eyes from the setting sun as he tried to make out the port, which had served Alcifer long ago, among the dense forest covering the shore. Could that blocky shape down to the left be it? He adjusted the sail of the dinghy, and then the tiller a fraction. Surely it had to be.

His escape from Fiz Gorgo had been uneventful, as had his trip up the west coast of Meldorin, east through the passage between Meldorin and Qwale and south again halfway down the Sea of Thurkad. It had taken longer than it would have done to walk from Fiz Gorgo across the width of Meldorin, but at least it had been safe. The lyrinx rarely attacked ships on the open sea, while anyone foolish enough to pass through the swamps of Orist into enemy lands would have been killed and eaten on sight. Gilhaelith had taken to the dinghy just that morning, for the ship's captain had refused to go within a league of the fabled, haunted city, much less the lyrinx's underground labyrinth of Oellyll, delved into the living rock beneath Alcifer and home to at least seventy thousand of the enemy.

Besides, Gilhaelith could not have walked across Meldorin to save his life. He hadn't regained the strength he'd taken for granted in the hundred years and more he'd dwelt at beautiful Nyriandiol, and perhaps never would. Every stone of that great edifice had been chosen for its geomantic properties. Each had been shaped and placed so as to enhance the natural magic of the mountaintop, and to support him in his life's endeavour – to understand the nature of the world and the forces that made it so. Without Nyriandiol, Gilhaelith was not a shadow of the master geomancer he'd been while he dwelt there.

He still yearned to complete his life's endeavour, though Gilhaelith now doubted that he ever would. While trapped in sticky tar deep in the black pit of Snizort last summer, as the node had been about to explode, he'd done the only thing he could to save himself. He'd created a phantom, mathemantical crystal in his mind and used it to draw the power he'd needed to escape. He'd managed to drag himself to safety but in doing so the crystal had burst asunder, spearing its fragments through his brain and damaging part of it. The injury had further reduced his capacity for geomancy. What once had been effortless he now did only with the most prodigious labour, while some things he could not do at all.

But that had not been the worst of the damage. The phantom crystal fragments remained and whenever he drew power, even for the most trivial purpose, they burned more of his brain. Gilhaelith was faced with the worst of all choices. He could hope to prolong his life by never drawing power again, though without practising his Art, his life would be meaningless. Or he could attempt, by geomantic means, to locate and unmake every fragment of the phantom crystal. There lay his only hope of restoring himself to the greatness he'd once had, or at least to what shadow of it he *could* regain.

In that endeavour he'd spent his previous months at Alcifer refashioning his geomantic globe. He'd made it into the most perfect representation of Santhenar he could create, its lands, seas, mountains, rivers and icecaps, even down to the nodes themselves. It would give him the focus he needed to repair himself, though the work had done him more damage, of course. He'd completed it little more than a month ago, an unparalleled, agonising labour and, in the circumstances, a phenomenal work of genius. But then Matriarch Gyrull had sent him outside to take measurements of the field for her.

172

In reality she'd used him as an unwitting decoy to try to capture Tiaan and the thapter, and had almost succeeded. Instead, Tiaan had captured Gilhaelith and taken him to Fiz Gorgo. Without the geomantic globe, his agony had been complete and his death, or descent into irreparable brain damage, certain.

Unable to face that prospect, Gilhaelith had single-mindedly set out to get back to Alcifer, unwittingly betraying Fiz Gorgo to Ghorr in the process. He didn't want to think about that.

He adjusted the sail again, taking advantage of an easterly wind-shift to speed towards the scrub-covered oblong that was undoubtedly the end of one of the breakwaters of the port. What would happen now? Even if he recovered his geomantic globe, using it to find and unmake those crystal fragments risked destroying his mind completely. He could scarcely bear the thought of his greatness reduced to a mindless, drooling vegetable – lyrinx fodder. Assuming that the lyrinx would allow him access to the globe at all. Matriarch Gyrull had been spying on him all the time he'd worked on the globe and had probably seized it in his absence. If she didn't need him any more, he'd be sent to the slaughtering pens.

The thought checked him for a moment, for Gilhaelith had a horror of being eaten. It wasn't right that a man so great as he could come to such an undignified end. Dare he go on, confronting such a fate? He took the numbers, to see what kind of omens there were for this choice. The once effortless calculations were now a great strain but the omens proved to be neither good nor bad. It was up to him to tilt fate one way or the other. He would go on. He would risk all to get back what he had lost, no matter what the consequences.

Gilhaelith brought the dinghy in to the eroded stone jetty and tied the painter to a gnarled root that had forced the stones apart. After heaving his canvas holdall up onto the barnacle-covered stone, he pulled himself after it, and froze.

Four lyrinx stood there, back against the shrubbery so that they had been out of sight from below. He recognised three of them: a young wingless male called Ryll; Liett, a young female with outer skin that was quite unarmoured and colourless, so that he could see the purple blood flowing beneath it; and Matriarch Gyrull, big and old with pouched eyes, battle-scarred armour and segments missing from her crest. And, further back, almost concealed by the shadows, the biggest lyrinx Gilhaelith had ever seen – a vast coal-black male with a golden crest. He was one and a half times Gilhaelith's own majestic height, and probably five or six times his bulk. His folded wings drooped as though he was tired, though the lyrinx held himself erect and his golden eyes seemed to miss nothing.

'I hoped you would come back,' Gyrull said, reaching out and encircling Gilhaelith's bony wrist with her clawed fingers. 'Come with me, Tetrarch.'

When Gilhaelith had been safely penned in a stone chamber of the underground city, and a pair of zygnadrs, or sentinels, set to watch him, the four lyrinx repaired to an empty dining hall. There the coal-black male selected the lower half of a dead human male from a meat tray and tore it into two haunches, one of which he politely offered to the matriarch.

Gyrull shook her head. 'I'm not hungry. I have much to think about. Go ahead, Anabyng. You must be hungry after your long flight.'

'I confess I am,' he replied. 'I didn't settle once in the last two days, so anxious was I to get home.'

Liett took the haunch and bit a chunk from the thigh muscle with her sharp grey teeth. Ryll reached into the tray for a lower leg joint. He hadn't eaten human flesh for a good while, since there were few humans left in Meldorin. He absently twisted the foot off and tossed it back into the tray, then went across to the table with the others. He was about to tear into the tasty calf meat when Gyrull spoke.

'I don't like it, Anabyng. Why has the tetrarch come back?'

The black male chewed and swallowed before answering. Golden speckles broke out on his chest, in appreciation of the quality of the meat. 'For the geomantic globe. It means more to him than his life, and he is a dead man without it.'

'Were it up to me,' said Liett, 'he would be a dead man now, though I wouldn't care to dine on his tainted flesh.' Gilhaelith favoured the most exotic of diets: salted slugs, pickled wood-roaches and other kinds of vermin that not even the lowest of the lyrinx would have eaten but to save their lives.

'We need him,' said Ryll, putting down the leg joint untasted.

'How is the flisnadr going?' asked Anabyng, referring to the power patterner that Ryll and Liett had been trying to create for many months. 'Have you made much progress since I left?'

Ryll took up his joint again, stared at the red flesh for a moment, then all at once let it fall on the table. For some reason he couldn't fathom, human flesh, which he had enjoyed all his life, had lost its appeal. 'There hasn't been *any* progress, Great Anabyng. We're bedevilled by the same problem that we've had from the beginning: linking the individual patterners, with their humans inside, to grow the flisnadr. And we still haven't worked out how to use Gilhaelith's geomantic globe to solve this problem.'

'Then you'd better torture it out of him.' Anabyng stripped the rest of the meat off the upper thigh, then bit off the pro-truding bone and crunched it noisily. 'We've got to have it by the beginning of spring.'

'What's the matter, Anabyng?' said Liett, devouring her haunch with gusto. 'Why so soon?'

Anabyng's head jerked up and his eyes glowed, though he did not speak.

Matriarch Gyrull struck the table with her fist. 'Be so good as to use Anabyng's proper title, daughter. He is our greatest hero of the battlefield, and the greatest in the Art, too. He earned his honour the hard way.'

Liett dipped her head in a perfunctory manner. 'But I'm the daughter of the matriarch!' she said sulkily.

'Then it's incumbent upon you to observe the proprieties, more than anyone.'

Liett's eyes flashed. 'You said we had to recreate ourselves to suit the new world once the war is won. That's what I'm doing.'

'Have you learned nothing?' cried Gyrull. 'You expect me to choose you as matriarch after me, yet you display few of the necessary qualities. Your lack of respect diminishes you, daughter.'

'Name one person more suited to the honour than me,' Liett said with an imperious tilt of the head.

'Even Ryll is more suited to the honour than you,' Gyrull replied deliberately, 'and he is *male*.'

Anabyng spread his great maw wide, making a choking noise that Ryll could only interpret as a laugh. Ryll wasn't laughing. To even compare him to a candidate for matriarch was mortifying. 'Matriarch, you mock me,' he said, hanging his head. His skin colours flashed red and purple and he felt an unusual burning sensation in his cheeks.

'And insult *me*,' cried Liett, giving him a savage look, as if he had deliberately undermined her.

'By millennia-long custom we are led by a matriarch,' said Anabyng, 'and none of us would seek to change that.'

'Nor I,' said Gyrull. 'I merely point out that, in the half-year since we returned from the fall of Snizort, the wingless one has set an example in the mastery of his Art, in strategic thinking about the war and the future, and in unassuming leadership. When he speaks, the common folk set down their tools and listen. You'd be well advised to follow Ryll's example, daughter.'

Liett, incredulous, flashed out her beautiful wings and bared her teeth at Ryll, for all that she had long sought permission to mate with him, and he with her. Theirs was a volatile relationship.

'Assuming you *do* wish to be a candidate for matriarch,' said Gyrull. 'On that display, I doubt it. Leave us, Liett.'

'What?' said Liett, belatedly folding her wings.

'Leave us!' Gyrull snapped. 'I wish to speak about matters of importance with those mature enough to offer worthwhile opinions.'

Liett began to flounce away. She caught Ryll's eye and he gave a little shake of the head. She snapped her teeth at him, a last display, then slunk out, head bowed.

'I truly don't know what I'm going to do with her,' sighed Gyrull.

'Send her to the battlefront,' said Anabyng. 'If she survives, it may make a leader of her yet. She does have a great talent, though it's wilfully misdirected.'

'I need her here,' said Ryll hastily. Though he knew it made good sense, he couldn't bear the thought of losing Liett. 'To send her to battle, unarmoured as she is, would be to condemn her to death.'

'Perhaps your feelings for her overpower your good sense,' observed the black lyrinx.

'No, Ryll is right,' said Gyrull. 'We do need Liett to complete the flisnadr; she has special abilities. Enough of that. What news from your scouting, Anabyng? Why do we need the device by the end of winter? I thought we had months more.'

'The humans are too clever and cunning,' said Anabyng. He crunched the rest of the thigh bone and slurped up the marrow. 'I'm worried that they'll come up with some fiendish new strategy over the winter.'

'We have them on the run,' said Gyrull. 'We've defeated them time and again, and by spring we'll have another ten thousand to set against them. I'm not afraid –'

'There have been developments. The whole Council of Scrutators attacked Lord Yggur at Fiz Gorgo a few weeks ago but the chief scrutator was killed, along with many others. Only seven of their sixteen air-dreadnoughts escaped.'

'I heard,' said Gyrull. 'But that's something to celebrate, surely?'

'Fusshte has taken over,' said Anabyng, 'and he'll pursue us more relentlessly than Ghorr ever did.'

'But he's no leader,' Gyrull said, dismissing the threat. 'And leadership is what they need most desperately.'

'I think . . .' began Ryll tentatively. 'Er, Great Anabyng . . .' He squared his shoulders and tried to meet the male's eyes boldly, though Ryll was only too conscious of his physical deficiency, his lack of wings. 'This power in Fiz Gorgo, that can defeat the entire Council and all their soldiers and mancers, must be a threat to us. We've got to find out who they are and what their plans are. If a great leader should emerge from the present chaos we could have a hard time of it, since we've failed with the flisnadr. Gilhaelith –'

'Indeed.' Anabyng's eyes met Gyrull's. 'I believe that's the kind of strategic thinking you were talking about, Matriarch. We must extract everything Gilhaelith knows about Fiz Gorgo, without damaging him too much, then put him to work.'

'Quite,' said Gyrull. 'What of the other humankinds?'

'Lord Vithis has gathered all his Aachim around him. They've built camps near the Foshorn, by the south-western edge of the Dry Sea, planted gardens and harvested enough fish from the Sea of Thurkad to see them through the winter. Now they're building vast stone structures at the Foshorn.'

'Are they preparing for war against us?' said Ryll.

'There's little sign of it,' said Anabyng, 'though I can't say what they *are* up to. And if driven to it –'

'Since they've broken with the old humans, at all costs we must avoid provoking them,' said Gyrull. 'Or the Stassor Aachim. Or the exiled ones, for that matter. What was their name?'

'Clan Elienor,' said Ryll. 'Though without their constructs, and reduced to beggary on the shores of the Sea of Thurkad, Elienor can't threaten us.'

'If we attack them, Vithis might come to their aid despite sending them into exile. We must do nothing to provoke any of the Aachim, for we cannot fight them *and* the old humans. But it's the old humans that worry me. They adapt too quickly, and they're deadly inventive. We'd better step up the attacks on their manufactories.'

'Indeed. And now I must rest for an hour or two,' said Anabyng. 'It was a wearying flight and I'm spent. After that, we'll see what the tetrarch can tell us.' He bowed to the matriarch, nodded to Ryll and went out.

'You haven't eaten your meal,' Gyrull said to Ryll, glancing at the joint on the table.

He walked across and tossed it back in the tray. 'I no longer enjoy the taste of human flesh, Matriarch. I'd like to talk to you about that .... if you have the time. I've begun to feel that it's wrong.'

'Wrong?' she said without emphasis.

He had no idea what she was thinking. 'To eat the flesh of another sentient species, one that is, despite outward appearances, not so very different from ourselves, it just seems . . . I feel that it reduces us to the level of beasts. *And we're not beasts!*' he cried. Then he went on, more tentatively, 'Are we, Matriarch?'

'No, Ryll,' she said softly. 'We were artists once, and philosophers, with a noble culture that stretched back a thousand years. In those days our identity did not depend on warriors' arts. We were once great, and we lost it all. No,' she said reflectingly, 'our ancestors abandoned the past so that we could survive in the void. We had no choice.'

'This war stopped being about survival long ago,' said Ryll. 'It's become *existence*, and it's not enough. I want our culture back, Matriarch. I feel hollow inside, as if I've lost my soul. And I'm not the only one.'

'Many of us have begun to feel that way,' she said. 'And we matriarchs are doing what we can to shape our people for the future, ill-fitted as we are for the task.'

'Don't say that, Matriarch,' said Ryll. 'You are the best of us; our guiding force.'

'We *were*, in the void, and even in the early days here. But the world is changing too quickly, Ryll, and we're too fixed in the old ways. We can't guide you much longer. We must make way for a new generation, and I'm afraid . . .'

'You, Matriarch?' he said uncomprehendingly.

'The war may soon be over but the peace will be even more dangerous for us, for our warrior caste is not fitted for it. Many of our people can conceive of nothing but war and don't want to give up its glories, even for peace.'

'We must find a way to change their minds,' said Ryll.

'They know nothing but war and if we take it away without giving them something else, they'll be broken; people without a purpose. It'll tear us apart. We matriarchs of the six cities have had much mindspeech on the topic this past year. We're starting to try to shape the thinking of the progressives, like you . . .'

'What about the warriors?'

'The warriors too, as best we can,' she said, 'though with limited success. But they are disciplined and obedient to our edicts – in the void, anything else meant extinction. If all else fails, we will have to issue a Matriarchal Edict. It's not been done since we made the decision to come out of the void, but I think they'll obey. I *think* they'll lay down their arms, but what happens after that I cannot say.'

'We must replace our warrior culture with a sounder one, fitted for peace.'

'With what we had before? How can we, Ryll?'

'We can't return to the past, Matriarch. All we can do is discover what we once were, and use the best of that heritage to shape our future here on Santhenar, after the war.'

Gyrull was smiling, and now she put an arm across his shoulders. 'Your forethought constantly surprises me, Ryll. Come, let's take a walk and you can tell me more.'

NINETEEN

'How is he?' said Nish from the doorway.

Four healers were gathered around the shrouded figure of Xervish Flydd, blocking Nish's view, and he was reluctant to go closer for fear of the horrors he might see, to say nothing of the righteous wrath of the healers. Cryl-Nish Hlar, artificer, who had faced down the mighty, who had defied the greatest figures on Santhenar including the late and unlamented Ghorr, was afraid of these diminutive healers. He had no place here and no right, and he knew it.

The chief healer turned, regarding him with hard black eyes that saw all men as brutes. Her dark hair was pulled back so tightly that her brow and cheeks were shiny taut. Evee was younger than he, and only chin-high to Nish, who was a small man, but she had such presence that he stepped backwards.

'I'm sorry. I – I was worried, you see. He – he's an old friend and . . .'

'Had you any part in this?' she said, snapping back the sheet.

Nish didn't look but still the red registered. Flydd was a ruddy brown colour between the lower belly, where the flaying had begun, and mid-thigh.

'I – I wasn't there,' he stammered. 'I couldn't sleep, you see, and I went for a walk. I was in the tower when the air-dreadnoughts descended on us . . .' Nish realised that he was babbling.

'Boys' games,' she said scornfully, drawing herself up to her insignificant height. Evee, who was little, plain, stringy and completely covered in freckles, dominated him in every respect. 'Men destroy and women are left to put it all together again.'

It isn't like that, he wanted to shout, our whole world is at stake here, but there was no point in saying it; his pride didn't matter. Nothing mattered except that Xervish Flydd should survive and be made whole again so that he could lead them against Nennifer. No one else would do.

'I'm sure you'll do everything you can for him,' he said quietly, and went outside.

On their return, Yggur had assembled the soldiers, artisans and crew left behind when the scrutators had fled. There were nearly three hundred of them: about a hundred and fifty soldiers and almost as many artificers, artisans, prentices, deck hands, junior cooks and other workers both skilled and unskilled. He had offered each a choice: to enter his service at Fiz Gorgo, or money and free passage aboard the next trading vessels going to Lauralin. Most had opted to return to their homelands and families, though some fifty soldiers and forty workers had accepted his offer of service. Yggur questioned each of them, rejecting several, who were also given passage east, then took the oaths of the remainder. They, plus carpenters and masons hired from Old Hripton, were immediately put to work repairing Fiz Gorgo and strengthening its defences.

Nish had a more important obligation to attend to. It had taken him a day to find a place to bury Ullii, on a little rise covered in trees overlooking the bay, and another day to dig a deep enough grave through the heavy clayey soil. It was painful work with his gashed arm but he wouldn't allow anyone to help. He had to set Ullii to rest by himself. He'd spent most of the third day gathering stones for a cairn and hauling them to the gravesite, for there were none nearby, then sitting by the mound afterwards in silent contemplation of what they'd had and all they had lost.

At the end of that day, Yggur called the company together after dinner. Malien was talking as Nish entered, late. Instead of eating he'd walked to Old Hripton and back to clear his head for the urgent work to come. It hadn't worked – he couldn't concentrate – he just kept reliving that desperate day in the tower and up on the amphitheatre, and the way it had ended.

Ullii was dead and he couldn't come to terms with it. He kept seeing her as she'd been the first time they'd met, crouched in the corner of that dark room in the manufactory, rocking on her bare feet. And all the times afterwards: hiding in her basket in the balloon as they'd set off to try and track Tiaan down; climbing the slopes of Mount Tirthrax; making love in the balloon after they'd fought off the nylatl. Escaping Snizort with Flydd, many months later, when she'd been so angry with him about the baby and Nish hadn't even known she was pregnant. And then the ultimate horror: Myllii with his arms around Ullii as if trying to carry her away, and Nish trying to stop him, and the knife sliding into Myllii's back. The moment that had changed both their lives and surely had led inevitably to her death.

He'd talked to Irisis about that, and Malien. Ullii had been glad to go, they'd said. There had been nothing left for her in this world, and she'd wanted to atone for betraying them to Ghorr. Nish knew that as well as they did, but it didn't help. He missed Ullii, with all her frailties and all her strengths, more than he could ever have imagined. Even though they'd had no future together, there had never been anyone like her. She'd been the mother of his dead son and, now she was gone, he had nothing left of Yllii either. Every time he thought about them, tears welled up under his eyelids. If he'd only done things differently they would both be alive.

Yggur cleared his throat and Nish realised that he'd stopped in the doorway, lost in his thoughts. Malien was beckoning him – he was late.

'We have to decide today, *now*,' she said in a low voice, once

Nish was seated and the door sealed, 'whether to go through with the attack on Nennifer. If we are to go, it must be now or not at all. Gilhaelith knew of our plan, and while I don't think he would betray it deliberately, we can't rely on it remaining a secret.' She inclined her head towards Klarm.

The dwarf scrutator was sitting on the edge of the table with his legs dangling, toying with an enormous goblet of Yggur's finest purple wine, for which he had a capacity entirely out of keeping with his small stature. He took a hearty swig, rubbed a trickle of wine off his chin, leaving a mark like a purple bruise, and nodded. 'Aye. Now or never.'

'What news of Flydd?' said Yggur, scowling at the dwarf. Hospitality demanded that he offer wine with meals but, being a man of modest and constrained appetites himself, Klarm's indulgence and sheer gusto aroused his ire. 'It was his plan and I don't see how we can succeed without him.'

'The healers have wielded their Arts as only they can,' said Klarm, setting down his goblet with a sigh of contentment. He took pleasure in provoking stern, conservative Yggur and in another frame of mind Nish would have been amused by it. 'The damage to his body will heal after a fashion . . .' Klarm trailed off, as reluctant as everyone else to talk about the true nature of Flydd's injuries. The matter was too private and personal – as if, by talking about what had been done to his body, they were taking the flaying blades to his soul.

'But the scars carved into his psyche may not?' said Malien.

'He won't be the man he once was,' said Klarm, not meeting her eye.

What did he mean by that? Nish thought. That Flydd would no longer be a man at all? Just what *had* the torturers done to him? No one would say.

Yggur rose and paced the length of the room, limping badly today. The blisters on his face and arms had disappeared but he was covered with dead, flaking skin. He rubbed at an arm and flakes rose on a current of warm air from the fire. 'Can we do it without him?'

'I'm not sure we can,' said Malien. 'The plan relied on Flydd's knowledge of Nennifer, gained from working there for many years.'

'I dwelt there for a good while,' said Klarm, 'and had charge of its security. I know Nennifer as well as any man, so if his plan relied on a flaw in the defences –'

'We don't know if it did or not,' said Yggur. 'We planned to talk about that on the way, to ensure that there was no chance of the secret being revealed. But Flydd was sure he could get us in.'

'Fusshte will soon be as strong as Ghorr was,' said Irisis, 'and he's even more cunning and treacherous, but he can't win the war either. We have no choice, Yggur. The Council must be brought down without delay. If Flydd's incapable, we'll have to work out a plan with Klarm.'

'I can't say I'd be confident of the outcome without Flydd,' said Yggur, 'but I agree we have to try.'

'When?' said Klarm.

'Our equipment and supplies haven't been touched,' said Malien. 'It will only take hours to load them into the thapter and make ready for departure. We could go tomorrow afternoon if you wanted to.'

'Let's give Flydd a few days,' said Yggur. 'I'll talk to the healers again. If fortune is on our side, he'll be on the road to recovery by then.'

'Fortune is a chancy beast,' said Klarm. 'I can't say I've seen many of her smiles this past year.'

In the event, Flydd had emerged from the healers' coma the day after the meeting and insisted on coming. He stated that he would be ready to go in two days' time, curtly overrode the healers when they'd protested, and had not spoken a word since. He'd turned away all visitors, even Yggur. There was much speculation about his state of mind and health, though not even Irisis, normally so adept at ferreting out secrets, could glean anything from the healers.

'I've got a bad feeling about this trip,' Nish said to Irisis the night before they were due to depart. They were checking the supplies yet again. 'How can he be in any state to go?'

185

'He's a tough old coot,' said Irisis, who had been unusually quiet lately.

She'd hardly spoken to him since he'd come back from burying Ullii, though Nish often caught her giving him cool, assessing glances. She was much more reserved than previously and he couldn't fathom why. He'd expected that, after all he'd done to save her and everyone else, she would have been more grateful, and he felt a little hurt.

'From what I saw on the first day –' Nish began.

'I'd rather not talk about it, if you don't mind,' snapped Irisis. 'If Flydd doesn't want us to know, we should respect his wishes and mind our own business.' She went out, keeping her back to him the whole time.

Nish stared after her, uncomprehending. Surely, on such a desperate mission, Flydd's health, mental and physical, *was* their business?

The chief healer, Evee, insisted on accompanying Flydd and no one could dissuade her, which meant that the thapter no longer had room enough to carry everyone. On a long journey it could accommodate fourteen in considerable discomfort but with Flangers and six soldiers, and Klarm and Evee, they were now sixteen. And Evee's supplies took up a lot of space.

The problem was solved by leaving Fyn-Mah behind to take charge of Fiz Gorgo, and by throwing together a dirigible sled to carry their gear and supplies. It was a small, semi-rigid airfloater with a cabin on the underside, which they planned to tow behind the thapter. It would greatly reduce the thapter's manoeuvrability as well as slowing it, and was bound to make it cumbersome to take off and land, but they could see no other solution. And because it used the controller from Inouye's airfloater, she would have no trouble coping.

And all the preparations had to be done in the utmost secrecy. Yggur had taken the precaution of caging up his skeets and sending them on a sea voyage, to be sure that no one could send a message to Nennifer after they'd gone. The name had never been mentioned in front of the soldiers and servants; in fact, the attack itself had never been discussed. As far as everyone in Fiz Gorgo knew, they were simply going on a long trip. Nonetheless, it was impossible to be too careful.

A week after Ghorr's attack on Fiz Gorgo, on a windy, miserable autumn morning with sleet spitting at them from the west, all was ready. They assembled in the yard, waiting for Xervish Flydd.

They stood there for more than an hour, stamping their feet in a vain attempt to keep them warm, and blowing into their gloves. Finally even Yggur, who had been a model of patience ever since Flydd's injury had been revealed, was driven to say, 'Where the devil is the fellow?'

Shortly Flydd appeared, supporting himself on the shoulders of Evee and Fyn-Mah, and walking in a wretched grimacing shuffle. His skin was completely bloodless and with each halting step every muscle in his face shivered as he tried to prevent himself from crying out in agony.

Nish couldn't bear to see the scrutator, who had once seemed to carry the whole of Santhenar on his scrawny shoulders, reduced to such emotional penury. 'Surr!' he cried, and ran across the yard to offer his arm.

As he approached, the scrutator wrenched back some control over himself and with a supreme effort shook off the pain, or at least drew it into himself. He stood up straight as Nish, realising belatedly what a blunder he'd made, stumbled to a halt in front of him. But he and Flydd had been through much together; they'd been comrades in the desperate times after the fall of Snizort, and surely Flydd would understand. Nish tried to make the best of it.

'Surr,' he said quietly. 'May I assist you into the thapter?'

Flydd looked right through him. 'Did I ask for help, Artificer?' he ground out. Shaking off Evee's arm, and then Fyn-Mah's, he lurched unaided across the black paving stones in an appalling travesty of a careless stride. Every movement of every muscle showed the pain he was enduring, though his face was like stone.

Fyn-Mah cried, 'Xervish –' but broke off and put her hands over her face.

Evee let out an almost inaudible cry and ran after him, but he slashed at her with one hand and she fell back, biting her knuckles. She directed a furious glance at Nish. 'Are you the biggest fool that ever was?'

Nish was beginning to think he was. Flydd had now reached the thapter but he didn't stop there; he forced himself up the rungs of the ladder. The pride of the man was awesome, though Nish had to avert his eyes as Flydd struggled all the way up. It took him three attempts to get his leg over the side into the hatch, and heaving the second leg in wrenched a cry of anguish out of him, swiftly cut off. Nish thought he saw blood running down Flydd's ankle, then he disappeared inside as if he'd fallen through the lower hatch.

After a brief hesitation Evee ran after him. The others followed, except for Fyn-Mah. Normally so cool and reserved, she was grinding her knuckles into her eyes. She turned away and walked back inside Fiz Gorgo, closing the door like a silent accusation.

'That went well,' observed Irisis as Nish came up to the side of the thapter.

Nish wanted to weep. 'I was trying to help him.'

She relented and put her arm around his shoulders. 'You know what a proud man he is, Nish. And you saw what Ghorr did to him. How do you think Flydd must feel, knowing that his friends are talking about his deepest torment and shame?'

'If it were me, I'd want the support of my friends.'

'Not if you'd been a scrutator. It's a solitary profession and you have to hide your feelings. And especially your weaknesses.'

He said no more. They took their places in the thapter. Pilot Inouye stood at the controller of her dirigible, cast off the ballast and the little craft rose gently in the air. Yggur hadn't wanted anyone inside in case something went wrong, but Inouye was happier that way and it eased the cramped conditions a trifle.

Nish stood with Irisis and Malien in the upper compartment of the thapter, looking out as they lifted off into the scudding cloud. Yggur was on the shooter's platform at the rear, legs spread, cloak flapping behind him, appearing to relish the icy wind in his face.

Nish didn't relish anything about the coming journey, though at least the war had gone quiet and there shouldn't be too many disasters before the spring. The lyrinx didn't fight in winter unless they had to.

He had enough to worry about. Evee had said that Flydd had been *repaired*, whatever that meant, though clearly he was far from recovered, and must be more hindrance than help on such a dangerous mission.

Nish had also begun to fret about Gilhaelith, the only outsider who knew of the planned attack. Since he'd made a fortune trading with the enemy, Gilhaelith was unlikely to have qualms about betraying them to the Council and, given the way Yggur had treated him from the moment they'd met, Nish wasn't sure he'd blame him. Nish had doubts about the dwarf as well. Klarm had broken his oath to the Council, so why wouldn't he break it again? The reward for betraying them would be unimaginable.

'I overheard the healers talking about Flydd last night,' Irisis said an hour or two later.

They were now sitting on the top of the thapter with their legs dangling down into the upper compartment. Irisis was swinging her long legs, quite at home there. Nish held on grimly, afraid that a sudden lurch could send them over the side. The thapter was dipping in and out of layers of cloud like wet, clinging fluff, and it was unusually bumpy.

'Oh?' Nish said sharply. He let go with one hand to wipe the cold condensation off his brow, then slapped his hand down again as the machine jolted in an updraught.

'They don't know what to make of him. He won't talk. He won't even look at them. They're . . . they're afraid for his sanity.'

'Marvellous!' said Nish. 'And Flydd didn't tell Yggur the details of the attack. It's all in his head . . . Or *was*.'

'He had hours of discussions with Malien and Yggur just before Ghorr attacked Fiz Gorgo,' Irisis said.

'But they only went through generalities, never the plan in detail. They agreed not to until we were on the way, just to be safe.'

'Well, I just thought you should know.'

'I'm glad you told me,' said Nish. 'It drives all the other worries right out of my head.'

TWENTY

'So what's Nennifer like, anyway?' Nish asked Irisis.

It was late on their third day of travel and the thapter had just settled, as it must each night, onto the most isolated and desolate peak they could find. Only Malien could pilot the craft and she was still so weak that each day's flying required long hours of recuperation.

She had taken all possible precautions to avoid being seen, flying in cloud wherever possible, and keeping clear of towns and densely inhabited areas, though there was always a chance that someone had spotted them. And if they had been seen, the Council's unparalleled network of spies and informers would soon hear of it. Even now a skeet or a courier air-floater could be racing towards Nennifer with the news that the thapter had been seen in the sky over the Peaks of Borg.

'You can't imagine it,' Irisis replied, climbing down the side of the thapter onto moss-covered rock. The night's camp was halfway up an isolated ridge in the middle of the Ramparts of Tacnah, a series of rearing slopes of tilted greywacke, layered against the western edge of the Great Mountains like a leaning stack of cards. The high parts of the Ramparts caught moist breezes from the west and were, consequently, wet and cloud-covered for most of the year. A fine place for hiding, though dank, mosquito-ridden and inhospitable. 'Nennifer is as hostile a place as anywhere on Santhenar, except the middle of the Dry Sea. It never rains there.'

Flangers and the other soldiers were already fanning out up and down the slope, making sure that there was no habitation nearby, though none had been seen before they settled. Nish watched them go, then moved into a cleft where a boulder bigger than the thapter had split in two. It was marginally sheltered from the wind. 'Never rains? How can that be?'

A frog croaked from the dark recesses beneath the boulder. Another answered it from not far away. Irisis looked down and smiled.

'Nennifer lies hidden in an angle between the Great Mountains and the range running down the east coast of Lauralin.' She squatted down and drew on the mossy rock with a fingertip. 'There are higher mountains all around and they catch all the moisture. I can't think why the Council made their home there, save that it's so isolated that no land attack could possibly succeed. Even in mid-summer there can be frosts, but at this time of year it's hellish cold.'

'Where do they get their food from?'

'It used to be brought in, at fabulous expense, on great supply caravans that could only move for eight months of the year, though most now comes in on air-floaters. And their indentured peasants grow what crops they may in the valley bottoms, where there's soil and water – turnips and other charming delicacies. Do you want to share a tent tonight?'

'It's a bit cold for camping, isn't it?'

'Better the cold than being cooped up in the thapter for another night. What with all the snoring, the whispering and Flydd's nightmares, I've hardly slept a wink since we left. I like to sleep alone.'

'If I was in your tent you wouldn't be alone,' said Nish.

'You don't count. If you dared to snore I'd thump you in the ear.'

He smiled. It seemed they were friends again. 'With an invitation like that, how could I refuse?'

192

Two days later they were flying between the peaks of the northern Great Mountains. Not even the thapter could rise high enough to pass over them, and the air would have been too thin to breathe anyway. The barren valleys below were filled with concealing cloud. Though they were now close to Nennifer, Malien felt confident that they would not be seen. Most of the game animals had long since been killed for the scrutators' tables, so she didn't expect to encounter even a solitary hunter.

Flydd still hadn't said a word, but at every stop he went further and further, driving himself relentlessly, though his characteristic crab-like scuttle had been replaced by a stiff-legged, twisting dance, the oddest walk Nish had ever seen. He supposed the healing skin, replaced by the healers' Art, had pulled taut and was troubling him.

Malien called down the hatch to Yggur and Klarm, who came up. 'We're within four or five leagues. Dare we go closer?'

'I think not,' said Klarm after a brief glance at the forbidding mountainside passing by. 'Set down wherever you can find a safe place.'

Malien curved around in a circle, signalling her intentions back to a fur-shrouded Inouye, before heading for a relatively bare, relatively flat patch on the rock-littered slope. The thapter settled, gravel grating underneath. Ten spans back the dirigible came to ground silently.

Irisis opened the upper hatch and gasped at the frigid blast that swept in. Nish pulled his fur-lined coat more tightly around him, the earmuffs down over his ears, and climbed out. As soon as his boot touched the ground he felt a pang of unease, but dismissed it. How could he feel otherwise, so close to Nennifer?

He had never been anywhere like this place. The surface was utterly barren, just shattered rock and grey gravel and grit as far as his eye could see. He saw no living thing: no birds in the sky, no animals on the horizon, no plants anywhere. There weren't even lichens on the rocks.

'What a wasteland!' Nish said to Irisis, who had walked away a few steps and was nudging stones over with the toe of her boot. There was nothing underneath them either.

193

'The perfect place for the arid souls of the scrutators,' she said.

'Shh!' Nish gave her a meaningful glance.

Klarm stood behind her, his bowed legs braced against the wind. He'd had the calipers removed before they left Fiz Gorgo, though he still put his foot to the ground gingerly. 'Take no mind of me,' he said. 'I always hated Nennifer and was never more glad than to see the back of it. And –'

'What?' said Nish.

'To me, the choice of location was not suggestive of unparalleled strength and supreme majesty, as the Council would have it. It indicated a deep-seated insecurity and I always wondered . . .'

Again he trailed off, as if he scarcely dared to speak what he was thinking – a survival strategy, surely. Ghorr had not encouraged people to speak their minds, and that included the host of lesser scrutators who weren't members of the Council.

'What did you wonder?' said Yggur, coming up beside the dwarf and turning his back to the wind.

'What the Council is most afraid of,' said Klarm. 'It isn't the lyrinx, for all that we're losing the war. And certainly not their own people, thoroughly cowed after a century of the scrutators' iron rule.'

Nish and Irisis exchanged glances but neither said anything. It wasn't their place.

The wind gusted up, howling around the thapter and lifting the tethered dirigible a span into the air. They ran and held it down with their weight, and the effort of running those few steps left them breathless.

'We can talk about that later,' said Yggur. 'Get the dirigible tied down before it blows away.'

'There's nothing to tie it to,' said Nish. 'You can't drive a stake into this grit.'

'Then it'll have to be anchored to rock. Is something the matter, Malien?'

She had her hands over her eyes and was walking back and forth, taking tiny, sliding steps that rasped across the surface. Her

194

head was bowed. She continued for another ten steps, rotated slowly on the ball of her right foot and came rasping back.

'Malien?' Yggur said sharply.

'I'm not sure about this place.'

'This campsite?'

'No, Nennifer itself. I'm sensing a strain on the node.'

'You'll have to explain,' said Yggur. 'Your Art and mine are totally different, remember?

'I learned to be sensitive to such things,' said Malien, speaking breathlessly, 'while guarding the Well of Echoes in Tirthrax against the amplimet.'

'Is the amplimet doing something to the node?'

'No ... At least I don't think so. I feel that the amplimet has been *contained*, yet the node is under strain ... like a ball of rubber squeezed between the heels of one's hands.'

'Irisis,' said Yggur, 'would you take your pliance and tell me what the field is like here?'

She withdrew it from between her breasts and squeezed it in her right hand. 'It's incredibly strong,' said Irisis. 'I can almost see it. *With my eyes*, I mean. I've never experienced such intensity.'

'We're close to one of the greatest nodes in the world,' said Klarm. 'Another reason why the Council chose to build Nennifer here.'

Nish was still feeling uneasy. He closed his eyes and a shimmering silver loop drifted across his inner vision. He tried to focus on it but it eluded him and disappeared.

'The fields have been drawn right down,' said Irisis. 'They weren't like this when I was here before. It's as if the node is being sucked dry ...' She gave a spasmodic jerk. 'Aah!'

Nish saw, or felt, a bright flash of blue; his eyes sprang open.

'What is it?' said Yggur.

'It flared up,' said Irisis shakily. 'So strongly that I couldn't keep it out. But now it's died again.'

'Can it be the node?' said Yggur. 'Is it bound to explode?'

'No – it doesn't feel like the time we went into Snizort.'

'It's not the node,' said Flydd, lurching up behind them.

195

He was staring over the edge of the mountain. 'It's nothing like that time . . .'

Everyone stared at him. 'You spoke!' said Irisis, her eyes lighting up. 'Xervish . . . surr, you're better!'

'Am I, Crafter?' He turned his eyes to her and they were as bleak as chips of stone. 'I'm glad you think so.'

She quailed, and that did not happen often. 'I – I –'

He turned away as if she wasn't there and Nish saw the hurt, quickly veiled, in her eyes.

'Then what's going on?' said Nish, memories of that dark time in Snizort rising up to choke him. 'Why would the scrutators be using so much power?'

'I think . . .' Flydd seemed to be straining hard to see the unseeable. He bared his teeth. 'They're probing the amplimet, I'd say, hoping to master it and gain undreamed-of power. And there may also be a power struggle between the scrutators. Not a battle, but certainly intrigues and undermining of each other.'

'But the chief scrutator –'

'Ghorr was a thug and a bully –' said Flydd. He broke off, rigid with rage, and had to force himself to calm down. 'But he was also a natural leader, and he knew how to use the authority of the chief scrutator. So, despite his failures, he was unchallenged until the end. Fusshte has neither charisma nor natural authority. He repulses people and can only maintain power through terror.'

'He's capable of it,' said Klarm, with an involuntary and uncharacteristic shudder.

'The Council won't vote Fusshte as their chief, for he doesn't have the strength to dominate them. He may have seized the position after Ghorr's death but, safely back in Nennifer, every scrutator will question his legitimacy. And after the fiasco at Fiz Gorgo, every ruler on Santhenar must be querying the fitness of the scrutators to rule the world.'

'Will they rise up to overthrow the Council?'

'Not yet,' said Flydd. His eyes met Nish's for a moment, though without any sign of warmth or fellow-feeling. 'For a hundred years the scrutators have cut down every mancer, army officer, governor and provincial leader who showed signs of personal ambition. Subservience to their rule has been a prerequisite for survival and no one in Nennifer would have the initiative to mount a coup. But if the struggle isn't resolved quickly, rebellion becomes a certainty, and that would be worse than having Fusshte as chief scrutator. Once authority is lost at the centre, the outskirts will swiftly fall.'

After the dirigible had been fastened to steel pegs driven into rock, Yggur sent two soldiers to look over the other sides of the ridge and report back. They soon returned, reporting that nothing could be seen but the same dismal vista in all directions. He set out sentries, relatively close to the thapter for their safety in case a blizzard swept in, and everyone else went below for dinner, after which they sat down to plan the attack.

'Nennifer has but two entrances, front and rear, and each will be strongly guarded,' said Flydd, who was sitting on the bench with a folded fur coat under his backside, though he still winced every time he shifted his weight. 'They had a thousand troops here previously, of which Ghorr took four hundred to Fiz Gorgo. We think about a hundred returned, so they must still have seven hundred.'

Irisis studied him surreptitiously. Despite Evee's claims, Flydd was just a grim husk of his former self. Every time she tried to speak to him the barriers went up, which hurt after all they'd been through together. But it wasn't just her – he kept everyone at bay. Flydd was a driven man and the only thing keeping him going was his lust to smash the Council and grind them into the frozen gravel.

'Every entrance and exit is watched,' Klarm added. 'Even the sullage tunnels that discharge over the precipice into the Desolation Sink, since Irisis and Ullii's escape that way last year.'

'What are they really afraid of?' said Irisis.

Flydd's eyes met hers and she knew he was remembering his drunken revelation about the Numinator, long ago at the manufactory. For a moment he seemed almost like his old self, but the shell closed over.

'Nennifer's only weak point is the roof,' he said. 'We'll –'

'It's been strengthened since air-floaters were invented,' said Klarm. 'And further reinforced since the first thapter appeared.'

'Then what are we doing here?' said Yggur. 'Flydd, all along you claimed that you had a way in. If that's been closed off . . .'

'We're going in,' Flydd said savagely, 'if I have to tear the roof off with my bare hands.'

He looked around him like a jackal and for a moment his eyes flashed red. No one met his gaze. He was a man possessed by a demon.

After a minute or two his fists unclenched and he went on more calmly, 'There's a weakness in the roof defences. It occurred to me after we escaped last spring.'

'What weakness is that?' said Klarm sharply.

'The sentinel covering the west fourth, fifth and sixth garrets was incorrectly built into the roof cavity. Its sensing crystals look sideways, not up, leaving a gap large enough to allow the thapter to land on the roof. It would have to be piloted with exquisite precision, of course, but –'

'The gap isn't there any more,' said Klarm. 'After your escape, Ghorr had the mancer responsible for the watch flayed alive and abandoned in the centre of the Desolation Sink to die. Afterwards I personally checked the roof sentinels, replaced the one you refer to and doubled their number, just to be sure. To be very sure,' he added, rubbing one horny hand up the other arm. 'I'm partial to my skin the way it is – in place . . .' He trailed off, realising what he'd said.

Flydd's stare was like shards chipped off the front of a glacier.

'I beg your pardon, Xervish,' said Klarm, but Flydd did not reply.

'So we don't have a way in,' said Nish bitterly. 'We've come all this way for nothing –'

No one said anything. Everyone was pointedly avoiding Flydd's eye. Irisis studied him from the corner of hers. His seamed and puckered face became even more mask-like, though Irisis thought she could see through the cracks. Rage was the

198

one thing keeping him going, and he'd just lost the only chance of dealing with his enemies. He was so overcome that he hadn't even heard Nish.

'So we can't break in and we can't sneak in,' said Yggur. 'I suppose it's too much to ask that either of you know of a secret entrance or exit for the Council's convenience?'

'If there is, none but the Council knows of it,' said Klarm. 'But I doubt it very much. There's no way in or out but the front and rear doors.'

'What about a gate?' said Irisis. 'A portal such as those used in olden times to travel instantly across the world.'

'All portals failed after the Forbidding was broken,' said Yggur. 'And no one knows how to create them anew, or even if it's possible.'

'Except the one Tiaan made in Tirthrax to bring the Aachim here. Malien knows how it worked,' said Nish.

'That doesn't mean I could make one, even in Tirthrax,' said Malien. 'And here it would be quite impossible.'

'Yggur, you made a gate during the time of the Mirror,' Nish persisted. 'I've read about it in the Histories . . .'

'Once the Forbidding failed two centuries ago, that way failed with it,' said Yggur dismissively. 'I know no other.'

'Then we're beaten before we begin,' said Nish.

No one spoke. The wind shrilled around the hatch of the thapter. Flydd's head was sunk in despair.

'What a miserable place,' said Irisis, shivering. 'I'm not looking forward to my turn on sentry duty.'

'I'd better make sure they've changed the watch,' said Yggur, rising painfully and going up the ladder. 'A man could freeze to death outside without realising it.'

'He's looking very weary,' said Nish after Yggur had gone.

'I feel the burden too,' said Klarm.

Malien was sitting on the floor, cross-legged, peeling a warty green fruit the size of an orange. Inside, blood-red pyramidal segments were packed together in pairs, one up and one down, separated by yellow pith. She seemed far away as she arranged the segments neatly on an enamelled plate.

Shortly Yggur returned, clapping his gloves together. He took off outer and inner pairs and began to rub his hands over his face. 'Malien,' he said at last. 'You've been quiet lately. What have you got to say?'

'What makes you think I've anything to say?' she said, selecting the smallest of the segments and popping it in her mouth.

'I know you of old, remember. You have a plan in mind, don't you?'

'I wouldn't call it a plan.' She chose another segment.

'An idea, then.'

'A possibility occurred to me earlier but I dismissed it out of hand. It was too perilous to consider further.'

'I don't see how we can be in more danger than we're already in,' said Nish.

'Do you not, Artificer?' Malien looked at him, into him and through him with those ageless green eyes that had seen everything. 'But of course, you're barely out of childhood. You could not understand.'

Nish flushed and turned away. Irisis smiled inwardly. He never knew when to shut up. She noticed Yggur watching Malien with tense expectation.

'More perilous than losing the war?' he said at last.

'I don't know!' she said forcefully, losing her calm for a moment. 'That's the problem.'

'Then let's hear your idea. Between all of us, we should be able to see the good and the bad in it.'

'We don't know what we're doing, and we *can't* know. I – no, it's too perilous. Better we give up and go home, rather than attempt it.'

'And leave the world to the scrutators?' cried Nish.

Yggur waved him to silence. 'What's your idea, Malien?'

She arranged the remaining segments in a star shape, then moved the points in until they formed a circle, an unbroken barrier with a single segment in the middle. 'Very well. There's no way in from outside. But what about from *inside*?'

'I don't follow you,' said Irisis.

200

Malien looked as though she regretted having it prised out of her. She glanced up the ladder as if to make sure that no one could overhear her, then lowered her voice. 'I had in mind to try and wake Tiaan's amplimet.'

TWENTY-ONE

'I don't understand,' said Irisis. 'No crystal can be used until it's
been activated, which we artisans call waking, so surely the
amplimet has to be awake already.'

'We Aachim use the word in a different way,' said Malien.
She let out a heavy sigh and her years fell upon her. 'Since the
moment Tiaan revealed the amplimet to me in Tirthrax I've
been afraid of it, and I'm not the only one. Vithis was against its
use from the beginning, and had not his people stood in peril of
extinction he would never have allowed it.'

'Then why did you let Tiaan keep it?'

'What would *I* have done with it? I could not have remained
in Tirthrax once the amplimet began to communicate with the
node, nor taken it to any other place with a powerful node.
Tiaan had used it safely for half a year and I judged it was better
off in her hands.'

'Until someone took it from her,' said Nish.

'I cannot see the future,' said Malien frostily, 'and *I'm* not so
arrogant as to think I know better than everyone else.'

But you *do* think that, Irisis thought. It's one of the defining
characteristics of the Aachim, even you.

'Besides,' Malien went on, 'back then I was just serving out
my days, bidding a prolonged farewell to Santhenar and all I'd

202

loved in it, before going to the Well. If not for Tiaan I would have left this world by now.'

'A path I've also thought about taking,' said Yggur. 'Lives can be *too* long. What's the point, when you've seen everything and done everything?' he ruminated. 'What changed your mind, Malien?'

'By the time Tiaan returned to Tirthrax I'd seen just what a dangerous path the world was on. I had to act for the good of my own kind, and all humankind. That's why I took Tiaan to Stassor, and why I subsequently disobeyed the edict of my people and carried her to safety.

'But on our way west, I stopped to give succour to Clan Elienor, my distant kin, exiled for allowing Tiaan to escape from their custody. I sat down with the leaders of Elienor and they told me what they knew about amplimets.' Her voice dropped. 'And then I knew fear, as I've not known it since the time of the Mirror.'

'What did they tell you?' said Irisis in a whisper. It would have felt wrong to speak in a normal voice.

'This isn't the first amplimet to have been found. There was another, in the distant past of our own world, and it nearly brought my people undone.'

'Really? What happened?' said Yggur.

'I don't know, exactly. It was long before Clan Elienor's time. Even their elders haven't been able to uncover the details, though they discovered that the sacred Histories of Aachan were changed to hide the truth. There are bitter enmities behind the rivalries of the clans,' Malien said. 'Very bitter and longstanding ones. It's no wonder Vithis's plan to seize half of Santhenar has come to naught – the clans can't even agree on the conquest of another world.'

'Was it the crystal that was perilous,' said Yggur, 'or the bickering over it?'

'Both, I think,' said Malien. 'But certainly the amplimet woke and began to draw power for itself, and no one could control it.'

'Well, that was thousands of years ago,' said Yggur. 'The Art has moved on a long way since then. Maybe we *should* consider waking Tiaan's amplimet, if it's the only way we can get into Nennifer.'

'We've always known that it needed a strong hand,' said Flydd, a glint in his eye. 'We've plenty of strong hands here, so let's get on with it.'

'Let's not be hasty,' said Yggur mildly. 'I'd want to know what we're letting ourselves in for, first. Explain what you mean about *waking* it, Malien.'

'When Tiaan first saw the crystal,' said Malien, 'she said that it was *awake*, meaning that it was drawing power by itself. Not much power, only enough to make it glow, but some. Who knows how long it had been doing that? A thousand years? A million? And perhaps at some stage in that aeon, or later when Tiaan began to use it, it developed a kind of crystalline awareness. At Tirthrax it began to communicate with the node. I don't know why, but it wouldn't allow Tiaan to take it away in the thapter and later, when she tried to defy it near Nyriandiol, it caused the thapter to crash. It also communicated with the node at Snizort, though it hasn't acted up since Tiaan fled. I dare say Vithis drove it back to its previous suspended state . . .'

'From which you plan to rouse it,' said Irisis, trying to understand. 'What will happen if you succeed?'

'I *hope* it will reach out to the node that sustains Nennifer,' said Malien.

'How is that going to help us?'

'I think I can see what you've got in mind,' said Klarm. 'At the best of times, Nennifer uses most of the field. Now they're using almost all of it; that's why the node is under such strain –'

'Once the amplimet reaches out to the node,' said Flydd, 'their devices will start to fail. They won't know what's going on and we'll attack in the confusion.'

'What if Fusshte realises it's the amplimet?' said Yggur. 'He must have interrogated Tiaan by now.'

'He won't know what's happened,' said Flydd.

'Wait on!' Yggur was frowning. 'What happens after the amplimet is roused?'

'How do you mean?' said Klarm.

'Why does it communicate with the node? What's it trying to do and how can it be stopped once we're inside? How is it put to sleep again?'

'That's why I was reluctant to mention the idea in the first place,' said Malien. 'No one knows why it communicates with nodes, but it can be stopped by taking it out of range – twenty or thirty leagues in this case – or by putting it inside a sealed platinum box, which the field can't penetrate.'

'Have we such a box?' said Yggur.

'No, but we have the materials to make one,' said Flydd. 'It wouldn't take long.'

'And how do we wake it?'

'I think I can do that,' said Malien. Flydd's eyes bored into her but she did not elaborate. Evidently she did not plan to share that secret.

'What if they already keep it in a platinum box and we can't wake it?' said Yggur.

'Then we're beaten and will have to think of another plan,' said Flydd. 'But remember who we're dealing with, Yggur. The Council is greedy and they've always seen sheer power as the way to win the war. Having finally got their hands on this wondrous amplimet, they'll be working night and day to find out how they can use it.'

'Cautiously, perhaps.'

'When it comes to the Art, their mastery of devices has made them arrogant. They're the most powerful group of mancers ever assembled for a common purpose, and they have hundreds of skilled mancers to do the dirty work and take the risks. So,' Flydd said, 'when the amplimet does wake, they'll have no reason to assume that the interference has come from outside.'

'How is waking it going to advantage us?' said Yggur. 'We can't know *what* the amplimet will do, so how can we know *where* to attack Nennifer?'

'We'll have to be ready to take advantage of whatever opportunity comes our way,' said Flydd.

'That's not good enough,' said Yggur. 'Even if the amplimet

were to disable every sentinel and device in Nennifer, there will still be seven hundred guards to deal with. We can't fight our way in.'

'We've got to have a clear and specific plan.' Klarm scratched his belly. 'Would it be possible to *direct* the amplimet, so it creates an opportunity we can use?'

'I'm reluctant to do that,' said Malien.

'Why?'

'It . . . I'm afraid it might try to take control of me.'

There was a long silence. Xervish Flydd finally broke it. 'Is there something you aren't telling us?'

Malien looked anywhere but at him. It was the first time Irisis had seen her at a disadvantage.

'Malien?' said Yggur.

'The one found on Aachan got out of control,' she said with evident reluctance. 'Whole clans were wiped out in a great cataclysm, though whether it was caused by the amplimet, or the clans fighting over it, no one will say.'

'But you're afraid it was the amplimet?'

'I'm very afraid. That a crystal – an inanimate lump of rock – should communicate with a node is an abomination. This one has already woken once, so *what does it want?*'

'A serious question,' said Flydd, 'though not one we can answer. We must rely on our own judgment, and I say we use the amplimet. What's our alternative? Only to run away and hide until the Council's incompetence finally brings our world to an end.'

'How can an inanimate piece of crystal want anything?' said Nish. 'It's absurd.'

'How can it communicate with a node?' said Malien. 'I agree, the notion is preposterous. Nonetheless, the amplimet has done so, and that surely isn't the end of it. It's deadly and it can turn on you in an instant, as Ghaenis, son of Tirior, found to his cost.'

'I'm going to destroy the Council and I'm prepared to take my chances on the amplimet,' said Flydd. 'If it takes control of me my troubles will be over. But I sense there's more, Malien.'

The thapter creaked as the wind, which was increasing as nightfall approached, battered at its left flank.

'There's more,' she said.

'So if we follow Flydd's plan,' said Yggur, 'we not only have to overcome the scrutators and all their forces; we've got to find the amplimet and shut it up in your platinum box with the utmost dispatch.'

'Yes,' Malien said faintly. 'Why don't we continue after dinner? I'm more fatigued than I thought.'

Flydd put on his coat and gloves, lurched up the ladder and went out into the dark.

After dinner Irisis had restless legs from being cooped up too long, so she went outside, pacing across the gritty ground. The night was overcast though not completely dark, and shortly the outline of one of the guards loomed up. 'Flangers?' she said softly.

'Yes. What brings you out here?'

'A need to stretch my legs. And too much company.'

'I know what you mean,' he said. 'In truth, I'd sooner spend the whole night on watch than crammed into the bowels of the thapter.'

'Quite. Which way did Flydd go?'

He pointed to the left. Irisis went right. She'd had enough of the scrutator for the moment. She climbed the slope for a few hundred paces but soon felt short of breath and sat down on a rock shaped like a toadstool. The thapter was out of sight, the world reduced to a few dark outlines.

She felt sure that this attack would fail. Logic told her that they'd have little chance even with the best plan in the world. But this shambles - it couldn't be called anything else - was laughable. They'd be killed or captured, and falling into the hands of the scrutators again filled her with dread.

She heard the footsteps long before she saw the shadow, and Irisis could tell by the sounds that it was Flydd, dragging himself up the slope. He took every opportunity to walk, forcing himself through the pain to recover his strength and mobility. She debated whether to say anything or not, but he was coming so close that she could hardly ignore him.

'Scrutator,' she said.

Flydd stopped a few paces away and she could just see his head move as he sought her out. 'Ah,' he said and came towards her.

She stood up. 'You seem better, surr.'

'Do I?' he said bitterly.

'Don't start that with me,' she snapped. 'I'm fed up with it.' Irisis wasn't unfeeling by any means, but they desperately needed the old Flydd back.

'I beg your pardon?' he said coldly.

'You know what I mean. We all know you've suffered. You don't have to rub it in our faces every moment of the day.'

'You don't know anything about it, Crafter.'

'That's because you won't talk about it.'

'Do I have to expose my deepest torment to the world so people can sneer behind my back and use my shame against me?'

'We're not your enemies, Flydd. They're inside Nennifer.'

'Well, I can't talk about it.'

'Then I will,' she said. 'They castrated you, didn't they?'

He stopped suddenly. 'Is that what they're saying?'

'*They're* not saying anything. But I am.'

'Yes,' he said. 'They've unmanned me. I'm just a hollow shell.'

'You look the same to me,' she said. 'A little more battered and scarred, a lot more angry, but still Flydd. Still the same man I used to admire.'

'But not one you'd have for a lover, eh?'

Irisis sighed. She'd been hoping not to have this discussion. 'That was over long ago and you know it, Xervish, so stop using it against me. More to the point, stop using it to whip yourself.'

'I can't,' he said. 'And nor would you, if the heart of your womanhood had been cut from you.'

'Look, surr,' she said. 'We can't understand what you're going through, but you've got to get over it. We can't do without you.'

'So what I'm feeling inside doesn't matter?'

She ignored that. 'We're all here because of you. It's been your plan, and your object, ever since Snizort. Without you at

208

your best, the attack can't succeed. We'll fall into the hands of the scrutators and what they'll do to us next time . . .'

'I see,' he said coldly. 'Walk on, Irisis.'

'Surr?' she said.

'Leave me!'

'I'm going!' she snapped. 'And when you're done with feeling sorry for yourself, be done with the whining as well.' And then she ran to escape his outrage.

Flydd returned an hour later. His face was pinched from the cold but he said nothing to Irisis, just sat down and took a sparing portion of bread, cheese, sausage and pickled vegetables.

'If we're going to do this, let's put the plan together,' said Yggur. 'There's still an army to be overcome, in the unlikely event that the Council and all their mancers are distracted by the amplimet. How do we get past that army?'

Malien didn't answer.

'What if we were to allow the amplimet to take control?' said Irisis.

'I presume you mean *get out of control*?' said Yggur.

'Yes.'

'How do we know that it will?'

Everyone looked at Malien.

'It must,' said Irisis, 'otherwise Malien wouldn't have suggested it. She knows more than she's letting on . . .'

'Malien?' said Yggur

Malien gave Irisis a cold stare. 'Yes, that's what I had in mind – the amplimet trying to take control of the node.'

'Why didn't you say so?' snapped Yggur.

'I'm constrained by my oath not to speak about our secrets,' said Malien. 'Already I'm treading a finer path than I care to.'

'Considering that your people exiled you and sentenced you to clan-vengeance, you seem overly fastidious. How do you know the amplimet will do what we require?'

Again Malien hesitated before answering. 'I don't know *what* it will do if it's unleashed. Amplimets are capricious.'

'What if we were to threaten it?' said Nish.

Irisis was amazed at Nish's audacity. How could he, with neither talent for the Art nor any sensitive abilities, presume to tell the mighty their business?

'That's a good idea, Nish,' Flydd said thoughtfully. 'A very good idea. Provoke it and make it lash out. It'll either go for the node, or attack what it perceives as the threat. The scrutators won't know what hit them, and in the chaos we go in.'

'I don't like it,' said Yggur. 'We've no idea what we're doing.'

'It could do anything,' said Malien. 'And what if we can't get to the amplimet, to put it in the platinum box?'

'Our troubles will soon be over,' said Flydd. 'Unfortunately, it's our only option so let's vote on it right now. Do we provoke the amplimet and risk the consequences, or run home and let the Council drag the world to ruin?'

He went around the table one by one and wrung reluctant agreement out of them. 'We're all in save one. What say you, Malien?'

'We do it,' she said after a long hesitation, 'and if it goes terribly wrong, I pray none of us live long enough to realise the enormity of our folly.'

TWENTY-TWO

As soon as the platinum box was finished they gathered their gear, shrugged on their heavy packs and climbed down the ice-crusted ladder into the darkness. They dared not take the thapter closer; the Nennifer field was under such strain that any drain of power from outside the fortress must arouse suspicion. It would take most of the night to get close enough to wake the amplimet. And even if they succeeded, they had to attack on foot, and in the blackest of nights, when not even the sentries on the watch-towers could see beyond their noses. That meant before midnight tomorrow night, when the moon rose.

Nish heard a series of clicks: Malien locking the thapter. They couldn't spare any guards for it, not that a couple of guards could defend it anyway if a patrol came upon them. Nish shivered. Leaving the thapter so far away seemed like burning their boats behind them. He took a couple of noisy, crunching steps. It was impossible to move quietly on the loose gravel.

'Hold on,' said Irisis, taking him by the arm. 'Flydd wants to say something.'

'Why didn't he say it inside?' Nish grumbled, for his breath was already freezing on his moustache.

The dullest of glows appeared, lighting up the faces of the group. She pulled him into the circle, facing the wind. Nish's eyes began to water and the tears to freeze.

'Fusshte knows we have the thapter,' Flydd reminded them. 'He probably isn't expecting an airborne attack but he'll certainly be prepared for one. The only thing he can't be expecting is an attack on foot.'

'Because only the biggest fools on Santhenar would think of it,' said Yggur sourly. 'If we are to go for this folly, let's get moving.'

'Once we approach, we must be exquisitely careful,' said Flydd. 'The guards are always watching. Always waiting.'

Nish gathered his cloak around him, feeling out of his depth. There had been a long debate as to the safest method of waking the amplimet, or threatening it, most of which had been so arcane as to be incomprehensible. He wished he'd slept instead. His head throbbed from the stale air in the thapter and he had a leaden feeling behind his temples.

'Flydd must be out of his mind,' he muttered to Irisis. 'Lust for revenge has blinded him to reality.'

She didn't reply.

'Malien is afraid,' he went on. 'Even Yggur is against it. I –'

'We voted,' she said in a dead voice. 'We're going in.'

'But I –'

'Shut up, Nish!' Irisis hissed in his ear. 'We've got a long march ahead and you're not helping.'

'And a horrible end when we get there.'

She must have picked up his despair, for Irisis turned and put her hands on his cheeks, looking into his eyes. 'Oh, come on, Nish,' she said more kindly. 'You've been working towards this day since you escaped from Snizort.'

'Doesn't mean I'm not terrified,' he muttered.

'We all are. Anyway, I'm supposed to be the doom merchant. Don't push me into the caring role – you know I'm not comfortable with it.' Giving the lie to her words, she linked her arm through his and they set off.

It was a long and miserable trudge across the slopes of the mountain, as cold as anything he'd experienced, though nothing happened to distinguish one gritty, sliding step from another. Because of the altitude, walking was hard work and he was soon so short of breath that talking at the same time wasn't worth the effort.

Near the tail end of that exhausting night they ran into a steep ridge of quartz that puckered the mountainside vertically like a badly healed sword slash. Klarm had noted it from afar, from the thapter. They felt their way up it in the dark, eventually finding a fissure large enough for the fifteen of them to hide in. Nennifer lay below and to the east, little more than a league away. They could go no further until Malien had done her work on the amplimet.

They put up a pair of tents, set out the guards and crawled in for whatever rest they could steal before the attack.

Malien cleared her end of the tent by the simple expedient of creating a golden bubble from her fingertips and allowing it to expand until it enveloped her completely. Whatever else it touched was pushed out of the way.

'What's she doing?' whispered an awed Inouye.

Malien was dimly visible inside, sitting cross-legged with her eyes closed and her long fingers extended along her thighs. The shimmering luminescence of the globe cast moving lights and shadows across her face and body. She looked ageless, cunning, fey.

'She has her own unique form of the Art,' Yggur said quietly. 'As do I. Hers doesn't rely on the field, so she can scry without the scrutators detecting her.'

'At least, we hope so,' said Irisis.

Yggur glared at her, then went on. 'We can, of course, draw on the field at need.'

'How long is it going to take?' said Nish.

'However long it takes,' snapped Flydd from his sleeping pouch. 'Now keep your trap shut. I need my sleep.'

Flydd must be in constant pain, Nish thought charitably. He'd always been irascible, but now he was angry all the time. Nish wriggled around against the side of the tent, trying to find a comfortable position. Irisis elbowed him in the ribs. He sighed.

The golden bubble popped. 'I've located the amplimet,' said Malien.

'What, already?' The words burst out of Nish.

Everyone turned to stare at him. He flushed. 'I thought it would take hours,' he mumbled. 'Thought there'd be time for sleep.'

No one said anything, which was worse than if they had.

'It's not sealed away,' Malien said. 'And, judging by the peculiar orientation of the field, the scrutators are working on it now. They must have barriers up to prevent the amplimet taking more than a trickle of power.'

'Then they know the danger it represents?' asked Yggur.

'We have to assume that they've discovered everything Tiaan knows about it,' said Flydd.

'Tiaan has a way of revealing only what she wants to,' said Malien. 'But I agree – it's safer to assume that.'

'Then you'd better get to work,' said Flydd.

Malien took several deep breaths, knitting and unknitting her fingers, but didn't move.

'You *can* wake it?' said Flydd roughly.

She nodded stiffly. 'I just don't think I should.'

'We've been through all that. Just get on with it!'

Nish had never heard anyone speak to Malien that way before. Her lip curled as she looked at the meagre old man. 'In the circumstances, I will forgive that. Ah, but you know so little of what you're asking.'

She regenerated her bubble, though this time it took on an opalescent translucency that reduced her to a hunched shape inside.

'You can have your precious sleep now, Artificer,' said Flydd.

Nish lay down and dozed off at once, only to be woken by a mutter from the other side of the tent. As he began to sit up, Irisis gripped his arm, warningly.

'It worries me that the field is so strained,' said Yggur. 'One misjudgment –'

'Let's not speculate about that,' Flydd said. 'Get some sleep. You too, Klarm. You'll need it before this is over.'

'As will you,' said Klarm. 'We're relying on you, Flydd.'

'I don't need much sleep these days. Master Flenser pruned me of all that was superfluous. Perhaps he did me a favour.' He laughed harshly.

Yggur made no reply.

Nish closed his eyes and tried to get back to sleep, though now an image kept recurring – the red ruin which Flydd's healer had revealed so fleetingly, and with such rage at man's inhumanity to his own.

A long time later Yggur put his head out of the tent, looking up at the dark sky. A high overcast blotted out the stars and moon. 'It's coming dawn.' He rubbed his stubbled cheeks. 'Aah, it's cold out.'

Flydd was sitting with his hands on his knees, exactly as he had been hours earlier, watching Malien.

'Doesn't look as though she's having any success,' said Yggur.

'It's taking too long,' said Flydd, 'and there's nothing we can do to help her. This is Malien's great task and if she can't do it, no one can.'

Before dawn the sentries were drawn back inside the ends of the fissure. Everyone else spent the day cooped in the tents. This close to Nennifer they dared not go outside, for the risk of being seen was too great.

In mid-morning, Malien dissolved the bubble and crawled across to the food bag, where she made a scant meal of mouldy bread and hard cheese, and another of the knobbly fruits. She had trouble eating it; her hands and arms shook unceasingly. Washing the morsel down with gulps of water that spilled down her front and froze instantly, she flopped onto her sleeping pouch and fell into sleep.

Yggur and Flydd exchanged glances. Yggur jerked his head at the tent flap and went out. Flydd followed. They could be heard conversing in the fissure, though Nish didn't catch a word.

'What do you think they're talking about?' he said quietly to Irisis.

She rolled over, irritably pulling the sleeping pouch up around her ears. Nish turned onto his back, staring at the roof of the tent.

Ice crystals were growing down from the ridgepole. He shivered and drew his fingers down the canvas wall. They left trails in the growing frost.

'This is too big for any of us.'

Klarm's voice, though soft, came from just behind Nish's ear. He jumped. 'What do you mean ... er, Scrutator?' Nish still wasn't sure how to address the dwarf. In truth, despite Klarm having saved his life, Nish still felt uncomfortable with him. He rotated so he could see Klarm's face.

'Malien has just realised that what she's trying to do isn't possible. It's too much for any mancer, or all of us together. Go to sleep,' Klarm said abruptly. 'It's what you wanted.' He got up and went out. The tent flap, stiff with ice, crackled as it fell back into place.

Nish, feeling vaguely uneasy, said softly, 'Irisis?'

She didn't reply. Irisis was asleep; Malien too, judging by the gentle snores issuing from the other end of the tent. There was no one to share his fears with. Inouye and Evee had been sent to the other, larger tent, occupied by Flangers and the soldiers.

He went across the litter of gear and sleeping pouches on knees and elbows. A buzz of conversation came from outside. Nish eased his head through the flap. Klarm sat hunched in his cloak just before the bend in the fissure, head tilted to one side as if listening.

Flydd and Yggur must be just around the corner – Nish could see the edge of Yggur's long cloak draped over the rock. Unfortunately Nish still couldn't hear. And what was Klarm up to? Had everything just been a plot to lure them here? Did he plan to betray them as the price of admission to the Council?

Long fingers wrapped around Nish's ankle. 'What do you think you're doing?' Malien said, soft and low.

He whirled, cracking his ear on the tent pole. A stalactite of ice fell on his head and shattered. Nish sat down, picking ice out of his hair. 'Klarm's up to something.'

She let go. 'Do you think of Yggur and Flydd as fools?'

There was ice in his ear as well. He tried to get the fragment out but it melted, sending an icy trickle down to sear his eardrum. 'Of course not.'

'Then leave the worrying to them.'

'What if the Council's quest succeeds, and they learn to control the amplimet?'

'They'll have enough power to annihilate us.'

'And if they fail and the amplimet gets ... whatever it's looking for?'

She looked him in the eye and for an instant Nish saw beyond the stern, almost ageless face. What was she thinking? Did she pity him?

'Worse,' she said almost inaudibly, and turned away.

TWENTY-THREE

Two frustrating days dragged by, and Malien spent most of that time isolated in the bubble, working at her incomprehensible task of locking onto the amplimet and forcing it to wake. When not doing that she lay in her pouch, panting or tossing in a restless sleep.

The conferences in the fissure became longer and more harried, Yggur more remote and imperious, Flydd more insanely driven. He would not be talked out of the attack, though after all this time no one saw any chance of it succeeding. To get away from them, Klarm had taken to climbing up the rocks in the dark. At least, that was what he'd said he was doing, though Nish wasn't sure any more. He didn't have any good reason to suspect the dwarf scrutator, but with so much time to fill in he'd come to doubt everything. And every hour the probability of chance discovery grew greater, as did the risk that the scrutators would master the amplimet first. Or the amplimet master them.

As the third night fell Malien was still going, but when she broke for a brief rest Yggur had to lift her into her sleeping pouch. Her skin had begun to wrinkle like a dried olive, and her shrunken eyes had a dull opacity as if she were developing cataracts.

'Why is she so worn out?' said Nish to Irisis, after Flydd and Yggur had just slipped out again.

'Because she daren't take power from the field. Malien is using an older Art but she has to draw it from herself, and she's at her limit.'

'I can't do it,' Malien said an hour later, pushing away the mug of honeyed tea Irisis was holding out for her. 'Aftersickness is wearing me down and there's no time to recover from it.'

'Get some more sleep,' said Yggur. 'Flydd and I have been discussing another way.'

'One that doesn't require me?' she said, lying down and closing her eyes.

'We'll still need you but we'll be taking some of the load.'

They went out to discuss their plan. Klarm wasn't there either. He'd gone climbing up the quartz ridge at dusk and still wasn't back. He could have walked all the way to Nennifer by now, Nish thought.

'Now I'm really worried,' he said to Irisis.

She was sitting in the corner, sleeping pouch up around her waist, weaving a couple of dozen silver and gold wires into a complicated braid, part of a piece of jewellery she'd been working on for days. Being a jeweller had been her life's ambition, stifled when she was a little girl by a mother who had invested the Stirm family's future in her clever daughter. Irisis still planned to become a jeweller, 'after the war is over'.

'You started worrying the day you were born, Nish. Have a nap or something.'

'I've had about forty naps since we've been stuck here. I couldn't sleep to save my life.'

'Then be quiet. I'm trying to work.'

'Your fingers do the work by themselves,' he observed. 'You don't need to think about it.'

'That doesn't mean I don't work better without interruptions.'

'I'm *really* worried.'

Irisis cast a glance over her shoulder at Malien, who was twitching in her sleep, and set her work aside with, charitably, just the gentlest of sighs.

'What about?'

219

'I think Klarm's leading us into a trap.'

'But he's not leading us; Flydd and Yggur are.'

'They call upon his knowledge of Nennifer all the time.'

'I'm sure Flydd and Yggur are keeping an eye on him.'

'They're too distracted.' Nish, realising that he was panting, took a deep breath. It didn't help; he could feel panic rising and it was worse than he'd felt in other tight situations, because he was so helpless to do anything. 'It's out of control, Irisis, and there's nothing you or I can do to stop it.'

'In which case there's no point worrying.'

She was almost supernaturally calm these days, or fatalistic. 'That's not like you,' he said accusingly, as if she were letting the side down. 'You hate waiting for things to happen, and you hate –'

'Well, I'm sorry if I'm acting out of character!' Irisis turned her back, pointedly taking up her braid again.

'Sorry,' Nish said automatically. 'I – I'm out of my depth. This idea about waking the amplimet . . . it's bound to go wrong.'

'It's the only plan we have, Nish.'

The flap was thrust open, scattering ice across the floor. Yggur came in, bent low, followed by Flydd and Klarm.

'Time to go,' said Yggur, going to his knees to shake Malien's shoulder.

She sat up, bleary-eyed. 'Already?'

'I'm afraid so. We've got about half a league to go. We go over the ridge and down into the little valley where they grow their crops. We'll get a bit of cover there. When we're in place, we'll work together. It'll be easier down there, closer to the amplimet. If you seek it as before, I'll lend you my shoulder when you need it.' He hesitated. 'That's the idea, anyhow.'

'Great,' Nish muttered when they had gone out. 'Now when it goes wrong we'll lose them all.'

'It's no use,' said Yggur a couple of hours after midnight, wiping hard granules of blown snow off his brow. He'd been working with Malien for ages, without success. 'It's hopeless.'

'Let's give it one last try,' said Flydd.

'The moon's up. We'll have to leave it until tonight.'

'We must go on,' said Flydd.

'We've got to have darkness.'

'Another day and neither you nor Malien will have the strength. And I'm not turning my back on the Council again.'

This time they were just above the valley floor, which was networked in dark and light greys by its dry irrigation ditches and the tufted remnants of the harvested autumn crop. They huddled in the long moon-shadow behind a cluster of hip-high boulders, while the wind shrieked all around them. To their left, a frozen stream in the bottom of the valley disappeared over the precipice into the abyss of the Desolation Sink.

'Aftersickness is killing me,' croaked Malien.

'One more time,' Flydd said grimly.

Malien grew the golden bubble around her and became a blurred outline. Yggur stood facing her, his hands at his sides. He whistled under his breath and a series of golden threads extended from the sphere towards his face.

Malien shifted her weight, Yggur threw up his arms as if off-balance, and for a moment the rock Nish crouched behind faded to translucency. His vision blurred then returned to normal, but his anxiety only intensified. He let out his breath in a loud hiss.

Flydd jabbed him in the ribs. 'What's the matter with you tonight?'

'The amplimet is waiting for us,' Nish burst out, 'and it's angry.'

Malien stood up on tiptoe, shuddering with the strain. Yggur turned his head as far as the filaments would allow. He seemed to be holding his breath.

'It's just a mineral,' said Flydd. 'It can't feel anything. You're projecting your own fears onto it.'

Malien seemed to be beckoning to Nish, as if saying, 'Go on.'

'It's real,' said Nish.

Everyone stared at him. 'What do you mean?' Flydd rasped.

Nish had no idea how he knew it, until the words formed and he spoke them aloud. 'I can sense something . . . just as I did that

221

night above Gumby Marth, after Father cast his alchymical spell on me and I saw the lyrinx stone-formed into the pinnacles. It's a . . . a brittle rage, a *crackling* fury like a box of crystals being ground underfoot. The amplimet is tormented, and it hates the scrutators for shackling and probing it, and for blocking it from the field it so desperately needs. They've fenced it in with ice and now they're forcing it . . .'

'To what end?' said Flydd.

'I can't tell.' Nish slumped to the ground and it was all gone. He was just his normal prosaic self, with not a trace of the Art in him.

'Ice,' Yggur muttered, the golden threads twanging as his jaw moved. He swayed on his feet and nearly fell.

'Heat quickly destroys any kind of hedron,' said Irisis. 'Cold never can, but it can slow it to a murmur. Why didn't I think of that? That's how they've made it safe to use.'

Flydd gave a mirthless snort. 'And to think we've spent days trying to wake it without killing ourselves. To unshackle it, all we have to do is warm it up. It'll lash out at the scrutators and then we go in.'

'It may lash out at us,' said Malien, slumping to the ground. 'You can never tell what an amplimet will do.'

'We don't have any other option,' said Flydd. 'We must go on, no matter what the risk.'

'You're insane,' she said in a wisp of a voice.

'We – go – on!' he ground out.

Another still silence.

'If Malien can find it again I *might* be able to warm it up,' said Yggur finally. 'Though I'd have to be closer. I've not got much strength left.'

'How close?' said Malien, lying on her back on the frozen ground with her arms flopped by her sides.

Yggur joined her, breathing heavily. 'Ideally, against the outside wall of Nennifer.'

'The sentinels would pick you up before you got within a hundred spans,' said Klarm.

'How close can we get?' said Flydd.

'Five hundred spans is the closest I'd dare,' replied Klarm, 'and even that's . . .'

'Not good enough,' said Yggur. 'I can't do it from so far away.'

'Then we risk everything and go on,' said Flydd in tones that would not be denied.

'No closer,' Malien begged as they crawled up the edge of the shallow valley towards the flat-topped promontory, out of which the foundations of Nennifer had been carved. Here there had been enough moisture to freeze the gravelly soil into an iron-hard aggregate, brutal on their hands and knees. 'Please.'

'I can't do it from here,' said Yggur as he'd said half a dozen times already. He could barely hold himself on all fours now. Aftersickness was crushing him and Malien was little better.

'Hold him up, Nish,' said Flydd, working some kind of illusion with the fingers of one hand. It made no difference as far as Nish could see but, after a whispered consultation, Malien and Yggur agreed to keep going.

They continued crawling up the side of the valley, thence onto a fluted ridge of sharp rock. The sky had clouded over but now the moon came out momentarily and Irisis, beside Nish, caught her breath. The sudden brightness lit up the paved parade ground and mooring field which extended from the vertical slash of the thousand-span-high precipice that fell into the sunken lands of the Desolation Sink, all the way, as flat as a table, to the front wall of Nennifer. Two air-dreadnoughts were moored in the central part of the parade ground, one not far from this end, the other midway.

Nennifer's monumental bulk reared up before them, the biggest building in the world and one of the most brutal in its sheer functional ugliness. It made no concession to beauty, harmony, proportion or setting: in a world devoted to war, nothing mattered but the power of those who told the world how to fight and die. Behind Nennifer, mountains black and bare rose up to pierce the glowing sky.

They were no more than five hundred spans from the front of the building. From here they would be exposed every step of the way, and within range of the great javelards and catapults mounted on the walls. If the sentries saw them, they would be shot without warning.

'Where's the amplimet, Malien?' said Flydd.

'Somewhere in the middle of the building,' she replied. 'I can't tell more from here. The third floor, or perhaps the fourth. No closer, please.' She choked.

'What's the matter?' said Nish.

'Something is very wrong. We must turn back.'

'We have to go on,' grated Flydd.

'No further. I'm begging you.' Malien's face was stark in the moonlight. 'Take another step and the mission will fail.'

'If we turn back, we've already failed. Neither of you have the strength for another attempt.'

Yggur raised his head, which was nodding like a puppet's. 'What's that?' he whispered, looking at a small stone structure a couple of hundred spans ahead and to their left, not far from the edge of the precipice.

'It's a shed where they keep the mooring cables for the air-dreadnoughts,' said Klarm.

'Will anyone be there now?'

'No reason why there should be.'

'We'll do it in the lee of the shed,' said Flydd, 'if we can't get inside.'

They went on their bellies across the ice-glazed paving stones, and every wriggle of the way Nish expected to feel the pulverising impact of a javelard. He could make out guards moving on the upper walls. Surely Flydd's meagre illusion couldn't conceal them from such an unceasing watch?

The shed was built of flat slabs of gneiss laid in courses like long thin bricks, the mortar deeply raked so that the joints were half a fist deep and wide. The door proved to be locked so they took shelter against the end wall, whose shadow provided partial screening while allowing them to see the front of Nennifer.

'Keep still,' whispered Flydd. 'I'll have to release the illusion now, and the guards never fail in their alertness at Nennifer.'

'They fail at times,' amended Klarm, 'but then they die horribly, as an example to their fellows. And rightly so.'

Nish gave him a shocked glance.

'A guard's duty is to guard,' Klarm elaborated, 'and all may rest on it.'

They put their backs to the rough stones while Yggur and Malien did their best to overcome their aftersickness, then made ready for the final attempt.

The night grew wilder. The wind, howling around the angles of the shed, rasped at exposed skin with abrasive particles of ice. The last of the cloud blew away and the moon appeared, brilliant in the thin mountain air. Then, as they watched, a pair of rings grew around it, the spectral colours little more than shades of grey.

'Two rings around the moon,' said Klarm. 'Not a good omen.'

'It's better than a moonbow,' grunted Flydd.

'Not much, and we may see one as it rises.'

'Let's get on with it,' said Yggur. 'Malien?' The moonlight gave her face a bluish cast.

'Are you all right?' said Nish.

'Just thinking,' Malien said, 'of all the ways it could go wrong.'

As soon as she and Yggur began, the crystal's inanimate fury hit Nish like a blow to the stomach. For a minute he struggled to draw breath and, when it passed, his belly throbbed. They had no idea what they were dealing with.

Yggur and Malien were sitting side by side, she sagging in her bubble, he propped against the wall with his face enveloped in pale filaments. The bubble was dull this time, else it would have been visible in the shadows.

'Ready?' Yggur's jaw moved oddly, as if the threads were working it like a puppet.

Malien's affirmation was just a distant echo.

'The amplimet is hungry for power,' said Flydd. 'All you have to do is melt the ice wards surrounding it.'

'If we alert Fusshte's mancers,' said Malien, 'they'll shut it in a shielded box and we won't be able to reach it.'

225

'Then flood it with power directly. That'll warm it up. But whatever you're going to do, do it *now*. The guards patrol this area and they could come by at any time.'

Nish heard Malien's inrushing breath, the bubble darkened and she let out a pained grunt.

'Withdraw!' gasped Yggur, but there was no reply. The bubble had gone black and nothing could be seen inside.

'Come back, Malien, wherever you are,' Yggur choked. He tried to get up and fell forward, right into the moonlight.

Everyone went still, knowing that the guards on the wall must have seen the movement. All at once Irisis leapt up, grabbed Yggur's legs and began to drag him back.

A klaxon sounded from one of the corner guard towers. It was answered by half a dozen others, then a javelard spear screamed off the paving stone where Yggur's head had been a moment before. Nish grabbed a leg and heaved, heedless that Yggur's face was being dragged across the ground.

Another spear dug a span-long groove in the stone before Nish and Irisis got the big man around the corner.

'And now we're dead,' Nish said.

'Like hell!' Irisis said savagely. 'Run, while we still can. Maybe we can attack from the rear of Nennifer.'

'We can't carry Yggur and Malien,' said Flydd.

'Then leave them behind!' she snapped. 'I thought you were a ruthless scrutator, not a puling defeatist without any balls.'

Nish froze, holding his breath. Flydd gave a strangled gasp of outrage, but then a hail of heavy spears slammed into the far wall, flinging shattered rock everywhere.

'Come on!' she hissed. 'The soldiers will be on their way.'

'It's too late –'

Malien's sphere expanded then shrank again as if she was breathing it in and out. Its surface roiled, solidified like the shell of a nut then turned transparent again. They could now see her inside, working desperately with her hands as if trying to contain something too hot or bright to touch.

A catapult ball tore half the roof off the shed, showering them with broken tiles and splinters of wood. One of the soldiers, hit on the head, slumped sideways without a sound.

'Another couple of those and there'll be nothing to hide behind,' said Flangers, flicking fragments of tile out of his crossbow. 'They can pick us off without risking a man.'

'The scrutators don't care about risking a thousand men,' said Klarm. 'Now that the shock has worn off, they'll want us alive.'

Malien doubled over, holding her midriff, but forced herself upright and extended her fists in front of her. The shell burst into fragments that fizzed to nothingness in the air. She brought her fists together with a spray of light and stood swaying on her feet for a moment before sliding into a crumpled heap.

'The amplimet was waiting,' she said faintly. 'I couldn't contain it.'

In the distance something went *crack*, like a long, brittle crystal being snapped in two.

'What happened?' asked Flydd.

'I don't know.' Malien could barely speak. 'There was no resistance at all. As soon as I pushed, the wards gave way like rotten ice . . . as if they'd been eaten away from inside.'

'The amplimet must have already woken,' said Klarm. 'It had set a trap for the scrutators but got us instead. Now there's an irony for you.'

'So we just wait for Fusshte to take us?' said Irisis.

No one said anything. The barrage had stopped; now the klaxons were cut off in mid-cry. The guards were equally silent. Not a sound came from the length and breadth of Nennifer.

Nish could feel the tension building. His skin prickled and his diaphragm began to thud back and forth like a beaten drum. He swallowed and his ears popped, but the pressure on his eardrums was still there. He did it again and again. It made no difference.

The moonlight faded like a slowly lidded eye. When it shone out again the double rings were brighter than before.

'Why haven't the guards come after us?' he said.

'They're afraid to move,' said Irisis.

Nish's diaphragm was beating so hard he could barely draw breath. Afraid?

'What was that?' hissed Flangers.

The wind had died down too, and they heard a curious noise.

'It sounds like rushing water,' said Irisis, looking towards the precipice only a dozen spans away.

'Any water on the ground would be frozen iron-hard at this time of year,' said Nish.

She wriggled across to the edge, keeping within the shed's shadow, but came straight back.

'It's rushing out of a fissure in the cliff and freezing as it falls.'

'Funny we didn't hear it before,' said Nish. The ground gave the faintest tremor. 'Did you feel that?'

'Earth tremblers are common here,' said Klarm.

Again they heard that brittle crunching, though this time it was like a clanker's metal feet grinding across a field of crystals and crumbling them to shards. There came a drawn-out, subterranean rumbling and the ground shook hard enough to toss Irisis off her feet.

'We're not finished yet,' said Flydd, standing up and lurching back and forth with a maniacal glint in his eye.

'What have we done?' gasped Malien. 'Yggur . . .?' She looked around wildly.

'He's unconscious,' said Flydd dismissively. 'Overcome by aftersickness. He'll be no further use tonight.'

'The amplimet's broken free,' said Malien, climbing to her feet and bracing her back against the shed as the vibrations grew stronger. 'We've got to stop it before it gets out of control.'

'How can we, Malien?' Turning away, Flydd gave a series of low-voiced orders to the troops and they readied for action.

'You don't understand. It's . . . It's . . .'

'What?' At the expression on her face he spun around and caught her by the lapels of her coat. 'What is it?'

'I . . . think it's come to the second stage of awakening,' she said, then her eyes rolled back in her head.

Flydd cursed and let her fall. 'Two down.'

Nish was shocked by his callousness, even in this desperate situation. The Flydd he'd once known so well had been replaced by a ruthless stranger.

228

'*Second* stage of awakening?' said Klarm. 'What's she talking about, Flydd?'

'I don't think I want to know.'

There came a tearing screech, like metal being torn apart, followed by a low shudder that shook more fragments of roof slate onto their heads and shoulders. They moved down to the corner where the structure was still sound, and Nish peered across the mooring ground. The shuddering grew stronger; then, with a deafening roar, a boiling shaft of light the width of a room burst up through the roof of Nennifer. Coloured particles whirled around and up until the column faded against the bright moon. And then the whole world moved.

'What the hell was that?' said Flydd, picking himself up. The ground beneath their feet was still quivering.

'I don't know,' said Klarm. The whites of his eyes were showing. 'But I suggest we run for our lives.'

'We'll be seen,' said Flydd.

The rings around the brilliant moon had given way to a gigantic moonbow. The ground shook again and parts of the moonbow disappeared as if washed away. The parade ground wrenched sideways, hurling them against the wall. Nish's hand went straight through a crack, to his bemusement. He wrenched it out just before the crack snapped closed, losing the skin along his right thumb. The soldier who'd been hit on the head got up, shakily.

'Move!' roared Flangers, hurling Nish out of the way. He picked up Malien and ran with her as the shed collapsed behind them.

Nish lay where he'd been thrown, unable to believe what he was seeing. A series of ground waves spiralled out from Nennifer, heaving solid paving stones in the air and shaking the tethered air-dreadnoughts like balloons in a storm. The first wave threw him up and backwards, and it was like being hit by a moving clanker. He'd just landed on his shoulder when the second wave tossed him head over heels. Falling head-down, he saw the ground coming up and threw out his arms to break his fall, but it dropped away again.

'Run!' Flydd heaved Nish to his feet. Irisis had taken Malien from Flangers, who was struggling to lift Yggur.

'Which way?' Nish gasped.

'Towards Nennifer, you bloody fool. This is our chance.'

But they'll see us! Nish thought. He watched them go, thinking they'd lost their minds, until another shock knocked him down and the outer edge of the parade ground began to tilt beneath his feet. And then he ran until his heart was bursting. Ahead, a knife-edged crack appeared, curving out from the centre of Nennifer. The inner side rose and the outer fell, leaving a cliff a third of a span high. Irisis pushed Malien up it, then went over in one great bound, her bright hair flying in the moonlight. Flydd scrambled over, followed by several of the soldiers. Nish made a last effort and smelt a whiff of brimstone as he sprang.

The crack opened visibly beneath him and clouds of misty dust boiled out. The groaning in the depths was like the prisoners in the dungeons of Nennifer suffering their daily torments.

He landed on the high side, skidding on his knees, out of breath. Surely he was the last? No, one of Yggur's soldiers was labouring up the slope carrying another, who looked to have broken his leg.

He was almost to the cliff when the outer section of the parade ground dropped sharply. The man with the broken leg screamed. His partner, straining with all his might, lifted the injured soldier above his head and tossed him up onto solid ground. Reaction sent him sliding the other way, down the steadily increasing slope of the falling slab.

The soldier put his head down and even made a little ground before the slope grew so steep that he could gain no traction on it. He clung on with hands and knees, looking up at them in despair as the whole great slab of parade ground, fifty spans wide and about two hundred long, ground off, carrying him over the cliff into the vast abyss of the Desolation Sink.

TWENTY-FOUR

'What have we done?' said Nish, lying on the ground with his hands over his face.

Flydd jerked him to his feet. 'I don't know, but we're going to make the best of it.'

The whole of Nennifer was shaking and, it seemed, the mountains behind them. More slabs of parade ground fell into the Desolation Sink and springs burst out of the ground, freezing instantly to brittle fountains. The tethers snapped on the nearer of the air-dreadnoughts, which lifted sluggishly on its flabby airbags.

Spiralling lines of force appeared in Nish's inner eye, radiating out from the point whence that column of light had originated. His head whirled and he felt a sudden attack of nausea, like lying down when very drunk. Weird visions fleeted through his mind – the vast bulk of Nennifer as transparent as a glass maze; magnified views of one part of it, then another. Distant cries carried to him as if the people were standing close by. Then the enormous building was cut into curving slices and slowly forced apart by a boiling white nothingness.

It had to be an hallucination, but how come he could still think clearly? Klarm let out a cry of disbelief. Nish blinked, turned towards the dwarf scrutator and the vision was gone.

Klarm raised his right arm, pointing with one finger. With

wrenching shrieks, like blades piercing his eardrums, Nennifer was sliced into dozens of segments along the spiralling planes he'd seen earlier. For a moment the segments stood in place, slightly offset from each other, their edges as sharp and sheer as razor cuts. It wasn't right; it could not be real; but there they stood.

Then in an instant the planes or dimensions shifted, but Nish couldn't take that in – his mind refused to believe his eyes. He doubled over, trying to retch out the head-spinning nausea.

Irisis wiped his face with his coat sleeve. 'Are you all right?'

He had to lean on her for a moment. Nennifer still stood but the segments had been rearranged, as if they had been withdrawn into another dimension, shuffled like a deck of cards then put back in place. Curve lay perfectly against curve but Nennifer was no longer rectangular. It now resembled a spoked wheel and some of the segments – the layers of the original building – were exposed like slices through a cake.

The air shimmered and the front of the building warped as though a distorting lens had passed along it. Dust devils whirled up. Sections here and there, now unsupported, crumbled to rubble, while the rest of the edifice stood as solidly as if it had been built that way. In the brilliant moonlight, people could be seen at the windows, up on the battlements and in sections that had been sliced open.

The subterranean noises became a grinding roar that blocked out every other sound. Nish smelt the earthy pungency of ground-up rock. Clouds of dust billowed out, obscuring parts of the building, and by the time it began to clear they were all coated.

'Did the amplimet do all that?' whispered Flydd, his self-possession gone.

'The Council didn't throw Nennifer down,' Klarm replied shakily.

The ground shook again, hurling men and women from the battlements. One of the surviving front doors was flung wide and people – servants, soldiers, mancers in capes and gowns – boiled out of it, fleeing for their lives. Others climbed out of every hole and crack, threading the front of Nennifer with figures like ants from a stirred-up nest. A few jumped from upper floors, though they did not get up again.

The cracked remnants of the parade ground gave a last, self-satisfied shudder and all was still once more. In the distance, someone was shouting orders but the fleeing people took no notice.

'Look out,' said Nish, brushing dust from his nose. His eyebrows were thick with it. 'They're coming our way.'

'Just act terrified and aimless,' said Irisis, blinking dust out of her long eyelashes.

A battered group of people stumbled by, not giving them a second glance, and disappeared. Others followed.

'Do we have to go in?' said Nish. 'Surely this means the end of the Council.'

'I should have listened, Malien,' Flydd sounded as if he had a throat full of gravel. 'It's woken. What's the amplimet going to do now?'

Malien, lying on the ground with her eyes closed, did not reply.

Irisis reached out and caught hold of Nish's fingers. 'I'm scared,' she said quietly. 'I don't want to go in there.'

Coming from the bravest person he knew, that was chilling. He slid his cold hand into hers. 'Neither do I.'

Klarm waddled across to Flydd. 'I don't see what we can do, Xervish. It'll be like a maze inside.'

'One where every path leads to a blank wall,' said Flydd. He thought for a moment. 'We must go in. We've got to make sure of the Council – you can bet they've survived – and attempt to secure the amplimet. And find Tiaan.'

'If she's alive!' growled Klarm.

'You'd better hope she is,' whispered Malien. 'She may be the only one who can restrain the amplimet now.'

'We'll never find it in that chaos,' said Klarm. 'Or her.'

'I will lead you,' said a vaguely familiar voice from the crumbled rock along the edge of the cloven parade ground.

Klarm whirled, groping for his short blade.

233

'Hold!' cried Flydd. 'Hold, damn it.'

Klarm slowly lowered his arm.

'Come forth,' said Flydd. 'Slowly.'

A man emerged, empty hands out in front of him. His back was to the moon and Nish could make out no more than an outline. He was of middle height and slim.

'Surr,' said the man.

Suddenly Nish knew him. 'Eiryn Muss!'

'Or someone taking his shape,' said Irisis.

'No, it's Muss all right,' said Flydd. 'Where the hell have you been all this time, Prober Muss? I sent you to do a job months ago and you didn't report back.'

'You sent me to find news of the flying construct, surr,' said Muss. 'And I followed the webs of lies and rumour to Lybing where, unfortunately, I came to the notice of Scrutator Fusshte. He knew I served you, of course. And my worth.'

Flydd grunted, which could have meant anything.

'Fusshte offered me a choice,' Muss went on. 'To serve him, or die the death prescribed for the trusted servant of a traitor. What could I do, surr? Dead I would be no use to you. I chose to serve Fusshte, for that was the only way to discharge my oath and duty to you. And, after all, much of the scrutators' intelligence flows through him.'

'He's a master of lies and deceit,' said Klarm. 'As are you, Prober Muss. Any man sworn to Fusshte is no good to us.'

'Surr,' said Muss. 'I –'

'Eiryn Muss served me faithfully for a very long time,' said Flydd, though in a neutral voice.

Klarm just looked at him. Flydd met his stare. Finally Klarm said, very dubiously, 'And *in all that time* he gave you no cause to doubt him?'

'Not in the least degree,' said Flydd.

What was Flydd playing at? In Nish's travels with him after fleeing Snizort, Flydd had more than once wondered at Muss's personal agenda.

'Explain yourself, Muss, *if you can*,' said Flydd. 'And be quick about it. Time presses upon us.'

'I'll save you more time than you'll lose by questioning me, surr. Fusshte brought me here to assist him and, in time, made me his Master of the Watch. I learned much about flying constructs, surr, and other matters of interest to you.'

'You conveyed not a jot of it to me,' snapped Flydd.

'Fusshte did not allow me access to the message skeets,' said Muss.

'How could he stop a man of your talents?'

'He put a specific ward around their pens, proof against whatever guise I might put on. I did everything I could to find a way –'

'Fine words,' said Klarm, 'but they mean nothing.'

'Neither could I leave Nennifer by air-floater or mountain camel caravan,' said Muss. 'All escapes were warded against me, and I'm not hardy enough to cross the mountain paths alone.'

'Few are,' said Flydd. 'This seems enough –'

'Without proof of loyalty his words are empty,' said Klarm. 'I spent months here after my leg was smashed, and this man seemed all too close to Fusshte then. He even admits that he's Fusshte's sworn servant.'

'What say you, Eiryn Muss?' said Flydd. 'Can you offer any proof to convince my doubting companions?'

'Only this,' said Muss. 'I detected your coming yet did not give you away.'

'Prove it,' said Klarm.

'You did not come straight here in the thapter,' said Muss. 'You flew by in the cloud before turning to approach from the west. Your thapter towed another craft, a balloon of some sort, and landed some four or five leagues beyond the mountain to the north.'

Klarm rocked back on his heels. 'Really? When was this, Prober Muss?'

'Four days ago,' Muss said without hesitation. 'Late in the afternoon.'

'And how did you detect our coming, Prober?'

'My profession has its secrets, surr,' said Muss with dignity, 'and I'll no more reveal them than you would yours. I will say

235

only that, in addition to my own talents and devices, as Master of the Watch I monitor all the sentinels in Nennifer.'

'Who else knows of our coming?' rapped Klarm. 'The entire Council, or just Fusshte?'

'I told no one. Indeed, I kept the knowledge from them.'

'Which makes you a treasonous oath-breaker,' cried Klarm, vindicated. 'And no doubt a liar as well.'

'My oath to Scrutator Flydd remained valid,' Muss said simply. 'Subsequent oaths were made under duress and therefore had no force.'

'Flydd had been cast out by the Council,' said Klarm, 'which unbinds all oaths.'

'My oath was to the man as well as the scrutator,' said Muss. 'I deemed that it held.'

Klarm did not relent. 'Flydd was condemned and made a non-citizen. By law, no oath to a non-citizen can remain valid.'

'It remained binding to me. I can say no more.'

'I cannot trust –'

'Enough, Klarm!' snarled Flydd. 'It is, as you point out, a matter of trust. I choose to trust my man and there's an end to it.'

Klarm inclined his head and stepped backwards. 'As you will,' he said, though his eyes did not leave the face of the prober.

'Well, Muss,' said Flydd. 'I expect you know why we're here. What can you do for us?'

'If you would give me a moment, surr,' Muss turned away, consulting an instrument he kept concealed under his cloak. Coloured gleams briefly illuminated the fabric.

'Hey!' cried Klarm, grabbing his arm. 'What are you doing?'

'My eidoscope is linked to the sentinels,' said Muss, pulling away. 'It enables me to see truly, even in this chaos, though the sentinels are failing now.'

'What do you see, Muss?' said Flydd.

'The scrutators have survived the collapse and guard the amplimet still. You won't easily get to either.'

'But it is *possible*?' said Flydd. 'You can lead us to it?'

'I believe so,' said Muss. 'Though even for me, the *dislocation* of Nennifer will not be easy to track through.'

'What about Artisan Tiaan? Does she live?'

'Unless she died in the dislocation. I expect I can find her.'

'Tell me about the amplimet. What is its state?'

'Ah!' said Muss pregnantly. 'Not being a mancer, surr, I cannot say.'

'What do you know, Muss?'

'The Council has been probing the crystal, very carefully, ever since they brought it back from Fiz Gorgo. And I *understand*, surr, though I've not been able to confirm it with my own eyes, that they've contained it to prevent it drawing more than a trickle of power.'

'With ice wards,' said Flydd. 'But they've been melted; that's how it got free.'

'Ice was just the inner ward,' said Muss. 'There were outer wards as well.'

'What were they?' said Klarm eagerly.

'I know no more than that,' Muss said. 'And beyond the wards was a circle of adepts, just in case . . .'

'In case?' said Flydd.

'I was unable to discern the contingency they were guarding against.'

'And you call yourself a spy,' said Klarm.

'The Council guards its secrets jealously,' said Muss. 'Though I dare say it bears upon what you've done to destroy Nennifer, for all that you had no idea what you were doing.'

'Thank you, Muss,' snapped Flydd. 'Such speculations exceed your mandate. Lead us within, if you please.'

'Hold just a moment,' said Klarm. 'I think this fellow knows more than he's telling us. Prober Muss, pray enlarge upon your previous statement. What do you know about our doings?'

Muss glanced at Flydd but found no relief there.

'Well?' said Klarm. 'What does a humble prober know about the Art?'

'Nothing, surr,' said Muss, his normally impassive face showing the faintest sign of discomfort.

'Come now, Eiryn Muss,' said Flydd. 'Don't treat us like fools. You're far more than a humble prober, *aren't you?*'

'I don't know what you mean, surr.'

'Of course you do. One of the reasons you're such a brilliant spy is that you have a *hidden* talent, in the true sense of the word. You're a mancer too, Eiryn Muss, but of a very rare kind.'

'I –' Muss shook his head. 'No, surr . .'

'You're a morphmancer, Muss – you can take on the shape and appearance of any human, or any creature, roughly your own size. You can go anywhere, and disguise yourself as anyone, and no one will ever know it's you.'

Muss, who had regained his self-control, scarcely reacted this time. All Nish caught was a slight tightening of the fists, a momentary flexure of the brows.

'I can take on certain shapes and appearances, surr,' Muss said, 'but my essential nature remains unchanged. Therefore any ward or sentinel set against me will keep me at bay no matter how I change my shape. I tried to enter the chamber where the amplimet is held, but the sentinels would not allow it. Therefore I know not, of my own eyes, what went on in there.'

'You just said your eidoscope was linked to the sentinels,' said Klarm.

'Only to read them. I can't change their settings.'

'What does your eidoscope tell you about what we did?' said Flydd.

'I believe,' Muss said carefully, 'though I do not *know*, that you managed to bypass the wards and the rings of mancers surrounding the amplimet. You melted the ice wards –'

'That was our intention, but the ice wards had already been eaten away from within,' said Flydd. 'The amplimet must have done that, so it must have already woken, secretly.'

'You forced power into the amplimet,' said Muss, 'allowing it to take control of the field for an instant. It lashed out, killing the ring of adepts and causing the dislocation of Nennifer, before the Council brought up another ring of ward-mancers to reinforce the wards that now contain it again.'

'Are you sure they've contained it?' said Malien, trying to sit up but failing. She lay down, cradling her head in her hands. 'It's under their control?'

'For the moment,' said Muss. 'Though it may not remain so. Once they tire, or if Fusshte decides that there's no more to lose . . .'

'Are the Council united in this?' said Klarm shrewdly. 'One would have thought that Fusshte . . .'

'They *weren't*,' said Muss. 'Had you chosen subterfuge over action I would have led you inside. You might have taken advantage of their intriguing to seize control. That's not possible now – they're united by their fear of the amplimet. Your rash stroke has made your task far more difficult.'

'You forget yourself, Prober!' snapped Flydd.

'You taught me to speak plainly,' said Muss.

'There's a difference between plain speaking and insolence. Does the Council know we're here?'

'They must do,' said Klarm. 'The guards fired on us.'

'The guards fired on a shadowy movement,' said Muss. 'I explained it as a mountain goat wandering onto the parade ground.'

Flydd regarded him dubiously. 'Really?'

'False alarms aren't uncommon. The guards are taught to shoot on sight, then go and see what they've shot.'

Flydd nodded. 'So even in this supposedly impregnable fastness the Council feels insecure. How interesting. Can you get us inside without alerting the guards?'

The spy consulted his concealed instrument. 'The sentinels have failed now and we can get in anywhere, if we're quick. Once the guards recover from the dislocation they'll renew their watch on the perimeter.'

'Very well. Lead us in, Prober, without delay.'

'Where do you wish to be taken, surr?' said Muss.

'To the chamber where the amplimet is held,' said Malien from the ground. 'Before anything, we must put it –'

'Can you help us?' said Flydd. 'Are you fit, Malien?'

'Alas,' she said, 'I can't even stand.'

'And Yggur is still unconscious,' said Flydd. 'Aftersickness won't release him today, so we can't take on the amplimet yet.'

'The Council are close by the warding chamber,' said Muss.

'And they'll be in disarray, so we'll try to overpower them. Only then can we attempt to deal with the crystal.'

'Once you bring them down,' said Malien quietly, 'their hold on the amplimet will fail and you may not be able to control it.'

'I can see no other way,' said Flydd. 'We can't delay any longer. Where can we safely leave our disabled, Prober?'

'There, surr,' said Muss, indicating a corner section of wall jutting out from the front of the building. 'It's solid and sheltered from the wind; as safe as anywhere.'

Which isn't saying much, Nish thought. They left Malien and Yggur inside, along with the soldier with the broken leg, plus food, drink and cloaks to cover them, and Evee to do what she could for their hurts.

'Splendid,' said Flydd, visibly gathering his resolve. 'Take us within, Muss.'

TWENTY-FIVE

The stream of fleeing people had dropped to a trickle, now following an ant trail of refugees that led around to the rear of Nennifer, where there would be shelter from the biting wind.

'This way will be quicker,' said Muss. 'Try not to attract attention.'

'What about a disguise?' said Flydd.

'Your own mother wouldn't recognise you under all that dust, surr.'

Muss led them across the tilted, shattered stones of the parade ground, keeping to the low side of an upthrust bank of rubbly rock that curved towards the former entrance of the fortress. In the drifting dust and smoke it was hard to follow him. Though Muss was undisguised, he tended to blend into his surroundings.

'He's almost as weird as the rest of the place,' Irisis said quietly to Nish. 'I don't trust him, despite his fine words.'

Nish didn't have the energy to worry about anything else. 'He knew we were here. He could have betrayed us any time in the past few days, had he wanted to.'

'He's up to something,' she muttered.

Muss, ten or fifteen paces ahead, stopped and looked directly at her, before heading off again.

Irisis shivered. 'And he's fey.'

Nish put an arm around her but the sudden movement made his head spin again. He gagged and pulled away.

'Are you all right?' Irisis said sharply.

'This place makes me dizzy.'

'I feel it too.' She touched her pliance with a fingertip. 'Whatever the amplimet did to the dimensions, they haven't quite gone back to normal.'

Where the rubble bank branched into two, Muss stopped for everyone to catch up. 'Best if we go in here.'

The curving slice of building in front of them was shaped like a fingernail paring cut in half. The short straight end still had its outer wall, but the exposed side, which protruded several spans further than the neighbouring slice, revealed a section through all the above-ground floors of Nennifer. The lower floors were intact and contained their original contents, but the upper two levels were in disarray, their floors and ceilings partly crumbled.

Muss sprang lightly up onto the lowest floor, which stood two-thirds of a span above the ground, and disappeared.

'What –?' said Klarm.

The spy reappeared, his image wavering as if seen through the surface of a rippled pond. Nish felt an almost overwhelming urge to throw up.

Irisis steadied him until the nausea faded. 'Perhaps if you close your eyes?'

'Fat lot of use I'll be then, when we're attacked.'

'You won't be any use if you're hurling your breakfast up all over yourself.'

'We didn't have any breakfast!' he said miserably.

'You'll be fine then. Hold my hand while we go through.'

Klarm looked back, frowned, then flipped himself up onto the floor. This time Nish couldn't control his stomach. Once he'd finished, Irisis took his hand and led him to the edge. 'Close your eyes,' she hissed as Flangers swung himself up.

Nish did so. 'Ready?' Without waiting for him to answer, Irisis took him under the arms and heaved him up, grunting with the effort.

His stomach tied itself in knots as he passed through a chilly, wetly-clinging barrier, but the nausea faded as he landed on the floor inside. He stood up, steadfastly looking the other way as Irisis came through.

The room appeared to have been the sleeping chamber of a senior mancer, or possibly a scrutator, for it was lavishly appointed with rugs, tapestries and furniture made of inlaid ebony and other rare timbers. An ivory wand lay in the middle of the rug, broken in half.

'Which way?' said Flydd, moving in behind Muss and taking him by the upper arm.

Muss went still. 'I don't like to be touched, surr,' he said stiffly.

Flydd didn't let go, and the pair stood frozen for a full minute before Muss gave a slight dip of the head and Flydd stepped back.

'I still have to find the way,' said Muss, looking around. He glanced down at the eidoscope in the folds of his cloak, then opened a door and slid through it. They waited. His head appeared around the door. 'This way.'

Irisis muttered something rude. Flydd directed a fierce scowl at her. 'If you are to lead, you must also learn when to trust.'

'I'd trust Muss more if he had a personality,' she retorted. 'I've known him for years, yet I have no idea what he thinks or feels, about *anything*. He's a machine.'

'One who's served me faithfully and well, and never let me down, which is all that matters. Now be quiet. This place could still be full of enemies.'

'They've all run away save the scrutators and their pet mancers.'

'Really?' said Flydd, thrusting at her his seamed and puckered face, all bone and gristle. 'A good seven thousand people dwelt in Nennifer and there could be many still inside.'

She pulled away, scarcely abashed, but drew her sword. Oddly, Flydd had lost the bitter fury of the past days. The duress seemed to have driven him back to his normal irascible self, which she was used to dealing with. Nish moved closer to her.

The dust made everyone else look grubby but it only heightened her beauty.

He'd expected to be fighting his way in, but the monumental corridor proved empty apart from blocks of stone, scatterings of plaster and overturned pieces of furniture. One or two wall globes still glowed further on, and moonlight streaming in through fissures provided irregular slashes of illumination. The walls and ceiling were webbed with cracks, while pieces of plaster were falling all the time.

'One more shock and the rest of this will come down,' Flydd said with unsettling good humour.

It was the first time Nish had seen a smile on the scrutator's face since the rescue at Fiz Gorgo. 'You look awfully cheerful about it.' It was incomprehensible in such a situation.

'I've been looking forward to this day since Snizort. I feel almost restored.' A momentary spasm distorted his features, but he overcame it.

'Do you think there are going to be aftershocks?'

'Bound to be,' said Flydd. 'Muss?'

Muss had stopped in a corner of the wall, again scrying under his cloak. 'That way.' He pointed to the right, across a mess of rubble and timber that marked the junction with the next building slice.

The rubble contained three partly crushed bodies; none had died pleasantly. 'It doesn't look too safe to me,' said Nish, averting his eyes. 'There could be a crevasse below that, or anything.'

'Or *nothing*,' Muss said cryptically.

'What if we crossed up there,' said Irisis, pointing to the next floor. 'See the beam that's fallen across?'

They went out and along to a stair that led to the next floor, then walked the beam in single file, a miniature nightmare to add to the rest of Nish's horrors. It was precariously balanced on shifting chunks of stone and every movement made it wobble.

They passed diagonally across part of a prentice artisan's training room, or so Irisis judged from the boxes and displays of crystals and other artefacts, each with its crudely lettered instruction cards. The front right and rear left corners of the room had been shorn off, replaced by a masonry wall on the one hand and a triangular section of room containing only a pair of butcher's blocks on the other. The second block, illuminated by a puddle of moonlight, held a partly carved ham and a neatly severed hand and arm, still holding the carving knife. The arm had hardly bled at all, though the fingertips were as white as the ivory wand Nish had seen earlier.

At the door, Muss checked his instrument. This time Irisis, who had been watching for it, caught a quick glimpse of brass rods and mottled lenses. Muss pointed to the right, down a narrow hall.

They were just gathering behind him when Klarm said, 'We're being watched.'

'What do you mean?' Flydd asked in a low voice.

'I don't know, precisely, but I can feel it.'

'*It?*' whispered Flydd.

'I believe so.' Klarm cast a quick glance across the displays of crystals on the far side of the room.

Irisis followed his gaze. The reflection off one particular crystal, a deep green tourmaline, gave it a predatory look. 'I think we should get out of here right away.'

No one argued. On the other side of the door, Flydd said, 'I can *feel* the amplimet now. It may be contained but it's not controlled. It's extending a web of filaments throughout Nennifer. And it'll use any crystal or device capable of drawing power. We'd better hurry.'

They hastened along the hall, but had just turned the corner when they heard a distant screaming that sounded as if it came from dozens of throats. Muss stopped so suddenly that they ran into him. He sniffed the air. 'Phantoms and spectres from the dungeons. Nothing to worry about.'

Irisis shivered and moved closer to Nish. 'I saw more than enough of them in Ghorr's cells. Such torments the scrutators' prisoners have suffered here.'

He took her arm. And we'll be joining them before long.

'The amplimet's blocking us,' said Flydd as they stumbled

down another dark, shattered hall only to be confronted by yet another dead end.

'How can it?' Klarm replied. 'We're just following *him*.' He directed another suspicious glare at Muss's back.

'Perhaps it's blocking his eidoscope,' said Irisis. She still hadn't seen the device clearly, for Muss only used it in the shadows.

Eiryn Muss turned to face them. 'Not even an amplimet can influence my eidoscope. Its Art is designed to see true, no matter what.'

'How can you possibly know what an amplimet is capable of, and you a mere *prober*?' Klarm said coldly.

The derogatory emphasis made Nish flinch.

'I chose to remain a prober because that was how I could best serve my scrutator,' said Muss without emotion. 'Had I wished otherwise, I could have attained the highest position any spy can aspire to.'

'More words,' said Klarm.

'But in this case, true words,' Flydd interjected. 'Muss could have been a master spy a decade ago. I recommended him many times.'

'Does your eidoscope see the webs and meshes the amplimet has drawn throughout this place to spy on us?' said Klarm. 'How else could you know that it's not controlling what *you* see?'

'It's not,' Muss said stolidly.

'Lead on, Muss,' said Flydd.

'It's not far now, surr,' said the prober.

'Let's plan our attack,' said Flydd. 'How many soldiers are guarding the warding chamber?'

'None, surr. No one would dare enter that place without authority, and the entrance is closed with scrutator magic.'

'Ah, but can we break it?'

'Between you and me, I think so,' said Klarm.

'Fusshte will have his guard on call,' said Flydd.

'Many died in the dislocation,' said Muss, 'and others have been ordered to their posts, but certainly some will be nearby.'

'Can you get us past them, Muss?'

'I believe so, but you'll have to be ready to fight.'

They went on, though after about ten minutes Muss stopped and stood to one side with his arm pointing down the corridor. 'Go down there.' He gave a series of directions. 'Then follow your nose as far as it takes you, and go straight up.'

'Muss?' said Flydd.

'You're close, surr. You'll smell the place before you go much further.'

'Lead on, Prober,' said Flydd.

'I can't go on,' said Muss with a distracted look.

'Why not?' Klarm said.

'I only spy. I don't go into dangerous places.'

'The hell you don't –' cried Klarm.

In a second, Muss morphed from his normal self into a shaggy, ape-like creature. As Klarm leapt at him, Muss skin-changed to the appearance of the wall behind him and vanished.

'Grab him!' Klarm yelled, but Muss was gone. Klarm stood there with clenched fists, breathing heavily.

'You shouldn't have pushed him,' said Flydd.

'He's run, Xervish, which proves that my doubts were well founded. He brought us here for a purpose and the more I think about it, the more it worries me. What if he's told Fusshte we're here?'

'I don't think so,' said Flydd. 'I believe what Muss said.'

'And what he left *unsaid*?' said Irisis. 'He hasn't brought us here to serve you. He wants something and he can't get it from the scrutators.'

'That's what I'm worried about,' said Flydd.

TWENTY-SIX

Flydd hurried them across a series of dark rooms that had been chopped in half, stumbling over bodies on the floor. They did not stop to look at them. They climbed down into the next segment of the building, a dining hall that had been turned upside down and fitted neatly back into place, though what had been the ceiling was now strewn with upside-down trestles, benches, trenchers and cutlery. Oddly, the globes on the walls were still working. The place smelled of boiled turnip, the vegetable Nish hated most. It had been a staple back in the manufactory.

Something squelched underfoot. He had trodden in a bowl of yellow gruel, as sticky as glue. He kicked it aside and it skidded across the floor to shatter against a bench.

'Quiet!' hissed Flydd, appearing to look every way at once. 'What was that?'

'I didn't hear anything unusual,' said Klarm in a low voice.

To Nish's mind, every sound was unusual and some were uncanny. The groan of timbers deformed under weights they were never intended to bear; the sporadic crash and crumble of plaster or masonry; the trickling rivulets of dust and grit; the alternate soughing, whining and whistling of the wind across the severed edges of stone and tile; the cascades of water from twisted pipes and the surging ooze and plop of waste from shattered drains. And then there were the wails and groans of those trapped in the wreckage and the shrieking of the spectres forced from their dungeon homes. The cries seemed to come from every direction.

They went on, Nish's boot sticking to the floor with every step, through the far door into a frigid stone canyon. The roof was gone, as well as the floors above, while the walls to either side stretched up, bare and unclimbable, for a good twelve spans. The opposite wall was crusted with frozen runs of brown muck that had a sewer stink. Moonbeams angled along it, touching silver gleams here and there.

'Help!' came a distant cry. 'Please ... help me. Oh please, please.' It sounded like a child.

Flangers turned that way, searching the darkness.

'No, Sergeant,' said Flydd, laying a hand on his arm. 'If we stop to render aid to one, all may fail.'

'But it's a kid, surr,' Flangers said in a choked voice.

'I know,' Flydd said gently, 'but we must go on.' He looked left, then right. Then left again. 'Bloody Muss! I don't know which way.'

'Left,' Klarm said without hesitation.

No one asked how he knew. At the far end they clambered up a pile of rubble two storeys tall, over a precariously founded stone arch and onto a bridge formed by a crumbling stretch of lath and plaster ceiling that had fallen from somewhere above. It spanned a chasm at least three storeys deep. Something flickered redly in the depths, though there was no smoke.

'I don't think that's going to support our weight,' said the biggest and heaviest of the soldiers. 'Better look for another way.'

'We haven't time,' said Flydd. 'It looks solid enough. A couple of beams are holding it. Just tread carefully.'

'That's all right for you,' Irisis grumbled. 'You don't weigh more than a cupful of fleas.'

'I'd better go first then, in case you fall and carry the lot with you,' said Flydd callously. He stepped out onto the bridge, which was mottled white and black in the moonlight, the black patches barely distinguishable from the holes.

Klarm followed, stepping confidently. Nish went after him, trying to place his feet precisely where the dwarf's had gone, though it was awkward owing to the greater length of his stride. Four steps out from the edge, his right foot went through a patch of plaster. Nish tried to scramble back but was too far off-balance. He fell forwards, his left knee punched a hole through more plaster and he fell. He threw his arms out and managed to hook the left over the supporting beam.

'Help!' he roared, but the others were well back and Flydd five or six steps ahead.

Nish was flailing desperately, the weight inexorably straightening his arm, when Klarm sprang, landed with his stumpy legs straddling the two beams and caught Nish by the collar. Legs spread-eagled like a gymnast, Klarm strained until his eyes stood out of his head.

Nish knew the little man couldn't do it. The beams slipped, Klarm wobbled back and forth and threw out his free arm to balance himself.

Flydd took a step towards them. More plaster crumbled.

'Don't move!' cried Klarm.

Flydd froze. Klarm bellowed like a buffalo. His face and neck had gone purple and there was a bead of saliva on his lower lip. His arm trembled; then, with agonising slowness, he lifted Nish's dead weight a fraction.

'Reach up with your right foot, lad,' he said after he'd raised Nish a couple of hand-spans. 'You'll have to take the strain. I'm not tall enough to lift you all the way, and if the beams slip again we're both gone.'

Nish felt for the beam, stretching sideways and up, but his calf muscles knotted. He couldn't allow them to cramp. He eased back, stretched again and his foot touched the side of the beam.

'You'll have to get your foot on top,' said Klarm, the sinews in his neck standing out like cords. 'Push sideways and you'll force the beam away – and I'm already doing the splits.'

Up, up Nish reached. The beam slipped again and he saw

the agonised expression on Klarm's face as he was forced to stretch even further. Nish hooked his heel over the top of the beam, took a little of the strain and, almost miraculously, the beam came back towards him. He levered, Klarm lifted and with a heave and a shudder Nish was on the beam, clinging to it with his legs dangling down either side.

He was drenched in sweat, his heart hammering, and his knees had turned to rubber. Nish looked back at the silent group. No miracle at all. Irisis and Flangers had linked arms around the beams, taken the strain and pulled them together.

'Thank you,' he said quietly.

Klarm extended a hand and lifted Nish to his feet. Nish wobbled after him, this time stepping exactly where the little man had and, ten or twelve steps later, reached the other side. He turned to watch the rest of the party.

'What's that funny smell?' said Irisis when she was halfway across. She stopped to sniff the air, no more troubled by the crossing than if she'd been walking down a path.

'I can't smell anything,' grunted Flangers as he edged his way after her, looking green.

'It's a sweet, gassy odour.' Irisis took another breath. 'Not unpleasant.'

'Round here, nice smells can mask . . . other things,' said Klarm, kneading the muscles of his calves. 'I'd not breathe too deeply if I were you.'

'Muss did say to follow our noses,' said Irisis.

'And you know what I think about his advice.' He sniffed the air. 'It's coming from that direction.'

They went along a narrow service hall, relatively free of debris, then up a steep, straight staircase that ran on for three floors. In several places the steps were covered in rubble or broken plaster, and further up by a large, intricately carved soapstone cabinet that had fallen on a stout, muscular woman with closely cropped grey hair. Blood trickled down the steps from the back of her head.

'She's dead,' said Flydd after a cursory examination. 'Was she carrying it to a place of safety?'

'Stealing it in the confusion, more likely,' said Klarm, 'else she'd have had someone to help her.'

'It's hard to see how she could have hoped to profit from it. She could hardly carry it through the mountains.'

'People don't always act rationally in a disaster.'

'I'll bet the scrutators did,' said Flydd, moving around the dead woman and up. 'They'll have a refuge somewhere in here.'

'I doubt if any hiding place could be proof against what's happened here,' said Klarm. 'The force that sliced Nennifer up and rearranged it came from outside our three dimensions.'

'Where are all the people?' said Nish.

'Probably sucked through a dimensional wormhole into the void,' speculated Irisis gloomily. 'Like we're going to be before too long.'

'Nonsense,' said Flydd. 'They would have fled through the rear doors and windows. If they've any sense they'll be in the air-dreadnought yard around the back. Even if the walls collapse, it's sheltered from the wind and they can make fires there.'

'Getting back to the amplimet,' said Klarm, 'how are we supposed to master it without Yggur or Malien?'

'I don't know,' said Flydd.

'Seems as though we came all this way without a proper plan and we still don't have one.'

'There's no point to having a plan, since we don't know what we're going to find.'

Klarm looked unconvinced. The statement did nothing for Nish's confidence either. 'It's awfully quiet,' he said. The creaking had stopped, the cries for help faded long ago. There was no sound but the distant wind.

They kept climbing, only to be confronted by an appalling stench on the fourth floor.

'Slowly now,' said Flydd.

The air was hot up here. Klarm pressed open an iron door with a fingertip, and reeled back. If the smell had been bad lower down, it was revolting here, and the walls were covered with a greasy film of soot.

'It smells like burnt meat, or leather. Or hair.'

252

'Perhaps all three,' said Flydd, crumpling a corner of his cloak in his fist and breathing through it.

Nish pulled his sleeve down and held it over his nose, which didn't help much since the cloth stank of vomit. He glanced at Irisis, who looked green.

'What do you think has happened?' he whispered.

'Be quiet,' hissed Flydd.

Irisis allowed him to move ahead, then said out of the corner of her mouth, 'The scrutators aren't roasting us a welcome dinner.'

Nish couldn't even smile. They went through a second iron door, which was ajar due to the warping of its frame. The third door had been sealed with scrutator magic which it took Flydd and Klarm a considerable effort to break. The gap between door and floor was coated with soot.

A fourth door confronted them, this one partly open. It was made of chased bronze, soot-stained in places, elsewhere banded with swirling patterns of colour from being overheated.

The smell was even more nauseating. Flydd reached out to the bronze door but drew back before his fingers touched the surface. 'It's still hot!'

He tried to force it with his boot but the hinges were stuck. Flangers levered it open with the hilt of his sword and carefully put his head through. He beckoned behind him with one hand.

They passed through into a large, open space and stopped as one. There was just enough light to show that the chamber was shaped like a hemisphere. The charred reek was overpowering. Klarm made a muffled noise in his throat. Nish wanted to be sick, though fortunately he had nothing left to bring up. Behind him he could hear someone spewing liquidly.

His eyes began to pick out details. An oval central dais, about five spans long, was partly shielded by head-high blades of faceted rose quartz, preventing Nish from seeing what lay within, though he assumed it was the amplimet. Water had trickled down the sides where the inner ice wards had melted, and there were puddles on the floor. A metal column, the size of a substantial tree trunk, ran from one end of the dais up

253

through the ceiling. So Muss hadn't sent them to the scrutators' lair after all. Surrounding the rose-quartz walls stood what Nish had thought were nine statues carved out of ebony, or obsidian, though their surfaces were rough and dull. It was only when Flydd put up his hand and light streamed forth that Nish realised his mistake.

The statues were the remains of nine men and women, the scrutators' chief mancers, he presumed.

'Just as Eiryn Muss said.' Flydd gave Klarm a significant glance.

They had been turned to charcoal where they had stood, anthracised in place as they strove to work some mighty magic on the amplimet. No, not charcoal. It looked like black, honeycombed flesh, as if the living bodies had turned to char where they stood and escaping gases had foamed it up before it solidified. The statues were perfect replicas of the humans they had once been, save for the empty eye-sockets and various glistenings and dribbles, like wax that had run down the sides of a candle. Imagining the horrors they'd been through before they died, Nish's skin crawled.

'They must have been probing the amplimet,' said Klarm. 'And it didn't like it. It's a warning to us all.'

TWENTY-SEVEN

Something skittered along the curved far wall. Irisis couldn't see what it was. She moved further out into the room, though shadows lay all around and she still felt exposed. The scrutators could be anywhere.

'A warning to the Council, too,' said Flydd. 'Fusshte must be paralysed with terror.'

'He'll get over it,' Klarm said dryly. 'He's the ultimate opportunist. Well, do we go for the crystal or the Council?'

Irisis looked the other way, only then seeing, in the semidarkness around the circumference of the room, another ring of mancers, each standing with left arm outstretched and hand up, as if holding the whole world at bay. There were fifteen of them, and the right hand of each clutched a device that vaguely resembled her pliance, though presumably much more powerful. The mancers stood as still as the carbonised statues, apart from the faint tremble of an outstretched arm here, a pulse throbbing in a throat there; and apart from the wide, staring eyes, which revealed such terror in their hard and rigid souls as Irisis had never before witnessed. The mancers knew what their fate would be once the concentration of any one of them faltered, as sooner or later it must.

'If we go for the amplimet we may be caught in the cone of control these ward-mancers have over it,' said Flydd. 'Yet, if we attack the Council, their hold could fail and the amplimet break free.' He considered for a moment, gazing at one of the ward-mancers though not seeing her. 'The Council would be less risky, I think.'

'How so?' said Klarm.

'Given the fate of the inner ring, would *you* put your shoulder to the same wheel? Or would you stand back and let your man-cers take the strain?'

'I'd stand with my people,' said Klarm. 'How could any man do otherwise? Better it cost me life than honour.'

'Quite,' said Flydd, 'though Fusshte would see it differently. Better the limb be amputated than the whole body die. Nothing is more important than the Council, so the Council must survive even at the cost of everything and everyone surrounding it. Can we attack Fusshte without risking their hold on the crystal?'

'I don't know,' said Klarm.

They moved through the ring of ward-mancers, Irisis passing by a dumpy, white-haired woman whose eyes did not even register her. The ward-mancers' vision was turned elsewhere.

'How can we find Fusshte in all this chaos?' said Flydd. 'Curse you, Eiryn Muss.'

'I'm sensing something above us,' said Irisis, crushing her pliance in her fist, the better to *see*.

'Are they drawing on the field?' said Flydd.

'The reverse . . .' Irisis tried to make sense of what she was seeing, which wasn't easy. The patterns were weirdly truncated, as if the dimensional dislocation that had sliced up Nennifer had done the same to the fields. 'There must be hundreds of little devices still working here – globes and so forth. I can see where they're drawing on the field all over the place.'

'Then what's the problem?' said Klarm roughly.

She screwed her eyes closed, furrowing her brow. 'That's just it. It all looks normal except, directly above this room –' she nodded upwards, '– it's completely blank. It's as if the field doesn't extend through that space. And that's impossible.'

'The Council has shielded its bolthole,' rapped Klarm. 'They're afraid to come out. Come on.'

Flydd didn't move. 'If they're afraid to use power, so should we be.'

'So we rush them and overwhelm them with physical force,' said Klarm. 'It's the one thing they won't be expecting.'

'Let's hope Muss was right about the guards,' said Flydd, eyeing their little group.

He went back through the four metal doors and looked around. 'Straight up, Muss said. Ah!'

He headed for a set of coiling metal stairs that looked as though they'd been jammed diagonally down through the roof. As he stepped onto the first tread the stairs shook as if the only thing holding them was the shattered hole through the ceiling. A span below that, the outside curve and rail had been shorn away leaving the treads dangling precariously.

Klarm followed, then the four surviving soldiers and Flangers, Nish and Inouye, who carried a short sword as though it were a walking stick. She'd be no use in a battle. At the first coil of the stairs Nish looked down at Irisis, who had stopped on the bottom step. 'Is something the matter?'

She shook her head but couldn't clear away the after-images of the field. 'I . . . think so. Everything's so strange here; I can't get my bearings. And . . .'

'What is it?'

'I can't help feeling that we've missed something.'

'I feel the same,' said Nish. He looked up. The others had passed the damaged part of the stair and were disappearing through the ceiling.

Above the ceiling the stair continued, more wobbly than before, eventually terminating just below a broken hole in the slate-clad roof. They scrambled up and through onto the roof. Not far away, the remains of an open-sided, glass-roofed passage led into a broad dome that stood some twenty spans above the roof on pillars of basalt. The dome, although tilted at a slight angle, was intact, but the roof surrounding it had been sliced and reassembled in many places.

'Careful now,' said Flydd as they headed for the passage and the entrance to the dome. 'There could be guards inside.'

The wind howled around the dome, though not loudly enough to block out the cries of the injured in the rear yard. A bonfire blazed in the far corner and throngs of bewildered, bedraggled people stood around it, staring at the flames.

With a crash and a shudder, a section of Nennifer to their west collapsed. The mass of people surged away towards the far wall of the yard.

'Poor devils,' said Flydd. 'Without food or water they can't last long, and they know it.'

'They're brutes, all of them,' said Irisis, recalling her previous treatment here.

'Aye,' said Klarm. 'Corrupted by cruel masters, but human beings nonetheless.'

Seeing no guards, they pressed on, acutely aware that the amplimet could overcome the ward-mancers at any moment. At the entrance to the dome, Flydd and Klarm laid their bare hands on the door, sensing the magic that closed it. Flydd asked Klarm a question which Irisis didn't catch. Klarm shook his head. Irisis crept closer. Flydd moved his hands across the door, taking one position after another. He looked down at Klarm, who gave another shake of the head.

Flydd swore, stepped back and bumped into Irisis. 'Would you get out of the way?' he snapped.

She gave him room. 'Will it warn them if we break the magic?' he said to the dwarf.

'Very probably,' said Klarm.

They put their heads together, low down, and Irisis couldn't see what they were doing, but shortly the door came open. No klaxon went off, though that didn't mean there was no alarm. Flydd beckoned and they went through. 'I'll seal it to any but us,' he said. 'It won't keep scrutators or mancers out but the guards won't be able to get through.'

He did so, looking haggard as he turned from the door. After-sickness was wearing him down and there was so far to go, the worst yet to be faced.

The space inside the dome consisted of a single open chamber, some fifty spans across, dimly lit by globes suspended from the ceiling on long chains. The central area was divided up by a maze of long tables, workbenches and cabinets, while the outer ring of the chamber was completely empty. Irisis wondered why. The walls contained tapestries and paintings glorifying the Council, and there were statues and busts of scrutators everywhere. Irisis saw many busts of Ghorr, carved in marble, obsidian and even granite. She wanted to knock them off their pedestals.

From the look of the devices laid out on the benches, the chamber was the Council's private workroom. In the centre a spherical turret was mounted on a metal stalk five or six spans high. Clusters of conduited bell-pulls ran out from one side of the turret, as well as flared pipes that Irisis assumed to be speaking tubes. Through the wide windows, standing at sloping tables, she saw five scrutators.

Fusshte, identifiable at a distance by his meagre, misshapen frame, had his back to them and stood by himself. The other four scrutators made a tight group on the other side of the turret. Irisis recognised Scrutator Halie, a small dark woman who'd once been a kind of ally of Flydd's, and Scrutators Barbish, Ying and Eober.

'The four surviving scrutators have been forced to side with him,' said Flydd, 'and they don't like it. Now, if we can just –'

Too late. They'd been seen. The group of scrutators leapt for their consoles. Fusshte stood frozen for a moment, staring in disbelief as Flydd waved jauntily at him, then disappeared from view.

They dived behind the benches. 'Did you see the swine?' crowed Flydd. 'He had no idea we were within a hundred leagues of Nennifer.'

'He'll soon realise that *we* were behind the amplimet's liberation,' said Klarm. 'That'll terrify him.'

'Until he works out that we don't know what we're doing,' retorted Flydd. 'Come on – we've got to attack while he's still off-balance. Soldiers – split into two pairs. Narm and Byrn, go around to the right; Yuddl and Qertois, take the left flank. Weave through the benches to attack the turret from the sides with

259

crossbow fire. I'll hit it from our left front. Flangers, come with me. Klarm, take the right front approach. Inouye, go with him as a messenger.'

'What about us?' said Nish and Irisis at the same time.

'Stay here. Irisis, keep an eye on the field and watch for the unexpected. Nish, guard her back.'

They scattered.

'I've just had a horrible thought,' said Nish after a minute's inactivity.

'So have I.'

'What is it?'

'You go first. We're probably thinking the same thing anyway.'

'Fusshte has another option Flydd didn't think of: to divert the amplimet's attention to us. While it's attacking us, Fusshte's ward-mancers might be able to permanently contain it. And then he can use all the power he wants.'

A long interval of silence was punctuated by the creaking of the foundations, a distant collapse, and then the thunder of thousands of terrorised people in the yard stampeding again.

'Let's hope he doesn't think of that,' said Irisis, holding her pliance against her temple. 'Though of course he will.'

Nish waited, but when she didn't go on he said, 'Was that what you were thinking?'

'Unfortunately not. The scrutators won't dare direct power from the field against us. If they did, the amplimet could ride it back and overwhelm them. But they can still use devices that *store* power, and there are plenty here. Nennifer reeks of the Art.'

'So Flydd and Klarm could be walking into a trap.'

'They're bound to be.'

Something whirred across the room, high up, and a chilly eddy touched the back of Nish's neck. 'What was that?' he whispered.

'I don't know.' She moved closer to him. 'Can you see what's going on?'

Nish eased his head above the bench and caught a fleeting

scuttle from the left of the turret, though he couldn't identify it. 'I haven't got a clue.'

The whirr sounded again, and closer. A serrated flash of light was followed by a mechanical shrilling that set his teeth on edge. Someone far off cried out.

'That sounded like Klarm!' Irisis's eyes were closed and her pliance was enclosed in her hands, which were extended in front of her as if in prayer. He'd never seen her look so uncertain.

Another flash, a thud, a scream, and then a grinding sound like metal teeth cutting through bone.

'Get back!' Flydd roared. 'Baaack!'

'No!' one of the soldiers roared. 'Behind you –'

Swords clashed on metal, then something shot straight up from beside the turret. The light caught it as it revolved in the air – a small object, toothed like a cogwheel. A glassy sphere with a brown circle on one side, resembling a mechanical eyeball, arced after it. It seemed to look down on them, a yellow light blinked back the other way, and the sphere disappeared behind the cabinets.

The speaking tubes gave forth a deep, throbbing blast that shook dust down on Irisis's hair. It went on and on, and only at the end did Nish realise that there were words in it.

'Guards! Guards! To the scrutators' dome at all speed.'

'What are we supposed to do now?' said Nish, risking another glance over the bench.

Pfft! A crossbow bolt scored a groove across the timber, embedding dozens of splinters into his right cheek. He ducked down and began to pick them out.

'I don't know. The scrutators have outwitted us.'

'Should we go to Flydd's aid?'

'Better to die in battle than fall into Fusshte's hands. Let's do it. A last stand together, Nish.'

She was about to stand up when Nish heard a low clattering sound in the alley of benches and cabinets to their left. He jerked her down. Three bolts screamed through the space where she'd been about to lift her head.

Clatter, rasp-clatter came from around the corner.

'What's that?' He cocked his head.

It came darting this way and that, a device like a metal ball with rubber tyres running around it in three directions, and a pair of whirling scythes the length of knife blades sprouting from either side. It bumped against a cabinet and the blades chopped straight through the wood. It then spun around twice, thumped against the outside wall, turned and headed straight for Nish.

'How the hell are we supposed to fight that?' said Irisis.

'I don't know, but I sure hope there aren't more of them.'

TWENTY-EIGHT

'Keep your head down!' Irisis hissed.

Nish ducked but this time no one fired. They didn't need to; this whirring menace would cut them off at the ankles.

Nish stepped forward like a batsman facing a bowler and swiped at the spinning ball with his sword. It darted the other way, bounced off the wall and came at him, blades whirring.

He stumbled backwards, was stopped by the bench and lashed out. Again the ball shot sideways; his sword tip just missed the scything blades. Before he was ready for another swing it spun towards his right foot, turning at the last moment. A blade chopped through the side of his boot into his foot.

Nish yelped and leapt high. The ball rolled back then raced at him again. He bounced on one foot, hacking at his attacker, left, right then left again. His second blow dug into one of the circular tyres, sending the ball whirling like a top, but the tyres spun the other way, bringing it to a smoking stop, and it went at him again.

Nish tripped over a fallen chair and landed flat on his back. The ball, its blades clacking, darted up between his legs. He couldn't get his sword to it in time.

Whoomph. Irisis's heavy cloak smothered the deadly blades. Nish propelled himself out of the way, sliding on his back. Lifting a granite bust of Ghorr off its pedestal, she turned it upside down and dropped it on the still quivering bundle, which smashed satisfyingly. The nose broke off the bust.

Irisis eased her cloak away and the blades fell to the floor. The ball lay on its side, crushed, an ooze of green grease coming from inside. She turned a bench over in front of them and another behind, walling off the lane, then put the slashed cloak on.

'Thanks.' Nish poked a finger through the gash in his boot. The injury didn't seem too serious. He got up.

Another of those eyeball objects arced across the room. A series of flashes – red and green, followed by an eye-searingly brilliant white – came from one side of the turret. Others burst from its rear.

'At least they're still alive,' said Irisis. 'Well, some of them.'

'But for how much longer? And when the guards get here . . !'

'I don't hear anyone running,' said Irisis. 'Perhaps they can't find a way through the dislocation.'

'I wouldn't bet my life on it.'

The bright lights faded, returning the chamber to its previous gloom. Along to Nish's left something scraped against timber. 'Did you hear that?' he whispered. 'They're coming.'

'I've been expecting it.' She gave him her hand. 'Ready?'

He clasped it, gulped and nodded stiffly. Drawing his sword, he swung it through the air a few times. A bolt whistled over his head and smacked into the wall, releasing a little cloud of plaster dust that drifted around the circumference of the chamber.

There came a rustle from the direction of the scrape; an odd, tentative sound. 'That didn't sound very scary,' said Nish. 'Shall we go at them?'

'Can't hurt.'

I'll bet it can, Nish thought. 'All right.' He stepped over the bench, ducked low as he passed a gap, then crept forward, sword out. What was waiting for them? Soldiers in ambush? More of those scything balls? Or any of a myriad of uncanny devices of war the artificers of Nennifer had created in the past decade, some under the supervision of Xervish Flydd himself?

The suspended globes faded to a dull yellow; the gloom thickened. The scratching came from just ahead. A lump throbbed in the pit of Nish's stomach and the sword slipped in his sweating fingers.

Courage! he told himself. Die like a man, if you must die. He took a step, hesitated, then another. It was just around the corner. Nish glanced over his shoulder at Irisis. She was crouched low, her sword flicking from side to side like a viper's tongue.

The speaking tubes rumbled again. 'Guards!' came Fusshte's voice. 'To me, to me.'

Nish went another step. Something rustled in the darkness and he went up on his toes and sprang.

'Stop!' Irisis hissed.

A small pale face and huge dark eyes looked up at him and he stayed his stroke at the last instant. It was Pilot Inouye, crawling along the floor, a trail of blood coming from her left leg.

Nish sheathed the sword and dropped to his knees beside her. 'What's happened?' he said.

'Guards came from – behind. Two of Yggur's men – dead. Flydd and Klarm – pinned down. Can't get free.'

'And they sent you for help?' said Nish, drawing up the leg of her pants. Inouye's slender calf had been cruelly gashed, probably by another of those scything balls. 'They want us to come to their aid?' He already knew it was hopeless.

'No,' she gasped. 'You can't do anything . . .'

Nish tore off the hem of his undershirt. It was none too clean but he had to stop the bleeding. He began to bind the wound. Inouye winced, and tears sprang to her eyes, but she made no sound.

'What does Flydd want us to do?' said Irisis.

Inouye was growing paler by the second. 'Flydd can't use power . . . nor scrutators against him. But . . . soldiers coming. Flydd says, find Tiaan and bring her . . . bring her . . . Must not let her . . !' Her head flopped sideways to the floor. 'Malien . . !' Her eyes closed. She was breathing shallowly and her lips had no colour at all.

'What's she trying to say?' said Nish.

'I'm not sure,' said Irisis.

'Why does Flydd want Tiaan?'

'No one else can hope to control the amplimet,' Irisis conjectured. 'If Tiaan can, it'll break the stalemate and Flydd can attack.'

'Doesn't sound like much of a plan,' said Nish. 'Where the bloody hell is Tiaan anyway?'

'Muss . . !' whispered Inouye, opening her eyes momentarily.

'We'll have to find the sneaky little bastard first,' spat Irisis. She jerked her head at Nish and moved away. He followed. 'What are we supposed to do?' Irisis went on. 'We can't carry Inouye and she can't walk.'

'She's lost a lot of blood,' said Nish, not understanding what she was getting at.

'We'll have to leave her here, Nish.'

He shook his head. 'I can't.'

'What's the matter?'

'We've turned our backs on too many people already. I keep hearing their cries for help, just as I did at the battle of Gumby Marth. I had to leave them to die and I swore I'd never do that again.'

'This means survival, Nish, for all of us, and all our hopes.'

'But Inouye is one of us. She's done all that's been demanded of her and we've given her nothing in return.'

'Do you think I don't know that?' she said between her teeth. 'You've got to steel yourself, Nish. This is just like any other battle. It's cruel, but the injured have to be left behind. If we stop to help them we'll all die, *in vain*.'

Her words roused memories he wasn't strong enough to face. Nish had left Gumby Marth a hero, though that had been diminished by the hundreds of soldiers he'd had to abandon because they'd been too badly injured to walk. He could still see the agony on their faces, but what he most remembered was their bewilderment – that their sacrifices had been repaid so cruelly.

'Nish?' she shook him.

'What if it were me?'

She looked away. 'It isn't.'

'All right!' he said furiously. 'But we can't just leave her lying on the floor.'

Irisis hesitated, then nodded. 'I'll find a hide for her.'

Nish turned back. Inouye opened those tragic eyes and reached up to him with one hand. 'Don't leave me,' she said in a cracked voice.

'I'm sorry,' he said, picking her up.

'Don't let me die,' she whimpered. 'My children –'

'You're not going to die, Inouye.'

'In here, Nish.' Irisis was pointing to the top shelf of an open cabinet. 'It's the best we can do.'

Nish carried Inouye across. 'Don't leave me,' she whispered. 'Don't leave me, don't leave me.' She was shuddering with terror.

He tried to ignore it, sliding her onto the shelf and pushing her to the back. She reached out to him but Nish ducked out of the way. He couldn't meet her eyes. 'We'll be back soon.' They probably wouldn't be back at all.

Inouye began to wail in a low scratchy tone.

'Bloody little fool!' hissed Irisis. 'Do you want to attract them to you? Lie still and shut up and you may yet survive.'

Inouye kept on wailing until Irisis whacked her. The noise stopped immediately.

'Come on,' Irisis muttered, red in the face.

They hurried towards the entrance, keeping low. 'Did you have to hit her so hard?' said Nish. 'The poor little . . .'

'You can shut up as well, Cryl-Nish Hlar, unless you want the other hand,' Irisis said savagely.

It heartened him to discover that she wasn't as unfeeling as she made out. They slipped out through the mage-locked door, which plucked at them like a thousand rubber fishhooks. Irisis stopped on the landing, one hand to her ear.

'Can you hear anything?'

'Only people groaning in the yard, poor devils,' said Nish.

'No, the reinforcements are on their way. Let's get out of their path.'

They moved off the stairs into a narrow space, a sliver of

267

green-tiled floor between two moss-covered outer walls. 'How are we supposed to find Muss?' said Nish.

'I imagine he'll find us. I didn't believe his story for an instant. He left Flydd months ago because he was no longer useful. Then, when Flydd turned up here and the scrutators' downfall looked likely, Muss changed sides again. He does it as easily as he changes his shape. He led us in because he wanted something that he couldn't get himself. The amplimet, presumably.'

'Why would he want it?' said Nish. 'He's not –'

'For decades he concealed that he was a powerful adept,' she said in a low voice. 'What else is he? No one knows. Muss will be close by, waiting to see who gets the upper hand and working out how he can use them to his advantage.' She lowered her voice. 'He'll tell us where to find Tiaan. The stalemate won't suit him any more than it does us. But the *instant* he tells us, we grab him.'

Grabbing a morphmancer didn't seem like a very good idea to Nish. 'What then?'

'We bind his hands and stop his mouth so he can't morph into another shape, and take him with us. I want the wretch where I can see him for the rest of our time here.'

'He could be rather a handful.'

'Then club him over the head! Whoever isn't with us is against us, Nish.'

They were nearing the warding chamber when Nish heard the sound of massed footsteps, below and to their left. 'That must be Fusshte's reinforcements.'

Irisis pulled him into a rubble-choked cavern where two walls had fallen against each other to form a space shaped like a tent. While they waited, Nish couldn't help wondering how solid the structure was.

A squad came tramping along the gritty corridor, ten men led by a stocky captain, followed a minute later by a second squad and then a third. The captain stopped, looking around in puzzlement at the dislocated walls and the stair which patently had crashed through the roof. 'Which way?'

No one seemed to know. They turned back down the corridor, stopped again and the captain called, 'Master Muss?'

He came towards them, reluctantly, and after a brief exchange pointed back the way they had come. The soldiers tramped off and Muss came on, stopping directly outside Nish and Irisis's hiding place. 'Well?' he said.

'It's a stalemate,' said Irisis. 'Flydd and Klarm are pinned down. They can't get to the scrutators' turret and the scrutators can't reach them. They're afraid to use power.'

Muss stared into her eyes as if he suspected her of holding something back. 'Then Fusshte will take them sooner or later.'

'And that doesn't suit you, Muss?' said Irisis.

'We've got to find Tiaan,' Nish burst out. 'She may be able to control the amplimet.'

'Tiaan . . .' Muss stared into the dusty distance. 'I don't think – she's not been treated well. Unless she trusts you, you may not get anything out of her.' His eyes seemed to look into Nish's head.

Nish coloured. 'Well, she's all we have left.'

Taking the eidoscope out from under his cloak, Muss turned away. Nish peered around him. The morphmancer pushed in one spangled lens and rotated it, pulled out another, spun a third and peered through the end. He scratched his ear, performed more rotations with his eye and cheek to the end lens, then said, 'Follow me.'

After some minutes of trekking quite as dangerous as the trip in, and rather more crowded with wailing spectres, they reached the solid wooden door of what, from the dank smell, had been a basement dungeon cell. It now lay two floors above ground level.

'Tiaan's cell,' said Eiryn Muss.

Nish tried the door but it didn't budge.

'It's held fast by scrutator magic,' said Muss. 'You'll have to break the door to get inside.'

'It's solid ironwood,' said Irisis. 'It'd take half an hour to get through it with an axe. And we don't have an axe.' She stared at him expectantly.

After a long hesitation, Muss used his eidoscope again, this

269

time not seeming to care that they saw it. Nish didn't think that was a good sign. Muss frowned, shape-shifted a couple of times, returned to his normal form, then reached out and seemed to put his arm right through the stone beside the door. He did something on the other side and the door came open.

They pushed in. Tiaan lay on a straw-filled palliasse, staring at the ceiling. She was filthy, her clothes even filthier, and her black hair formed a tangled mass. Her arms and legs were shaking. Nish approached her tentatively, for Tiaan mistrusted him, and with good reason. And she felt the same way about Irisis.

'Tiaan?' he said softly.

She turned her eyes toward him, without recognition, then looked back at the ceiling. A louse the length of Nish's fingernail crawled up her neck into her hair. She didn't appear to notice.

'Tiaan?'

She turned, and this time her eyes widened. She lurched to her feet, batted feebly at a point to the right of Nish, gave a gasp of horror and tried to climb the wall behind her.

Nish caught her as she fell back on the palliasse. 'It's like she's seeing ghosts.'

'Perhaps she thinks we *are* ghosts.'

'What do we do with her?' said Nish.

'I have no idea. And to add to our troubles, bloody Muss has disappeared again.'

TWENTY-NINE

They carried Tiaan back through the spectre-infested chaos, taking turns. She did not resist. Indeed, Tiaan hardly knew they were there.

'What's the matter with her?'

Nish had stopped for a breather on a floor made of smashed slabs of pink gneiss that crunched and crackled underfoot. In the distance, a segment of Nennifer crumbled with a roar that shook the walls. Glass objects, warped like figures in a torture chamber, fell off a shelf. Collapses were happening all the time now.

'She's been in the depraved hands of Fusshte,' said Irisis, frowning at the three corridors that led on. 'It would drive anyone out of their mind.'

'He's slimy and squalid, but he's not a fool. Tiaan can do things no one else has ever been able to, and he wouldn't break her and lose that talent.'

'I'll take her now.' Nish hefted Tiaan off his shoulder onto Irisis's. Irisis grimaced. 'She stinks.'

'And that's not all.' Raking his fingers though his short hair, Nish plucked off a fat louse which he flicked away with his thumb. He scratched under his arm. 'I think she's given me fleas as well.'

'Poor Nish. How you must be suffering.' She looked around. 'Surely we're getting close to the warding chamber?'

271

'I think so. It's not easy to remember the way.'

They continued on, struggling between head-high piles of rubble, or over them. Confronted by a particularly large heap, with beams sticking out of it like the spines of a sea urchin, Nish said, 'This wasn't here when we came through.'

She picked her way around to the left, Tiaan flopping on her shoulder. 'There's not much holding Nennifer up. Once any slice fails, the ones on either side of it are doomed to follow. The whole lot could come down without warning.'

He stayed where he was, unsure if they were going in the right direction. 'You don't have to be so damned cheerful about it.'

'The joys of fatalism, Nish. When you have no expectations, every extra moment of life is a blessing and a wonder.' She gave him a beatific smile over her shoulder.

'Humbug!'

'I think it's this way,' she said, moving around the other side of the rubble pile.

Nish climbed up onto the heap and peered over into the gloom. Their path was blocked by tilted slabs of floor and ceiling which had collapsed on one another like a deck of cards. 'No, we'll have to go back to that junction where we went right, and take the middle way. Do you need a hand?'

Irisis hefted Tiaan higher onto her shoulder and turned back. At the junction she checked the other corridors. 'I don't think it was either of these. Bloody Muss! What's he up to?'

Nish was too weary to answer. He put his hand on the wall and a small section collapsed, revealing a cavity than ran in to the limit of sight. He hopped backwards in case the rest came down, but the wall didn't move. Once the dust had settled he sniffed the air coming from the hole. 'I can smell that stink again. The warding chamber must be this way.'

'Surprised you can smell anything over Tiaan,' Irisis grumbled, coming up to the cavity. 'Can you take her?'

Nish hauled Tiaan through, heaved her onto his shoulder and set off, following his nose.

Tiaan let out a low moan and began to thrash. Nish, who was

negotiating a pile of rubble higher than his head, landed hard on one knee on a broken piece of stone and cried out. Tiaan jerked herself out of his arms. Crouching on all fours, she gave him a strange sideways glance and scuttled up the pile.

'No you don't!' Irisis threw herself after Tiaan and caught her by the ankle.

Tiaan let out a thin squeal and kicked furiously. Irisis clamped her other hand around the smaller woman's calf, holding her until Nish twisted one arm behind her back, whereupon Tiaan ceased to struggle and her eyes fluttered closed.

'What's the matter with her?' he panted.

Irisis shrugged. 'Do you think we should tie her up?'

He shook his head. 'We need her to cooperate when we get there and . . . you know how she feels about us.'

'We'd better keep moving. We've taken too long already . . .'

Time may well have run out, Nish thought. A small war could have been fought at the other end of Nennifer and they wouldn't have been aware of it.

They struggled on. Tiaan wasn't a big woman but the strain of carrying her was telling. Nish ached in every muscle.

'We must be nearly there,' said Irisis as they stopped briefly, 'though I don't recognise this place.' The burnt-flesh smell was sickening.

'I think we're approaching the warding chamber from the other side.' What were they supposed to do once they got there? 'So the scrutators' workroom and turret must be above us. Now what?' said Irisis as if she'd read his thought. 'Did Flydd want us to take Tiaan to him, or to the warding chamber?'

'The chamber, surely? We've no way of getting to him.'

'Inouye was trying to tell us something,' Irisis recalled. 'But she couldn't get it out. Should I go up and ask her?'

'She's probably unconscious,' said Nish, guilt rising up to overwhelm him. What had Inouye ever done to harm anyone?

They were pressing on towards the final door into the amplimet chamber when Tiaan's eyes sprang open. She quivered in Nish's arms then said clearly, 'Put me down.'

Nish did so gladly. Tiaan wavered on her feet, steadied herself and looked around, as alert as she had previously been apathetic. She glanced at Irisis, then Nish, without seeming to recognise either of them. Tiaan faced the door, cocking her head as if listening, then smiled.

What's going on? Nish mouthed to Irisis. She signed that she didn't have a clue. He pointed to the door. Irisis puffed out her cheeks, looked back the other way, then ruefully scratched herself.

A stub of wall collapsed behind them, sending a cloud of dust billowing in their direction. Someone called out in the indeterminate distance. Tiaan started.

'That sounded like Flydd,' said Irisis.

'I don't think we'd hear him from here.'

They listened but the cry was not repeated. A crystalline crackle came from inside the chamber and Nish suddenly knew that they'd made the wrong choice.

'It's waiting for us!' he hissed. 'We've got to go up to –'

The crackle sounded again, peremptory this time. Tiaan stopped quivering; a joyous smile spread across her dirty face and she bolted for the last door.

Irisis threw herself forward and got two fingers into Tiaan's collar. Tiaan swung around, clenched her two hands into a mallet and clubbed Irisis across the side of the head. Tiaan tore free and darted through the door into the warding chamber.

Nish cursed and raced after her. 'That's what Inouye was trying to tell us. To keep Tiaan away from the warding chamber.'

He crashed through the door. Tiaan was nowhere to be seen.

'All the signs were there,' said Irisis, 'and we missed them. Fusshte hadn't mistreated Tiaan, he'd only neglected her. Tiaan was suffering withdrawal from the amplimet and the first thing she'd do would be to go for it.'

The room was noticeably warmer than before, and the reek of burnt flesh and hair even more overpowering, if that was possible.

'I don't see her,' said Nish, taking a couple of steps.

Irisis dragged him back. 'Remember what happened to the inner ring of mancers.'

'But if we don't stop her –'

'Tiaan may be suffering withdrawal, but she's seen other people die through the amplimet. She'll make sure it recognises her before she goes too close.'

'There's no saying it will allow her near. What are we supposed to do?'

'I – I've got no idea, Nish. I can't make sense out of anything.'

Irisis had always been a leader and her indecision dismayed him. 'I'll stay here and see if I can catch her. Run up to the dome chamber and shout a warning to Flydd.'

She smiled at that. 'Don't be silly, Nish. There's nothing *you* can do here, but I may be able to. Go up. Run as though all our lives depend on it. And . . . be careful. You've got the most dangerous job.'

Nish ran, though it was not until he'd passed through the last door and was halfway up the shuddering metal stairs that he realised she'd deceived him. The safest person in the warding chamber, if anyone could be safe from the amplimet, was someone who had neither talent for the Art nor ability to draw power from the field.

He stopped, afraid for her, but then went on. Irisis had made her decision and it wasn't up to him to undermine it. Besides, there was no time. He could feel the tension building second by second.

Nish was just stepping off onto the roof when the back of his neck crawled, as if someone was watching him. He looked left, then right, but saw nothing. He headed for the walkway, cursing an over-active imagination.

The attack came without warning – a colossal thump in the back that drove him face-first into the roof. He tried to scramble away but was struck in the back of the neck and around the sides of the head by someone who was kneeling on his back, pinning him down.

The weight wasn't inordinate – a woman or a compact man, and not one with much experience of fighting. The blows hurt but had done no great damage, apart from his nose which felt as if it was broken.

275

He took a deep breath, tensed and heaved with all his strength, rolling at the same time. His attacker went flying. Nish kept rolling, came to his feet and threw himself at the man. It *was* a man, a young fellow not much bigger than Nish. Nish didn't waste time. He punched his assailant in the belly, kneed him in the jaw when he doubled over, lifting him to his toes, and followed that with a left hook that rattled the fellow's teeth. His head hit the wall and he *shifted* right before Nish's eyes, becoming a shaggy, dazed, but very small bear.

Nish hit him and he shifted again, into a small wingless lyrinx. 'Muss, you bloody treacherous bastard!' Nish roared, clamping his fingers around the leathery throat and banging the crested head against the wall.

Muss shifted to a much smaller person, a beautiful, buxom young woman, black of hair and eye. Nish lost his grip and hesitated for a moment. The code against harming women was so strong that it momentarily overrode his reason.

Muss brought his knee up into Nish's groin, thrust him out of the way and bolted for the stairs. By the time Nish recovered, the spy was out of sight. Nish didn't go after him. Trying to ignore the agony in his groin, he staggered across the roof towards the dome.

He eased through the door, keeping a sharp lookout. The chamber was as gloomy as before, though an occasional fitful burst of light came from the direction where Flydd and Klarm had been pinned down. At least one of them must be at large.

Nish didn't try to get to them; he would certainly be captured. All he could do was shout, which would alert Fusshte as well. Nothing he could do about that. He raised his voice and roared, 'Flydd!'

The flashes stopped. The room went dark, then he heard Fusshte's voice. 'That's Cryl-Nish Hlar. Get him!'

'About time!' yelled Flydd. 'Where's Tiaan?'

'She got away. She's in the warding chamber.'

Flydd cursed. 'You damn fool – I told you – never mind. Nish, we got two of the scrutators but the other three are blocking us. Run down and smash the warding barriers – the rose-crystal blades around the amplimet. Hurry!' He paused, then said in a lower voice, as though to his comrades, 'Now!'

A gigantic flash of purple light illuminated the chamber and the dome. Thunder reverberated back and forth. Nish was starting for the door when he felt the floor move underfoot. At first he thought that the whole chamber was collapsing, but the movement was constant and only in one direction. The floor was moving, drawing back underneath the walls. That was why the outer ring of the chamber had been empty.

It slid away from the centre in radial sections, revealing that the scrutators' turret was founded on a column that ran down through the floor. It looked like the column that ran up from the warding chamber. Sections of false floor rotated out and up and snapped into place, creating circular ranks of seating as in a stadium, or a theatre with a central stage. That's what it was – a theatre for displays of power and terror. The scrutators loved their public spectacles.

Ducking low, Nish made his way to the edge. The warding chamber, several floors below, now formed the stage of the theatre. He could see the dais with its rose-crystal barriers, and outside them the shadows of the nine anthracised mancers. Tiaan was standing between them, staring at the barriers.

She could get to the amplimet before anyone else could reach the warding chamber. What then? Disaster, he suspected. And doom for Irisis, wherever she was. His heart turned over at the thought.

Flydd had ordered him to smash the rose-crystal barriers. He couldn't jump – the dais was a good twenty spans below. Nish turned and bolted for the door.

THIRTY

Once Nish had gone, Irisis began to creep around the circumference of the warding chamber behind the ring of fifteen mancers, who were standing as silent and motionless as before. Her stomach hurt. Fatalist that she was, she was still vain enough that she didn't want to be slain in some grotesque or disfiguring way.

A swift sword thrust between the ribs, or in through the back, she found herself thinking. That won't make too much of a mess. But no severed limbs or spilled guts, and definitely not anthracism. The sight of those oozing, foamed-up statues of char and bone, once men and women as proud as herself, filled her with unspeakable horror.

Irisis heard a footfall off to her left and shook herself free of morbid reflections. She'd spent far too much time wallowing in that sort of thing lately. How was she to capture Tiaan while preventing the amplimet from destroying them both? If she drew no power at all, not even the tiny amount required to check on the state of the field, she might be all right. But then again, the amplimet might be able to take control of her pliance and direct power straight at her. She didn't know what it was capable of.

She passed in front of one of the living ward-mancers – the dumpy old woman she'd noted earlier. Her whole body was shuddering now, and her eye had a deranged, unblinking stare. Her mouth hung open on the left side but was twisted closed on the right, as if she'd had a stroke. Saliva ran down her chin, sliming the breast of her robe. Surely she couldn't hold out much longer.

Irisis circled the room. The other fourteen mancers were in a similar condition. Though none had yet failed, they were close to cracking. When they did, they would die as gruesomely as the inner circle, and so would she.

She circled the room again but saw no sign of Tiaan. At all costs she must stop the amplimet breaking free until Flydd got here, though how was she to do that?

She couldn't do anything to support the ward-mancers. Tiaan was the key, but would Tiaan try to contain the amplimet or help it get free? Another unknown. Irisis went down on hands and knees and began to crawl towards the dais. The stench was truly revolting, and as she eased between two of the carbonised mancers, her head brushed a hanging hand. A finger tangled in her hair and broke off. Irisis raked it out furiously. The crunchy, bubbly feel of the remnant made her gag.

She still hadn't seen Tiaan, though surely she would be close to the rose-crystal barriers. Irisis didn't think Tiaan would have gone inside yet – she'd sound out the amplimet first. She could be patient now; this close, her withdrawal would ease.

And then the unexpected happened. The ceiling shook and, with a whirring of oiled rods, separated into radial segments that moved fractionally apart and began to slide away from the centre, exposing a twelve-sided hole. It slowly enlarged to reveal, far above, the scrutators' turret with its elongated speaking trumpets, surmounting its column like a flower at the end of a tall thick stalk.

As the ceiling opened, benches concealed within it rotated up and locked into place, creating a theatre whose central stage was the warding chamber with its two rings of mancers, the outer ring scarcely more alive than the black inner one. And central to it all, the oval ward-walls of rose quartz guarding the as yet unseen treasure, and the steel column ascending from inside.

Flashes lit up the distant curve of the dome, the bell-pulls and speaking trumpets disengaged from the scrutators' turret and then, silently, the turret began to inch down the column. Did the scrutators now have what they'd wanted all along? It seemed so. They must have planned some great spectacle once they'd mastered the amplimet.

Shouts and battle cries echoed down from above, along with the sound of sword on sword and the clang of crossbow bolts on metal. Craning her neck, Irisis saw a small group of people running around the circumference of the upper chamber, darting between the seats as they tried to find a way down. She thought she recognised Flydd. And yes, that small, rolling shape was definitely Klarm.

But without a rope there was no way down. The walls of the warding chamber were intact, for it had been protected from the dislocation. Flydd and Klarm would have to take the precarious metal stair, but before they were halfway down, the turret would have reached the dais.

Turning back to the dais, Irisis caught a glimpse of a dark head moving along the base of one of the tall blades of rose crystal. It was Tiaan, down on hands and knees. A glimmer grew inside the wards at the opposite end to the column; a blue-green flicker made patterns on the walls. It seemed the amplimet was responding to her nearness. Calling her?

The flicker became a pulse, and each time it brightened the ring of mancers let out a collective groan. They wouldn't be able to hold the amplimet back this time. Its light seemed to shine right through the small crawling figure. Once Tiaan found a way past the wards it would either be the end of her, or of everything.

Irisis hesitated only long enough to think of what was going to happen if *she* passed between the wards. Taking a deep breath, she followed.

As Nish came through the dome door onto the roof he was caught from behind and his arms pinned. He struggled to get free but was held too cunningly.

'The game has been set up,' Eiryn Muss's voice was soft in Nish's ear. 'No one can stop it now. Let them work it through.'

Nish threw his head back, trying to ram it into the spy's face. Muss held him and drove a knee into his kidneys. The pain was so excruciating that Nish fell to his knees. Muss tied his hands using a length cut from a coil of rope that hung from his hip.

'Why are you doing this?' Nish ground out.

'I have my reasons and they go back a long way. And, no, I'm not a traitor. I no longer serve anyone but myself.'

'Why, Muss?'

Muss hauled Nish up a narrow ladder that ran up the outside curve of the dome. Muss had learned from his earlier defeat. This time he wore the guise of a stocky, muscular man in a soldier's uniform.

At the top, he levered open a small service hatch and pushed Nish through onto a balcony covered in icicles. He tied Nish's hands to the semicircular cast-iron railing. Where Nish's wrist momentarily touched the frigid iron, his skin stuck to it and tore as he jerked away.

'Aah!' he yelped.

Muss looked down and, to Nish's surprise, lengthened the rope. Not from compassion, Nish felt sure. He'd not seen Muss evince any such emotion, but neither was he one to inflict needless suffering.

'A fine spy nest,' Muss observed, glancing into the warding chamber. 'One can see everything from here. I've often used it when the scrutators were at their meetings.'

Nish looked down but couldn't see Irisis or Tiaan. 'Who are you?' said Nish.

'Eiryn Muss, the perfect spy.' There was a hint of emotion in his voice. Bitterness?

'The morphmancer,' said Nish. 'How did you come to be a mancer and no one knew about it, in this place dedicated to the perfection of the Secret Art?'

'I never wanted the things they wanted,' said Muss. 'Not gold, nor power nor domination, nor the gratification of the senses. I had no need to show off my Art. I was content to bide my time.'

'For what?' Nish cried in frustration. Muss was a creature of shadows, an illusion. Whenever pushed, he retreated to places no one else could go.

'Shh!' said Muss. 'The pieces are moving into place.'

The scrutators' turret was halfway now, still inching down its column. On the far side of the upper chamber, among the seats, Nish made out a hobbling Flydd and several companions, trying to find a way down to the warding chamber. They looked in bad shape.

'What's Fusshte up to?' Nish said aloud.

'I suppose he wants Flydd to *think* that he's going after the amplimet . . .'

Flydd and his companions had disappeared. Nish hoped they'd made a break for the stairs.

'But Fusshte isn't?'

'He's too scared,' said Muss. 'He now knows that he can never understand the amplimet. What man can? It's inanimate, a crystal that has somehow, over the aeons, *woken*. Its needs, desires, *urges* are incomprehensible.'

'And Fusshte's purpose is?' said Nish. Muss's words were as confusing as everything about him.

'He wants to force the amplimet to strike at Flydd. As soon as Flydd draws power to defend himself, the amplimet will turn that power against him. And while it's diverted, Fusshte surely hopes to bind it to himself. If he succeeds, he'll have all the power he could ever want. And all his opponents will be dead.'

'How is Fusshte going to do that?' said Nish, to keep Muss talking while he tried to think of a plan. Muss avoided fighting so he could hardly be good at it. Nish had to attack violently, without warning.

Muss, peering down at the dais through his eidoscope, permitted himself the faintest of smiles. 'He's got scores of mancers and artificers. He'll have them attack the amplimet while making it appear that Flydd is doing so. There's no risk to *him* that way.'

'But plenty to the mancers and artificers, I'll bet.'

'What does any scrutator care if his servants live or die, as long as he gets what he wants?' Again that hint of bitterness. 'And now, *they come.*'

Flydd and another man close behind, possibly Flangers, eased in through the door of the warding chamber and seemed to be trying to sneak between the circle of juddering mancers. The darting figure of Klarm appeared, then a second soldier.

A hatch flipped open on the far side of the chamber and Flydd threw himself down, cursing as a purple ray lanced past his head. It illuminated the tip of one of the rose-crystal wards, the light slowly spreading down until the whole ward glowed pink.

Nish could feel tension building, charging up everything from the floor of the lower chamber to the tip of the dome. His hair and beard were drawn upwards and a shock leapt from the metal rail to his hand. Below, someone let out a moan of horror.

Behind the hatch from which the ray had come, a man screamed, his voice rising higher and higher until it became a cracked falsetto which was abruptly cut off. Something burst with a pulpy splat, like a melon dropped from a great height.

Red mush began to ooze from the partly open hatch, then brown fumes. Nish averted his eyes. The scrutators' turret had stopped some five spans above the dais and he could see Fusshte inside, seeming to direct his forces like a concertmaster directing musicians.

The tension began to charge up again. Another ray zapped from an aperture beside the first hatch, followed by a third from the other side of the room. Each just missed Flydd's hand before lighting up the rose-crystal wards. It was intended to look as if Flydd were attacking the wards, but the amplimet wasn't deceived. The consequences in each case were just as quick, bloody and horrible.

The speaking horns boomed. 'Guards, guards! To the warding chamber.'

Flydd scuttled for the rose-crystal wards, dived over the fallen corpse of one of the carbonised mancers and lay still. The corpse exploded to fragments. Flydd rolled out of the way.

'The amplimet isn't fooled,' said Nish. 'It's not attacking Flydd.'

'He's clever,' said Muss. 'He's not defending himself.'

'Why doesn't the amplimet attack the turret?' said Nish.

'It's shielded with platinum.'

Flydd appeared and disappeared like a dolphin swimming in the surf. Corpses, benches and other paraphernalia burst all around him. Fusshte had given up on the wards and was now directing the attack at Flydd.

'He'll soon have nowhere left to run,' said Nish.

An enormous flash lit up the chamber and Fusshte began waving furiously. Several dozen apertures opened at once and rays stabbed across and across, like solid rods of light in the enveloping darkness.

The amplimet struck back. The rays of light bounced back and forth, then froze solid a couple of spans above the floor, forming a network through which the turret could barely be seen. Fusshte looked dismayed; he didn't seem to be able to communicate with his people. His mancers and artificers died gruesomely behind their hatches. More red mush oozed out, and more brown fumes, then the attack faltered.

Flydd, crouching between two carbonised mancers, fell to his knees. His hands were moving though Nish couldn't imagine what he was trying to do. Tiaan was lying on the dais, turning her head one way and then the other.

One carbonised mancer was blown apart at the shoulders, the other at the waist. Flydd was thrown backwards and something small, cubic and shiny flew from his hands – the platinum box. He felt around on the floor but couldn't seem to find it in the gloom.

The attack entered a new phase. The few surviving hatches opened and their occupiers came forth. Flangers began duelling with an artificer mounted atop an articulated device like an iron caterpillar. Klarm was running through the obstacles in figure-eights with a giant of a man in close pursuit. One of the carbonised mancers fell on Flydd, its black chest shattering on his head. He rolled out from under, spitting out char.

The speaking horns boomed again, and this time there was a panicky note in the cry. 'Guards, guards! To the warding chamber.'

'They're not coming,' said Muss. 'I've laid illusions all around to keep them out.'

The huge soldier darted, caught Klarm by the ankle and lifted him high, one hand around each leg as if to tear him in two. Flydd went after him and the giant backed out the door, swinging the dwarf in one hand and kicking the door shut in Flydd's face. Flydd heaved at it with his shoulder. Flangers ran to his aid and they went after the giant. The artificer pursued them, crashing through the iron doors in his iron caterpillar.

The room was empty apart from Irisis and Tiaan, and the silent ward-mancers. Tiaan came to her feet, moving in slow-motion, her eyes fixed on something Nish couldn't see. She extended her arms towards it and took a step forwards, where-upon a long shadow flashed between the wards and took her around the knees. It was Irisis. Nish's heart seemed to be blocking his gullet. What was Irisis doing inside? *She* couldn't pass safely through the wards.

Tiaan began to struggle furiously and one foot caught Irisis on the jaw. Her head cracked into the rose-quartz ward behind her. Irisis slumped to the floor and Nish lost sight of her in the shadows.

Tiaan stepped over her and rose to her feet, reaching out with both arms. A sullen red glow illuminated her face. She looked like a rapt sleepwalker moving slowly towards the ampli-met and Nish knew that, once she got it and lifted it high, the crystal would be free.

And Irisis would be its first victim.

THIRTY-ONE

Nish acted instinctively. If he didn't save Irisis, no one could. Bracing his back against the rail he kicked out with both feet, striking Muss so hard in the chest that he slammed into the wall.

Sliding his rope around the rail, he tore the knife from Muss's belt and awkwardly hacked himself free. He had to get down to the warding chamber and there was only one way to reach it in time.

He snatched the coil of rope and fled down the ladder, then into the dome. Knotting the rope around his waist, he ran around the inner edge of the room, looking down into the dome chamber. A third of the way around the circle Nish skidded to a stop, whipped the free end of the rope around a bench and tied it tight. He gauged the distance to the dais, ran on for ten steps and hurled himself over, praying that he'd judged correctly. If the rope was too long, he'd hit the floor hard enough to snap his thigh bones, or worse.

Nish fell free for an awfully long time, passed through the network of frozen light then swung in an arc across the chamber. He curved down, his feet almost touching the floor, then up straight towards one of the remaining carbonised mancers, a broad, shapeless woman wearing a pointed leather hat, now mainly char.

There wasn't time to try and sway out of the way. He smashed side-on into the corpse, shattering it into stinking fragments that clung all over him. The blackened head went flying across the floor.

The impact set Nish spinning on the rope as he shot up towards the far wall and through the beams again, trying to clear the char and muck out of his eyes. He got one eye open just before he reached the top of the wall. He saw Tiaan move, calculated the necessary swing and pushed off with one foot. Now on a different trajectory, he flashed between the rose-crystal wards just as Tiaan, arms outstretched, sprang for the amplimet. He cannoned into her chest and she went flying off to the left. Nish spun the other way and thudded into the base of another of the wards.

Low down, it was solid as rock. Something went *crack* and a brilliant pain shot up Nish's right arm. He'd broken it. Momentum gone, he orbited around the inside of the wards, passed out through a gap then in again, and rotated on the end of the rope several times before grounding against the ward that had broken his forearm.

The amplimet sat in the middle of a small alabaster pedestal, its central spark throbbing balefully. Tiaan was nowhere to be seen. Nish wiped crumbly bits of black foam from his face and looked down. Irisis lay directly below him, staring up.

'How are you?' he said haltingly, supporting his arm.

Irisis sat up, rubbing the back of her head, and winced. She inspected her fingers, which bore a faint bloody smear. 'Just a bump on the head. What's the matter with your arm?'

'Broken.'

'That wasn't very smart.' She grinned and unfastened the rope from around his middle.

'I didn't do it deliberately.' Nish could hardly think for the pain shooting up his arm.

Again the speaking horns trumpeted their plaintive cry for help, but it wasn't answered. The turret could no longer be seen through the frozen light which, oddly, shed no illumination downwards.

'What do we do now?'

'We find the damn platinum box,' Irisis said quietly. Tiaan wasn't in sight, though she couldn't be far away. 'We get the crystal into it any way we can, wire the lid on tight and chuck the box into the hottest fire we can make.'

He glanced back at the amplimet. 'Not so loud.'

'It can't hear, Nish. It isn't alive.'

'Heat will end it.' Despite all the trouble it had caused them, Nish was uneasy about destroying such a precious thing.

'It's the only solution, but no one else is going to do it. They all want to make use of the wretched thing, though it's too dangerous for *anyone* to use safely. Even Malien is afraid of it, Nish. Doesn't that tell you all you need to know? Once it's gone, there will be nothing anyone can do about it.'

'Flydd will crucify you,' said Nish. 'And me.'

'I'd do it anyway. Some objects are just too deadly to have around. I'd better look for the box.'

'It fell over there.' He pointed.

Irisis began to crawl out between the wards. Nish tried to keep to her heels, but it wasn't easy to crawl with a broken arm.

'What if it's watching us?' he said, supporting himself on his left hand. His right clutched at his coat buttons in a vain attempt to take the weight off his forearm.

'I don't think it can do anything to you, since you have no talent for the Art whatsoever.'

'So people keep telling me,' he murmured. 'Can you see the box?'

'No.'

'Do you think Flydd's still alive?'

'How would I know?'

'What if everyone's dead but us? It might be better if the scrutators *do* succeed.'

'*What?*' she hissed in outrage.

'If we can't replace the Council with honest leaders, because they're all dead, what's the point of bringing it down? That can only result in anarchy, and the lyrinx will defeat humanity all the sooner. *You* can't seize power, Irisis, and neither can I.'

Irisis stared at her long and elegant fingers for a moment and Nish regretted airing his worries. What could be gained by putting his fears on her?

'Since we don't know that our friends are dead,' said Irisis, 'we must assume that they're not. We hold true to our purpose, Nish.'

She began to worm her way through the debris. It seemed darker than before. Nish couldn't keep up and was resting on his good arm when it occurred to him that they'd left Tiaan unwatched. She was the key, and always had been.

'I'm going back to keep an eye on Tiaan,' he said.

Irisis didn't answer. He couldn't see her and didn't know if she'd heard. Not daring to shout his intentions, in case Fusshte could hear, he made his painful way back to the rose-crystal wards.

He couldn't see her at first, for Tiaan lay on her belly at the base of the alabaster pedestal, looking like any other bit of debris littering the blasted room. It wasn't until Nish eased his head between the wards, and her dark eyes moved, that he realised she was there.

Tiaan was taking a more cautious approach this time. She raised herself to her hands and knees, her eyes darting around the room, then up. The turret was becoming visible again as the frozen light faded. Her shoulders quivered. She looked like an animal ready to pounce. What would she do once she got the amplimet? Could she control it, or was it already controlling her? Judging by the feral look in her eyes, it could be, in which case it was just an arm's length away from its goal.

As she stared raptly at the crystal on the pedestal, Nish slipped through the gap. He had to be ready. The instant she sprang, so must he, whatever it cost him.

Up in the turret, a movement caught his eye. Fusshte was leaning out, almost as rapt as Tiaan. Whatever she was up to, he was waiting for it. He had something in his hand – a net or a metal basket. Fusshte dared not touch the amplimet, and he'd failed to force it to attack Flydd, but once it was in Tiaan's hands it would be different.

Tiaan quivered. She was going for it. Nish swayed forward and pain shot up his arm. He had to ignore it.

She sprang and so did he, but too late. Her upstretched hands closed around the amplimet and tore it from its mounting. She let out a cry of bliss but, even before Nish crashed into her, Tiaan went rigid and her eyes became blank.

He threw his good arm around her slender waist. Tiaan flopped like a doll, then her eyes focussed. 'Get away!' she cried, beating at his face with her free hand.

Nish bent his head and took the blows, since he had no way of defending himself. Tiaan had gone into a frenzy, clubbing him over the ears.

She hit him on his broken nose and the agony made him let go. Tiaan raised the amplimet above her head, took three small steps and light streamed out, illuminating the chamber so brightly that he had to shade his eyes. Nish felt, rather than heard, a brittle crackling that might have been interpreted as laughter.

Fusshte froze halfway out of the turret; even the ring of ward-mancers ceased their violent shuddering. Chills oscillated down Nish's spine. The amplimet had what it wanted at last.

Tiaan's black hair stood straight up, she went as rigid as the carbonised mancers and her eyes bulged from their sockets as if poked out from the inside. Her mouth fell open. Steam wisped out, followed by a liquid gurgle, an attempted cry for help.

A shining net of woven platinum mesh fell from an embrasure of the turret to envelop her and was jerked sideways, toppling her off her feet. As Tiaan hit the floor the light from the amplimet faded, before flaring even brighter and more ominously.

In an instant the warding chamber went wild. The faintly glowing globes on the walls exploded, flinging chips of stone in every direction. The rose-crystal wards flushed a brilliant pink. The ward-mancers fell to their knees, their faces contorted as they struggled for control. Their terror was absolute – they were going to die as hideously as the inner ring had and there was nothing they could do to prevent it.

In the turret, Fusshte and two other scrutators were desperately flailing the wires to the platinum net, trying to get its opening over Tiaan's feet so they could pull it closed and cut the amplimet off from the field. Unfortunately the mesh had caught on Tiaan's heels, they couldn't free it and the amplimet was surging ever closer to complete control.

Flydd hadn't come back and Nish couldn't see Irisis, so what was he to do? If he did nothing, the amplimet would take control. Or he could pull the mesh over Tiaan's feet, stopping the amplimet but giving Fusshte all he wanted. Which should it be?

Tiaan began to kick and struggle, tearing at the unyielding mesh and trying to pull it off her, though her movements were uncoordinated. Perhaps it was the crystal telling her what to do.

'Nish!' Irisis was hissing at him from the shadows.

He spun around, trying to make her out in the smoky gloom.

'Nish, you bloody fool. They're trying to lift her up. You've got to stop them.'

'Have you found the box?'

'Not yet.'

Tiaan's feet were already half a span in the air. Fusshte had realised that if he lifted the mesh by the drawstring wires, there was a good chance Tiaan's feet would slip in.

Nish stumbled across the rubble. Halie and another female scrutator were leaning out of the embrasure of the turret, struggling to lift Tiaan and the heavy platinum mesh by its wires while Fusshte tried to hold the opening closed. They were making hard work of it.

Nish threw himself onto the net and the sudden load proved too much for the two slight women. One, not Halie, cried out, thudded head-first to the floor and didn't move again. The mouth of the net fell open.

The amplimet flared dark, then bright. Panicking, Nish pulled the mesh down over Tiaan's feet and drew the drawstring tight, whereupon Fusshte let out a cry of triumph and hurled a blast of light that set fire to Nish's coat. He let go of the drawstring. The hole eased open and Fusshte froze, arms outstretched. The flames were singeing the hair on the back of Nish's neck as he shrugged out of the coat.

'Irisis?' he yelped. 'What am I supposed to do?'

'Hold her until I get there.'

That proved more difficult than it sounded, for Tiaan was thrashing in the net, and the amplimet letting out blinding rays. Nish ended up sitting on her, jerking the mouth of the net closed then open again, hoping to prevent the amplimet going all the way or Fusshte using his Art.

Irisis staggered up, bruised, bloody and covered in dust and char, but she had the platinum box open in her hand. 'Pull it off her, quick.'

Nish slid off and began to heave at the platinum mesh. It was incredibly heavy and Tiaan's furious thrashing kept tearing it out of his good hand. He took the other end, Irisis stumbled round to join him and together they got the net up past Tiaan's ankles. Her calves emerged. The mesh came up over her thighs, and the further they lifted it the more overpowering the light from the amplimet became.

As they drew it up Tiaan's chest she let out a cry, half pain, half ecstasy, and raised her right hand high inside the mesh. Irisis gasped, dropped the box and began staggering around in a circle, tearing at her coat and shirt, ripping it in her desperation. She got her hands inside, pulled out her pliance and jerked the chain so hard that it snapped. She threw her pliance onto the floor and leaned against one of the rose-crystal wards, panting. A trail of smoke wisped up from her shirt.

Fusshte was hanging over the embrasure, mouth gaping open. He flung a metal goblet at Nish, but it missed. Nish hauled the net up and over Tiaan's head. Only her arm to go.

The circle of ward-mancers wailed and collapsed. Only Tiaan's arm and wrist, and the amplimet, were covered. Just the platinum mesh bunched around her arm held the amplimet back. She whipped her arm out and the crystal, in a roaring, cataclysmic crescendo, drove for the third stage of awakening it so urgently craved.

The skin of Tiaan's fingers began to smoke but she was in

292

such ecstasy that she wasn't aware of it. Nish stood frozen in horror, thinking that it was going to anthracise them both, like the gruesome remnants all around. He threw his good arm around Tiaan's chest, crushing her against him, and even tried to hold her with the broken one. Tiaan struggled listlessly.

'Irisis, the box!' he screeched.

In a wild instant, reality was overturned. Irisis took one step towards Nish and fell into the floor. Waves passed through the walls, floor and ceiling as if they were rubber. The solid walls became transparent, revealing the shadowy, sliced-up jumble that was the rest of Nennifer. It seemed to stretch to infinity like reflections in a pair of mirrors.

Irisis caught hold of Nish's trailing cloak and pulled herself out. Parts of the floor were solid, other parts like jelly. She turned towards Tiaan, though it was like trying to push against a hurricane. Irisis leaned forward into the blast, put her head down and forced with all her strength.

Something rang off Nish's skull and a soldier's metal helm clattered onto the floor – Fusshte again. Nish staggered under the blow but didn't look up. He just concentrated on holding Tiaan.

Irisis was nearly there. Tiaan began to struggle furiously, to kick and scream. Irisis reached out and caught her by the coat, dragging Tiaan and Nish to her. She tried to pull down Tiaan's arm but it was as straight and hard as a metal rod. Tiaan belaboured Irisis with her other hand, stabbing at her face with stiff fingers. One blow caught Irisis in the eye and she gasped and had to let go.

Tiaan tried to wriggle free. She slipped in Nish's grasp and in desperation he butted his head at the inside of her elbow. Her arm folded, the amplimet fell from her numb fingers and Irisis scooped it out of mid-air, thrust it into the platinum box and slammed the lid down.

The tension, and the impossibilities, cut off abruptly. All the lights went out in Nennifer as the Art that sustained it failed. Tiaan's knees collapsed and she subsided gently on the rubble, wailing as if her heart was broken. The moon shone down through the dome onto the still, silent figures in the centre and the ring of ward-mancers crumpled around the periphery. Everyone was waiting for something to happen.

'Now what?' said Nish, hanging onto Irisis to prevent himself from falling.

'The ward-mancers are free to use power without risking instant annihilation. Fusshte too. They'll try to get the box.'

'Take it!' shouted Fusshte.

Nish prepared for the hopeless defence, but the fifteen ward-mancers came to their shaky knees and began to crawl away.

'What are you doing?' screamed Fusshte. 'Attack them. Kill them and bring the box to me.'

The ward-mancers took no notice. They kept on crawling towards the door, head to tail like a line of caterpillars on a branch.

'He asked too much of them,' said Irisis. 'They've broken. We've got a chance. Come on.'

Before he could move, Scrutator Fusshte stood up on the sill of the embrasure, a rope in his hands, preparing to slide down. Nish watched helplessly. He couldn't fight scrutator magic and, with the amplimet at the third stage, he dared not open the box.

Fusshte had one leg over the side when a bloody, wild-eyed Flydd hurled himself through the door. He stopped there and Fusshte did too, staring at him. The crawling ward-mancers froze.

Flydd hobbled across the chamber and extended his hand. After a long hesitation, Irisis put the platinum box in it and Flydd raised his arm, holding the box high. Fusshte's eyes followed it but he did not move.

'We've been enemies since the day you bribed Ghorr to admit you to the Council,' Flydd said, loud enough for the whole room to hear. 'Oh yes, I know all about that, and before I've finished with you the whole world will know your other dirty secrets, Fusshte. You schemed, bribed, lied and slaughtered your way to power. I might even have forgiven you that, had you used your talents to help win the war, but you were happy for the war to go on forever. It kept your kind in power and you used that power to be rid of anyone who threatened you. Especially me.'

Fusshte said not a word, nor did his eyes leave the platinum box.

'You condemned me to be flayed alive,' Flydd went on, 'you and Ghorr. You laughed at my agony and sneered when the torturers cut my manhood away. But a man can still be a man without his male parts, as a man can have them and be no true man at all. I swore I'd bring you down for that alone, no matter what it cost me, to show that I was more a man than you.'

Fusshte made no reply. The ward-mancers began coming to their feet. He gestured frantically at them but one by one they folded their arms and stood there in a line.

'Here is the amplimet you so craved, Fusshte.' Flydd shook the platinum box. 'I challenge you for it – man against man. None of these witnesses will interfere.'

Beside Nish, Irisis drew in a sharp breath. Nish's heart began to pound. Fusshte's snake eyes glittered. His bony hands tightened on the rail of the turret and he leaned over, dark tongue darting through his lips. He was surely planning some treacherous attack that Flydd wouldn't anticipate.

Nish glanced at Flydd, a small, battered and bloody old man who was practically collapsing with weariness. Yet Flydd would not give in and he used that iron will to drive himself upright. His eyes never left his enemy's and his stare never faltered. Nish could hardly breathe as the moment was drawn out to its snapping point.

Fusshte moved blindingly fast, bringing his concealed hand up and hurling a dagger. It caught the light as it flashed across the room and Nish was sure it was going to plunge into Flydd's right eye.

Flydd tilted his head to the left, the dagger skimmed his ear and embedded itself in the wall. Fusshte reached down for another weapon but Flydd flipped open the platinum box and the flickering glow of the amplimet lit up the room. Holding the box in front of him, Flydd reached in, plucked the crystal out and raised his fist. It glowed blood-red.

'Xervish!' cried Irisis. 'Put it back. It'll anthracise you.'

Flydd did not hesitate. How can he dare, Nish thought. Isn't he afraid? Surely he can't hope to hold the amplimet back by himself?

Flydd's fist began to pulse, pink to blood-dark. The strain showed in the muscles of his face – would he control the crystal or would it turn him to reeking char?

No one moved. Fusshte's tongue flickered across his lips again. A minute passed. Two. Three.

Flydd's arm trembled; his body jerked, and suddenly Fusshte had a crossbow in his hand and was drawing a bead on Flydd's forehead. Nish looked for something to throw but couldn't find anything save chunks of charcoal.

'Surr!' Nish cried. 'Get out of the way.'

Fusshte wound the cranks and the bow creaked as it bent. His finger moved for the lock lever.

Before he could fire, Flydd roared, 'You're mine, Fusshte. Mine!' He thrust his arm high and strained until the tendons in his neck stood out.

Fusshte had his finger on the lever but before he could release it the wire of the crossbow glowed red and sagged away.

The amplimet flared and faded. Steam burst from Flydd's nostrils. He strained again, his fist rock-steady though his arm had the faintest tremor. Flydd grunted, groaned, steam or smoke burst from his mouth and for a moment it looked as if his fist was dripping blood.

'You're mine!' he cried, rising up on tiptoes. 'Mine. Back, I say – all the way back.'

The crystal flared to coruscating brilliance, Nish gasped, and then the glow went out completely.

Flydd staggered and nearly fell, but recovered and extended his hand towards Fusshte, the amplimet pointing from his fingers. The central spark wasn't blinking at all. 'Mine!' he roared.

Fusshte dropped the useless crossbow as if it had grown too hot to hold. His black-rimmed mouth gaped open and a mewling cry of terror issued forth. He threw himself backwards into the turret, which shook free and began to slide down the column until it crashed into the dais.

Flydd slipped the dull crystal back into its box and softly closed the lid. He headed for the turret, staggering in his weariness. Nish and Irisis followed warily, but when they peered in Fusshte and Halie were gone.

Flydd closed his eyes and pounded the sides of the turret in his anguish.

'I expected more of Fusshte,' said Nish, 'after the way he faced down Ghorr at Fiz Gorgo.'

'The chief scrutatorship was within his sights, back then,' said Irisis. 'But Flydd's towering attack on the amplimet has crushed Fusshte's hopes forever. He can't hope to match the strength Flydd has just displayed, and the ward-mancers have repudiated him. If Fusshte can't command their loyalty, all he can do is run.'

Shortly, Nish picked out his spidery shadow, high on a rope ladder that ran up the other side of the column. Fusshte was too high to attack and soon disappeared into the darkness. Halie, the other surviving scrutator, was close behind him.

'They can't get far,' said Nish, leaning back against Irisis. 'It's over.'

'That was the bravest, most reckless deed I ever saw,' Irisis said to Flydd. 'You could have –'

'And I so very nearly did,' said Flydd. 'I was sure it would be the end of me.'

'And yet you did not falter.'

'I told myself I had to keep going, that there was no other option. And to my shame, there was a touch of pride in it as well. I had to prove that I was still a man.'

'A *touch* of pride isn't such a bad thing,' said Irisis.

'It was so near. And yet, it's still not over.' He looked up but Fusshte and Halie had disappeared.

Flydd climbed onto the top of the turret, turned to survey the ward-mancers and extended his hands towards them, then to the others in the chamber.

'The two surviving scrutators have fled,' he said so softly that Nish had to strain to hear, 'abandoning Nennifer to the fate they brought upon it. Their Council is disbanded. Scrutator Klarm and I will take their place until a new regime can be installed. Does anyone challenge our edict?'

None of the ward-mancers spoke, though they bowed their collective heads. 'Then it is done,' said Flydd. 'Go, inform the guards that a new council is in charge, and that Scrutators Fusshte and Halie must be held for trial and execution. Tell everyone to assemble in the air-dreadnought yard, well away from the walls, for the remains of Nennifer will soon collapse. Everyone must collect what food and clothing they can gather on the way.' He turned to Nish, Irisis, Flangers and Klarm.

'It's not over yet. We must make sure that the amplimet has been driven back to the lowest stage of wakening, where it was when Tiaan found it. I've done the first part of the job, but it's mancer's work and none of you need be bothered about it.'

'Let's go home,' said Irisis.

One of the seats rattled up above, and Nish looked up to see Muss's slender figure disappear from the rail of the dome chamber.

'First we have a mite of unfinished business to attend to,' said Flydd. 'After him, and be quick about it.'

'What's going on?' said Klarm.

'That's what I'd like to know. All I know is that Eiryn Muss has been waiting for this moment for a very long time.'

'And probably engineered it,' said Nish.

Flydd gave him a keen glance. 'He probably did.'

'He's a chimaera,' said Irisis.

Flydd started. 'Ah!' he said. 'Unwittingly, you've put your finger on the very key to his nature, though you don't realise it. He *is* a chimaera and I don't know how to deal with him.'

THIRTY-TWO

Tiaan was secured and one of the soldiers carried her out to where Yggur, Malien and Evee had been left. Everyone else went after Eiryn Muss at the best pace they could muster. It wasn't impressive – they were all beyond exhaustion – but the cold spurred them on. In exposed areas it was crippling, for the Art sustaining Nennifer had completely failed now. All the globes had gone out and what remained of the structure was crumbling visibly in the moonlight. Not a minute went by but that another segment fell into ruin.

'Where would Muss go?' said Flydd, the only one of them who wasn't staggering. His hair was white with dust, his lips like bloodless worms, his scarred and puckered skin glassy tight. He had bloodstains small and large all over him and his clothes were in shreds, but his eyes were gleaming beacons. The impossible victory had been achieved and he'd exacted a partial revenge for his torments. The amplimet's box hung from his hip in a net made from a section of platinum mesh, just to be sure, and both were secured to his waist with a fine steel chain.

Klarm shrugged. 'I've no idea.'

Something occurred to Nish. 'Xervish, at Gumby Marth you said –'

'When I want you to blab about my affairs I'll let you know,' Flydd said coldly.

'Aren't you being a bit hard on the lad, Xervish, after all he's done?' said Klarm, lurching on the leg that had previously been in calipers.

'Humph!' Flydd snorted, casting Nish a piercing glance from beneath his single brown and hairy eyebrow. The mad grin of triumph came back. 'If our subordinates are to earn our trust, they must learn when to keep their mouths shut. Which way here?'

Klarm held up an oil-fed lantern he'd found in the upper chamber and passed it back and forth over the dusty rubble. Nish couldn't make out anything from its flickering yellow glow.

'This way,' said the dwarf, gesturing with the lantern towards a crumbling opening on their left.

They followed him in silence, too worn and weary to speak. Nish's broken arm hadn't been set yet, and indeed, he wasn't sure anyone but Irisis realised that it was broken. Irisis was stumbling along with her eyes almost closed. There had been no time to eat, drink or rest before the pursuit had begun. Nish was in such pain that he couldn't think, and every step up onto the rubble, or down off it, sent another spasm up his arm. The pain ran all the way to the base of his skull, where it lodged as a brilliant, white-hot glow.

'I've got a feeling he's heading for the chief scrutator's strongroom,' Klarm went on after they'd scrambled through another three half-collapsed building segments, following Muss's trail through the dust. 'Which is off his private mancing chambers – at least, it used to be.'

'How can you tell *where* he's going?' Flydd said wearily. The grin was fading.

'Just a hunch.'

'I've never been to the strongroom. Have you?'

'Once,' said Klarm. 'Though only to the outer door, and the inner was sealed with potent scrutator magic all the time I was there. *Chief* scrutator magic, at that – I could sense it from the other side of the room. It pleased Ghorr for me to know about it, I think. He liked to emphasise his superiority in little ways as well as big.'

'It's surprising that you got on at all,' said Flydd, 'considering . . .'

'Considering that he despised anyone with physical imperfections,' chuckled Klarm. 'Ghorr sneered at everyone less imposing than himself, and loathed those who had a greater physical presence.'

'An insecure man, despite all his natural gifts. Unlike yourself.'

'I came to terms with what I am long ago. It's the inner man that counts, not the fragile shell that carries it around.'

Flydd paused a moment, as if pondering that. 'You say the strongroom was locked with chief scrutator magic,' Flydd ruminated, 'the secret of which is passed on to the new chief scrutator only when the old one is on his deathbed, or in some equally dire extreme. Are you thinking what I'm thinking, Klarm?'

'I'm not sure I am,' said Klarm.

'I am,' interjected Irisis, suddenly perking up. Her wits were many steps ahead of Nish's. 'None of the scrutators were with Ghorr when he died, so the secret can't have been passed on. Fusshte wouldn't have been able to discover what lay inside the chief scrutator's strongroom.'

'That would have driven him into a fury,' Flydd chuckled. 'Being chief but not having the keys to the treasure chest. But now the Art sustaining Nennifer has failed, perhaps the scrutator magic has failed as well. Yes – that's why Muss is heading for the strongroom. He's after something inside. Is this what he was trying to engineer all along?'

'I presume so,' said Klarm.

'Does that mean we can expect a visit from Fusshte as well?' said Nish, plodding dully along. He couldn't contemplate yet another struggle. He was utterly, utterly burned out. How was it that Flydd could drive himself on?

'After Flydd's awesome display to overpower the amplimet,' said Klarm, 'Fusshte will be running as fast as he can.'

'That will be the strongroom ahead,' Klarm said a while later, heaving himself up a pile of stone blocks towards an imposing steel door, once concealed by maroon velvet drapes which now

301

hung from the left side, all tattered and covered in dust. The door was ajar. 'Quiet now. It looks like he's already within.'

They eased up behind him: Flydd followed by Flangers, Irisis and Nish, nursing his arm. Flydd put his head around the door, then beckoned.

Nish slipped through the gap in his turn. He was standing in a gloomy hall made of some dark stone that soaked up the glimmers of moonlight coming through the cracked roof. After much eye-straining he discerned a square door at the far end. It seemed to be moving – no, it was the hall that appeared to stretch and contract before his eyes. He couldn't look at it.

It's an illusion, Nish told himself, a deception meant to keep out those who don't belong here. So the scrutator magic hasn't completely faded. He moved forwards a step and ran into Irisis's back. He hadn't even seen her.

'What's going on?' he whispered.

She put a hand on his arm – the good one, fortunately – and the illusion faded somewhat. 'Eiryn Muss is up at the far door,' she whispered right into his ear. 'He's trying to get in.'

As Nish's eyes adjusted he made out the faintest shadow there, though it didn't have Muss's outline. It was taller and broader, and with a hint of wings, like a very small lyrinx. Why that shape?

'Ah!' said Flydd as gently as a sigh. 'He's done it. He's through.'

The shadow disappeared, though Nish did not see it move. Flydd held up his hand. 'Give him a moment. We don't want to scare him off.'

There came a distant rumble – another collapse – and the floor heaved subtly beneath them. Flydd waited until it had stopped, then moved on. A yellow glow appeared in the strong-room and brightened sufficiently to light up the hall and dispel the illusion.

They reached the inner door, which was made of black steel a hand-span thick, bonded to the solid stone wall on steel hinges thicker than Nish's upper arm. Both walls and door were scorched as if great heat had been applied in an attempt to force the lock.

'Looks like Fusshte's work,' said Flydd. 'How it must have vexed him not to gain access to Ghorr's treasures.'

Approaching the door, Nish was assailed by a powerful feeling of wrongness, then every muscle in his body went rigid. He couldn't even move his tongue; he was like a living statue. Flydd turned, wove his hand in a circle above him, and then above Irisis and Flangers, and they could move again. Klarm had not been immobilised, though he walked as if his joints had rusted up. Flydd did the same for him.

'This is a forbidden place,' said Klarm in a croaky whisper. 'No man or woman, bar the chief scrutator, has passed this door in the hundred years since it was built. And though the old Council has fallen, its edict freezes my very marrow now that I pass it.'

'Ah, but the Council *has* fallen,' said Flydd, equally quietly. 'No edict of theirs has power any more. We may do whatever we have the strength to bear.' He eased through the door, though not without a wrenching shudder that gave the lie to his words.

Nish passed through without further effect. The strongroom proved larger than he had expected, and was still intact. It was illuminated by the soft yellow glow of an oil lantern. Nish could smell the sulphurous tang of the quick-match Muss had struck to light it. There was enough light to reveal gorgeously patterned marble- and travertine-clad walls that could have graced an emperor's palace.

The strongroom formed a perfect cube some seven or eight spans on a side, though it proved empty apart from a small square table carved from green serpentine, polished to bring out the oily sheen of the rock, a throne-like chair cut from a single emerald, and a large glass sphere, mirrored on the outside, suspended from a frame like a globe of the world.

Eiryn Muss stood with his back to them in the middle of the room, the eidoscope up to his right eye, scanning back and forth across the far side of the room. He flipped one lens out, another in, rotated the ones on either end and scanned that part of the room again.

'What's he doing?' whispered Nish.

Flydd reached back and crushed his good wrist. Nish fell silent, though Muss gave no sign of having heard. He made a minor adjustment to one lens and scanned a third time.

'Ah!' Muss groped around in the air like a blind man. His probing fingers touched something and he shaped the air around it, murmuring under his breath.

The air suddenly swarmed with phantoms: lost spectres or ghosts of grim Nennifer. Muss dissolved from the vaguely lyrinx shape to that of the grossly fat, bald-headed halfwit, the guise in which Nish had first known him. It stirred uncomfortable memories.

Muss morphed again, this time into an unfamiliar figure, a stocky merchant clad all in green apart from a brown hat shaped like a pudding bowl. Colours streamed across his back as the garments adjusted to his new shape. Nish wondered why he was doing it, or if he even realised that he was.

The merchant's stubby fingers cupped the air above the chair as if feeling his way around a pair of spheres the size of melons. He sighed, clapped his hands and a metal case, shaped like two round balls joined together, appeared on the chair. The outside, mirrored like the globe on its stand, revealed distorted images of Muss, though each image was different. The left-hand one showed a short, round man, the right a puny, deformed lyrinx. The group of watchers in the background were not reflected at all.

'How very curious,' Klarm breathed. 'Can the outside be a reflection of the interior?'

'Perhaps when you called him chimaera, Irisis, you saw more truly than you knew,' said Flydd. 'Be ready to rush him as soon as he opens it.'

'Why not rush him now?' said Nish. 'Just to be sure.'

'We may not be able to open the case.'

Eiryn Muss inspected the double case, turned it over and around, and scanned it from end to end with the eidoscope, muttering under his breath all the while. Another swarm of phantoms appeared up near the ceiling. He set the eidoscope down on the green table, passed his hands over the locks of the double case, caressed them with his fingertips as if playing a keyboard, then pressed down hard. *Snap, snap.*

'Don't move until he opens it and takes out what's inside,' said Flydd.

Gingerly, Muss lifted the top of the right-hand spherical case. There came a reflected flash. The inside was mirrored just like the outside.

Muss let out a choked gasp, then threw up the top of the other case.

'Nooooooo!' he wailed, as though all the demons of the underworld were clawing at his soul.

THIRTY-THREE

'Take him!' hissed Flydd.

They rushed him, though they need not have bothered. Muss was in such agony that he was oblivious to their presence. Even when they seized his arms and bound them behind his back, he made no attempt to resist.

'It was all a lie,' he said, writhing and twisting as if his intestines were full of thorns. 'They weren't there at all. Ghorr never had them.'

'What isn't there?' said Flydd. 'Out with it, Muss.'

'The tears,' Nish said suddenly. 'The tears created by the destruction of the Snizort node.'

The scales fell visibly from Xervish Flydd's eyes. 'You bloody deceitful bastard, Muss!' he said savagely. 'So that's what you were after all along. You weren't my faithful servant at all. You were just using me until your opportunity came.'

Eiryn Muss looked like a man with the disembowelling hooks deep in his belly. The impassive prober that Nish and Irisis had known, the spy who'd not shown a flicker of emotion no matter what, had disappeared. Muss was in agony and showing it.

'Forty years I sought for even the tiniest piece,' he wailed. 'Forty wretched years, and all for nothing.'

'Piece of what?' said Klarm.

'Nihilium,' Flydd grated. 'The purest substance on Santhenar and the very fount of the Art. The tears of the node are made of it. Why would you betray me so, Muss?'

Muss looked up at him. 'Betray *you*? I embarked on this search before I ever heard your name.'

'You gave me your oath, to serve me truly and me alone.'

'And so I have, whenever it did not conflict with my prior purpose.'

'I begin to understand,' said Klarm. 'It was you, Muss, who tampered with the node-breaker after the Council gave it to Flydd. It had to be you, for I saw it, tested it and found it perfect, then sealed it under scrutator magic into its case. Those seals weren't broken until Flydd took the node-breaker into the tar pits of Snizort. No one else could have broken the magic that sealed that case, for no one else ever had charge of it. No one but you, Eiryn Muss, morphmancer or whoever you are.'

Flydd went purple in his wrath and Nish stepped hastily out of the line of fire.

'*You* deceitful, treacherous wretch,' Flydd raged, seizing Muss by the throat and shaking him like a rat. 'You stinking hypocrite. You changed the node-breaker so that it would destroy the node, and almost certainly the man who had been ordered to use it. Me, Muss!' He shook him again. 'You were happy for me to die as long as you achieved your goal, and you *dare* claim to have served me faithfully. Why, Muss, why?'

'To create the tears, of course,' said Irisis. 'Muss needed nihilium for some purpose of his own, and the only way he could gain any was to destroy a node in a particular manner. But you thought the tears would form at the node-breaker, didn't you, Muss? That's what you were searching for so desperately when we met you in Snizort, after the node exploded.'

'I created them,' said Muss insistently. 'The tears were mine.'

'But you couldn't find them,' said Nish, 'and by the time you realised that they'd been created at the node itself, they were gone. Flydd, Ullii and I saw my father take them, leaving no witnesses alive – at least, none that he was aware of. Father took the tears to the ruinous defeat at Gumby Marth and lost them to the lyrinx.'

'Jal-Nish was an alchymist,' mused Flydd, 'and the tears were an alchymist's dream. No substance holds the print of the Art more tightly.'

'Father practised with them every night,' said Nish, 'and his mastery grew apace, though not as quickly as his hubris. He led the army into the cul-de-sac of Gumby Marth to lure the lyrinx in after him, planning to boost his alchymical Art with the tears and crush the enemy utterly. Not for the sake of a mighty victory, just to gain a place on the Council of Scrutators.'

'And had he done so, with all that nihilium at his disposal,' said Flydd, 'not even Ghorr could have stood against him. Jal-Nish would soon have dominated the Council, and then suspended it to rule the world in his own name. But, unfortunately for him, his Art was not up to his ambition.'

'He was a minor mancer, no more,' said Klarm. 'And yet he very nearly succeeded.'

'He came up against a mighty opponent,' said Nish. 'The greatest mancer-lyrinx I've ever seen. And went within an ell of defeating him.'

'And that's why you went to Gumby Marth after the battle,' said Flydd to Muss. 'You came looking for the tears, but again you were too late. Jal-Nish was dead and the tears were in the hands of the enemy, beyond even your talents to find.'

'Ghorr boasted that he'd found them buried in the battlefield,' said Muss brokenly. 'He was cock-a-hoop about it.'

'I'll warrant he never showed them to anyone,' said Flydd.

'He never did. Though once, just before the fleet left to hunt you down, he displayed the sealed cases to the Council of Scrutators.'

'He was lying to bolster his shattered reputation,' said Flydd, unable to conceal his contempt. 'How did he survive so long?' He swung around to Muss. 'Tell me, Prober, how long have you secretly opposed me? You were accused even back at the manufactory, as I recall . . .'

'It was *you* all along!' Irisis almost lost control and took a step towards Muss. 'You sabotaged Tiaan's work and put the blame on me. You drugged her, then killed the poor stupid apothek to conceal it, and Nish and I were whipped to the bone for your crimes. We'll bear the scars until the day we die.'

'You weren't whipped just for that,' Flydd said mildly. 'You two weren't entirely blameless. Enough, Irisis. Leave him to me.'

Irisis dropped her fists and turned away into Nish's arms, tears running down her dirty face, and only then did he realise how deeply the whipping had cut into her soul. She'd pretended it didn't matter, and had even fought with her scarred back bare during one attack on the manufactory, exposing it to a thousand people. He should have known better. To have her beauty so marred had hurt her far more deeply than the whipping.

Flydd's face hardened. 'The only man who recognised you for what you were, Muss, was Foreman Gryste. He threw you into a cell, but no cell could hold a morphmancer. You used your Art to break out, concealed the pieces of platinum in his room that condemned him as corrupt, and fled.' His voice quavered. 'And I convicted poor unhappy Gryste on that tainted evidence. I was so sure he was the traitor that I refused to listen. I failed my own standards of justice and executed an innocent man.' Flydd was shaken. 'Why, Muss?'

'You were never going to give me what I was looking for. I had to have an aggressive, ambitious master, one who would do anything to become scrutator. Jal-Nish was the only candidate.'

'So you decided to undermine the manufactory to discredit and destroy me.'

'It wasn't personal,' said Muss. 'I liked and admired you, but you just wouldn't do.'

'I wondered how Jal-Nish always seemed to anticipate me,' said Flydd. 'You were spying on me and reporting to him.'

'You don't know what it's been like.'

'What *is* it like?' Flydd said savagely. 'Who are you really, Muss, apart from a liar, a murderer and a traitor?'

'I was a prentice mancer once, here at Nennifer, or rather, a mancer's prentice – a lesser creature entirely. I was young, handsome and clever, and I thought I had the whole world in front of me. Fool that I was, I didn't realise what my master really wanted me for. I meant nothing to him. I was no more than a living body to be used and discarded once his Art had ruined me. I wasn't the first – who knows how many boys and girls were brought to this place, to advance the scrutators' twisted Art.'

'He was trying to create a weapon of war from you?' guessed Irisis.

'A chimaera.' Muss nodded in her direction. 'You think of a chimaera as a phantom: a horrible, unreal creature of the imagination. But there's another, darker kind of chimaera: a creature made by blending the tissues of two distinct species into one.

'My master bound me to a drugged lyrinx and used one of the Great Spells, a spell of regeneration, to create a chimaera from us – a human with the strength and chameleon ability of a lyrinx. A bastard creature that could be bred like maggots, grown to adulthood in a decade and trained into an army powerful enough to take on our enemies on the battlefield.'

'But it didn't work,' said Flydd. 'It couldn't have.'

'I survived the transformation but I was no stronger than before, and wracked by pain. My blended tissues, seemingly integrated, were constantly at war with each other. My mind was outwardly human, inwardly a blend of human and lyrinx, and it could never be at peace. I didn't know whether I was human or lyrinx, but I understood that I was a beast and a monster. And the joke was not yet played out. The failed spell had reproduced neither the lyrinx's female organs of generation, nor my own male ones. It left me sexless, the worst cruelty of all, and made me useless to my master. He blamed me for the failure of his spell, mocked me for the monster I was, then had me knocked on the head and hurled out of Nennifer onto the kitchen middens for the swine to tear to pieces.'

Muss met their eyes, one by one, and continued.

'But I survived, for two qualities of the lyrinx I had in abundance. I could flesh-form far better than any lyrinx, for it was part Art and part innate ability, and I could do it to myself. It hurt brutally at first, but I persisted until I had gained enough mastery to assume any form roughly my own size, and use my

310

chameleon ability to mimic whatever external appearance I cared to. To survive inside Nennifer I had to become a morphmancer beyond compare, and I had to go back in. I couldn't live outside, nor cross the mountains alone.

'I killed a lowly prentice and took his place. I regretted the necessity but, after all, I'd saved the lad from a fate as bad as my own. And then I set out to learn everything I could about the spell that had so disastrously transformed me, in the hope that one day I might undo it. Years passed; a decade. In one guise, then another, I learned everything there was to be known about the regeneration spell. Even how to reverse it.'

'Why didn't you?' said Nish.

'It wasn't enough to just know how. Being a mancer only moderate talent, I needed great power, perfectly focussed, to work the smallest of charms, and on my own I could never hope to use any Great Spell. But then, by pure serendipity, I hit upon another way. If I could gain a small piece of nihilium, I could imprint the spell on it, then attempt to undo what had been done to me. But not even the Council of Scrutators possessed such a treasure. After years of spying I was unable to discover nihilium anywhere on Santhenar. I had, however, learned that it might be created if a node were destroyed in a particular way, by feeding power back into it.'

'Why didn't you do it yourself?' said Irisis.

'You privileged people think everything is easy,' he snapped. 'But fate distributes talents thinly, and seldom where they're most needed. I lacked the Art to control the destruction of a node, and no amount of hard work or self-belief could change that. I had to find a great and powerful patron to do it for me, but I feared the Council members too much to try and influence them. I had to leave Nennifer, but in the outside world there was only one position I was suited for. So I became a prober, a junior spy to Scrutator Xervish Flydd.'

'I wouldn't have thought . . .!' began Nish.

'I made a perfect spy, for in addition to my morphmancing talent, I was stoic, patient and painstaking. After all I'd been through, I had to be. Having two minds in one, as it were, I read

311

character very well. And being a chimaera, I find it easy to unravel what is hidden, confused, concealed or enciphered. To bolster that talent even further I made my eidoscope, to see the true forms of things, to make sense out of what is confused or hidden, and to find the true path through a maze.'

'But you weren't a fighter,' said Nish.

'Despite being part lyrinx I was physically weak, and my warring tissues magnified the least injury into a debilitating agony. I had to be careful to avoid conflict. My best defence was to hide.'

'Well, it's all over,' said Klarm. 'Tie him up, someone, then let's collect our wounded and go home. I've had enough of Nennifer.'

'You spent years spying on the scrutators,' Irisis said thoughtfully. 'What do you know about the Numinator, Muss?'

'Not here, you bloody fool!' snapped Flydd, quelling her with a glare of such ferocity that Irisis stepped backwards out of the way.

Eiryn Muss let out an inarticulate cry and skin-changed to the swirling patterns of the marble wall behind him. Within thirty seconds he was practically invisible. He cast a glance over his shoulder in the direction of the emerald throne and began to back away, his skin tones shifting to match whatever he passed in front of.

'What's going on?' Klarm seized Muss by the wrist and held him easily. 'What is this Numinator, Flydd? Are you telling me that there's a higher power?'

'Not here, Klarm,' Flydd said warningly.

'Why not?' Klarm's voice rose. 'Start out as you mean to go on, Flydd. No more secrets. After what we've gone through, we deserve an answer.'

'I'll tell you once we get back to the thapter,' said Flydd. 'It's not . . . safe.'

'Poppycock!' said Klarm. 'We're the only power left in this place.'

'And as the chief power, I say *not now*. If we don't collect our injured friends soon they'll freeze to death. I'm at the end of my

312

strength and we've got a lot of work yet to do.' He tapped the platinum box pointedly and trudged to the door.

Klarm didn't budge. 'Eiryn Muss, you're the perfect spy, and were spying long before you left this place to go into Flydd's service. There can't be any secret you didn't delve into in all your time here. Tell us about this mysterious Numinator.'

Muss wiped cold sweat off his brow with his free hand. He tried to shape-change but Klarm did not let go and, after several transformations, the prober reverted to his customary form.

'I don't think –' Muss broke off at the rumble of a distant collapse. The mirrored globe shuddered on its stand and the deformed reflections danced.

'Now!' Klarm snapped.

'I'd also like to know,' said Nish, feeling that he'd earned the right to defy Flydd this once. 'I heard . . .' Flydd had told him but he dared not say it, '. . . that the Council of Scrutators danced to the Numinator's tune. How can the most powerful people in the world be cowed by someone no one has ever seen?'

Muss licked lips so dry and fissured that they crackled.

'And be quick about it,' said Klarm. 'If I never see Nennifer again after today, it'll be too soon.'

'The Numinator created the Council of Scrutators in the first place,' said Muss.

'What?' cried Flydd, who was halfway through the door. He came back slowly, now showing his age and aftersickness with every dragging step.

'It was well over a hundred years ago . . .' said Muss. 'The Numinator – he or she, no one knows – took over the existing Council of Santhenar and shaped it to his own purposes . . .' another glance over his shoulder, '. . . only one of which was to win the war. The war wasn't going so badly then. The lyrinx were few and didn't threaten the whole world.'

'What were the other purposes?' said Klarm.

'Controlling the world was one. Rewriting the Histories, in particular the *Tale of the Mirror*, was another. A third was collecting information on every person: their ancestry, looks, family traits, habits and talents, and compiling the bloodline registers.'

'What for?' said Nish.

'No one knows,' said Muss. 'A copy of each register was placed in this room, and from here it vanished.' His head jerked up and he stared at the emerald throne as if expecting the dread personage of the Numinator to materialise there.

The emerald throne remained as it was. Muss was gazing up at something, unblinking, and his eyes widened perceptibly. He was looking at the mirrored globe.

Nish glanced at it and the little hairs stirred on his arms. The room and its contents were still reflected there, but none of the people were. He edged towards the door. 'As Flydd said, there's Tiaan, Malien and Yggur to be recovered, and little Inouye, if she's still alive. We can sort this out later.'

'I think so too,' said Flydd, who had come back into the room. 'Let's go, Klarm.'

At a faint humming sound, like a swarm of bees a long way away, Muss's mouth gaped open and his eyes bulged. With a convulsive jerk he tore free of Klarm's hand and bolted for the door.

'Don't let him get away!' yelled Klarm.

To the distant music of tubular bells the mirrored globe became as clear as glass, revealing a roiling sphere inside as bright and burning as the sun. A ray of light burst from it and fingered the surface of the table before creeping along to the eidoscope, which was still lying there. The lenses rotated of their own accord; a mass of coloured rays shot from the other end and touched Muss on the back.

Just inside the door, Muss gasped, turning slowly and with evident unwillingness, until he faced the eidoscope. The rays expanded to cover his entire body. His clothes faded and were revealed as flesh-formed protrusions of skin and tissue, mimicking the colour and texture of the real thing. They dissolved back into him and Muss stood naked and sexless, a neuter with the body of a human but the massive crested head and toothed maw of a lyrinx.

And then he shifted into two, the images superimposed. One was a weathered man of some sixty years, the other a small, aged female lyrinx. The images separated fractionally, blurred together again then sprang apart. The lyrinx image went into a crouch; the man turned as though to flee, but only managed a couple of steps before the other was on him, attacking him savagely, clawing and biting.

The two images merged, blurred and faded back into Muss, though the battle continued as his body went to war on itself. The skin of his chest bulged out as if pushed from inside. Wounds appeared without any seeming cause – three long tears across his belly like claw marks; a chunk out of one shoulder; a gouge on his lower thigh. A bulge moved down from his diaphragm, pushing his stomach out until the watchers could see the shape of his organs outlined against the stretched skin.

It moved up through his chest while he choked and gagged, then the skin burst at his throat and he was torn apart from the inside out. Muss fell into a bloody heap on the floor, the light from the eidoscope faded and the mirror became reflecting once more.

They looked at one another, their faces taut with horror.

'What was that?' said Irisis.

'The vengeance of the Numinator,' said Flydd. 'A mancer of surpassing power and, it appears, one who guards his privacy jealously.'

'But what –?' Irisis continued.

'Do you really want to ask that question here, after what we've just seen,' said Flydd.

'All things considered,' said Klarm, 'I think we should go now.' He was nearly knocked down in the rush for the door.

Outside and well away from the strongroom, they stopped to splint Nish's broken arm. Dawn had broken by the time they reached the place where they'd left the injured. Malien had recovered from her aftersickness and volunteered to go and bring back the thapter.

'Where's Yggur?' said Flydd.

'He recovered suddenly an hour ago and went off, saying he had business to attend to,' she said.

'You'd think this was a birthday party,' Flydd muttered. 'I suppose we'll have to drag him out from under the rubble. As if we don't have enough to do.'

Before he could organise a search team, Yggur came limping in, carrying Inouye in his arms.

'She had a panic attack when she was left in the cupboard,' he explained. 'I could sense her pain from down here.'

He passed her to Irisis, who hefted the slight burden in her arms. Inouye moaned and reached out for Yggur. He laid a hand on her brow, her eyes closed, and with a little sigh she settled into sleep.

'What about Tiaan?' said Nish relieved of his fears for Inouye.

'I locked her in that little room at the back,' said Malien. 'She wasn't rational and I didn't have the strength to deal with her.' She went out.

'Tiaan is in withdrawal,' Flydd said quietly. 'Artisans have sometimes gone mad from it. Leave her to Evee. We've got work to do. The survivors will be dead within days unless we take command.'

'We?' said Klarm.

'The scrutators were led by a chief with absolute authority, so we must replace him with a different kind of rule. A council –'

'They called *themselves* a council,' said Klarm. 'If we use the same name, people will think that nothing has changed.'

'If we change it, we'll spend years fighting usurpers and opportunists instead of the enemy. I propose that the new council's members be myself, Klarm, Malien, Yggur and –'

'I won't be part of any council,' said Yggur. 'And I suspect Malien won't either.'

'I'll do my best to persuade her when she gets back,' said Flydd. 'Have the guards taken Fusshte?'

'Unfortunately he got away in an air-dreadnought,' said Yggur, 'along with Scrutator Halie and more than a hundred soldiers.'

'He would have needed more than one air-dreadnought to carry them . . .' Flydd said slowly.

'Fusshte took them all, including the one moored out front. Seven, I believe.'

Flydd cursed loud and long. 'I should have cut him down while I had the chance. Why didn't I?'

'Because Muss seemed a greater threat,' said Nish.

'I suppose he'll head for Lybing,' said Klarm. 'To damage our victory in any way he can.'

'The truth will out,' said Flydd. 'We'd better get to work or there won't be any survivors.'

It proved a brutal day and a bitter night, as hard as any Nish had ever experienced. He laboured with the rest of them, as best he could with a broken arm, and was still working when the thapter finally appeared overhead around the middle of the following day, towing the dirigible. They'd rounded up more than four thousand survivors, organised them to construct flimsy shelters inside the walls of the air-dreadnought yard and recovered enough rations to feed them, and firewood to keep them warm, for the next few weeks. Only then was Nish able to lie down on a deck made of loose planks with hundreds of other people, as close to a fire as he could get, and snatch a few hours of glorious sleep.

He'd just woken, late that afternoon, when Irisis, who was looking up at the sky, said, 'I think that's an air-dreadnought coming in.'

'Who can it be?' Flydd said. 'Flangers, bring a detail armed with javelards, on the double.'

They hurried around to what remained of the parade ground, for the air-dreadnought was coming down in a rush.

'Looks like it's been through a storm,' said Irisis. 'The rigging is all tangled and one of the airbags has been torn open.'

'I can't see anyone but the pilot,' said Nish.

'It may be a trick. It'd be just like Fusshte.'

'Pilot looks half-dead,' said Inouye, who had limped after them. She shouldn't have been walking at all, but her professional curiosity had been aroused. 'She's going to crash.'

Nish thought so too. The air-dreadnought swept in upon a strong wind, trying to land on the narrow strip of parade ground that remained at the southern end, but the wind swept it sideways. For a moment it looked as though the craft would come down on the precipice and tumble into the Desolation Sink, but the pilot corrected in time and the great craft lumbered towards the collapsed front of Nennifer.

Nish held his breath but she managed to turn it and the keel slammed into the ground with just ells to spare. The pilot didn't get out. She had collapsed at her controller arm.

'It's the air-dreadnought that was shaken free in the earth tremblers,' said Irisis. 'The pilot must have been asleep on board at the time. It looks like it was blown halfway across the mountains before she could turn it.'

'Then she's the greatest pilot I've ever come across,' said Klarm, 'to bring that wreckage back without a crew, and no rest in a day and a half.'

'Flangers, gather a work gang and get it tied down,' Flydd shouted, hobbling towards the craft.

He lifted the collapsed pilot out and kissed her on the cheeks, left and right, to her bemusement. 'Thank you, pilot. You'll make a big difference. Nish, run and find the air-dreadnought artificers. I want this craft repaired by midnight, ready to fly east with as many of the survivors as we can cram into it. We won't beat Fusshte to Lybing with the news, but we'll spread it north and south as far as we can. His lies won't stand up in the face of so many witnesses. And see what other craft were being built, and get them finished. There are a lot of people to be moved and little time.

'Klarm, would you find all the pilots here who still have their controllers? I'll round up the surviving chroniclers, artists and tale-tellers. There's a new order in the world and we've got to get the word out right away.'

'And as soon as we're beyond the corrupted influence of the Nennifer node,' said Yggur, 'we must join forces to drive this baleful amplimet back to the state from which it woke.'

'We have the amplimet and we have Tiaan,' said Flydd. 'And the Council has been overthrown. Now the long fight-back can begin.'

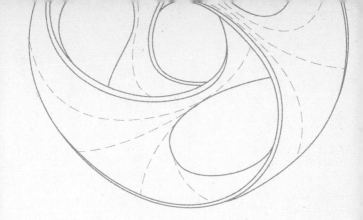

PART THREE

FARSPEAKER

THIRTY-FOUR

Irisis was surprised at how smoothly the transition had gone. The occupants of Nennifer were so cowed by the long rule of Ghorr's council, and Fusshte's brief reign of terror, that they accepted the orders of the new council unquestioningly. Flydd and Klarm were well known to them as hard, uncompromising men, but fair ones.

The air-dreadnought was sent east to Fadd, the closest city to Nennifer. It carried three pilots so as to travel non-stop, and a contingent of artists and tale-tellers whose task it was to broadcast news of the fall of the old Council, and the succession of the new one, all along the rugged east coast from Einunar to tropical Taranta. Flydd sent a guard with them, and plenty of the Council's gold to buy their passages. With fast ships and the wind behind them, the whole of the populous and wealthy east coast could be alerted in a few weeks.

Nish spent his days helping to retrieve survivors and supplies from the rubble. He wasn't much use with a broken arm but working was better than sitting around in the cold. It was freezing, dirty and ultimately thankless work, for after the second day they uncovered only dead. He saw little of Flydd and Klarm, who had gone back into Nennifer time and again, recovering what they could of the old Council's most precious devices and secrets, and destroying the rest. A large number of crates were

321

loaded into the thapter and dirigible, which were guarded night and day.

Irisis was frantically busy, digging with teams of labourers into the workshops and storerooms to recover air-floater controllers, floater-gas generators and all manner of other crystals, devices and tools that would be needed for the fight-back.

About a week after Fusshte fled, they'd done all they could do. Flydd climbed onto a platform built from firewood to address the multitude in the rear yard.

'The air-dreadnought is expected back from Fadd at any time,' he told the four thousand survivors, who were still camped around their meagre fires. They'd recovered plenty of firewood but it would have to last for months. 'It will begin ferrying you to Fadd, the closest place we can send you, but it's going to take a long time. Even if we can pack one hundred into the air-dreadnought, it'll take forty trips to carry everyone to safety, and the evacuation won't be completed until next summer. In the meantime you must organise yourselves for survival, for we have to get on with the war.

'There's enough water in the cisterns, but you'll have to dig out the storerooms to feed yourselves until supplies can be ferried back.' Flydd looked up, searching for the source of a faint whirring. 'That'll be the air-dreadnought now.'

He stepped down. The refugees were already streaming out towards the broken parade ground on the other side of Nennifer. Flydd headed around the left-hand side, which was longer but would be quicker.

'Laden with fresh fruit and vegetables, I hope,' Nish said quietly to Irisis. They had been managing on hard tack for so long that eating dinner was like gnawing on a saddle.

'They need it worse than we do,' said Flydd. 'You'll have to wait till we get home.'

'It's funny to think of Fiz Gorgo as home,' said Irisis. 'Though I suppose it is.'

As they reached the front of Nennifer, the air-dreadnought, which had been slowly descending on its path to the parade ground, used the wind to turn sharply.

322

'That was an odd manoeuvre,' said Nish. 'The pilot must be exhausted . . .'

Fire arced across the sky and disappeared over the lip of the Desolation Sink. No one reacted for a moment, then Flangers shouted, 'That was a fire spear from a javelard. We're being attacked!'

Three air-dreadnoughts broke out of the cloud where they'd been lurking. The one that had been landing was so close that Irisis could see the pilot's terrified face. It turned away but half a dozen fiery spears struck its airbags and all five exploded in a stupendous conflagration. The boom echoed back and forth.

For a moment she thought the occupants might have a chance, the craft being so low, but it fell like a stone onto the fractured edge of the parade ground, broke in two and both pieces dropped into the Desolation Sink.

'Like shooting a bird in a cage,' gasped Klarm, who had pounded around the other side of the ruined fortress.

They stood together, wondering what was going to happen now. The three air-dreadnoughts put their noses down and raced for the rear of Nennifer. 'It's Fusshte!' said Irisis. 'He's come for the thapter.'

'If the refugees switch allegiance again, we're done for,' cried Flydd. 'Why, why wasn't I ready for this?' He set off in his awkward stagger that covered the ground deceptively quickly.

'You weren't to know that Fusshte would come back,' said Irisis, running beside him.

'There was a skeet missing from its cage the other day,' panted Klarm, who was having trouble keeping up.

'And you didn't think to mention it?' cried Flydd.

'I thought someone had eaten it.'

'A spy must have been keeping Fusshte informed,' said Flydd. 'Once he realised I wasn't going to use the amplimet he got his courage back. I should have cut him down like the vermin he is.'

He turned as he ran and Irisis saw a fury in his eyes that was close to insanity.

'Where's Malien?' panted Yggur, limping up to join them.

'I haven't seen her all morning,' Irisis called over her shoulder.

Flydd swore a ghastly oath. 'We're going to lose the thapter.'

They turned the rear corner of Nennifer and the first air-dreadnought was just a hundred spans from the ground. Its sides were lined with soldiers, all with crossbows at their shoulders. Javelard operators at front and rear were sliding spears into position.

'Keep to the shadows,' said Flydd. 'They'll be watching for us.'

'They'll be hard pressed to pick us out of four thousand people,' said Nish.

'Care to bet your life on it?' Yggur grated. 'Fusshte won't take chances this time. Their orders will be to shoot us on sight.'

'Can't you spin an illusion around us?' said Irisis.

'Not on the run, out of nothing. I haven't got the tiniest crystal on me.'

The thapter had been left about three hundred spans away, in an alley between piled rows of timber recovered from the wreckage for firewood. It was covered by a tarpaulin and, since there were canvas shelters all over the place, Irisis hoped that it wouldn't attract the attackers' immediate attention.

She edged through the heaps of rubble at the back of Nennifer. The air-dreadnought was hovering, its rotors roaring to keep it in place against the strong wind. A man at the bow – Fusshte himself, the stinking cur – had a speaking trumpet up to his mouth. Oh for a crossbow, Irisis thought, but hers was inside the thapter.

'Where is the traitor Flydd and his treacherous companions?' Fusshte shouted. 'Where is the flying construct? Point them out and you'll be well rewarded.'

'We're finished,' said Nish.

'Keep moving,' hissed Flydd. 'They don't know where we are.'

They crept on. The low sun cast deep shadows behind the standing remnants of Nennifer and they took advantage of the cover to get closer.

'Speak!' roared Fusshte, 'or I'll shoot you down like the treasonous dogs you are.'

Evidently no one had betrayed them, for Fusshte turned to his archers, pointing down inside the walls of the air-dreadnought

324

yard. Judging by the collective roar, they'd fired into the crowd. Fusshte's signalmen exchanged signals with the other two air-dreadnoughts, hovering above, and they separated. One headed around the far side of Nennifer, the other over the rubble in their general direction. Someone had given away the location of the thapter.

'See how easy it is to do your duty,' Fusshte said.

'Run!' gasped Flydd.

Irisis put on a final burst, her long legs carrying her ahead. There wasn't far to go – just down to the far corner of the rubble wall and around to the left, into the firewood alley, then along it for fifty or sixty spans.

Her breasts were thumping up and down painfully. Had she been expecting action she would have bound them. She looked back for Nish, who was labouring along, red in the face, about thirty spans behind.

Irisis didn't wait, for the nearest air-dreadnought had suddenly altered course, the long airbags wobbling in their rigging as it tried to turn at right-angles. They had been spotted. The soldiers were lined up on the sides, crossbows at the ready. They weren't within range but the javelards probably were.

Thud-crash. A spear buried itself in the timber just behind her. She raced on, weaving from side to side, risking a quick glance over her shoulder. Javelards weren't accurate at that distance, but once within crossbow range the craft would turn side-on to fire a fusillade at them. They had a minute to get to safety.

Irisis turned the corner into the firewood alley and stopped in dismay. The canvas cover lay on the ground but the thapter was gone.

THIRTY-FIVE

'It's not there,' Irisis was saying as Nish rounded the corner.

'Malien must have seen them coming,' panted Yggur, who had turned grey, 'and gone looking for us in the thapter.'

'We'll be dead before she finds us,' said Nish.

Irisis was running back along the jumbled windrow of timber, trying to see over it, but it was too high.

'Keep going, to the other end of the alley,' gasped Flydd. 'She can't be far away.'

Nish set off again, with Irisis, but the brief respite had sapped his stamina. He hadn't run in a long time and every step felt leaden now. The middle of his back itched as if a javelard was lined up on it.

The leading air-dreadnought had completed its turn and was approaching rapidly. The one that had fired into the crowd was coming their way too. There was nowhere to hide.

'Malien!' Irisis screamed, though even if Malien were nearby, she wouldn't hear over the whine of the thapter. She stopped halfway up the alley where a gap in the heaped timber allowed access into the adjoining alley.

'No point running any more,' Irisis gasped.

Nish edged into the gap, which provided some shelter from the attack, and watched the two craft moving in. 'Malien wouldn't go looking for us,' he said. 'She wouldn't know where to look.'

'She wouldn't stay and risk losing the thapter,' said Yggur.

'I never thought she'd abandon us,' said Irisis.

'She hasn't,' said Nish more confidently than he felt. 'And she wouldn't leave Tiaan either, after all the time they've spent together. That's probably where she's gone, to get Tiaan.'

'She'd better make it snappy,' said Flydd.

The first air-dreadnought was now inching into a turn against the strong wind, getting ready to fire a crossbow broadside that would cut them to pieces.

'Can't you blast them out of the sky?' cried Nish. 'Yggur? Flydd? Klarm?'

'If we had that kind of power we would have used it at Fiz Gorgo,' said Yggur. 'There's nothing we can do to air-dreadnoughts from this distance.'

'Through here into the next alley,' said Nish, pointing with his splinted arm. 'It'll buy us a minute.'

They scurried through the gap into the next alley. 'Spread out and keep low,' said Nish, 'and press right up against the timber. They're having trouble staying steady in the wind. Make their shots as difficult as you can.'

'What's that?' hissed Irisis, cupping her ear.

'I can't hear anything,' said Nish. With the whistling wind, the clatter of rotors and the cries of refugees, it was a wonder that anyone could.

'It's the thapter coming back,' said Irisis.

'Which way?' snapped Flydd.

'I can't tell,' Irisis wailed.

'They'll cut us down before we can get to it,' said Flydd.

Without a word, Flangers leapt to his feet and scrambled up the timber pile.

'What does the bloody fool think he's doing?' said Flydd. 'They'll shoot him –'

It was the atonement Flangers had been searching for ever since he'd shot down Klarm's air-floater at Snizort. 'No, Flangers,' Irisis screamed. 'Get down!'

'I see it,' Flangers shouted. 'Three alleys across. Malien!' He roared out her name, leaping in the air and waving his arms. 'She's –'

The impact of several crossbow bolts threw him onto his back. Irisis cried out and covered her face. Nish pulled her in under the tangle of timber. The others had taken what shelter they could. Bolts thudded into the firewood all around them and whined off the paving stones. A javelard spear smashed into a beam above his head, snapping it in half.

'That's the broadside,' said Nish, looking up. 'We've got about thirty seconds until they reload. Come on – through to the next alley.'

They ran through the gap, emerging just as the thapter appeared at the other end. The mechanism shrilled as it shot towards them, stopped, and the hatch sprang open. They scrambled up the ladder.

Nish was coming up, one-handed, when he realised that Irisis wasn't behind him. Had she been shot as well? He leapt down, looking around frantically. She was staggering down off the pile with a limp and bloody Flangers over her shoulder.

'You imbecile!' Nish wept. 'He's dead. Leave him.' Both air-dreadnoughts were turning into position, carefully maintaining a safe distance from each other in the wind, which was pushing them to the east. He threw himself up the ladder. 'Malien? Have you a crossbow?'

She handed it out to him, carefully, for it was already loaded and cocked. Irisis wouldn't make it before the archers were ready to fire. Nish hooked a leg inside the hatch to brace himself, steadied the bow with his splinted arm and aimed, trying to do deliberately what he'd once done by accident.

He fired at the left-hand rotor of the upwind air-dreadnought. It was more than a span across and at this distance he could hardly miss, though that wasn't what bothered him. His worry was that the bolt would pass straight between the blades of the rapidly spinning rotor and out the other side.

Fortunately it did not. It struck one of the wooden blades,

which shattered, and the unbalanced rotor immediately tore itself to pieces. With the other rotor going full bore the air-dreadnought slewed around, caught the wind and drifted towards the downwind machine. Its pilot turned as hard as she could, the outer airbags touched but unfortunately did not tangle, and it raced out of the way, downwind.

The damaged craft was full-on now, and the soldiers might have fired their broadside, had they not fled from the near colli-sion. By the time their officers had cursed them back to the rails the craft had been carried out of range.

Nish climbed down, keeping a wary eye on the third air-dreadnought, now racing their way. He assisted Irisis up the ladder as best he could and Yggur helped her to carry Flangers below. Nish clambered in last.

Malien lifted the thapter off and curved away from their pursuer, raising an eyebrow at Flydd. 'To Fiz Gorgo?'

'Not while Fusshte is alive,' he said grimly.

'I don't see what we can do about him.'

'Just circle round while I think. Make the thapter go eratic-ally, as if there's something wrong with it. Nish, get ready with the crossbow.'

Malien shrugged and did as Flydd had asked. The damaged air-dreadnought rotored away, then dropped grapnels onto the far wall of the yard, holding the machine in place while the crew tried to make running repairs. The other two air-dreadnoughts were circling, keeping their distance for the moment, watching the thapter.

'Which one is Fusshte's?' said Flydd, holding himself rigidly upright. His eyes glittered and a muscle was twitching at the corner of his mouth.

'The one on the left,' Nish said carefully, realising that Flydd was so angry he was barely in control. He wound the crossbow awkwardly.

'Are you sure?'

'I can see him standing at the bow.'

'Would you go closer, Malien?' said Flydd.

'The thapter isn't invulnerable,' she said. 'A heavy javelard spear, fired from close range, could smash right through the mechanisms.'

'I know!' he snapped, 'but we've got to finish the old Council, utterly and forever. Go closer.'

She circled around Fusshte's air-dreadnought. He stood boldly at the rail, watching them with a contemptuous sneer. Fusshte knew Malien wouldn't dare come close enough to shoot him and, armed only with a crossbow, they couldn't do appreciable damage even if they fired into an airbag. The huge floater-gas generators would make up any loss from a tiny hole in the fabric of one of its five airbags.

Malien circled again. Fusshte gave orders to his signaller, who began to wave a series of flags. The two air-dreadnoughts turned in the thapter's direction, approaching from either side. The javelard operators readied their weapons; the archers raised their bows. The third machine had rigged a canvas rudder behind its remaining rotor, and now it cast off its grapnels and came at them from a third quarter.

Malien began to turn away.

'Stay!' snapped Flydd.

'They'll shoot us down,' said Malien, giving him an imperious Aachim stare.

'Stay, damn you,' said Flydd.

She ignored him. 'When I'm in command I take orders from no man.'

Flydd jerked his hand out of the pocket of his cloak, thrust it in Malien's face, and snapped. A glass phial burst in his hand with a white spray of light and an acrid stench that burned Nish's nose for a moment.

When his eyes had recovered, Malien was sagging at the controller, barely able to stand, and the thapter was zigzagging across the sky.

'Surr!' Nish cried in horror. 'What are you –?

Flydd thrust him out of the way and slammed his hand down on Malien's right hand before it slipped off the controller. He jerked it over so hard that the thapter turned on its side.

Malien slammed into the wall, eyes closed. She reached up blindly with her free hand, caught the rail and tried to pull herself up. 'Nish, stop him before he kills us all.'

What was he supposed to do? Nish wasn't going to attack the scrutator. He uncocked the crossbow and dropped it behind him so there could be no misunderstanding, then stepped towards Flydd, uncertainly. 'Surr,' he said.

'Get out of the way, Nish,' snarled Flydd. 'I should have done this the first time and no one is going to stop me.' The thapter's mechanism spun up to a roar and it shot forwards.

'Nish!' Malien said frantically. 'Stop him. He's gone mad.'

Nish reached for Flydd, but Flydd kicked sideways, striking him in the knee. Nish went down, but managed to catch Flydd's foot and tried to pull him down as well.

Flydd fought him off. His teeth were bared in a savage grimace; he was like a man possessed. He kneed Nish out of the way, pinned Malien's other hand, turned the thapter and roared straight at Fusshte's air-dreadnought.

'What are you doing?' cried Nish, sure that Flydd had gone out of his mind.

Flydd didn't answer. There came a clamour of voices from the lower hatch and Irisis came running up the ladder, but Nish couldn't tear himself away from the sight in front of him. They were approaching the stern of the air-dreadnought at frightening speed. Flydd was flying directly at Scrutator Fusshte and he wasn't going to stop.

Fusshte realised it and a spasm of terror crossed his face. For Nish it was almost worth it, to see Fusshte turn and run, then understand that there was nowhere to run.

One or two bolts struck the thapter though most of the archers couldn't shoot for fear of hitting the huge rotors. The thapter hurtled towards the air-dreadnought. Fusshte glanced over his shoulder; Nish saw the whites of his eyes and, caught up in the madness of the moment, felt a surge of savage glee. The thapter wiggled at the last second and shot past the rotors, its slipstream making them flutter. Flydd twitched his hand and the machine struck the side of the air-dreadnought, knocking it

331

sideways in a hail of shattered timbers and shredded ropes and canvas. The archers were thrown off their feet; three went over the side.

Flydd moved the controller again and the thapter smashed into the bow of the air-dreadnought, tearing part of it off and sending more of Fusshte's troops plunging to their deaths. The thapter turned so sharply that Nish was crushed against the side. He got to his feet in time to see Fusshte dive into the central cabin.

Flydd, teeth bared in a maniacal rictus, turned the thapter directly towards the cabin. More bolts hit its front and a javelard spear screamed off the rim of the open top hatch. There wasn't time to reach up and pull it over. Flydd didn't even flinch.

Nish did, as Flydd drove the thapter straight into the air-dreadnought, amidships, smashing its flimsy timbers. A length of canvas wrapped itself around the front of the thapter, cracking in the wind as it shot out the other side. Nish couldn't see anything out the front. Neither could Flydd, though it didn't seem to bother him.

Nish climbed up onto the side and looked back. The air-dreadnought had broken in half, its two hull sections swinging wildly from the tangled rigging of the five airbags and spilling the remaining crew down into the walled yard.

Flydd shook the thapter from side to side until the canvas tore away, then turned again. 'Where is he?' he grated. 'Did you see him fall?'

'No,' Nish said quietly, not wanting to assist Flydd in this madness. Malien's eyes were open but she wasn't resisting him either. Irisis stood at the back of the cockpit, saying nothing at all.

Flydd tore through the wrecked craft again and again, after each impact standing off and searching the floating remains for his enemy.

'He's dead,' said Nish. 'He must have fallen long ago. You can stop now, surr.'

'If he was I'd know it,' said Flydd. 'He's still – ahhhhh!' he sighed.

332

Nish saw it too. The air-dreadnought had been reduced to a tangle of rigging, two deflated air-bags and one that was still full of floater-gas. It was drifting across the yard towards the rear of Nennifer, with a dark-clad, meagre man clinging desperately to the ropes below the airbag.

Flydd brought the thapter up beside the rigging, matched its motion and stood on tiptoe to look over the side. Fusshte, battered and bleeding from mouth and nose, stared defiantly back at him. His feet rested in a tangle of loops and knots. One arm was twisted through the rigging, the other hand resting on a rope.

'Surrender?' said Flydd.

'To be tried by you?' spat Fusshte. 'I'll die first.'

'Either way,' said Flydd. The madness had passed, leaving him worn out and wasted.

'But surr . . .' said Nish, troubled in spite of his loathing for Fusshte.

'He has to die,' said Flydd. 'While any of the old Council remain alive, the foolish and greedy will rally to them, and we'll be fighting them instead of the enemy. Let's put an end to it.'

Fusshte looked as though he was going to beg for his life, but steeled himself and nodded. 'Would you grant me a dead-man's boon?'

'You mocked my agony as my manhood was cut away. I'll grant you nothing but a quick end.'

Fusshte's grotesque face crumbled. 'Aaah!' he wailed. 'It's not for me. It's for my crippled mother . . .' He reached out one hand in entreaty. 'Once I'm dead, she'll starve.'

'Begging doesn't become you, Fusshte,' said Flydd.

'Surr,' said Nish, thinking of his own mother, whom he hadn't seen in years. 'Surely you can –'

'What do you want, Fusshte?' Flydd snapped.

Fusshte reached into his coat and held up a small object, like a jewelled bird's egg. 'It's all I have now. Would you sell it and give her the coin?'

Flydd nodded stiffly and held out his hand. Fusshte sent the egg spinning across. Nish caught it and was about to hand it to Flydd when Irisis sprang up and batted it over the side.

333

'What did you do that for?' cried Nish.

As he finished speaking the egg burst asunder, peppering the base of the thapter with glassy shards that would have torn straight through their living flesh.

Without a word, Flydd spun the thapter around, curved away then drove it straight at the centre of the full airbag. Fusshte was begging, pleading, weeping, but nothing could save him this time.

Irisis pulled Nish down into the corner, pressed his face against her chest and bent her own head over his. There was an enormous bang and a flare of blue flame. He felt his hair crisping, his ears and the back of his neck burning. Irisis pulled him harder against her and then they were through it and out the other side. He smelt burnt hair, opened his eyes and Flydd was standing up at the controller, as bald as an egg. Every hair had been burnt from his head.

He turned and even his continuous eyebrow was gone. 'It's done.' He released the controller to Malien and slumped to the floor. 'It's done at last.'

Nish looked over the side and saw Fusshte's remains hit the ground. There was no movement but the people on the ground swarmed over the corpse and didn't let up until there was nothing left of it. The other two air-dreadnoughts were hovering now, and the soldiers had their hands up. Nish signalled them to go down.

'How did you know, Irisis?' he said.

'I didn't. I just knew that Fusshte could *never* be trusted.' She helped Flydd up. 'You'd better say something to the crowd before we go.'

Blisters were rising on his cheeks and the top of his head, but the haggardness had gone from his face. Flydd had been relieved of his greatest burden. Still on his knees he turned to Malien, bowing so low that his forehead touched the floor.

'I apologise most abjectly,' he said. 'I lost control.'

'Never ask anything of me again,' she said, so cold that Nish couldn't look at her, 'for I will not grant it. I've suffered enough from men like you for more than one lifetime.'

334

She set the thapter down next to the dirigible, which was packed with all sorts of gear recovered from Nennifer. Inouye went aboard and made it ready for flight. Nish fastened its tether, then Malien took the thapter over the yard and Flydd stood up on the rear platform. The people were spread around the walls of the enormous yard, apart from the few on their knees beside the bodies of those slain in Fusshte's initial attack.

'The old Council has finally been extinguished,' he said, not loudly but in a carrying voice. 'And the new one must fly to fight the enemy. These two air-dreadnoughts are yours – use them to ferry everyone to safety, then prepare to fight with us again, until Santhenar is free.'

He raised one fist. Every individual in the crowd raised their own with a great roar of acclamation.

'Take us home,' said Flydd and, with a nod to Malien, went below.

THIRTY-SIX

Flangers was still clinging to life, though only because of Healer Evee's Arts, when Nish and Irisis came down the ladder.

'How is he?' Nish said.

'He may live,' said Yggur, 'though with two bolts through the ribs and one that's smashed his thighbone, I doubt if he'll walk again, much less fight.'

'You stupid, brave fool,' Irisis said several hours later as Flangers came round after the bolts had been removed and the bone set.

'I had to atone for my crime,' said Flangers. 'You knew that.'

'And have you finished atoning?' she said gently. 'Or can we expect more such follies next time?'

'I laid down my life, and it wasn't taken. Only a fool would do it twice.' He closed his eyes and slept.

'You can't talk!' Nish accused her. 'Going after him was the stupidest thing I've ever seen.'

'The line has to be drawn, Nish,' said Irisis. 'In this bloody war I've done a hundred things I've regretted, and I expect I'll do more before the war takes me. But I won't turn my back on my friends ever again. That's all there is to it.'

She must have been thinking of Inouye. 'Flangers should have been dead, with three bolts in him.'

'But he wasn't.' Irisis leaned against him and closed her eyes.

Nish was exhausted but his mind was too busy for sleep. He looked around. Tiaan was sitting in the corner, staring fixedly at him. She looked angry, lost and desolate in equal parts. Did she hold him to blame? Perhaps she did – he'd robbed her of the amplimet she'd striven so desperately to regain.

He had avoided her since, thinking that his presence could only make things worse. Tiaan had been in good hands. Malien had taken charge of her, bathing and delousing her and spending long days and nights talking to her, working to bring her out of her withdrawal psychosis. It seemed to have worked. Tiaan had been almost her normal reserved self by the time the air-dreadnought returned from Fadd. Nish had seen her laughing and joking with Malien, and once even with Yggur, though whenever Tiaan's eye fell on Irisis or Nish he knew that she'd forgotten nothing and forgiven even less.

Nish looked away with a mental shrug. What did it matter? They didn't need to work together.

Malien was so angry that she kept flying all night, only setting down at dawn for a brief rest stop before heading on. Her fury began to wear off during the day and at sunset she set the thapter down on a slaty hilltop in an unknown land. Flangers was out of danger and sleeping, so they left him inside with Evee and Inouye.

'Let's talk about the war,' said Flydd at the campfire that night.

'I've been putting together a plan,' said Yggur.

'So have I,' said Flydd. 'But let's hear yours first.'

Nish was a little surprised at Yggur's forthrightness. When they'd first come to Fiz Gorgo, about six months ago, he'd professed little interest in the war. But of course, the Histories told that Yggur had been a great warlord once.

'Humanity is still strong, but its people, manufactories and armies are scattered across thousands of leagues and can't easily be coordinated. But if they *could* be, we'd be a formidable force and many of the lyrinx's advantages would evaporate.'

'Intelligence and communication are the keys to victory,' said Flydd. 'To win we have to beat the enemy at both.'

'The lyrinx avoid war during the winter mating season, and immediately after it,' said Klarm. 'So we have till early spring to prepare ourselves for the final phase of the war – just over three months.'

'And in that time,' said Yggur, 'we must do a number of things. First, we must draw together all our allies, near and far.'

'It would take a month to contact them all by skeet,' said Klarm, 'assuming we had enough skeets. And another month before the replies all came in.'

'With the thapter we can visit them all in weeks . . .' said Flydd. He gave Malien an abashed glance, which she did not acknowledge.

'But the next time you want to consult them it'll take just as long,' Yggur said reasonably.

'And the time after,' Klarm chimed in. 'You can't be tied up as a messenger boy, Flydd. And if something goes wrong with the thapter, or we lose it, or it's needed elsewhere –'

'We must have more of them,' said Yggur, 'which is my second point. We'll come back to the first. Are you prepared to share the secret of making thapters with us, Malien?'

After a brief hesitation she said, 'With some disquiet.'

Yggur bowed his head. 'Thank you. That raises another problem, of course. We can't build thapters, or any kind of flying machine more complex than an air-floater, at Fiz Gorgo. We'd need an entire manufactory for that and it would still take years to construct one.'

'Then the second problem is as insoluble as the first,' said Klarm. He drained his goblet, which had been half full of a fine wine from the Council's cellars. One of his crates had contained several small barrels. Klarm lived life to the fullest. 'Why go back to Fiz Gorgo anyhow? Why not Lybing, for instance?' Klarm had been the provincial scrutator for Lybing before his leg injury.

'Lybing doesn't have manufactories either,' said Yggur.

'But it does have skilled workers.'

'We can bring skilled workers from anywhere,' said Flydd. 'In Fiz Gorgo we have an establishment and complete control.'

'If you're going to take on the role of head of the Council,' said Klarm, 'you need to be seen. Otherwise the generals and governors will seize the chance to intrigue against you. You've got to show them you're just as tough as Ghorr.'

'In Lybing I'd be pestered constantly by people wanting favours,' said Flydd, 'and I've no time for it. There's a war to win.'

'Don't say I didn't warn you,' said Klarm. He sighed, presumably for the fleshly delights of civilised Lybing. 'Pass the barrel, Flydd. This is thirsty work.'

Flydd rolled it across.

Yggur scowled. He didn't like indulgence, in any form. 'Some months ago we recovered parts of a construct abandoned at Snizort, including its flight controller. With Malien's advice, we ought to be able to make the controllers needed to turn constructs into thapters.'

'Why didn't I think of that?' said Flydd. 'You'll take charge of that work, Irisis, and Tiaan can help you. If you require more artisans, we'll press them from a manufactory.'

'And the moment the flight controllers are ready,' said Yggur, 'we'll fly to the battlefield at Snizort, put them in the best of the abandoned constructs and fly them back.'

'But the node exploded,' said Irisis. 'There's not enough field at Snizort to flutter a handkerchief.'

'Leave that to me,' said Yggur. 'I dare say I can think of a way.'

She regarded him dubiously. 'How many controllers will you need?'

'As many as twenty, certainly,' said Yggur. 'More, if you can make them in time. We'll need as many thapters as can be made to fly.'

'So you'll need to take a small army to Snizort,' said Klarm. 'And dozens of trained pilots, though I don't see how you're going to train them.'

'And we'll need a means of getting them there,' said Yggur, standing up and circling the fire before sitting down again. 'The plan is coming together. First we must train artificers to fix those constructs that aren't too badly damaged, and pilots to fly them. That's going to take a long time. Meanwhile, we'll need enough air-floaters to carry everyone to Snizort. Cryl-Nish, you will command this operation.'

'I don't see how it can be done in time,' said Nish.

'You'll have to find a way – we've got to have the thapters before spring.'

'It takes time to train people.'

'It has to be done, Nish, and you've got to do it.'

Nish gritted his teeth. 'If I had a year and a hundred people I couldn't do it all,' he muttered. 'I can't just wave a magic wand like some people. I have to do *real* work.' Irisis squeezed his arm, warningly. Yggur was glaring down his long nose at him. Nish buried his face in his goblet.

'That's only the first stage,' Yggur said coldly, 'but everything else relies on it. Coming back to my first point, of finding a way to talk to our distant allies and our scattered forces, there's *this*.'

Yggur withdrew a glass globe, the size of a grapefruit, from a leather case at his side. He held it up. 'Some of you may have seen it before. Fusshte stole it from Fiz Gorgo and it was the first treasure I went looking for in Nennifer. It's one of the few surviving farspeaker globes of Golias the Mad.' Flydd cleared his throat. Yggur continued. 'Or if not, it's closely based on his original. It doesn't work, unfortunately. The secret was lost with Golias's death.'

He glanced briefly at Nish. 'I plan to rediscover Golias's secret and, once I have, our skilled artisans will craft as many globes as we need. You may give one to each of our allies, Flydd. Such a gift, and the hope of greater ones, will do more to unite us than all the former Council's threats and punishments.'

'Many have sought Golias's secret,' said Flydd, 'but none have succeeded.'

'But they worked as individuals for their own greed or glory, sharing neither their discoveries nor their failures. For us, it's our very survival. And around this campfire, Flydd, are people whose grasp of the Art is as great as any who have ever lived.'

'I thought you said *you* were going to do it,' Flydd said.

'It's my task,' said Yggur, 'but I plan to call upon everyone here. Everyone with a talent for the Art, I mean. We now have the greatest secrets and Arts of the Council, and they'd made many breakthroughs the world was never told about. If we can work as a team, and we must, together we will be greater than the greatest individual. We must crack Golias's globe. We cannot win the war without it; not even with a hundred thapters.'

'The Council didn't believe the war could be won at all,' said Klarm.

'I do,' said Flydd. 'Is that your entire plan, Yggur? You haven't given me much to do. Or Malien. Or Klarm, for that matter.'

'Klarm will be poring over the Council's Arts and devices. Malien . . . can speak for herself.'

'I expect I'll be at the controls of the thapter most of the time,' said Malien.

'You're the head of the new council, Flydd. You must lead our embassy-at-large,' Yggur went on, 'since you know everyone in the east. While the air-floaters and thapter controllers are being built, and their pilots and artificers trained, you'll need to fly east and north to rally our allies.' Yggur looked around the fire. 'That's my plan.'

'It's a good start,' said Flydd, 'but we must also plan the second stage. The lyrinx have had it far too easy in the past. They've attacked and we've defended; and *lost*. The Council's response has always been predictable, so we've got to be unpredictable. I want to mount a surprise attack on the enemy in early spring, before they're ready to fight. I want to shock them; to make them worry about what we'll do next and how strong we really are.'

'Good idea. Incidentally,' Yggur said casually, 'Tiaan, I believe you attempted to map fields from the air, in the east.'

Tiaan, who was staring blankly at the fire, came out of her introspection with a start. 'I – I spent a long time at it, surr. I've mapped the fields north and south from Stassor for a hundred and forty leagues, east to the sea and west for another eighty leagues – perhaps a tenth of Lauralin. My map is still in the thapter, if you'd care to see it.'

Yggur gaped. 'You're making a fool of me, surely?'

'I never joke about my work, surr.' She went into the darkness with her head high, returning a few minutes later with a rolled map drawn on coated linen.

Tiaan unrolled it on the rough ground and weighted the ends with rocks. A chart of north-eastern Lauralin, it extended from Guffeons in the north to Tiksi in the south, and as far west as the desert of Kalar. The mountains were drawn in relief and shaded pale grey. Overlaid were a series of black marks, with symbols beside them, each surrounded by coloured haloes of various shapes and sizes, some in single colours, others like rainbows.

'These represent the nodes,' said Yggur, touching one of the black shapes with a fingertip.

'Yes. There are 317 of them in the area of this map. Most, as far as I can tell, were not previously known.'

Yggur glanced at Flydd, whose astonishment was nearly as great as his own. 'But this is priceless! Why didn't we know about this?'

'You didn't ask.'

'And the symbols?' asked Flydd. 'The kind of node, presumably?'

'Yes,' Tiaan said faintly. She hated being the centre of attention. 'This symbol denotes a normal node, this a spiral node and this a double.'

'A double node?'

'It quite disturbed me, passing over it.'

'How did you manage such detail?' said Yggur.

'Oh, this is nothing. I have larger maps of many of the nodes, back in Fiz Gorgo, showing how they changed the various times I passed over them.'

'But –'

'I see each field as a coloured picture,' she said. 'And once seen, I can remember it forever. For example, this one,' she pointed to a dot in the Kalar Desert, 'I can show you how the field changes over a day and –'

'We can talk about the details at another time,' Yggur said. 'Tiaan, such maps may be vital to the war. *Will* be vital, I should say, especially if the lyrinx expand their attacks on nodes. Would you care to do more of it?'

'I want to map all the nodes in the world,' said Tiaan, her eyes glowing. 'I – I long to understand how the fields work. But . . . don't you want me to work on thapter controllers . . .?'

'This is more urgent. If Flydd agrees, I'd send you with him when he goes off on his embassies.'

'She'll have to come anyway,' said Flydd gracelessly. 'Flying the thapter is hard work and Malien can't do it all by herself.'

'Assuming I agree to take you,' said Malien quietly.

Yggur ignored the exchange. 'Tiaan, wherever Flydd goes, you shall go too, and map the fields of all the lands you pass over. Then, should the war resume sooner than we expect, at least we'll have maps to go by.'

'Thank you,' said Tiaan in a low voice, and turned back to her contemplation of the fire.

'I believe you're up to something,' Flydd muttered to Yggur.

'I'm thinking ahead,' Yggur replied. 'We make more use of the fields each day, as do Vithis's Aachim, and Malien's people in Stassor. Malien is worried that we're taking too much from them. We talked about it some time back. And the enemy uses fields far more than they did before. Now there's talk of nodes failing of their own accord, and nodes being drained dry by overuse. If it gets worse, whosoever knows the fields best will have the upper hand. That task is yours, Tiaan, and it's a vital one.'

Tiaan was so transformed by the responsibility Yggur had given her that she declined to fly the thapter when Malien offered her the amplimet. Irisis, who was in the cockpit at the time, saw the longing in Tiaan's eyes. She gazed at the softly glowing crystal for a moment, then edged it away with the back of her hand. 'You fly. I want to map.'

All the long hours that it took to get home, Tiaan sat with the relevant section of the map unrolled on her lap, making annotations on a pad in a tiny hand, and coloured markings on an overlay. Each night by the campfire she wrote up her notes and refined her master map.

Klarm was working just as hard. He sat in his corner of the

thapter, studying the sheaves of papers he'd taken from Nennifer and writing in a series of rice-paper books with different-coloured bindings. He worked by the campfire too, until dinner, after which he got roaringly drunk every night.

THIRTY-SEVEN

They returned to Fiz Gorgo twelve days after the beginning of winter, having been away for a little over three weeks, and for once it wasn't raining.

Fyn-Mah came running out before the thapter had set down. Irisis, who was sitting on the rear platform, smiled to see the perquisitor. Normally so austere and controlled, that small, dark-haired figure was staring up at them, fists clenched at her sides. Fyn-Mah didn't seem to take a breath until Flydd's head appeared, whereupon she bolted to the ladder. At the bottom she hesitated, no doubt remembering the hideous scene at their departure. She looked up at Flydd, and he down at her, and then she smiled and went up to him in a rush. Shortly afterwards they went inside, ignoring everyone else.

Fiz Gorgo was in very good order. Fyn-Mah had the walls manned day and night and the damage repaired, apart from the upper sections of the blasted towers. The larders were provisioned for the winter and squads of soldiers were carrying out drills on the other side of the yard.

Four days after their return, Yggur called everyone together to discuss new intelligence about the war. Irisis sat up the front, next to Nish. Yggur scanned all the faces, frowned and said to Flydd, 'Where's Klarm?'

'He's gone out in the air-floater.'

345

'What, *again*? Why wasn't I told? I suppose he's ransacking the cellars of ruined Garching this time, the sot.'

'Klarm has work to do, as do we all,' Flydd said pointedly. 'Shall we get on? Now winter has ended hostilities, we must urgently plan our spring offensive. Time is running away on us.'

'Since the lyrinx don't like to fight in winter,' said Irisis, 'surely it'd be a good time to retake the lands we've lost?' It was a question she'd often wondered about.

'It's too wet and cold,' said Flydd. 'Our clankers and supply wagons would bog, and soldiers don't fight well with wet feet and empty bellies. And, while the enemy *prefer* not to fight at this time of year, they'll aggressively defend what they have.'

'I thought they hibernated in winter?'

'Only for a month, and not all at the same time, except where they feel very secure.'

'Oh!'

'Is there anywhere else we can look for aid?' said Irisis. 'What's Vithis up to?'

It was a much debated question. The behaviour of the invading Aachim seemed to be inexplicable. Why *had* they suddenly retreated north and walled themselves in?

'There's been no news since he went to the Hornrace,' said Yggur, 'though rumours persist that he's raising a fortress there. But after the craven way he held back his forces at Snizort, I'd be wary of relying on him.'

'What about the Aachim of Stassor?' said Flydd.

Yggur glanced at Malien, who said, 'I know what their reply would be. They don't involve themselves in the affairs of old humans.'

'They may find it in their interests to do so this time,' said Flydd.

'I wouldn't count on it,' said Yggur dismissively.

'Is there any hope for us, surr?' said Irisis. 'Give us the truth.'

'The enemy don't yet have our numbers but they surpass us in strength,' said Flydd, 'and in toughness and mobility. They have the advantage of flight, those who are winged and can use the Art, and lyrinx need less supplies, since they can live off our fallen.'

'It'd be more profitable to consider their weaknesses,' said Yggur.

'The enemy seem to rely on strength more than intelligence,' said Irisis, 'but I'm not sure they're very adaptable.'

'They adapt well enough when they have the time,' said Flangers from his litter by the fire. 'But not in the heat of battle. When hard pressed, they fall back on their same old tactics, where we would work out new ones.'

'Then whenever we're fighting them, we must shape the battle plan to make them uncomfortable,' said Nish.

'They suffered from the heat in Kalissin,' said Tiaan in a hesitant voice. Irisis looked around and found her sitting in the shadows of the far corner, as if she were hiding. 'They prefer cool weather, though they don't like bitter cold any more than we do. And another thing . . .'

'Yes, Tiaan?' said Yggur.

'It seemed to me that they weren't quite at home in their bodies.'

'How do you mean?'

'It was the way they kept working their limbs, shrugging their shoulders and plucking at their outer skin,' said Tiaan. 'They seemed uncomfortable a lot of the time.'

'That's hardly surprising,' said Flydd, 'considering how greatly they flesh-formed their unborn young, to survive in the void. For every strength that served them well there, they must have a weakness we can exploit here.'

'How do they *feel* in themselves?' said Fyn-Mah, who was sitting close to Flydd, as always since his return. 'Are they happy with what they've become?'

'Not all of them,' said Tiaan. 'Many are born malformed. Some never develop wings and others lack pigment or the armoured outer skin.'

'Do they treat these ones badly?' asked Flydd.

'Not as badly as humans would,' said Tiaan, 'though they *are* regarded as inferior. They're rarely permitted to breed.'

'Anything else?' said Yggur.

'Snizort had some other significance for the lyrinx,' said Nish, 'and it was more important than fighting us. They delayed the battle so they could complete it.'

'Why hasn't anybody mentioned this before?' said Yggur sharply.

Nish shrugged. 'They made a tunnel into the Great Seep and took a lot of relics out of it. Gilhaelith helped them to find the relics, I'm told.'

'A *tunnel* into liquid tar?'

'They froze the tar first,' said Tiaan. 'We saw the entrance as we escaped from Snizort.'

'And I've thought of something else,' said Nish. 'Tiaan was with a man called Merryl, a freed slave who'd been held by the lyrinx for many years and spoke their tongue. If anyone knows the enemy's secrets, it would be him.'

'What happened to this fellow, Tiaan?' said Yggur.

'I haven't seen him since we escaped.'

'Chances are that he was put to work, hauling clankers,' said Flydd. 'If he survived that, he could be anywhere.'

'I'll tell my spies to keep watch for him,' said Yggur, 'though I doubt he'll be found. Pity. Are we finished?'

'Gilhaelith once mentioned that a lyrinx had developed a dreadful inflammation between its skin layers,' said Flydd. 'It clawed its armoured skin off and they had to put it to death. They buried the body and left hastily, as if afraid of infection.'

'When was this?' said Yggur, his mouth tightening at mention of the geomancer.

'He came to visit me at the healers, before Fiz Gorgo was attacked.'

'How curious,' said Yggur. 'Tell me, did he say *why* the enemy were tunnelling into the Great Seep?'

'No.'

'What did they find?'

'The remains of an ancient village – wooden walls, floors, furniture, and a lot of bodies preserved by the tar. Also some large crystals of brimstone in boxes. They called one "The Brimstone".'

'*The* Brimstone?' said Yggur. 'What did they say about it?'

'Gilhaelith didn't know.'

'Or wouldn't tell you,' Yggur said darkly.

Not even in that slave-driven time in the manufactory a year ago, after their return from the fatal trek across the ice plateau, had Nish laboured as hard as he did now. The expedition to Snizort required three more air-floaters, which had to be built from scratch in a month. He'd given a list of essential items to Klarm, thinking that they'd be obtainable in Borgistry, only to be told that the old Council had stripped Borgistry clean to make its sixteen air-dreadnoughts. He'd already searched the sites where air-dreadnoughts had crashed and burned but the intense fires had consumed everything, and no one knew what had happened to the other four Fusshte had fled with.

Nish worked in a cramped stone shed in a southern corner of the yard. Being built against the outer wall, it never saw the winter sun. His sole source of warmth was an open brazier fed with chips and wood shavings, when he had the time to gather them. He started work at five in the morning, seldom finished before midnight, and was often so tired that he slept on the floor.

He didn't see Irisis from one day to the next for she was just as frantic, directing Tiaan and four other artisans in the making of all sorts of devices they'd need before the spring offensive. They'd recovered air-floater controllers, floater-gas generators and all manner of other bits and pieces from Nennifer, but still the work was endless. Nish missed her.

Yggur had sent Fyn-Mah off in the air-floater with Klarm to conscript artificers, smiths, carpenters and all the other workers needed, but she hadn't yet come back. Some might be found at Old Hripton but others would have to come from Borgistry.

And making air-floaters was the easiest of his jobs, for at least Nish knew what to do and he had the original air-floater to use as a template. He also had to find skilled artificers to carry out whatever repairs would be needed to get the abandoned constructs running. Among the survivors of the amphitheatre's collapse were a number of artificers who had experience with

349

clankers, but constructs were very different. Nish would have to conduct most of their training without a thapter to work on, as it was about to leave on Flydd's embassy to the east coast. Nish had the construct mechanism recovered from Snizort some months ago, but for the rest he had to make do with wooden models and drawings, which he knew were not good enough.

But his most challenging job was finding and training pilots to fly thapters from Snizort to Fiz Gorgo. If his other tasks were difficult, this one looked impossible. Few people had the talent to draw power with a controller, and most became air-floater pilots or clanker operators. Once trained for a particular machine it was difficult for an operator to adapt to another; the emotional bond usually got in the way.

Nish discovered that two air-dreadnought reserve pilots had survived the collapse of the amphitheatre. Unfortunately one had gone insane when her craft had exploded. The other, distraught at being separated from her machine, had stepped off the outer wall of Fiz Gorgo while he'd been away on the trip to Nennifer. After much searching, Nish despaired of finding a single pilot.

'It's hopeless,' he said to Flydd after days of frustration and failure. 'We'll never be ready for spring, surr. I'm letting everyone down.'

'Just take it one step at a time, Nish. Don't think about winning the war, or even being ready for the spring offensive. Just concentrate on getting the next task done. And then the one after that.'

The following day there was a knock at the door of his shed. Nish fed the last of his wood chips into the brazier, held his blue fingers over it for a moment and went to see who was there.

It was Yggur's newly appointed seneschal, Berty, a small, round, bustling man, not much short of eighty, with wings of frothy white hair on either side of a pink, bald skull. He was accompanied by a pair of downcast, bedraggled and red-eyed men, one big, pockmarked and hairy, the other small and completely bald.

'Cook found them in an inn at Old Hripton,' piped Berty.

'They lost their machines in the battle at Snizort, then became separated from the army. They were pressed into service as sailors, deserted and worked their way from port to port around Meldorin. Gorm and Zyphus are their names.' He nodded and hurried out.

'Operators,' Nish said hungrily, ignoring his misgivings. Since they'd lost their machines so long ago, retraining might be possible. 'Let's see what we can do for each other.'

When he took them to see the controllers Irisis's team were working on, Gorm and Zyphus broke down and wept, and Nish had to leave them for an hour. When he returned, the hairy operator, Gorm, the ugliest, roughest fellow Nish had set eyes on in a long time, threw his arms around Nish and kissed him on the cheek.

'You might change your tune when you see what you'll be operating,' Nish said. He led them to the side yard where the thapter stood, ready to depart.

The operators' eyes stuck out like toadstools. 'Not sure I could operate one of them alien craft,' said Gorm. The small bald man, Zyphus, looked equally askance. 'Used to clankers, we are.'

Nish cursed under his breath. Operators couldn't be forced. They had to be cajoled, and if there was no bond with the machine they would not be successful. 'We don't have any clankers. What about piloting an air-floater?' He needed three more air-floater pilots, plus reserves.

'Don't know,' said Gorm, rasping at the wiry bristles on his chin.

'It's an air-floater or nothing,' said Nish.

'Used to watch them soaring above us at Snizort,' said Zyphus. His skin broke out in goosepimples. 'Always fancied one of those. Come on, Gorm, you'll love it.'

'Expect I won't,' said Gorm, 'but it'll be better than nothing.'

That was Nish's feeling too, so he took them on and Irisis began to tailor two of the Nennifer controllers to them. That afternoon, Nish was sitting head in hands at his bench, despairing of ever finding anyone to become thapter operators, when there came a tentative knock at the shed door.

'Enter,' he said. Again the knock. 'Come in,' he roared, and a small, sweetly pretty girl who looked about thirteen put her head and shoulder through the crack.

Her straw-coloured hair was done in dozens of small plaits, her cheeks were red from the wind and her frosty grey eyes had a liquid shine. Unusual eyes around here; where had he seen their like before?

'Please, surr,' she said in a whispery little voice, 'Lord Yggur sent us.'

'Did he?' said Nish. 'What for?'

'Operators, surr.'

Nish almost laughed aloud, but restrained himself. Yggur was not known to be a joker. 'Really? Come inside. Put this on your head and tell me what you see.' He held out a contraption of wires and crystals, like a jewelled skullcap, that Irisis had made up for him. With such a device, even a no-talent like Nish could identify people who might become operators.

She pressed it onto her head and immediately cried out, her eyes as wide as her charming bow-shaped mouth. 'Oh, surr, it's like all the rainbows in the world, spinning round and round. Surr, you must see.' She held out the device to him.

'I don't have the talent,' he said gruffly. 'All right, that's enough.'

Her lower lip wobbled. 'Am I no good, surr? I thought you would at least . . .'

'You'll do,' he said. 'What's your name?'

'Kattiloe, surr.' She made a clumsy but fetching attempt at a curtsy.

Nish smiled behind his hand. 'And where do you come from, Kattiloe?'

'Old Hripton, surr.'

'I'm sure we'll make an operator of you. Now, all I need is another twenty-nine.'

'My big sister Kimli is outside, surr.'

'Is she?' Sometimes the talent ran in families. 'Send her in.'

In she came. Kimli was minutely taller and nearly as pretty as Kattiloe, though her hair was an ashy brown. Her eyes were also that familiar frosty grey, and she too had the talent, though not as strongly as her sister. 'Two!' said Nish. 'I don't suppose you've got any more sisters?'

'There's seven of us,' said Kattiloe, curtsying again. 'Not counting the twins, of course, but they're only fourteen.'

'How old are you, Kattiloe?'

'Twenty, surr.'

'Are you really?' Nish felt middle-aged, though he wasn't much older. 'Well, tell them to come and see me.'

They all possessed the talent of seeing the field, and most had it strongly. Chissmoul, a black-eyed, sturdy young woman of twenty-three, was so shy that it took hours to coax her into taking the test, though she turned out to have the strongest aptitude of all. Nish took on the lot, even the twins, who might have been fourteen but looked about ten. He suppressed his anxiety about using such young girls. Boys that age were dying in battle all the time.

'Any brothers, uncles, aunts, cousins?' he said hopefully.

The sisters turned out to be equipped with relatives of all sizes, shapes and ages. Most had those penetrating grey eyes. Yggur's eyes! The old hypocrite.

Nish recruited thirty-seven of them, mostly young women and girls, before he'd exhausted the family tree, and then consulted the expert, Irisis. The majority had the talent so strongly that they probably would make operators, so he abandoned the search for more. Now all he had to do was work out how to train them. It wasn't going to be easy – Nish knew no more about using a controller than he did about childbirth. But it *must* be done so, with the aid of his two trained operators, and Tiaan and Irisis, he would get it done.

Only after their flight controllers were tuned to them, and the operators had completed the lengthy process of familiarising themselves with them, could the real training begin. But of course they did not have flight controllers for thapters yet, and Malien's machine was soon to take Flydd on his embassy to the east coast. Nish planned for his prentices to begin practising with Yggur's little beetle flier, all too conscious of its inadequacies.

Would he have the courage to get into a thapter flown by someone who had only practised with a toy?

The evening before Malien and Flydd were due to leave, Inouye's air-floater touched down in the yard and Klarm scrambled out. Nish looked out the door of his shed and saw Flydd waiting on the steps outside the front door. The two scrutators held a hurried conference in the middle of the yard, Klarm handed Flydd a sealed packet which he slipped inside his cloak, they shook hands and Klarm scuttled back to the air-floater. It lifted at once and rotored off in the direction of Old Hripton.

The front door opened and Yggur came out. 'Was that our peripatetic head of intelligence, favouring us with another of his flying visits?'

'It was Klarm,' said Flydd, turning to pass him by.

Yggur caught him by the arm. Nish stopped in the shadows, hoping to hear some news. Yggur and Flydd had been even more tight-mouthed than usual, lately.

'What news from Borgistry?' said Yggur.

'I haven't read his dispatches yet.' Flydd was trying to pull free.

Yggur did not let go. 'So Klarm has actually done some work this time?'

'He's been frantic, though I don't propose to discuss it on the front porch.'

'As far as I can see, all he's done is spend my gold as though it flows down the river like water, drink himself witless night after night, and cavort with women half his age and twice his size, though why any woman would want –'

'Klarm is the closest friend I have left,' Flydd said coolly, breaking away and heading up the steps, 'so be careful what you say about him. Spying on the enemy takes rivers of gold. Besides, most of the coin he spends came from the treasury at Nennifer.'

Yggur spun around. 'I wasn't aware that it had been found!'

'It must have slipped my mind,' Flydd said smoothly.

'There's still the matter of his general debauchery. I don't see why we should fund –'

'Klarm is a man of lusty appetites,' sighed Flydd. 'I was that way myself before the knife –' He gave another sigh. 'In his case, take away the appetites and you destroy the man. He's doing good work, the very best, and that makes up for the other.'

'Then why am I being kept in the dark?'

'You're not,' Flydd said. 'Come inside and we'll go over his dispatches.'

'All of them,' said Yggur, 'or just the ones he's prepared for my consumption?'

'Don't be ridiculous,' said Flydd. 'We're all in this together.'

'Are we?' Yggur turned to the door. 'How does he do it, anyway?'

'Do what?' said Flydd.

'How does a sawn-off runt like Klarm attract women the way he does? I wasn't an unattractive man in my prime, but they didn't care for me.'

'Most of Nish's prentices have your eyes, you old dog.'

Yggur looked abashed. 'A brief liaison two generations ago. She didn't care for me either.'

'What do you expect?' said Flydd. 'You keep people at a distance and give nothing of yourself.'

'I gave once,' Yggur murmured, 'and look what came of it.'

'They don't see Klarm as a threat. He charms them and makes them laugh. And, er . . .' Flydd gave a delicate cough.

'What other amazing talent does the man have?'

'It's said that he's not a dwarf in all departments. Quite the contrary, in fact.'

Yggur made a disgusted sound deep in his throat. 'Don't tell me any more!'

THIRTY-EIGHT

Yggur, Malien and Flydd had spent fruitless days studying Golias's globe, trying to coax the mad mage's secret from it. They attempted to probe it with Fyn-Mah's scrying bowl, with a variety of other devices, and even with Muss's eidoscope. All proved fruitless. Flydd and Yggur tried a dozen spells of seeing, divining, scrying and controlling, none of which had any effect.

For long days they ransacked each other's Arts, revealing secrets that they'd kept to themselves for all of their long lives of mancing, trying to find a way to understand the globe. They brainstormed over flasks of the potent wines of northern Meldorin, now unobtainable because the vineyards had been abandoned. They tried hypnosis and trance states; they scoured the mouldering records of ancient times in Yggur's library, but came up with nothing.

As the thapter was about to lift off, Yggur slipped the globe into Tiaan's hand. He had developed a fondness for the young artisan with the faraway sadness in her eyes. They had something in common.

'Take this with you,' he said quietly. 'You've as much chance of solving it as any of us.'

She looked down, surprised, and her fingers caressed the silky smooth surface of the globe. She gave him a fleeting smile, which reminded him that he had once been young, slid it into her pocket and turned away.

'Do well in the east,' said Yggur and went inside.

Tiaan hated Fiz Gorgo and couldn't wait to be gone. It was too crowded and noisy, and too full of unpleasant memories. Every time she walked down the hall it brought back the morning of Ghorr's attack. She'd been dragged from her bed, still half-asleep, and beaten black and blue by Fusshte's soldiers before they realised who she was. She'd seen terror on their faces then; they'd be brutally punished for injuring such a valuable prisoner. A hand had been thrown over her mouth and nose, Tiaan had smelt a sickly-sweet odour; then, oblivion.

From that moment until she'd been hustled out of Fusshte's air-dreadnought into Nennifer, Tiaan remembered nothing but a few shredded images: darkness punctuated by lantern gleams, faces she didn't recognise leaning over her, doors opening and closing. And always in the background had been the ticking of the rotors as the scrutators fled for their lives, not stopping night or day.

Her time in Nennifer had been almost as confused – cold and darkness, rats and cockroaches writhing in a halo around her dinner bowl, Fusshte giving her viscous potions that disconnected her mind from her eyes, then questioning her for hour after hour about her talents and about the amplimet. Tiaan had no memory of what she'd told him, for something he'd done had woken the withdrawal she'd not felt since the portal between the worlds had been opened in Tirthrax.

Once withdrawal began, it had grown until those desperate feelings of longing overwhelmed her. She remembered little else. Not even the squalor of her imprisonment had registered once withdrawal reached its peak. Her next memory was of Nish and Irisis leading her towards the warding chamber, where the proximity of the amplimet had roused her again.

Remembering that moment still brought tears to her eyes – the pain and the ecstasy of communing with the amplimet, and the agony and loss when Irisis and Nish had robbed her of it, as they'd robbed her of her previous life at the manufactory. How she *hated* them. It was unbearable to be trapped in Fiz Gorgo with the two of them. She would have agreed to anything to get away.

Malien had spent days with her in Nennifer after Fusshte fled, patiently talking through all that had happened. Despite what everyone else thought, Tiaan was no longer troubled by it. The past weeks were just another trauma and she'd overcome many in the past year. Now all she wanted was to escape. There were too many people in Fiz Gorgo and she'd never been good with people. She was afraid of Yggur, terrified of Flydd and had nothing to say to anyone else. If only it were just she and Malien going in the thapter it might be like the good old days mapping the fields near Stassor – one of the most pleasant times of her life.

Tiaan had the amplimet back now but her longing for it had faded. Driven back to the lowest stage of awakening, it seemed so insignificant that she wondered at her previous longings. Had Flydd and the other mancers erased all that had made it unique?

After flying due east to Tiksi, a journey of more than five hundred leagues which, now that Malien was fully recovered, they hoped to do in six days, Flydd planned to head all the way up the east coast to Crandor. That long coastal strip contained half the population of Lauralin and most of its greatest cities and armies. He planned to stop at Tiksi, Maksmord, Gosport, Guffeons, Roros, Garriott and Taranta, before returning via the west coast of Faranda, the only part of that arid island with cities of any significance. The journey would take at least three weeks, if the weather was good and nothing went wrong, but they were expecting to be away for a month. Tiaan couldn't wait to lift off so she could turn to her field maps.

'We won't be able to visit every important city in the east,' said Flydd as the thapter's entrails whined, 'but we'll do much good nonetheless. No one can have seen a thapter before, and the common people will marvel at it. The enemy may be able to fly but they don't have thapters.'

358

'It doesn't mean the east will rally to you,' said Malien, rolling her palm across the flight knob.

'They can't give us men or clankers; they're simply too far away. But our visit is bound to do good for morale – theirs and ours. We'll all feel that we're not alone, and that's as good as another army.'

'I thought we were heading directly to Tiksi?' said Tiaan an hour after they'd left Fiz Gorgo.

'It's impossible to fool someone who sees a map once and never forgets it,' smiled Malien. 'I'm taking a slight detour to visit my exiled clan, Elienor, on the coast of the Sea of Thurkad.'

'Have you told the scrutator?' Flydd was down below, deep in his papers.

'Not yet.'

'Do you . . . think it's a good idea to keep him in the dark?' Tiaan put it tentatively, knowing that Malien could be prickly.

Malien sighed. 'I still can't forgive him for taking over my thapter at Nennifer.'

'We've all done things we've later regretted, Malien. If you and Flydd don't trust each other, I don't see how we can succeed. And . . .'

'What is it, Tiaan?'

'I won't be able to concentrate on my mapmaking.'

Malien stared straight ahead for some time, clenching her jaw. Finally she said, 'You're right, of course. We Aachim have a strong sense of our own importance and we feel insults more deeply than we should. I'll set things right with him.'

During Tiaan's time at the manufactory, Flydd, as scrutator for Einunar, had been the supreme authority figure of everyone's life. She still saw him that way and, not knowing what to say, avoided him whenever she could. In the cramped confines of the thapter that wasn't easy so she sat up on the rear shooter's platform in the icy wind, swathed in blankets and scarves, alone but for her map, which she'd mounted on a board to protect it in high wind, and her crystals. The platform on Malien's thapter was surrounded by a knee-high coaming, and had a harness to keep her in place in bumpy weather, but it was miserably cold even in the mildest conditions. Tiaan mapped the fields all the daylight hours, and for as much of the evening as they travelled.

Flydd came back once to see what she was doing, but she said, in her most polite talking-to-the-scrutator voice, 'I can't talk to you just now, I'll miss part of the field.'

Early the following morning, Malien crossed the Sea of Thurkad and settled the thapter outside a palisade of sharpened timber at the end of a narrow, rocky inlet. The ridges rose up steeply on either side and straggly forest ran east into the distance. Guards on the walls had spring-fired catapults and crossbows trained on them. Malien stood up and raised a blue flag. After some time it was answered by a flag from the wall.

'Do you want me to hide, as I did last time?' said Tiaan. They'd stopped briefly here on the way to Alcifer, after escaping from Stassor.

'No; you'll come with me and Flydd,' said Malien.

'But . . .' said Tiaan. 'What if –?'

'This is an embassy and you're under my protection. You'll come to no harm.'

But you're an exile too, Tiaan thought, dreading the meeting. Her escape and Minis's maiming had ruined Clan Elienor, for it had been held responsible. Vithis had confiscated their constructs and sent them into this precarious exile.

Gates in the palisade were creaking open as Tiaan climbed down, following Malien and the scrutator. As she put one foot on the ground, seven Aachim came through the gate. With their red hair, compact stature and pale skin they were strikingly different from all other Aachim.

'The first is Yrael, clan leader,' said Malien to Flydd as they approached. 'Next his wife Zea and daughter Thyzzea . . .'

Yrael, whose hair was the glowing flame-red of sunset in a smoky sky, stopped just outside the gate, waiting for them to come to him. His arms were crossed, his face expressionless. Tiaan felt a spasm of panic.

Malien introduced Flydd and Yrael shook his hand, as did

each of the others. There was no need to introduce Tiaan, who had remained several steps behind – every one of Clan Elienor's five thousand knew her. She would forever be in their Histories.

Yrael stepped around Flydd and came towards Tiaan, and her heart missed a beat.

'Tiaan,' he said, studying her with his head to one side. 'You look worn.'

'I'm sorry!' she burst out. 'I had to do it. I was afraid for my life –'

Zea, a small woman with kindly eyes, came up beside Yrael. 'But of course you did,' she said, 'and though your escape cost us dearly, how could we blame *you* for it?'

'It was your duty to escape,' said Yrael, 'and the negligence of our guards, and Vithis's, that allowed it.' He put out his hand.

Tiaan took it, tentatively, the long fingers wrapping right around her hand, but at the moment of contact a wave of relief swept over her. She shook hands with Zea and then her daughter, Thyzzea, remembering their kindness and Thyzzea's impish good humour during what had been a desperate time for them. Thyzzea, who wasn't even an adult, had stood up to Vithis to protect her. All at once, Tiaan felt as though she had come home.

'Come within,' said Zea, indicating the gate with a sweep of her hand.

They took refreshments in a small pavilion made of carved white wood, set on a grassy rise by the stream that wound into the end of the inlet. The camp, a mixture of tents and small timber buildings, was neatly laid out and the walkways paved, though it looked impoverished. It was also precariously close to Oellyll, just across the sea, and must have been miserably cold and damp at night. The Aachim were thinner than Tiaan remembered, though they looked no less cheerful.

'We are glad to see you, Malien, but why have you come?' said Yrael once the formalities had been exchanged.

'To find out where you stand,' said Malien. She explained what had happened at Fiz Gorgo and Nennifer, and Flydd outlined their plan to win the war, or at least such parts of it as he cared to reveal.

361

'I realise that you must feel bitter towards us, because of your exile,' began Flydd. He glanced at Tiaan but she avoided his eyes. 'And that you won't dare –'

'On the contrary,' Yrael broke in, 'Tiaan did us a favour. We've lost much, it is true, but we've been cut free of the other clans who, many millennia after Elienor founded our line, still can't accept us. To them we're a nagging reminder of the greatest failure in our Histories, and we'll never go back. Henceforth we will make our own way on Santhenar, and our own friends, beholden to none.'

'I'm prepared to offer –' began Flydd.

'We cannot be bought,' said Zea. 'What we give, we give in friendship.'

'And obligation,' said Yrael. 'We were twice shamed at Snizort. Shamed because Vithis made alliance with you, Scrutator Flydd, then held us back when your soldiers were overrun by the enemy. And shamed again by the shabby way Matah Urien and Lord Vithis treated Tiaan, who made the gate and saved us all. In payment of those debts, and in friendship between our species, you may call upon us at need and we will answer the call with a thousand men.'

'What of the other Aachim?' said Flydd, once they were in the air again. 'Will they give us anything?'

'My own people in Stassor will not,' said Malien. 'Sadly, they can think of nothing but their own security, though how they can imagine it's threatened in such an impregnable refuge, I don't know.'

'That's what the Council thought about Nennifer,' Flydd reminded her. 'What about Vithis and the other clans? They've more than ten thousand constructs. If we could just –'

'Not while Vithis remains leader,' said Malien. 'I know his kind. Once set on a course, he will follow it to destruction rather than turn aside.'

'How secure is his tenure? Are the other clan leaders likely to challenge him?'

'I talked to Yrael about that – they've had word of Vithis's doings. There's much dissension among the clan leaders, but also much rivalry, and Vithis survives because of it. The other clans won't give any leader the support to topple him. Clan rivalry is one of our longstanding weaknesses.'

They planned to stop briefly at Tirthrax, where Malien would gather certain materials needed to turn constructs into thapters, then head to Tiksi, which had been under siege for a year. Tiaan had been born there and knew it well, since her mother Marnie, the champion breeder of the breeding factory, still lived in Tiksi. Though Tiaan did not get on with her mother, she missed her terribly.

Unfortunately, as they were travelling across Mirrilladell, they encountered a blizzard so fierce that Malien had no choice but to put the thapter down and wait it out. She turned for Tirthrax, which was not far away, and they spent days there, unable to go outside the entrance for fear that they would not find their way back again.

'I think we'd better pass Tiksi by and go straight to Fadd,' said Flydd on the third day, when conditions showed no sign of abating. 'It's bigger and more important.' He looked to Malien as if for affirmation.

'Whatever you say,' Malien replied indifferently. 'I know nothing about the politics of old humankind.'

Even Tiaan knew the untruth of that statement, but Flydd didn't challenge it. 'We simply can't spend more than a month on this trip and we've already used up most of our contingency time.'

Tiaan scrunched herself up in a corner and pretended to be asleep so Flydd wouldn't talk to her. Long anxious about her mother, she was bitterly disappointed that they weren't going to Tiksi. She felt lost and Flydd's presence inhibited Tiaan in her friendship with Malien. Tiaan did the only thing she could do. She withdrew into her work.

The following day the blizzard eased and they headed north-east across the mountains to Fadd, a city on the coast some eighty leagues north of Tiksi. It had been besieged by the enemy for most of the autumn, so Flydd hoped their visit would be doubly welcome. Tiaan resumed her mapping and, when they reached Fadd, pleaded women's troubles so Flydd would not require her to go with him. After Fadd they had a long flight along the seaward edge of the rugged coastal mountains to Maksmord, where her excuse still served, though judging by Flydd's expression it would last no longer.

They continued north-west up the coast and the cities blurred into one another. Their visits were brief, normally just overnight. Malien would circle the city several times in daylight before setting down in the main square, or outside the governor's palace, making certain that they were seen by the maximum number of people. They would meet with the governor, the army command and other notables, and the provincial scrutator.

The first questions were always about the legitimacy of the new council and the lack of eastern representation on it. The story of Flydd's earlier condemnation was well known, as was the humiliation of the Council at Fiz Gorgo and the destruction of Nennifer. Yet here Flydd was, accompanied by an Aachim out of the Great Tales and carrying a charter signed by the legendary Yggur himself, and travelling in the astounding flying machine that the whole world was talking about. Once they saw that marvel, few could sustain their doubts. Flydd's council was the new power in Santhenar and not even those scrutators who had been loyal to Ghorr put up further resistance.

Flydd made a point of meeting the common soldiers and townsfolk, to reinforce his message that the new council was different from the old one, and hoped that word of mouth would do the rest. At last, after receiving assurances of fellowship and support from the governor (if nothing else), the thapter would lift off early the following morning and crisscross the city several times, flying low, before heading to the next destination.

Finally they reached Roros in Crandor, the largest city in the world since Thurkad had been abandoned, only two days behind their original schedule. They planned to spend two days here. There would be many meetings, which Flydd required Tiaan to attend, though she did not have to say anything.

On the second afternoon, bored out of her wits with political manoeuvrings which meant nothing to her, Tiaan was feeling for an apple in her bag when her hand touched Golias's globe. She hadn't thought about it before – there had been too much on her mind. Tiaan made a mental note to study it in her room tonight, since all her maps were up to date.

Her thoughts turned back to her mother. There had been no news about Tiksi in Fadd, or anywhere else. Anything might have happened to Marnie in the past year. As the governor finished her interminable address, Tiaan slipped in beside Flydd, plucking up the courage to ask him. He shook the hands of a pair of noblewomen in silk robes and went with them towards the doorway. Tiaan went after him and was just reaching out a hand when he turned away to speak to the governor. Tiaan's hand fell to her side.

'Is something the matter?' said Malien.

Tiaan even felt estranged from her now. She stared at the floor.

'Tiaan, what is it?'

'It's my mother,' Tiaan said mournfully. 'I was hoping to see her in Tiksi. I'm so worried. Tiksi has been under siege for months . . .'

'You should have mentioned it at the beginning,' said Malien. 'I would have talked Xervish into going there instead of Fadd. Come on. I'm sure he knows what the situation is in Tiksi.'

Tiaan could not imagine calling the scrutator by his first name. 'He's far too busy. I don't want to bother him.'

'He can spare you a moment.' Malien went across. 'Xervish . . . Excuse me,' she said to the governor, 'but I must speak to the scrutator for a moment.'

Even from where she was standing, Tiaan saw the flash of annoyance on the governor's face, though it was swiftly hidden. 'Of course,' she said, bowing to Malien and to Flydd, and turning away.

They came across. Tiaan was mortified. 'I'm s-sorry,' she said, expecting the scrutator to be furious. 'It wasn't important –'

Flydd smiled, which didn't make him any the less fearsome. 'Governor Zaeff is the most tedious old bore I've encountered in a decade, and I'm delighted to be rescued from her. What can I do for you, Tiaan?'

'It's nothing really,' she said. 'It's just that, I'm worried about my mother . . . Of course you wouldn't know her, but she lives in Tiksi . . .'

'Marnie Liise-Mar,' he said. 'The star of the breeding factory. Of course I know her.'

'*You* know my mother?'

'When I was scrutator for Einunar, which I still feel myself to be, morally, I tried to know about everyone important in my realm.'

'Oh.' She could not imagine why her mother would be considered important. There were many breeding factories. 'Is Tiksi . . .?'

'I had news in Fadd, and all was well then, so they're safe until spring. Tiksi was besieged three times over the last year, and much damage done, but they've repulsed several attacks since. Ah . . .' He gave her a keen glance from under his continuous eyebrow, now grown back to brown bristles that stuck straight out. 'In the first attack the breeding factory was burned to the ground.'

Tiaan gave a little cry. 'Oh, poor Marnie.'

'I was there soon afterwards in an air-floater. It wasn't long after you left Tirthrax in the thapter, the first time. As I recall, the women of the breeding factory had been evacuated, and all were accounted for.'

'Marnie spent her whole adult life there,' said Tiaan. 'It *was* her life. What will she do?'

'I'm sure it's been rebuilt. It's vital work, breeding, and I dare say she's back at it.'

'She may be past it by now.'

Again Flydd smiled, and even touched her on the shoulder. He didn't seem quite as fearsome after all. 'Then she'll be having an honoured retirement. Marnie is, after all, one of the richest people in Tiksi. Excuse me, I'd better get back to the governor.'

'There you are,' said Malien. 'I'm sure she's perfectly all right.'

'I suppose so,' said Tiaan. 'Marnie always did know how to look after herself.'

She wondered, momentarily, if she dared ask the scrutator about the bloodline register, a human stud book she'd seen in the breeding factory the night of her escape. Tiaan decided not to. Scrutators didn't appreciate people prying into their secrets.

THIRTY-NINE

In another tedious meeting that afternoon, Tiaan found herself involuntarily stroking Golias's globe. Taking it out of her bag, she surreptitiously inspected it under the table.

The inner spheres revolved with the slightest movement, as if bathed in oil. She squinted at them, trying to see how many there were. One, two, three, four, five . . . six, seven. She shook the globe and something moved in the depths. Eight – in Gilhaelith's mathemancy, a perfect number.

She shied away from the thought of Gilhaelith. They'd been more than friends at the end of her time in Nyriandiol, but he'd not been able to take the next step. He couldn't overcome his troubled past, and in the end greed for the amplimet had outweighed his regard for her. She still felt the betrayal, and Ghorr's attack on Fiz Gorgo suggested that Gilhaelith made a habit of betrayal. Damn him. She dismissed him from her mind.

Each layer of the globe was different. The outer one was clear glass with, here and there, a few faint swirls of smoky grey, like wispy clouds in a clear sky. The next layer was also clear except for faint lines running around it that shone like silver metal.

The globe was very heavy, heavier than it should be if it were just made of glass. The third layer was faintly swirled with blue, embedded in which was a red band. Copper, she presumed.

Someone cleared their throat and Tiaan looked up. Malien

was glaring at her. Tiaan put an attentive look on her face until Malien turned back to the governor, who was still droning on about clasped hands across the world and other such nonsense. It was what people did that counted, not what they said.

The device was a puzzle and Tiaan loved solving puzzles. It drew her in. Each of the succeeding layers was different, but all were combinations of clear, patterned or engraved glass which had been banded, woven or partly masked with metals of different kinds. The outer layers covered so much of the inner ones that she could see virtually nothing of the seventh and eighth layers, at least in this light. And what lay at its core?

A crystal that could draw power from the field? Or one charged by its maker before it had been put into the farspeaker an aeon ago? If charged, its power must have faded long ago, in which case the globe was useless. Each layer of glass was seamless and there was no way to take the device apart without breaking it.

Malien jabbed her in the ribs and Tiaan nearly dropped the globe. One or two people were giving her curious looks. She slid it into her bag and tried to concentrate on what the governor was saying.

'. . . we will, of course, do all we can. But as you can see we are hard pressed ourselves . . .'

'I'm not asking you to come to our aid,' said Flydd in his best diplomatic tones. 'Clearly that's not possible. I'm asking that we all cooperate. Together we're strong. Separately, *nothing!*'

'Of course!' The governor spread her arms. 'But so far away . . . and skeets are so unreliable.'

'We may soon have a better solution,' said Flydd. 'A faster, secret means of communicating.'

'Oh?' The governor half-rose to her feet, her eyes on him.

'More of that when we have it. But in the meantime –'

Governor Zaeff stared at him, calculating. Even Tiaan could read her expression. *What's in it for me?*

'If you had a thapter, or two, it would make all the difference to your war,' Flydd said, very quietly. 'Not to mention the subsequent peace.'

Naked greed flashed in Governor Zaeff's eyes this time. 'You only have one, and you're not giving it away.' If she could have seized it with no danger to herself, she probably would have.

'By winter's end we expect to have several more,' said Flydd, 'enough to reward our most loyal allies.'

'And none more loyal than Crandor,' she said smoothly. 'We've been friends with the west for two thousand years and that alliance is sacred to us.'

'I'm delighted to hear it,' said Flydd, 'for it means just as much to us.' Rising, he gave her his hands across the table. Everyone else did the same, to seal the agreement.

Tiaan, who was holding the globe again, didn't know what to do when the man across the table extended his hands to her. She let it fall into the bag then took his hands, in her embarrassment not meeting his eyes. It was a minor breach of protocol, but forgivable in a foreigner. Everyone bowed to everyone else and they made their farewells.

'Would you really give her a thapter?' said Malien once they were safely in the air. 'When the war is over, Governor Zaeff will use it to enrich herself immeasurably.'

'Undoubtedly,' said Flydd. 'She's as greedy as anyone I've ever met, and therefore a valuable ally. She'll do everything in her power to protect her wealth, and no one could take better care of Crandor. It's the richest nation in the world, and the strongest. She's well armed, her troops well trained, her people well fed. Yulla Zaeff knows that the way to maintain her position is to keep everyone happy, and she does. I have great admiration for her, even though she's like a sow in the trough. I'd give her a dozen thapters if I had them to spare.'

On they went, heading north-west across jungle, mountain, desert and the unimaginably vast canyons that led down to the bed of the Dry Sea. This terrain was unfamiliar even to Malien. Tiaan stared at the salt-covered desolation in wonder, for its nodes were unlike any others she'd seen.

That night, two-thirds of the way to Taranta, they camped in the drylands far from any habitation, and it was warm enough to sleep under the stars. Tiaan lay in her hammock, with the globe clutched to her chest, rocking gently in the warm breeze. What could be at the core of the globe that powered it and weighed so much?

Tiaan wondered if she might induce some aura in it with the amplimet, in the same way she'd once tested the failed hedrons back at the manufactory. That seemed a lifetime ago. Unfortunately she didn't have the amplimet. Malien had taken to using it in her flight controller, and at other times it was always kept in the platinum box. Flydd was taking no chances with it, and perhaps not with her either.

The others were asleep, the night still, apart from the swish of wings as a colony of bats streamed in and out of caves in the escarpment just behind the thapter. The globe had been carefully designed and each layer must have a purpose. But how could she tell without seeing the details of each?

Tiaan brought to mind an image of the globe as she'd seen it earlier that day, in bright sunlight. She slowly rotated the image, one of the talents that made her such a brilliant artisan and geomancer. She could recall, as clearly as a picture, anything she had ever seen. If it was any kind of mechanism, like the workings of a clock, she could make it operate in her mind so as to identify the flaws in it.

Recalling the outside of the globe was trivial. Next she brought to mind the second layer, rotating it until she had put together a complete image of the surface. The third layer proved more difficult, since more of it was obscured by the upper layers. But soon she assembled the separate views until she had that too.

The fourth was more difficult again. Large sections were covered by the copper band, and when she mentally moved the globe to rotate all the inner layers, she tended to lose the image she already had. It took most of the night before she was sure she had it perfectly. Thinking about the fifth sphere, Tiaan fell asleep.

The following day she was too exhausted to do more than her mapping as they crossed the mountain range to tropical Taranta, although Tiaan did remember to take out the globe and inspect it under bright sunlight. After much rotating of the inner spheres she felt sure she had seen the entirety of the fifth and sixth layers. That night, after the meeting, she fitted them into her mental model of the globe and felt that she had achieved a feat no one else could have done.

The following day, not even her beloved work was able to keep her awake, so a swathe of country along the north-eastern rim of Faranda went unmapped. She hoped the omission would not prove costly.

They reached Nys, a large town on the north-west coast of Faranda, which marked the turning point in the journey. After this they would be heading south, back towards Fiz Gorgo and winter. It took all her spare time to complete her image of the seventh layer and fit it into the mental model. The eighth would be almost impossible, for it was dim and almost completely obscured by the seven layers rotating above it. She was looking forward to the challenge.

Completing the surface of the eighth sphere was like doing a jigsaw puzzle through a pinhole. She had hundreds of separate tiny images in her head, but could not see enough at a time to fit them together. In despair, she put Golias's globe away and went back to her mapping.

Towards the end of the odyssey, Tiaan was sitting, as usual, on the platform at the back of the thapter. Malien had followed the coast all the way south, and then south-east. Here Faranda became a narrow, mountainous peninsula like the handle of a spoon, extending down to Tikkadel, midway along the Foshorn, which resembled its bowl. To her right was the Sea of Thurkad, then the island of Qwale. Running towards her was the short Sea of Qwale which separated the island from Meldorin.

On her left, clearly visible beyond the mountains from this altitude, lay the white-crusted immensity of the Dry Sea, so vast, arid and hot that seldom had it been crossed. Tiaan had eyes for it whenever she could spare them from her mapping, though that was seldom. Unfortunately she had little time for spectacles at the moment. A chain of powerful nodes ran down the handle of Faranda, so close together that many fields overlapped at once, and it was difficult to sort out which was which. Malien seemed to be having trouble too – the note of the thapter kept swinging high then plunging low.

What kind of fields were out there, in the Dry Sea? The urge to investigate was overwhelming. Tiaan could see the rainbow shadows of a number of odd, elongated fields, but their sources were too far off to discern.

At Tikkadel, Malien turned right to cross the Sea of Thurkad, intending to pass over Qwale, which as far as they knew still resisted the enemy, and thence on to Meldorin Island.

As the thapter turned, Tiaan felt a bulging pressure in her head, as if a balloon was being inflated inside it, and a momentary shearing pain. Purple lights began to pulse behind her eyes and more bright spots drifted across her vision, resembling the migraines she sometimes suffered after overusing her talent. Colours exploded in her mind. 'Aah. Help!' she groaned, putting her hands over her eyes to shut out the light.

The wind was blasting at them and Malien did not hear. 'Malien!' Tiaan screamed.

Malien's head appeared up through the hatch. 'Tiaan, what is it?'

'I don't feel well. Can you go down?'

'We're over the sea. I'll have to turn back to the Foshorn.'

They landed on a grey, wind-tossed plateau overlooking the Sea of Thurkad. As the thapter came down it crushed the salty shrubs, releasing pungent herb oils that were like a tonic to her abused senses. Tiaan hung over the side, panting.

Malien climbed up to her. 'Are you all right?'

'I . . . don't know. The field –'

Malien helped her into the shade by the side of the machine. 'You've been overdoing it. Come inside. You can lie down in the dark and sleep all the way to Fiz Gorgo if you need to. It's only two days, with this wind behind us.'

'I'm not ill,' said Tiaan shakily. 'I feel all right now, but I sensed something strange up ahead.'

Flydd came down the ladder, rubbing stiff joints. He looked

as though he'd been asleep. 'What did you feel?' He squatted beside her.

'A monster node, bigger than the one at Tirthrax, but its field was unlike any I've ever sensed before. And there was something else.'

'I don't see why a field should trouble you,' said Flydd, 'no matter how huge.'

'I'm sorry – I'm not explaining it very well. It felt dangerous.'

'That's easily dealt with,' said Malien, smiling. 'We won't go near it. Let's get you inside.'

'Something isn't right,' said Tiaan. 'I have to put it on my map.'

Malien and Flydd exchanged glances. 'I don't think –' Flydd began.

'I must,' Tiaan insisted. 'If something's wrong, I've got to see it.'

'All right,' said Malien. 'We'll go down to the tip of the Foshorn.' Then, unaccountably, she shivered.

'There, you're feeling its wrongness too,' said Tiaan.

'Not at all,' said Malien. 'Just remembering the last time I was there.' She did not elaborate.

'Go carefully,' said Flydd, giving her another meaningful look.

Malien withdrew the amplimet and Flydd closed the lid of the platinum box over it. She made adjustments to the way she controlled the thapter, to make up for not using the amplimet, and lifted off, just skimming the shore. The field of the monster node grew in Tiaan's mind until it swirled all around her.

'Can't you see it?' she said to Malien, who did not seem to be troubled now.

'I've never been able to see the field; at least, not the way you do.'

'Really?' Tiaan was astonished. 'Then how can you use the thapter?'

'My Art is very different to the Arts that other mancers use. I think I mentioned that once. I know where power is, and using this controller I can draw upon it, but I don't see anything.'

'So what's at the other end of the Foshorn?'

'The Hornrace, a chasm five hundred spans deep that separates Faranda from the continent of Lauralin. I'm sure you've heard it mentioned in the Great Tales. The chasm was once spanned by the Rainbow Bridge, the most beautiful of all our works on Santhenar, but it was thrown down by Rulke during the Clysm. He caused the very earth of the Foshorn to move, tearing the Rainbow Bridge asunder and toppling it into the chasm. The remains of the bridge can still be seen, tangled up in the rocks of the Trihorn Falls at the eastern end of the Hornrace. Only the four pillars of the bridge still stand, to remind us of what we have lost. I never thought I'd see them again.'

'They must be mighty falls,' said Tiaan.

'Indeed, for the Foshorn is like a dam holding back the weight of the Sea of Thurkad and the Western Ocean behind it. The bed of the Dry Sea lies two thousand spans below the Sea of Thurkad, which has a powerful urge to reclaim it. The water races down the Hornrace as fast as this thapter can fly, but compared to the vastness of the Dry Sea it's no more than a dribble down a lunatic's chin.'

'Perhaps I'm seeing a node associated with the chasm,' said Tiaan. 'No wonder it's so huge, and so different.'

'No wonder,' said Malien, though there was a wary look in her eye. 'Let's see.'

They kept to a slow pace in order to lessen the strain, so it was late in the afternoon before they finally came in sight of the Hornrace. The thapter crept along the coast, which was incredibly rugged here, the mountains rising directly from the sea. They passed by one black headland after another and Tiaan felt her nerves tighten, as if each headland represented another turn of a clock spring. She already felt overwound.

The swirling patterns were everywhere now; she could hardly think for them. Flydd came up with a mug of tea, which she drank in a single draught. It tasted of ginger and the bitterness of willow bark, and shortly her headache began to ease.

Malien rounded another jagged headland and the tension snapped so tight that Tiaan could hardly draw breath. Malien took her hand, and Flydd – the scrutator himself – put his arm around her and held her up. Another dark headland loomed ahead.

'The next will be the last,' said Malien, controlling the thapter expertly with one hand. 'Brace yourself.'

They rounded the last headland and the field struck Tiaan in the face like a flail. She cried out. Flydd opened the platinum box, Tiaan reached in and touched the amplimet, just for a moment, and the tornado of light and colour eased enough for her to open her eyes.

Just below them, the sea swirled in a series of whirlpools between rocks that stuck out of the water like the teeth of sharks, only black. Beyond, the current raced towards a dark slot in the cliff.

'Go up a little,' said Flydd as air currents buffeted them violently. He closed the platinum box, to Tiaan's regret.

The thapter rose a few spans and the eddies grew less. They crept forward, rocking in the air. Forward, forward, and suddenly the chasm of the Hornrace opened up in front of them. The black cliffs towered so high that Tiaan had to crane her neck to see their tops.

A wild gust – a gale of air – struck the thapter and sent it tumbling. Had not the hatch crashed down they might all have been thrown out.

'Straps!' yelled Malien, clinging grimly to the controller.

Flydd put his arm through one of the sets of straps hanging from the back wall, then whipped two others across Tiaan's shoulders and buckled her in. He did the same for Malien, and lastly for himself.

Malien gained control of the thapter but a wilder gust immediately flipped them upside down. She righted the machine and it was tossed the other way.

'Get out of here,' roared Flydd. 'The torrent is drawing a gale of air through the Hornrace and it'll smash us on the Trihorn.'

Malien had gone pale. She tried to turn the thapter but it shook violently, swung towards the black cliffs, rotated one hundred and eighty degrees but kept going, hurtling backwards down the Hornrace. Below, Tiaan could hear compartments flying open and gear crashing everywhere.

'The gale is too strong,' said Malien, fighting the controls.

'Give the thapter more power.'

'I'm doing the best I can. It's hard to take it from the node I've been using.'

'What about the big node?'

'I can't sense it.'

'Tiaan?'

Her skin crawled at the thought of trying to draw power from such a field. It would turn them all inside out.

'I dare not,' she whispered. 'It's beyond me.'

'What do I do?' cried Malien. 'Flydd?'

'Turn around,' said Flydd through gritted teeth. 'Don't fight the wind. You'll have to go with it.'

In turning, an eddy flipped the thapter over and a down-draught hurled them at the torrent of black water. Tiaan bit down hard on a scream. Malien pulled up on the flight knob, the thapter struck the water and skipped like a stone, the blast from its base sending steam corkscrewing up all around them like miniature tornadoes.

'Go up! It's deadly this low,' he yelled.

'I know it!' she snapped. 'It . . . doesn't want to go up, Flydd. The downdraught is too strong.'

'Try to get out into the middle.'

'I'm doing all I can,' Malien said, fighting the controller.

The thapter edged toward the middle of the Hornrace. The wild air eddies were fewer there but the gale was stronger, hurling them from side to side. They skated across to the southern side on a rising column of air. Tiaan closed her eyes, sure they were going to strike the basalt wall.

Malien took advantage of another eddy to carry them away, and managed to lift the machine a little. The dark cliffs of the Hornrace were rushing past. Tiaan had never gone so fast. How could Malien control the little craft?

Somehow she did. 'We're nearly halfway down the Hornrace,' said Flydd. 'Better try and get out.'

'I *know*,' Malien said crossly.

'Sorry.' Flydd explained to Tiaan. 'At the other end, three pinnacles stand up in the middle of the stream, breaking it into four torrents. Beyond the pinnacles, the race plunges over the mightiest precipice in the world.'

'The Trihorn Falls,' said Malien. 'Misnamed now, for the tip of the third peak collapsed when the earth moved and the Rainbow Bridge fell.' She eased the thapter upwards. The buffeting grew less for a moment, until a gust plunged them down again. 'Not as easy as it seems.'

The wild dance continued for another few minutes then, suddenly ceased as, in the distance, a pair of fanged peaks and a stump, almost as tall, rose out of the water. The craft hurtled towards them.

'Now!' cried Flydd.

Malien jerked the controller hard. The thapter shot up and with a momentary shudder broke free of the streaming gale above the water into slightly calmer air. She kept going up, though the pinnacles seemed to rise out of the water just as quickly. The thapter was going like a rocket and she couldn't slow it.

Tiaan held her breath. One minute it looked as though they were going to make it, the next that they would smash straight into the left-hand peak.

'Up!' Flydd roared.

'I'm doing my best,' said Malien, tight-lipped.

She climbed, curving toward the gap where the third peak had been. An air whirlpool threw the thapter back toward the left peak. The controller was shuddering as if it lacked the power to lift the weight. It felt as though the whole machine was going to come apart. Malien tried again and again but the thapter wouldn't turn. She just couldn't reach the gap.

'We'll have to try and go over the top.'

Tiaan reached into the box, took out the amplimet and held it against her heart. They shot toward the tip of the peak; they were going to smash into the rock. At the last second Malien coaxed a little extra from the mechanism, the airflow over the pinnacle bumped them up and they soared over and out toward the Dry Sea. The buffeting ceased: they were sailing in clear air.

Malien slowed the machine, curving around so they could

take in the majesty of the Trihorn Falls in their wild plunge, a whole sea full of water, down and down, fifteen hundred spans to the floor of the sea. It was magnificent, glorious, unsurpassed in the Three Worlds.

But Tiaan's eyes were drawn beyond it, back along the top of the Hornrace, to where four black pillars stuck up, two on either side of the chasm. They were all that remained of the Rainbow Bridge.

Around each pillar were immense stacks of cut stone, the foundations for some monstrous structure that was even now being built. One of the piles on the Lauralin side of the Hornrace was already half as high as the bridge pillars, and five times as wide.

'What on earth is that?' Tiaan whispered.

'So that's what Vithis has been up to all this time,' said the scrutator. 'But what's he building?'

'And why?' Malien said grimly.

FORTY

'Whatever Vithis is building,' said Malien, 'he's doing it with the utmost urgency. What he's done in a few months is extraordinary.'

Flydd took the amplimet from Tiaan's fingers and put it away. As they climbed, enormous camps became visible. Roads had been carved across the drylands, ravines dammed and aqueducts were being constructed.

'He has the best part of ten thousand constructs, even after the losses he suffered at Snizort,' said Flydd. 'He could do a mighty lot of carrying, hauling and lifting with all of them. And don't forget he has well over a hundred thousand disciplined adults to do his bidding.'

'As long as he can compel their loyalty,' said Malien.

'Would you go over the biggest structure, Malien? I'd like a closer look.'

'Be careful,' cried Tiaan. 'I went over another camp once and Vithis did something to the field. I nearly crashed.'

'I remember you telling me,' said Malien. 'They won't find this craft so easy to deal with.'

Nonetheless, she kept well up, circling while Flydd peered over the side with a powerful spyglass. 'I wonder what he's doing?' said Malien. 'Can Vithis be trying to span the Hornrace itself? That would eclipse the Rainbow Bridge and every other structure in the Three Worlds, but I don't see the point of it. It would be a monument to hubris, nothing more.'

'Or a way of staking claim to their portion of Santhenar,' said Flydd. 'In a manner that no one could dispute.'

'And perhaps,' Malien pursed her lips, 'they plan to tap the great node here for some purpose we know nothing about.'

'Or one we'd rather not know about,' said Tiaan.

The headache and the visions returned at twice their former force and she doubled over, holding her hands over her eyes. Then, as they passed above the largest structure, for a fraction of a second it was as if they'd flown through a vertical beam of light. Tiaan saw right through Malien, her bones just shadows, even through the wall of the thapter to the world outside. She blinked and the spectral image was gone. The whine of the thapter stopped, and just as suddenly rose to a scream before settling back to its familiar whine. Tiaan closed her eyes but could still see the images.

'What was that?' came Flydd's voice from beside her. He did not seem to be overly concerned.

'Something to do with the node, I suppose,' Malien replied, no less casually.

'Did you see the light?' said Tiaan.

'What light?'

'A boiling column of it. I saw something similar the first time I flew over an Aachim camp, before I crashed on Booreah Ngurle. It wasn't as big as this one though.'

'Curious,' said Flydd; then, after a moment, added: 'We've seen enough. Head for home, Malien.'

The pangs eased once they were over the sea. Tiaan went below and lay on the floor with her eyes closed. She could not work the node out. Its field radiated away in a perfect oval centred on the Hornrace, but inside that it gained strength in a series of concentric ovals whose fields were reversed to each other.

Still thinking about it, she fell into sleep and didn't wake until the following morning. She couldn't map at all that day, and fell asleep before Malien stopped for a few hours' rest in the afternoon. She'd spent so long puzzling over the eight layers of the globe and how they fitted together that, even in sleep, her mind would not turn off. It ran the mental model over and over, rotating each layer this way and that. In the early hours it began to fall into place. The first and the second layer clicked together. The third.

The thapter hit a bump and Tiaan threw out her arms in the darkness, as if for balance. Shortly she turned on her side, pillowed her head on her hands and the dream continued. The fourth and the fifth layer snapped to the others, just a few seconds apart, then there was a long pause to the sixth, but straight after that, the seventh.

The last layer eluded her as she drifted from restless sleep to dream, to deep sleep and back again several times. But finally, not long before they began to pass over the swamp forests of Orist, the eighth layer slid into position. *She had it.*

Tiaan smiled in her sleep and turned the other way, giving a little sigh. She woke just as the thapter settled to the yard at Fiz Gorgo.

Tiaan wavered across the yard, still half-asleep. The great space was practically full now. Sheds had been erected everywhere, there were piles of dressed timber and rolls of canvas, stacks of firewood and cauldrons with black runs of tar down their outsides. On the other side of the yard stood the timber frames for the cabins of three air-floaters. And there were people all over the place: hundreds of labourers, carpenters, sail-makers, artificers and every other kind of craft worker imaginable.

Everyone was staring. Hadn't they seen a thapter before? She supposed most had not. As she headed toward the front door, Nish came out, looking harried and thinner than before. He went to go around her then started.

'Hello, Tiaan,' he said distractedly. 'How was your trip?'

'Very good, thank you,' she said formally.

She dodged around him and went inside, longing for a bath and time to herself. As she passed through the doors, something made her look back. Nish stood on the step, looking at her. She tossed her head and continued on. Going by the kitchens, she cadged some chunks of brown bread and a couple of boiled eggs from the red-faced, perspiring cook, and went to her room.

There Tiaan took off her boots and sat at the little table, munching bread. She idly spun one of the eggs on its pointy end, spun it the other way, then laid it aside uneaten. Taking out Golias's globe, she weighed it in her hands. There was one final puzzle to solve but it still wasn't clear how to begin.

She scratched her head. She'd not had a bath since Taranta, itched all over and hated it. After Nennifer, she couldn't bear to be dirty. But she had to solve the puzzle first. She got out a box of crystals and her artisan's tools and began to work. Then she planned to bathe, lock the door and luxuriate in being completely alone for at least a day.

Tiaan didn't get the solitude she craved. Her hair was still dripping when she was called down to Yggur's meeting chamber. She sat right up the back, in the corner, hoping no one would notice her, for she had much to think through.

'You've done well,' Yggur said after the scrutator had summarised their trip.

'It went better than I expected,' said Flydd, toying with the goblet in front of him. 'Everyone knew about Ghorr's fall and the destruction of Nennifer. They have a great hunger for news in the east and took great pleasure in hearing how the downfall of the old Council came about, though they were anxious about the new one. I believe I allayed their fears and gave them something to hope for.'

'Splendid,' said Yggur, leaning back and folding his arms. 'Please proceed.'

'We've made some friends, learned much useful intelligence about the enemy and done wonders for morale in the east.'

'That's all very fine, but how many clankers have you come back with? How many soldiers?'

'None apart from Clan Elienor's one thousand,' Flydd said grudgingly. 'And that was Malien's doing. But I never expected to. Even if the east had men and clankers to spare, we can't march them across the continent.'

'The war will be won or lost here in the west, Flydd, and

we can't do it without armies. Have you got *anything* we can fight with?'

'I have agreement that we can use a number of manufactories in the south-east to make the devices we need. And there are a few matters we need to discuss later, Yggur. Privately.'

'I'll look forward to it.'

'Where's Klarm?' said Flydd, looking around the room.

'Away in Nihilnor, or perhaps Borgistry by now, spending gold by the bucket. Truly, the man is a profligate.'

'But worth it.'

'We can talk about that later, too. Thank you, Flydd. I'll give you a report on our progress, which *will* advance the war effort. Nish?' said Yggur.

Nish came out the front. 'I've got two experienced clanker operators presently training to operate air-floaters, as well as thirty-seven prentices, four training for air-floaters, the remainder for thapters. Most of the prentices show promise though the real test won't come until we put them in thapters. I also have eight experienced clanker artificers, and thirty prentices training to maintain thapters. Lacking a thapter, I'm doing my best with drawings and models.

'You saw the air-floater vessels outside; they'll be ready in a few days. Unfortunately I can't get enough silk cloth for the airbags. We've made one with silk gleaned here and in Old Hripton, but we can't finish the others without cloth and there's none to be had, even in Borgistry. Silk comes from the east but Ghorr used the lot for his air-dreadnoughts.'

'What about the ones that crashed in the swamp forest?' said Flydd.

'They either burned or their airbags floated away. We haven't recovered enough silk to make a pocket handkerchief.'

'Well, Thurkad was the centre of the western silk trade for a thousand years,' said Flydd. 'There's bound to be silk cloth in its abandoned warehouses.'

'If the lyrinx haven't burned them,' said Nish. 'Or moths eaten the cloth.'

'The lyrinx aren't wanton destroyers, despite their reputation.

And the warehouses would have been protected against the moth, for a while at least.'

'We can discuss an expedition later,' said Yggur. 'Irisis, your report.'

She stood up tall and confident and beautiful, and Tiaan slipped down in the seat, avoiding her eye.

'My people have been busy making the assemblies to turn construct controllers into controllers for thapters,' said Irisis. 'We've completed seventeen assemblies so far, apart from the special parts Malien was going to bring from Tirthrax.' She glanced at Malien, who gave the slightest of nods. 'As well, we've readied the controllers and floater-gas generators, brought from Nennifer, for two of the three new air-floaters, should we obtain the silk.' She sat down again next to Nish and casually draped an arm across his shoulder.

'I've not been idle either,' said Yggur. 'I've had artificers going over various battlefield devices we recovered from Nennifer, and they're ready to hand over to the manufactories.'

'What about your own project?' said Flydd. 'You were going to tell us how to move the thapters from Snizort. There's no field there, remember? At least, only enough to power an air-floater.'

'I'm still working on it,' said Yggur.

'What progress do you have to report?'

'None that I care to speak about in a general gathering.'

'If we can't move the thapters once we make them,' Flydd said with deliberation, 'there's no point to any of this.'

'I've said it will be done,' Yggur said frostily. 'Is there anything else?' His eye fell on Tiaan and he gestured for her to come up.

She did so reluctantly, hating to be the focus of everyone's attention, and she hadn't even had time to brush her hair.

'I've extended my node maps,' Tiaan burst out, but couldn't think what to say next. She hastily unrolled her master map so they'd look at it and not her. Everyone did, and the tension eased.

Yggur took the other side of the map and beckoned to Nish, who held her side. Tiaan outlined the thapter's flight track across to Tirthrax and Fadd, up the east coast to Roros, west to Taranta and back down the west coast of Faranda to the Foshorn.

'I've learned a lot,' she said, 'as you can see from the map. It shows another seventy-eight nodes, some of them powerful, and the extent of their fields. Many were not previously known, as far as I can tell. Of course, this wasn't a proper survey and there are many gaps. I had to sleep,' she said apologetically. 'All it really tells us is how little we know.'

'It almost doubles what we know about the nodes of the world,' said Flydd.

'Some were very strange,' she went on. 'The one at the Hornrace –'

'We'll come to that later,' said Flydd hastily. 'Malien or I will tell that tale, if you don't mind.'

Tiaan did not mind at all. She looked at Yggur, then hesitated.

'Would you like to go down?' he said kindly.

'There's . . . something else.' She gasped it out.

'About fields?'

'No.'

'Oh? Well, please go on.'

Tiaan had her hand in her capacious pocket, clutching the globe for comfort. 'Before we left, you gave me Golias's globe.' She held it high and the lamplight gleamed off it. 'You asked me to look at it in my spare time.'

'Never mind,' said Yggur. 'I've decided to begin again from scratch.' He put out his hand.

Tiaan held onto the globe. She glanced around the room. Flydd was staring at her in puzzlement. Fyn-Mah was writing notes on a scrap of paper. Irisis played with a controller apparatus in her lap. Nish was staring into the fire.

'Yes, Tiaan?' Malien said encouragingly.

Tiaan flicked her wrist as if spinning a ball, but held the globe tight. Its internal spheres revolved, darting reflections in all directions, then she squeezed her fingers and the layers froze as if they'd been locked in place.

'I've solved the puzzle,' she said softly. 'I know how the globe works.'

There was dead silence. Yggur set his goblet down with a clatter, looking to Flydd and Malien as if he suspected them of organising a joke at his expense. 'How did you get it apart, and back together?'

'I didn't need to. As we were going along,' she said, 'I observed it closely and made a model of all the layers, in my mind. The first few were easy enough. The sixth, seventh and eighth proved rather difficult.'

'We'll take that as a modest understatement,' said Yggur.

'Once I knew how each of the layers was formed,' Tiaan went on, confidently now, 'and how they related to each other, it was a matter of using my artisan's experience, and what I'd learned of geomancy from Gilhaelith and the Aachim, to work out how the globe could be used to farspeak. I like solving puzzles. *Things* are so much easier than people . . .'

'Only to you, my little artisan.' Yggur was smiling now.

'But that was only half the problem,' Tiaan said. 'I knew there was something else at the core, but there was no way to see it without breaking the globe. It's a lot heavier than the glass and metal foil the layers are made from, so the core had to be something very heavy. I weighed the globe, then again in water, and discovered that the core had to be heavier than iron, or even lead. But what elements are heavier than lead?' She looked at each of them but no one spoke. 'Only gold, platinum, and quicksilver.'

Putting the globe down on the table, Tiaan spun it hard. 'It didn't spin like a solid globe would. See how it wobbles? The core has to be liquid, and the only liquid metal is quicksilver.'

They were all staring at her now. Tiaan could feel a hot flush rising up her throat. 'But there was one last problem to be solved. The globe contains everything needed to act as a farspeaker, but how was it powered? There had to be a crystal at its core, in the quicksilver. What sort of a crystal? I could see nothing through the liquid metal.

'I channelled power into the globe – so much power that even a dead crystal would have to respond. But this crystal wasn't dead, and it gave forth such a strong aura that I could read it with my pliance. That told me what kind of crystal it had to be. It's monazite.'

'What's monazite?' said Irisis.

'A stubby, hard yellow mineral Gilhaelith showed me once.'

'It's the first time I've heard of any mancer using monazite,' said Flydd sceptically. 'It doesn't hold power at all.'

'It doesn't need to. Monazite has a particular and unique virtue,' Tiaan said. 'It generates power from within itself. Not much, but enough to power a farspeaker, and it lasts forever.'

'Forever?' said Malien.

'Thousands of years, at any rate.'

'But no one has ever been able to use the globe,' said Flydd. 'Some of the best mancers in the world have wasted their lives trying to.'

'Including me,' growled Yggur. 'I can't believe –'

'I read some of their writings in Gilhaelith's library,' Tiaan replied. 'In ancient times, mancers tried to recharge the globe, but the power was dispersed by the liquid metal. Besides, monazite can't hold a charge.'

'And recent mancers, such as my humble self?' said Yggur. 'Why did they not discover the answer?'

'You know as well as I do, surr.' The flush now covered her face up to the roots of her hair. Tiaan just wanted to get away.

'Indulge me, artisan.'

'Since fields were discovered a century ago, mancers seldom think of any other kinds of power. Malien and yourself are the only ones who still use the old ways. But the globe employs an entirely different force, forgotten aeons ago.'

'Then why doesn't it work?' cried Yggur in frustration.

'It's a puzzle.'

'A puzzle?' he echoed.

'No one else knew how to solve it because no one else could see all the layers at once, or understand how they worked together to create a farspeaker.' She squeezed the top and bottom of Golias's globe, then flicked her hand. The eight layers revolved. Tiaan stood with her eyes closed, visualising the moving layers, squeezed again, and all froze into place. 'There.'

She held the globe out to Yggur but he did not take it, so she went on.

'I work out the required alignment in my mind, spin the globe and, when the layers come to the right alignment, I stop them in place. The globe is ready to be used.'

'So you say,' said Malien. 'But how can you prove it?'

From her other pocket, Tiaan took a small piece of crystal wrapped around with fine wires in intricate patterns. She carried it to the back of the room, sat it on a chair and returned to the front. Holding Golias's globe close to her mouth, she said, 'How can I prove it?'

A hollow, scratchy voice came from the crystal at the back of the room, fractionally delayed, 'How can I prove it?'

Yggur's eyes shone. 'Oh, this is glorious! How far can you separate them, Tiaan?'

'I don't know. This is the first test.'

'How did you know it would work?' he exclaimed.

'I didn't. I almost didn't mention it, I was so afraid of looking a fool.'

'Let's try it now, at once. This is marvellous, marvellous.' Yggur leapt up and began striding back and forth in his excitement. 'Tiaan, write something on a piece of paper and give it to Nish. Don't tell us what it says.' Yggur took up the wire-wrapped crystal. 'Come on, everyone. We'll go right to the other end of the fortress.'

Tiaan scribbled something on a piece of paper and handed it to Nish. Everyone else trooped out after Yggur. Nish remained in his chair.

Tiaan wished he had gone too, but he didn't budge. She gave them ten minutes to get to the other end of the building, then said, slowly and carefully, 'I just want to go to bed.'

Five minutes later Yggur reappeared, panting. He'd run all the way. '"I just want to go to bed",' he quoted.

'That's correct,' said Nish, showing him the paper.

'And as strongly as if you had spoken in my ear.' Yggur came across and shook her hand. 'This is it – the missing piece of our plan. You may just have won the war for us, Tiaan. Let's sit down

389

in the morning and work out a design for more farspeakers. Skilled artisans at one of Flydd's manufactories can make them for us. It won't be easy but it's within their skills, Irisis tells me. And monazite isn't a rare mineral. Tell me, can we use those to communicate with each other?' Yggur held up the little wire-wrapped crystal.

'It's not that simple,' said Tiaan. 'Golias's globe is the master farspeaker, while the other is just a slave, if you like.'

'Go on,' said Yggur.

'The master drives the message out, but can only be used once the key has been set. The slave farspeaker only responds to that setting. It can call the master farspeaker, if the master is set to it, but it can't call another slave. If someone with a slave farspeaker wants to talk to someone else with another slave, the message must go through the master.'

'An excellent idea,' said Flydd. 'We must maintain control over what people say to each other. Free speech is a wicked thing.'

Tiaan, who had been imagining all the good things one could do with a farspeaker, such as talking to her mother, was so shocked that she couldn't speak.

'Spoken like a true scrutator.' Yggur clapped him jovially on the shoulder. 'Klarm will be tickled pink when he gets one. It'll save him months of travel and give him so much more time for drinking and wenching.'

'Presumably a message from the master farspeaker can be heard by all the slaves,' said Flydd, frowning.

Tiaan didn't want to answer, though the question was an interesting one. She thought for some time before replying. 'It could, if all slave farspeakers were the same. But an artisan could tailor them so they only respond to one particular setting. Then you simply lock Golias's globe at the correct setting and speak, and only the person you're talking to will hear your message.'

'Oh, very good,' said the scrutator.

'The message isn't instantaneous,' said Yggur. 'I wonder why?'

'Who knows what tortuous route it takes, via the ultra-dimensional ethyr,' said Flydd. 'Who cares if it takes hours to get from one side of Lauralin to the other, or even a day? Not even a skeet can beat it, and it can't be intercepted.'

'Nor will it tear your throat out, like a skeet will if you step too close to its cage,' said Flangers.

They all gathered around, excitedly discussing the device and how it might alter the balance of the war. No one noticed Tiaan slip away quietly.

Malien realised that Tiaan was missing and went to her room.

'I wasn't joking,' said Tiaan. 'I just want to go to bed.'

'I know. But tell me, you didn't seem quite as pleased as everyone else, at the end.'

'It was the way Flydd was talking about it,' she said. 'Wanting to control what people say. Farspeakers could be wonderful things. If only we all had them I could talk to Marnie now.'

'You miss her terribly, don't you?'

'She's the most annoying woman in the world, and we fight constantly when we're together. She says the most awful things to me. But I *do* miss her – she's the only family I've got. And I'm worried. She's too old for the breeding factory now. What will become of her? She has no idea how to look after herself.'

'She can afford a house and servants.'

'If they'll put up with her.'

'I'm sure she's all right. And Xervish *is* a good man.'

'The way he talks frightens me. The powerful wouldn't use farspeakers to help people, but to control them.'

'But when the war is over, the whole world will be transformed.'

'But how?' said Tiaan. 'For good or for ill?'

Later that evening, Malien, Flydd and Yggur met secretly, and Flydd told Yggur about what they'd seen at the Hornrace.

'I don't understand why the Aachim broke off their plans for conquest,' said Yggur. 'With all those constructs they could have swept from one side of Lauralin to the other.'

'We Aachim have never been empire builders,' said Malien. 'Security has always been more important to us. And often, after a setback, instead of fighting back we've simply cut ourselves off from the world.'

'Have you any idea what Vithis is constructing?' asked Yggur.

'It's either a bridge – a gigantic arch – or a building spanning the gulf,' said Malien. 'Though I can't imagine why anyone would go to such an immense labour.'

'Any building to span the Hornrace would be a mighty one indeed,' said Yggur. 'I'd have thought it beyond the capabilities of any civilisation.'

'We used to be fond of extravagant symbols,' said Malien. 'Vithis may simply be putting his mark on Santhenar in the strongest way possible.'

'Do you think so?' Yggur wondered.

'If he is, it masks a deeper purpose,' said Malien.

'Such as?'

'A gate to ferry the rest of the Aachim from Aachan? A device to change the weather and make the desert bloom?'

'Could it be a weapon?'

'It could. They are greatly advanced in geomancy. They taught Tiaan how to make a gate, something no one on this world could have done. They built eleven thousand constructs on Aachan in a couple of decades. They may be building a weapon that we cannot even conceive of.'

FORTY-ONE

Nish went back to his room that night, fretting more than usual. Everyone else seemed to have achieved wonders but *his* students weren't trained yet, nor the air-floaters ready, through no fault of his own. Now that the thapter had returned he could do some work with his pilots and artificers, but there was nothing he could do about the air-floaters. Ghorr's air-dreadnoughts had consumed all the suitable silk cloth available in Meldorin, and only silk would do. Nothing else was light yet strong enough for an air-floater gasbag.

Unfortunately, he was in charge and neither Yggur nor Flydd was interested in excuses. They simply expected the problem to be solved, and quickly. Nish could see no alternative but to make a raid on the silk warehouses of Thurkad, dangerous though it would be.

He went to see Flydd and Yggur about it in the morning and asked if they knew which warehouses contained silk cloth.

'I've no idea,' said Yggur. 'Thurkad had thousands of warehouses. Klarm would know but naturally he's not here. I'll put a discreet word around in Hripton, and also up at The Entrance, where all the thugs and pirates dwell. Someone there will know.'

'And I'll need to take the air-floater and a crew to Thurkad to steal the stuff,' said Nish.

'Klarm's using it at the moment,' said Flydd.

'Is he ever not?' said Nish. 'It's ironic, don't you think, that I need the air-floater so I can make more of them, and train more pilots, but I can never get access to it.'

'It's generally the work done behind the scenes that wins the war,' Flydd said, 'rather than the armies slaughtering each other. Very well, put a plan together and, if you locate the silk, we'll see what can be done. One step at a time, remember?'

Two days later, Seneschal Berty brought a villainous-looking old fellow to Nish's shed. He had two teeth in the bottom jaw and three in the top, whose purpose seemed solely to hold the blackened pipe that never left his mouth. He certainly never used them to chew his food, his diet being entirely liquid. It was a foul-smelling brew, too, even worse than the turnip brandy the miners used to drink around the back of the manufactory. It smelled as though it had been distilled from the cook's compost heap, a festering mound of vegetable peelings, food scraps, burnt fat and bones that even the dogs turned their noses up at.

'This is Artificer Cryl-Nish Hlar,' said Berty, keeping well upwind. 'He is known to his friends as Nish. You are not his friend, Phar, and never will be. You may call him Artificer Hlar.'

'Yerz, Nish,' said Phar.

'Hello,' said Nish. 'Come inside. No, let's go out in the fresh air.'

The air in the yard was anything but fresh, reeking as it did of wood smoke and hot metal, sweaty labourers and bubbling tar. All were ambrosia beside Phar, who was small, bandy-legged, red of eye and so foul of breath that it signalled his arrival from five paces away. Nish could not imagine being cooped up in the thapter with him, if it should come to that. Phar's sandals revealed splintered black toenails and ankles from which the grime could have been peeled with a knife. He was missing two toes, one thumb and half his left ear. He was, in short, the most repulsive individual Nish had ever seen.

Nish had already heard about Phar, who had a single redeeming feature. He had, through more than sixty years of crime centred around the waterfront of Thurkad, developed an encyclopaedic knowledge of the warehouses and their contents.

He loved the ancient city, in his own squalid and inarticulate way, and nothing would have induced him to leave it. Nothing, that is, but the threat of being eaten by a lyrinx. So Nish gleaned eventually from Phar's rambling and incoherent discourse, punctuated regularly by slugs from his putrid leather flagon.

You were never in any danger, thought Nish, looking him up and down in disgust. There wasn't a lyrinx in Santhenar that would have touched him, not even to feed its starving children.

'I understand that you know the warehouses of Thurkad well, Mr Phar. I wonder if you would be so good –' He stopped at the seneschal's slashing gesture.

'Allow me, Nish,' said the seneschal. 'Phar. We want silk cloth. Strong cloth, best quality. Long bolts of it. Where do we get it?'

Nish passed Phar a map of the waterfront which Yggur had given him. 'Can you read, Phar?'

'Maps. Not words.'

Nish spread the map on the paving stones. Phar squinted at it, picked his nose then turned the map upside down. He grinned broadly, his wagging pipe spilling clots of tarry ash on the map. Nish brushed it off hastily. The disgusting stuff stuck to his fingers.

'Here,' said Phar, pointing with a snotty fingertip. 'Street of the Sail-makers. All these buildings behind are warehouses. This, this and this, all silk.'

'You're absolutely sure?' said Nish.

'Bah,' said Phar, picking the other nostril and parking the residue on the edge of the map.

'Disgusting brute,' piped Berty, cuffing him over the half-ear. 'Wipe that off, you pig.'

Phar smeared snot halfway across the sheet. Snatching the map, Nish rolled it up and said, 'We'll go at first light.'

Phar began to shamble off. 'Not likely,' said the seneschal. He called a pair of guards over. 'Look after this fellow for the night, will you? And take good care of him; he's escaped more times than you fellows have changed your underwear.'

'Never change my underwear,' said the first guard, evidently puzzled by the comparison. 'Only when it falls to pieces.'

'You're in good company then. Lock him up tight. If he escapes you'll be explaining why to Lord Yggur.'

The mission seemed doomed from the first second. When the guards went to the cell for Phar in the morning he wasn't there; despite all the precautions, he had got away.

'What the blazes were you doing?' Nish roared, practically incoherent with rage. It did not matter that Seneschal Berty had given the orders and the guards carried them out. He, Nish, was in charge and there was no excuse for failure.

Berty looked worried too, which was unusual. He was always the picture of control. He hastily roused out the guards and soon a hundred people were looking for the thief.

An hour later Nish was sitting on the step to his shed, head in hands, a position he'd spent a lot of time in lately, when Yggur came stalking out the front doors of Fiz Gorgo, holding a crumpled, twitching object as far away from him as possible.

'I believe you're looking for *this*,' he said, dropping Phar on the ground. The villain splatted, like a cow defecating. Lying on the paving stones, reeking, he did rather resemble a pile of droppings.

'You won't run away again, will you, Phar?' said Yggur.

Phar covered his face, making a ratty squeal. He shook his head vigorously.

Yggur inspected his fingers, seeming to find some distasteful residue there, for he crossed to a wash trough and scrubbed his hands with sand-soap and water.

'*You* won't let us down, will you, Nish?' Without waiting for an answer Yggur went inside.

No, Nish said to himself, I won't, and he finished stowing his gear in the thapter. Yggur would not let him take the airfloater to such a dangerous place, deeming it too slow and vulnerable to lyrinx attack. Nish heartily agreed. They were to leave immediately.

'Where's Malien?' he said to his crew after they had been waiting for half an hour. She was to pilot the thapter to Thurkad.

No one had seen Malien. He found her in her bed, looking wan.

'I'm sorry, Nish. I've been throwing up all night. I don't think I can even stand up.'

'Was it something you ate?'

'No. I'm afraid I overdid it, flying the thapter all that time. I've been feeling poorly for days. Maybe tomorrow . . .'

'Well, look after yourself.' He went out. Tomorrow was going to be too late. Nish was acutely conscious how time was fleeting by. It was mid-winter and they had to be ready for war in less than two months. At this stage, even a day could make the difference between success and failure.

In an emergency, Nish supposed Flydd and Yggur would agree to his taking the air-floater, though it was exquisitely vulnerable to attack by lyrinx. A single tear in the gasbag meant the loss of the craft and everyone on it, and any chance of recovering thapters. And though it was the mating season, when the enemy avoided all-out war, there would be plenty of lyrinx about who were neither hibernating nor mating. No, it had to be the thapter and they must go today. Flydd needed it in a few days' time, to visit the manufactories in the south-east, which were to make farspeakers and other devices for the spring offensive.

None of Nish's trainee pilots had ever been at the controls of a real thapter and there was no possibility that they would be allowed to take this one to Thurkad. He needed the best for such a dangerous mission. He would have to ask Tiaan.

Nish had kept clear of her ever since her return, for Tiaan made it plain that she loathed him. She only spoke to him when she had to, and avoided him whenever she could.

And if she refused, as he expected her to? Nish had no idea what he would do.

He knocked on her door. She did not answer. He knocked again. Still nothing. It was early and she could be asleep. He turned the handle.

'Tiaan?' he said quietly.

Her bed was empty. Perhaps she was down the hall having breakfast. Then Nish heard splashing, realised his error and, too late, turned to go. Tiaan appeared around the corner, naked from her bath, towelling her dark hair vigorously.

Had he slipped out at once he might have got away with it, for the towel was over her face. Nish hesitated just long enough for her to open her eyes and see him staring at her.

She fled back into the bathing room. Nish went the other way, scarlet with mortification. Now what was he supposed to do?

Irisis laughed herself sick when he confessed his folly. 'What a prize clown you are, Nish. You can't do anything right, can you?'

It stung, even from his best friend. 'Not with Tiaan. I was trying to do the right thing.'

'But Nish, she's such a repressed little chit, and you sneaked into her bedroom. How could you imagine she was going to react?'

'I didn't sneak. I knocked twice.'

'It was her *bedroom*. You should have knocked loudly and not gone in until she answered.'

'I was trying not to disturb her.'

'And she didn't have any clothes on?'

'Completely naked,' he said miserably, 'and still gleaming wet from her bath . . .'

'Remember who you're talking to,' Irisis snapped.

'Sorry.'

'She'll never forgive you, not if she lives for a hundred years.'

'I know. I've ruined everything.'

'Not necessarily. Just because she despises you and holds you in deepest contempt –'

'You're enjoying this, aren't you?'

She sniggered. 'Of course I am. You were being a rotten little perv and now you've got your just desserts.'

'I wasn't!' he said plaintively. 'Why won't you believe me?'

'Because I don't want to. It'd spoil the story, for me and for everyone.'

'You're not going to tell the others! No, please don't, Irisis.'

'Of course I am. We can all do with a good laugh. But, just to show good faith, I'll get you out of your little problem.'

'How?' Nish said suspiciously.

'As I was saying, just because Tiaan despises you more deeply than –'

'Thank you! I got the message.'

'– it doesn't mean that she won't fly the thapter.'

'But . . .' He looked at Irisis in sudden hope.

'If you hadn't caught her at her bath, and she had agreed, would she have done it as a favour to you?'

'Of course not. She loathes me.'

'Well, there you are. Now she just loathes you a little more. Er, a lot more, actually.'

'Thanks! But I still don't see –'

'Go and talk to Malien. Confess your folly and get her to ask Tiaan to do it. Malien is her only friend.'

Malien looked a little better, and she also laughed when Nish shamefacedly told her what he'd done. 'That's worth two hours with the healer, Nish. How do you get yourself into such messes?'

'Will you plead with her?'

'I'll ask Tiaan. She's been working night and day on the far-speaker designs, but I believe they're finished now.' She pulled the bell cord and asked the servant, who appeared straight away, to fetch Tiaan at once.

'I'll go,' Nish said hastily.

'No, stay. Time is precious. Sit over there.'

He took a chair by the window.

Shortly Tiaan appeared. 'How are you, Malien? They said you weren't well.'

'I've felt better. Dare say I'll be all right in a day or two.'

'If there's anything –' She caught sight of Nish and a flush mounted up her cheeks. 'You vile, disgusting, repuls–'

'I gather you had a small incident this morning,' Malien said mildly.

'He sneaked into my bedroom so he could spy on me at my bath!' she cried. 'He's always been a squalid little pervert.'

399

Nish, even redder in the face than she was, wanted to die. He couldn't think of a single thing to say. Between her and him, his words had always made things worse. He opened his mouth but Malien signalled, hand up, for him to say nothing.

'I believe he thought you were asleep,' said Malien, 'and did not want to wake you suddenly.'

'If you believe that –' Tiaan cried, then broke off. 'I'm sorry, Malien.'

'I've been insulted by the most powerful people in the land, Tiaan. There's nothing you can say to upset me. Now listen – I'm ill and can't fly the thapter to Thurkad. It must go today or it will be too late. Nish went to your room to ask if you would do it.'

Tiaan opened her mouth to refuse, but Malien went on. 'No one else can do it, yet it must be done. So I'm asking you, Tiaan. Will you fly the thapter?'

After a long hesitation, she said, 'Of course, Malien. But let it be known I am not doing it for *him*.' Turning to Nish she said formally, 'I will be ready in one hour. Will that be sufficient?'

'Yes, thank you.'

Still red in the face, Tiaan went out.

'Sounds as though it's going to be a jolly trip,' said Malien, 'what with you, Tiaan and Phar. Tell me all about it when you return.'

Tiaan turned up as the last grain of the hourglass fell, when the soldiers and Phar were already below. Nish took his place beside her. It was going to be a hideous trip. Tiaan, at the controller, was like an iceberg that, instead of thawing, seemed to get colder by the second. Nish tried to apologise.

'Don't say anything. Your apology means nothing, since I know you're only offering it to get what you want.'

'But, Tiaan, I didn't mean –'

'Do you think I don't know your character by now?' she hissed. 'You're a true son of your father. I have nothing to say to you. Just tell me where you want to go and what you want to do.'

He did so, since the soldiers were already muttering among

themselves. Morale was critical to the success of any mission. Someone began to bang on the lower hatch.

'What's that disgusting smell?' said Tiaan, edging away from him. 'That wasn't you, was it?'

'Of course not!' Flushing again. Nish lifted the hatch. He didn't need to take a step down the ladder to discover that he'd made a gross mistake. The stench was so appalling that even the soldiers looked green.

'Get him out of here,' said the first, 'or none of us will still be alive when we get there.'

'Phar!' snapped Nish. 'I should have put you in the cauldron and boiled the filth off you. Grab hold of him, lads. We'll take him up the back.' He climbed up. 'Would you set down, please, Tiaan? We'll have to take this villain up to the platform and tie him on.'

'You should have thought of that before we left,' she said without looking at him. Tiaan directed the thapter toward a mud island in the swamp forest, taking it expertly down between the trees. She stood to one side, wrinkling her nose, as the soldiers manhandled Phar over the side and back to the shooter's platform, where they secured him with ropes.

The stink lingered, and even after the long flight to Thurkad, Nish could still smell the fellow. They arrived over the city around one in the morning. Tiaan was standing at the controller, practically asleep on her feet. She was swaying from side to side.

'Are you all right?' he asked.

'Of course I'm all right!' she snapped. 'Why wouldn't I be?'

He began to unroll the map of the city. Tiaan touched a panel globe above her head, which illuminated the binnacle with a soft white glow. Nish spread the map out as best he could over the irregular surface.

'These three are the silk warehouses.' Nish pointed to the buildings behind the Street of the Sail-makers. 'Any will do.'

'Just tell me which one you want to go to,' she said curtly.

'The easternmost one,' said Nish.

'Thank you. You can go now.'

'I'll leave the map –'

'I don't need it. Once I see a map I never forget it.'

He didn't see how that could be possible, for Nish was used to poring over maps for hours and still getting lost. However, he rolled it up and went below. The place still reeked of Phar.

Shortly the thapter settled with a bump on a sloping roof. Timbers creaked underneath them and several slates cracked. Tiaan lifted the thapter off again, hovering just above the roof.

'We're here,' she called down the hatch.

'Time to go,' Nish said to the soldiers. 'Vim and Slann, would you bring Phar? He's a burglar and it's his job to find us a way in. I hope he can, otherwise we'll have to make a hole in the roof and I'd rather avoid that. Tiaan, if you would keep watch . . .'

'What if the enemy appear?'

'If they see you and attack, go up at once. Come back every hour on the hour if you can, but don't risk yourself or the thapter for us.'

For the very first time, some kind of feeling showed in her eyes, as if she'd realised that he was, after all, a human being not completely without redeeming features. To be abandoned in a city possessed by the lyrinx was not pleasant to contemplate.

'I won't,' she said.

They gathered on the sloping roof beside the thapter with all their gear: packs full of tools for breaking and entering, coils of rope, a small hand winch, weapons. It was as dark as a cellar full of coal and the roof was wet and hard to stand on.

'Ready?' said Nish. 'Come on, Vim,' he hissed in the direction of the rear platform. 'Get a move on.'

'Phar's not here.'

'What?' Nish scrambled up the back. The stench lingered in the open turret but it was empty. Nish felt along the rails, encountered the ropes and ran his fingers down them. The ends had been neatly severed.

'He must have had a blade hidden away, and jumped off as soon as we touched down,' Nish raged. 'Why didn't anyone search him?'

'We searched him,' said Vim. 'But, well . . .'

'I know,' said Nish. It was a disgusting job. There was no point blaming anyone. But it was not a good start.

FORTY-TWO

'I dare say he'll come back once he's done his bit of pilfering,' said Slann. 'He won't want to stay here.'

'If he does I'll kick his arse right out into the middle of the bay.'

They had to break in through the roof. It wasn't difficult but pulling up slates in the dark made more noise than Nish liked.

'If there are any lyrinx about,' he said, 'they now know we're here. And they'll see us even though we can't see them.'

'It'll be a quick death then,' said Slann, who had a melancholy disposition.

'Though not a painless one,' said Vim. 'Better get down there, quick.'

He fixed a rope around a roof beam. They climbed down it and, after breaking though a ceiling, ended up in the top floor of the warehouse. It was empty.

'Suppose the silk will be in the basement,' said Slann, 'and we'll have to carry it up ten flights of stairs.'

'Shows how much you know,' scoffed Vim. 'They wouldn't keep precious silk in the basement where it'd go mouldy. It'd be up high, where it's warm and dry. Naw, I reckon the place is empty.'

'It'd better not be.' Nish gloomily headed for the stairs.

Before long they were on their way up again. The warehouse contained nothing but rat droppings.

The thapter was still there, thankfully. Phar was not. They climbed in.

'Empty,' said Nish.

Tiaan did not look surprised. 'Shall I go to the next one?'

'Please.' He sat on the floor and put his head in his hands. Nish had a pretty good idea what he would find in the second warehouse. Nothing. Phar must have been extracting a petty revenge, and now that he was gone they had no hope of finding the right warehouse.

The second warehouse took a long time to break into, but proved as empty as the first. Nish was in a sick despair by the time he returned. Tiaan said nothing at all, just carried them to the third.

Nish consulted the stars as they got out. It was three in the morning. Dawn was around seven-thirty. Plenty of time if the warehouse was empty. Not long at all if they found what they wanted and had to lift it through the roof.

The top floor proved to be empty. So did the one below that. Halfway down the stairs, Nish paused. 'I can smell something.'

'So can I,' said Vim. 'Frying onions.'

It had not occurred to Nish that there might still be people living in Thurkad. He'd assumed that the lyrinx would have driven them away, or eaten them all. But unless the enemy had become vegetarians, there were people below.

'Where's it coming from, do you think?'

Slann sniffed the air. 'Can't tell.'

'Be as quiet as you possibly can. If they find us, they're bound to want a ride to somewhere safe.'

Nish shuttered his lantern to a slit and crept around the corner onto the next level. He slid open the door, shone the light around and could have wept for joy. The whole floor was packed with rolls of cloth.

'Come on,' he hissed, running to the first stack. It proved to be cotton, and so did the second, but the third was silk. Beautiful silk.

404

Nish sorted through the rolls. It didn't have to be the finest cloth but it needed to be strong. All the rolls at the top turned out to be too fine, no use for anything but scarves and nightwear. 'The best stuff is right down the bottom,' said Nish. 'Pull that one out, would you?'

The soldier, whose name he could not remember, hauled at the roll. It did not budge. 'We'll have to shift the ones up top first.'

Vim climbed the end of the stack, which was a couple of spans tall, and began hurling rolls down from the top. They thumped onto the floorboards.

'Don't do that!' Nish waved his arms frantically. 'If there are people below, they'll come up to see what's going on. Hand the damn things down.'

They were all panting by the time they'd uncovered the bottom of the stack, and the dust was tickling their noses. Nish resisted the urge to sneeze. 'Help me unroll this one.'

They spread it out along the floor. It was good strong cloth, better than anything they'd been able to obtain at Fiz Gorgo. There were no flaws, no rat or moth holes. He paced out the length and width, calculating, then rolled it up again.

'We'll need eight of these to make three airbags. Vim, Slann, take this one. Leave it upstairs at the rope and come straight back.'

'It's bloody heavy,' said Slann, a weedy man, as they heaved it to their shoulders.

'Just get on with it.'

They went out, the cloth sagging between them. Scarcely had they turned the corner when there came a cry of rage.

'Hoy! Put that down, you. Neahl, Roys, they're stealing our cloth.'

The other four soldiers pelted to the door. Nish drew his sword and followed with the lantern. Opening the shutter wide he flashed it down the stairs.

About three flights down, a crowd of at least thirty people, ranging in age from dirty children to withered oldsters, had gathered. A good few of them looked fit, though they were only armed with an assortment of knives.

'What are you doing here?' said Nish.

'We live here,' replied a snaggle-toothed old man.

'But the lyrinx –'

'Don't bother us and we don't bother them, any more'n the rats do.' The oldster gave a squeaking kind of laugh.

'Well, we've just come for some of this silk.'

'Can't have it,' said the old fellow. 'It's our'n.'

'You're not using it.'

'We will one day, now clear orf!'

'We can pay you for it,' said Nish, feeling the ground sinking beneath him.

'Get lost! Can't eat yer stinkin' money.'

'You fellows get your crossbows ready,' Nish said in a low voice.

'They are,' a soldier replied. 'Just give the word.'

'Don't shoot unless there's no choice.' Nish raised his voice. 'Whether you accept the money or not is up to you, old fellow. We're taking the cloth anyway – for the war.'

Fingering a small bag of silver out of his pocket, he tossed it down the steps. It landed halfway and burst, scattering coins everywhere.

The old fellow did not look down. Nor, to Nish's surprise, did anyone else. Not even the children scrambled for the silver. The cold feeling in the pit of his stomach grew colder.

'We don't give a damn about the war,' said the old man. 'The lyrinx leave us alone.'

'Raise your weapons, lads,' Nish said softly. Then louder, 'Come any closer and we'll shoot.' Nish drew back to give the soldiers with the bows a clear shot, though he still hoped that they could intimidate the crowd into running away. To the others he said, 'Take it up, Vim and Slann. You two, get the next bolt. *And hurry!*'

Vim and Slann thumped up the stairs. The second pair of soldiers hefted their bolt of silk. The crowd were a quivering mass of indignation. Nish darted in and tried to pick up the third bolt. It was extremely heavy, and when he got it onto his shoulders the ends of the roll bent to the floor. He'd never carry it up the stairs on his own.

'Don't move!' said the soldier on the left.

Nish staggered to the door. The old man was slowly creeping forward. 'If you have to shoot, try not to hurt him,' said Nish. 'This is their home, after all.'

The crowd moved up behind the oldster. One step; two; three. They weren't looking at the two soldiers. Every eye was on Nish.

'No further!' Nish shouted. 'Soldiers, shoot if they go one more step.'

The old man looked Nish in the eye and kept coming.

'Stop or we'll shoot!' said the soldier on the left.

The old man ignored him. The crossbow snapped, the bolt taking him in the middle of the forehead and hurling him backwards into the throng. A woman wailed. Children screamed. Two men took the oldster under the arms and dragged his body down the stairs into the darkness. The rest moved down to the limit of visibility and remained there. The soldier frantically reloaded his crossbow.

'You bloody fool!' Nish raged, dropping his roll. 'I said don't hurt him.'

'And then you said to shoot if he went any further,' said the soldier, as if that made it all right.

Vim and Slann came thumping down the stairs, followed by the second pair of soldiers. 'What's happened?' panted Vim.

Nish told them.

'Not good,' said Slann. 'I wonder what they'll do now?'

'I don't dare think. Come on. Get the rest of the rolls up. We need another six.'

The soldiers went up with another three rolls of silk, the second pair dragging a bolt each. Silence fell.

'It's very quiet down there,' said Nish. 'I wonder what they're up to?'

'Running for their lives,' said the soldier who had fired. 'Vermin.'

407

Disgusted, Nish returned to the silk floor and began to drag the remaining bolts toward the entrance. He was lifting the third when the soldier who had fired clutched at his throat and toppled down the steps. The other soldier threw himself in through the entrance.

'What was it?' said Nish.

'A slug from a sling, I'd say. Caught him in the throat.'

'Do you think he'll be all right?'

'If the slug didn't kill him, or the fall, *they* will when he gets to the –'

Slaughtering noises came up from the darkness. Nish looked around the corner. The lantern still glowed in the middle of the step. He ducked back hastily as another slug smacked into the side of the doorframe.

The soldier picked it up. It was a piece of tightly rolled lead sheet, about the size of a plum. 'Enough to kill a man if it hits him in the right place. Are they coming?'

'Couldn't see anything.'

'Makes it worse. Should I put the bow around the corner and send a bolt down at them?'

'Might as well,' said Nish. 'Aim high. I don't want to kill anyone else. Though I don't suppose they'll be so scrupulous now.'

The soldier fired. A yelp was followed by sounds of people fleeing down the stairs.

Vim and Slann came creeping down and sprang in through the doorway.

'Where are the others?' said Nish.

'Roping the rolls and winching them up,' said Slann.

'All right. Let's get these last three.'

Before they could load them onto their shoulders, something clattered on the steps and began to rattle and *sploosh* its way down again. Something else followed it, then a third object.

'Sounds as though they're throwing buckets of water at us.'

'Why would they throw water –'

Nish smelt turpentine; then, with a *whoo-whoomph*, fire exploded up the stairs, licking in through the entrance and coiling around into the room. Nish's dangling sleeve began to smoke. He hurled himself backwards away from the door, dashing the flames out against the floor. Vim's hair was ablaze.

Nish whacked it out with his hands and they moved further away, staring at the flames which were roaring up past them. The three bolts of silk on the floor began to burn.

He tried to drag one out of the way but it was already well ablaze and the silk would be ruined.

'Can we get up the stairs?' called Slann, who was furthest from the door.

'Not a chance. Nor down.'

'If we close the door it'll keep the fire out.'

'For a while,' said Nish, who already suspected they were doomed.

They kicked the blazing silk down the stairs and dragged the door closed. It was solid wood and would take a while to catch, but burn it would. Nish sat down on the pile of silk rolls. The others took seats as well.

'Seems a stupid thing to do,' said Vim. 'Setting fire to the stairs.'

'The fire would go up before it went down,' Nish said wearily. 'They'd have plenty of time to get away.'

'But it's their home.'

'Plenty more warehouses in Thurkad.'

'That old man Welmi killed must have been an important fellow.'

'Must have been.'

'Any chance the fire will just go out?' said the soldier who had fired last.

'These old buildings are dry as tinder,' Slann replied. 'If there's a decent wind it could burn half the city down.'

'Good riddance. Thurkad always was a stinking place.'

'The outside of this building is stone,' said Nish.

'Makes no difference,' said Slann. 'Everything else will burn and the stone will fall down.'

'Any chance we can break through the outside walls?' Nish said a while later. The floor was growing hot and smoke had begun to wisp up through cracks in the boards.

Vim inspected the stone. 'Not a hope.'

'So we're going to burn to death?' said Vim.

'Looks like it,' Slann replied.

'Never thought I'd be going this way.'

The conversation petered out.

FORTY-THREE

Nish and the soldiers had been a long time. Tiaan's eyelids were drooping when she heard a cry from below.

'We've found it.'

She peered over the side of the thapter and saw lamplight through the hole. One of the soldiers had come up the rope with the hand winch slung over his shoulder. Another rope trailed down through the hole in the roof onto the ceiling. Climbing onto the side of the thapter, he attached the winch to the carrying racks that had been mounted at the back, pulled the rope through, tied it and began to wind.

'Heavy work,' he said conversationally.

'Looks like it,' said Tiaan, who'd never been good at idle talk.

'Could you bring the flier round a bit, d'ye think? The way the rope's hanging, we're likely to catch the silk on the hole in the roof.'

She rotated the thapter into position. 'How's that?'

'Perfect.'

'Did you find enough silk?'

'Plenty,' he grunted, winding slowly and panting with each circle of the handle.

The rolls came up, two lashed together and hanging vertically. The soldier pulled the top ends onto the racks, took a bight around the lower ends and slowly hauled them on.

'I'd help you if I could,' said Tiaan, 'but I can't leave the controller.' She didn't want him to think she was a shirker.

'I'm used to it. I don't know why the others are taking so long.'

He tied the bundle on, threw the end of the rope down through the hole and shortly began to heave the second bundle up, three bolts this time. No sooner had he finished, and was binding it to the racks, than the second soldier came hand over hand up the rope, roaring at the top of his voice.

'What's he saying?' said Tiaan.

'Fire!'

'Where?'

The second soldier pulled himself onto the racks, gasping. 'There were people living in the warehouse. There was a fight. Welmi's dead, and some of the natives, and now they've set fire to the building.'

'Where are Nish and the rest of the soldiers?' said Tiaan.

'Three floors down. Fire's coming up the stairs and they're trapped on the silk floor.'

'And there's no other way out?'

'Warehouses don't have windows.'

The horror of their situation made her bowels tighten. To be burned alive ... 'I don't see what we can do,' Tiaan said reluctantly. Yggur and Flydd had made her duty plain to her before she left. Firstly, and at all costs, she must bring back the thapter – it meant the difference between survival (if only for a time) and ruinous defeat. And it was their only hope of victory, faint though that seemed.

Secondly, Tiaan had been instructed to protect herself even at the cost of the lives of any or all the others, because her talent was irreplaceable. Doing so went against her feelings, but she would follow orders. Thirdly, she had to ensure that whatever silk they found got back to Fiz Gorgo. And finally, lowest in importance, she must do her best to protect the lives of her crew, including Nish.

Nish, her nemesis. And yet, how could she think of him, or any of them, trapped by the inferno and knowing that they were going to be burned to death? Tiaan couldn't allow that to happen, even to her enemy, if there was any safe way to prevent it. She came to a decision.

'Get the silk inside!' she rapped. 'Quick as you can.'

They obeyed, squeezing the rolls through the small lower hatch and dragging them below, and went back for the winch.

'Where are the breaking tools?' she said.

'Below, on the ceiling.'

'Get in.'

They climbed through the hatch. Tiaan pulled it down and latched it. Taking hold of the controller, she allowed the thapter to fall onto the roof.

Smashed tiles flew everywhere and the roof timbers emitted a wrenching groan, but didn't break. She hadn't hit them hard enough. Lifting the thapter again, she went a little higher and dropped the machine onto the same place.

More flying tiles; torn timbers flashed across her view, then part of the roof gave way and they were through, still falling. She brought the machine to rest just above the ceiling beams in a rain of splinters and tiles.

'Pick up the tools and get back in.' She eyed the ceiling timbers. They were not heavy ones.

Using the same approach, Tiaan dropped the thapter through the ceiling. It gave way easily, ceiling joists being lighter than roof beams. The room below was wreathed in smoke and the thapter struck the floor before she realised how close she was. The impact shook the building but the floor held. These were much stronger timbers and she didn't dare try to crash the thapter through them. It was solidly built but not indestructible.

'Get out,' she yelled. 'Chop holes in the floor on either side of that joist – there where the line of nails runs. Hack into the joist as well, and the next one.'

The soldiers threw themselves out and began chopping furiously. Tiaan went below and rifled through one of the compartments, looking for a steel towing cable with an eye on each end, which she had seen previously. She threw it down.

'Put one end through the first hole and bring it up through the second. Pass the second eye through the first and put it over the hook at the back of the thapter. Then stand clear.'

When that was done Tiaan took the thapter up hard. The cable twanged tight, the floorboards bowed. She had hoped to pull the floor joist out from the stone at the wall end, but it held. She reached out for the field, took more power; the joist bent then snapped in a fountain of broken floorboards, exposing the joists to either side.

'Chop through the joists,' she ordered. 'Quick!'

They cut them halfway, but even then it needed several thumps to break through the floor. She put the machine down on the floor below and the soldiers got to work with their axes. Tiaan climbed out and inspected the thapter with a lantern. The metal skin was bent and buckled in several places, gouged and scratched in others, but no serious damage had been done. She silently thanked the Aachim for their workmanship. Clankers were strongly built but this kind of treatment would have wrecked one.

This room was even smokier and Tiaan didn't see how anyone could have survived further down. She wadded up her sleeve and tried to breathe through it. Her eyes were stinging.

'Is there any point us going on?' she said to the furiously chopping soldiers. 'Surely they'll be dead by now.'

The taller of them, a dark-haired man with a circle of hairy moles on his chin, laid down his axe to wipe streaming eyes. A fit of coughing doubled him over.

'I'd imagine so. But if they're not, they'll be real pleased to see us.'

They broke through. The other soldier put his head down one hole. 'Hoy?'

There was no answer. 'That's bad,' he said.

Tiaan checked the other hole. 'The smoke isn't much worse than here and I can't see any fire.'

'Smoke can kill just as quickly.'

'Maybe they didn't hear us over the noise of the fire,' said Tiaan. 'They could be right down the other end of the floor.'

'Could be,' said the dark-haired soldier. 'That's where the entrance is.'

Tiaan used her cable again, but this time, as soon as the strain went on it, it snapped. She cursed and dropped the thapter hard onto the floor. The building shook but the beams hardly moved.

'These floors are built to carry a heavy load,' said one of the soldiers.

It was past time to give up. She'd already gone further than she should have. Flames were visible through cracks in the far door and the smoke oozing in was black and choking. But having come this far, Tiaan did not want to give up until she knew that they were dead. 'Is either of you game to go down through the hole?'

'I will,' said the shorter of the two. 'Nish is a good man. I know he'd do the same for me.' He looked Tiaan in the eye and his were moist, though perhaps it was the smoke. 'You should hear the stories about him.'

Again it made her stop and think. In the past, she'd deliberately absented herself whenever people had talked about Nish's deeds, not wanting to hear anything that would change her ill opinion of him.

The soldier tied the rope, threw it over, wrapped rags around his hands and slid down. As he reached the floor below, the building shuddered. The floor timbers squealed, and a crack zigzagged its way up the stone wall beside the thapter.

Tiaan felt cold inside. The building was going to collapse. She scrambled back into the thapter.

'Where are you going,' cried the soldier holding the rope.

She could see the whites of his eyes. He thought she was going to abandon them. 'I've got to be ready. Can you see them?'

He put his head down the hole. 'Not a thing.'

'Give your friend a shout. We can't wait any longer.'

'Hoy, Plymes. Come on! The bloody building's gonna fall down.'

He listened at the hole. 'I can hear him! He's coming up.'

'Is there anyone with him?'

'Can't see. I don't think so. Yes! Yes there is. There's Vim and Slann.'

'What about Nish, and the other soldier?'

'Can't see them.'

Again the building shuddered and the wall beside Tiaan seemed to move fractionally outward. This was madness. She lifted the thapter off the floor, one eye on the hole that she'd have to rise through, if she could find it in the thickening smoke, the other on the rope.

Again that white-eyed look from the soldier – and then he screamed, 'They're coming! Don't go, they're coming.'

Not nearly fast enough. She rotated the machine in the air, watching the cracks enlarging in the wall, the quivering of the floor above. If either collapsed on them, not even a thapter could get out. She'd been unforgivably stupid. She should never have come down.

Heads appeared through the hole: Vim and Slann, another soldier, then Nish. They scrambled through.

'Get in,' she screeched, waving her arms at them. 'I've already disobeyed my orders. I can't wait any longer.'

Vim and Slann took over the rope. The others climbed onto the racks. 'In,' she screamed. 'If you're not inside when we go up, you'll be scraped off like muck from a boot.'

They fell through the hatch, crowding the cockpit, gasping for breath. Nish came last and his eyes silently thanked her, but she had no time for that.

'Go below! You're in the way.' Tiaan revolved the thapter around the holes. 'What's the matter?' she yelled to Slann.

'Plymes has fallen off the rope. I'm going down.'

'I can't wait, Slann.'

He went anyway but stopped, just below the hole. Tiaan could still see his bald head. There came a tremendous roar as though something had collapsed below him, flames shot up through the hole and the floor buckled. Again the wall seemed to move outwards. Slann's clothes caught fire, then the rope. He stared up at them, his face riven with agony as he tried to climb the burning rope. As it flamed up over his hands, he had to let go.

416

'Vim! Come on!'

Vim was staring at the hole. He shook his head and leapt for the side of the thapter, catching hold of the racks. Tiaan, looking up, saw the floor above them move.

'Hang on,' she yelled. 'The upper floor's going to come down.'

She spun the thapter around and headed up towards the hole, which was moving. That meant the whole floor was slipping. There was no time to pull the hatch down. She manoeuvred through the belching smoke. The floor below suddenly collapsed and flames swirled towards them and over Vim, now clinging desperately to the racks.

She zigzagged the thapter up through the hole as the upper floor fell. Something struck the side of the thapter, making it lurch sharply. The smoke was even thicker on the next level and Tiaan hit the wall without realising it. Where was the ceiling hole? She had to go back and forth three times before she found it. Her lungs were burning. She shot up though it, up again and out through the roof to safety.

Hovering above the roof, she looked for a place to set down so Vim could come inside. The adjacent roof had a low pitch. She drifted across to it, settled down and put her head through the hatch.

The whole area was illuminated by the flames, which had ignited the timber wall of the neighbouring building. The racks were empty.

'Vim?' she yelled.

'Where is he?' said a soldier beside her.

'He must have fallen off when we struck the wall,' said Tiaan.

They looked back at the roof. Flames were coming up though the hole.

'He's dead,' said Nish beside her. 'They're all dead. Let's go home.'

He looked ghastly – soot-streaked, eyes running, a tremble in one arm. 'I led them to their deaths,' he said. 'It's not right that I got out and they didn't. I failed them.'

For the first time, Tiaan saw the man inside Nish and pitied him. She put a hand on his shoulder. 'We all did our best, Nish.

There's no more that anyone could have done.'

He nodded his thanks. 'You risked your life for us. You shouldn't have come down.'

'I know. I disobeyed my orders and could have lost the thapter. I'll be in trouble when I get back.'

'I dare say. Why did you do it?'

'I brought you here. I couldn't leave you behind, no matter who you are or what you might have done.'

FORTY-FOUR

Things were never the same between Tiaan and Nish after that. Saving his life had transformed the way she felt toward him. On the long trip back to Fiz Gorgo, battling fierce headwinds all the way, Tiaan mulled over every aspect of their relationship, to see if she might not have been as wrong about him as he had been about her.

There was no chance to speak to Nish in private, then or later. When they finally landed in the yard, in the early morning more than a day later, the entire population of the fortress was waiting for them.

'What's the matter?' she called as she climbed down the side.

The smile faded from Malien's face. 'What have you done to my thapter?'

'We had a . . . few problems.' Tiaan put her feet on the ground, which seemed to be heaving, and had to clutch at the racks to avoid falling on her face.

'Are you all right?'

'I've not slept in forty-eight hours.'

'You failed then,' said Yggur, eyeing the empty racks.

'Four of the soldiers were lost, and Phar got away at the beginning.'

'I was talking about the silk.'

419

'It's inside. Five bolts. Not as much as Nish wanted, but it was all we could get.'

The others came out, still filthy, ragged and smoke-stained, but proudly bearing the precious rolls of cloth between them.

'You've done well,' said Yggur. 'I didn't think you would return at all, least of all actually bring back any cloth.'

'Then why did you send us?' said Nish.

'I didn't send you. This was your mission, Nish.'

'But you permitted it, even at the risk of the thapter.'

'If we dare not take risks we'll never win this war.'

'Nor if we take foolish ones,' said Flydd, but he was smiling too.

'You took the best team in the world,' said Yggur. 'If you couldn't succeed, no one could have. Come inside. Breakfast is ready.'

Tiaan was seated next to Irisis at breakfast. The crafter seemed unusually friendly, or perhaps Tiaan could now allow her to be.

'Is there no challenge you cannot rise to?' said Irisis, open in her admiration.

Tiaan didn't know how to answer. 'I just did my best. I couldn't leave them to die.'

'Not even Nish?' Irisis said, but Tiaan knew she was joking. 'Thank you for saving his life, Tiaan. He's my dearest friend and everything to me.'

'I've been wondering about him all the way back from Thurkad. Wondering if I might not have been wrong about him. In *some* things.'

'Perhaps you were, in some things,' Irisis said. 'We did you wrong, Tiaan, back at the manufactory, and I'm very sorry. It was my failing, more than his. I was a nasty, inadequate woman and I used him against you.'

'You, inadequate?'

'Another time,' said Irisis. 'But since we hunted you across the mountains and lost you to the lyrinx, and Nish's father was so terribly injured . . .'

'I remember that day all too well,' said Tiaan.

'Ever since, Nish has been a changed man. He grew up that day.'

'I'll never forget the way he treated me in Tirthrax,' said Tiaan with a flash of fire.

'But there was a good reason for it. Flydd sent Nish after you and, when he reached Tirthrax, he saw you bringing the Aachim through the gate. He truly believed that you'd betrayed our world.'

'He was cruel . . !' Tiaan trailed off, replaying the scene in her mind.

'If you knew how he has suffered this past year, Tiaan, and all the great things he's done, you would think differently of him. I know you would. But I'll say no more than that. Talk to him, if you care to, and he can plead for himself.'

Flydd fell in beside Nish as they went inside. 'Remember your despair after we came back from Nennifer and you couldn't get anything done?'

'I remember,' said Nish.

'Look how far you've come since. And keep it in mind, Nish, whenever you wilt under the burden of all we have to do – as I do. We just go one step at a time, and no matter how low we're brought, we never, ever give up.' He squeezed Nish's shoulder and passed inside.

Nish stood there for a moment in reflection. The plan *had* come a long way, and so had he. One step at a time. He smiled and followed.

Two days later, with twenty people sewing the silk, the air-floaters were complete. He'd reclaimed the silk from the dirigible, and Inouye had discovered part of an air-dreadnought airbag hanging in a tree ten leagues away, giving them just enough to complete the airbag of the third air-floater. There had even been a little time to use the thapter for training the pilots and artificers. Every pilot had made at least one flight under Malien's stern guidance. No one had crashed it, though there had been sufficient incidents to make Nish fear for what would happen if they did recover any machines from the battlefield.

'Everything's ready,' he said to Yggur, after having worked all night. 'We can go as soon as you say the word.'

'Excellent!' beamed Flydd. He shook Nish's hand. 'And *on time*, too. It's a pleasure to deal with a man who's as good as his word. Well, Yggur, if you would just explain to Nish how he's to move the thapters without access to the field, he can be on his way.'

Yggur looked as though he'd had no more sleep than Nish. 'My devices aren't ready yet.'

'What?' said Flydd, putting on a show of surprise. 'But you said you were nearly finished a week ago.'

'I am nearly finished, but I haven't tested them to my satisfaction.'

'Why not?'

'There are a few wrinkles still to be ironed out.'

'But everything depends on them.' Flydd seemed to be taking a malicious pleasure in Yggur's discomfiture. It was a weakness in his character that Nish could only appreciate, in the circumstances. The two mancers might be working together but they would be forever rivals.

'I'm aware of that,' Yggur said, stone-faced.

'And the least delay to the schedule could be fatal to our chances of being ready for the spring offensive.'

'Yes,' said Yggur. 'It could.'

'Well, I won't pretend that I'm not disappointed,' said Flydd. 'Bitterly disappointed, in fact. It's a major setback.' He gave Yggur a sly glance, then said cajolingly, 'When do you think it will be ready?'

'I don't know.'

'Tomorrow?'

'Not tomorrow!' Yggur snapped.

'What about the day after?'

Flydd had such a strange, coquettish look on his craggy face that Nish wouldn't have been surprised if he'd batted his eyelashes.

Yggur cracked. 'I don't know, damn you.'

'Then I won't keep you,' said Flydd. 'I'm sure you're anxious to get back to your workshop and try to make up for lost time. Good day.' He nodded and turned away, taking Nish's arm and pulling him after him. 'Wipe that grin off your face, Artificer,' Flydd said sternly. 'Show some respect for your betters.' But as soon as Yggur was gone, Flydd clapped Nish on the back, taking the sting from his words. 'Well done, lad. You can go to bed now.' He went off, whistling a cheerful air.

The following day the thapter set off for the south-east, carrying the patterns for various devices that were to be made up by manufactories there, including Tiaan's plans for master and slave farspeakers. It was to be a lightning trip, both Malien and Tiaan taking turns and going night and day, as Flydd hoped to be back in just over a week.

The trip proved uneventful, apart from their first brief call at Tiksi, where Tiaan hoped to see her mother. Unfortunately Marnie was not at the rebuilt breeding factory.

'She lost everything in the fire,' said Matron. 'I haven't seen her in nearly a year.'

'Poor Marnie,' Tiaan wept. 'Cast out on the streets with nothing. Doesn't anyone know what happened to her?'

She was unable to find out, for the city's records had been lost in the fires.

Thence they turned west to her old manufactory. Tall, dark-skinned Tuniz was still overseer, and she reminded Flydd of his promise, that if she met all her targets for a year he would send her home to Crandor, to the children she had not seen in two years.

'I remember,' said Flydd. 'And have you met all your targets, Overseer?'

'Not all, but nearly,' she said, anxiously baring her filed teeth.

'Then the condition has not been met and I owe you nothing!' She winced. 'Nonetheless,' Flydd went on, 'I do want to send you home, and will if you complete this last task to my satisfaction. I have here a number of samples.' He showed her Golias's globe, several different slave farspeakers Tiaan had made, plus her detailed designs of each. 'Can you make me, say, ten master farspeakers, and one hundred of the slave variety, in a month?'

'The slave farspeakers will be no trouble,' said Tuniz, after a careful study of both. 'The master globes are another matter.' She ran her fingers through her frizzy hair and asked Tiaan a number of technical questions. Once they'd been answered to her satisfaction Tuniz said, 'If I divert all of my crafters and artisans to the task, I believe we can do it, surr, though I'll need to talk to my chief crafter to make sure.'

'Call her. I plan to return in a month, more or less. Have them ready and I'll take you home to Crandor in this thapter.'

Her eyes shone. 'It will be done, surr. You can count on it.'

They went to several other manufactories nearby, where Flydd left other commissions, and headed directly home.

'I've done as much as I can, for the moment,' Flydd told Yggur when they arrived back at Fiz Gorgo on schedule. 'Though to make a difference in the spring I have to give our allies more than words.'

'I hope we can give them much more. Nish left just an hour ago for Snizort.'

'Was he prepared?' said Flydd, meaningly.

'As well as could be managed. Though of course –'

'I meant, did he have some way of moving the thapters in the absence of a field?'

'Of course,' said Yggur airily, as though it had been the most trivial of tasks, hardly worth discussing. 'He could not have gone, otherwise.'

'How is it to be achieved, as a matter of interest?'

'Oh, I made up some little devices that store power,' Yggur said in an offhand manner. 'Enough to drive a thapter for leagues. I charged them up from the field just before he left.'

'I noticed it was drawn right down as we came in,' said Flydd. 'Malien had more than a little trouble getting the last couple of leagues, and at one stage we thought we were going to come down in the swamp. What kind of devices?'

'Just something I put together with a little tinkering,' said Yggur.

'Sounds like they could transform the war,' said Flydd. 'With enough of them we could make our craft independent of the field. Let the lyrinx attack the nodes as they dare, then.'

'Unfortunately, the core of my devices relies on a most rare crystal, the only one known capable of storing the amount of power required. I had the only three in existence and I used them all.'

'Might I know the name of this crystal?' said Flydd casually, though he knew Yggur wasn't going to tell him anything useful. Noble and dignified he might be, as a rule, but Yggur couldn't resist the urge to get his own back.

'Inkspar.'

'I've never heard of it.'

'It's rare, as I said.'

'Only three devices? That's going to limit the number of thapters we can recover.'

'If they recover more than three, which I doubt, they'll have to shuttle the devices back and forth in the air-floaters. It's inconvenient, but not a fatal problem.'

'It could be if they're under attack.'

'It was the best I could do.'

'Oh well,' said Flydd. 'It's out of our hands now. They'll either come back or they won't. No point worrying about it.'

'Plenty of point, just no use,' said Yggur. 'Oh, and I've found Merryl.'

'Merryl?' The scrutator frowned. So many names in the past couple of months. So many faces. 'Ah, the one-handed prisoner. The fellow who speaks the lyrinx tongue. How did you find him?'

'One of *my* spies was asking around and someone knew him. Merryl was in a refugee camp south of Gnulp Forest.'

'Was?'

'Well, he's here now.'

'Why didn't you say so?'

425

Hurrying down to the other end of the fortress, they ran into Tiaan, who was talking to Malien. 'We're going to talk to your friend Merryl,' said Flydd. 'Would you like to come along?'

Her face lit up. 'Merryl is here?'

'Yes,' said Yggur. 'He came in with one of my spies on the air-floater this morning.'

Tiaan had a lump in her throat. Merryl had cared for her in Snizort, asking nothing in return, and she would always think kindly of him for it.

He was lying on a straw-filled pallet, asleep. His left arm, the one lacking a hand, hung over the edge of the bed. Merryl stirred as they entered, and sat up. He was very thin.

'I am Yggur,' said Yggur, 'the master of this place, which is known as Fiz Gorgo.'

'I know who you are, surr.' Merryl's eyes turned to the smaller man.

'This is the scrutator, Xervish Flydd, and . . . where has she got to?'

Tiaan stepped out from behind Yggur.

'Tiaan!' Merryl reached out to her. 'I saw the Aachim take you. I was so afraid.'

'That's a long time ago now. What have you been doing these past months?'

'Surviving. I became a slave for my own kind, hauling clankers out of the mud.'

'Me too,' said Flydd. 'Not an occupation with much to recommend it.'

Merryl gave him a curious glance. 'After it was over, most of us were abandoned to our own devices. Some of the slaves joined the army, but I did not.'

'Not willing to do your duty, Merryl?' said Yggur.

'I never shirked my duty, surr,' Merryl said mildly, as if nothing anyone said could touch him. 'And I've spent the past twenty years paying for it. Not liking what I saw of the scrutators, I pretended to be one of the peasants pressed into hauling duties, and afterwards I disappeared into the countryside.'

426

'You must have had a lean time of it,' said Flydd. 'The armies had scoured the land bare.'

'I went hungry more times than I ate, but I wouldn't have changed anything. I've been a prisoner of the lyrinx for half my life. They treated me well enough but I lived with the threat of being eaten if my usefulness expired. After that, even the freedom to starve was a precious gift. Why did you bring me here?'

'We need to know about the lyrinx, Merryl,' said Yggur. 'Particularly any weaknesses we can use against them.'

'I'll write out a list for you.'

'Just tell us!' said Flydd.

'The thoughts don't flow, with mancers and the like staring at me,' said Merryl, unperturbed. After surviving all the enemy had done, no mere human could bother him. 'I work better in solitude.'

'Whatever gets us the list the quickest,' said Flydd, turning away.

'Just a moment,' said Yggur. 'Why did they make a tunnel to the centre of the Great Seep, and what did they find there?'

'The remains of a village of ancient times, under edict for sorcerous practices, I understand,' said Merryl. 'Apparently the village sank into the tar and the lyrinx wished to recover some relics that had been lost at that time.'

'Why?'

'I don't know. Since I knew their language, they were always careful what they spoke about in my presence.'

'And what did they find?'

'Bodies, young and old, preserved in the tar, and other household items of that time. Some yellow crystals which, I heard, they were excited about. I didn't see the relics, for the node exploded.'

'Do they have any diseases or illnesses?' asked Flydd.

'Not many. They're healthy, robust creatures, generally.'

'But their children are sometimes born malformed, lacking the ability to develop wings. Sometimes they're born without armour, skin pigment or claws.'

427

'That's so,' said Merryl. 'Such malformations are common, but not all survive to adulthood.'

'I heard,' said Yggur, leaning forward, 'that one lyrinx working in the tar tunnel developed a dreadful skin inflammation that rendered him helpless.'

'I saw several with that affliction,' said Merryl thoughtfully. 'They were in such torment that they sloughed their outer skin, though that was as agonising as if the layers of our skin were peeled away.'

'The less said about that the better,' said Flydd, rubbing his upper thigh.

Merryl gave him a puzzled look. 'Sometimes grit gets in between the armour and the inner skin, which is irritating to them. But this inflammation was much worse.'

'Do you know what caused it?' said Flydd. 'Was it the tar?'

'I believe it was a mould, or fungus.'

'Do they often get this kind of complaint?'

'I never saw it before, in all my time with them. It may have come from one of the relics they found in the tar.'

'Thank you,' said Yggur. 'That's most interesting.'

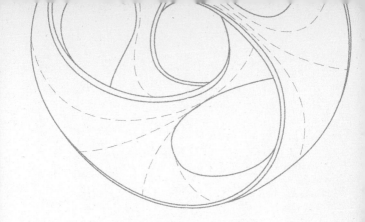

PART FOUR

GEOMANTIC GLOBE

FORTY-FIVE

Nish breathed a sigh as the last air-floater lifted. They were finally on their way to Snizort. Though the expedition was well behind schedule, no one could have done it more quickly, and what they'd achieved was nothing short of miraculous. All the pilots had flown Malien's thapter, though few more than twice. That was his biggest worry, apart from the state of the abandoned constructs. He was afraid they would be too damaged to repair.

They arrived over the battlefield just before dawn. Everything had been rehearsed. The four air-floaters would fly low across the site as soon as it was light, while Nish and the other artificers identified those constructs in the best condition. The pilots and artificers would go to work and three air-floaters would wait on the ground. The fourth would take a wandering path over the battlefield, to raise the alarm if the enemy appeared. Snizort seemed to be abandoned but Nish wasn't taking any unnecessary risks. There were too many necessary ones.

'How long have we been working towards this day?' he said, leaning on the rope rail of Inouye's air-floater. The east was growing light, though there were still some minutes until sunrise.

'It's two months since we got back from Nennifer,' said Irisis.

'I never thought we'd get this far.'

'Nor did I. But then, I try not to expect anything. Saves disappointment.'

'How many constructs were abandoned here, do you recall?'

'Tiaan said about five hundred.'

'And how many of those could have been repaired,' Nish wondered, 'if the node hadn't been destroyed?'

'I wouldn't have a clue.'

'Imagine if we could bring a hundred thapters back,' he said dreamily.

'That would certainly be a marvel,' she said dryly, 'since you've only managed to train thirty pilots.'

He came back to reality. 'True; but just imagine the look on Yggur's face.'

'If we manage to recover three he'll be over the moon.'

The sun slid over the horizon like a jelly across a greased tray. The battlefield consisted of a series of hummocks, their tips just touched by light, surrounded by seas of shadow. 'Not much snow left,' said Nish.

'It's been windy in these parts.' Klarm came up beside them and rested his forearms on the lower rail. He had a small bound volume in one hand.

'Have you been here recently?' Nish said carefully. Klarm did not talk about his spying missions.

'Not in more than a month.'

'But we wouldn't expect to run into the enemy?' They'd been over this before but Nish felt in need of reassurance.

'Lyrinx could be anywhere,' grunted Klarm, 'though they haven't reoccupied Snizort. The area is a wasteland, the tar's still burning underground and the native people fled long ago. There's been no sign of the scavengers here either.'

The light was advancing swiftly now and Nish began to distinguish the bones of the wrecked machines. Most were clankers, but scattered among them, particularly on the western side of the battlefield, he made out the distinctive smooth curves of constructs.

'Over there,' Klarm called to Inouye. 'Some ten constructs were abandoned close together, formed into a group.'

The air-floater drifted westward. 'I don't see them,' said the pilot. It was the first time she'd spoken in ages. Inouye went about her work in silent, tragic despair, and it wrenched Nish's heart. Separation from her children and her man was eating her alive.

'Just to the left of that little hill,' said Klarm.

Inouye took them over the hill, then circled around it.

'You must be mistaken,' said Irisis. 'I can only see three.'

'I kept careful records,' said Klarm, consulting his book, 'because the constructs weren't badly damaged.'

'Well, there's only three now. Maybe Vithis came back and dragged them away. Could you go a little lower, Inouye?'

The air-floater came down to within ten spans of the ground. 'I can't see any tracks,' said Nish.

'The surface snow has been blown away.'

'Constructs are very heavy. If they'd been hauled off, you'd expect to see drag marks.'

Inouye hovered over the site. 'They *have* been taken,' said Irisis. 'Look, you can see depressions where they were lying.'

'They must have flown –' Nish began furiously. 'Oh no!' He clutched at her arm as a chill ran down his spine. 'They've *flown*. Vithis converted them to thapters and flew them away.'

'Or hovered them.'

'I don't think so,' said Klarm. 'The only thapter my spies have sighted near the Hornrace was Malien's.'

'What if Malien's people have been here?' said Irisis slowly. 'They already know how to build thapters, so it'd be no trouble to fix these ones. In fact, that's probably what's happened.'

'How many have gone?' Nish choked. 'Please, let it only be these seven.'

They rotored back and forth across the battlefield. 'There's another depression,' said Klarm, pointing. 'It contained four constructs a month ago.'

'And two more have gone from the south of it,' Irisis called.

As they went back and forth, and the count rose, Nish fell deeper into depression. 'How many is it now?' he asked drearily as they completed the last run.

'Thirty-one,' said Irisis.

Despair. 'I'll bet they've taken every construct that could possibly be repaired.'

They spent all day trudging through the remnants of rust-coloured snow, checking the constructs one by one. There was not a single usable machine among them. The controllers had been broken with a hammer.

Nish studied the innards of the last machine, grim-faced. 'There's no chance that our pilots could fly it with one of your controllers?'

Irisis shook her head. 'Ours are just designed to fit into theirs. If we'd had to make new controllers from scratch, we'd still be working on the first one.'

'What am I going to say to Yggur and Flydd?'

Night fell. Nish set up camp and sent an air-floater home with the bad news. He was too depressed to eat and the trainee pilots, highly strung as were all operators, had taken it hard. Many were in tears, including one of the best, pretty little Kattiloe with the dozens of blonde plaits. Sturdy, dark-eyed Chissmoul, too shy to speak about her distress, had simply walked off into the night. The artificers and their prentices were of a more phlegmatic disposition. Glad of the opportunity to employ their talents on real machines, they were pulling one of the constructs apart in the firelight.

Nish felt like screaming at them, but resisted. Let them have their moment. Let them hone their useless skills.

'We might as well go home.' Funny how he could think of forbidding Fiz Gorgo as home.

'The air-floater pilots need their rest,' said Irisis. 'They flew all night, Nish.'

'In the morning then. At first light.'

Irisis prodded the fire. 'I've been thinking. This might not be an absolute disaster yet.'

'How do you mean?'

'Remember the first time we came here, when we ran into

434

the scavengers? I took away a complete controller and used it to design all my flight assemblies. I'm sure I brought the controller with me, so at least we can bring one thapter home. Kimli can fly it.'

'One lousy thapter,' said Nish in melancholy tones.

'Oh, come on. It's twice what we have now.'

After his glorious daydreams about bringing back fleets of fliers, it took an effort for Nish to see that even one thapter was infinitely better than none. None meant that the past months had been wasted. With none, the war could not be won. With one, added to the one they already had, it was still possible to hope.

They worked all night fitting the controller into the least damaged of the machines close by. It took a team of artificers and artisans, for whoever had smashed the controller had done other damage and they had to take parts from a second construct to fix it. The work was not yet completed when the sun came up. As it lifted above the horizon they heard an approaching, unmistakable whine.

'It's a thapter!' Nish cried. 'The Aachim have come back. Are you nearly finished?'

'Not nearly enough,' came Irisis's muffled voice from inside.

'Get your weapons!' Nish raced for the air-floater, where he'd left his gear. A short sword banged against his hip but he'd be at a disadvantage against a tall Aachim. He reached over the side for his crossbow and pouch of bolts.

The thapter shot out of the north, flying low, banked and circled around them. The soldiers raised their crossbows. 'Do we shoot?' called their sergeant.

'No!' hissed Klarm. 'Find out if they're hostile, first.'

'Not until I say so,' Nish yelled.

The thapter banked again. 'Don't shoot!' roared Irisis from on top of her construct. 'That's Tiaan.'

Nish shaded his eyes and squinted. 'How can you tell?'

'It's all scratched and battered about the base.' Irisis waved furiously, pointing to the ground.

The thapter jagged sideways, dropped sharply and came

sweeping in to settle on the ground just a few spans away, the blast from underneath whirling dust and crunchy fragments of snow up in their faces.

'How can Tiaan fly, *here*? We've got the only power storage devices.'

'With the amplimet she can draw on a distant field,' Irisis reminded him.

Of course. That's how she had got them out of the burning underground labyrinth. 'What are you doing here?' Nish called.

Tiaan climbed out, followed by Merryl, a hobbling Flangers and another soldier. 'We had to do a little job nearby,' said Tiaan. 'So we thought we'd see how you were going.'

'Terribly,' said Nish, rubbing red eyes. He explained.

'Have you had breakfast?' Tiaan said abruptly.

'We haven't had time,' he snapped.

'Neither have I, but I'd appreciate something hot if you can manage it.'

She turned away to the campfire, where a large pot of chard was simmering. Pilot Kattiloe, who had been eyeing Tiaan's machine enviously since its arrival, offered her a mug of the red brew. Tiaan wrapped her hands around it and stood with her back to the fire, looking down at the dirt. Taking what looked to be half a dried quince from her pocket, she nibbled at one edge. Pilot Chissmoul appeared silently from behind a mound. She kept apart from everyone, but pressed her cheek against the side of the thapter and closed her eyes. Flangers limped over and stood leaning against the thapter. He said something to her. Chissmoul didn't answer, but she didn't go away either.

'Let's get something to eat,' said Irisis. 'I'm sure we'll feel better for it.'

Nish suppressed his irritation and shortly, warming his hands on a bowl of stew, did feel as though he could cope with the world after all.

'There's no possibility of repairing any of the smashed controllers, I suppose?' Tiaan said.

'Not with what we have here.'

'What about assembling new ones from the undamaged parts?'

436

'The Aachim did a pretty thorough job of breaking them . . .' Irisis said; a spot of colour appeared high on each cheek. She seemed to be going through some internal struggle. 'But maybe we could check them again, if you've got the time. Together.' It came out in a rush.

Tiaan seemed to be having trouble breathing. 'We could.' She put out her hand.

Irisis clasped it, then looked up at the sky. 'Shall we get started?'

A crushed skull protruded from the frozen mud where the construct had lain. The size and shape told them that it was Aachim – one of the few bodies not recovered and buried before Vithis left Snizort. The eye-sockets stared mournfully at them.

'I don't like this place,' Irisis said.

Tiaan shivered. 'Neither do I.'

Though Tiaan and Nish were friends now, Tiaan still felt uncomfortable with Irisis. They had disliked each other since they'd been small children and it would take a lot to come to terms with their history.

'None of these controllers can be repaired,' said Irisis that afternoon, as they finished surveying the last of the constructs in the third area. The short day was nearly over, the sun declining swiftly.

'Where to next?' Tiaan looked around.

'The last area is a good league further west.'

'We'd better take the thapter.'

Irisis had been making a map as she went along and marking the location of each construct so she wouldn't miss any. 'That last one was 429.'

'How many more are there?' said Tiaan.

'Thirty-six. It'll be after dark by the time we finish.'

They whined slowly along, hovering, not flying. Ahead, in a depression, three or four clankers lay in a tangled mess. They'd hit so hard that they were welded together by the impact.

'I wonder how that happened?' said Tiaan.

'When the node exploded,' said Irisis, 'it sent out wild surges of power that tore the legs off a good many clankers. They were the lucky ones; the ones that weren't so well built. The ones that didn't break were uncontrollable, and a lot of constructs were wrecked the same way. We landed in the middle of the battlefield just after it happened, Flydd and I. And Ullii. It was horrible. You haven't known real fear until you've stood in the middle of a battlefield with uncontrollable clankers and constructs rampaging at you.'

'I've known fear,' said Tiaan with an involuntary look over her shoulder.

She curved around to get a better look. 'No one could have survived that impact. Hey! What's that underneath? It looks like –'

'A construct.'

Tiaan set the machine down and they scrambled out. From this angle, though no other, one curved flank was visible beneath the mess. 'It is a construct, badly damaged. I wonder if I can squeeze through that gap?'

'Might be better to drag the clankers off first,' said Irisis.

'That could do more damage. I'll risk it.'

Tiaan squeezed in then stuck her head out. 'Could you grab a lantern from the thapter, please?'

Irisis came back with it and pushed in after the smaller woman. 'If the Aachim have missed something, I want to see it too.'

The top of the construct was badly damaged but the hatch had been sheared right off, leaving an opening framed by jagged metal. Tiaan wriggled inside. Bones were visible down below, though there was no smell. Scavenging beasts had done their job. Irisis pushed in beside her.

'The controller's still here. What do you think?' said Tiaan.

'It looks intact.' Irisis couldn't keep the elation out of her voice.

'Let's get it out.'

By the time they'd finished it was dark. Outside, Tiaan spread the mechanism on her coat while they inspected it with the lantern. 'I think it's good,' said Tiaan.

'So do I.' Irisis threw her arms about the smaller woman, and after the briefest hesitation Tiaan hugged her back. She felt as though she might have made another friend.

Tiaan set her thapter down beside the other. 'How's your thapter going?' Irisis called to Nish. He looked worn out.

'We've put the controller in, and it works, though not very well. I'm worried we won't get it home. Our pilots aren't experienced enough to be flying good thapters, much less faulty ones. They won't know what to do if something goes wrong. Still, things are looking better than they were this morning. How did you get on?'

'Pretty well, considering. Look at this.' Irisis took the controller out of her bag. 'Isn't it the most beautiful sight you ever saw?'

It was worth all the labour for the look on Nish's face.

After dinner they put it into another construct, slipped in the flight assembly tailored to Kattiloe, and one of Yggur's power-storing devices, and the thapter worked straight away. Kattiloe danced a little jig on top of the machine. Chissmoul whirled and ran into the darkness again but this time Flangers followed.

Tiaan and Irisis continued their survey at first light, and among the last of the constructs found two controllers that were not as badly damaged, as if the wrecking work had been abandoned in haste.

'The crystal in this controller looks all right,' said Tiaan. 'It's chipped, but should still work. Do you think, if we put it in the second controller, it might just be good enough?'

It was, and Chissmoul wept for joy.

'Three!' said Nish, who had perked up considerably overnight. 'Plus your thapter, Tiaan. If only it were five.'

'You're getting ideas above your station,' said Irisis, grinning like a loon. 'Shall we go home?'

'Wait a minute,' said Tiaan. 'I think I know where we might find another controller. Or even two.'

'We've been through them all now,' said Irisis. 'Twice.'

'As I escaped from Vithis there were several, er, accidents involving constructs.'

'Accidents?' said Irisis.

'I'd prefer not to talk about it,' Tiaan went on. 'People died because of what I did. The constructs were wrecked but it's possible the controllers were left behind. Do you want to come, Nish? It'll take a fair while.'

'Let's get these ones organised first.'

Yggur's devices were inserted in the other two machines and they were hovered north to the nearest field. Nish then took the devices back, just for luck. He left the three lucky pilots, Kattiloe, Chissmoul and Kimli, practising hovering and low flying under Klarm's watchful eye, gave orders for everyone to be ready to depart as soon as they returned, and climbed into the thapter after Irisis.

'Can either of you swim?' Tiaan said.

'Not very well,' said Nish.

'Like an eel,' said Irisis. 'We used to go to the seaside in summer, when I was little.'

'I'm not much good,' said Tiaan. She put her head out the hatch. 'Hoy. Are any of you good swimmers?'

'I am,' said Flangers.

'Do you think your leg's up to it?' said Irisis.

'It works better in the water than on land.'

'Come on then.'

He limped across and climbed in. Tiaan went south, following the path she'd taken when towing the constructs to the node. At the place where she'd crippled Minis during the accident with the towing cable, Tiaan began to circle.

'A few constructs were damaged here, though not badly. They may have taken them away.'

'Looks like it,' said Irisis, scanning the area with the spyglass. They found nothing. Nish looked crestfallen.

'Never mind,' said Tiaan. 'I didn't really expect to find anything here.'

She continued south into Gnulp Forest, on the winding route she'd taken last summer. It wasn't hard to remember. At the top of a steep hill she stopped and closed her eyes, imagining every detail of that desperate flight, and remembering her state of mind – thinking that she'd killed Minis and blaming herself for it.

'I was here,' she said. 'They came at me up the hill, dozens of constructs led by Vithis. I'll never know how I escaped.'

'Nor I,' said Nish, 'had I not seen you in action.'

The undergrowth was still battered down in a line along the path of her flight, though autumn growth had begun to cover it up. 'That's where I hit a tree.' She was pointing to a gouge out of the bark, a couple of spans in height. 'And there's where Vithis crashed. I was hoping his machine might have been abandoned, but they've taken it. On to the next.'

Nish said nothing but his shoulders were beginning to sag again.

Tiaan flew west to the Sea of Thurkad and turned left, following the shoreline south. Some half an hour later she slowed.

'Somewhere around here they tried to catch me in a net held by five constructs. I know there's a construct underwater, not far from shore, though I think it'll be in pieces.'

Gentle waves broke over black rocks and dark sand. Gulls shied away as they approached. It took a long time to find the place, for the shore looked much the same for a league or two. Tiaan had to go inland, locate the trail she'd smashed through the scrub and follow it to the beach.

She stopped at the shoreline. 'It was just out there. The construct went underwater and blew apart.' More deaths on her conscience. There had to be a better way of solving people's problems.

'Could be hard to find the pieces,' said Irisis.

'Go up a fraction,' Flangers said. 'The sun's fairly high. We may able to see through the water.' He climbed up to the back platform.

The sun wasn't high enough for them to see much, though occasionally Nish caught glimpses of the bottom, between dark rocks.

'There it is,' Flangers called. 'At least, part of it.'

Tiaan hovered. 'Looks like it's in two pieces,' said Nish.

'There's the top section,' said Irisis. 'Now for the chilly part.'

Tiaan hovered over the water while Irisis demonstrated to Flangers, with the thapter's controller, what they were looking for and how to remove it.

'Is that clear?' she said. 'We don't want to break the controller getting it out.'

Flangers nodded. They stripped off and jumped into the water. Irisis ducked under but soon came up again.

'What's it like?' Nish called.

'Bloody freezing!' Her teeth chattered.

'I meant the construct.'

'Thanks for your concern, Nish. It's down two and a half spans, which is fortunate – that's about as far as I can dive. Couldn't see if the controller was still there. Ready, Flangers?'

He raised a thumb and went down, legs rising out of the water. Irisis slid straight under.

Nish counted the seconds aloud. At thirty-eight Irisis reappeared. Flangers did not.

'It's there,' she said, 'and looks to be in one piece, but I can't hold my breath long enough to get it out.'

Tiaan wasn't surprised. Removing the controller was a complicated process and she knew she couldn't have done it underwater.

On one hundred and five, Flangers reappeared. 'Cold!' He took three deep breaths and went down again.

'S'pose I'd better help him,' said Irisis, pretending nonchalance, and submerged.

After eight dives, Flangers surfaced and trod water. 'I'll have to get out. I'm frozen to the core.'

They let down a rope and hauled him up. His skin was blue. 'Coming, Irisis?' Nish called.

'I'll keep going as long as I can.'

She went under. This time Nish had counted down two minutes and few seconds more, and was about to dive in after her, fully clothed, when Irisis surfaced, blowing like a walrus.

'Have a rest, Irisis,' said Tiaan. 'I've got hot soup here.'

'I'll have it afterwards. Once I get out I'm not going back in, even for a whole bag of controllers!'

After Flangers had been given a brisk towelling and drunk a mug of hot soup, he felt able to go down again.

'I feel the cold more than I used to,' he said, noticing Tiaan's gaze on his scars. His right thigh was smaller than the left and the right leg noticeably shorter.

'It's coming,' said Irisis as he dived in. 'Won't be long now.'

They went down together. The seconds passed. A minute; a minute and a half; two minutes.

'Do you think I'd better –?' Nish began.

The surface erupted, Irisis marginally before the soldier, and her arm was held high with something dangling from it.

'We've got it!' she roared. 'Now get me out of here.'

Back at the battlefield they quickly fitted everything in place in the soundest construct they could find and the machine whined into life.

'Four thapters!' said Irisis, who was still blue and shivering two hours after coming out of the water. 'And that's all you're going to get, Nish, so don't get that mournful look in your eyes again.'

'I won't! I'm happy now.'

'Actually there *was* one more,' Tiaan said. 'The one I escaped in. I just managed to get it to Tirthrax, though I suppose the Aachim have taken it long since.'

'No doubt,' said Irisis, whose teeth were still chattering. 'I want to go home.'

'I'm beginning to think you've left the whole of Lauralin littered with wrecked machines, Tiaan,' said Nish.

Tiaan started, then gave an abashed grin. 'I had forgotten about the one I brought here from Booreah Ngurle – the original thapter Malien and I made. I hid it among the rocks on a hilltop over that way.' She pointed east. 'I wonder if it's still there?'

'How *could* you have forgotten that?' said Nish.

'I took out the parts that allowed it to fly. It was just another construct then. The original machine *might* still be there,' Tiaan

443

ruminated. 'It was well hidden among rocks and scrub, on a barren hill. There's no reason why anyone would climb up it. And with one of your assemblies, Irisis, it could be made to fly. Let's go and see.'

They took the best of the remaining pilots with them, just in case. The construct turned out to be exactly where Tiaan had left it, covered in dust and a layer of leaves, untouched. An hour later they were flying it back.

'That's five,' said Nish. 'I'm the happiest man in the world. Let's go home!'

FORTY-SIX

After the air-floater returned with the initial bad news, Yggur and Flydd had been in despair, which redoubled when Tiaan failed to return from her own mission. They held an anxious meeting, and another the following day when there was still no sign of anyone. They were sitting gloomily by the fire when Fyn-Mah came running with the news that a thapter had been sighted, flying slowly and erratically.

Yggur ran all the way along the long hall to the front doors and threw them open. Flydd came scuttling after him. As they went down onto the steps, a thapter wobbled in, to thump onto the paving stones.

'That's definitely Tiaan's,' said Yggur. 'What's the matter with her?'

The hatch was pushed open and Kattiloe's head appeared, beaming to split her face in two. 'I did it!' she cried, capering about dangerously on top of the machine.

'Report, if you please,' said Yggur sternly, though it was undermined by the delight he couldn't suppress.

Before she could jump down they heard the scream of a second thapter travelling at high speed. It shot across the yard and, with reckless insouciance, carved an ascending spiral around one of the horned towers, a descending spiral around the next, then hurtled towards the front door. Yggur and Flydd

445

ducked as it banked sharply just over their heads, spun in a circle and dropped neatly to the paving stones beside the first, so lightly that it would not have crushed a feather.

'Who the devil is that?' cried Yggur.

Two guards staggered down the ladder, ashen-faced and holding their bellies. Then Chissmoul, so quiet and shy that few people had ever heard her speak, sprang up onto the open hatch, laughing like a drain. Catching sight of the astonished mancers she broke off at once, though she didn't look repentant.

Soon two more thapters were scattered across the yard, these rather untidily. The fourth, flown by Kimli, had almost taken off Yggur's first-floor balcony as it came in. Yggur was grinning broadly now, though he could not relax yet. Finally, a few minutes later, a fifth thapter appeared, shepherding the sixth – Tiaan's battered machine – though it was evident that she wasn't flying it. They landed in the middle and Tiaan waved. She had elected to fly the faulty one.

'The air-floaters are on their way,' said Nish, springing out after her and grinning as if he'd just won the war by himself. 'I'm sorry that we only managed five thapters, surr, but we did it without the loss of a single man or woman.'

Yggur was so overcome that he embraced Nish, and then the lot of them, even Chissmoul. There was something suspiciously like moisture in the corner of one eye, though he pretended it was a piece of grit. 'After the bad news, I would have been happy to see a single thapter,' he said. 'This is more than I could have hoped for.'

Tiaan came up beside him. 'How about you, dear Tiaan?' Yggur said quietly. 'Did you get what you went for?'

'It's down below, in the lead casket.'

'Splendid. Leave it there; we'll retrieve it after dark. And then, I think, the first banquet Fiz Gorgo has seen in a thousand years.'

Nish was hovering, just down the hall. 'Could I ask a favour?' he said.

'Just name it,' smiled Yggur.

'It's Pilot Inouye. She hasn't seen her little children in a year, and she's in despair. Could we send her home now? We don't need her air-floater any more.'

'Of course,' said Yggur. 'She's served us faithfully and well, and we can do no less for her.'

It was worth all the pain and trouble of the past months to see the look on Inouye's face when Nish gave her the news.

The next few weeks passed swiftly. Tiaan was away with Malien for most of the time, completing her node survey of Meldorin and subsequently the part of Lauralin lying between the Sea of Thurkad, the Karama Malama and the Great Chain of Lakes.

Flydd raced east in Kattiloe's thapter, taking two of her sister pilots as well, so as to fly day and night. He'd gone to the manufactory to collect the ten farspeaking globes and hundred slave units ordered from Tuniz, and to order many more. He planned to take half to allies in the east, then bring the remaining sets home for the imminent spring offensive. He returned a fortnight later to be confronted with another problem. The farspeakers did not send as far as Golias's globe, and were much less reliable. After conferring with Yggur and Irisis, he sent her back to the manufactory to sort out the problem.

And in practice, even Golias's globe proved not to be quite the panacea Flydd had expected. There were limits to how far a message could be sent, though they varied all the time. One day the governor might be contacted in Lybing, the next Flydd could have trouble speaking to someone as close as Old Hripton. And messages could rarely be directly to farspeakers as far away as Tiksi or Roros. To speak to people at such a distance the message might have to be relayed several times, but often it did not get through at all.

On the first day of spring, Yggur began to mutter about Klarm's absence. They were waiting for him to return with the latest intelligence so that the offensive could be planned. He was well overdue and they were beginning to fear that he'd been taken by the lyrinx, which would have been a disaster. Klarm knew too much and, tough though he was, the enemy had ways of extracting the truth from anyone.

He arrived with a bang at lunchtime the following day, the air-floater coming in so quickly that it scraped varnish off its keel going over the wall, before skidding across the paving stones between the sheds and piles of timber.

Nish looked up from the thapter mechanism his artificers were repairing, said, 'Keep at it, you're doing well,' and wiped his greasy hands.

Klarm was over the side before it stopped, taking the steps three at a time and crashing through the front door. Nish followed.

'I've got it!' Klarm shouted up the hall.

'Got what?' said Yggur, emerging from his office polishing Golias's globe with a scrap of airbag silk.

'I've discovered where the lyrinx from Snizort and Gumby Marth have been hiding all this time. The ones who didn't fly back to Meldorin.'

'Come in here and tell me about it.' Yggur took the little man by the arm and began to steer him into his workroom. 'And you can start by telling us where the blazes you've been. You should have been back weeks ago.'

'Not in there. We'd all like to hear the news,' said Flydd, hurrying up the hall with his hands still dripping from the wash-tub. 'Nish, would you call everyone together?'

Nish collected Flangers, Fyn-Mah and Merryl. Tiaan and Malien were away, mapping, and Irisis was still in the east. They assembled in the dining hall, neutral territory as it were, and Klarm began.

'We've always wondered where the bulk of the lyrinx army went after the battles of Snizort and Gumby Marth. Most of the fliers returned to Oellyll but the others disappeared, as did the armies that had been terrorising Taltid and Almadin since the spring. They simply vanished at the beginning of winter. It was thought that they'd taken ship back to Meldorin, though we could find little evidence for it. I now know that they did not.'

'Where did they go?' said Flydd.

'Underground,' said Klarm. 'They made their winding way by night, in small groups so as not to attract attention, to the sea caves of Rencid. They went into the caves but they didn't come out again.'

'Sounds a bit far-fetched to me,' said Flydd. 'They'd have to cross running water just to enter the sea caves, and a lot more inside.'

'That's why we didn't look more closely,' said Klarm. 'We knew it was against their nature, but there's no doubt about it. The leaders must have fed their people an elixir to overcome their terror of water.'

'I'd be more convinced if you could tell me where they went,' Yggur said dubiously.

'I know exactly where they went. At some stage, perhaps decades ago, they found or made an underground connection between the sea caves and the deep caverns that honeycomb central Rencid, a good hundred leagues away.'

'They couldn't have *made* a connection all that way,' said Flydd. 'It would be the work of a thousand years.'

Klarm shrugged. 'It's mostly limestone country and no one knows how far the caverns run. They've never been explored. But that doesn't matter – the lyrinx now lie hidden in their tens of thousands, deep underground, within a stone's throw of Worm Wood.'

'How can you know?' said Yggur. 'How do you know they went through the sea caves, for that matter?'

'My spies have been scouring the area between Nilkerrand and Snizort ever since we came back from Nennifer,' said Klarm. 'Talking to the hunters and scavengers, and the nomads who used to wander those plains. It's surprising how many people still live in those lands. Most useful were the scavengers who roam the west coast of Lauralin. A rat doesn't scurry from one side of a ribcage to the other without them knowing about it.

'My spies have talked to thousands of people over the past months, and very expensive it was. I felt positively *profligate*.' Klarm's eyes flashed at Yggur. 'And when I wasn't wenching and boozing like the dissipated sot you think me to be, I put together a picture from all those tiny fragments of information, and it told me where to search.

'We identified the right sea cave a month and a half ago, and I checked out the signs for myself. There was nothing at the entrance; the enemy had wiped it clean of tracks, but there were plenty inside. They'd gone in and there were no tracks coming out again. Where had they gone and how would I find them? Even ten thousand lyrinx, hibernating deep underground, would produce no sign that could be detected from above.'

'So how *did* you find them?' said Flydd, signing to an orderly. The fellow went out silently.

'The only way I could. I followed their tracks.'

'What, underground?' cried Flydd. 'You bloody fool, what if you'd been caught?'

The little man bowed in his direction. 'It had to be done, Xervish, and I couldn't send anyone else to do such a dangerous job. Besides, no one was more suited to it than myself, my father being a caver. I was born underground.'

'And had they caught you, you would have died underground,' said Yggur, 'though not before telling them every secret we have.'

'I carried a poison pill set in wax inside a hollow tooth,' said Klarm. 'If taken, I would have bitten it in half.'

The orderly reappeared with a flagon of black beer and a large tankard, which he placed in front of Klarm before withdrawing. Klarm nodded his thanks and filled the tankard. 'It's surprisingly thirsty work, following a lyrinx army underground.' He downed half the tankard in one swallow.

'And frightening too, I dare say.'

'Aye.' Klarm took another pull at the tankard. 'It was that. In truth, I had little expectation that I'd come out alive. There's bad air in places, and fast streams, and it wasn't unguarded either. That was the hardest part of all. I couldn't kill the guards, nor harm them in any way, or they would have known someone was spying on them. All I could use was my natural cunning and the odd small illusion.

'But illusions work better underground, and the enemy were

450

more frightened than I was, despite their elixir. They had to cross many subterranean streams and their terror gave me heart. But, terrified or not, they'd gone on, and so must I. That's why I was so late back. I followed them the whole winding way, at least a hundred and twenty leagues underground, through one system of caverns after another. Many a marvel I saw that no man has seen before, and in the end I found them, hibernating in groups of thousands, unguarded apart from sentries at entrance and exit.

'There were more lyrinx than I could count – thirty thousand at the very least, and there could be other groups I didn't find. They're hiding three hundred spans underground not far from the abandoned town of Strebbit. They'll be coming out of hibernation any time now. They're less than a night's march from Worm Wood, the perfect cloak for their movements, and they'll be ready to attack within weeks. Once they reach the forest they can go anywhere, unseen.'

Flydd swore. 'I'd assumed they would come from the coast, and that we'd hear of their march a good week in advance.'

'What do we do now?' said Yggur.

'We must attack them the moment they come out,' said Klarm.

'How do we know where they're going to come out?' said Flydd. 'If my memory serves me, those caves have dozens of outlets.'

'But the cavern they're hibernating in has only one dry exit,' said Klarm. 'All the connecting caverns are partly flooded. Their elixir allowed them to endure the terror of the water, but I'm betting they'll avoid it on the way out. All elixirs take their toll and they won't want to be suffering from it on their way to war.'

Klarm's voice went hoarse. He drained his beer, licked the foam from the rim of the tankard, and filled it again.

'The dry passage opens out into a natural bowl.' He shaped it in the air with his hands. 'If we can get our forces into position in time, we can ambush them as they come out, still sluggish from hibernation.'

'And if they retreat?' said Flydd, smiling as if he already knew the answer.

'We drive them into the underground streams and cut them down in their panic.'

'Have you been in contact with General Troist?' asked Yggur.

'I have, and he gave me heart. His troops are well armed, well trained, and he has supplies stockpiled. Moreover, he has a keen eye for the weaknesses of the enemy and how best to attack them.'

Yggur looked questioningly at Flydd. Flydd nodded.

'If they take Borgistry,' said Yggur, 'western Lauralin must fall and then sooner or later the whole continent will be lost. But while Borgistry survives, the enemy can't control the west. We'll do it.'

'How soon can we be ready to strike?' said Flydd. He went over to study the map that covered half of one wall. Yggur joined him, measuring distances with a length of string. 'Troist could be there in nine days.'

'Two weeks for us,' said Nish. 'All the thapters need work, and three of the air-floaters. They can't go to war the way they are.'

'Two weeks!' Flydd cried. 'What if the enemy come out sooner? Why do they hibernate anyway? Merryl?'

'In order to survive in the void,' said Merryl, 'they flesh-formed their unborn to the limit. They made themselves the most formidable fighters ever seen, but it came at a cost. They have to hibernate for at least a month every year to repair the damage the past year has caused.'

'So it's a necessity, not just a custom,' mused Flydd. 'Good – all the less likely that they'll cut it short. Even so, we've got to be ready sooner.'

'Well, Nish?' said Yggur.

'If all our work goes perfectly,' Nish said, 'and we get just the right weather when we're flying, we *might* be ready to attack in ten or eleven days. But things never go perfectly, so I can't possibly promise less than twelve.'

'Perfect!' Flydd conferred with Klarm and Yggur. 'A strike in ten days will catch them still lethargic from hibernation.'

'But I just said –' Nish began desperately. Allowing three days for the slow air-floaters to fly there, it meant he only had seven days rather than the nine or ten he needed.

'The attack is set for ten days. Be ready!'

The first thapter flight left eight days later, and Yggur wasn't pleased at the delay. It carried Klarm, an advance guard and a number of devices that had been made in the eastern manufactories. The destination was an isolated valley north-east of Strebbit, where everyone would rendezvous with Troist's army, then march down to encircle the bowl-shaped depression in which the cave mouth lay.

Now it was the following day, and Nish hadn't slept for two nights. One of the thapters was still being repaired after crashing into a small tree in darkness, and the floater-gas generator on Gorm's air-floater had failed and had to be completely taken apart, though even then no one could work out what was wrong with it. Yggur came down to Nish's shed every hour, demanding to know when they would be ready, which only made matters worse.

'I knew this would happen,' Nish raged when Yggur turned up for the fifth time that morning. 'I told you it couldn't be done.'

'I don't like excuses,' said Yggur frostily.

There were plenty when your work wasn't done on time! Nish thought, though he was wise enough not to say it. 'It's not an excuse. It's reality. Things go wrong and you have to allow time for it. I'm not a magician –'

'When will the last machines be ready?' Yggur snapped.

'Tomorrow morning, at the earliest.'

Yggur scowled. 'That's not good enough.'

Nish had had enough. He threw his tools on the ground. 'If you can do better, you're welcome to try.'

To his surprise, Yggur merely said, 'Get it done,' and disappeared again. Then he ducked his head around the door. 'Where's Tiaan?'

'She's still not back from her node survey with Malien.'

'But they knew we needed Malien's thapter for the offensive. We've been planning it for months.'

'It wasn't supposed to be for a couple of weeks yet.'

'Does she have a farspeaker with her?'

'Yes. Flydd tried to call her again last night. He couldn't make contact.'

'Better try again.'

As if Nish didn't have enough to do. He ran his fingers through his tangled hair. He hadn't eaten since this time yesterday, nor bathed in a week. Slamming the door of his shed, he headed across the yard. Piles of supplies were stacked wherever space could be found. Dozens of lean-to sheds had been constructed against the walls. Two more thapters were being loaded. Three air-floaters, being much slower, were long gone. People were running everywhere.

Weaving through the yard, Nish was stopped a dozen times by people who needed to be told what to do. He finally climbed the steps with a sigh of relief, but as he went through the doors someone called his name from the other end of the hall. Not recognising the fellow, Nish turned left into a cross-passage that was mercifully empty, then left again to the circular stair that ran up to one of the repaired horned towers.

He was panting by the time he reached the top, a round chamber of naked stone with arrow slits, through which the drizzle-laden wind whistled. Nish pulled his coat around him. The spring weather was the same as winter's, only wetter.

He peered through a slit that was out of the direct path of the wind. The rain came in waves. Nish shook his head, which felt as though it was full of spiderweb. The farspeaker operator's bench was between two embrasures, fenced off with flapping walls of canvas that broke the worst of the wind. Merryl was sitting there.

'Oh,' said Nish. 'I was looking for ... whatever his name was.'

'I've taken over for the day. Do you want to send a message?'

'I didn't know you had the talent.'

'Neither did I,' said Merryl cheerfully, 'though farspeaking doesn't take much. You could probably do it yourself.'

'I doubt it. Anyhow, I don't have time to learn.'

'My father was a bit of a sensitive, so Yggur had me tested

and found I could use the globe, and here I am. The only tricky part is changing the settings.'

'I was trying to contact Tiaan,' said Nish. 'She's supposed to have been back days ago. We need her thapter; and her field maps.'

'I tried earlier, but no luck. I'll change to her settings and have another go.'

Merryl consulted a sheet covered in cryptic symbols. He selected one, took Golias's globe in his hand, steadied it against the table with his stump, pressed and twisted. The inner globes spun, the light flashing off them in dozens of colours. Merryl squeezed and the layers locked.

He held the globe up, inspecting it minutely. 'No, that's not right. Sorry, Nish. It's a bit tricky.'

'Take your time,' said Nish, sitting down in the other chair. 'I'm glad of the break. I can't remember when I last had a full night's sleep.' He leaned back against the cold wall and closed his eyes, listening to the globes spinning, again and again.

'That's better,' said Merryl. 'Hello, Tiaan, this is Merryl, calling for Nish. Are you there?'

He repeated his call over and over, until Nish, lulled by the softness of his voice, drifted into sleep.

'Hoy, Merryl?' It was Yggur, calling from the stairs. 'You haven't seen Nish, have you?'

Nish's feet struck the floor. 'He's here with me,' Merryl called back after a decent pause. 'We're trying to contact Tiaan.'

Yggur entered the room. 'I assume you've had no luck. Nish, half the yard is looking for you and it seems none of them can wait.'

Nish levered himself up, rubbing sleep out of his eyes.

'No luck at all with Tiaan,' said Merryl. 'Nor anyone else.'

'I spoke to Klarm earlier, in Strebbit,' said Yggur.

'But Klarm has a master farspeaker,' said Merryl. 'Tiaan only carries a slave. Master to master goes a lot further.'

'Keep trying; we need her thapter. And give Klarm another call; find out if he's rendezvoused with Troist yet.' Yggur went down the stairs again.

Nish was halfway down too when Merryl called him back. 'It's Klarm,' he said in a dead voice when Nish entered the chamber.

'What's the matter?'

'Lyrinx were seen moving north last night, in large numbers, so Klarm rotored straight down to the ambush site.' Merryl stopped for a deep breath.

Nish knew what he was going to say. 'The enemy aren't there any more.'

'There were plenty of signs of them in the hibernation cavern,' said Merryl, 'but it was empty apart from bones. They've gone and he doesn't know where.'

Bootsteps came back up. It was Yggur, with Flydd. 'From the way Merryl called you back, Nish, I figured it was important,' said Yggur. 'Did I hear you say the enemy have fled, Merryl?'

'Not fled,' said Merryl. 'Marched to war. They've outflanked Troist's army and Klarm reckons they'll be attacking Borgistry within a week. He's trying to get a better estimate of their numbers.'

'So what do we do?' Nish was so tired that he couldn't think straight.

'We'll have to go to Lybing and put our backs to the wall with everyone else,' said Flydd. 'Borgistry can't be allowed to fall. And that's my big worry.'

'Why?' said Nish.

'It's too rich, complacent and soft. Borgistry hasn't been threatened before. It has a big army but not many of its troops have seen combat, and its generals are fat and complacent. We're going to have to take over.'

'How will the governor of Borgistry react when you do?' Nish wondered. 'I heard the Council was unpopular there.'

'The old Council was,' said Flydd, 'but we're held in high regard, and we have Klarm to thank for that. He was like a will-o'-the-wisp, fleeting back and forth across Borgistry in the first month of winter, spreading his propaganda about the old Council and bolstering ours. There's not a soul in Borgistry who hasn't heard about Fusshte's dirty little secrets.'

'I haven't heard anything about them,' said Nish.

'Do you really want to know?'

'I don't suppose I do.'

'But do you know the single thing that has legitimised our Council?' said Flydd, smiling grimly.

'Thapters,' said Nish. 'Or farspeakers.'

'It was that grisly relic Klarm picked up in the swamp.'

'What relic?' said Yggur.

'Remember how Ghorr was blown out of his skin in the airbag explosion, and we found it hanging in a tree? Klarm had Ghorr's skin tanned and inflated to make a full-sized balloon of the former chief scrutator.'

'How revolting,' said Yggur. 'Is there no depth to which the little man won't sink?'

'Klarm knows how to move the common people,' said Flydd. 'He carried Ghorr's blow-up under his arm to every gathering, setting it up beside him like a saggy, disgusting naked puppet. When the people saw what kind of a man Ghorr had been, or rather how *little* a man he was, they rallied to us because we'd brought the brute down. There's nothing quite like ridicule.'

'I'm prepared to admit that I was wrong about Klarm,' said Yggur, 'though he wenches and drinks far more than is proper.'

'If the tales of this war are ever written, which seems increasingly unlikely, there'll be a Great Tale in Klarm's exploits and escapades over the past three months. He's the bravest man I've ever met.'

'That he is,' said Yggur. 'But a libertine nonetheless.'

FORTY-SEVEN

Lybing, from the air, was a fairytale city built at the confluence of three rivers. The old, walled town spread across five hills that surrounded the confluence like the points of a squashed star. Water formed the heart and arteries of the city, and its citizens had built no less than nineteen bridges, each beautiful, each different, across the rivers. Nish had counted them as the air-floater flew in.

The city now extended well outside the walls, for Borgistry was packed with refugees from the west, while a couple of leagues upstream, thousands of tents marked the camp of Borgistry's largest army.

That was all Nish saw of the place, for the thapter was directed to land on the lawn of the White Palace, a rambling, grotesquely ornate building of indeterminate age or, rather, many ages. It spread across a trio of mounds between the upstream arms of the two largest rivers, and was built of white marble.

Nish had just climbed out onto a springy, daisy-starred lawn when he was called into the palace. He had expected to be part of a vast conclave, but Nish found himself in a grand reception room fitted for the deliberations of emperors that was practically empty. Up the far end, by a roaring fire spitting sparks over the screen onto the tiled floor, stood an oval table and eleven chairs, all but one occupied.

'Artificer Cryl-Nish Hlar,' called the man in livery at the door.

Someone at the table was talking, and no one looked up as Nish made the long walk, his heels clicking on the tiles. He stood at the end, uncertainly.

'Sit down!' snapped Flydd.

Nish took the empty chair at the near point of the oval and looked down the table, which was piled with maps and papers. A farspeaker globe, its base encrusted with gems by a master jeweller of Lybing, sat in pride of place in the centre. He recognised a number of people there, including Flydd and, down at the far end, General Troist, who looked nearly as weary as Nish felt.

Nodding to Troist, Nish scanned the other side of the table. An elderly woman and man, both richly dressed, sat next to Troist. To their left was another general, a vast, choleric man bursting out of his uniform, his chest festooned with rows of shining medals. Beside him was a woman in black who might have been a merchant, then a tall, dark woman with frizzy hair and filed teeth – Overseer Tuniz from the manufactory. What was she doing here?

There were three more, two middle-aged men and a woman whose face Nish couldn't see as it was concealed by a dark veil. He picked up the papers in front of him.

The elderly woman extended a hand towards Nish. 'Good day to you, Artificer Cryl-Nish Hlar. I am Nisbeth, Governor of Lybing and all Borgistry. This is my husband, Argent of Borg. Next to him are General Orgestre, Grand Commander of the Army of Greater Borgistry, and Merchant Meylea Thrant. Overseer Tuniz you would know, of course, and General Troist and Scrutator Flydd. Beside Tuniz are Mancers Rodrig and Crissinton Tybe, and lastly, Mira Seliant, who has come from Morgadis.'

Nish dropped the papers, which scattered across the table. As he tried to gather them up the woman in the veil turned her face to him. It was Mira. He felt a flush moving up his cheeks. She looked at him without expression, then turned away.

Nish had an urge to run from the room, as he had fled Morgadis that night nearly a year ago. What must she think of

459

him? What would she say? It was as if all he'd made of himself over the past months was as naught.

'Cryl-Nish Hlar?'

Nish realised that Nisbeth had spoken to him and he hadn't answered. 'I'm sorry. I didn't catch that.'

'Your report, Nish!' snapped Flydd.

'Ah . . . ah . . . yes, my report. I –'

'Stop babbling, man, and get on with it. The enemy draws nigh.'

'We brought four thapters,' said Nish. Tiaan and Malien had the fifth and the other was about to go to Roros, to Governor Zaeff. 'And four air-floaters –'

He broke off, unsettled by the piercing stare of General Orgestre, who was regarding him as if he were the most lowly of worms. Orgestre's thin lips were pressed into a pale line that stood out against his red, broken-veined cheeks, and his bloodhound jowls wobbled as he turned his head.

Nish continued through his list of equipment, mostly weapons of war. What must Mira be thinking? Having lost her man and all three sons, she hated war and despised those who waged it.

'Very good,' said Flydd, turning away. 'Overseer Tuniz?'

'My manufactory has completed its commission on schedule and to Xervish Flydd's satisfaction. I've brought ten more master farspeakers and another hundred of the slave variety. There were some problems with the earlier ones but they've been sorted out by Crafter Irisis Stirm, who will remain in the east to make sure we don't have any more problems. We've also brought two hundred light blasters.'

Tuniz bared her filed teeth but Nish knew it to be a sign of good cheer. She had done all that had been asked of her and was going home to her little children as soon as the next thapter went to Crandor. Nish didn't feel as cheery. He missed Irisis and had hoped she would be coming back soon, though considering the state of the war perhaps it was better that she wasn't.

'What are light blasters?' asked Nisbeth.

'A battlefield weapon. I have one here.' Tuniz reached into a leather bag and held up a pod-shaped object, the length of her hand, made of opaque yellow glass. She threw it at the wall and it burst with a brilliant flash of light that hurt Nish's eyes. 'It's enough to daze the enemy for a minute or two. Their eyes are more sensitive than ours; that's why they avoid fighting in the middle of the day.'

'Very clever,' said Nisbeth, frowning at the blackened hole it had made through her intricate plasterwork, 'though you might have warned us.'

'The enemy will get no warning, Governor,' said Tuniz. 'These won't win the war but they'll give us a tiny advantage.'

'I doubt it,' grated Orgestre. 'We need clankers and stout men with long swords, not artificer's toys.' His eyes seemed to be accusing Nish of reckless frivolity, though it had nothing to do with him.

Flydd cleared his throat and the others at the table gave their reports. Counting Troist's forces, now making a forced march back from Strebbit, Borgistry would have an army of sixty thousand men and eight thousand clankers. They could rely on support from Tacnah, the land north-east beyond the lakes, though its eight thousand troops would take a fortnight to get here. Clan Elienor had promised one thousand, and they were already on their way, though they probably wouldn't arrive in time either. Borgistry's allies in Oolo had promised another fifteen thousand but they were a month's march away. The lands further south and west might be able to provide ten thousand raw troops who would have to be trained and equipped, though they would not arrive until early summer.

'We'll be at war within days,' said Flydd. 'Therefore, we can rely on nothing but our sixty thousand.'

'It's a mighty army,' said Nisbeth. 'What are the enemy numbers?'

'Estimates vary considerably. The lyrinx travel individually or in small groups, and mainly at night. Even in the daytime it's difficult to count them.'

'We know that,' snapped Orgestre. 'Give us your numbers.'

'General Troist?' said Flydd. 'You've just rotored in from Strebbit. What's your estimate.'

'At the end of autumn I had their numbers at twenty-eight thousand between here and the Sea of Thurkad, counting those that had gone into hiding after Snizort. There could be more to our north. As to how many might have come across the sea, I cannot guess.'

'So many,' said Nisbeth, 'after all their losses last year?'

'I'm afraid so.'

'General Orgestre?'

'My spies tell me thirty-two thousand,' said Orgestre, 'plus a few thousand that we guess will fly from Meldorin. A mighty force, but we're fighting for our homes and families and we have the numbers to defeat them. What about you, Flydd? Let's pray that your estimate falls in the middle.'

'It doesn't,' said Flydd. 'According to Klarm, who's counted them and was hoping to be here to present the details himself, the enemy numbers *at least* fifty-seven thousand.'

Nisbeth clutched at her heart, but after a minute the colour returned to her face. She took a sip of water, gripping the arms of her chair to stay upright.

'Go on,' Nisbeth quavered. 'If you've more bad news we might as well hear it right away.'

'That's it,' said Flydd. 'Each lyrinx is the match of two of our soldiers, so we're effectively outnumbered two to one. Surrounded as Borgistry is by forest, I don't see how we can defend its borders.'

FORTY-EIGHT

Someone drew a deep, shuddering breath. Nish thought it had been Mira, though she was sitting back and he couldn't see her. General Orgestre's mouth opened and closed. For the first time in his life, it appeared, the hard-faced man was directly threatened, and he was terrified. He began buffing his golden medals, as if to find comfort there.

'Then Borgistry will fall,' said Nisbeth. 'We must evacuate to our refuges.'

'Where we'll either starve in the drylands, freeze in the mountains or be eaten alive by midges in the stinking bogs of Mirrilladell,' said Meylea Thrant, the merchant. 'Had I known I was throwing my money away, I would have paid my military levies rather less cheerfully.'

'You never handed over a copper grint without shedding a tear,' General Orgestre said, now desperately polishing his chest ornaments.

'I'd gladly pay it to an officer who'd earned his commission, rather than bought it,' said Thrant.

Dead silence. Orgestre swelled up like a red-faced toad. His mouth opened but nothing came out.

'That's not helpful,' said Nisbeth, who was deathly pale. Her husband was supporting her. 'General Troist, may we hear your view?'

Troist, a neat man, apart from his mass of tangled, sandy curls, stood up. 'As far as I know, no human army has ever beaten the enemy when the numbers were equal; nor should we expect to. Yet,' he looked down one side of the table and up the other, 'the situation is different now.'

'Go on, General,' said Nisbeth. 'Do *you* have a plan to defend us?'

'I'm beginning to formulate one. Flydd and Yggur have given us new hope. Farspeakers are going to revolutionise warfare, though we're still working out how to make the best use of them. And with our thapters, essentially invulnerable to lyrinx attack, we can see the whole of a battlefield – indeed the whole of Borgistry – at once.'

'They'll attack in bad weather when you can't see further than you can throw a spear,' said Orgestre.

'Then we'll know when to expect them,' said Troist.

'But not *where*. Not *how many*,' said Orgestre with relentless despair. 'And both thapters and farspeakers are vulnerable to node-drainers. Only a fool would rely on such untested Arts at a time like this.'

'We're overusing the fields,' said Mancer Crissinton Tybe, who had the narrowest, most angular face Nish had ever seen on a man, and a mouth that gashed it in two as if the back of his head were hinged. 'It's as simple as that. We're abusing the natural forces, and so are the enemy, and there's got to be a reckoning.'

'I'm not sure I understand you, Mancer Tybe,' said Flydd.

'What he means,' said Mancer Rodrig, a small, deliberate man, 'is that one day the fields will let us down when we most need them.' His skin was starkly white but there were such dark rings around his eyes that he appeared to be wearing goggles. 'We must wean ourselves off the fields before it's too late. We've seen it in the stars.'

'*The stars!*' said Flydd, unable to contain his derision. 'Unfortunately, my dear mancers, this war is being fought on solid ground and to give up the fields is to give up existence. While the enemy uses power we have to match it.'

'Even to the ruin of the world,' Crissinton Tybe intoned.

'If the numbers are correct, we've lost the battle and the war,' said Orgestre. His red face was now blotched with ugly purple stains like birthmarks.

'It would almost be worth it,' came a low voice from behind the veil, 'to rid the world of the bloodless warmongers who send our young to die but never hazard their own lives. Have you ever seen *active* service, Orgestre?' Nish had never heard such hatred as there was in Mira's voice.

'Mira, please,' said Nisbeth. 'Would you go on, General Troist?'

'We have thapters, against which the enemy haven't yet found a defence. We have farspeakers – which aren't perfect, I agree – yet in this battle, in the limited compass of Borgistry, they're worth twenty thousand troops. If the enemy break though in some unexpected place, our captains will know in time to send reinforcements, or withdraw.'

'They have the numbers to overwhelm us,' said Orgestre. 'and they too can communicate over a distance.'

'Their mindspeaking is of the most primitive sort,' said Flydd. 'Only those most powerful in the Art can use it. There's still hope, since the lyrinx are just out of hibernation. They'll be lethargic and wouldn't normally do battle for another week. And they'll be wasted and hungry when they get here.'

'They'll fight all the more fiercely for it,' said Orgestre. 'We must withdraw.'

'They won't fight as well, or for as long. We must force them into battle before they're ready, and seize the advantage.'

'You've got to find them first,' said Orgestre. 'How are you going to do that?'

'We're training animals to sniff them out,' said Flydd, reluctantly.

'What kind of animals?'

'Pigs, as it happens. They can pick lyrinx even further away than dogs, and –'

'*Sniffer pigs!* That's one for the Histories. They'll still be laughing about it in a thousand years.'

'Enough, gentlemen,' said Nisbeth. 'We've got to decide on a plan.'

465

'Get rid of this fool before he leads us all to destruction. As Grand Commander –'

'No, General,' said Nisbeth. 'I bow to the Council and Scrutator Flydd's leadership. Xervish?'

Flydd set his jaw. 'We fight for Borgistry and the whole world,' he said flatly. 'We can do nothing less.'

Nish was out the door the moment the Council finished. He was running away, for he could not bear to see the contempt in Mira's eyes. He fully expected guards to come for him, and all day he had an itch in the middle of his back, as if a target had been painted there. He desperately needed to talk to someone about it, but Irisis was the only person with whom he could share such a delicate matter and he had no idea when she was going to return.

That afternoon he was summoned to Troist's rooms. Nish went expecting the worst.

'Come in,' Troist said. He was a reserved man and Nish couldn't read his expression. 'I didn't get the chance to congratulate you earlier, so let me do it now. You've done great deeds since I last saw you at Gnulp Landing. I wouldn't have thought any man could have accomplished so much. And now this new miracle: air-floaters built, thapters recovered from Snizort, pilots found and trained, and all unexpected but most timely. There's no man under my command who could have done it, Cryl-Nish.'

'It was . . . everyone worked very hard, surr.'

'And no one harder or more intelligently than you.' He gave Nish his hand, and Nish shook it in rather a daze. 'You've given us a chance that even I – and my wife Yara calls me an incurable optimist – never dreamed of having.'

'Thank you, surr.' Nish swallowed, still thinking about Mira. For all his bravery on the battlefield, he would never find the courage to face one small woman. 'I was wondering if I might come with you, surr, when you go to war? I might be more useful at the front than sitting here.'

Troist gave him a keen glance. 'I've need of an aide who can get things done. If Scrutator Flydd has no objection, I'd be delighted to have you. I'll be leaving in the morning.'

Scrutator Flydd had many objections, which he put strenuously, but Nish would not back down.

'You're a curious chap, Nish,' said Flydd. 'I recall a time, not so long ago, when you pleaded with me to keep you away from the front-lines. Now you're begging to go there.' He surveyed Nish just as keenly as Troist had. 'Are you sure you're not running away from something?'

Nish tried to pass it off. 'Well, I'm a different man now.'

'You're a man, not a boy pretending to be one. That's the difference. Oh, go on then. I dare say Troist needs you more than I do.'

Troist and his retinue of officers were heading for Clew's Top, east of The Elbow in southern Borgistry, where a small force of his army was stationed, to await the main army now racing back from Strebbit. Nish rode with them in a cramped, bone-jarring clanker. It seemed such an old-fashioned conveyance now, so noisy that he couldn't think straight, and joltingly uncomfortable.

'Did you happen to see Mira yesterday?' Troist said that afternoon.

'I didn't get the chance,' Nish lied.

'She was looking for you. And so were Yara and my twins.'

'I was working on the supply records until late.' Hiding, as it happened.

'I dare say she'll find you when we get back.'

If we get back. The lyrinx generally attacked the command centre from the air at night, with massive force, at the beginning of a battle. Just so had Troist gained his command after all the more senior officers were slain.

FORTY-NINE

Tiaan had spent weeks in the thapter, alone but for Malien, who flew it while Tiaan monitored the fields and refined her maps. She had now surveyed the whole of western Lauralin save for the northern sector of the Great Chain of Lakes, which roughly marked the boundary between the lyrinx-occupied lands to the west, Borgistry in the centre and impoverished Tacnah to the north.

Tiaan was now completing her lakes survey, after which they were to go to Borgistry to help with the coming war. They'd heard from Yggur the previous day, though perturbations in the ethyr had prevented them from replying with their slave farspeaker.

The Great Chain of Lakes lay in rugged, rifted and sunken lands bounded by great fault escarpments on either side, dotted with fuming volcanoes and boggy geyser country. Complex lines of nodes ran along the rift valley and the area had proven troublesome to map, but now, almost a week later than Tiaan had expected, the first rough chart was finished.

Malien was flying across Warde Yallock, the longest and deepest of all the lakes, and the cradle of civilisation on Santhenar. 'Let's set down there, by the water. I'm so weary of flying.'

'I'm not surprised,' said Tiaan. 'You've been doing it for months with hardly a break.'

Malien headed towards an open area on the western side of the lake, landing at the top of a long green slope that ran to the water's edge. Patches of forest spread over the hills behind them like dark green eiderdowns. Beyond the lake, twinned volcanoes smoked. They strolled out to the edge and Tiaan bathed while Malien kept watch. The water was surprisingly warm for the season. Afterwards Tiaan dried her hair in the sun and Malien swam out until she was just a dot in the distance.

They had lunch in mid-afternoon, in the shade of the thapter. They could see all the way across the lake, where the setting sun illuminated tall cliffs of red stone.

'It's peaceful here,' said Tiaan. 'I'm so sick of the war.'

'You've never known anything else.'

'It must seem like the blink of an eye to you.'

Malien laughed aloud. 'Not even in my advanced years could I consider one hundred and fifty years to be the blink of an eye. But it has been a bad time, the worst I can remember, though my people have scarcely been involved in the war. We leave the lyrinx alone and they don't trouble us.'

'What was it like, in olden times? Was it as good as the tales say?'

'No, nor as bad, in my lifetime, anyway. There was peace, of a sort, before the Forbidding was broken and everything changed. Oh, there were always little wars going on somewhere, but few people were affected by them. Most lived their lives without ever seeing an army, save during a ceremonial march. But the big difference was the freedom.'

'How do you mean?' Tiaan had never known freedom before leaving the manufactory, and could not imagine it. The Council organised every aspect of people's brief lives from the moment they were born until their untimely deaths.

'Well, people were free to move to another place or another country, if they wished to. They might not have been welcomed, but there was no law to stop them. They could do whatever kind of work they could make a living at. There were no examinations and no Council of Scrutators telling everyone what to do.'

'And no breeding factories,' said Tiaan.

'Certainly not! Women could choose to have children, or not. It wasn't a crime to prevent conception then.'

That reminded Tiaan of a puzzle she'd often thought about. 'When I was held in the breeding factory, I saw something that I've wondered about ever since.'

'What was it?' Malien lay on the grass and closed her eyes. 'Can you keep an eye out, in case I doze off?'

Tiaan climbed onto the shooter's platform and scanned the country. There was no living creature in sight. She sat beside Malien again.

'I don't know who my father is and Marnie wouldn't tell me. But one time in the Matron's office I happened to see a book – the bloodline register for the breeding factory at Tiksi.'

'Bloodline register?'

'Yes. It was like a human stud book.'

'You old humans are obsessed about your family Histories. The breeding factory would have to have records of the parents.'

'But it was what was *in* the records,' said Tiaan. 'The talents of the parents . . .'

Malien yawned. 'You should ask Flydd about that. I've never understood why old humans do the things they do. I suppose we'd better find a place to hide for the night. I'm too tired to fly all the way to Borgistry.'

In the morning they flew due south over the unending expanse of northern Worm Wood, and in the early afternoon Tiaan saw a cluster of volcanoes in the distance.

'There's a place I've not properly surveyed,' she said. 'Booreah Ngurle, the Burning Mountain.' It stood at least a thousand spans higher than the other volcanoes in the cluster and was belching dark grey clouds of ash.

'We might as well have a quick look at it on the way to Lybing.'

Before they reached the lowest of the peaks, as they were flying across dense forest, Tiaan looked up from her map. 'That's funny!'

'What?'

'There's a strong node here but the field is really tenuous.' She peered over the side but saw only the same untracked forest they had been crossing for hours. It was getting dark.

'Fields fluctuate,' said Malien.

'Not as much as this.'

'We can go back and forth if you want to take a closer look.'

'No.' Tiaan felt uneasy without knowing why. 'We're supposed to be heading for Borgistry.'

'There's time. Yggur said they wouldn't be fighting for a few days yet.'

'In that case, go on to Booreah Ngurle. It has a double node that I'm interested in.'

Malien flew around the peak, then back and forth across it, to either side of the ash clouds.

'All finished, Tiaan?'

'Um, can we go back to that weak field now? I want to take another look.'

They flew north on the same track as they had taken south. Two small chains of hills ran to their left. The area that interested Tiaan lay a little to the east of them. 'Now turn around and go back.'

'Again?' said Malien when they had returned to their starting point.

'No! Just keep going. I've got to think.'

'Perhaps if you were to think aloud . . .'

'Sorry, Malien. The fields down there are all wrong. The nodes are strong ones but their fields are just points.'

'Meaning that something has almost drained them dry?'

'Exactly,' said Tiaan. 'But why would the enemy put node-drainers in the middle of trackless forest. We'd never fight in such a place. It doesn't make sense.'

'How many fields have shrunk?'

'All of them, over an area of forest ten leagues square.'

'All of them?' Malien stared at her. 'It would take an army of lyrinx flying over the forest to drain that much from the field.'

'And there aren't any fliers in sight.'

'An army moving through the forest then?'

471

'They don't use the field when they're marching. Unless . . .'

'Unless they're travelling under a vast concealment,' said Malien, 'even greater than the one that stone-formed thirty thousand of them into the pinnacles above Gumby Marth. And it would have to be *much* greater to conceal an army on the march. We'd better get back. Whatever Flydd's expecting, I'm sure it's not an attack from the north, between Booreah Ngurle and the Peaks of Borg.'

'They must have done a forced march all the way from Strebbit, to have got here so quickly.' Tiaan measured distances on the map. 'They're only twenty-five leagues from Borgistry and lyrinx march faster than soldiers. They could do it in a couple of days, even through the forest.'

'Try the farspeaker again.'

Tiaan did so, but heard nothing except a shrill whistling. 'What are we going to do?'

Malien jerked the thapter around in mid-air. 'We're going to Lybing.'

They arrived over the city at the darkest hour of the night. 'Do you know where to go?' said Tiaan as they approached.

'I haven't been to Lybing in a couple of hundred years.'

'I've *never* been here.'

'There's the Great North Road,' said Malien. 'I'll set down at the northern gate.'

The terrified guards did not know whether to fire their crossbows or run screaming as the thapter whined into the pool of light outside the gates.

'Hoy!' roared Malien. 'The enemy is nigh. Where can we find the governor?'

The guards each pointed in a different direction.

'General Troist?' said Malien. 'Scrutator Xervish Flydd? Lord Yggur?'

'The White Palace,' gasped the guard. 'Where the three waters join. If you run that way –'

'Run,' said Malien. 'At my age?'

The thapter screamed and shot off, directly over the gates.

They landed hard on the manicured lawn outside the front door of the White Palace, skidding on the dewy surface and carving out a streak of crumpled turf three or four spans long. Tiaan gathered her maps and threw herself over the side, Malien following just a little less hastily.

Tiaan pounded on the bronze-studded doors with her free hand. A sleepy guard opened the left-hand one.

'Where is Scrutator Flydd? Or Lord Yggur?' Malien rapped out.

'Inside,' said the guard, 'but they'll be sleeping now.'

'I am Malien!' she said briskly. 'Matah of the Aachim. My name is written in the Great Tales.'

He took a step backwards, calling out to his fellows.

'The enemy is almost upon us,' said Malien. 'Let us in at once.'

No one else could have done it, but such was her authority that the guard did allow them through. 'Take the stairs straight ahead. Turn left down the corridor. The scrutator's door is at the end.'

'Thank you,' said Malien.

Tiaan ran. Her back was troubling her and her legs felt weak, but she soon outdistanced Malien. After scooting up the stairs, she turned left and ran along the hall. Which room? She couldn't remember what the guard had said. At the end, or near the end?

She pounded on the first door she came to, and then on several others. 'Scrutator, Scrutator! Wake, wake! The enemy is nigh.'

There were cries of panic, shouting and an occasional scream, as if people thought the lyrinx were inside the palace. Shortly Xervish Flydd appeared at the end door, pulling a robe around his gristly frame.

'Scrutator, surr?' said Tiaan.

'Where the bloody hell have you been?' he snapped.

'Delayed,' she lied. 'We know where the enemy are, surr. They're coming under a concealment of surpassing power, down through the forest on the north-eastern side of Booreah Ngurle.' She partly unrolled her main map. 'Here, surr. Their fliers could

473

attack as early as tomorrow, and the whole army could enter northern Borgistry within two days.'

'Attacking from the north,' he breathed. 'I never would have expected that. How can you be sure?'

Malien came hobbling up. 'There's so many of them that they've drained all the fields in a huge area, about ten leagues square, down to pinpricks.'

'How do you know they haven't put in node-drainers, to fool us?' said Flydd.

'Why would we check the fields in such a remote place?'

'Come down to the war room. We'll take a look at the big maps. I hope you're right, Tiaan. If I direct our forces north, and they strike somewhere else . . .'

Two days after leaving Lybing, Nish was working in the command tent at Clew's Top when Troist's farspeaker gave forth a hollow tapping, like the flicking of a fingernail against a blown egg. He looked up. Troist was not there.

Nish did not know how to use a farspeaker, or even if he was capable of doing so. Putting his head through the flaps of the tent he bawled, 'General Troist?'

A soldier standing a few paces away grinned and said, 'He's gone to the privy. He'll be a while. The general suffers from a flux —'

'Thank you, soldier!'

Nish ran to the farspeaker, which was still tapping, though more loudly. If it was already set, maybe all he had to do was talk. He tapped back. The farspeaker gave out a squelching noise, then a voice rumbled forth. It did not come from the farspeaker, rather from the air above it, and had an echoing, unearthly quality that made it hard to identify.

'Troist? Is that you?'

'Scrutator? It's Nish. Troist is out at the bogs.'

'Run and get him. We've found the enemy and they're only days away.'

A spasm twisted Nish's entrails. The moment had finally come. 'Where?' he cried.

'From the north, east of Booreah Ngurle, if Tiaan is right.'

'I'll get Troist right away, surr.'

Nish ran down to the privies and yelled through the wall. 'General Troist. Flydd is on the farspeaker. It's urgent.' He didn't want to say more, since there could be a dozen men in the privies at any time and morale could easily be damaged.

'I'm coming.' Troist appeared after a short delay, holding his stomach.

Over the farspeaker, Flydd repeated what he had told Nish.

'What are your orders, surr?' said Troist. 'What if Tiaan is wrong?'

'Then we're in as much trouble as if she's right and we do nothing. Bring your army north to Ossury. How soon can you be there?'

'My main force has only just got here from Strebbit, in their clankers,' said Troist without consulting the map. 'I'll bring them north without delay, leaving the rest here. I can't leave this place undefended. On good roads, going night and day, we should be able to reach Ossury in two and a half days, as long as we don't have too many breakdowns. And as long as the fields last. There have been a few failures around here lately. How about there?'

'The same,' said Flydd. 'We haven't lost a node yet but the fields grow more unreliable by the day. Take the usual precautions and spread your clankers out. We can't afford another loss like Hannigor. Goodbye.'

'No surr,' said Troist. 'We cannot.'

'What was Hannigor?' said Nish.

'It's a village down south, between Saludith and Thuxgate. Fifty-four clankers were travelling close together at full speed, coming to the aid of a smaller force that had been ambushed by the enemy last autumn. They must have taken more from the field than could be borne. A sphere of light formed around them, collapsed, and they vanished. Even the ground they were travelling over was gone, annihilated down to bare rock.'

'I heard a similar tale back at the manufactory. Do you think we're in danger now, just travelling in a convoy of clankers?'

'I don't know, lad,' said Troist. 'Fields have never been perfectly reliable, but lately it's become worse. Some mancers think we're drawing on them beyond their capacity, but what can we do? Without the Art we would already have lost the war.'

'And yet, each time we make a new advance, they counter it with one of their own that also uses power. What will it be next?'

'I don't dare think.'

Within two hours camp had been broken and they were heading north up the Great North Road as fast as the clankers would go. Every machine was packed with food and supplies, and most towed sleds or carts, piled high. More soldiers sat on the shooter's platforms or clung to the sides. Troist had left behind two thousand soldiers and a token force of eighty clankers to help protect them. The goodbyes were sombre. Whether the enemy appeared in the north or the south, everyone knew that they were unlikely to see their friends again.

They were plagued by breakdowns and field failures on the way north, and by the end of the second day of travel were half a day behind schedule. They bypassed Lybing on the west and continued. Troist was in and out of the jolting clanker, either urging his operators and artificers on, or darting behind a bush or hedge to relieve himself. He drank flagons of a thick green liquid with an offensive odour, trying to quell his troublesome innards, but to little effect. The race had taken three and a half days, and morning had broken, before they came in sight of the towers of Ossury, the northernmost town in Borgistry.

'I don't see any sign of fighting,' said Nish to Troist as they climbed out the rear hatch of the clanker and stretched their cramped muscles.

'I'm not sure if that's good or bad.'

An air-floater hung in the sky above the town. As they turned off the road towards a river, to make camp, a thapter screamed overhead. Judging by the exuberant swoops and rolls, Chissmoul was at the controller. Nish smiled, imagining the joy of his shy protégée.

476

'How far away were the enemy when Tiaan sighted them?'
Nish asked.

'The scrutator didn't say.'

'We'll soon know. That looks like him now.'

A small man came cantering through the gates on a tall white
horse. It seemed incongruous, after months of travel by air.
They went to meet him.

'Good day, Scrutator Flydd,' said Troist. 'What can you tell us?'

'We believe they're quite near,' said Flydd, without so much
as a greeting or a glance at Nish. 'The depressed fields were no
more than a day's march away last night.'

'What about now?' said Troist.

'I don't know. I'm keeping Tiaan away, in case we alert them
and they attack somewhere else.'

'So we don't know if they're coming this way or not?'

'Sadly no.'

'Any news from the pig sentries?' Nish said. 'Not a sausage,
I suppose.'

'Very funny!' Flydd said coldly. 'We'll just have to pray that
Tiaan is right.'

'If she's not . . .' Troist began.

'We've been through that already,' Flydd snapped.

They spent a long and anxious night, during which a hundred
messengers must have come in and out of the command tent.
No one knew what was going on. Nish retired at midnight but
his tent was next to the command tent and he couldn't sleep.
Every minute he expected to hear the cry, 'To battle!'

When a call finally came, it was something of an anticlimax.
Nish stamped his feet into his boots and ran next door. 'What
is it? Are we under attack?'

Troist looked like death and Flydd was not much better.
'Unfortunately not,' said Flydd. 'The enemy has attacked from
the east, fifteen leagues south of here, and are driving directly
for Lybing.'

'The east?' said Nish. 'How did they get *there*?'

Flydd just shrugged.

'How many of them?'

'We won't know until dawn. Hopefully it's just a feint by an isolated band of fliers.'

The farspeaker belched like a cow and a deep voice exploded from it. 'We're under attack, surr!'

Flydd rapped on the globe. 'Identify yourself, you fool. How the bloody hell am I supposed to know who you are?'

'Sorry, surr,' came back after a considerable pause. 'It's Captain Maks, of Troist's detachment at Clew's Top.'

'The south as well!' Troist knuckled his bristly cheeks. 'I knew it was the wrong –'

'You forget yourself, General,' hissed Flydd, turning away from the farspeaker. 'Morale, dammit.'

Turning back, he tapped the globe. 'Captain Maks, this is Scrutator Xervish Flydd here. How many of the enemy are there?'

Again that over-long pause. 'Ethyr must be very slow tonight,' Flydd muttered.

'Or the fields overly drained,' fretted Nish.

The farspeaker belched again. 'Maks, surr. Can't tell their numbers. Seems like a good few.'

'What the hell does that mean? Hundreds? Thousands? Tens of thousands?'

'Hundreds at least, surr.'

Flydd conferred with Troist, who tapped on the globe. 'It's Troist, Maks. Don't engage the enemy. Take to the constructs, all that can fit inside, and retreat slowly north towards Lybing, protecting the infantry.'

'Don't engage ... retreat ... Lybing,' Maks repeated, and faded out.

'Troist, call for a general report,' said Flydd.

Troist contacted the detachments of Borgistry's other forces, one by one. Another squad, this one on the western side, also reported being under attack. 'What are the enemy up to? Are they going to attack along a hundred and fifty leagues of border, or is this just a distraction until the main force is in position?'

'It's going to be a long time till dawn,' said Flydd.

'Why don't you see if you can contact Tiaan, Scrutator?' said Nish.

478

'Good idea.' Flydd ordered her to fly north, keeping so high that the sound of the thapter could not be heard. 'And don't fly over them. As soon as you detect them, turn back.'

An anxious half-hour went by, during which a stream of couriers ran in and out. Flydd was constantly interrupted by representatives of the villages surrounding Ossury, terrified that the enemy was about to fall on them. Finally he ordered the guard to keep them away. Troist pored over his maps, his back bent.

Tiaan eventually reported back. 'The depression in the fields is still moving south, in the direction of Ossury.' Her voice was clear, though there was a bell-like ringing of the ethyr in the background.

'If it's a feint, it's a magnificently coordinated one,' said Flydd. 'How can they do that over such distances?' No one answered. 'We'd better get the other thapters armed and in the air,' he went on.

'Everything's ready,' said Troist. 'We just don't know where to send them.'

By mid-morning it had begun to rain, and it became heavier as the day wore on. They still had no idea what was happening. The attacking lyrinx could have numbered hundreds, or thousands. More conflicts broke out until the borders of Borgistry were ringed by skirmishes.

Finally, around the middle of the day, came the news they had been dreading.

'General!' Even through the rumble of the farspeaker they could hear the terror. 'It's Captain Maks. We're still well south of Lybing. There are enemy everywhere.'

'Are you using the light blasters?'

'Yes, but we don't have enough to make a difference. There's thousands of the enemy, surr! They're coming –'

The farspeaker cut off and they could not raise him again.

'Doesn't mean they're lost,' said Troist eventually, but there was a blank look in his eye that Nish had not seen since they'd first met, just after the ruinous defeat at Nilkerrand.

Flydd seized the globe. 'Thapters, report! Who's the nearest to Clew's Top?'

A full minute passed before a youthful voice said, 'It's Chissmoul, surr.'

'Who's Chissmoul, Nish?' Flydd said out of the corner of his mouth.

'Chissmoul is the one who doesn't have Yggur's eyes. The rather . . . exuberant flier.'

'Oh, *that* one. Downright reckless, I would have said. What's she doing down there?'

'Patrolling.'

Flydd turned back to the globe. 'Chissmoul, go down carefully to where the soldiers are. Tell me what you see.'

They heard nothing for a good half-hour, then Chissmoul called back. She wasn't exuberant now. Her voice quavered. 'I've found them, surr. I have them with me.'

'What the blazes are you talking about, Pilot?' said Flydd.

'The survivors. I have both of them.'

'*Both?* There were two thousand soldiers and eighty clankers!'

There was a long silence.

'Chissmoul?'

'None of the clankers are moving, surr. All the soldiers are dead and the enemy has gone.'

Troist turned to Flydd, but Flydd couldn't meet his eyes.

'Gone where?' said Nish, leaning towards the farspeaker globe.

'They're heading north, towards Lybing,' said Chissmoul.

'How many?'

'More than two thousand. Surr.'

'Follow them, but keep out of catapult range,' said Troist, tapping the farspeaker to indicate that he'd finished. 'What do we do now?' he cried. 'Do we let them slaughter our scattered forces, man by man, then fall on defenceless Lybing while we sit here watching for phantoms?'

'Lybing is a walled city defended by an army of ten thousand,' Flydd said.

'If the enemy send just half of their fifty-seven thousand against Lybing, they'll take it before we can get there!'

'Tiaan?' called the scrutator after changing the setting of the farspeaker. 'It's Flydd. What's happening?'

'The depression in the field is still moving towards Ossury.'

Flydd paced back and forth, his lips moving. He cast a glance at the general, who was staring at the wall. Flydd sat down with head in hands. Nish was glad the decision wasn't his to make.

'My men are dying, Scrutator,' said Troist. 'If you're wrong, the three rivers of Lybing will flow red for a week. You're gambling everything on Tiaan and, to be frank, her history doesn't inspire confidence. Wasn't she out of her mind in Nennifer?'

He pressed his knuckles into his stomach, his face grey with pain. Nish passed over the flask containing Troist's latest remedy, a noxious yellow potion. Troist swigged half a flask, though it seemed no more efficacious than the green sludge he'd resorted to previously.

Flydd bit his lip. 'Tiaan has never let me down. Besides, Malien is with her. We hold firm for another hour.'

The farspeaker emitted a farting burp. 'Xervish Flydd,' said a deadly voice whose tones came through quite unchanged. 'Grand Commander Orgestre here. This is madness. Will you twiddle your thumbs until the enemy have destroyed us all?'

'It's a feint,' said Flydd desperately. 'As soon as we turn south they'll be onto us.'

'You've lost your mind. You are dismissed from command of our forces.'

'I don't hold command, and if the governor and the generals no longer have confidence in me they can say so.'

'General Troist,' said Orgestre, shrilly. 'I order you to take Flydd into custody and render him up to me. You are to come south at once and defend Lybing.'

'You don't have the power to give orders to me, Orgestre,' said Troist, who had gone the colour of his elixir. 'My army is not from Borgistry.'

'Then who *do* you obey, surr?' Orgestre ground out. 'Think carefully before you answer. You know the penalty for treason.'

Troist took a long time to answer. 'I do know the penalty, surr, and I take my orders from Xervish Flydd, the head of the

Council of Scrutators. He has asked me to wait another hour, and wait I will.'

'You will regret this, General Troist.'

'We may all regret it, surr, though not for very long.'

'I hope I can repay your trust,' said Flydd after Orgestre had gone.

Troist sank the rest of the potion and continued to knuckle his rebellious belly. The hour passed with agonising slowness. More reports came in, of isolated squads slaughtered to the last man.

Nish turned the hourglass, setting it down with a clatter.

Flydd's eyes flicked to the glass. 'I'll contact Tiaan again.'

'And if there is no concrete news?' said Troist.

'I fear we must turn back to Lybing. Tiaan?' he called.

'Still the same,' Tiaan's voice came clearly over the whine of the thapter.

'Can I speak to Malien?'

'Yes, Xervish?' said Malien.

'The enemy are attacking all around the borders. We've lost thousands of men already and if they're really heading for Lybing . . .'

'Are you asking me to back up Tiaan's report?'

'If she's wrong, Lybing will be destroyed and the west will fall. I need confirmation.'

'I'm not able to see the effect that Tiaan has reported,' said Malien, 'but I have no reason to doubt her.'

'In any respect?' A river of sweat ran down Flydd's cheek.

'If you're questioning her sanity, have the goodness to speak plainly.'

'The world is at stake here, Malien.'

'Then you have quite a decision to make,' she said coldly. The farspeaker cut off.

Flydd wiped his face with a rag that was already drenched with sweat. 'What am I to do, Nish? How am I to decide?'

'I don't know, surr.'

'The effect Tiaan's seeing must be a decoy – a spread-out group of lyrinx carrying node-drainers. They've lured us here so they can destroy the rest of Borgistry unhindered. That has to be it. I can't delay any longer. Order the turnabout, General.'

Troist sprang to the farspeaker and changed the setting. 'Captains, this is General Troist. Turn back to Lybing immediately. Follow Plan Three.'

The orders had just been repeated when the farspeaker squealed.

'This is Tiaan. I can see the enemy, surr. *Surr?*'

Flydd jumped out of his seat. 'Where are they?'

'They're coming out of the forest in their thousands, from the point where the Great North Road meets the forest, then west for a couple of leagues. There's thousands of them.'

After a long pause, Malien added, 'I'd say tens of thousands.'

'Thank you! Thank you, Tiaan and Malien. Stay on watch.' There were tears in Flydd's eyes. He embraced Troist and then Nish. 'To war!'

'To war,' said Troist, then snatched the farspeaker globe.

'Captains. General Troist again. Ignore the last order. The enemy are coming from the forest north of Ossury, from the Great North Road west for several leagues. This is the main attack. Put Plan Six into action.' He broke off and ran to the door. 'Guards, the war begins. Ready the command-centre defences.' He came inside and buckled on his armour, made from boiled leather, and his steel helmet.

'I think I'll go up in one of the thapters,' said Flydd. 'Even in this weather we might see something useful. Will you join me?'

'My place is here, with my men. I'll send up my best tactician, Orbes, and he can report back.'

'Very good.' Flydd called down the nearest thapter. 'Nish?'

'I'm with Troist, at least until the battle is over,' said Nish, shrugging his armour over his shoulders.

FIFTY

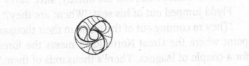

The sun came out and the clouds blew away, but it was going to be a desperate day.

'They're not fighting as hard as in other battles I've seen,' said Nish around midday. The command circle had been set up on a bald hill overlooking the battlefield. He was standing at the edge, within the ring of guards, acting as an observer.

'They do seem a little wasted after their hibernation.' Troist had just come from the command tent to join him.

'I wonder why they're fighting now?'

'After Klarm discovered their whereabouts and we sent the army to Strebbit, I suppose they had no choice.'

'Then why didn't they attack there? They had the numbers.'

'They were just out of hibernation and needed the past week to recuperate.'

'Why not take a fortnight and recuperate fully?'

'How the blazes would I know, Nish?' snapped Troist. 'They may have been afraid to wait, in case we discovered them. It's not easy to hide that many lyrinx and they wouldn't want to be forced into battle at a ground of our choosing, as they have been here.'

'I suppose not.' Nish scanned the battlefield. 'Our light-blasting weapons don't seem to be having much effect.'

'There are few miracle weapons in war. They've worked

about as well as I'd expected. They are making a difference.'

'Not much.'

'A lot of small advantages make a big one. We're fighting the lyrinx on our terms. Good visibility, open land and bright sunshine. We can use our new tactics to best effect.'

The soldiers were fighting in tight formations, making it difficult for the lyrinx to get through their walls of spears and shields. And when the lyrinx attacked in groups, as they had to, they were vulnerable to the clankers, which could fire their catapults and javelards from the side or the rear, over the heads of the soldiers. The thapters were also taking a toll, maintaining a height from which they could fire at the enemy but above the altitude where the enemy's catapults could reach them.

'I do believe we're gaining a little,' said Troist in the early afternoon, watching the battle through a spyglass and relaying orders over his farspeaker. 'They don't seem to be fighting quite as ferociously as I remember.'

'I was thinking the same. We've taken heavy casualties though,' said Nish, gingerly feeling a shoulder wound. A small band of lyrinx had broken through the lines just before noon and gone straight for the lookout. It had been a brief but vicious struggle. He hadn't killed the lyrinx that had attacked him, but fortunately one of Troist's guards had.

His shoulder was throbbing. It was not a bad wound, as battle wounds go, just three long claw marks. Nothing like the blow that had practically taken his father's shoulder off a year and a half ago. Another ell, though, and Nish would have been in the same situation.

Troist was going through the latest tally sheets. 'We've lost nine thousand men, and as many injured. They've about twelve thousand dead, so it's evened the odds a trifle, but they still have the advantage if they dare to press it. Pray that they break soon, Nish. They can take these casualties better than we can.'

He called Flydd on the farspeaker. 'Scrutator, we can't manage much more of this.'

'I agree,' said Flydd. 'It's time for a different approach. A strike at their morale.'

485

Shortly, five thapters appeared in the west, flying in a line, low and slow. As they passed over the enemy formations a soldier on the shooter's platform of each machine emptied a bag of what looked like brown flour over the side. Dust clouds slowly sifted down onto the lyrinx. At the edge of the battlefield the thapters wheeled and came back on a different track, flying just above catapult height. They kept this up until they'd covered the bulk of the enemy troops and all the bags of dust were gone.

At the end of that line, four thapters turned away and resumed the bloody work with their javelards. The fifth went back and forth across the battlefield again, a second man standing on the rear platform, though he didn't appear to be doing anything.

Nish raised an eyebrow. 'What's that all about?'

'Something Yggur came up with,' said Troist. 'Did you hear about those lyrinx at Snizort that caught a dreadful skin inflammation?'

'I did. The creatures had to be put out of their misery.'

'Klarm discovered where they'd been buried, and Tiaan thaptered there and recovered one of the corpses.'

'So that's what she was doing,' said Nish.

'I beg your pardon?'

'She showed up at Snizort when we were trying to make thapters from the wrecked constructs. Tiaan didn't say what she was doing there, and I was so pleased to see her I didn't think to ask.'

'The disease was some kind of fungus. Yggur grew it on offal, harvested bags of spores, and that's what we've just dumped all over the enemy.'

'A fungus could take weeks to infect them,' said Nish. 'It's not going to make any difference today.'

'What does it look like that second man is doing?' smiled Troist.

'It's a bit hard to tell from here.'

'Take a closer look.'

Nish focussed his spyglass. 'It looks like he's holding a flagon to his mouth. No, it's a speaking trumpet. He's giving them a message. He's got only one hand. Is it Merryl?'

486

'It is. He's telling them, in their own tongue, what the dust is and what it will do to them.'

'To break their morale.'

'Hopefully,' said Troist.

'I wonder what they'll do in retaliation?'

Another hour went by. Whatever the effect of the dust, the enemy continued to fight, though it did improve morale in the defenders. The advantage turned their way, then back to the enemy after a furious counterattack.

Nish was working his spyglass back and forth, counting casualties, when something small and dark streaked across the bloody ground and hurled itself into a formation of soldiers. There were screams, the formation collapsed in the middle and broke up. It reformed quickly, though with three fewer members than before.

'What was *that*?' said Nish.

'I don't know,' said the scribe who was tallying Nish's figures and sending them with a runner to the command table.

A second creature lunged into a formation and broke it as well. By the time it had reformed the little beasts were everywhere. One raced up the hill towards them, as if directed to the command post. Nish dropped the spyglass and reached for his crossbow but the creature disappeared.

'What was that?' said Troist, hurrying down from the chart table.

'I don't know,' said Nish, 'though I've got a nasty suspicion . . .' There had been something about the way it had scuttled, low to the ground. The hairs rose on the back of his neck. *Flesh-formed.* Was it another nylatl, or something even worse?

Fortunately he'd prepared a remedy in case of this eventuality. Reaching into his pack, Nish withdrew a small metal phial with a tight stopper that had been wired on for safety. Carefully taking the stopper out, he touched it to the tip of the crossbow bolt, stoppered the phial even more carefully, twisted the wire over it and packed it away.

'I don't much go for poison,' said Troist. 'It's a dirty way of fighting.'

487

'Don't see what the difference is,' said Nish. 'War's a dirty business. This stuff is an easier death than the fungus, by all accounts. Besides, if those little creatures are what I think they are, we'll need every advantage we can get.'

Troist turned away to the farspeaker and began calling urgently. Nish crouched low, the crossbow cocked. Where had it gone? The creatures could camouflage themselves almost as well as a lyrinx.

It shot out of the low grass, a spiny, toothy creature the size of a dog. Scooting across the bare earth of the path, claws scrabbling and raising puffs of dirt, it leapt at Troist.

'Surr, look out!' cried Nish.

The general turned and the nylatl, or a near cousin, struck him in the chest, knocked him down and lunged for his throat. Troist desperately tried to fend it off with the farspeaker globe but it was knocked out of his hands and rolled away. The claws tore his chest and arm, and Nish could not shoot for fear of hitting him. Soldiers were running from everywhere but they wouldn't get to the general in time.

Nish dropped the crossbow, which fortunately did not go off, sprang and grabbed the nylatl by its tail. Its spines went through his palm and the venom burned. Nish bit down on the pain, heaved with all his strength and tore the creature off. It tried to go for him but he swung it around his head and hurled it at a rock three or four spans away.

It rolled into a ball in mid-air and the spines took the impact, bending then springing erect. The creature twisted to land on its feet and streaked for the general again. Nish grabbed the crossbow and, as the nylatl sprang, put the bolt in through its open mouth.

The bolt must have torn all the way through it. The nylatl screamed, turned over in the air and landed hard on its back with its legs spread. It kicked twice then went still, though its eyes remained open and its flanks heaved for a minute or two.

'Don't go near it!' cried Nish as a bloody Troist wavered towards the beast. Troist froze.

Nish wrenched the sword out of the general's hand and came

488

up behind the creature. It rolled over and raised its bloody maw to snap at him. Its back legs scrabbled on the ground. With a savage blow that buried the blade a hand-span into the turf, he cut it in half lengthways.

'*Now* it's dead,' he said after a careful look. 'They're flesh-formed creatures, surr. The spines drip poison and they can even spit venom at your eyes, if they get close enough.'

'You've fought one before?'

'I have, and it was one of the defining moments of my life. Aah!' Nish wrung his hands, which were already swollen and burning. The pain grew until they felt as if they'd been skinned and dipped in vinegar. He wiped them on the grass, which did no good at all.

'I owe you my life,' said Troist, signalling behind him. A healer was already running towards them.

While she was attending to Troist, Nish took up the spyglass again to scan the battlefield. He could barely hold it. 'I'd say they had about a hundred of these creatures, surr. Aah, Aah!' The spyglass fell from his hands and he couldn't pick it up again. 'They've savaged hundreds of our troops. And hundreds more have been killed after their formations collapsed and the lyrinx attacked. If they'd had a thousand nylatl, it might have won them the day.'

'It might anyway, the way things are going.' Troist sat down suddenly.

'How are you, surr?' said Nish, wincing as a second healer began to bathe the poison off his fingers.

'I feel . . . a little faint.' Troist lay back and closed his eyes.

'Is he bad?' Nish asked the healer.

She pulled back Troist's shirt. 'He's been clawed about the chest, but he'll recover. Unless the poison takes hold or infection sets in.'

'It knew how to pick its target, surr,' Nish said to the general. 'It went straight for you.'

Troist didn't answer. 'Bring the farspeaker, quick,' he said in a faint voice. 'And get me Flydd.'

An attendant ran up with it.

Flydd answered immediately. He knew about the nylatl attacks. 'It's not looking good, Troist. I think we'd better go with the dust again, just to reinforce the idea.'

'I think so,' said Troist, and closed his eyes.

The five thapters repeated the operation, exactly as before, except that this time one flew a little too low. Four javelard spears caromed off the sides and a fifth went just over the head of the pilot, who was flying with the hatch open. The sixth and seventh spears converged on the soldier hurling the dust from the rear platform, sending him spinning into space, dead before he hit the ground.

The battle swirled back and forth. The thapters finished their work and the four swept around and back, firing their javelards furiously. The fifth flew across as before, Merryl repeating his message with the speaking trumpet.

Nish looked down at his casualty sheets, adding up the dismal numbers. It was clumsy work with his bandaged hands, but when he finally looked up there was hardly a lyrinx to be seen.

'Where have they gone?' he said. When the nylatl had been released there had been more than twenty thousand of the enemy. 'Troist? *Troist?*' It must be another trick.

Nish swept the spyglass across the battlefield. The remaining lyrinx changed colour before his eyes until they blended with the grass. They'd had enough.

'It's over, surr!' he roared. 'The battle's over. They're running away.'

The healer helped Troist to sit up, and he took the spyglass in shaking hands. 'A strategic withdrawal, I would say. There they go, back into the forest. We haven't exactly beaten them, but we've severely damaged their morale. It's the first time we've overcome a superior force on the battlefield. We've shown that it can be done.'

'And we have Klarm to thank for it,' said Nish. 'Had he not forced them to battle we'd never have done it. And Yggur's fungus spores have won the day.'

Troist chuckled. 'Indeed, the fungus.'

'I could use a laugh, if there's some secret I'm not aware of.'

'Yggur was only able to collect a cupful of spores. The rest was just flour stained with tea.' Troist roared with laughter.

The victory turned out to be far greater than they'd first thought. On the east coast, from Tiksi north all the way to Crandor, every lyrinx force in the field withdrew on the same day, as if the reversal had shaken confidence in their tactics.

'Their mindspeech must be better than we'd imagined, to call all the way to the east,' said Flydd four days after the battle. They were back in the White Palace in Lybing, reviewing the struggle to see what could be learned. 'I'd like to know more about it.'

'I don't know how you're going to find out,' said Yggur.

'Did anyone notice any difference in the lyrinx this time?'

'They didn't seem to fight with as much conviction as before,' said Nish. 'I'd put that down to the after-effects of hibernation but . . . I'm no longer sure.'

'You're not the first to note it,' said Flydd. 'And I thought so too.'

'And this time they didn't feed on our dead,' said Flangers. 'Not a single body was despoiled, though there were plenty they could have fed on during respites.'

'Now that is odd,' said Flydd. 'Something's changed. I wonder what it could be?'

'Judging by the personal hygiene of most of our troops –' Nish began, grinning.

'This is serious, Nish. Find out why they've changed and we may have the key to the war.'

'I hope so,' said Troist weakly. His wounds had become infected and he'd been brought to the meeting on a stretcher. 'We may have won the day, but the cost was unsustainable.'

The smile left Nish's face as he looked down at the final list. 'Thirteen thousand dead, another five thousand seriously injured. Many of those will die and half the remainder will never fight again. We've lost almost a third of our forces in Borgistry.'

'But saved two-thirds,' said the scrutator, 'while the boost to morale, all over Lauralin, is worth another army the same size.

491

And there's one other thing: Klarm's spies report a number of lyrinx dead in Worm Wood, infected by the fungus.'

'How many?' said Yggur. 'I hadn't really expected there'd be any, spreading it out in the open like that.'

'Three or four, and I dare say there are more we haven't found. It's not the numbers, it's fear of the disease that's done the damage. But the most interesting thing of all is their reaction to the defeat. To have withdrawn from all the other conflicts, we must have profoundly shocked them. For the very first time, they're afraid of us.'

'Our new tactics unsettled them,' said Nish.

'They're conservative fighters. They prefer to use their own well-tried methods,' said Troist, trying to sit up and grimacing at the pain in his clawed chest. His healer put two pillows under his back. 'If they're overturned, the lyrinx normally take a while to formulate new ones. It's the first time we've taken the advantage, and we must capitalise on it. We must formulate new tactics for each battle, so as to unsettle them again and again.'

'Dare we take the battle to the enemy and attack them in their cities?' said Yggur.

'We dare not,' said Flydd. 'We'd need at least a four-to-one advantage for that, and we'd have to be prepared to sacrifice most of our troops. It's not worth it.'

'How many cities do they have?' said Nish. 'And where are they?'

'They have six main cities that we know of,' said Klarm. 'All underground, plus a number of smaller ones. They're not comfortable living permanently in small groups, and never breed in such places, though they can live almost anywhere for a time, for some particular purpose.'

'Such as the group living in the spire at Kalissin,' said Flydd with a glance at Tiaan, who was sitting quietly up the back as usual. 'Is that not so, Tiaan?'

'It is,' she said.

'Seldom do they build structures above ground,' Klarm went on, 'and then only small and temporary. But underground they construct massive complexes of tunnels and chambers. Their warren of Oellyll, beneath Alcifer, is vast. They have two main cities in the west – one at Alcifer and another in caves in the escarpment west of Thurkad. From those they control the whole of Meldorin and reach out to threaten us here.'

Yggur cleared his throat.

'Almost the whole,' Klarm amended. 'Alcifer is thought to hold seventy thousand. The city west of Thurkad, at least as many.'

'What about those in the east?' said Yggur.

'We don't know their precise locations because we've never been able to get near them. That may change once our thapters are free to search from the air. One city lies in the mountains west of Roros, in Crandor. Another two are somewhere in the wildness of the Wahn Barre, or Crow Mountains, one west of Guffeons and the other west of Gosport. The sixth, and I believe the last, is somewhere in the coastal range south-east of Stassor. As many as forty thousand lyrinx are thought to live in each of those four places.'

'Why don't we know exactly where they are?' said Yggur. 'I find that hard to comprehend.'

'They cleared the land of settlers from the very beginning,' said Flydd. 'And guarded the borders before they went underground. The cities are all in rugged country, heavily forested. Even with all the Council's efforts, which have been considerable, we've not been able to get a spy into any of those places.'

'What can't be seen from outside may be perfectly clear from above,' said Yggur. 'So many lyrinx, coming and going, will have beaten paths which must converge on their cities. Finding them must be one of our priorities.'

'It must,' said Flydd. 'And that's all, Klarm?'

'As far as we know.'

'What are their total numbers?'

'Counting those away from their cities at any time, and those we know of in small settlements, around three hundred and fifty thousand.'

'I had not thought quite so many,' said Troist.

'That includes infants and children, pregnant females, and

old ones. The number of adults capable of fighting would be a little over half that number. Two hundred thousand at the very most, though they couldn't put all of them in the field at any one time.'

'So the army we've just defeated was a quarter of their fighting force, and perhaps half of the troops they have in the west.'

'I should say so,' said Klarm.

'Maybe we despaired when we should not have,' said Flydd. 'The enemy know we have six thapters and many farspeakers. After this defeat, they may be afraid that the war is turning our way. And if we were to ally with Malien's people, and Vithis with his ten thousand constructs, unlikely as that seems to us –'

'With all the advances we've made over the winter, they're vulnerable in ways they could not have imagined last autumn,' said Klarm. 'Back then they were definitely winning the war. But by the dawn of spring their spies and informers would have told them about our thapters and farspeakers. They must have been really worried, to risk so much on the premature strike against Borgistry.'

'Let's not get carried away by one inconclusive victory,' said Yggur. 'They too have made brilliant advances in the past few years. They'll come back from this reversal with new tactics and new weapons, and they could snatch back our gains just as easily as we won them.'

FIFTY-ONE

Gilhaelith paced his cell, a watermelon-shaped chamber exca-vated out of the shale underneath Alcifer. He'd been back for months, he'd finally been able to test the geomantic globe, had made the last changes and thought it perfect. He'd begun the dangerous experiment of scrying out and dissociating the fragments of phantom crystal from his brain, but to his dismay it hadn't worked. He soon discovered why. Gyrull had deceived him last autumn, fed him some false details about nodes. The globe was wrong in several small but important aspects that made it useless to his purpose, while not affecting hers. He was trying to uncover the errors when Gyrull and Anabyng seized him and cast him into this cell deep within Oellyll. The only way out was through a long, narrow and winding crawl passage, like the stalk of a watermelon, but the entrance was closed off with crisscrossing bars socketed deep into the rock.

And here he had remained, cut off from his Art and feeling his intellect fading every day. He'd pleaded with Gyrull to be allowed to fix the globe and repair himself but, afraid of what he might do with the globe, she would not even allow him to see it. Gilhaelith was in despair.

Occasionally one or other of the phantom fragments would grow hot, or sing a fractured note that seemed to echo back and

495

forth inside his skull. It was a resonance induced by the globe, which meant that the lyrinx were using it to try and solve the problem of their flisnadr, or power patterner. Gilhaelith knew about that. He knew what the power patterner was intended to do, the problems they'd had making it and, he believed, the reason why they'd failed.

The knowledge did him no good, for Gyrull did not trust him. She made no response to his frequent pleas to the guards and eventually replaced them with two ever-watchful zygnadr sentinels: strange, twisted objects like a ball wrenched into a spiral. Their surfaces bore traces of a crab-like shell and segmented legs, reminiscent of the fossils found everywhere in Oellyll, including the walls of his prison.

The weeks went by but no one came near Gilhaelith except a human slave, the lowest of the low, who once a day slid food and water beneath the bottom bar, and took away the wooden pan containing his waste. The man did not speak Gilhaelith's language, or indeed any of the many languages Gilhaelith knew.

Helpless, Gilhaelith paced his reeking, claustrophobic cell and brooded, and his resentment festered.

A half-grown female lyrinx came running into the main chamber of the eleventh level, where Ryll was working with the patterners. These were large pumpkin-shaped devices, chin-high to a lyrinx, whose gelatinous outsides also bore fossil-like traces, though in this case they were plant fossils: leaves, cones and bark. There were twelve patterners, and inside each was a human female with only her head exposed. Writhing vines or tubes, not unlike the fissured stems of pumpkins, ran from each of the patterners to a barrel-shaped object made of yellow glass, within which a tapered object roughly the size and shape of a bucket was suspended in aqua jelly. The object's exterior was leathery and covered in nodules the size of peas. Waves of colour passed constantly across it, like a lyrinx's skin-speech, though the colours never settled. The sides bore a number of irregularly spaced slits that a small human child might have inserted a hand into. It was the growing flisnadr. At least it had been growing –

it had stopped a long time ago, well before maturity, and no one could work out why.

'Master Ryll, Master Ryll?' said the girl.

'Yes?' Ryll said sharply, for he'd made no progress in months and was keenly aware of his failure. Had the flisnadr been ready at the end of winter they would never have been forced into the recent battle in Borgistry. And when they *had* done battle, with the flisnadr they would have had a glorious and overwhelming victory, not this humiliating defeat that had sapped the morale of everyone in the great underground city.

'Matriarch bids you come to the nylatl breeding chambers.'

'I'll be there directly,' he said, rubbing his aching back. He'd been on his feet for two days, without sleep or any kind of progress to give him the least encouragement that he was on the right track.

The girl wrung her hands. Soft hands, he noticed, and she'd applied some kind of pearly lacquer to her nails, which had been trimmed down to uselessness. Her armour had hardly grown at all, though her chest had.

'Er, Master Ryll,' she said diffidently, 'Matriarch said to bring you without delay.'

He sighed, exposing hundreds of teeth. 'Very well, Oonyl. Take me there.'

She turned away, walking several steps ahead, and he followed. Ryll extended his finger claws, which he kept sharp enough to tear through leather. They were yellowed, not very clean, and there was old blood under one of them. He studied the girl from behind. She was smaller than most, and slighter, and her wings were just nubs that would never develop. But then, once the war was over, what need would there be for fearsome clawed and armoured creatures like him? Perhaps *she* was the future and his time was passing as well. Assuming there was a future. Suddenly, after years of successes, he had begun to doubt.

Up on the seventh level, he followed Oonyl into the breeding chamber and was immediately struck by a strong, festering odour. Ryll sniffed the air and detected the tang of blood and rotting flesh. The nylatl always smelled that way, but this time

497

it was worse. Diseased. He spied the matriarch over next to the cages on the far side of the chamber, talking to Anabyng, Liett and several other important lyrinx.

'Ryll!' said Gyrull peremptorily. She beckoned.

Ryll hurried over and eased between the matriarch and Liett to see what the matter was. 'Not another failure?' he said. 'The nylatl went so well in the battle.'

'They're dying!' Liett said accusingly, as if it were his fault, though Ryll had nothing to do with nylatl these days.

Though Ryll loved Liett dearly, sometimes he wanted to throttle her. She could be brilliant, even inspiring at times, but so often spoiled it by saying the first thing that came into her head.

'It's a flesh-eating infection,' said Gyrull, moving aside. 'The keepers have tried all the potions they know but none have made any difference.'

Ryll studied the savage, spiny creature, which lay on its side, whining and licking at itself. The muscles of its back legs were a putrid eruption of rotting flesh. 'Put it to death, then carry it outside and burn it,' he said. 'Are there any others?'

'Hundreds,' said Anabyng. 'Near a third of the breeding stock, and more are looking sickly.'

'They'll all have to be put down,' said Ryll. 'It's impossible to control an infection in such a confined space. Take the healthy ones up into Alcifer and keep them out in the open air, in their cages. They may live. Incinerate all the dead and infected ones, then seal this floor and burn brimstone inside until the whole chamber is filled with its fumes. Wash the ceiling, walls and floor afterwards. That may be enough to kill the infection.'

'If we put down the sickly ones,' said Gyrull, 'we won't have enough breeding stock for the next battle.'

'If you don't put them down,' said Ryll, 'we may lose the lot. The nylatl all spring from one ancestor, so an illness that kills one will probably kill all of them.'

Gyrull and Anabyng conferred for a moment, then the matriarch said, 'Let it be done. Come, Ryll, Liett; we must talk.'

They left the others and went up to the matriarch's chamber, a large round room, sparsely furnished with a broad low bed, a shelf containing a number of books, a table and stool, and several charts on the wall made from human leather. Gyrull closed the door. They sat on the mats and she took a leather flask from a peg on the wall, pouring a milky liquor into small bone cups.

They raised the cups as high as their extended arms could reach, then lowered them and downed the liquor in a single swallow. It carved an acrid track down Ryll's throat and the rising fumes burned the passages of his nose like hot mustard.

'What are we to do?' said Gyrull. 'This reversal in Borgistry – no, this *defeat* – has shaken me.'

'The old humans are deadly cunning,' said Anabyng. 'I don't like to say it, but they're cleverer than we are.'

'Never say cleverer,' said the matriarch. 'Yet they adapt their plans more quickly than we do. In battle we're stuck in our old, tested ways, while they change their tactics constantly. For the first time since becoming matriarch, I don't know what to do.'

'Attack them with everything we have,' growled Liett. 'They're weaker than they seem.'

'And so are we, daughter. I dare not risk it. What if that's been their plan all spring, to entice us into all-out war on their terms?'

'They don't have the numbers. We'll overpower them through sheer force of arms.'

'They don't need the numbers when they can track us from above with their flying machines. And when they can talk to each other and coordinate their forces with these devilish far-speakers, far better than we can with our halting mindspeech. Two brilliant discoveries in less than a year, Anabyng. What will they come up with next?'

No one spoke.

'And then there's Vithis's army down at the Hornrace,' said Anabyng. 'His massive beam spears across the heavens every night. I don't know what kind of a weapon they're developing there, but I know one thing. If they can perfect it, and mount it on their constructs, they could wipe out our entire army before we get within catapult distance. I was with foolhardy Tyss when he flew into the beam, to see what it was made of. It crisped him like a moth in a candle flame.'

'And there's no doubt they'd side with the old humans, if pressed,' said Ryll.

'None whatsoever. Have you mastered the principle of their farspeakers yet, Anabyng?' the matriarch said.

'I've cut apart the globe we captured, though I still don't understand how it works, or how to reproduce it.'

'And we've no further progress on the flisnadr,' said Gyrull.

'None worth talking about.' Ryll lowered his head, ashamed of his failure, so costly to the hopes of his people. 'Though I wonder . . .'

'Yes?' said Gyrull.

'Gilhaelith understands the geomantic globe far better than we do. Can we use him to help ourselves?'

'Gilhaelith is a lying, treacherous villain and I fear the consequences if he puts his hands to his device. To say nothing of what he may learn about the flisnadr itself.'

'I know,' said Ryll. 'But on my own I can do no more. I think it's worth the risk. If we guard him suitably. Say . . .' He lowered his head at his temerity, but pressed on. 'Say if he were guarded by Great Anabyng, surely he could do no harm.'

The matriarch and Anabyng exchanged glances.

'It would be worth the risk, since we've come this far,' said Anabyng. 'Though . . .'

'And as soon as the flisnadr is complete, grown to maturity and tested,' Ryll said hastily, 'we put Gilhaelith to death.'

'Very well,' said Gyrull. 'Let it be done.' She bowed her head, deep in thought. 'How could it have come to this?' she mused. 'At the end of autumn we were close to victory. Four months and one battle later, and I'm thinking of defeat.'

'Never think of defeat,' cried Liett, flashing out her iridescent wings so they touched the ceiling. 'We came to Santhenar for a great and noble purpose, remember?'

'I have not lost sight of it, daughter,' said the matriarch.

'Everyone has lost sight of it,' Liett said savagely. 'Oellyll is rife with despair. But I say, *never*! We cannot go back to the void.

We came here to grow and discover ourselves, and I cleave to that purpose. But if it should prove to be beyond us, if defeat should become inevitable, let us not go tamely to our deaths. Let us not suffer the ultimate indignity – to be caged and paraded like circus animals for the amusement of these human savages. We are warriors from a line of warriors, and in the ultimate extreme, *let us die like warriors!*

'It hasn't come to that,' said the matriarch uneasily. 'I too cleave to our dream: a new future on this beautiful world. A future where we don't have to fight to survive, where we can grow beyond our warrior past, as we've already begun to grow.'

'As do I,' said Liett, springing to her feet. 'But should that prove impossible, should all hope fail, let's make a last, desperate plan,' she said in ringing tones. 'Let the entire lyrinx nation, women, men and even children, come out of our cities and fight to the death, holding nothing back. Let there be nothing in between.' She thrust her fist as high as it would reach. 'Let us have victory, *or annihilation!*'

Ryll felt the blood rush to his face, and the matriarch and Anabyng were equally fired. He had never loved Liett more than at that moment, nor been more inspired.

'Yes,' said the matriarch, filling their bone cups. 'That is the only way, should we be put to it.' She stood up and they all raised their cups high.

'Victory or annihilation.'

FIFTY-TWO

The bolder of the refugees began to reoccupy the borderlands of Almadin and Nihilnor, putting in what crops they could. They had no choice: Borgistry was rich but it could not feed them all.

Spring passed into summer, and summer into autumn. The crops planted in the borderlands began to ripen. It had been a good season, and the settlers hoped that they might, after all, harvest enough to get them through the winter.

There had been no more battles like the one for Borgistry. The lyrinx had gone back to the guerrilla tactics they'd perfected in ages past, melting away at the first signs of resistance. But they did considerable damage and everyone knew that the terror campaign had a darker purpose – to keep humanity from taking back more of the lands they'd lost during the war. To keep them afraid until the lyrinx trained a new generation to replace those that had been lost, and perfected whatever new weapons they were working on in Alcifer.

As soon as that was done, the savagery would be unleashed.

The company had returned to Fiz Gorgo in mid-spring, where Yggur and Flydd began working on a secret project, aided by Flydd and, at times, Malien and Tiaan. Nish didn't know what it was – no one would say a word about it.

Irisis was still in the east, now overseer of her former manu-factory in place of Tuniz, who had gone home at last. Nish missed Irisis terribly. He'd tried speaking to her over Golias's globe once or twice, relayed via several farspeakers on the way. Each time he spoke it took minutes for Irisis to reply, and her voice was so distorted by crackling sounds, whistles and gurgles that it was unrecognisable. Finally he gave up and wrote to her instead, sending his letter with the next thapter to go east. He received a brief, scribbled and unsatisfying reply when it returned. Irisis was not one for writing letters.

Nish had spent the past months making more air-floaters, now that the new season's silk was becoming available, and training more air-floater pilots and artificers.

Tiaan spent her time refining her maps of nodes and fields, sometimes with Malien, more often with one or other of the thapter pilots. Each time she returned, Tiaan went directly to Yggur's workroom, briefing him and Flydd on her latest dis-coveries and how they fitted into her overall picture of the fields and the nodes. By the end of summer she had surveyed all the known world save the Dry Sea, the reefs and islands of the equatorial north, and the frigid lands south of the Kara Agel, or Frozen Sea.

Flydd had made good his promise to Governor Zaeff of Roros, in Crandor, sending her a thapter and two pilots, as well as an artisan in case anything went wrong with the controller, and three artificers to keep the machine in good order. Tuniz, who came from Crandor, had been made overseer of the most troubled manufactory there and was busy restoring it to order, aided by Mechanician M'lainte, the genius who had built the very first air-floater. Flydd had also provided the Stassor Aachim with far-speakers, though they'd not offered any support in return. His embassies to Vithis at the Hornrace had been turned back at the borders.

Then in early autumn, after six months of running and hiding, an overwhelming force of lyrinx ambushed a column patrolling the Westway near Gospett, destroying thirty clankers and two hundred soldiers in twenty minutes of bloodshed. It was on again.

'We've lost another node,' said Klarm, who'd just been flown back from inspecting the scene of the massacre.

He was having dinner in a secluded corner of the refectory with Yggur, Flydd, Malien, Nish and Irisis, who had finally been recalled from the east after more than half a year, to Nish's joy.

'Whereabouts?' said Malien sharply.

'South-west of Gospett, in Gnulp Forest. Tiaan took me by it on the way back, and the node had disappeared.'

'Exploded, like the Snizort one?' asked Flydd.

'No. It had just faded away. That's three in that area now.'

'Do you think it's got anything to do with the massacre?'

'No,' said Klarm.

'Is it some new kind of node-drainer?'

'We couldn't find any sign of one.'

'Then why is it happening?' Yggur said in frustration.

'Everything is connected to everything else,' said Malien cryptically.

The table fell silent. Yggur took a small goblet of wine, as was his wont. Flydd half-filled a large goblet, as was his. Klarm filled his goblet to the brim but did not drink at once. Malien, unusually, had nothing at all.

'That's it!' cried Yggur, springing to his imposing height and spilling wine across the table.

People on the far side of the room looked up. Flydd mopped the droplets with a grubby sleeve. 'I presume it's no secret, since you see fit to tell everyone in Fiz Gorgo about it.'

'Everything *is* connected to everything else,' said Yggur. 'If you draw on a node too heavily, it affects its neighbours.'

'It doesn't explain how the node near Gospett failed. No one's drawing power down there.'

'Nodes *need not* be linked to their neighbours. Maybe they can be linked to distant ones.'

'There are thousands of nodes, Yggur,' said Flydd. 'If they can be linked to any others, anywhere, we could never hope to work out the connections.'

'But we can observe them. At least, Tiaan can.'

Tiaan spent a week going through her records before talking to Yggur and Flydd. 'I've found something strange,' she said. 'When Vithis draws heavily on the massive node at the Hornrace, a field near Morgadis dies down, as does another on the southern end of Lake Parnggi, and a third at Hardlar, on the coast of the Karama Malama. They must be linked in some way. And these nodes between Gnulp Landing and Gospett have completely failed.'

'Will they regenerate?' asked Yggur.

'I have no idea.'

'Anything else?'

'A group of four nodes in the Tacnah Marches, here, seem to be affected by power you're drawing in Fiz Gorgo.'

'Is that so?' said Yggur. 'What about the lyrinx?'

'Doubtless they're affecting other nodes,' said Tiaan, 'but I don't know enough to tell. Wait! I remember a node way down south that was fluctuating wildly.'

'Where was that?' said Flydd, who had a large leather satchel slung about his neck and was fiddling with the fastenings.

'Near the Island of Noom, in the Kara Agel, in late spring. I could take another look at it, if you like,' said Tiaan.

'There isn't time to go so far,' said Flydd. 'Klarm tells me that the enemy have made a great breakthrough.'

'When did this intelligence come in?' said Yggur. 'And how does he know?'

'He reported just a few minutes ago. I don't know how he's done it but Klarm even has spies within their cities. He believes they're planning a massive strike in early spring, to overwhelm all our defences.'

'What kind of breakthrough?' said Yggur.

'Klarm didn't know, but they've made great strides in flesh-forming lately,' said Flydd. 'The nylatl they let loose last spring were just a trial, since perfected.'

'Where did you hear that?' said Yggur.

Opening the satchel, Flydd slid something onto the table. Tiaan screamed and leapt halfway across the room.

'It's dead!' said Flydd. 'Klarm sent it back from the city west of Thurkad.'

505

'Sorry,' she said, feeling shaky. 'I still have nightmares about the nylatl.' Tiaan peered at it from a distance. Nothing could have induced her to go up close. 'It looks . . . different.'

'They call it an uggnatl, I believe. The skull is flatter, the armour thinner, while the legs aren't armoured at all. It's leaner, longer, and much faster.'

'It looks like a spiny, short-tailed rat,' said Tiaan. 'A rat the size of a small dog.' The teeth were large, sharp and angled back. 'Once it gets hold of you, it won't let go. You'd have to cut it off.'

'The nylatl were designed to take a lot of punishment, but it made them slower and less agile,' said Flydd. 'These little beasts have been formed for one purpose only: to inflict as much damage as they can. The venom is stronger and they're as agile as a rabbit.'

'Easy to kill,' said Yggur.

'But hard to hit,' Flydd retorted. 'Ten thousand of them would turn any battlefield into a slaughterhouse, and they'll have a lot more than that by spring. Klarm believes they're breeding them in all six cities.'

'What can we do about them?' said Yggur.

'Nothing. Absolutely nothing.'

'We don't have any choice. We'll have to attack first,' said Flydd that night, when they were all gathered in Yggur's workroom. 'Soon; well before winter.'

'How ready are your forces, Troist?' called Yggur.

'Borgistry's army, and my own, have replaced most of our casualties. We number fifty-six thousand, more or less.' Troist's voice came from the farspeaker globe on the centre of the long table. 'Plus a thousand from Clan Elienor, and the levees and volunteers from north, south and east. We didn't get all we were promised but they've sent another twenty thousand. Though few have combat experience.'

'That's considerably less than the enemy can field in the west,' muttered Flydd, 'if they send all their fighters out at once. And they're not wasted from hibernation now. They're well-fed and fit.'

'How do we stand on the east coast?' asked Yggur.

'They're as prepared as they can be,' said Troist. 'Between them they can field one hundred and twenty thousand troops, and twenty-five thousand clankers. Formidable forces, but they're a continent away and have their own enemies to fight.'

'Roros has the thapter I sent to Crandor,' said Flydd, 'and the eastern manufactories have built dozens of air-floaters. And they have many farspeakers now, though the enemy numbers are vast.'

'Wasn't your overseer working on making more thapters?' said Yggur.

'Tuniz has had a manufactory given to her for that purpose,' Flydd said. 'But even with Mechanician M'lainte's help, it'll be at least six months before they can produce the first thapter. There's too much to learn.'

'What do you think about attacking their cities, Troist?' said Yggur.

'To attack a well-defended city we'd need *at least* a four-to-one advantage,' said Troist. 'Even if we could gather together all our armies in Lauralin we wouldn't have enough men to attack Oellyll, and even if we won we'd lose most of them. And that's not even considering these uggnatl creatures, against which we have no defence.'

'They're what I'm really worried about,' said Flydd. 'We can't allow the enemy another six months to breed them. We simply have to act before winter . . .'

'Are you absolutely sure?' said Yggur. 'If we implement the plan, there'll be no going back.'

Nish looked from one to the other. 'I hadn't realised it had come to this.'

'It's come,' said Flydd. 'What if they were to release uggnatl into our cities? Can you imagine the horror if they were let loose among our children, our unarmed mothers?' Flydd didn't go on. He didn't need to.

'Then we'll have to go with the plan,' said Yggur.

'What plan?' said Nish and Irisis together.

'An aerial strike, simultaneously, on each of their cities.'

507

'With what?' said Irisis, puzzled.

Flydd took a deep breath, let it out, then motioned to Yggur.

'We plan to drop a barrel of fungus spores down the airshafts of each of their underground cities,' said Yggur.

'Is *that* all? It wasn't all that successful when we used it last spring,' said Nish. 'Except on their morale.'

'That was out on an open battlefield,' said Yggur. 'Underground, the conditions are perfect for the fungus to grow and with luck we'll infect most of them – enough to destroy the lyrinx threat and force them to capitulate.'

'Is there any danger to us?' said Nish.

'We've been working with it since mid-winter and it hasn't infected anyone yet.'

'I don't think it's right to use that kind of a weapon,' said Malien.

'Nor I,' said Tiaan uncomfortably. And after they capitulate, then what? Are you going to kill all the survivors?'

Flydd and Yggur exchanged glances. 'They'll have to go into camps,' said Flydd at last.

'Prisons?' said Tiaan.

'Well, yes.'

'For how long?'

'Forever. Either that or . . .'

'So you're planning to pen them up, and then wipe them out?' said Tiaan, her fists clenched on the table.

'We're not planning anything that far ahead,' said Flydd. 'Look, Tiaan and Malien, what else are we to do with the lyrinx? Uggnatl aren't just another battlefield weapon – they're living, *breeding* creatures born for one purpose only – to slaughter. They can wipe us out, and if we give the enemy time to breed up their numbers, they *will* wipe us out. Once they're released, the lyrinx won't have to fight. These uggnatl will hide and breed until they sweep like a plague across the land, consuming everything in their path.'

'It's not right,' Tiaan repeated.

'It's not right to use uggnatl against mothers and children either, but the enemy will. We've got no choice, Tiaan. We've got to attack their cities first. *Now*, before the creatures can be bred in numbers. What do you say?'

'I've fought nylatl twice,' said Nish. 'The first time was the most terrifying of my life. If these uggnatl are faster and more agile, I couldn't possibly beat one. Who could?' He shuddered at the thought.

'Well, Tiaan?' said Flydd. 'You assisted in the making of the first nylatl.'

Shadows crossed her face. 'I saw what it did to three defence-less women. I – I can imagine the horror of an uggnatl in my mother's nursery. If there's no other choice, I suppose we must attack their cities.'

'There's no other choice,' said Flydd. 'Believe me, we've tried to think of one.'

'Let it be done,' said Yggur, and one by one everyone agreed.

FIFTY-THREE

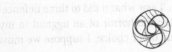

Rather to Tiaan's surprise, Irisis and Nish had asked if they could accompany her to Alcifer, where she was to drop a barrel of spores into one of the air vents. Flydd had allowed it and, to her own surprise, Tiaan had agreed. Though they were friends now, she preferred her own company. But then, she had to take someone.

'What do you think of the morality of this attack?' she said once the three of them were settled on their course from Fiz Gorgo to Alcifer.

'I can't say it bothers me,' said Irisis. 'How can it be worse than what the enemy has done to us, and hope to do with these uggnatl?'

Not long after dawn, Tiaan settled on a misty mountaintop a few leagues away from Alcifer, where they could hide unseen. The thapter sank a little way into powdery autumn snow, whirling it up all around. The snow hissed as it turned to steam, which burst out on all sides before drifting away on the keen southerly.

'How long do we have?' said Irisis, yawning.

'About five hours,' said Tiaan. 'I left early, just to be sure. All six cities have to be attacked at the same moment, otherwise the lyrinx would send out a mindspeech alert.'

Nish and Irisis dozed for most of that time. Tiaan was tired but too tense to sleep, and it was too cold at this altitude to make walking pleasant. She closed the upper hatch, sat on the warm floor above the mechanism and studied the plans of Alcifer, working out how she was going to carry out the attack. It was not going to be easy.

They could only attack in daylight, of course. Tiaan's attack was timed for noon, as was the attack on the city west of Thurkad. There was a three- or four-hour time difference between here and the lyrinx cities on the east coast.

'It won't be long now,' she said later, as they descended towards the sea, north of Alcifer. 'Alcifer is down to our right.'

'And well protected,' said Irisis, shading her eyes. 'I can see lyrinx in the air from here. Look.' She counted them. 'At least fifteen.'

The farspeaker belched. 'Where are you, Tiaan?' The voice was unidentifiable.

'Who's asking?' she snapped, bending over the slave farspeaker attached to the binnacle.

'Xervish Flydd!'

The way he said his name identified him, though passage through successive fields had dragged his tones out to something between a bark and a croak.

'We're approaching Alcifer now, surr. Just ten minutes away. There are a lot of lyrinx in the air.'

'Also west of Thurkad. Perhaps they know we're up to something.'

'Or *they* are,' said Irisis.

'Call when you've done it.' The farspeaker squelched and Flydd was gone.

The magnificent ruined city spread out before them, just like the map impressed in Tiaan's mind. 'I'll circle a few times, as we do whenever we're spying on them. We'll locate the air shafts, then I'll hurtle down and hope to dump the spores into one on the first attempt. We can't afford to have them guess our intentions. If we have to make a second attempt there'll be fliers everywhere and it'll be ten times as difficult.'

511

'And deadly,' said Irisis.

'Where are the air shafts?' asked Nish as Tiaan began to circle. He was looking down as if he expected to see them boring through the hillside.

'We know of three, though they're not easy to see. Two are concealed within partly ruined buildings in the centre of Alcifer. The third is at the base of a cliff, under the trees over there somewhere.' Tiaan pointed to her left, where a series of grey cliffs fell into the forest that had grown over the rim of the city. 'There may be others.'

'What do they look like?'

'They're shafts bored through rock, about a span across. One has a giant bellows outside, to pump in fresh air. It would be the best place to dump the spores but it's the hardest to get to, so I won't risk it.'

As they curved around the edge of the city, the wheeling lyrinx began to climb towards them. 'Which shaft are you going for?' asked Irisis.

'The two within Alcifer will be easiest to find. I'm going for the one beneath the dome – see the sun shining on it? The dome is open underneath, so I'll go down to the left, come in between the columns and see if I can get close enough.'

'I thought we'd just fly over and drop it in,' said Nish.

'I may not be able to get that close. One of you will probably have to jump out and heave it in. Keep an eye on the fliers. And you might want to get your crossbows ready.'

The lyrinx closed the gap.

'Ready?' said Tiaan.

'We're ready,' said Irisis.

'Hang on!' Tiaan turned sharply left and dived steeply.

Nish let out a muffled cry as the thapter hurtled towards the dome. The lyrinx folded their wings, diving after them.

Tiaan felt the Secret Art fizzing in her brain. 'They know we're up to something,' she shouted over the shrieking of the mechanism and the roaring of the wind. 'They'll be everywhere in a minute.'

'How are you going to get to it?' said Irisis.

Tiaan pointed to the right as she curved around the dome and its many extravagantly carved columns. 'In there.'

The dome was about two hundred spans across and supported on many slender columns. She couldn't see far inside, though the tiled floor was scattered with rubble and rectangular piles of stone blocks.

Tiaan turned sharply, slowed and darted in between the columns. It was much darker inside and her eyes were slow to adjust. She clipped a cairn of blocks, sending loose stone tumbling across the floor, jolting the thapter sideways.

'Can you see the shaft?' she yelled. 'Irisis?'

Irisis was standing up on the side. 'No, I can't. Are you sure this is the place?'

'I'm sure it's the one Klarm told me about.' Tiaan turned in a figure-eight inside the dome. 'But I'm beginning to think he got it wrong, or his spy did.' She turned again, her stomach already knotted up. The lyrinx would be here in seconds. 'He said the air shaft was in the middle but we've been across twice and there's nothing here. We'll have to go to the next.'

She shot out the other side, but as they passed between the columns Irisis cried, 'It's just there.'

Tiaan saw it out of the corner of her eye as well, though too late to stop. The vent was right on the edge, hidden between two walls of stone. The thapter shot into the sunlight and there were lyrinx everywhere. Several landed just outside; others flew in under the dome, and dozens more were approaching. What to do?

'I don't dare go back,' she said. 'They'd be onto us before we could get the barrel to the opening. We'll have to try the one with the bellows.'

She shot across the abandoned city, carving a curved trail to the other side, hoping thereby to confuse the enemy about her destination. There were flying lyrinx everywhere now, hundreds of them, and more appearing all the time.

She turned down a broad boulevard where ruined, half-ruined and intact buildings towered on either side, screamed left into a smaller road and turned right into an alley. From there she flew

513

up, soaring over the thoroughfare ahead, turned left again and headed towards a pentagonal pavilion with steepled roofs, set on a stone platform reached by broad steps on all five sides.

'How do you do it?' Irisis said.

'What?'

'Know exactly where you are, despite all the twists and turns. It's as if you have the whole map in your head.'

'I do,' said Tiaan. 'The second air shaft is in the building with the steeples. We've got to do it this time or they'll close off all the shafts.' The sky was dark with lyrinx now.

She roared straight up over the steps, across the forecourt and inside.

'To the right!' Irisis yelled in her ear. 'I can see the bellows.'

Tiaan turned sharply, swept around in a circle and came to a stop directly before the enormous bellows, which consisted of a concertina-like timber and canvas structure, three times the size of the thapter, that was squeezing and expanding, powered by a series of phynadrs. The multiple intakes opened and closed as the bellows worked, directing a roaring blast into a long canvas funnel that ran down into the vent. 'Nish,' said Tiaan, 'see where it sucks the air in? I can't take the thapter in under there – you'll have to carry the barrel. Hurry!'

He threw himself over the side of the thapter, not bothering with the ladder. Irisis lowered the barrel. Nish heaved it onto his shoulder and ran, staggering under its weight. Irisis fitted a bolt to her crossbow.

Tiaan darted a look over her shoulder. The first lyrinx was already sweeping in. She edged the thapter closer to the bellows.

Irisis fired, so close that the snap of the bow hurt Tiaan's ear.

'I hope you got him,' Tiaan said irritably. Even at close range it wasn't easy to kill a lyrinx with a crossbow.

'I got him.' Irisis was already reloading.

'Get a move on, Nish!' Tiaan screamed over the hiss and whoosh of the bellows. 'They're here.'

He had reached one of the intakes but was struggling to get the lid off the barrel. The suction of the bellows was so strong that with every blast it pulled him across the floor.

514

'I can't get the lid off,' he yelled. 'It's too tight.'

'Hold it out to the side,' said Irisis.

He did so. Irisis took careful aim, fired and the bolt stove the lid in with a puff of spores that was whipped into the bellows intake.

Nish slipped, caught hold of the side then tossed the barrel into the intake. The movement sent him off-balance and he began to slide towards the aperture. Tiaan squeezed her controller so hard that it hurt. The suction was going to pull him in too, and she was surprised at how much she cared.

Irisis cursed, leapt over the side in a single fluid movement and ran. Tiaan edged the thapter a fraction closer. Another lyrinx flew in, followed by a third and then two more.

The bellows sucked so hard that Nish's legs went from under him. He landed on his side and was jerked towards the intake, fingernails scratching against the glassy floor. Before he could get to his feet the bellows sucked again, pulling him halfway in. He threw his arms out, managing to jam himself in the opening. The bellows sucked and Nish's arms shuddered with the effort of holding himself in place. The next pump would suck him through and send him plummeting fifty or a hundred spans down the shaft.

Without even thinking, Tiaan spun the thapter, jerked it forward and thumped the front into the tapering canvas funnel of the bellows, pushing it almost flat. With a gruesome farting noise air rushed back the other way, ejecting Nish straight at Irisis. They both went down, Nish landing on his forehead.

Tiaan looked over her shoulder. The lyrinx were approaching rapidly, two in the air, two on the floor. Was there time to pick up Nish and Irisis? She didn't think so.

Whirling the thapter on its axis, Tiaan scooted straight at the lyrinx in the air. As soon as she did, she knew it was a mistake. This pair were moving slowly, while the ones on the floor were racing towards Irisis and Nish.

Thinking swiftly, she shot by so close that the thapter's wake collapsed their wings and the lyrinx fell out of the air. Tiaan spun the other way, knowing she wasn't going to make it. The

515

running pair of lyrinx were practically on Irisis, who was in the lead, waving her sword. Nish was staggering, clearly dazed, and appeared to have dropped his weapon.

The farspeaker blurted. 'Tiaan? Where are you?'

She thumped it with her fist, screaming, 'Not now!'

The running pair of lyrinx checked and one turned its head towards her, its mouth wide open as if in pain. The other threw its hands over its ears. The ones that had fallen thrashed their wings. Tiaan slid the nose of the thapter in between them and Irisis, tilting it as far as she could to the left. Irisis took Nish under the arms and boosted him up the side, where he clung to the ladder as if he could go no further.

The four lyrinx were recovering. Letting go of the controller, Tiaan pulled herself up onto the hatch, caught Nish's hand and he managed to drag himself the rest of the way. He fell over the lip and lay on the floor, making a low noise in his throat. She sprang down and caught the controller.

Irisis came scrambling in and dropped to the floor beside him. 'You can go now,' she said unnecessarily.

'I'm going!' said Tiaan.

One of the lyrinx sprang but she jerked the machine backwards and the creature landed short, on the smoothly tapering front of the thapter. Its claws scratched furiously but there was nothing to grip and with a shriek of claw against metal it slid off.

Which way now? One of the fallen lyrinx was back in the air, another limping across the floor, favouring one leg. Where was the fourth?

'Hurry!' screamed Irisis, 'before they have the pavilion surrounded. They're coming from everywhere.'

Lyrinx were dropping from the sky all along two sides – three. Tiaan turned for the fourth but it was already blocked. There was one small gap on the fifth side. She headed for it.

Something thumped at the rear and the thapter lurched sideways. 'What's that?' Tiaan cried, though she knew full well.

'The fourth lyrinx,' said Irisis. 'It's on the shooter's platform. See if you can throw it off.'

'Shut the hatch!'

'I can't. It's got one foot on the far rim.'

Tiaan hurled the thapter from side to side so rapidly that Nish slid down through the lower hatch. He cried out, just once.

'Any good?' said Tiaan.

'No.' Irisis was loading the crossbow again.

Tiaan pushed the controller forward and streaked towards the remaining exit. The back of the thapter kept wobbling as if the heavy creature was throwing its weight from side to side. It was going to spring through the top hatch, right onto them.

'Shoot it, Irisis,' Tiaan screamed. She couldn't help herself.

Outside, lyrinx were falling from the sky in their hundreds. Tiaan raced for that small remaining gap, holding her breath. A lyrinx crashed into the side of the thapter, shaking it, but could not get a grip, and suddenly they were out into the open.

The crossbow sang but Irisis cursed. 'Got it in the shoulder, not the throat. Where the hell are my extra bolts?' Not finding them, she cast the bow on the floor and went for her sword. 'Nish, get up here!'

Nish, blood running down his forehead and into one eye, began to pull himself up the ladder, crossbow in hand. He tried to aim it but the bow was wavering all over the place.

'Careful!' said Irisis. 'You'll shoot one of us.'

Nish gritted his teeth, let go of the ladder and tried to aim the bow two-handed. He closed the eye that was wet with blood.

'Look out! It's –'

The rear of the machine jerked as the lyrinx sprang. Nish's crossbow went off at the same time. Tiaan jerked the controller sideways, knowing she'd moved too late. She tried to get out of the way but there was nowhere to go. The lyrinx came crashing through the hatch, smashing the binnacle and the screen in front of it, and knocking the farspeaker to the floor. One huge arm and shoulder slammed Tiaan against the side wall and she lost hold of the controller arm.

A thud signalled that Nish had fallen down again. The creature's great legs thrashed, slamming Irisis against the rear of the compartment. She cried out.

Something hot and wet spurted against Tiaan's back and the

517

creature's weight pinned her against the smashed binnacle and the mass of knobs and wheels. It gave a feeble roar. Reflected in the broken glass, its mouth was open, the grey teeth menacing, but its eyes were staring. Purple blood flooded from the bolt wound in its neck, drenching her.

'Tiaan,' cried Irisis. 'Take the controller.'

Tiaan couldn't turn her head far enough to see out. They could have been heading for the sky or towards the ground. She couldn't budge. All she could see was the floor and part of the side wall.

'We're heading straight for a building!' Irisis screamed.

Tiaan tried to reach the controller but her arm was pinned. The lyrinx was ten times her weight. She tried to push it off but it didn't move an ell.

'I can't move,' she gasped.

'Nish!' Irisis yelled.

No answer, apart from groaning. Irisis forced herself along the side, put her shoulder under the creature and shoved. 'Any better?'

'No,' said Tiaan, panicking.

'Reach out. The controller's just here.'

'I can't turn my head that far.'

'But you know where it is, Tiaan.'

Irisis heaved the lyrinx and pulled Tiaan's hand. It slipped free and Irisis slammed it onto the knob of the controller. 'There.'

'Where am I supposed to go?' Tiaan gasped. 'I can't see out.'

'Left and up.'

Tiaan tried to move her hand but could not. Irisis put her hand on top, jerking Tiaan's the required way. The thapter banked right and the weight on Tiaan eased enough for her to lift her head. Stone columns flashed by.

'Ten more seconds and we would have piled straight into that,' said Irisis, directing Tiaan's hand in uneven motions. Something rolled across the floor and down the hatch.

'How are we going to get the lyrinx out?' Tiaan whispered. She felt as if the life had been crushed out of her. 'I can hardly breathe.'

'I don't know. Nish?' A weak groan from below. 'Are you all right?'

'Bloody farspeaker landed on my head.'

'Just when we needed you, too,' said Irisis unsympathetically. 'Grab hold of something and hang on.'

The lower hatch clanged – Irisis must have kicked it shut. She began fumbling around below Tiaan.

'What are you doing?' said Tiaan.

'Strapping you in. You'll have to turn the thapter upside down.'

'I don't think I've ever done that.'

'Then learn fast. Look out – there's bloody enemy everywhere and we can't stop to hurl this fellow out. Wiggle the controller.'

A crashing thump at the rear made the whole thapter shudder.

'What was that?' said Tiaan weakly. She didn't think she could take much more.

'They're dropping rocks. You'll have to bank to the right until the thapter's on its side. That should drop the weight off you. Then take the controller and turn us upside down. I'll make sure the corpse doesn't catch on anything. Sounds easy, doesn't it?'

If Irisis meant to be reassuring, she wasn't. Tiaan had no idea what would happen if she turned the thapter upside down. Would the controls work the other way?

Something smashed into the front, knocking the craft sideways. 'That was close,' Tiaan said to herself.

'Ready, Tiaan?'

'Yes,' she gasped.

Irisis pushed her arm to the right as far as it would go. It wasn't far enough.

'It's times like this,' said Irisis, 'that I wish controllers could be used by more than one person.'

'I can see the virtue in it,' said Tiaan dryly.

'Is the weight easing at all?'

'A little.'

Irisis put her shoulder under the dead creature and heaved. It moved fractionally. 'See if you can squeeze out.'

'Not yet.'

Irisis managed to push Tiaan's arm across a bit further, then jerked it back sharply. Another building flashed by.

'Oops!' Irisis said. 'Wasn't looking.' She pushed it over again, the thapter banked and the lyrinx slid against the right-hand side of the compartment, dragging Tiaan with it. Irisis pushed Tiaan's arm a fraction more. The weight eased.

Tiaan wriggled free. 'I feel as though I've been crushed flat.'

A blow struck the thapter, forcing it downwards. Clinging to the controller arm, Tiaan pulled it over as far as it would go. They plunged down and to the right. She had to do it now.

'Hang on,' she gasped. 'I'm going to flip.'

The thapter banked even more and the ground appeared, upside down and very near. Irisis shoved and grunted and the dead lyrinx slid out, dragging her with it – a claw had caught in her pants leg. She clung desperately to the straps. The claw tore her trousers down to the knee and came free; the lyrinx fell out of sight.

Tiaan flipped the thapter back to level and was gasping so hard that she had to close her eyes for a moment. When she opened them, thousands of enemy were converging on the thapter.

'Oh, it hurts,' whispered Irisis, sliding down onto the floor.

Her leg was drenched in blood. Red blood, not purple. It was typical of Irisis to say nothing about her own injury. 'What happened?' said Tiaan.

'Dying spasms,' Irisis whispered. 'Its back claws raked up and down my leg.'

'Is it bad?'

'It hurts like hell. I think I'll have a little rest.' She pillowed her head on her hands and closed her eyes.

She's bleeding to death like the lyrinx did, Tiaan thought. And I can't do anything about it.

As she traced a zigzagging path across the sky between the enemy, Tiaan tapped on the lower hatch with her toe. 'Nish!'

After a long while the hatch lifted. 'Yes?' His voice was as pale as Irisis's face.

'See to Irisis's leg. She's bleeding badly.' Pushing the controller forward as hard as it would go, she streaked for the safety of the clouds.

Nish came up and began to tear cloth into strips.

'Tiaan,' squelched the farspeaker. 'Tiaan?'

Flydd again. 'We're alive and we got the job done,' she said. 'We're coming home.'

'We lost the other thapter west of Thurkad,' said Flydd sombrely.

'What happened?'

'A flying lyrinx shot Pilot Mittiloe with an aerial crossbow as they were coming in for the attack; can you believe it? The others got a message off before the thapter crashed. They didn't get near the air shaft.'

Mittiloe had been Kattiloe's little sister, one of the fourteen-year-old twins. She'd been so proud of her machine. The other pilots would be devastated, as was Nish. He was weeping in dry spasms.

'What?' said Tiaan, realising that Flydd was still speaking. 'I didn't catch that.'

'I said, have you still got the spare barrel of spores?'

Tiaan was tempted to say no. How could he ask more of them? 'It's down below.'

'Good. Go to Thurkad and do the job there.'

'Can we come home then?' she said with a hint of sarcasm.

'Of course not. You'll have to keep watch, at least a week, and tell us what the effects are. *If any.*'

'What do you mean?' she said.

'I'm not confident that it's going to work,' said Flydd.

'Oh. How did the other attacks go?'

'Against the cities in the east? Well enough – they all got their spores in. So if you can do the same . . .'

'We'll do our best,' she said and thumped the farspeaker to end the conversation. 'Whatever we do, it's never good enough. How's Irisis?'

'She'll live,' said Nish, who looked ghastly. He had two cuts across his forehead, still ebbing blood, one eye had a crusted red ring around it, and more blood was smeared across his cheek and the back of his hand.

'And how are you?'

'My head's still ringing but I'm all right. Is any of that blood yours?'

'No,' she said. 'Ugh! It reeks.'

FIFTY-FOUR

Tiaan flew north at full speed until the lyrinx turned back, then kept going. The mountains curved away to the west, rising ever higher. Some hours later she passed over an enormous river that flowed to the sea, far to the right, debouching through a delta five or six leagues across, with many mouths. A broad road ran slightly east of north, and beyond sight in either direction. The land between the sweep of the mountains and the sea consisted of fertile plains cut by large rivers, though the country was already being reclaimed by forest. Abandoned cities and towns studded the plain. Tiaan counted the remains of a hundred villages below her, but there was no sign of human life.

'This is Iagador,' she said without consulting her map. 'That great river is the Garrflood and the city covering the island between its branches would be Sith. The hilly country ahead to the left, bordering the mountains, is Bannador.'

'Where's Thurkad?' asked Nish, who hadn't been this way before. On the silk-stealing mission to Thurkad they'd travelled up and back on the western side of the mountains.

'About sixty leagues up the coast, before the mountains curve back towards the sea. The lyrinx city is almost due west of Thurkad. Hours yet.'

'Are we going straight there?'

'We can't get there before dark. Besides, none of us are up to it today. We'll have to work out a plan to attack the place tomorrow. I'm going to set down at Sith.'

Shortly the thapter settled on one of the many jetties that ringed that once great trading city. 'I don't think there'll be any enemy here,' Tiaan said. 'I've flown over Sith quite a few times and never seen them. Still, from here we'll get a good view if they are coming.'

Nish roused Irisis, who was lying on the floor, and they carried her down onto the wooden deck. There they laid her in the shade of a ramshackle building, once a customs booth, stripped her off and bathed and rebandaged her wounds. Five deep claw marks ran down her thigh, one extending to her shin. She'd lost a lot of blood.

'They'll scar,' said Tiaan. 'We can't do anything about that.'

'I've so many scars now that a few more won't make any difference,' Irisis said wanly. She tried to perk up. 'And mostly because of you, Tiaan.'

'Me?'

Irisis rolled over and pulled her shirt up. Her creamy back was crisscrossed with scars, once purple but now faded to pale red and blue.

Tiaan put her hand over her open mouth. 'You were whipped?'

'Overseer Gi-Had did it, on the orders of Nish's father. He flogged us naked, out in the snow, in front of everyone.' Irisis managed to grin, though Tiaan couldn't understand why. 'Show Tiaan your scars, Nish.'

'I'd rather not,' said Nish. He looked deeply ashamed.

'Because of me?' said Tiaan.

'Because of the way we undermined you. And for what Jal-Nish thought we'd done, though it was actually due to Eiryn Muss's treachery.'

'I'm sorry you were whipped,' said Tiaan. 'I hated you both but I wouldn't have had you suffer that.'

'It doesn't matter,' lied Irisis, deliberately offhand. 'I can hardly remember it.'

524

'I remember every stroke,' said Nish. 'Not to mention the humiliation of being punished in front of the entire manufactory. It scarred me deeper than the whip.'

'We earned it,' said Irisis. 'It's not important.'

Nish's face told a different story, but thankfully it wasn't directed at Tiaan.

It was a sweltering autumn afternoon and so humid above the water that it was hard to breathe. Nish lay in the shade beside Irisis and went to sleep. Irisis closed her eyes but every so often gave a convulsive shudder of pain. Tiaan didn't have anything she could give her for it, and she couldn't bear to watch.

She wandered to the far side of the wharf, out of sight, and climbed down a decaying wooden ladder to the water. It was deliciously cool and inviting so she took off her boots and went in wearing her clothes. The river was low at this time of year and she could see pebbles on the bottom a couple of spans below. She scrubbed the lyrinx blood from her clothes, wishing she could wash the experience away as easily.

'How are we going to attack the next shaft?' said Irisis the following day, long before they were in sight of the northern city. 'They'll be waiting for us, and if they get the chance they'll close it off or form a living wall over it.'

'I was wondering about that,' said Tiaan, who was already feeling anxious. 'I think we'd better go in as fast as the thapter can fly, and hope to reach it before they can react.'

'After their success in killing the pilot of the other thapter they'll be waiting for us. Can you fly in with the hatch closed?'

'Not in such a tight space, I've got to be able to see all around.'

'How can we drop the spores and protect you at the same time?' said Nish.

'I'll just have to take the risk. You two will be in more danger than I am.'

'Nonsense,' said Nish. 'If they kill one of us, the others can still go ahead. If they kill you they kill us all – and deprive humanity of another priceless thapter.'

'What's the site like?' said Irisis. 'Have you seen it before?'

Tiaan recalled the maps to mind before answering. 'The entry tunnels run horizontally off a series of sandstone cliffs. The air vents lie above the tunnels, disguised as caves, and they won't be easy to get to. They're sheltered behind a series of pinnacles rising up in front of the cliffs.'

'How are we going to reach them?'

Tiaan had to think about that too, for she still hadn't worked out the best means of attack. 'I think – I think the best approach would be to fly along the face of the cliff at high speed, really close to the rock so we'll be hard to detect from on high, and come hurtling around the end of the ridge just south of the city. We'll appear without warning, hopefully, heading directly for the openings. That'll give them the minimum time to react.'

'Won't it be dangerous, flying so close to the cliff?' said Nish.

'Very, but I don't see any other choice.'

'What if I took one of the curved side panels off and fixed it halfway over the hatch?' said Nish.

'What good would that do?'

'If I angled it up from the back, it'd protect you from crossbow shots from behind and above, and even a bit from the sides, but you could still see. Except directly behind, of course.'

'You'd have to fix it pretty solidly or the wind would tear it off,' Tiaan said dubiously.

'I'll see what tools are below,' said Nish. 'Why don't you set down?'

Tiaan settled under the trees and Nish went to work. It didn't take long to remove a piece of metal from the side, shaped like a shield bent into a shallow curve along its long axis. However, it proved impossible to fix tightly in place, and eventually he had to tie it down.

'Better than nothing, I suppose,' Nish said gloomily as he surveyed his work.

'If it stays there,' said Tiaan. 'When we're going quickly the wind might tear it away.'

'We won't be any worse off,' said Nish.

'We will if the wind drives it into the person who's dumping the spores from the rear platform,' said Irisis. 'That'll be –'

'Me, of course,' Nish said hastily.

'It'll be me!' Irisis said. 'You hit your head, twice.'

'And you pumped a couple of flagons of blood out of your leg.'

'It was no more than an eggcup and I'm going up the back.'

'You're not!'

Nish and Irisis were glaring at each other.

'I can't believe you're fighting over who's most likely to be killed,' said Tiaan. 'You're like a pair of children.'

'We are not!' they said together, and burst out laughing.

Tiaan found them incomprehensible. How could anyone joke at a time like this? 'It's my thapter and I say who does what. Nish, you'll dump the spores from the back, and you'll also be under a metal hood. Irisis, you've lost too much blood. You might faint at the critical time.'

'I've never fainted in my life!' Irisis exclaimed.

'Anyway, I need you in with me. You'll probably have to hang onto the hood to stop it flying off, and you can do that easier than Nish could, since you're taller. No, don't argue. It's settled.'

Tiaan's palm was sweating on the controller. The thapter was hurtling along just a span away from the cliff, and maintaining that distance was much harder than she'd imagined. She hadn't flown along here before and had no mental picture to rely on. The cliff looked smooth from a distance but, close up, ledges, rock outliers, pinnacles and angled trees appeared out of nowhere. She had to react by instinct to avoid them – there simply wasn't time to think about it. Moreover, it was another sweltering day and the updraughts and eddies along the cliff could hurl the machine in any direction. Thunderheads were already forming in a line along the escarpment.

'It's just around the point of this ridge and back about a quarter of a league,' said Tiaan. 'Ready?'

'Yes,' said Irisis. Her left arm was upstretched, holding the hood, which was jerking up and down in the wind, threatening to tear the ropes away.

'What about Nish?'

He was lying prone on the rear platform in his rope harness, under a curved sheet of metal taken from the other side of the thapter. Tiaan hoped the enemy wouldn't realise he was there until he got up and hurled in the barrel of spores. If they did shoot at him, the black metal *ought* to protect him from a crossbow bolt, even one from a powerful lyrinx bow.

Irisis looked around the side of the hood. 'He's ready.'

As Tiaan reached the end of the rocky point she flung the thapter around in a tight turn, bouncing on the eddying up-draughts. Irisis made a muffled sound in her throat as the hood was flung upwards and one foot lifted off the floor. She hauled the hood down again.

Something banged at the back. 'Is he still there?' Tiaan said.

'Yes. Threw him around a bit, though.'

'The main entrances to the city are just around the curve of the cliff to the right. See the caves?'

'I see them. And that must be the air opening above them, where all the lyrinx are.'

A globe-shaped mass of flying lyrinx were circling around a smaller opening, the second of five in a row, some twenty spans above and a hundred to the right of the main entrances. In front, three jagged rock pinnacles rose up hundreds of spans from an outlier of yellow sandstone. Between cliff and pinnacles the cleft was only ten spans at its widest point, and half that at its narrowest, through which the thapter would have to nego-tiate at speed. There were lyrinx on the tops of the pinnacles, too, though from here Tiaan couldn't tell what weapons they might have.

'I don't see any bellows,' said Tiaan.

'It could be inside the air vent,' Irisis replied.

'There's something wrong.' Tiaan pushed the levers forward and the thapter rocketed along the cliff face.

'What is it?'

'I don't know.'

The sphere of lyrinx turned in their direction. 'They've seen us.'

'Ask Nish if he's ready,' Tiaan said, clenching her jaw so tightly that the muscles cramped.

'I already did.'

'Ask him again!' she snapped.

Irisis called out. Tiaan couldn't hear any answer but Irisis said, 'He's ready.'

'Fifty seconds,' said Tiaan.

Irisis relayed it to Nish.

An updraught sent them flying towards the yellow cliff, so close that Tiaan was sure they would hit. She corrected, the thapter sheered along the cliff and through a veil of water trickling from above, shaving off ferns growing in crevices on the wet surface.

'That was close,' said Irisis, seemingly unperturbed.

Tiaan's knees had gone weak. 'Thirty seconds.' You trust me more than I trust myself, she thought.

She lined up with the cleft between the cliff and the pinnacles. At this speed there was no room for error or, hopefully, for a successful counterattack. Two lyrinx on the pinnacles had rocks above their heads, the third a javelard. The sphere of lyrinx in the air were armed with crossbows or other weapons.

'Ten seconds.' Irisis relayed it to Nish at the same moment, then counted them down.

'Five, four, three, two –'

'No!' Tiaan screamed, pulling the thapter up so hard that her stomach churned. 'No, Nish, don't throw the spores.'

She flicked a glance at the openings as she passed. With an almighty crash, a boulder struck the left flank of the machine, which lurched sideways towards the cliff. There was a lyrinx right in front of her, aiming a crossbow. No time to turn or climb; the thapter ploughed straight into the creature as it fired. Purple blood streaked the screen but Tiaan had no idea where the bolt had gone. A clatter-clatter at the back told her that the machine had been hit several times. She prayed that they hadn't got Nish.

She shot through the circle of lyrinx, up and over the cliff, streaking away, wavering because her hand was shaking so much.

'Report!' she said roughly.

'I'm all right,' said Irisis. 'And I *think* Nish is, though his hood was hit by crossbow bolts a couple of times.'

'Did he throw out the dust?'

'No. What was the matter?'

'I knew something was wrong,' said Tiaan. 'It was a decoy. They were waiting outside a shaft they'd already closed off.'

'It's going to be mighty hard to make a second attempt,' said Irisis.

FIFTY-FIVE

They set down in the mountains a few leagues away to discuss tactics. Nish was unharmed, though a crossbow bolt
had dented the metal above the back of his head.

'If your head had been touching the metal it probably would
have killed you,' said Irisis, hugging Nish. The dent was half the
depth of her thumb.

'If Tiaan hadn't insisted on the hood you'd be scraping my
brains off the platform now,' said Nish. 'So which opening was it?'

'The fourth – I could see all the way in. The others were
blocked off.'

'Do you think it's possible to make a second attempt?'

'Let's think it through. We'll give it a while. They've probably
closed that opening off as well, in case we come straight back,
but they can't close all the openings off for long. If the others
have been closed since the attack yesterday the air will be
getting bad by now.'

They had something to eat and drink, washed their sweaty
faces and hands, and sat down to plan.

'There's just one chance left,' said Tiaan, looking up at the
sky. The thunderheads were joining up to form a continuous
mass of storms, just east of the escarpment, with lightning
flickering inside them. 'We drop out of one of those clouds and

fly at the cliff head-on, then swerve between the pinnacles, straight into the air vent and chuck out the spores.'

'It'd better be big enough,' said Nish.

'It should be, and a little to spare, but there won't be any room for error.'

'Or another rock that knocks us out of line,' said Irisis. 'Anything short of dead centre and the thapter will be wrecked.'

'And we'll be killed,' said Nish.

'And then what?' said Irisis to Tiaan.

'Straight out again, backwards, and try to get away.'

'Be surprised if we can.'

'We don't *have* to have another go,' said Irisis. 'Flydd doesn't expect us to commit suicide. More importantly, he won't want to lose another thapter.'

'I think we can do it,' said Tiaan.

Nish and Irisis looked at one another. 'If you think so, that's good enough for me,' said Irisis.

'And me.'

Tiaan went south and lifted up into the clouds, flying in and out of their black and chilly tops so she could see where she was going. She looked at Irisis, who nodded. 'Nish's ready too.'

Tiaan gulped. 'If the air currents don't move us too far out of line we'll burst out of the cloud about five hundred spans above the opening and the same distance from the cliff. I'll line up and head for it as fast as I can possibly go, slowing only as we approach the pinnacles. They won't have much time to get ready for us, but it'll be enough. They'll hit us with everything they've got. I'll try to dart through between the pinnacles but, the more I think about it . . .'

'Then don't think about it,' said Irisis. 'It's too late for that. Just do it and if we don't make it, well, I'm glad we're friends now.' Impulsively, she reached forward and hugged the smaller woman.

Tears came to Tiaan's eyes and she hugged Irisis back, one-handed.

She turned away, wiping her eyes. Lightning flashed to the right, rather close. Tiaan wondered what would happen if the thapter was struck. Don't think, she told herself. Just go. She headed down at a steep angle, ridding her mind of the negative thoughts and just flooding it with her mental picture of the cliffs, the pinnacles and the approach she had to take to slip between them into the air vent. She allowed her hands to do the flying.

A spatter of hail rattled on the hood and the skin of the thapter. A chunk slid down the back of her neck, startling her at first, though the cold was not unpleasant. The clouds billowed around her. Can't be far to go now, she thought, and then the thapter exploded out of the cloud and the pinnacles were below and ahead, lined up perfectly.

She streaked for the opening and made it halfway there before the lyrinx reacted. They must have been expecting her to approach along the cliff, as before. The pinnacles loomed up and Tiaan could feel the tension coming from Irisis. Tiaan felt no anxiety now, nothing but a gritty determination to get the job done and survive it if she could.

The lyrinx were spreading out, fanwise, as they realised that their formation was wrongly oriented. So was the hood, Tiaan noticed belatedly. It gave no protection at all, head-on.

She plummeted towards the pinnacles, slowing so she could dart between them. The lyrinx were lining up their weapons. She swerved left, then right.

'Keep your head down, Irisis!'

Irisis ducked just in time as bolts spanged off the sloping hood. She made a muffled noise in her throat and let go of the hood, pulling her hand down to reveal the blood welling from her wrist. The bolt had gone straight between the arm bones, leaving a hole that she could have slipped her little finger through.

The hood slammed up and tore half-off, flapping back and forth against the hatch cover. Tiaan almost allowed herself to be distracted, almost hit the pinnacle. She slipped between it in a positive cannonade of bolts and flashed towards the vent.

The lyrinx were pulling a cover across it, a frame covered in fabric painted to match the colour and texture of the rock. They weren't quite in time. Tiaan struck it head-on and fortunately the frame was timber, not metal. It smashed, the fabric tore on the sides of the thapter and they were in.

'Nish,' she shouted over the scream of the mechanism. 'Do it now. Irisis, what's going on?'

Irisis pulled herself up on the side and blood dripped on Tiaan's cheek.

'He's down! Ah, Nish, Nish!' Irisis scrambled up onto the back platform, heedless of her bloody wrist.

Tiaan clambered up as far as she could go while still holding the controller. The rear hood looked crushed against the platform, as if a boulder had been dropped on it, though Tiaan could have sworn she hadn't heard any impact, and two javelard spears had gone through it as well, pinning it to the platform. She couldn't see Nish, who was below the coaming around the platform.

There had been no dust flying past them in the suction from the bellows, so he hadn't got the spores away. They'd failed and she couldn't see the barrel. It was time to go.

Tiaan jerked the thapter backwards. 'Hang on, Irisis!'

Irisis was inside the coaming, tearing at the crushed hood, trying to lift it, but couldn't budge the spears. You'll never get him out, Tiaan thought. Anyway, he's better off there, if he *is* alive.

The thapter went backwards as Irisis came to her knees and she nearly fell off. She hung on, dragged the barrel out from under the hood and punched the top in with her fist. She hurled it over the side just as Tiaan accelerated backwards and shot out of the vent, the rush of wind buffeting three lyrinx out of the way as if they'd been hit with the end of a piston.

The barrel struck the rocky rim of the vent, letting loose a cloud of spores, but fell outside. Tiaan didn't see what happened after that, for Irisis lost her footing as the thapter accelerated. She slid head-first down towards Tiaan's flapping hood and managed to wrap her arms around it.

'Hold tight!' Tiaan screamed, spinning the thapter in a semicircle. Irisis's legs were thrown over the side and Tiaan could see the strain on her face as she struggled to hang on.

There was nothing Tiaan could do except tilt the thapter the other way and pray, for lyrinx were coming from every direction. The gap between the pinnacles came into view and she went for it.

Clang, clang, smash. The binnacle that had been broken the previous day now shattered, sending glass, crystal and what she thought were drops of quicksilver flying in all directions. Fragments of glass stung her face and she closed her eyes, involuntarily.

For a second Tiaan lost sight of the gap and had to keep going from her mental image, praying that it would take her through. The gap wasn't wide and she felt a horrible moment of panic that Irisis's dangling legs would be torn off between the thapter and the stone.

She opened her eyes and Irisis was clinging grimly, desperately, to the flapping hood. The thapter was moving too quickly for the lyrinx to catch it, though it was still within range of their weapons. Tiaan didn't dare weave around in case she threw Irisis off.

There were more crashes, thuds and spangs as the thapter was hit by everything the enemy could fire at it. At least one bolt ricocheted off the hood that partly protected her now.

It wasn't protecting Irisis. What if the lyrinx targeted her? She had to do something. Tiaan put the nose down so sharply that Irisis's legs went up in the air, and directed the thapter towards the canopy of the forest out of which the pinnacles rose.

'How are you doing?' Tiaan yelled.

'I can't hold on much longer,' Irisis said through gritted teeth. 'I've got no strength in my injured wrist.'

Her arms were wrapped around the hood, and she had managed to twist her bloody wrist through the rope that was barely holding the hood on, but her fingers were slipping as the hood flapped up and down.

What if it tore away? It looked as if it might. Tiaan reached up on tiptoe and took hold of her friend's wrist, the uninjured one. It was more reassurance than security, but Irisis managed a smile.

'Just a few seconds more,' Tiaan said. 'We're nearly down. Just hang on a few seconds more.'

The crowns of tall trees loomed up. Tiaan slowed, directed the thapter towards a gap and risked a glance over her shoulder. A host of lyrinx were heading after her like a swarm of wasps, and she could see dozens more threading their way down the steep slope below the cliff. She'd have to be quick.

The hood pulled free of the fastenings Nish had fixed to the rim of the hatch. The wind threw it backwards, and Irisis with it, until it was brought up by the ropes. Tiaan lost her grip on Irisis's wrist. Irisis slammed into the rise leading up to the rear platform, was held there momentarily by the wind, then began to slip inexorably down the side.

It was still a long way to the ground. Tiaan couldn't reach back to Irisis now; couldn't do anything but head for the steeply sloping forest floor and hope she got there before Irisis fell.

She didn't quite make it. The thapter was still five or six spans up when Irisis's fingers were pulled free and she went over the side.

FIFTY-SIX

Tiaan threw the thapter at the ground, which sloped steeply here. The base of the machine hit wet, clayey soil and kept sliding, and she had to spin it around to avoid trees and rocks. She slowed, stopping against the base of a giant tree whose trunk was wider than the thapter was long.

She couldn't see Irisis anywhere. A fall from that height onto solid ground could well have killed her, but the slope was so steep here, and the ground so slippery, that it would have helped to break her fall.

The sky had clouded right over now and grown ominously black. Lightning flashed, thunder roared and it began to rain. A spatter of hail struck the thapter.

'Irisis?' she yelled.

No reply. Tiaan could hear the lyrinx crashing down the slope above her. They'd be here within minutes. The fliers would be even quicker.

Her orders had been made more explicit after she'd nearly lost the thapter in the burning silk warehouse. Tiaan was not to risk the thapter, or herself, more than was necessary to complete the job. And once the mission had succeeded, or failed in this case, she must not risk the thapter to save any life but her own.

Her duty was absolutely clear. If she couldn't find Irisis in the next minute she had to abandon her to whatever fate the lyrinx had in store for such a continued thorn in their side. And there still hadn't been time to check on Nish. Tears pricked at her eyes and she dashed them away furiously. There wasn't time for that either.

'Irisis?' she shouted.

Tiaan calculated where Irisis should have fallen and circled up and across the slope, looking for a body. She didn't find one though she did discover a long yellow streak where Irisis had hit the slope, tearing though the thin grass and exposing the clay underneath.

Tiaan followed it down. Irisis must have slid a long way, and fast enough to smash bones or skull if she hit an obstacle. The minute was up. She hesitated, then decided to give Irisis another thirty seconds. The enemy couldn't be that close yet, surely?

She headed directly down and saw a pair of clay-covered feet sticking up in the air some twenty spans below. Irisis had skidded all that way, then fallen over a couple of embankments before embedding herself in a wiry bush.

'Are you all right?' Tiaan called, settling the thapter against a tree trunk to prevent it from sliding. She was afraid to get out in case it slipped.

The feet moved. Irisis began to pull herself out of the bush. 'Just wonderful,' she said sarcastically. 'Apart from ten thousand bruises, a badly wrenched ankle and a hole in my wrist I could thread a needle through.'

'Can you hop?' said Tiaan. 'They're after us.'

'I heard them.' Irisis stood up, holding her left foot up. 'What's that?'

It was a crashing and a rumbling that was growing ever louder. Tiaan spun around, staring up the hill. 'It sounds like a landslide.'

'It's not,' said Irisis. 'They're rolling boulders –'

The ground shook and a rock half the size of the thapter came thundering though the trees, bouncing ten spans high. Passing to Tiaan's right, it struck the trunk of a big tree, smashing it into jagged splinters as long as Tiaan was tall. Leaves and wood rained down, fortunately below them, then the upper part of the tree toppled and fell down the slope. The boulder, hardly slowed by the impact, kept going and they heard more ground-shaking crashes before it disappeared beyond their ken.

'Go!' cried Irisis. 'You know your orders. Don't risk the thapter. You can't get me in by yourself.'

Tiaan hesitated. She was obedient by nature. But then again . . . She leapt over the side, slid down the greasy slope and gave Irisis her shoulder. The rain grew heavier, running into her eyes until she could barely see. It had been warm at first but the drops now felt like melted ice.

'Hop as if the fate of the world depended on it,' she said, terrified that the thapter would slide away and be lost.

Irisis did so, ignoring the pain, and they slipped and staggered up towards the thapter. Another boulder came crashing down, smaller than the first and not bouncing as high, but all the more dangerous because of that. It followed the path of the other and disappeared.

They reached the side just as there came a rumble of thunder, though there was no lightning. The ground shook. Another crash and it shook again; the thapter moved.

'That's one hell of a boulder this time,' said Irisis, putting her good foot onto the ladder. 'Sounds like half a pinnacle.'

Tiaan felt a spasm of fear. *Thump.* She boosted Irisis up and pulled herself up the ladder after her. Thankfully Irisis had the presence of mind not to hesitate at the top. She simply went through the hatch head-first, heedless of her injuries.

Thump-thump. The ground shook so hard that the thapter began to slide.

Tiaan fell in on top of Irisis, who let out a groan as Tiaan landed on her wrenched ankle. Tiaan pulled herself up using the controller.

Thump thump, thump thump. Thump-thump.

She jerked up on the flight knob and the thapter lifted, with agonising slowness. One span, two, three. And then she saw it coming and could not contain herself.

The lyrinx had toppled half of one of the pinnacles, which had broken into two gigantic boulders, bigger than houses, plus a host of smaller, thapter-sized ones. They were thundering down the mountainside, spreading into a fan of devastation hundreds of spans across, smashing trees and rocks to fragments as they came. The thapter was right in their path and from a standing start she couldn't see how she could get high enough to escape.

Thump. Thump-thump.

Tiaan wiped her eyes with her free hand and tried to see where she could go. The two huge boulders were bouncing twenty or thirty spans high, the smaller ones five or ten. She couldn't rise above them in time.

The only chance was to fly up the slope, between the biggest boulders, until she gained enough speed to sweep upwards. Tiaan turned that way, knowing that neither the height nor direction of the bounces was predictable. Just as dangerously, the air between the fan of boulders was full of fragments of rock and pieces of shattered wood, a hailstorm of it.

She had to fly on instinct, as she had before. Tiaan went left so as to put herself between the two big boulders, which were roaring towards her. She rose to avoid a pair of trees and corrected again as the right-hand boulder bounced in towards its twin. The next bounce took it out again and for an instant her hand froze on the controller, seeing that it was heading directly for her.

An instinctive wiggle took the thapter sideways; the boulder whistled past, its windstorm buffeting the machine wildly, and smashed off the top half of the tree just below her. She took the machine up and curved away as the smaller boulders, carrying a landslide of rocks, clay and wood with them, rumbled underneath.

The flying lyrinx, who had been hanging back to see the result of their handiwork, now turned towards her in an angry swarm, but it was too late. Tiaan peeled away and fled into the now freezing rain as fast as the battered machine could go.

Ten or fifteen leagues away, out of sight of pursuit, Tiaan set down on the first hill that had a clear view in all directions. She was still shaking.

'What about Nish?' she said softly. 'How did he look?'

'I don't know,' said Irisis, who had overcome her injuries enough to pull herself up onto the side. 'But he hasn't moved.' There was such a stricken look in her eyes that Tiaan had to turn away. She didn't feel very good either.

'I'll go and see. Keep watch.'

'I'm coming too,' said Irisis. 'I'm so afraid. I – I love him, Tiaan. I swore I'd never submit to such a folly. Not me; I was too strong for it. But I do love the little squirt, with every cell of my body, and now I'm terrified that I've lost him.'

'Did . . . does he know?'

'Of course not,' said Irisis. 'He's the thickest man on Santhenar. He understands nothing.'

Tiaan smiled at that. Nish understood a great deal. 'Then perhaps you should spell it out for him.'

'And perhaps you should mind your own business,' said Irisis. 'If you could give me a hand.'

Tiaan wasn't offended, though once she would have been. She was beginning to understand people too.

She helped Irisis up onto the back platform. The hood was flattened around Nish's body and head, squashing him face down against the deck, leaving only the top of his head exposed. The hood was deeply dented in four places from crossbow bolts. Moreover, two javelard spears had pinned it in place, one angling in towards his left side, the other between his knees. If either had gone through him he could have bled to death.

Irisis slid a hand under the hood onto Nish's cheek. 'He's icy cold. He's *dead*!'

Tiaan eased her out of the way. 'Of course he's cold. He's soaking wet and we've been flying fast. It's lucky he hasn't got frostbite. Nish?'

He didn't answer, so she felt his cheek. He was so cold that it was hard to believe that he could be alive. She forced her hand through the narrow space and down to his neck, which proved just as chilly. Tiaan wriggled her fingers underneath his shirt, where his skin was protected from the wind. She found a trace of warmth there. Was that a pulse? She couldn't be sure.

'I think he's alive, Irisis. Talk to him; hold him. I'll get something to prise the hood off.'

When she returned with a bar, Irisis was crouched down, her hand on Nish's cheek, her forehead touching the top of his head. Her eyes were screwed shut.

Tiaan began to lever from the side. It was hard work. The black Aachan metal, although thin, was intensely strong and inflexible. It proved impossible to bend out of the way. In the end Tiaan had to whack the spears one way and then the other with the bar until they came free, knowing that if either had gone into Nish she would be greatly aggravating the wound.

The second spear came out. Tiaan tossed it over the side and lifted the sheet of metal, which sprang back to its original shape. Nish gave a groan and turned his head. His nose was running with a mixture of blood and mucus and his lower face was wet with half-frozen saliva.

'You took your bloody time,' he said through bruised and swollen lips.

'Are you all right?' Irisis said, scrubbing at her eyes with the back of her hand. 'You look disgusting.'

'Thanks.'

'If you were all right, why the hell didn't you say so! I thought you were dead.'

'I couldn't move a fingertip. Couldn't open my mouth, or close it. Do you think you could wipe my nose?'

'The things I do for your dignity.' Irisis took off her shirt and began to clean him up with it.

Tiaan walked away across the wet tussock grass and left them to their cheerful bickering.

Once Irisis's twisted ankle had been immobilised by strapping it to shaped pieces of wood, her wrist bandaged and Nish's body-length bruises marvelled over, Tiaan said, 'What now?'

'Flydd wants us to check on the cities again, to see what's happened,' Nish reminded her. 'If we go back to Alcifer in three or four days, we should be able to see if the spores have had any effect. In the meantime, let's find somewhere to hide. With no lyrinx.'

'Somewhere tranquil,' said Irisis. 'With decent food.'

'And wine,' said Nish.

'Neither will be easy to come by,' said Tiaan, 'in a land that's been empty of humans for years. I'll see what I can find.'

They flew south-west, skirting along the foothills of the mountains. Below, they saw many manors and fastnesses, once sited to protect the fertile valleys from mountain marauders, but now abandoned and some already falling into ruin.

'What about that one?' said Irisis.

It was a small manor set on the edge of a grassy upland plateau. A stream meandered across the sward, passed by the rear of the manor then curled around like a sickle before tinkling over a waterfall, five or six spans high, in a crystalline shower. The grass was green, fragrant herbs grew on the edge of the plateau and in the distance a forest barred the way to the higher mountains. Stock grazed on the grass: cattle with long, twisting horns and sheep whose fine crinkly wool was a purple black. Goats stood sentinel on rock stacks here and there. The Sea of Thurkad was just visible in the east. They hid the thapter in a stone barn, pushed the doors closed and hobbled off to look for something better than the hard tack they had in the thapter.

'I wonder who lived here, and what happened to them?' said Tiaan. The place had a melancholy air. 'Whoever they were, they lost everything, and probably their lives as well.'

'A story that's been repeated a hundred thousand times across Santhenar since the lyrinx came,' said Nish, supporting Irisis with his shoulder.

The front door was closed but not locked. They went inside. The owners had either been killed or had fled carrying only what would fit on their backs, for the manor was full of precious things. Silverware, cloisonné lamps of the most exquisite workmanship, silken tapestries and other fineries remained in place as though the house was still occupied, though there was a film of dust over everything.

'How long ago would this place have been abandoned?' Tiaan wondered.

'It must have been one of the last, since it's not been looted,' said Irisis, hopping across to a leather chair and sitting down. 'No more than three years, I'd say. I'm going to stay right here. You can wait on me for a change, Nish.'

'There could still be food in the pantries, and drink in the cellars,' said Nish. 'Beer wouldn't be much good after three years, but wine should have lasted, and cheese.'

'You keep talking about food,' smiled Irisis.

'I haven't had anything decent to eat since you went east at the end of the winter. Cooking is a lost art at Fiz Gorgo.'

'Yggur's food is a little stodgy, I'll agree, but it's a damn sight better than I've been eating in the eastern manufactories.'

Nish and Tiaan found a larder with a vermin-proof door, and there was food in it: hanging hams, cheeses, pickled onions and other preserved vegetables and fruits. He found wine in a cellar too: an immensely strong red wine, as well as small barrels of fruit liqueurs. Nish lugged one of each up and outside, while Tiaan carried out the most comfortable chairs. Irisis was carving herself a crutch from a forked stick.

They had a picnic on the terrace, overlooking the lands of Iagador, while the sun went down behind them. It hadn't stormed here and they lingered outside in the balmy evening.

Tiaan toyed with a mug of wine, then put it aside. It was too strong, and wine did uncomfortable things to her head. She lay back and studied the stars.

Nish and Irisis had gone inside, Irisis hopping on her crutch. Tiaan knew what they were up to. Good luck to them; they might as well enjoy what little time they had left.

She was thirsty but felt too lethargic to go all the way to the well for water. Irisis had decanted part of the liqueur barrel into a jug so Tiaan took a sip. It was thick and sweet, more to her taste. She had another, then lay back in her armchair again, pulled her coat about her and watched the stars wheel across the sky.

She woke as a crescent moon rose over the distant sea. All was quiet inside the manor and her bare hands were cold. Somewhere behind her, an owl hooted. Moonbeams lit up the mist above the falls like a fairy veil drifting in the wind. Dew glittered on the grass. It was so peaceful; so beautiful. It must often have been like this, before the war began.

She felt a tear in the corner of her eye. This place would always be as lovely, but there would be no one to appreciate it. These attacks were a folly, and suddenly she felt sure that they were going to lose the war.

Tiaan had an urge to call Flydd and tell him so. She considered it, but the drink had left her lethargic. It was easier to snuggle up in the chair and close her eyes again.

Despite having unlocked Golias's globe all those months ago, she still didn't understand how a message could travel from one field to another. Even less, how it could loop and whorl its way across lands a dozen nodes apart one day, yet on the next, not even reach someone in a nearby town.

Nothing was as simple as it seemed. Tiaan wondered if the erratic performance of farspeakers could have anything to do with the interlinking, or failing, of the nodes. Could she put farspeaker globes at each end to study how the signals changed as power was drawn from the nodes?

What if? There were too many questions and never enough answers, while each answer raised new questions. In a lifetime she wouldn't be able to answer a fraction of them.

The moon travelled higher; the illuminated veils of mist danced over the waterfall like the restless spirits of those who once lived here. She wished she knew who they'd been, and what had happened to them. Did they still pine for this place and long to come home once the war was over? Or were they dead and eaten by the enemy long ago?

The morbid thoughts disturbed her. As a distraction, Tiaan went over the events of the past few days, still marvelling how they'd survived the attack at Alcifer. Had it not been for the lyrinx suddenly checking as they raced for Irisis and Nish at the bellows . . . Now, why had they done that?

For a few seconds, they'd all acted as though they'd been in pain. Could it have something to do with the way she'd been operating the thapter? She'd often flown it near lyrinx and never seen such a reaction before.

Tiaan replayed the scene, back and forth. It had happened just as she had screamed into the farspeaker at Flydd. Could that have hurt them? She'd not encountered anything like it. Or had she?

Nearly two years ago, when Besant had carried her off to Kalissin, Tiaan had felt a strange sensation whenever Besant drew powerfully on the Secret Art. It had been like sherbet dissolving and fizzing behind her temples, and Tiaan had experienced it a number of times.

Poor Ullii had felt it much more strongly: Tiaan could still recall her anguished screams as Besant took off. It was equally possible that lyrinx could be affected when humans used the Art in certain ways.

Had anyone else noticed? She went inside, intending to ask Irisis and Nish. The lamp had burned low in the front room but its dying flickers showed them lying together on a rug on the floor, fast asleep. Tiaan looked down at Nish's scarred back, which he had been so anxious to conceal. It was worse than Irisis's. How it must have hurt. Pulling a fold of the rug over them, she blew out the lamp.

She went into the barn and sat in the thapter, in the dark. It was the closest thing she had to home and a place of her own, though it still stank of lyrinx blood. Tiaan wanted to talk to Flydd or Yggur about her observations, but her slave farspeaker could only call when Flydd's master globe had been set to speak to her.

Setting up the farspeaker, she leaned back in her seat. What would Flydd and Yggur do if the lyrinx did come out of their underground cities? It now struck Tiaan as an absurd plan – surely the enemy would fight twice as hard if they had no home to return to. Using the spores now seemed reckless and she wished she hadn't been talked into it, though, if she hadn't, one of the other pilots would have done it.

She felt so isolated and alone that it was easy to imagine the world had already ended, for humanity. What if the only humans left alive were herself and the snoring pair inside?

In need of comfort, Tiaan took the amplimet out of its socket under the smashed binnacle. Flydd had given it back to her for the duration of this mission, after which it was to return to the platinum box. Tiaan didn't mind – since Nennifer she'd been purged of that tormenting withdrawal. Nonetheless, the amplimet was a comfort and reminded her of her first real friend, old Joeyn.

A tiny spark drifted slowly down the centre of the crystal. It was dull, which meant that there wasn't a strong node nearby. Tiaan knew that already – the fields were always in her inner eye now. She cupped the amplimet in her cold hands and warmth spread through her, out of all proportion to its size.

She focussed on her slave farspeaker, wondering yet again about the force that made such things work. Bringing up her mental image of Golias's globe, Tiaan revolved its inner spheres as if tuning it to speak with her farspeaker. The spheres turned as if coated in oil. Golias's globe had been so well made that the best artisans had not been able to equal it, and it still worked better than any of the copies. Messages went further and were just that little bit clearer.

The farspeaker burped, startling her. An uncanny coincidence, that the scrutator should call her just as she was thinking about him. She imagined him sitting at the long table, papers and maps all around. She waited for him to speak but he did not.

'Hello?' she said after a decent interval. 'This is Tiaan.'

'Tiaan?' Flydd cried in astonishment. 'What . . .?'

'What do you want, Scrutator?'

'I didn't call you. My globe was set to speak to someone else.'

'But, that's impossible.'

'It's supposed to be. What have you done, Tiaan?'

She didn't know. 'I was just sitting in the thapter with the amplimet in my hands, wondering what was happening back east. Thinking about your globe, and the settings needed for you to contact me, I just moved the spheres in my mind.'

'You did more than that. You actually changed the settings of my globe.'

'But . . .' said Tiaan.

'I saw them move.'

'I'm sorry.' Why did she always feel the need to apologise? 'I didn't mean to.'

'Don't be ridiculous,' he said delightedly. 'It's an important discovery. Where are you?'

'Somewhere in the hills of Bannador. We're resting on the way south to Alcifer.'

'Good for you. I presume you got the job done at Thurkad?'

'Not entirely.' She explained what had happened. 'Some of the spores could have been sucked inside but the barrel fell out. There was nothing we could do about it.'

'You did better than I dared hope, and survived. And who knows, fear of the fungus may do our work for us.'

'Why didn't you call before?'

'I tried,' said Flydd. 'But two more nodes have gone down and we're having a lot of trouble with our farspeakers.'

She was about to say, 'I have a theory about that,' but decided not to. It was probably nothing. She still hadn't thought it through properly. 'Scrutator?'

'What is it, Tiaan?'

'Something unusual happened during the attack on Alcifer. If you recall, I shouted at you on the farspeaker.'

Flydd chuckled. 'It's not often I'm shouted at. Most people are too afraid.'

'The lyrinx attacked Nish and Irisis as they tried to throw the spores in, and I couldn't get to them in time. But as I screamed at you, the enemy reacted as if in pain, and one lyrinx put its hands over its ears. Have you ever seen that kind of thing before?'

'Can't say that I have, though I've never been close to the enemy when using it. You've given me an idea. I'll order some trials with lyrinx prisoners.'

After he had gone she lay back in the seat, utterly exhausted, and slept.

Two days later they were high over Alcifer, above the height that any lyrinx could reach, watching and waiting. There was a little more activity on the ground and in the air than usual, but no sign of an army in readiness for battle. The scrutator called twice a day but there was nothing to report, apart from the odd flaring and fading of the exotic node-within-a-node at Alcifer, and a corresponding fading and flaring in the node associated with the nearby volcano. They had to be linked in some way. Tiaan made a note to mention it the next time he called. She hadn't attempted to contact him again, so she did not know if she could reproduce what she had done before.

Time went by. It was now a week since they'd dropped the fungus spores, without any discernible effect, and it was the same at the other cities. Every time Tiaan spoke to Flydd he sounded more depressed.

'What a waste of time this has been!' Irisis said irritably.

Nish was peering over the side with a spyglass. 'Hello, I think they're coming out. Yes they are. I can see hundreds of lyrinx, assembling in the great square not far from the white building with the glass dome.'

'Hundreds won't bother us,' said Irisis, reaching out for the spyglass.

'Wait a second,' said Nish, leaning away. 'Go a bit lower, Tiaan.'

'What is it?'

'I'm not sure, yet.'

Tiaan began to spiral down. Normally the wheeling fliers would have turned towards her but they continued their patterns as if they were flying along wires.

'They're carrying something out,' said Nish.

Irisis took the spyglass from him and peered over the other side. 'Looks like dead lyrinx, to me. A bit closer, please, Tiaan.'

Tiaan went down another turn, anxiously watching the fliers, who were not far away. 'They're carrying bodies down to that embankment,' cried Irisis, 'and throwing them over.'

Tiaan felt cold inside. They'd brought plague upon the lyrinx and they were dying in agony. It wasn't right.

Irisis counted some sixty bodies being dumped. Not long

549

after that, more lyrinx appeared, carrying barrels which they also emptied over the embankment.

'Can you see what that is?' said Nish.

Irisis adjusted the spyglass. 'The bodies of small creatures. About cat-sized. Hundreds of them.'

'Could they be uggnatl?' said Tiaan.

'I think they are,' said Irisis. 'Yes, definitely.'

Many more barrels were brought out, then the pile began to smoke, the fliers turned towards them and Tiaan headed away. They had just flown across the glass dome when the sound of the mechanism vanished. She took power from another node and climbed a little higher.

'What was *that*?' said Nish.

'I don't know, but it was a lot stronger than when they tried to take my power a year ago.'

It happened again, though this time Tiaan was waiting for it and switched nodes instantly. 'I don't think they like us here,' she said, turning away.

A few seconds later, power was snatched from her again. Then again, and each time it was quicker than before.

'Fly!' yelled Irisis.

Tiaan tried to, but all at once time seemed to freeze. Nish, his mouth open, went as still as a statue. Tiaan's hand appeared to solidify in mid-air and the thapter itself to stop, though it did not fall. She tried to reach for the flight knob but her hand would not move. *What's . . . happening?* Her thoughts were so sluggish that she had to force herself to create each word.

After an agonised aeon, time reverted to its normal beat and she streaked away to safety, without having the faintest idea what had been done to them.

Flydd was revoltingly pleased to hear about the dead, and the uggnatl, and told them that similar plagues had been reported from two of the lyrinx's eastern cities, though the number of lyrinx dead was relatively small so far. He was not so pleased to hear about the strange attack on the thapter, though he couldn't make anything of it either.

The next day Tiaan kept at a safe distance, observing with the spyglass. The thapter was not attacked again, but a thousand dead were carried out of the city. The day after that Oellyll erupted, lyrinx boiling from it like ants from a broken anthill. They disappeared into the forest too quickly to count, though Nish did his best to estimate the numbers.

'Around twenty thousand,' he said when dusk cut off the scene.

Irisis laid down her tally sheet. 'I make it more like twenty-five.'

'Then we'll take the difference. Twenty-two and a half.'

They were back on station at dawn, and found the enemy fleeing Oellyll as fast as ever. By the end of the day Nish and Irisis had estimated another twenty-two thousand. That night was clear with a good moon and they saw that the evacuation continued all night, though it wasn't bright enough to count them. Finally, around lunchtime of the following day, it slowed to a trickle and the circling lyrinx, without so much as a glance at the thapter, flew east across the sea.

'Fifty-five thousand,' Tiaan said when Flydd called not long after. 'And that's just the ones we saw in the daytime. There would have been roughly as many again at night.'

'So a hundred thousand; maybe a hundred and ten,' said Tiaan. 'That's far more than Flydd expected.'

The scrutator could hardly speak when she told him the number. 'And how many dead?' he said after a long, long pause.

'A couple of thousand, in total,' she said soberly.

'Is that *all*?' he whispered. 'It's not near enough. If that's repeated at the other cities, we're staring at a catastrophe.'

'What do you want us to do?' said Tiaan through her far-speaker.

'When you're sure it's safe, take a look at the bodies, if they're not all burnt. Then you'd better go north and see if the same is happening there.'

That afternoon she landed by one of the main entrances to Oellyll. The bodies lay in great piles, adults as well as infants whose armour had barely formed. The outer skin was red and blistered, the fingers and toes hooked as though the creatures had died in agony. The threat of the uggnatl had meant there was no choice, but Tiaan felt sick. We did this, she thought. *I* did it, and for what? There's got to be a better way – a way we can all live together, without slaughtering each other and resorting to ever-increasing barbarities like this.

By the time they reached the lyrinx city west of Thurkad the following day, the smoking bodies were piled as high as houses between the cliff and the pinnacles. They saw no lyrinx about, which surely meant that this city had also been abandoned.

Tiaan landed the thapter so that Irisis and Nish could inspect the bodies, then took them up to one of the entrances, as they wanted to check inside. She did not. She sat at the very brink, looking down at the fuming corpses. Many of them were children and infants. Very many. How could peace ever be made between humans and lyrinx, after this?

But there had to be a way. Tiaan could not bear to think of the war going on in ever-increasing violence and depravity until the world had been utterly laid waste. One side would be annihilated and the other ruined by the legacy of its own viciousness and moral corruption, as it tried to justify more and worse depravities in the cause of victory. How could humanity – should it prove the victor – ever recover from such bloody Histories? It would taint every child born in this world, for as long as the Histories endured.

I can't be a party to it any longer, she thought. I must find a solution, *whatever it costs me.*

Nish and Irisis came out, pale and silent. They did not speak about what they'd found inside, though Tiaan could only assume it had been more dead, twisted in their last agonies. Neither did she mention to them her resolve – let Flydd get word of it and she'd be deprived of thapter and amplimet, and probably locked up for the duration. Her quest would have to be silent and secret. She could not afford to trust even her new-found friends.

'We'd better report to Flydd,' said Irisis.

'You do it,' said Tiaan. 'I'm not in the mood.'

Irisis nodded. 'I think I know how you feel.'

I doubt that you do, thought Tiaan, handing her the slave farspeaker. 'Let's go; I can't bear the smell any longer.'

'We can't tell how many there were,' Irisis said over the farspeaker once they were almost to Thurkad. It had taken ages to contact Flydd. 'Though . . .' She squinted into the distance.

'What is it?' said Flydd, his voice echoing.

'I can see clouds of lyrinx in the distance, flying over the sea towards Meldorin. There must be ten thousand fliers; or more.'

'And I dare say there's more that you can't see,' he said heavily.

'I dare say. And the harbour of Thurkad is full of boats, thousands of them. The enemy must have had them stored under cover. Some are already moving out. They'll all be across the sea in a few days.'

'I suppose we could pray for a storm.'

'I've never seen the sea calmer,' said Irisis. 'What's happening on the east coast?'

'The same,' said Flydd. 'Our estimates were low at each city. Their numbers are at least a third higher than we'd thought.'

'A third!' cried Nish, staring into the farspeaker. 'But that means . . .'

'I'd hoped we'd infect most of them, and wipe them out as a threat, but a few thousand dead is nothing.'

Tiaan was even more shocked than when she'd looked at the twisted corpses. 'It seemed a lot to me,' she said quietly.

'Tiaan, each of our armies is outnumbered by an enemy that doesn't need to outnumber us, and they've nowhere to go. They'll all go to war against us. We gambled and we've lost.'

'Can't you use the spores again?' said Nish.

'They're all gone.'

'What do you want us to do?' said Irisis.

'Do whatever you want,' Flydd said despairingly. 'You have my permission to save yourselves any way you can.'

'What would be the point?' said Nish. He looked questioningly as Tiaan, who was staring straight ahead, her jaw clenched, and gave no response. Irisis nodded. 'We're coming home to fight,' Nish added.

FIFTY-SEVEN

Gilhaelith had been working with Ryll for months before, in late summer, they made the breakthrough. The lyrinx watched him so carefully, and constrained his every movement so tightly, that he could not have lifted a finger without being noticed. On the first few occasions he was watched over by Great Anabyng himself, whom Gilhaelith knew to be a mancer of surpassing power. Gilhaelith was meekness personified, doing nothing without asking permission first. He would be patient. The lyrinx couldn't afford to waste Anabyng's talents on guard duties for long.

Sure enough, after several sessions Anabyng came no more, being replaced by a pair of lesser but still powerful mancers who never took their eyes off him. Gilhaelith kept up the pretence of total acquiescence. In fact they constrained him so tightly, out of fear, that he was almost useless to Ryll. Gilhaelith was happy to go along with that. Sooner or later they would have to give him more freedom, and he would use it to get what he wanted. In the meantime he kept his head down and let his resentment burn. He, a master geomancer, had been reduced to begging for the right to use his geomantic globe, just to save his life. Gyrull had not deigned to reply to his pleas, which made him bitter indeed. Once he got hold of the globe, she would pay. He'd rehearsed his plan so many times that even his reluctant, damaged brain had it down perfectly.

Eventually they had given him a little freedom – enough for Ryll to discover what he needed to complete the flisnadr, yet not enough for Gilhaelith to take control of his globe. And the instant Ryll had it, the guards had taken Gilhaelith straight back to his watermelon-shaped stone cell and locked him in.

This time Gilhaelith knew he was doomed. The damage caused by the phantom crystals was close to irreparable now, and in a month or two it would be. A few months after that, if he was still alive, he would be little better than a vegetable. And he probably *would* live that long. They would keep him alive until the flisnadr had been tested and was ready for use, just in case. But as soon as it was ready, he would go to the slaughtering pens. Apart from any other considerations, he knew too much about the power patterner to be allowed to live.

Liett hurtled into the patterning chamber, skidding halfway across the stone floor before she could stop herself. Her claws screeched on the shale, gouging pale marks across it. 'Ryll!' she screamed.

He set down the bucket of gruel with which he was feeding the human females sealed in the linked patterners, but didn't turn to her at once. Ryll was used to Liett's histrionics, and he was deep in thought. The flisnadr was the size of a beer barrel now, almost fully grown, and he'd already carried out most of the tests. The results were encouraging, though he wanted to keep testing for a month or two, just to be sure that he had mastery of it well before it was needed. 'What is it?' he said absently, watching the flickering chameleon colours on its skin.

'We've been attacked,' she cried.

'Attacked?' Ryll spun around. 'How?'

'One of the enemy thapters flew right to the main air shaft, the one with the bellows, and hurled in a barrel of the skin-rotting spores.'

Ryll's skin turned a dull, creeping yellow, fading to grey, and he felt an involuntary urge to scratch himself. He resisted. 'When?'

'Just ten minutes ago. Mother ordered the bellows shut down and the shaft sealed but . . . it may be too late. The spores could have blown anywhere by now. What are we going to do?'

'We don't panic,' said Ryll, heading for the door at a run. 'First, we burn brimstone in the sealed shaft.'

'Will that work with spores?' Liett was trotting beside him.

'I don't know. It saved a few of our uggnatl, but that was a different kind of infection. We seal all the floors the shaft blows air to, wash everything down into the gutters, and burn the washings outside. Did we get the thapter?'

'Almost, but the black-haired pilot got away in the end.'

His heart sank even further. 'Tiaan was the pilot?'

'Yes.'

For once Liett refrained from making the obvious accusation. Tiaan had thwarted them a number of times now, and all because he, Ryll, had allowed her to escape from Kalissin a year and a half ago. Shame made his stomach throb, for all that he'd followed his honourable instincts, and few could fault that. His mind was already projecting the worst possibilities from this attack, and they were very bad.

On the upper level they ran into a group of desperate lyrinx, milling back and forth, barely able to contain their terror. Recalling the fate of those infected by the spores in Borgistry, he could hardly blame them.

'Where's Matriarch Gyrull?' said Ryll.

A squat female, whose dark-green crest looked as though it had been chewed by a dog, pointed down the corridor. 'She's *receiving*. She can't be disturbed.'

'What about Great Anabyng?'

'Outside, strengthening the defences.'

'It's too late for that,' said Ryll. 'They won't come back.'

'If they're trying to frighten us,' Liett said savagely, 'they –'

'They're not trying to frighten us, Liett. They're trying to wipe us out.' Ryll headed up the corridor searching for Gyrull, and found her in a small room, crouched in the corner with her hands over her ears, her brow ridges knitted in concentration. She would be mindspeaking to the other matriarchs.

He waited silently, and after several minutes she dropped her hands and looked up.

'What did they say when you told them, Wise Mother?' said Ryll.

'All our cities have been attacked in the same way, at the same time. All the attacks succeeded save the one at Thurkad, where the pilot of the thapter was shot and those inside it were killed.'

The ice in his stomach developed needles that pricked right through him. 'Is this *the time*, Wise Mother?'

'For victory or annihilation? I don't know, Ryll. The spores may do nothing. We won't know for some days, but we'd better be ready.'

'Are you going to release the uggnatl?'

'Maybe in the east, where we have enough to make a difference. Not here. How is your work going?'

'The flisnadr has passed all but the final tests. I could use it now if I had to. Within weeks I'll have mastered it.'

Matriarch Gyrull smiled. 'Well done, Ryll. It's been a mighty labour, and few among us thought it could ever succeed. Even I had my doubts, but you've done everything I asked of you, and more. We may save something out of our ruin after all. It – it'll be the last thing I do for my people.'

'But, Matriarch!' he cried, aghast. 'No – we need you.'

'Don't be troubled,' she said. 'I'm not dead yet. But my time as matriarch has been a long one, and I'll be glad enough to hand on the flask and the cup to a younger leader. One who's fit to lead us into our new future – if there is one for us.'

'Have you chosen the new matriarch?'

'Not yet, though I'm close to it.'

'May I ask if . . . Liett?' Ryll didn't know whether to hope she was chosen or rejected. Either way Liett would be insufferable. And yet, Ryll felt she would make a good leader in time. Unfortunately, time was no longer on their side.

'You may not.' She smiled. 'It may be Liett, or another. I'll be watching to see how the favoured ones acquit themselves over our coming trials.'

Some days after the attack, six lyrinx guards came for Gilhaelith. This is it, he thought, they're taking me to the slaughtering pens. He tried to summon up some vestige of his earlier rage but, after the months of solitary confinement, he felt too apathetic. Could that be due to the brain damage? His every sense, his every emotion, felt damped down these days, and perhaps it was for the best. At least it would put an end to his troubles.

The guards said nothing, just stolidly led him up the ramps towards Alcifer. Other lyrinx ran past all the time, close to panic. Gilhaelith smiled grimly. It was clear that the city had been attacked and the lyrinx did not know what to do. It no longer concerned him. At least he was going to die out in the fresh air, not in a claustrophobic, reeking chamber down in the pit.

But they did not take him to the slaughtering pens. The guards kept going up the road towards the central point of Alcifer, the five-armed white palace with the glistening shell roofs, at the intersection of the seven boulevards. Just there, beneath the glass-domed roof, he had completed the geomantic globe last autumn. So they weren't going to kill him after all – at least, not just yet. They still wanted something from him.

Gilhaelith was led inside and, to his unparalleled joy, the globe stood on the stone bench where he'd last used it, under its dust cloth. Ryll was waiting beside it, along with one of the lyrinx mancers who'd kept watch over Gilhaelith previously. He felt another tickle of hope. Perhaps in the present crisis they couldn't spare the second mancer. The fellow's skin was flashing and flickering in all the colours of the spectrum, such was his agitation. Ryll maintained a studied calm, though he kept scratching his claws across the bench.

'I've brought you here for the final tests on the flisnadr,' Ryll said, indicating a barrel-shaped object covered with a canvas. 'Let's begin.'

'I need answers before I'll agree to help you,' said Gilhaelith, who was beginning to see the faintest possibility of escape.

Ryll extended his claws towards Gilhaelith's face. Gilhaelith didn't flinch. 'If you could do without me you would have killed me long ago. What's going on?'

558

Ryll didn't even think before answering, which meant that things were desperate and the need for the flisnadr urgent. 'The humans have attacked Oellyll with the spores of a fungus that causes us to shed our outer skin and tear ourselves to shreds in agony.' He explained the circumstances of the attack.

Gilhaelith recalled the infected lyrinx that had been put out of its misery as they'd fled from Snizort last summer, and saw the implications at once. Had humanity got the idea from him? He vaguely remembered talking to someone about the incident, at Fiz Gorgo, he thought. 'Are you abandoning Oellyll?'

'No decision has been taken,' said Ryll. 'Shall we begin?'

He had told Gilhaelith all he needed to know. Oellyll surely would be abandoned, either because lyrinx were being infected with the fungus, or for fear that they would be. This was the crisis – the moment upon which the fate of both lyrinx and humanity hinged. He had to take advantage of the first chance he got, for the instant he gave Ryll what he wanted, Ryll would put him to death.

That knowledge quite concentrated the mind, and Gilhaelith rehearsed once again the attack he'd been planning for months now. He was ready; all he needed was the opportunity.

Ryll went to the flisnadr, though he left the canvas over it so Gilhaelith couldn't see how it was used. They worked for a night and a day, then slept for a few hours. Gilhaelith was bound hand and foot and watched over by four lyrinx guards, then untied and they worked on. Ryll was methodical and took no chances. Neither did he allow Gilhaelith any.

On the afternoon of the following day, Gilhaelith heard the whine of a thapter not far above. 'What's that?' he said, hoping to distract Ryll.

Ryll cocked his head. 'Thapter. Go and see,' he said to one of the guards, and the lyrinx ran off.

'Perhaps they're going to attack with more spores,' Gilhaelith said.

'They'll get a surprise if they try,' said Ryll, pretending indifference, though his skin colours told otherwise.

They continued, Gilhaelith sliding the brass pointers on their circumferential rings as he tuned the geomantic globe to the field, while Ryll worked under the canvas. Gilhaelith couldn't see what he was doing, though he could feel the effects on the field, which kept drawing down then flaring up. So the flisnadr *is* working, Gilhaelith thought. And if Ryll can control *this* dark and dangerous field, formed around the perilous Alcifer node-within-a-node, he can control just about any field in the world. He can take all the power from it, to deprive the enemy, or give it all to his own kind. He can do anything he wants with it. How can humanity counter that?

Surprisingly, Gilhaelith cared. The knowledge that he truly was doomed had come like a blinding revelation. His own selfish interests, which had sustained him all his life, would never be satisfied, but somehow that did not matter any more. What did matter was the fate of humanity, and he might hold the key to saving them. It seemed it was time to throw in his lot with his own kind after all.

The lyrinx came running back. 'It's the same thapter that attacked the air shaft last week,' he said. 'It's not attacking, though; just circling.'

Tiaan's thapter, Gilhaelith thought. This is my chance. If I can just get free and signal her, she can take me away from here. He suppressed the thought that, after his previous behaviour, she might refuse.

He glanced up at Ryll, gauging whether it was the right moment, only to realise that Ryll had seen an entirely different possibility. With the flisnadr he could withdraw all the power from the thapter, no matter what node Tiaan tried to use. He could cause it to crash or bring it to ground just where he wanted it.

Ryll hurled the canvas out of the way and his big hands danced over the recesses and protrusions of the warty, chameleon-skinned flisnadr. He thrust his arms into two of the slits, up to the elbows, and the note of the thapter dropped sharply. Gilhaelith knew his opportunity had come.

He wasn't going to be rash about it, though. One word from

Ryll, even a gesture, and the mancer or the guards would slay him out of hand. Gilhaelith continued moving the pointers exactly as before, and kept the geomantic globe turning gently underneath them on its cushion of freezing mist.

The pattern of the fields – for the node-within-a-node produced two fields here – came into view, slightly blurred in his enfeebled mind. He had to focus the fields, and then, right here in this most perfectly designed place in all the world, wake the sleeping construct that was Alcifer itself. If he could correctly align the geomantic globe to do that, he would have power to blast his enemies into oblivion, drag the thapter to himself and make good his escape in it.

The thapter's mechanism screamed, died away and screamed again as Tiaan tried desperately to escape. She was jumping from one field to another, trying to preserve her power, as Ryll took command of the fields. Her strategy had worked when she'd escaped from Alcifer the first time, almost a year ago, but it could not work now. Tiaan could not hope to defeat the power patterner in the hands of the lyrinx who had designed it.

Hurry! Gilhaelith told himself. If Ryll takes the thapter, or crashes it, all is lost. Gilhaelith ignored his own imperative. He must stay calm and, above all, be controlled. His mind was far less than it had been but his unquenchable will was as strong as ever. He could still do it. Focus. *Focus the field!*

Its grainy strands sharpened but then dissolved into a blur again. He could feel control slipping. With a supreme effort of will, Gilhaelith wrenched it back in place. The field came perfectly into focus and, the instant it did, he reached down to Alcifer's core that had lain sleeping for over a thousand years, waiting for a master who would never return.

Gilhaelith reached out and down, deeper and deeper, and suddenly there it was. It faded; then, without any warning, the faint nodes beneath the glass surface of the geomantic globe lit up.

Gilhaelith drew a deep breath and willed himself to calm as Ryll spun around, staring at the globe.

'What have you done?' Gilhaelith cried, to forestall Ryll and

561

make him wonder if he had done it himself, with the power patterner.

Ryll gave him a suspicious glance, withdrew one arm from the flisnadr and beckoned the watching lyrinx mancer over. The male came at a run, close enough to see into the bowl, then froze. The nodes were glowing more brightly than before, each according to its true nature. Now a slender thread of orange light began to extend from Alcifer's node-within-a-node to another node, a quarter of the way across the globe.

'Ah,' breathed Gilhaelith. Tiaan had previously told him that nodes could be linked. He'd thought a lot about that but had never been able to work out how. At last he began to understand. The thread had now touched the second node, and other threads began to extend out from it towards yet more distant nodes. If he could duplicate in the world what he'd done on the globe, could the power of all the nodes become available to him? His mind reeled with the possibilities – survival, even reversal of the brain damage after all? He didn't know – it was too much for anyone to take in.

'Step away from the globe,' snapped Ryll. 'Then don't move.'

Gilhaelith wasn't quite ready, but it had to be now. He could feel power flowing into the globe and he drew on it to strike his enemies down.

Something low down in the bowels of Alcifer throbbed; he heard a low grinding note. To his geomantic ear it sounded like basalt grating across obsidian. The nodes grew brighter, the threads of light raced between them and suddenly Gilhaelith woke to something that had happened to him a long time ago.

He began to feel the tiny, invisible thread that the amplimet had drawn to the back of his skull when he'd been working for the lyrinx in the tar tunnel in Snizort. He'd forgotten it during the escape, but now he could feel it tugging at him. Abruptly it also seemed to light up, a fiery pulse ran up it into the ethyr and then he felt – oh, horrible, horrible! He actually felt it – the sleeping amplimet in Tiaan's thapter was driven over the threshold to the second stage of awakening.

'No!' he cried aloud. 'Not that!' and hurled every iota of power

562

he could at the thread to sever it. He succeeded, but then the strangest thing happened.

All the lights went out, though it was daylight. The world and even the lyrinx faded to frozen translucency, and Gilhaelith *shifted*. Everything went dull and dim except the geomantic globe; the roused core of Alcifer, which now glowed a baleful red; and somewhere above, frozen in flight, a tiny winking gleam that was the woken amplimet.

He moved a hand. It appeared real, solid, though when he dropped it on the stone table it sank partway into it before enough resistance built up to stop it. Gilhaelith had been shifted outside the dimensions of the world. Or almost out.

Free, he exulted. I'm free.

First of all, he would make his escape from this accursed place. No, before anything, he must exact retribution on Gyrull, for holding him against his will and for refusing him what was rightfully his. Gilhaelith looked around and then down, tracing through the layers of Oellyll as if it were a translucent cake. The matriarch wouldn't be hard to find, even among so many lyrinx, for few held such power as she did. She would stand out among the lesser lyrinx like a ruby in a tray of grey glass.

Ah, there she was, deep down, in a secluded little chamber, frozen in the act of bending over what appeared to be a coffin. Gilhaelith looked more closely. It was one of the relics she'd retrieved from Snizort, and they were more valuable than the whole city of Snizort had been. Behind her, two other lyrinx, no more than grey shadows, had coffins on their shoulders. They were moving the relics. They must be evacuating Snizort.

Time to be going. Gilhaelith reached out and exerted his new-found power. It was easy here, outside the real world. With no more effort than the wiggling of a fingertip, he pulled down the roof of the tunnel in front of Gyrull, then collapsed it for a few hundred spans, to make sure she would never get out. You did everything for those relics, he thought, including kidnapping and enslaving me. Now you'll have what remains of your life to regret it.

The floor shook beneath him, reminding Gilhaelith that he

knew little about the power he was using, or what the consequences would be. A sharp pang struck him in the heart, and by the time he'd recovered from it, he was back in his body in the glass-domed chamber. All remained as it had been, except that Ryll was now moving in extreme slow-motion. Whatever power had *shifted* Gilhaelith outside of normal space and time was lapsing. Time and reality would soon resume.

Gilhaelith raised his hand and drew power to blast Ryll and the flisnadr to pulp, but that pain stabbed him in the chest again. He must have taken too much already. Revenge would have to wait. He picked up the globe and staggered with it out to the main door of the palace, then outside. By the time he reached the intersection of the boulevards, the world was almost as solid as it had ever been.

He looked up, thinking that he could at least use power to pull the thapter down to him, but whatever he'd woken in Alcifer's core slipped beyond his reach. One minute the thapter was frozen in the air above him, the next it had streaked away and vanished. Perhaps he'd taken the globe too far from the centre, but there was no time to think it through. He couldn't go back; the lyrinx would kill him on sight. Hefting the globe in his arms, Gilhaelith ran for the port, praying that there would be some kind of boat available when he got there. If he made it across the sea, Flydd would be most interested to hear about the power patterner. It gave him something to bargain with.

Ryll.

Ryll was frantically searching for Gilhaelith, who had inexplicably vanished from the glass-domed chamber. Now he stopped abruptly, for it had sounded like the matriarch speaking inside his head. Ryll had little talent for mindspeech – few but the strongest lyrinx did – but he had occasionally picked up fragments of the mindspeech of others, and knew what it was like. This was far stronger, for it came from the greatest mindspeaker of all.

Ryll, I know you can't answer me. Don't worry – I can tell you're hearing what I have to say. Alas, Gilhaelith is free and is now on his way across the sea to rejoin humankind. His knowledge of our flisnadr will strengthen them immeasurably, if we allow them time to understand it. The moment has come that we have long been dreading, but at least we're prepared for it, and we have the flisnadr at last. Humanity is strong; maybe stronger than we are. Only time and courage will tell.

Our cities are lost and, with winter coming, we've nowhere to go. We can't allow humanity to defeat us. No lyrinx could submit to the enslavement and degradation it visits on its unhuman enemies. We will die before we become caged beasts for their amusement. Liett was right. Now is the time for every one of us – woman, man and child – to go to war. We will have victory or annihilation! And you must lead us, Ryll.

'Matriarch,' he cried. 'What's going on? Where are you?'

Gilhaelith pulled the roof in on me. I'm trapped with two companions, and the relics. We're unharmed, and we have food and water, but it will take weeks to dig ourselves out, and nearly as long for anyone to tunnel in to us. The war cannot wait else the advantage of the flisnadr will be lost. You must take charge of it and go over the sea at once. Safeguard it at all costs, for it's the key to victory. Take it to our secret lair in the caves of Llurr, do the final tests and master it. Liett and the advance guard will carry you, and when the tests are done, get ready for the final battle.

'Matriarch, why me?'

It was as if she'd heard him. *I've prepared you well, Ryll. This is the first battle of the new lyrinx, and we need new leadership. If anyone can do it, you can. You will be well supported by Liett, and Great Anabyng, when he has time from his special duties, and all the others.*

Leave a detachment of volunteers here, to dig us out. When we get out – if we get out – and have taken the relics to safety, we will join you for the final battle. But if the disease claims us, someone else must retrieve and guard the relics. Should that happen, Anabyng has my orders for the succession.

Go at once, Ryll. There is much to be done. Farewell. I've already spoken to the other matriarchs and they're agreed that this is our only course.

565

'What about the children?' said Ryll. 'Surely you cannot think to take them to war?'

We have no home now, nowhere to shelter our young ones, and I will not leave them behind to the cruellest of all fates – enslavement and degradation by the old humans. Far kinder that they live or die with us. We'll shelter them to the end, but if the end comes, we will die together.

'Yes,' said Ryll. 'Better that we all die than exist only as their beasts or slaves.'

And so the entirety of our kind will go to war. That is the Matriarchal Edict and everyone will follow it – to victory or annihilation.

'Victory or annihilation,' he said with furious resolve, and turned to get ready for war.

FIFTY-EIGHT

They returned to Fiz Gorgo only to discover that Yggur, Flydd and the others had just gone to Lybing. Tiaan didn't follow immediately, for Irisis's leg was infected and needed a healer's attention. By the time they reached Lybing a week later, the news from the east coast was immeasurably worse. Attacking the underground cities had proven the most disastrous blunder of the war. The dispossessed lyrinx had gone to war and fought with unparalleled ferocity, annihilating the human army at Gosport. Less than fifteen thousand of its fifty thousand had survived, and none of them uninjured. The armies at Guffeons and Maksmord had capitulated after similarly bitter fighting that had reduced them to half their number in little more than a day.

Smaller armies, protecting human settlements all the way up and down the east coast, had suffered similar fates. Many towns had been overwhelmed, their people killed or forced to flee into the countryside where they would be easy targets. The walls of the principal cities, greatly reinforced over the past six months, now sheltered huge numbers of refugees but would soon be besieged. Of all the nations of the east only populous Crandor had managed to stay the lyrinx tide. Its armies had fought the attacking hordes to a standstill but Governor Zaeff held little hope. Roros and the other cities of Crandor would soon be islands in a sea of the enemy. With no possibility of outside aid, in the end even proud Roros, the greatest city in the world since Thurkad had been overrun, must fall.

The west had seen little action thus far, but regular flights over Almadin showed that the lyrinx hordes had crossed the Sea of Thurkad and were advancing ever closer. Battle was only days away, but this battle could not be won. The enemy were simply too many.

Tiaan's thapter landed on the lawn of the White Palace after dark and they went straight to conclave. It was an open meeting and the extravagantly over-decorated audience chamber was packed with people, standing in little groups waiting for the proceedings to begin. Few were talking. Everyone seemed too stunned.

Irisis had never seen such luxury as was displayed in the hall, though she paid little attention to it. It seemed like a sad folly that would soon be gone. She threaded her way through the groups, looking for Flydd. He was not up on the dais with Governor Nisbeth and the other dignitaries.

Painfully standing on tiptoe, she saw Yggur over in the far corner and headed for him. Flydd was standing beside him, talking to Klarm. They made the oddest of trios: tall, broad-shouldered Yggur, his ageless features as though frozen in ice; withered, scrawny little Flydd who barely came up to his chin; and handsome, unflappable Klarm, not even chest-high to the scrutator.

Flydd didn't look as though he'd eaten since they'd left Fiz Gorgo weeks ago. Bone and gristle were all there was left of him. He nodded as Irisis approached, with Nish and Tiaan close behind, but kept speaking.

'I promised our people in the east that if we all worked together we had a chance,' Flydd said bitterly. 'Then I took this ruinous gamble, and lost.'

'Not you alone,' said Klarm, twisting strands of his beard together. 'Our Council voted on the attack, as did the eastern governors, and to take the blame on yourself devalues everyone else.'

'I did my best to talk you into it,' said Flydd.

'You're an overly proud man, Flydd, for such a meagre one,' Yggur said waspishly. 'You know we didn't have a choice. We had to destroy the threat of the uggnatl and I believe we've done that.'

'We can't resist this tide,' said Flydd in anguish. 'All my life I've fought to save humanity. Now I've brought about its destruction.'

Irisis stopped a few steps away. She'd rarely seen Flydd in such a state. Nish and Tiaan pulled up behind her.

'Better we left the east to their own devices,' said Flydd, 'than raise hopes so savagely dashed. Not only is the east defeated, it feels betrayed.'

'It's not defeated until Crandor falls,' said Klarm, 'and that may take longer and cost more than the enemy are prepared to pay. There's steel in the hearts of the dark folk from Roros, and their fingers wield a blade cunningly.'

'I don't doubt it,' said Flydd more steadily, 'but it would take whole forests of steel to make up for the new –'

'Not *here*!' hissed Yggur, looking over his shoulder.

'What is it?' Irisis asked, lowering her voice. 'Have the enemy succeeded in making more node-drainers?'

'Later,' said Flydd.

Why was he holding back? What had the lyrinx come up with now?

'Have you asked the Stassor Aachim for help?' Irisis asked.

'We gave them farspeakers but they're not answering,' said Malien. 'How can my people have come to such a state?'

'They've been heading that way for a long time,' said Yggur. 'Withdrawing further and further from the world.'

'Then why take all the thapters from Snizort,' said Irisis, 'if they didn't intend to use them?'

'So no one could attack Stassor with them,' said Malien.

'What about Vithis and his great beam weapon?' Nish said. 'We could beg him for aid.'

'We've already begged,' said Klarm. 'Our embassy was fired on at the border.'

Yggur, who was looking up at the dais, said, 'We're called.' He turned to the three travellers and put out his hand. 'Let's not have this crisis overshadow your truly mammoth deeds. Well done, Tiaan, Nish and Irisis.'

'Too well done,' said Irisis. 'It would have been better if we'd died in the first attempt.' She fell in beside Nish, who was more silent than usual. They headed up to take their places. The silent crowd were already sitting down.

Tiaan did not follow them. 'I'll wait for you outside,' she said to Irisis. 'I don't think I can bear to hear what they're going to say.'

'We can't do anything to help the east,' said General Troist after the situation had been summed up to the silent gathering. 'Let's concentrate on what we can do for ourselves.'

'Not much,' said Yggur. 'The enemy's numbers are far greater than we had estimated, and in the east they've used their flesh-formed creatures to devastating effect. They released thousands of uggnatl, and other creatures like it, onto the battlefields. They had a lot more of them than we'd thought.' Yggur signed to an aide standing to the side, who held up the stuffed body of Flydd's uggnatl. Irisis could smell it from where she sat, a breath-catching odour of decay. 'The little beasts are so fast and agile that they're difficult to hit. They brought down our soldiers by attacking their legs, and once on the ground they had no chance.'

'We still have no defence against them,' Troist said heavily. 'Apart from leather leg armour, yet another burden for our overburdened troops.'

'Leg armour was tried in the east,' said the scrutator. 'The uggnatl simply went for the groin, the one thing most men fear more than death. So would I have, in my day.'

That drew a smile or two around the room, for Flydd was such an ugly, withered old coot that no one could imagine him at the business of procreation. Those who knew what had happened to him at the hands of Ghorr's torturers did not smile, however.

'What about mail or plate armour?' called a uniformed officer from the front row.

'It's too heavy,' said Troist. 'It slows our soldiers too much against the lyrinx. Thankfully the ones bred in Oellyll succumbed to the fungus, so *we* won't be facing them.'

'My council has long feared it would come to this,' said Governor Nisbeth, after a quiet word to her councillors. 'We made a plan for the end last spring. Now we must put it into effect. We won't send your brave men to certain death, General Troist. Our soldiers have been dying for more than a hundred years, and it has availed us naught. Our beautiful land must be abandoned, since it is undefendable. We will evacuate Borgistry to the last peasant and go east into the Borgis Woods. There are vast cave systems in the Peaks of Borg, as well as along Lake Parnggi and in the southern arm of the Great Mountains, beyond the lake. It's rugged, inhospitable country, but we know it well. Let the enemy pursue us there if they dare. In the caves, we'll maintain what's left of our civilisation for as long as we can endure.'

'Nobly spoken,' Flydd declared. 'Where's Grand Commander Orgestre?'

'Packing his bags and slipping out the window,' someone in the crowd said in a low voice. No one laughed.

Flydd scowled. 'What of your army, Troist?'

'We'll form a rearguard to shield the escape, then make our way east by paths suitable for clankers.' He paused. 'What a sorry day this is.'

There was another silence. No one wanted to break it.

A very tall man at the back of the room stood up and threw off his hood, and a mass of woolly hair sprang out in all directions. There was a stir around him. It was Gilhaelith. He began to walk up to the front, and such was his presence that no one said a word. He reached the foot of the dais and stopped.

'How the devil did you get in here?' said Yggur, rising to his feet. 'Guards –'

'Sit down, Yggur,' Flydd said wearily. 'Gilhaelith is the one man who might tell us something we don't know about our enemy.'

'He betrayed Fiz Gorgo,' Yggur said savagely, 'and I won't have a bar of him.'

'You imprisoned me for no other reason than that you disliked me,' said Gilhaelith, almost serenely. Not a trace of his previous bitterness was evident.

'I imprisoned you for dealing with the enemy.'

'And I merely did my best to escape.'

'Which showed Ghorr the way. Without him –'

'Enough!' grated Klarm, and they both fell silent. 'You came to our Council for a reason, Gilhaelith. What is it? Have you anything to offer humanity in its final hours, or are you here as an emissary for your lyrinx masters?'

'I barely escaped from Alcifer with my life,' said Gilhaelith. 'They planned to eat me once they'd finished with me.'

'How *did* you escape?' said Flydd, with an edge to his voice.

'Your attack with the spores threw them into confusion. I acted with dispatch and was lucky enough to spot an air-floater, which brought me here.'

'Hmn,' Flydd said, as if sifting his words for any grains of truth. 'What do you have to offer us in this emergency?'

'Information.'

'In exchange for what?'

'A place on the Council.'

'Not in my lifetime,' said Yggur.

'You declined to be on it,' Flydd snapped. 'You have no say.' He looked up at Gilhaelith. 'First you'll have to convince us to trust you and, considering your history . . .'

'Very well,' said Gilhaelith. 'I'll give you this freely, as a token of my good faith. The relics the lyrinx took from the tar pits of Snizort are most precious to them.'

'We already knew that, but go on,' said Flydd.

'They stole me away from Nyriandiol to locate the relics. Indeed, the only reason they built their city underground at Snizort, decades ago, was to find them, and they prolonged the battle for Snizort for a day, at the cost of thousands of lyrinx lives, just so they could get them safely to Alcifer.'

'Why do they value these relics? What can they possibly mean to the lyrinx?'

'I don't know, but the matriarch personally took charge of them when Alcifer was being evacuated. If you can seize the relics, the enemy would bargain with you to get them back.'

'Where are they now?' said Flydd.

'She was trapped with them when part of the underground city collapsed.'

'And yet the other lyrinx left Oellyll?' Flydd said doubtfully.

'The infection was spreading and they dared not stay. But the relics are safe and Gyrull is still alive. It will just take some digging to get them out.'

'You seem to know an awful lot about it.'

'Yes,' said Gilhaelith without elaboration.

'It's valuable information,' said Flydd, 'though I'm not about to risk an army digging under Alcifer. As soon as the lyrinx discovered we were there, they'd wipe us out. Do you have any information that can help us stave off the enemy? Considering your record, Gilhaelith, nothing else will do.'

Gilhaelith opened his mouth, but closed it again as if he'd thought better of it.

'Come on, man!' said Flydd. 'I know you assisted them to develop a more powerful device than their node-drainers.'

After a long, reluctant hesitation, Gilhaelith said in a low voice, 'I was forced to it, and this is for the ears of your Council only. They've grown a new device which they call a flisnadr, a power patterner. A device for *controlling* the flow of power from a field, rather than just shutting it off.'

'Have they now?' said Flydd. 'I've been thinking along those lines myself. We must talk more about this privately, Gilhaelith.' He put out his hand. 'Welcome aboard.'

The evacuation of Borgistry began at once, the people melting into the uncanny Borgis Woods. General Orgestre's army, the smaller, had gone with them, while Troist's force remained behind to guard the rear, in case the enemy came on more swiftly than expected. The Council and the governor were relocating to Hysse, a fertile valley surrounded by almost unclimbable ridges, between Parnggi and the Ramparts of Tacnah. Irisis was to go with them, along with Tiaan. Nish was to remain as Troist's adjutant for the time being, though he regretted it now. There was no saying he'd ever see any of his friends again.

Three days later, Tiaan, Nish and Irisis were standing by Malien's thapter while the last of the refugees assembled. Nish didn't know what to say to his friends. He'd rehearsed his farewells a dozen times but couldn't find any words that fitted such a desperate occasion. Irisis wasn't saying anything either, and Tiaan just bore the faraway look she'd had since seeing the piles of lyrinx dead.

Nish, recognising several familiar faces in the crowd, waved. It was Troist's tall horsy wife Yara and the twins, Meriwen and Liliwen, who would be fourteen now. He'd last seen them a year and a half ago at Morgadis. What must they be thinking after being forced to abandon all they'd held dear?

'How long have we got?' said Nish, wondering if there was time to say hello and farewell. The Council's thapter stood inside a ring of clankers, the army camp was packed up, the latrines filled in and everyone was waiting for the order to depart.

No one answered, so Nish went across, a little tentatively. The twins sang out and ran to meet him. Yara didn't run, but her face lit up at seeing Nish. He shook her hand and embraced the twins, sturdy girls who took after their handsome father. Their wavy hair, the colour of copper wire, hung in plaits halfway down their backs. They were almost identical, though Liliwen had thicker, darker eyebrows.

'We're very cross with you,' said Meriwen. 'You were supposed to come and see us in Lybing last spring, before the battle.'

'Extremely cross,' said Liliwen. 'We cooked dinner and everything.'

'I'm sorry,' said Nish. 'I was called away. You know what it's —'

'We think you ran away from Aunty Mira,' said Meriwen, frowning at him.

'Because you were too scared,' said Liliwen.

'Like you did last time,' added Meriwen. 'With your pants –'

'Girls!' cried Yara, scandalised. 'How dare you speak to Cryl-Nish like that. He's a great hero and he saved your lives. Twice!'

'It's a funny kind of hero that runs away from little Aunty Mira,' sniffed Meriwen, then giggled.

'With his pants down around his –' chortled Liliwen.

'Right!' said Yara. 'I'm going to wash both your mouths out, and don't think you're too old to get a good whack on the bare backside, either.'

They sobered up instantly. 'Sorry, Mother,' they chorused. 'But please, please let us stay. After all, Nish did save our lives, *twice*, and we might never see him again!'

'Don't flutter your eyelashes at me, young ladies,' said Yara. 'Wherever did you learn such tricks? Your father will be horrified when I tell him. Now come away. Mira has something to say to Nish.'

And before Nish could turn and run, Mira stepped out of the crowd, right beside him.

'M-Mira!' he stammered. 'I – I –'

She took his hand. 'Nish, why didn't you come to see me?'

'I was too scared; too mortified . . .'

'But why? You did nothing wrong. We were just two lonely, unhappy people, taking comfort where we could, until I had too much to drink and my nightmares overturned everything.'

'But . . . the guards . . .'

'It was all a terrible misunderstanding. I'd called them back and explained before you even reached the river.'

'They weren't hunting me at all?' said Nish.

'Of course not. I was terrified you'd drown. They were trying to bring you back, as an honoured guest who'd saved my nieces from degradation and murder.'

'And all this time, I've been living in fear of you,' said Nish. 'And not just from that night. Whenever I did the . . . business of war, I imagined how disgusted you'd be.'

She sighed and took his hand. 'You met me at my lowest point, Nish. War is a horror, but do you think I don't honour my man, and my sons, for the way they fought and died? Of course I do. I hated the old warmongering Council with all my heart, but I respect the brave men and women who fight and die for us. And I honour you, too.' She kissed him on the forehead. 'Go now, they're calling for you. And go with good heart. We'll all be thinking of you.'

Nish turned away, turned back and waved, then strode to the thapter feeling better than he had in a long time.

Klarm, who had just returned from a surveillance flight in one of the thapters, came waddling up. 'The enemy are two days away to the west, streaming through the forest. And another lyrinx army, almost as large, draws near to The Elbow from the south, heading up the Westway.'

'Then we'd better get moving,' said Troist. After making sure the refugees were well away, he was planning to retreat up the Great North Road through Worm Wood, then east, since the Borgis Woods were too rugged for his clankers. 'If they send a sizeable force across Worm Wood by Booreah Ngurle, as they did last spring, we'll be cut off.'

Nish embraced Tiaan, then Irisis, who thumped him on the shoulder and turned away abruptly. She practically ran to the thapter and got in without looking back. Tiaan didn't even say goodbye – she seemed in another world altogether.

It wasn't until the thapter had lifted off that Nish realised what he wanted to say to them, but by then it was too late.

FIFTY-NINE

Hysse was a small, pretty but incredibly overcrowded town at the top of a green valley surrounded by knife-edged ridges. All of its homes and buildings were built from silver weathered timber, with steep, pointed shingle roofs and green painted doors and window sashes. There were flower gardens everywhere, though many had been trampled by the deluge of refugees from Borgistry.

Tiaan set the thapter down in the market square, opened the hatch and was assailed by the overpowering perfume of night hyssamin, for which the town had been named. She was breathing deep when Flydd came running up, with Yggur not far behind. The sun was just rising.

'Don't get out, Tiaan,' panted Flydd. 'We're going north right away.'

'Where?' said Tiaan, who had one leg over the side. She rubbed her eyes. They'd stopped in the middle of the night for a few hours' sleep but she was still tired.

'I'll tell you after we've gone. I've had an idea.'

She couldn't resist saying, 'I hope it's better than the last one.'

A pair of soldiers laboured up, carrying something heavy in a small wooden crate. A second pair followed with a larger crate, while a third were directed to another thapter, standing across the square next to a stall proclaiming the merits of yellow quinces, hard green pears and other mid-autumn fruit. Tiaan's mouth watered, but none of the stalls were open yet.

'Come on, Fyn-Mah!' Flydd roared over the side. 'Yggur, Irisis, go with Chissmoul in her thapter.'

'Where?' said Irisis, getting out gingerly. Her ankle and leg still troubled her.

'East. I'll call you on the farspeaker. Just go.'

Yggur and Irisis clambered into Chissmoul's thapter, which shot into the air as if booted by a giant, to disappear eastward towards the Great Mountains.

'That pilot has a distinctly reckless streak,' Flydd observed. 'Malien, would you take the controller, please? I need Tiaan to do something on the way.'

'But . . .' said Tiaan.

'Come on!' snapped Flydd. 'We don't have any time to waste.'

'Where to?' said Malien, as Fyn-Mah climbed in, carrying a heavy bag, and went below.

'We need to find a powerful node that isn't being used by anyone. Tiaan, where's the nearest one that fits?'

Tiaan thought for a moment. 'At the southern end of Warde Yallock.'

'Perfect,' said Flydd.

'What is your idea?' Tiaan asked when they were among scattered fluffy clouds.

'Actually, it was yours,' said Flydd. 'I'm going to test your idea about speaking back and forth between connected nodes. Before we get to Warde Yallock I want you to try something. First, to make a map in your head of all the nodes in this area, plus all those you know to be connected in some way.'

'I've been doing that for ages.'

'I thought you might be. Do you know of any nodes connected to the one we're heading for?'

She closed her eyes, mentally rotating her network of node symbols, field colours and interconnecting lines. It took some minutes before she was sure. 'There should be one at the foot of the Ramparts of Tacnah.'

578

'Where abouts?'

Tiaan showed Flydd on the map.

'That's eighty leagues from where we're headed. Isn't there anything nearer?'

'Probably, but without studying every node I wouldn't know.'

Flydd set up Golias's globe and called Irisis. 'Tell Chissmoul to fly to the Ramparts of Tacnah.' He gave instructions. 'Call on your farspeaker when you're in place.'

Malien veered to the left to pass over a mass of lyrinx, assembled near a lake beyond the forest. Flydd counted the enemy numbers, then called Troist and gave their position.

Once they were in place at the southern end of Warde Yallock, late that afternoon, Flydd dragged the crate into the shelter of a tilted plate of rock, one of a group of ancient standing stones dating from the dawn of civilisation on Santhenar, and prised the smaller crate open. Tiaan yawned as she looked inside. It contained a complex device made of green crystals linked into an open sphere with thick wafers of beaten platinum, silver, gold and copper foil.

'It's my version of the node-drainer that we encountered in Snizort,' said Flydd. 'Yggur and I have been working on it, on and off, for months. Irisis and Yggur have another. They'll call when they're ready.'

He lay down under the tree, tipped his hat over his eyes to keep out the sinking sun, and began to snore.

'You might have told me what I'm supposed to do,' muttered Tiaan.

'He likes to be mysterious,' said Fyn-Mah. 'Get some rest. You look exhausted.'

'I haven't slept well since we attacked Oellyll, but I won't be able to sleep until I know what I'm meant to do.'

'As I understand it, you're to send messages, using Golias's globe, to Irisis. She'll send back while we watch how weak or strong the messages are, how much delayed, and so forth. Afterwards we'll set the node-drainer to draw power from this node and send again. We'll take ever more power, and do it over

579

and over, while Irisis and Yggur will be doing the same at the linked node.'

'To what purpose?' said Tiaan.

'We hope to discover *how* the fields, or the nodes, are linked. If we can solve that problem it might just give us a chance.'

Flydd woke Tiaan in the middle of the night and she sat with Golias's globe on a flat rock, waiting, listening and sending, until dawn. The globe squelched periodically, conveying reports of lyrinx sightings all over the place, attacks in various spots, and details of the movements of the refugees and their escorts. Troist's army had taken heavy casualties before beating off their ambushers, and the report was gruesomely graphic. Tiaan's resolve to find a peaceful solution grew stronger.

They began again a few hours after dawn, though she could sense Flydd's frustration now. He didn't seem to be getting anywhere. Her head was aching from overuse of the amplimet and she was well aware of *that* danger.

'I'll have to stop,' she said not long before sunset. 'My head is killing me.'

'If we can do just one more test,' said Flydd, 'it will complete this set and we'll be finished for the day. Can you manage it?'

'I suppose so,' Tiaan sighed, knowing that Flydd would keep pushing until he got what he wanted.

'Do you want me to increase the draining?' asked Fyn-Mah, who was wearing an operator's wire-and-crystal cap, with her hands inside Flydd's node-drainer.

'Leave it as it is,' said Flydd. 'We'll send the message on another farspeaker setting.'

He told Tiaan what it was and she relayed that to Irisis.

'Ready, Tiaan?' said Flydd.

'As long as it doesn't take too long,' she whispered. 'I don't feel very well.'

'Why don't I send the message?' said Flydd. 'Can you set the globe for me first? You're a lot quicker at it than I am.'

'All right.' Tiaan slipped the amplimet down her front. It felt hot. She put her hands around the smooth surface of the farspeaker and mentally spun the globes to visualise what to do with her hands. Her head felt fuzzy and she couldn't recall the setting she was supposed to use.

She did it again but a different setting flashed into her mind, one far removed from any she'd ever used before. She turned to Flydd but he'd gone across to Fyn-Mah and had his arms deep in the node-drainer.

She tried to concentrate but could only see the new setting, not the one Flydd had given her. But then, what did it matter as long as Irisis's farspeaker was set the same? She didn't relay the new setting to Irisis – it was easier to change Irisis's farspeaker the way she'd reset Flydd's from Bannador a while ago.

Then, without thinking that Golias's globe was self-powered, Tiaan drew power through the amplimet, spun the spheres and stopped them one by one until they lined up correctly. As the innermost sphere slowed and stopped, the amplimet flared. Its light shone through her blouse and the crystal grew so bright that it burned her and she had to jerk it out.

The node-drainer let out a loud crackling squeal.

'What's that?' cried Flydd, whipping his hands out as if they were on fire. 'What's happening?'

He ran to Tiaan, shielding his eyes. 'Tiaan?'

She blinked, shook her head then closed her fist around the amplimet. She cut off power and the sound from the node-drainer stopped abruptly.

'What are you doing?' Irisis roared from the farspeaker.

Flydd went still, turned to Malien, eyes wide, then back to the farspeaker. 'What just happened, Irisis?'

'The node flared out of control. The field was twenty times as strong as before. I could see it with my eyes open.'

'But that's not possible,' said Flydd. 'It was stronger *here* too.'

'What did you do?' Tiaan heard Yggur say, hoarsely. He sounded uneasy.

'Tiaan did something with Golias's globe, and the amplimet.' Flydd turned to her. 'What did you do, Tiaan?'

She explained as best she could. 'Is something the matter?'

'I think,' said Yggur over the farspeaker, 'you've stumbled on

581

a way to control the nodes themselves.' The unease was gone; he let out an uncharacteristic whoop. 'It's a secret no mancer ever expected to find. Do you see the implications, Flydd?'

'I'm beginning to see the perils,' said Malien.

'If we *can* control the nodes,' said Flydd, 'we can snatch power from the lyrinx while maintaining it for ourselves, despite their power patterner. We'd have as much power as we wanted, and they'd have none. *Then* we'd take the battle to them.'

'As long as they don't get it first,' said Tiaan. 'I've seen a pair of nodes acting that way before, now that I think of it. It was in Alcifer, not long before Oellyll was abandoned.'

'So the enemy may also be closing in on the secret,' said Yggur. 'And it may not be such a large step for them, since they've had node-drainers for years.'

Flydd scowled. 'Just when I thought we'd made a breakthrough.'

'We may have, but it's a race,' said Yggur. 'To the winner, ultimate power. To the losers, oblivion.'

That's all you mancers ever think of, Tiaan thought despairingly. She wanted to run away with the secret and deny it to all of them. But of course she could not – that would be playing into the hands of the enemy. Surely there had to be another way.

'Let's not get ahead of ourselves,' said Flydd. 'How are you feeling, Tiaan?'

'A little better.' She wasn't, but she might as well get it over with.

'Are you up to showing us exactly what you did?'

'I think so.'

Tiaan did it a second time. The node-drainer and the amplimet reacted exactly as before, and the effects were felt, as before, at Irisis's end.

'What else do we need, to control nodes?' said Yggur through the farspeaker, once all was quiet again.

'Two things,' said Flydd. 'Firstly, a completed map of the fields, including the Dry Sea, which Tiaan hasn't even looked at. Tiaan, I think you and Malien had better get that done right away.'

'I'd prefer to be asked,' Malien said frostily. 'I'm an ally, not a lackey, as I believe I've pointed out to you before.'

'I'm sorry,' said Flydd. 'I forgot myself. Malien –'

'Certainly I'll do it,' she said. 'Tiaan, what about you?'

Tiaan had to be asked twice, for her mind had wandered a long way as she worked through the possibilities of this unexpected discovery. 'Yes,' she said absently. 'I'd be glad to survey the Dry Sea.'

'Irisis, Yggur,' Flydd called on the farspeaker. 'Pack up and meet us at the southern end of Warde Yallock.' He gave directions. 'Tiaan, go to bed before you collapse. We'll talk in the morning.'

'What's the second thing we need?' said Yggur.

'A field controller. It's a device I've been thinking about ever since Klarm and I went through the Council's secret workrooms in Nennifer. Ghorr's best mancers and artisans began working on a field controller as soon as they finished making the nodebreaker we took to Snizort. They built a rude prototype, though they could never get it to work. Klarm brought it back in the dirigible and I've also fiddled with it over the summer. It's in the other crate.'

'But you couldn't get it to work either,' said Yggur.

'No, but Gilhaelith, unwittingly, gave me some fresh ideas when he was telling me about the power patterner. Tiaan's discovery might be the missing piece of the puzzle. As soon as you get here, we'll go over everything. Are you there, Irisis?'

'Where else would I be?' she said.

'I want you and Tiaan to pull apart the failed field controller and work out how to rebuild it to make use of Tiaan's discovery. Just throw it together anyhow, for the time being. Tiaan can help with the initial tests, then be on her way to the Dry Sea.'

'And me?' said Irisis.

'If the tests work, I'll give you as many artisans as you need. You've got to produce a reliable field controller and you haven't got long. It'll be the challenge of your life.'

'It's for all our lives,' said Yggur.

SIXTY

Nish watched his friends fly away, unable to speak.
Once the last refugees reported that they'd met Orgestre's army and no longer needed Troist's protection, his infantry and its escort of clankers set off up the Great North Road, which here ran north-west. Worm Wood was about twenty leagues away, the edge of the forest curving east until it ran into the northern extremity of the Borgis Woods, a forest just as dark and tangled, and with a more dubious reputation, than Worm Wood itself. The road ran through the forest for twenty leagues, then beside it and the lands between the Great Chain of Lakes, before finally passing into the flat drylands to the north. In all, the army had to cross more than forty leagues of rugged country, ripe for ambushing, before they reached the relative security of the plains of Tacnah. Nish knew they would be lucky to get that far.

'Nish,' said Gilhaelith as they camped on the fringe of the forest, 'you're a resourceful fellow. Come with me.'

Nish wondered why Gilhaelith had remained behind with the rearguard instead of flying to safety with the Council. Was it because Yggur was so hostile to him? Whatever the reason, Troist wasn't bothered about it. He'd invited Gilhaelith to travel with him in his twelve-legged command clanker, often consulting him about the lyrinx's mancery and how they might use it to hinder the army's progress.

Nish followed the woolly-headed mancer down through the rows of tents and clankers to a larger tent, guarded by two soldiers, set in an isolated spot under the trees. They went inside. It was dark apart from a glowing globe with a bowl of smoked glass over the top, reducing the light to a glimmer. A folding table had been set up in the middle. Merryl sat on one side, a writing tablet before him, a pen in his hand. A young, dark-haired woman on the other side of the table had her hands around a master farspeaker whose interior globes were spinning. Her head was bent so far that Nish couldn't see her face, only a long, pointed nose.

Nish turned to Gilhaelith but he put a finger across his lips. 'Later.'

Nothing happened for some minutes, when there came a whisper from the farspeaker. The dark young woman froze the globes. Again the whisper. Merryl wrote something on his pad. They waited. Eventually, another whisper. Another wait, interminable this time.

'All right,' said Gilhaelith after more than an hour had passed. 'Take a break.'

They went outside. 'You're spying on the lyrinx,' said Nish.

Gilhaelith raised an interrogative eyebrow.

'Merryl's the only one who speaks their language,' he added.

'Very good, artificer.'

Nish had an uncomfortable feeling that the mancer was laughing at him. He'd never worked Gilhaelith out; he did not fit any of the kinds of people Nish had met before.

'Daesmie,' Gilhaelith indicated the young woman through the tent flap, 'has a talent akin to Tiaan's, though undeveloped by comparison. She was only discovered recently – one of many projects the Council has going behind the scenes, Flydd tells me. Daesmie is able to sense lyrinx mindspeech and tune the master farspeaker to pull it out of the ethyr. There's one problem, of course.'

'There are half a million lyrinx,' said Nish, 'and they'd be using mindspeech all the time. How can you pick out what's important in all that racket?'

'On the contrary, few lyrinx have the talent and it's exhausting to use. They employ it on the battlefield, or to signal danger or cry for help, so everything they say is of interest to us. And only the most powerful lyrinx can call for long distances, so if the lesser ones are mindspeaking further away, we don't hear it.'

'So what's the problem?'

'They seldom identify themselves or where they are. It limits the usefulness of spying on them.'

'Have you learned anything interesting yet?'

'Indeed. Twice we've had warning of attacks before they occurred. Only a minute or two, but it makes a difference. The attack this morning would have cut the army in half if I hadn't alerted Troist to it.'

Nish had wondered why Troist seemed so happy with Gilhaelith. 'So what do you want me to do?'

'Read everything Merryl and the other listeners write down.'

'What others?'

'There are five tents down here, all listening on different globe settings. Merryl has taught the listeners the most common words of the lyrinx language, and each listener is recording pages of messages every hour. I don't have the time to read it all, so you can do it for me.'

'I'm Troist's adjutant, surr, and I've a lot to do.'

'And he's made you over to me for the time being.'

'Really?' said Nish, unconvinced.

'Go and ask him,' said Gilhaelith. 'The work I'm doing is vital to the survival of this army.'

'All right,' said Nish. 'I'll take your word for it.'

'Excellent. If you see something strange, or something you don't understand, call me.'

Gilhaelith hurried away. 'But what are you looking for?' Nish called.

'Something they don't want us to know,' Gilhaelith said over his shoulder.

The next day was tedious and long. Nish sat in the tent, listening to the whispers in the background, which meant nothing to him, and reading though the pages as Merryl handed them to him. They were just a series of words, with annotations by Merryl, that did not make much sense.

Great Lake (scratchy voice)

Dawn! Dawn! (hoarse voice)

Too late.

Humans.

Fly west to the . . . (unintelligible. ?Burning Mountain)

(long pause)

Fire? (hoarse voice)

(short pause)

Node failing. Node failing. Node fai – (powerful voice. female. ?a matriarch)

What node? (scratchy voice)

Where are you? (hoarse voice)

(burst of unintelligible chatter, many voices at once, then a long pause)

Dawn? (hoarse voice)

Dawn! (scratchy voice)

Nish puzzled over the exchange. Were they planning an attack in the morning, as the army passed by a smaller lake between the two largest of the Great Chain of Lakes? Did it involve fire, or was that a completely separate remark? He scribbled two notes and sent them with the waiting runner to Troist and Gilhaelith. Let them agonise over it.

His pages were piling up. He wondered about the other cry – about the node failing – but not for long. Node failures were increasingly common these days. He made a note on his summary sheet and got on with his work.

Rubbing sore eyes, Nish shuffled his papers and stacked them in the pile. He'd been reading for eighteen hours without a break and every time he shifted his head vertigo made him feel as though he was falling off his seat. It had been hard enough in the tent, for one recorder's writing could have been made by a

587

spider crawling out of an inkwell, and another's was so tiny Nish had to squint to read it. In a jouncing, rattling clanker on a winding mountain road it was almost impossible. He prayed that the column would stop soon. He was desperate for sleep but would be lucky to get an hour. Even here, the pages were coming in faster than he could read them.

He had dozed off, in spite of the vibration, when the clanker stopped suddenly. There were shouts and screams outside, while a red glow lit up the sky ahead. The operator thrust up the top hatch, shouting to the shooter.

'What is it, shooter? Are we under attack?'

The shooter did not answer at once. The threaded rods of his javelard whirred and the mechanism creaked as he turned it this way and that.

'There's a big fire up ahead,' he said.

Nish reached for the rear hatch but Merryl put a hand on his shoulder. 'Remember what Gilhaelith said. We're to keep away from the fighting unless our lives are directly threatened.'

'I can't hide while soldiers are dying.'

'Their job is to fight, and if necessary to die. Ours is to do this work which may save many lives.'

Nish slid back into his seat. 'What's going on?' he said softly, with a glance at the farspeaker operator. Daesmie was asleep, her head pillowed on her small hands. She looked like a child. 'What's Gilhaelith really looking for?'

'I don't know.'

A roar echoed down the road from up ahead and flames billowed into the sky. The clanker's shooter cried out in terror. Nish felt the wash of heat through the front porthole, until the operator lurched his clanker forward, sideways and around. The clanker ahead of them was covered in what looked like burning pitch. Nish could hear the agonised screams of those trapped inside.

'Stop!' he cried. 'We've got to get them out!'

The clanker kept going. 'I have my orders, surr,' said the operator.

Nish wrestled with the handle of the rear hatch but Merryl

caught him by the arm. 'There's nothing you can do, Nish. Their rear hatch is covered in burning pitch; you'd never get it open.'

The sounds, and the smell, lingered long in Nish's nostrils. It reminded him of that awful night in the slave team at Snizort, when he'd salivated over the smell of the burning dead.

'That was a timely warning,' Gilhaelith said later that night, when the army had found a safe camp. 'Troist asked me to personally thank each of you. It saved countless lives.'

Nish nodded absently, his mind still on the horrors of the attack, which had gone on for an hour before the enemy had silently withdrawn. 'Did we lose many?'

'Hundreds,' said Gilhaelith. 'But it could easily have been thousands. Now, back to work.'

Two days later, in the sunken lands between the two great lakes, Nish was again in Merryl's tent, completing his summary of the day's listening, when he heard a shouted message. It had an urgency he'd not heard from the lyrinx before.

Thyllix musrr. Ing! Ing!

Merryl sat up, cocking his ear at the farspeaker. His hand was scribbling furiously.

Nish knew the word 'Ing'. It was a cry for help. 'What –?' he began, but broke off. He could not afford to distract Merryl.

Thyllix musrr. Ing! Ing!

Nish moved around behind Merryl so he could read the words over his shoulder.

Skin bursting. Help! Help! (powerful voice, female. ? a matriarch)

Dark-haired, demure little Daesmie swore an oath so vile that not even Nish would have used it in public, and spun the globes. 'Lost it,' she said.

Nish resisted the urge to yell at her to get it back. She was doing her best. Anything that troubled a lyrinx matriarch was of interest to them. There were only six as far as he knew; one for each of their cities.

'Skin bursting?' he said. 'Does that mean the spore disease?'

'I'd say so,' said Merryl. 'There have been cries about it

589

before. But this is different. If it's affected a matriarch...' He trailed off, deep in thought.

The globes froze in place. 'I think I have it,' said Daesmie. *Help. Save the Sacred Ones. This ... Matriarch Gyrull.*

'Get Gilhaelith,' snapped Merryl.

Nish did not move.

Where? (female, whispery voice)

Where? (female, raspy voice)

Where? (male, deep, rolls his r's)

'Now, Nish!'

Nish hesitated, wanting to know what they were going to say next. He ran out and around each of the other listeners. Gilhaelith was not with them. As Nish turned back, intending to look for him at the command tent, he ran past Merryl's tent and now heard Gilhaelith's voice inside.

The mancer was positively glowing. 'This is it. Gather your gear,' he said to Merryl and Daesmie. 'Bring all the record sheets. Meet me by the thapter in five minutes. You too, Nish.' He disappeared.

Nish looked down at the sheet. Nothing further had been written on it. 'What is it?' he whispered.

'I can't tell you, Nish.' Merryl stuffed the papers in his pack and hurried out.

Daesmie was doing the same with the globe and the rest of her apparatus. Nish put the paper down, hoisted his pack and headed for Kimli's thapter, which stood behind the command tent. It had come in only an hour ago, after studying the enemy's movements from the air.

When he arrived, the others were already inside. He passed up his pack and was just climbing over the side when Troist came running around the tent. He had Nish's sheet in his hand.

'Hey? What are you doing?' Troist cried.

'Go, Kimli,' Gilhaelith hissed, heaving Nish in.

She hesitated. 'But he's the general, surr.'

'And I'm your superior and a mancer of dreadful power. Do as I say!'

'Guards!' roared Troist.

'Now!' Gilhaelith screamed in her face.

Kimli's arm jerked on the flight knob and the thapter leapt in the air. The guards came running, arming their crossbows, but by the time they took aim it was too late. The thapter was out of range.

'Go north until we're out of sight,' said Gilhaelith, 'then sweep around to the west.'

'Where are we going?' she quavered.

'First to Nyriandiol, my former fortress atop Booreah Ngurle, if anything remains of it. And then, we shall see. Go swiftly.'

Four soldiers were sitting down below. Flangers was one of them. Nish sat beside him. 'What's going on?'

'No idea,' said Flangers. 'I'm just doing what I'm told.'

He looked unhappy but did not seem inclined to talk so Nish sat in a corner, closed his tired eyes and tried to work out what the geomancer was up to, and what he, Nish, should do about it. Clearly, Gilhaelith was following his own private agenda. Equally clearly, he was on to something important and, even if Troist wasn't aware of it, it might have been sanctioned by Flydd or Yggur. Well, probably not Yggur. Nish decided to keep his eyes and ears open and follow Gilhaelith's orders, for the time being . . .

He woke as they set down on the mountaintop. Outside, he looked around curiously. Booreah Ngurle was often mentioned in the Histories. It had been an important site two thousand years ago, though Nish could not remember why.

It was mid-morning. The mountain's crest was wreathed in steam and fumes which had a yellow cast and a sulphurous stench. Gilhaelith had made a fortune mining condensed sulphur from the floor of the crater.

Nish looked over the side. Not even the foolhardiest miner would have gone down there now. The crater lake was boiling, while up the other end red lava forced itself from a vent, surrounded by roiling black smoke and punctuated by small explosions that filled the air with wheeling, red-hot lumps of rock. The ground shook and grey ash filtered from the sky. His shoulders were already coated with it.

'This is the end for the mountain,' said Gilhaelith, leaning on a stone wall to look over the edge. 'It won't be long now.'

'Then hadn't we better do what you came for and get away?' said Nish.

'Humour me, Nish. I lived here a hundred and fifty years, all that time wondering when Booreah Ngurle would finally blow itself apart. The mountain is like an old friend to me, and I have to say goodbye.'

'Why are we here?'

Gilhaelith roused. 'Ah, yes. Because I left something here which will help us to find the matriarch, and more importantly, what she has with her. Kimli, Nish, come with me. The rest of you, stay with the thapter. We won't be long. Keep a sharp look-out.'

He laid his hands on the broken front doors, which had been rudely but strongly reinforced with iron bands, and they unlocked. Gritty hinges squealed when he pulled the door open. Nish followed him and Kimli fell in beside Nish. No doubt Gilhaelith wanted her along in case she couldn't be forced to fly the thapter away.

They headed down a long hall thick with dust and ash which long ago had been scalloped into ripples by the wind. There were no tracks apart from one set of boot marks going in and another back out, and the occasional trail made by a lizard's tail. The boot marks were Gilhaelith's. So he'd been back here after escaping from Alcifer.

'The earth has been my science and my Art, for all my adult life,' said Gilhaelith, his long strides puffing up ash at toe and heel. 'If I am to leave here forever, there's one small thing I have to take with me.'

They went down several floors. Nish was amazed at the wealth of the place, and the austere beauty. Both his father and mother had been wealthy but they'd possessed nothing like Nyriandiol. Even more amazing, it had not been looted. Perhaps Gilhaelith's reputation was too uncanny.

Gilhaelith opened a door into a dark room, touched a quartz

sphere above the door and soft light spread out. The room was empty except for a sphere, about half a span across, turning slowly in a metal bowl on a round wooden base set with brass graduated rings and pointers that could be slid around them.

'This,' said the mancer.

'Not so small,' said Nish. It appeared to be a model of Santhenar. The side facing them showed Lauralin and the ocean to the east, and part of another land, beyond the equator to the north. He walked around it, studying the islands and continents. 'I've often wondered what was beyond those seas.'

'So did I, Nish,' said the mancer. 'All my life I've wondered, and now I know.'

'It must have taken you a long time,' said Nish.

'Half a lifetime. I completed it only recently, in Alcifer, with the aid of the lyrinx. They'd flown the entire world in their early days here, mapping it on charts made from tanned human skin.'

'How did you get away?'

'The globe can be used for more than I told them. At an early stage I tapped into their sentinels and discovered what they had planned for me – among other things.

'I'd given up hope of escape when fate took a hand. You, Tiaan and Irisis attacked Alcifer with the fungus spores. A clever idea – I never would have thought of it, but nothing could have been more cunningly designed to panic them. On the night of your attack, their watch relaxed, I used the globe to conceal myself from their sentinels and walked out of Alcifer to the port. I'd left a boat there when I came from Fiz Gorgo, and I sailed it across the sea. Once in Taltid I signalled a passing air-floater and convinced them to bring me and the globe here. I left it here for safekeeping and they flew me down to Lybing in time for the conclave.'

The holes in his story gaped as wide as the front door, but Nish didn't question Gilhaelith further. He took a closer look at the globe.

It was exquisite. The surface appeared to be a kind of glass, and although the mountains were raised in relief, they were below the surface, which was smooth and so cold that when Nish touched it with a finger, his skin stuck to the glass and had to be eased off.

'Don't touch,' said Gilhaelith. 'There could be . . . unexpected consequences.' He drew on a pair of silken gloves and traced a fingertip across the surface, which had hardly any dust on it. 'It's my life's work.'

'Surely not?' said Nish. A skilled artisan, such as Irisis, could have made it in a few months.

'It's more than it seems,' Gilhaelith said mildly. 'This is not just a globe, Nish. It's a geomancer's model of the world, meaning that each part of the model corresponds to a part of the world. Had I power enough, I could change the world, within limits, by changing the model.'

'Is that why you want it?' asked the pilot in a meek little voice.

'No, Kimli. I've never sought to change the world, merely to understand it. But I have a different purpose today. That call Daesmie picked up was from Matriarch Gyrull, one of the six matriarchs, and pre-eminent among them on the rare occasions when a supreme leader is required, as at the moment. She must have escaped from the collapsed tunnels in Oellyll, but the infection has taken hold. She'll soon be incapacitated, if she's not already.'

'That must be the bitterest of blows to them,' said Nish.

'Not in the sense that we value a leader. The moment Gyrull became matriarch, she would have begun training successors. It's what she's bearing that's important.'

'What are the Sacred Ones?' said Nish. 'Her children?'

'The cultural relics of the lyrinx.'

'I didn't know they had any culture.'

'They gave up their ancient culture in their struggle to exist in the void. That's why the relics found in the Great Seep are so important. They'll do anything to protect them. The matriarch must have been ferrying the relics to a safe place, far away, but was struck down by the disease. Perhaps her escort is similarly afflicted; they're calling for help and we have the chance I never imagined would come.'

'Where is she?'

'I don't know.' He held up his hand as Nish began to speak. 'But my geomantic globe may tell me.'

'How?'

'If you keep quiet, you'll find out. Stay here.'

He was only gone a few minutes, returning carrying a small timber box which he set on the table. Inside were many lemon-yellow crystals, pyramidal on each end.

'Brimstone, or sulphur,' said Gilhaelith. 'Don't touch them.'

'Why not?'

Irritated, Gilhaelith picked out the smallest and placed it in the palm of Nish's hand. It lay there for a few seconds; then, with a crackling sound, shattered to pieces. 'That's why. Just the warmth of a human hand can fracture them. But if one is careful . . .'

With gloved fingers he stroked another crystal, faster and faster, then held it out between forefinger and thumb. He passed it back and forth over the surface of the globe, without ever touching it, sweeping a series of closely spaced lines from the Sea of Thurkad to the curve of the Great Mountains. Gilhaelith began in the south, at the shores of the Karama Malama, and continued north, every so often stopping to rub the crystal vigorously.

Nish didn't question him. Gilhaelith's attention was focussed on the surface of the globe. Nish did the same. Finally, as the lines swept across the drylands of the Tacnah Marches, between the City of the Bargemen and the Ramparts of Tacnah, a tiny lemon-yellow light winked through the surface.

Gilhaelith thrust the box of brimstone crystals in his pocket and gave him a triumphant look. 'That's where they are.'

'How do you know. What was all that about?'

'Like calls to like, Nish. Among the relics is a large crystal, and some smaller ones. The larger one is known as The Brimstone. My crystal called and The Brimstone answered.' Gilhaelith gathered the geomantic globe up. 'Bring that crate over, would you?'

Nish lugged the box across. Gilhaelith nestled the globe inside, carefully protected in folds of indigo velvet, packed the turned base, put down the top, took one of the rope handles and signed to Nish to take the other. They carried the crate out to the thapter.

'I know one should never become sentimental about material things,' said Gilhaelith, 'but I spent the most contented years of my life here. If you would give me a moment. Please wait in the flier.'

Nish and Kimli handed the crate up into the thapter. Gilhaelith stood on the stone wall, staring into the crater. Fumes were now belching out of it; an explosion sent boulders arcing through the air.

Gilhaelith watched them rise and fall. One landed on the crater's rim just a few hundred paces away. Another crashed through an outside walkway of Nyriandiol, tearing most of it away and sending it plunging into the bubbling lake.

He took something out of his pocket. It looked to be a smooth round rock with a hollow in the centre, though it was shiny, as if it had been polished. Gilhaelith weighed it in his hand, tossed it up and caught it, then drew back his arm and hurled it high, out towards the centre of the crater. As it fell he spoke five lines in a language Nish had never heard.

The stone disappeared into the roiling clouds. Nish realised that he was holding his breath. The ground shook, shook again and with a roar that hurt his eardrums the centre of the crater erupted upwards with colossal force, a cataclysm of steam, pulverised rock and red-hot particles of lava.

Nish bolted to the thapter. Gilhaelith followed with calm and measured steps. As he climbed inside, the debris was boiling towards them.

'To the Marches of Tacnah,' he said. 'And be quick about it.'

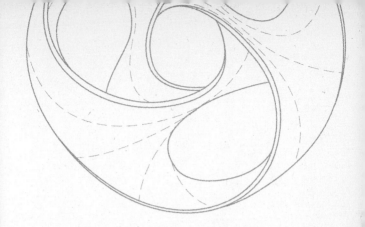

PART FIVE

WELL OF ECHOES

SIXTY-ONE

The following afternoon, Irisis and Tiaan were putting the core of their crude field controller together when Golias's globe belched. 'Flydd, Flydd? Troist here.'

Irisis didn't look up. Tiaan seemed to understand what she was doing but Irisis felt as though she were working blind and Flydd had been fretting at their lack of progress.

He ran to the globe. 'What is it? Are you under attack?'

'We've been under attack for two days, Scrutator. I've been calling and calling but couldn't raise you! *Why not*, was the unspoken implication.

'Sorry,' said Flydd. 'We've been using the farspeaker for something else. Is everything all right?'

'We're surviving. Tiaan's idea was a brilliant one.'

'What idea?' said Flydd distractedly.

'Shouting into the farspeaker, remember? It only works if the enemy are within twenty or thirty paces, but it knocks them down for a minute or two, and if we change the setting it keeps knocking them down. I've issued slave farspeakers to as many units as I could. We've driven off quite a few attacks that way, though with heavy casualties. Two thousand so far, and eight hundred of those are dead.'

'Two thousand . . .' said Flydd, unconsciously clenching one fist. 'It could have been worse, I suppose.'

'I weep for every life lost,' said Troist. There was a heavy silence, broken only by squelches and clicks in the background. 'But that's not what I've called about. Yggur was right about Gilhaelith. I should never have trusted him, though his timely warnings did save many lives. He's just played his hand.'

'What's he done now?' cried Flydd.

'He stole Kimli's thapter and flew north, just half an hour ago.'

'Has he gone over to the enemy?' Flydd asked dully.

'I've no idea, surr.'

Shortly Flydd set down the farspeaker and turned to Yggur. 'Gilhaelith took Nish with him in Kimli's thapter, as well as Merryl and four soldiers, one of whom was Flangers.'

Irisis dropped the assembly she was trying to put together. Crystals and tiny silver clips went everywhere but she didn't move to pick them up. 'Why did he take Nish?'

'He was helping Merryl to listen in to the enemy's mind-speech.'

'What's Gilhaelith up to?' said Yggur, who seemed to be resisting the urge to say 'I told you so'.

'Troist doesn't know,' said Flydd. 'Unfortunately, Gilhaelith took most of the mindspeech records. Troist has the last page, which mentions Matriarch Gyrull and some relics that seem to have precipitated his hasty departure.'

'The relics they took from Snizort?' said Yggur.

'I don't know. Pack everything up; we're going to Booreah Ngurle. That's probably where he's headed.'

'He'll be long gone before we get there.'

'Not if we hurry. We're not much further away.'

But it took longer than expected to pack the partly assembled field controller, and when they reached Booreah Ngurle late in the night it was erupting violently. They settled in the forest for a few hours' sleep, returning at dawn. They could not see the crest of the volcano for dust and falling rocks, and of course there was no sign of the thapter.

'That's the end of Nyriandiol,' said Flydd soberly as Malien circled at a safe distance. 'One of the most extraordinary places ever built. It's a shame.'

'Nothing lasts forever,' said Malien.

'Indeed not. Not even our kind.'

'Where do you want to go now?'

'I need to talk to Troist. Tiaan and Irisis can finish their work while we're there. And be careful. We're down to three thapters now.'

'*You're* down to two,' Malien pointed out. 'I still have mine, and I'm always careful.'

Work was the last thing on Irisis's mind but she continued mechanically, doing whatever Tiaan told her while she tried to understand what Gilhaelith could be up to. His actions didn't make any sense, though one thing was clear – he didn't care about people and Nish was in deadly danger.

Malien turned east and they met the army near a small lake between the great lakes of Warde Yallock and Parnggi. The surrounding grassland was clear of enemy so they felt relatively secure, though the lyrinx could not be far away. From here, Troist planned to head east, by paths suitable for clankers, then south to meet the refugees on the other side of Parnggi.

The four remaining mindspeech listeners had recorded intense message activity the previous afternoon and all morning, but in the early afternoon it stopped abruptly. The two thapters continued with the army. It was not attacked again, not even the solitary night raids from flying lyrinx to which Troist had grown accustomed.

'It's so quiet,' said Flydd the morning after that. 'Too quiet.'

They were camped on a gentle rise, a patch of barren ground with good views over the grassland in every direction. A small fire smoked between the thapters and Irisis was grilling gangrene-coloured offal sausages over it. She wasn't looking forward to dinner.

'I can practically *feel* the enemy's rage about their loss,' said Tiaan, who'd spent two days in the bowels of the thapter working on the field controller with Irisis, or by herself after Irisis had gone to bed. It had come together at last and they were going to begin testing after breakfast, Tiaan working as the operator.

Golias's globe sounded and a voice rumbled like a cow's belly, the words low and drawn-out.

'Who was that?' said Troist.

'It sounded like Governor Zaeff in Roros,' said Flydd in amazement. 'I've never spoken to her directly. The fields must be marvellously aligned today.'

'What did she say?'

'I couldn't make it out.' He turned to the farspeaker. 'This is Scrutator Flydd, north of Borgistry. Please repeat your message, Governor Zaeff.'

It came again, after a wait of two or three minutes. 'The enemy have abandoned the field of battle . . .' The rest was lost in noises like water bubbling in blocked drains.

'Please repeat that, Governor Zaeff. It sounded as if you said the enemy were retreating.'

'. . . were preparing to . . . walls of Roros . . . within hours of overcoming us . . . are streaming west . . .'

'Are you saying that the enemy have broken off the attack?' Flydd said incredulously.

'Yes,' said Zaeff. 'I don't believe . . . miracles . . . else can I explain . . .?'

'When did this happen?'

Another long wait. 'Yesterday morning. . . . felt sure it . . . a decoy . . . kept our silence until . . . knew what was happening.'

Flydd tried to call the other cities in the east, but could not raise any of them. Their fields were not aligned, so he had to go through the laborious process of having his calls relayed. It took hours, but in the end proved worth it. From Taranta to Tiksi, all had the same news. The lyrinx had broken off all attacks in the east and, accounting for time differences, at the same time.

'It's got to be a trick,' said Troist. 'They're trying to lure us out after them.'

'Strange kind of trick,' said Irisis.

'In the past weeks we've lost everything in the east but a few walled cities,' said Troist, 'and we've no hope of recovering it. The enemy can afford to forgo some of their gains if it means we capitulate sooner. Now the end is near they may want to limit their own casualties.'

'Abandoning sieges which will soon have to be renewed seems a strange way of doing it,' said Flydd.

'Governor Zaeff has a thapter at Roros. Ask her to find out what the lyrinx are doing.'

'She already has,' said Flydd. 'They waited out of range of the walls of Roros for the rest of the day and night, then headed south-west. The fliers were followed as far as the Wahn Barre, the Crow Mountains, which they were flying across when the thapter turned back. The lyrinx on the ground were marching in the same direction.'

'I don't believe it,' said Troist. 'The enemy must have found a way to seize control of our farspeakers. These messages are lies, to lure us out of our refuges – they've got to be. You know we've never been able to speak directly to Roros, Flydd.'

'You could be right,' said Flydd, frowning and pulling at his bristly chin. 'But we've got to know, either way.'

During the day, similar messages were received from the other eastern cities. Troist plotted the directions the enemy were said to have taken. They intersected in a broad area on the southern extremity of the Dry Sea, to the east of the area occupied by Vithis.

'What about the lyrinx who were besieging Borgistry?' said Yggur.

'They've gone into Worm Wood and we can't find them,' said Troist.

'There's only one way to uncover the truth,' said Flydd. 'I'll have to send one of the thapters east and confirm the flight of the lyrinx, with eyes I can trust.'

'That's going to take a long time,' said Yggur. 'If your observers can't report by farspeaker, they'll have to fly all the way back.'

'What's our alternative?' said Flydd. 'If we can't trust our farspeakers, we'll have to go back to the old reliable ways.'

Kattiloe's thapter was dispatched to the city it could reach quickest, Tiksi, with three pilots so it could fly non-stop. It would still take at least a week. More messages came in that day and the next. Hosts of fliers were reported to be streaming from the east, making no attempt at concealment. All were heading towards the same area, if the reports could be believed, though no one trusted anything heard through a farspeaker now, even when the voice was recognisable. Lyrinx were also reported flying north-east from Meldorin, and north from Borgistry.

Troist's map now had enough lines to show the destination: the old town of Ashmode, a port established an aeon ago when the Dry Sea had still been the Sea of Perion.

'Why Ashmode?' said Flydd. 'The lyrinx have never shown any interest in that part of the world.'

No one could answer the question. Initial tests of the trial field controller having shown promise, Malien and Tiaan were sent to the Dry Sea, to fill in the gaps in Tiaan's map. Irisis was assigned a team of artisans and told to get a reliable device made with the utmost speed.

SIXTY-TWO

Leaving Booreah Ngurle, now blowing itself to pieces behind them, Gilhaelith set off for the Marches of Tacnah, a flight of more than a hundred leagues.

'Get some sleep,' he said to Nish and the soldiers. 'I'm not planning to stop, and there'll be precious little time after we arrive.'

Nish settled down in a corner but couldn't sleep for worrying about the geomancer's intentions. He'd considered trying to foment a rebellion, but surely stealing the relics from the enemy was a good outcome?

Gilhaelith and Merryl were down at the other end of the thapter. Gilhaelith had a farspeaker on his lap and was spinning the globes, listening, then spinning again. Merryl sat in the corner, steadying a writing tablet with his stump while he took notes. Daesmie was asleep in the corner.

Nish got up and sat beside Merryl, so as to see what he was writing, but the fragments of mindspeech didn't mean anything to him.

'I'm not as skilled as Daesmie,' said Gilhaelith, 'but we have to keep listening. Every lyrinx who heard that call for help will answer it, and some are bound to be closer than us.'

'Why would they take the relics to Tacnah?' said Nish.

'They were taking them across Tacnah, to hide them. You

don't realise how insecure you've made the enemy feel. In a hundred and fifty years there wasn't one successful attack on their underground cities. Then Snizort was destroyed in a way no one could ever have imagined, and now their six remaining cities have been rendered uninhabitable for years, in a single day. They're homeless and winter is coming. They've lost everything except what they can carry on their backs.'

Gilhaelith kept working, but with little success – Merryl had only a few notes on his tablet by the time Nish began to doze off again. When he woke, Gilhaelith had his geomantic globe on the floor, its bowl resting on the crumpled indigo velvet from its box, and was scrying with the brimstone crystals again.

The light winked from the same place as before. 'They're not moving,' said Merryl.

'It might be a trap,' said Gilhaelith. 'Or a false trail.'

'How could they know about us?' said Nish.

'Never underestimate the enemy.'

Including you?

They flew into the night. Nish went up to stand with Kimli, who had begun to sag at the controller. The moon rose, near its full and mostly the dark side, an ill omen, not that Nish believed in such superstitions. Its slanting rays shone reddish silver off the dry plains grass. This was country the like of which he'd never seen before, even during his travels across Almadin. It was completely flat, bone-dry and empty.

'The City of the Bargemen,' said Gilhaelith, who had come up to stand on the other side. He pointed to their left, towards a lake shaped like a twisted teardrop. A meandering river ran in one end of it and out the other, its further reaches lost in the night. 'An odd name, since it's nothing like a city and the barges are run by the women. It's built out over the lake on poles of turpentine wood.'

'Then it's probably the only settlement in Lauralin safe from the lyrinx's vengeance,' Nish observed.

'I dare say. There's *nowhere* that the lyrinx will be safe from mine.'

'What did they do to you?' said Nish.

'They stole me away from Nyriandiol, the only place I've ever felt comfortable. They ruined me – I'm going to die the worst death a mancer can suffer . . .'

'You look healthy enough to me,' said Nish, who'd come to realise that Gilhaelith didn't always tell the truth.

'That is the worst death, Artificer. To have the body remain as strong as ever while the mind slowly decays from within. I've lost a quarter of my faculties already, because of the lyrinx. I might have repaired the damage with my globe but Gyrull denied it to me until it was too late and ensured there were flaws in it. My mind will be gone within a year. But worst of all, I'll never finish the great project I worked on all my life – to understand the world and the forces that move and shape it. My whole life has been rendered meaningless, and all because of the lyrinx.'

'So this is all about revenge?'

Gilhaelith was calm, almost good-humoured. There wasn't a trace of rage in him as he answered. 'The lyrinx robbed me of all that mattered, so I plan to take the relics that mean everything to them. I find revenge peculiarly nourishing. It's given me a new purpose.'

They began to pass over forest, though even in this light Nish could see how different it was from the forests he was used to. This was a woodland of scrubby trees, twisted by the unceasing plains wind. They were flying low now and once, as Nish looked down, he saw the moon-reflected gleam of a pair of eyes looking up. He shivered.

'How far to go?' he asked.

'Another twenty leagues,' said Kimli. She yawned. 'We should be there just after dawn.'

'Have you heard anything else, Gilhaelith?' said Nish.

'Not a whisper.'

'Maybe the matriarch is dead.'

'Or maybe they're waiting for us. *For every action, a reaction.* Everything we do with the Art leaves a trace, Nish, and a great adept may be able to find it.'

'First time I've heard of it,' said Nish.

'What you know about the Art would fit into a thimble,' Gilhaelith said crushingly. 'And you don't know any great adepts either.'

What about Yggur and Flydd, Nish was going to say. Not to mention Malien. He kept his mouth shut; Gilhaelith was baiting him.

'If a great lyrinx adept was watching when I scried with the brimstone crystals,' Gilhaelith went on, 'he's had plenty of time to close the trap.'

The moon dropped toward the western horizon, and as it sank the sun rose in the other direction, over the Marches of Tacnah. It was a featureless plain without rivers, lakes, or even a creek. Not a single tree could be seen; not a rock or a bush. The sparse tussock grass was grey, the soil red.

'What a bleak place,' said Nish.

Gilhaelith came up the ladder to see for himself. 'The lyrinx won't find it easy to ambush us here.'

But they can camouflage themselves to look like *anything*, Nish thought.

'Not long now,' said Gilhaelith. He went down to his globe, then called, 'A little more to the east, Kimli.'

'It should be just around here,' he said a few minutes later. 'Can you see anything?'

Nish was scanning the horizon with a spyglass. 'Only red dirt and grey grass.'

'Go higher, Kimli, and circle around.'

Kimli took the thapter up to a height of a few hundred spans. She could barely keep her hand on the controller now.

'Are you all right?' said Nish.

'So tired . . .'

'Anything?' called Gilhaelith.

'No,' Kimli whispered.

'What did you say?' said Gilhaelith.

'Lyrinx!' yelled Nish. 'In the west. Flying fast towards us.'

Gilhaelith shot up the ladder and took the spyglass. 'And more coming from the south.' He barked a bitter laugh. 'At least we know we're in the right place.'

'Can't you scry again?'

'To locate the matriarch precisely, I'd need a globe a thousand spans in diameter.'

They went around and around as the flights of lyrinx drew ever closer. With the spyglass, Nish estimated twenty in the western group, a few more in the more distant southern flight. 'They're coming straight for us,' he said, seized by a sudden thought.

Kimli, who had been sagging at the controller, let out a little squeak and stood up straighter.

'Of course they are,' said Gilhaelith.

'No, both flights are heading for *us*,' said Nish. 'You'd think one would be going to the matriarch, unless she's directly below and we can't see her.'

'She's had plenty of time to skin-change.'

Nish swept the spyglass around the horizon. While the lyrinx stayed still, skin-changing could conceal them, but once they moved they would be visible. He went all the way around, once and again, then a flying lyrinx flashed across his view, camouflaged to disappear against the sky.

He went around again and saw another lyrinx, or was it the same one? It wasn't flying towards him. It was streaking low across the grass to a point a little north of them.

'We're in the wrong place,' yelled Nish. '*There*, Kimli!'

Kimli, bright-eyed now, whirled the thapter around so fast that Nish was thrown against the side. She calculated the place the lyrinx was heading for, maybe half a league away, and accelerated towards it.

'Can we get there before it does?' snapped Gilhaelith.

'Yes,' said the pilot, 'but . . .'

'The others will get here before we can snatch the relics. Hoy, Flangers! Pass the farspeaker up here, would you. I may need it.'

It came up the hatch. Gilhaelith spun the globes, froze them and waited.

'There they are,' cried Kimli, changing course so abruptly that the farspeaker almost went over the side. The mechanism of the thapter screamed, she seemed to bounce it off solid air, put it sideways and stopped in a cloud of torn-up tussocks and a whirlwind of red dirt.

Nish was impressed. He'd had reservations about her skills in the early days, but Kimli was proving nearly as good a pilot as Chissmoul.

Five lyrinx lay on the ground. Three were dead and their skin had faded to an oily grey that stood out against the red soil. No, it was their inner skin, gone dry and wrinkly. They must have shed the armoured layer in their agony and then, exposed to the sun and wind, they had died. The fourth was still twitching, its fanged mouth opening and closing. It had torn its chest armour to shreds and crumpled pieces of bloody armour still clung to its claws.

The fifth, a huge green-crested female, was practically invisible, her skin matching the texture of the pebbly soil. Her wings, camouflaged the same colour, were spread out over several long crates.

'It's Matriarch Gyrull,' said Gilhaelith. 'Get the relics!'

Nish went over the side and ran toward the relics but one wing stirred and a fist of air thumped him in the stomach, knocking the wind out of him. It was more than just air, though. It had the Art behind it and Nish found it hard to get up again. All his nerve fibres were singing.

The matriarch lifted her head and tried to speak. Her armoured skin was blistered and had peeled away at throat and groin to reveal the sensitive inner skin, which looked as though it had been dipped in acid.

'Matriarch Gyrull,' said Nish, rising painfully. He bowed. She was a noble figure, after all, and he'd been taught respect at an early age.

He saw the dismay in her eyes. Mottled patterns chased each other across her chest and shoulders. The wing stirred and he felt another blow from her Art. This one was like a punch in the chest but not enough to hurt him. She was fading rapidly.

'I should have allowed Ryll to send you to the slaughtering pens,' she croaked. Her eyes were on Gilhaelith, who was on top of the thapter.

'You should have,' said Gilhaelith.

The soldiers leapt over the side and were racing for the crates when the first of the fliers shot across the bare ground towards them. Gilhaelith held the farspeaker close to his mouth and roared.

The lyrinx's wings locked; it let out a paralysed squawk and ploughed into the ground, skidding on its chest and belly armour. Another close behind it did the same, the pair coming to rest in a tangle of limbs and wings. They swung around, and in their eyes was the same distress Gyrull had shown – that the precious relics might be lost. Their clawed feet tossed red dust into the air as they tried to rise, but their legs wouldn't support them.

Two soldiers hefted the first crate, staggered to the thapter and slid it up onto the carrying racks. Flangers was limping for the second. Gyrull let out a despairing cry, her skin colours exploded into brilliant reds, yellows and blacks and she forced herself to her feet. Blood ebbed from the shredded skin. Her armour burst apart along the plates of her chest, revealing raw, bleeding flesh beneath. Red tears ran from her eyes but she took one excruciating step towards them. She would protect the relics whatever the cost to herself.

She took another step. Blood was running down her belly and thighs; her great maw was twisted in agony, but she reached out a hand and power fizzed from it. Nish froze in place, right foot upraised, the opposite hand outstretched. He couldn't move, and the soldiers were similarly afflicted.

Gyrull took another step. 'Come on!' shouted Gilhaelith, but none of the soldiers could move. He clambered onto the rear platform of the thapter, his right hand in a filigree basket, working some Art of his own.

Gyrull strained so hard that her chest plates burst away, but she took another step, and another. She was almost to the racks now.

Gilhaelith attempted a different working. Gyrull dismissed it with a flash of skin colours on what outer skin she had left. Forcing herself against the torture, she threw herself at the racks and caught the end of the crate.

Nish was still paralysed as Gyrull took the crate in both hands and tried to lift it off. Nish was struck with admiration, that she could overcome such agony to regain, against such odds, the most precious things in the world to her people. He felt sure she would, for the other lyrinx were only minutes away.

Gyrull hefted the crate onto her bloody shoulder and staggered back with it. Gilhaelith abandoned his Arts, which were clearly inferior to hers, leapt down through the hatch and reappeared with a crossbow. He slid in a bolt, clumsily wound the cranks and pointed it at Gyrull's back. The bow wobbled in his hands, but not even a novice could miss her from here.

He fired. She jerked, turned halfway around and the crate slid from her hands, raising clouds of dust when it hit the ground. Gyrull's claws scraped at the wound, fell to her sides and she thudded to the ground beside the crate. Though she struggled until the soil around her was purple with blood, she could not force herself to her feet again.

The paralysis vanished. Nish ran to help recover the first crate and tie it down, while the paired soldiers went for the second and third. The downed lyrinx were on their feet, wobbly but recovering rapidly. He felt for his sword.

Once more Gilhaelith roared into the farspeaker. The lyrinx collapsed again, though this time they were up rather more quickly. Each time the device was used, it seemed to affect them less.

He roared again. They checked, their mouths open in pain but they remained on their feet. Gyrull was still struggling, though weakly. She urged the lyrinx on in her own tongue, reinforcing her exhortations with fiery skin-speech on her rags of outer skin.

The second pair of soldiers were struggling to lift the last crate. They carried it a few steps, let it down hard then hefted it again. Flangers hobbled across to help them while his mate stood by with the rack ropes.

The two lyrinx struggled towards them as if walking through thigh-deep honey, but suddenly broke free and went for the last crate. The other fliers were closing rapidly and once they arrived all would be lost. Nish threw himself between the lyrinx and the crate, swinging his sword around his head, hoping to make enough of a diversion for Flangers to heave the crate onto the racks.

The two lyrinx stopped, cast a couple of blows in his direction, which he ducked, then went around him on either side. Nish whirled, attacking the one on his right from behind, though his blow did not penetrate its armour.

'Get aboard!' shouted Gilhaelith. 'We've got what we came for.'

The lyrinx were now between the thapter and Nish, running for the racks. Two soldiers took on the creature to Nish's left. One soldier went down from a backhanded blow to the side of the head but the second fought on.

Flangers and the fourth soldier were already climbing the ladder; the thapter began to move, stirring up clouds of red dust. The lyrinx on Nish's right sprang and landed on the racks, frantically slashing at the ropes with its claws and teeth, and tearing one of the metal covers of the thapter half off. Flangers armed a crossbow and jumped awkwardly onto the rear platform, landing just a span from the creature. His weak leg shook and he nearly went over the side, but the lyrinx didn't look around. It kept clawing at the ropes. Flangers shot it and it fell off just as the first flight of lyrinx came hurtling through the drifting dust. The second flight was close behind.

Kimli spun the thapter to approach Nish from the other side. Gilhaelith was shouting at her. The second soldier had fallen.

'Get aboard!' she screeched.

Lyrinx flew at the thapter from all directions, teeth bared and eyes wild.

'Go!' Gilhaelith roared. 'Leave him.'

Kimli nudged the machine across towards Nish, who took a running leap and managed to catch hold of the racks with one hand. The thapter jerked into the air, he lost his grip and fell hard.

'Get going!' Gilhaelith must have grabbed the pilot's hand and pulled up on the controller, for the thapter took off vertically through the lyrinx. It stopped in mid-air about twenty spans up and hovered while they desperately beat their way to it.

Gilhaelith climbed onto the rear platform and shouted down to Gyrull. 'Mindspeak this message to your people, Matriarch! Withdraw your armies from east and west or I'll burn your relics to ash and scatter them from one side of the Dry Sea to the other.'

'What would you have us do?' she croaked, barely able to raise her head.

The thapter lifted another ten spans to remain out of reach of the despairing lyrinx.

Gilhaelith raised his voice. 'Assemble your armies on the cliffs near Ashmode, at the edge of the Dry Sea north-west of here, and bring the power patterner with you. In exchange, I will return your precious relics.'

'We will not give up the flisnadr,' said the matriarch.

'I know your deepest secrets,' said Gilhaelith. 'You'll abandon everything else to recover the relics.'

'You know nothing about us, Tetrarch.'

Nish couldn't see how she found the strength to speak. And then a dozen lyrinx, diving out of the dazzle of the sun, plunged head-down straight for the thapter.

'On the contrary,' began Gilhaelith. 'No! *Kimli* –'

She'd already acted. The thapter shot sideways, flinging Gilhaelith to his knees. 'Bring the power patterner or lose everything,' he shouted. The thapter shot away, soon to disappear into the northern sky.

The lyrinx in the air formed a circle and let out a series of shrill, wailing cries, echoed by the creatures on the ground. What would they do now? They'd been driven from their homes and lost the relics that mattered most to them, so what did they have to lose? Had he helped to precipitate Armageddon?

The lyrinx on the ground turned to attend to him, and Nish discovered that he was alone – the other soldier no longer had a head. He put up his hands, but the closest lyrinx seemed in no mood to accept his surrender, while another score of lyrinx were even now surrounding him. They landed heavily, puffing up more red dust. Nish had never seen such violent and threatening skin colours.

The nearest lyrinx caught Nish around the chest in a crushing grip. Its claws dug into his ribs, the enormous mouth opened and green saliva sprayed his cheeks. It was going to bite his head off. He closed his eyes.

'Thlamp!' said a female voice. 'Inixxi rurr!'

The lyrinx dropped him on the ground and put its foot on him. Nish opened his eyes. The lyrinx that had spoken was unlike any of the others. It was slender, relatively speaking, with enormous pale wings that lacked pigmentation. Its skin was likewise uncoloured apart from the faintest tinge of green on its crest, indicating a mature female. Most unusual of all was the absence of armoured skin that protected the other lyrinx. Her soft outer skin, though coated with wax, was practically transparent. He could see her breasts through it.

'I am Liett, daughter of Wise Mother Gyrull, who is now dying in agony because of you,' the female said in the common tongue. 'You are my prisoner and I'm going to see the colour of your blood.'

Liett's wings caught the sunlight with a shimmering, pearly opalescence. Had he seen her before? Yes, he had. His eyes widened.

'Do I know you, human?' said Liett.

'You slashed my balloon near Tirthrax, the winter before last. I was lucky to survive.'

'Had I done the job properly,' she said savagely, 'we would not be here now. What is your name?'

He told her. She bent down and, though smaller and less muscular than the others, easily picked him up in one hand. Liett inspected him from top to toe. 'There is a vague memory. You humans all look the same – like the squirming grubs we hooked out from under the bark of trees to feed the despised tetrarch.'

Liett tossed him into the dust. 'Bind him tight,' she said to the other lyrinx, though in the common tongue. 'If he tries to escape you may eat his feet and lower legs, if you can stomach them,

615

but no more. I don't want him to die until after we have questioned him; *and he has answered.'*

Nish was bound hand and foot and left on the ground. Liett crouched beside her mother, spreading her beautiful wings to shade the dying matriarch. After giving Gyrull a drink from a canister on her hip, Liett spoke to her at length in low tones, in the lyrinx tongue.

She kept pointing to the northern sky and shaking one fist, as if counselling an all-out attack. The gathered lyrinx flashed the same aggressive reds and yellows as Gyrull had displayed earlier, but now Gyrull's colours were muted pinks and purples, in swirling patterns that Nish interpreted as soothing or conciliatory. Acquiescence to Gilhaelith's demands? More likely it would be feigned acquiescence until they recovered the relics, followed by an overwhelming onslaught to destroy the man who had so insulted them. And he, Nish, had been part of that sacrilege. He could expect no mercy either.

Liett glanced at him, her expression only marginally less threatening. She turned back to her mother, though this time she seemed to be presenting a different argument. She went to her knees, bowed low and spoke in a submissive way, looking up sideways at the matriarch.

Gyrull spoke so quietly that Nish didn't catch a word, though Liett seemed vexed at her reply. She began her pleading anew but Gyrull only shook her head.

'Ryll!' she said.

Liett stood up abruptly. 'Ryll?' she repeated, as if dumbfounded.

'Ryll.'

Liett turned away and stalked across the dirt, raising a storm of dust. She came back at once, trying to look contrite, and bowing until her head touched the ground. The matriarch said something in the lyrinx tongue. Liett called her fellows and they formed a tight circle, lifting Gyrull to her feet, supporting her and leaning over her with their foreheads touching. They began to chant.

Gyrull was beyond healing, as they must realise. He had the

impression that they were combining their powers to broadcast a sending to their brethren, telling them of the theft, and Gilhaelith's demand.

The chant built up until it became a thigh-slapping, foot-stamping roar. Finally, with a cry that went ringing across the plain, they broke apart and all flopped down, panting.

All but one. The matriarch swayed on her feet for a moment. She turned her head and her golden flecked eyes met Nish's, but she was already dead. The air rushed from her chest with a sighing sound and she fell into the dust.

Liett enveloped her mother in her wings, held her for a minute then let her go. She stood up and signed to the group, who began to excavate a grave with their claws.

Stalking across to Nish, Liett lifted him again. 'The call has gone out,' she said between her teeth. 'While we wait, I will talk and you will answer.'

SIXTY-THREE

Nish told Liett as little as he could without seeming unco-operative. Fortunately he had no idea what Flydd's plans were.

After the interrogation was over, the lyrinx separated. Liett picked Nish up in her claws and carried him, dangling like a rabbit in an eagle's talons, on a long flight north-west. She flew for the remainder of the day, stopping at dark in a nondescript range of hills where she tied him to a tree while she went hunting. He hung there miserably, the claw punctures in his back and sides throbbing. She soon returned with a small, black-haired goat which she skinned and ate, bones, entrails and all.

Once she'd licked the blood off her chin and hands, Liett freed Nish's hands and tossed a freshly skinned rabbit at him. It hit him wetly in the chest and fell to the dirt.

'What am I supposed to do with this?' he said.

'It's all the dinner you're getting.'

'But it's raw!'

She took it back and ate it with a few appreciative gulps, head and all. She retied his hands, lay down and went to sleep. Nish didn't sleep a wink. Before dawn they were off again, and even-tually he recognised the long expanse of Warde Yallock, the largest lake in Lauralin.

Near the northern end of the lake she wheeled over the

water several times before flying into a cave among hundreds that honeycombed vertical cliffs a hundred spans high. At the entrance she set Nish down while she folded her wings. He looked over the drop and his stomach churned. It was possible to climb up or down, if you were a lyrinx with clawed feet and hands, or fly in and out. Since he couldn't do either, the place was as secure as any prison.

Liett spoke to the guard by the entrance, who pointed around the corner to the next cave. Taking Nish under one gamy arm she climbed across the sheer rock face and inside. Not far from the entrance, working in the light, was a wingless male who was also vaguely familiar.

On seeing Liett the male's maw split into a smile of delighted surprise. He came striding out, arms spread, but Liett, scowling, thrust him away. After a heated exchange in the lyrinx tongue she threw Nish at the male, ran back to the entrance and hurled herself out. Her wings cracked and she raced away.

The wingless male stared after her, his skin colours flickering as if bemused, then turned to Nish. 'My name is Ryll,' he said, in an accent not dissimilar to Nish's own. 'And you, I'm told, are Cryl-Nish Hlar, son of the Scrutator Jal-Nish Hlar.'

'He was my father,' Nish said coldly, 'until you ate him.'

'*I* ate your father?' said Ryll. 'I don't think so, human. I would have recognised him.'

'Not you personally. Your people ate him at the battle of Gumby Marth.'

'Did they? I was not there. I'm sorry for the loss of your father, Cryl-Nish. I lost my own when I was young.'

'It was a mercy,' Nish muttered. 'After what you did to him two years ago, before you carried Tiaan away on that flying wing, he was never free of pain.'

Ryll inspected Nish. 'I recognise you now – small but valiant. You've grown face hair since our last encounter. As for your father, we fought each other and I did no more than he would have done to me.' Ryll spoke mildly, almost kindly, with none of the passion that characterised Liett. 'I hate this war as much as you do, human.'

'You started it!'

'Our records tell otherwise,' Ryll said. 'Still, we're not here to debate history, but for you to tell me everything you know about the plans of your leaders. Why did Gilhaelith the tetrarch steal our relics?'

'I haven't got the faintest idea.'

'Come, Cryl-Nish, you were with him at the time. You laid down your life so that he could escape.'

'We *are* at war,' said Nish. 'But I know no more than his parting message to Gyrull –'

'Matriarch Gyrull! Show respect, human.'

'Matriarch Gyrull. I'm sorry. Not everyone trusts Gilhaelith. Some people think he's on your side.'

Ryll let out what could only be interpreted as a honk of derision.

'He traded with lyrinx for many years,' said Nish. 'He helped you in Snizort and worked with you in Alcifer.'

'We did not find him entirely trustworthy at Snizort. Thereafter he attempted to make deals with us, and sold us one or other worthless secrets in exchange for his living, but he never worked *for* us. Indeed, I planned to send him to the slaughtering pens once he was no further use, though only a very hungry lyrinx would have gnawed on his rank bones.'

'I thought you lyrinx would eat anything,' said Nish thoughtlessly.

'And I thought you humans were treacherous, murdering scum,' said Ryll in his unemotional way, 'until I met Tiaan and discovered that humans could also be decent and honourable. There's a lesson for both our peoples. Anyway, we no longer eat humans. Enough of philosophy – how did you know our Wise Mother had the relics?'

Nish didn't answer at once, for he didn't want to aid the enemy. But then, Gilhaelith could also be an enemy. 'Gilhaelith found a way to eavesdrop on your mindspeech, with farspeakers.'

'Ahhh,' sighed Ryll. 'How did he know our tongue?'

'One of your former slaves, called Merryl . . .'

Ryll grimaced. 'We should have secured Merryl before we left

Snizort. Alas, in the chaos, many vital things remained undone. What did Gilhaelith do then?'

'He learned that your matriarch had the relics, but was dying. He kept it from everyone else, stole a thapter and fled.'

'Stole a thapter? So he *is* an outcast among you. How did he find our sacred relics?'

Nish hesitated.

'You can either tell me now or, with the greatest regret, I will torture you until you beg for death, and then you will tell me.'

The latter course seemed more virtuous, more noble, though Nish could not see a lot of point to it. 'He scried it out with his geomantic globe.'

'The same one he perfected in Alcifer using our maps – *or thinks he did.*'

Nish was not treated badly, though that did not surprise him. The lyrinx used torture where necessary to extract information, but did not torment for the sake of it, as humans did.

Ryll returned to his work, whatever it was, with a barrel-shaped device in a recess further down the cave. Nish didn't learn anything about it, for he was carried back to the adjoining cave. There he was given a wooden bucket and a fly-covered chunk of raw meat, so torn and filthy that he couldn't tell what animal it had come from. He felt sick just looking at it, but in the end he ate it, knowing that he'd get nothing else. He wasn't questioned further, and discovered only that he was a hostage.

After about a fortnight in the caves, the lyrinx abruptly departed late one afternoon. Nish was carried up to the top of the cliffs, where Ryll and a large band of lyrinx had gathered. Ryll carried the barrel-shaped object on his back, securely covered. Liett was there too. He gave it to her and she flew north-east with a large escort.

'We're marching to meet our fellows at the edge of the Dry Sea,' said Ryll. 'I trust you're well shod, Nish? You humans have such useless soft feet.'

'What are you going to do with me?' said Nish.

621

'We may exchange you, and other prisoners held elsewhere, if we get our relics back.'

'What if you don't?'

Ryll made neck-wringing motions with his huge hands.

Nish's boots were in good condition, though he wasn't much used to walking. His recent travels had been in thapters, airfloaters, constructs or clankers. The group set off at a pace he could barely maintain and, after an hour, when his legs had turned to rubber, he was taken on the shoulders of one or other of the lyrinx. It was not a position he found comfortable or dignified. They walked all night and until mid-morning the following day, and did the same every day.

The only rest they took was for the six hours in the middle of the day and, while he was carried for all but a few hours of the march, Nish was never anything but exhausted. However, the trip proved uneventful, and although he remained alert for opportunities to escape, they gave him none.

One day they were moving across a broad valley where the river was just a series of long pools up to a league in length, separated by gravel banks covered in tall reeds. Ryll and most of the lyrinx had crossed the gravel and Nish was stumbling along at the rear, with only a single lyrinx to guard him.

Without warning, a battered construct shot out of the reeds in front of them. Another construct pushed out behind and Nish heard a third moving in their direction, though he couldn't tell where it was. The guard, taken by surprise, darted into the reeds to his right. Nish went left and hid.

He heard the sound of a construct as it pursued the rest of the lyrinx across the river. Nish crouched down and did not move, hoping that the Aachim had not noticed him dart into the reeds, but unfortunately the other two constructs remained where they were. He could hear the gentle whine of their mechanisms now, and Aachim calling to one another in their own tongue. They began to tramp through the reeds and he debated whether it was better to remain where he was or to run. He stayed.

It wouldn't have made any difference, for they converged on

622

him from two sides – a thickset man with flashes of white at the temples, a dark-skinned woman with a badly scarred right arm. He recognised the woman's face, though not her name. He had seen her at some stage in his captivity a year and a half ago.

She recognised him too. 'Cryl-Nish Hlar!' she exclaimed. 'What were you doing with those lyrinx?'

'I was a hostage.'

'Lucky we were patrolling well outside our borders. Come, you look as though you could do with a ride. And Vithis will be pleased to see you, of course.'

'Of course,' Nish echoed. He could well imagine it.

The three constructs headed directly to the Hornrace, hardly stopping night and day, though it seemed to take a couple of days to get there. Nish could not be sure because he slept most of the time. In his waking moments, he wondered what the Aachim wanted of him. Information, no doubt. Nish was not sure that Vithis was much of an improvement on Ryll.

He woke before dawn of the second night of travel, sated with sleep, and went up the ladder. The woman with the scarred arm was at the controls but seemed disinclined to talk. Nish pulled himself up onto the top and sat with his legs dangling down the hatch, enjoying the cool breeze on his face and the sweetish, musky perfume of the little trumpet-shaped desert flowers that only opened at night.

The construct climbed up from a small depression and, straight ahead, he saw three lights in a line, one above the other. The highest was a good hand-span above the starry horizon. After an hour they did not seem appreciably closer.

'What are the lights?' he said.

'Vithis's watch-tower.' She absently stroked the writhen scars on her forearm.

'It must be a tall one.'

She didn't bother to answer. Shortly dawn broke and the shimmering heat haze obscured the land ahead. Nish couldn't see any sign of a tower.

In the mid-morning it suddenly sprang up out of nowhere

and the tower was so high that it could be seen across the arid plain an hour before they reached it. It was a needle of stone floating on a mirage which only dissolved when they were a couple of leagues away. Now the true enormity of the structure Vithis had built there was revealed, a vast rectangle of stone, hundreds of spans high, with stepped cubes forming a pyramid above that. The spire-topped needle tower rose from its top, suspended on five slender, arching wings.

Nish first heard the whisper of the Hornrace, an ocean flowing into an empty sea, shortly after that, and it grew ever louder. By the time the construct drew up at the foot of the building the music of the water had become a monumental roaring and crashing, so loud that it was difficult to talk over it. The building arched right across the Hornrace and was called simply the Span.

Ahead lay a door wide enough to admit the three constructs side by side. They whined into the bowels of the structure down a spiral path cut into stone, then stopped. Nish was led up a series of stairs whose sweeping shape was vaguely reminiscent of those in Tirthrax.

They emerged on an open floor paved with pale sandstone. The space was filled with the rush of flowing water. Nish was escorted across to the middle, where a slot in the floor wide enough to have engulfed a construct, though ten times as long, emitted wisps of vapour. He looked down and his head exploded with vertigo. He was directly above the Hornrace.

Nish felt himself leaning forward, almost as if he wanted to fall. The escort's fingers clamped onto his left biceps.

'The lure of the depths is powerful, but Vithis would be vexed if I allowed you to escape him that way.'

Nish took another glance at the torrent and shuddered. The roar was muted here, compared to outside. They went left, up a whirling stair into a perfectly circular room with glass walls that looked out on the Dry Sea, as well as down to the race and up to the stars. Vithis stood at the side, looking away. He did not turn as Nish entered, though Nish knew the Aachim was aware of him.

'You've come to gloat!' Time had only honed the bitter edge to his voice.

'It was not my wish to come at all,' Nish said.

Vithis turned. It was more than a year since Nish had last seen him, but he looked decades older. His hair was white, his face etched with such grief that Nish could hardly bear to look at him. Though Vithis had not treated him kindly and was a cold, unlikable man, Nish was moved by his suffering.

'Clan Inthis is *lost*. After all this time, I've heard no more than whispers on the ethyr.' Vithis spoke slowly, each word measured out as before, but he seemed a lesser figure than the man Nish had known.

'Do you mean,' said Nish, bemused, 'that you built all this just to search for your lost clan?'

'Why else would I have built it?' said Vithis.

'We thought . . . at least . . .'

'Go on. What did your friends Flydd and Yggur and treacherous Malien think?'

'After you went north so suddenly, after the battle of Snizort,' Nish said haltingly, 'it was thought that you'd made a pact with our enemy.'

'I don't ally with savages.'

Hadn't Vithis threatened to do just that in the early days? Nish could no longer remember all the twists and turns of the war.

'I left because Tiaan had destroyed Minis, my last hope,' Vithis went on, speaking so slowly that each word was like the grinding of an enormous mill.

'Is Minis *dead*?'

'What do you care for Minis?'

'I liked him,' said Nish softly. 'We were . . . friends.' Insofar as such a weak, flawed man as Minis could make friends.

'Minis is dead to me,' Vithis said dismissively. 'He's not a whole man any more.'

'So *that's* why you abandoned all plans for conquest and retreated here,' said Nish. 'With Minis disabled, the only way to restore your clan was to find the ones lost in the gate.'

'I wouldn't have thought that needed to be stated.'

'It does to us, surr. Humanity reads everything through the lens of our unending war. When you began to build this great tower, at such a powerful node . . . everyone . . . that is, Scrutator Flydd, believed that you were making a great weapon of war to strike down our army at a single blow.'

'What small minds you old humans have – I care nothing for your petty wars. This tower has one purpose and only one. It is a beacon, beaming through the limitless void, to tell my lost people that I'm searching for them. Its signal is so powerful that, if they can impress their cry for help upon it and bounce it back, I'll be able to find them. And once I do, I'll come for them if I have to tear the very void asunder.'

'You say "I",' said Nish. 'Is this the will of all your people?'

'Of course,' Vithis said. 'They voted me leader. Don't think to come between us, Cryl-Nish Hlar.'

'I wasn't. How do you know First Clan is out there?'

'Tiaan,' the name dripped like venom from his tongue, 'heard their cries and their lost wailing after the gate was opened. Later still, I too heard cries for help. Just twice, a long time ago, but I knew they were out there.'

'How will you get them back?'

'Another tower in another place will create the greatest gate that has ever been built.'

'But if you make a gate into the void,' said Nish carefully, knowing Vithis's rages of old, 'don't you risk more void creatures coming through? That's how the lyrinx got here in the first place.'

'There's *nothing* I won't do to get Inthis First Clan back.'

SIXTY-FOUR

Vithis questioned Nish about Flydd and Yggur's plans, in much the same way as the lyrinx had done, though he displayed little interest in Nish's answers. Vithis no longer feared the lyrinx and could not have cared less about the fate of humanity. First Clan was the only thing on his mind.

Nish was given a room with a window that looked south across the arid plains of Narkindie, and allowed to roam at will through the tower, so little did they fear him, though he was not permitted to go outside. After wandering on the first day he kept to the one floor, for the tower had been thrown up so quickly that it looked the same everywhere.

A few days later, he was eating black bread and spicy pickled fish in the open dining chamber when he heard the click of someone walking with a pair of crutches.

'Hello, Nish.'

The voice was Minis's, though the face was that of a stranger. Minis had aged more brutally than his foster-father. He was no longer an impossibly handsome young man, but one who'd been cast prematurely into a tormented middle age. The once smooth cheeks were now weathered like a desert hermit's and creased with vertical pain lines to either side of his mouth. He walked with an awkward twist of the hips and, though he wore robes, the stump of his right leg, amputated at mid-thigh, was clearly visible.

Nish rose abruptly, unable to keep the shock off his face. Minis faltered, then came on, forcing a smile.

'How are you, Minis?' Nish held out his hand and the Aachim's first finger and thumb wrapped right around it. The other fingers were gone.

The smile vanished. 'Even less a man than when last we met,' Minis said bitterly. 'And no man at all to Foster-father.'

'But . . !' Nish found his eyes drawn down to Minis's groin, then had to look away. He had no idea what to say.

'It's not *that*. Though my pelvis was smashed, in the *vital* respect I'm still whole. But to Vithis a maimed man is no man at all. He's given up on me and thrown everything into this insane search for First Clan. They're dead and gone but he can't see it – or won't. I think he's going out of his mind.'

'What do the other clans think?' asked Nish.

'The same, but discord would be fatal on this alien world so they've allowed him his way, for the time being.'

'Well, if he's given up on you,' said Nish carefully, for he'd had dealings with Minis before and knew how erratic he could be, 'you're free at last.'

'Free for what? What can I do like *this*? First Clan is extinct and no other clan would take in a maimed man. I have no future, Nish.'

'Perhaps, outside . . !' Nish began, only because he had to say something.

'Within days I would feed the lyrinx and, though I've nothing to live for, I cling to the rags of the life I have.'

'In time, Vithis may –'

'He'll *never* forgive me for calling across the void to Tiaan, or for her answering my call. He would sooner we'd all died in Aachan's volcanic fires than end up clanless on this accursed world. Neither has he forgiven me for instructing Tiaan in the making of the gate, because it went wrong.

'But most criminally of all, I allowed Tiaan to escape, causing many deaths, my own maiming and Foster-father's humiliation.

She took the secret of flying constructs with her, which everyone now has but us, and not even our brethren at Stassor will reveal it to us. It was my own fault – Tiaan feared for her life and begged me to help her escape. I promised to do so and yet . . .'

His eyes met Nish's and Minis flushed a ruddy brown. 'And yet, when it came down to it, I couldn't find the courage to defy Foster-father and betray our people. I did nothing and so, by default, betrayed the woman I love. This is my punishment. I am bile in Foster-father's mouth. And in my own, it need not be said.'

Nish had to look away to hide his contempt. Minis's dilemma had been a wrenching one, but Nish would have felt more respect for the man if he'd turned Tiaan in. At least he'd have made a choice, instead of doing nothing and whining about his regrets afterwards.

'Had it not been for you,' Nish said, to try to salvage something, 'none of your people would ever have reached Santhenar. The Aachim would be extinct on your home world. You saved them.'

'Foster-father does not count that to my advantage.' Minis clicked away, turned, then said suddenly, 'Have you seen Tiaan lately?'

'Not for some time, though we've had many adventures together in the past year. We've become friends, and I'm as surprised to be saying it as you must be to hear it.'

'I'm not surprised at all,' said Minis, and for the first time there was a spark of life in his eyes as he turned back to Nish. 'How did it come about? Tell me everything.'

Nish related his story from the time he'd last been with Minis, during their escape from burning Snizort, and how Tiaan had saved his life on more than one occasion.

'She's a wonderful woman,' Minis sighed. 'Tell me, does she have many lovers? I suppose she must.'

Nish resented the question and felt disloyal for answering it, though he did, curtly. 'As Tiaan is my friend, I wish you hadn't asked. But since you were . . . are also my friend, I'll do you the courtesy of an answer. As far as I know, she has no lovers at all.'

'Ah.' Minis looked away. 'Do you think there's any chance for a maimed man like me?'

Another question Nish didn't want to answer. 'Minis, how can I tell what is in Tiaan's mind? She keeps her feelings to herself.'

'Please, Nish. In your heart, do you feel she might ever consider me?' Minis's shiny eyes were on him, hope warring with dread.

Nish delayed his response for as long as he could. 'In all honesty, Minis . . .' He searched his former friend's face. What would be worse: to lie or to tell the truth? It had to be the truth, and in terms Minis couldn't possibly misunderstand. 'If she loved you, it wouldn't matter that you are maimed. But you betrayed her and that must have killed her feelings for you. I'm sorry. I wish you hadn't asked.'

Minis turned away, trying to compose his ravaged features. 'I – I suspected as much. Thank you for telling me. In some respects it makes my choice easier.'

Nish didn't ask what choice. He didn't want to know. He just wanted to get away and never see Minis again. They talked about other matters until the conversation petered out. Minis was returning to his work when the floor shook and there came a rumbling from below.

'What was that?' said Nish.

'The earth trembles here from time to time. We often felt it, when we were putting down the foundations.'

Two Aachim, deep in conversation on a bench across the room, also came to their feet but soon sat down again. Minis stood at the misty slot in the floor, looking down at the Hornrace for a drawn-out moment, before nodding curtly and stumping away on his crutches.

The afternoon dragged, as did the night. Nish was used to being busy all his waking hours but there was nothing to do here. He cadged some paper and spent the following day writing down his experiences with the lyrinx, and all the questions Ryll had asked him. Later he recorded Vithis's interrogation, just in case he escaped.

To ease the boredom, Nish began to do a sketch of the building, or at least the floors he'd been on, but soon put it away. His rudimentary drawing skills could not do the tower's wonders justice. He returned to the slot over the Hornrace again and again, staring down at the racing water and marvelling at the power of nature, which could reduce such a staggering work as the Span to insignificance.

Again there came that little shudder, but this time the water, hundreds of spans below, cusped up for an instant before the torrent flattened it out again. Three Aachim walking by stopped to remark upon the tremor, which struck Nish as odd if they occurred all the time.

Someone took him by the arm from behind and a deep male voice said, 'Come this way, please.'

'Where are we going?' said Nish.

'Vithis would like to see you again.'

'What about?'

The Aachim didn't answer. In Vithis's room, the same spherical one as before, the Aachim left him and closed the door.

'What's going on, Cryl-Nish?' Vithis was deadly cold now.

'I don't know what you're talking about.'

'Then you're a bigger fool than I take you for. Those two tremblers weren't like the normal ones we have here.'

'What do you mean?' Nish's voice had gone squeaky.

'Someone is sending me a warning. Who among your kind hates me the most, Cryl-Nish?'

'I don't know that anyone hates you,' said Nish desperately. Had Vithis finally cracked?

'One of your great powers is trying to bring me down. Who is it – Flydd? Yggur? Gilhaelith?'

'Maybe it's one of your own,' Nish snapped. He was taking a risk, but knew Vithis couldn't respect anyone who didn't stand up to him. He also knew of the longstanding bitterness between Vithis and Tirior of Clan Nataz.

'I have the full support of my people,' snarled Vithis, and Nish wondered if his guess had struck the mark. 'Come on; which one is it?'

'We're fighting for our lives, surr. No one has time to think about you.'

'What about Gilhaelith?' Vithis said menacingly.

'I hardly know the man.'

'He's a geomancer, is he not?'

'As I understand it,' said Nish, 'he wishes to comprehend the roots of the world and all the secrets that go with it.' He didn't see any point in mentioning the theft of the relics.

'Does he now?' There was a glint in Vithis's eye. 'And should he succeed in that impossible aim, what then?'

'Gilhaelith seeks knowledge and understanding for its own sake.' That may have been true once. Nish didn't have a clue what Gilhaelith wanted now.

'So pure a motive does not exist,' said Vithis. 'In my long life, there's one thing I can be sure of – once people have tasted real power, there are few who can give it up.'

Nish shrugged. 'Gilhaelith is an enigma.'

'Even more dangerous,' said Vithis. 'Leave now.'

Nish went.

That night he was lying in bed when the stones of the tower let out a groan like a ghost in torment and the room gave a long, sideways shudder. Nish's wiry hair stood up. He got out of bed, staring at the roof. The room shook the other way but this time it kept shaking. It felt as if the tower had been set vibrating and each oscillation plucked at the foundations of the Span.

Slowly the vibrations died away and did not resume, but sleep had fled. Nish went barefoot down the stairs, drawn to the slot above the Hornrace. The floor was dark but lights from the lower floors illuminated mist rising up through the slot.

He edged to the brink, fascinated by the torrent yet terrified of it. He went down on his belly and crept forward over the last distance.

'It compels, doesn't it?' said a low voice from the darkness. 'I come here every night, to think and to dream. To wonder if this will be the night when I take that way out.'

Vithis was sitting up the other end of the slot, his long legs dangling over the edge. The tone of his voice frightened Nish, who came to his feet and began to back away.

'Stay, Cryl-Nish. I mean no harm to you. Come and sit down.'

Nish did so, as far away as he reasonably could. His heart was thudding.

'They're trying to destroy me, you know.'

Mad and paranoid. Nish attempted to speak but nothing came out. He swallowed and tried again. 'Who?'

'Everyone. Yggur, Flydd, Gilhaelith –'

Nish wondered how the other clans allowed Vithis to remain leader. But then, from what he knew of Aachim Histories, insane obsessiveness was an all too common trait.

'You think I'm mad,' Vithis went on, softly. 'You think the loss of my clan has broken me. It hasn't, Cryl-Nish. I'm going to bring them back.'

'What if you can't find them, surr?'

There was a long, uncomfortable silence. Vithis's eyes caught the light and again Nish felt an urge to run away. 'I *still* have Minis,' he grated, 'despite what that little bitch did to him. He's pure First Clan. He'll build us up again.'

'Does Minis want to?' said Nish.

'Minis wants what I want.'

'How do you know?'

'He always has. He's never once tried to make his own life.'

'He's tried, but you would never allow it.'

'That proves that he never really wanted it.'

'You've broken his spirit,' said Nish.

'He didn't have any to begin with.'

'Then why did you adopt him?'

Vithis jumped up, swaying at the other side of the slot, his big hands held up as if he planned to leap it and throttle Nish. 'His parents were dead and I . . . could not have children of my own. Why was *I* so robbed?' he cried. 'My children would have been as strong as the founders of First Clan. Why am I cursed with this weakling who can never do anything right? Minis could have had his choice of a dozen women – all noble, all beautiful, all clever – but he wouldn't have them. He still pines after that sad little creature who brought him to ruin. Who would mate with him now?'

'Tiaan is a brilliant artisan and geomancer,' said Nish. 'She's brave and kind, loyal and generous.'

'She's an ugly, wretched little sow and no noble Aachim could see anything in her.'

'Among our own kind, Tiaan is considered a beauty. I think her –'

'An insipid kind of beauty, at best, and she has no family. Her mother is a breeding-factory slut; she has no father at all.'

'I've always thought the qualities of the person to be more important than the lineage of the family.' That was a lie. Until recently Nish had been as proud of his family's wealth and status as he'd been ashamed of his father's lowly ancestors.

'Considering your own lineage, I'm not surprised.'

'My mother and father –' Nish protested.

'Now you change your song. And who, I ask, were your father's parents, or your mother's? Nobodies! Minis can trace his lineage back ten thousand years. No old human on Santhenar can claim a quarter of that. Not one single person.'

'I dare say you're right,' said Nish, annoyed because he was sure it was true.

'Of course I am. I took the trouble to find out –'

The earth gave another wrenching groan, the building a grinding shudder. Vithis broke off and came around the slot. Taking Nish by the arm, he hauled him all the way up to the spherical room. By that time, Aachim were running everywhere in silent efficiency. Divided they might be over the construction of the Span and the great search, but a crisis instantly united them.

Tirior and Luxor appeared at the door. 'I see the Art in this,' Tirior said. She was in a blue nightgown which swept the floor, and her black hair formed a cloud of ringlets. Luxor was dressed but barefooted. He had extremely long and hairy toes, like brown caterpillars.

'Indeed,' Vithis said grimly. 'Do you know who it is?'

'Not yet.'

'Bring up the miasmin at once.'

Directly, an underling carried in an object roughly the size of a port barrel, shrouded in a green cloth. Tirior removed the cloth, revealing a glass bell jar mounted on an ebony base. There was something inside, obscured by fog. Tirior and Luxor worked their hands, eyes closed, with evident strain. The fog cleared and the object, the size of a large round melon, began to glow. The miasmin became brighter and brighter until it resembled the sun as Nish had once seen it through a smoked-glass spyglass. Its surface roiled and dark spots broke through, emitting flares and prominences that looped partway around it before plunging back into the surface.

Luxor whipped the bell jar off its base and the miasmin drifted up towards the ceiling, swelling to many times its size and boiling like a thunderhead. Red and black streamers were plucked out of it in one direction, then another, only to be resorbed. Tirior moved back, holding her arms spread above her head and making little movements with one hand or another. Luxor stood at right-angles to her and did the same, their hand movements seeming to keep the sphere away from the walls.

Vithis touched the lights on the wall to darkness. The surface of the miasmin smoothed, though it still roiled inside. A glowing filament arced from the top, twisted like a thread in the air and plunged back in halfway down the right side. Other filaments arose, whirled about and sank back into the mass. Dark, fringed spots appeared on the surface, slowly rotating.

'There are too many powers,' said Tirior with a shake of her black curls.

'I think not. That would be the scrutator, Flydd,' said Vithis, indicating a large spot from which the glowing filaments arose like sparks from a firework. 'And this, his chief lyrinx opponent. They seem too preoccupied with each other to be attacking us, though . . . the scrutator is cunning.'

'But not *that* powerful,' said Tirior. 'It's someone else, Vithis.'

'What's that one?' said Nish, pointing to another fringed spot that pulsed and spat black filaments, arcing out only to be sucked straight back in.

635

He shouldn't have interrupted. Vithis looked at Nish as if he'd just discovered a servant's nose hair in his wine.

'It's a node that's been sucked dry,' said Luxor. 'Not what we want to see, so close to our principal node.'

'It's being attacked, so as to drain our node,' said Tirior.

'Who by?' asked Nish.

Luxor consulted the miasmin, which was smaller than it had been. 'I can't tell.'

'Vithis,' said Tirior urgently, 'the field is falling faster than I've ever seen it. It's as if our node is being drained.'

'This reeks of the way Nennifer was destroyed.' Vithis's eyes were unfocused.

'The field is collapsing around us,' Tirior said. 'We're being attacked from the Foshorn!'

'It's the Council, but I have their measure.' Whipping an emerald rod from his belt, Vithis pointed it at the black fringed spot they'd just been discussing.

'No, Vithis,' cried Tirior. 'Not *that* one.'

Vithis spun the rod in the air, caught it, pointed it again. Momentarily a tight green beam burst from one end and illuminated the fringed spot, which sent out filaments in all directions before collapsing in on itself and disappearing. 'That's the end of them.'

While Nish stared, his mouth agape, Vithis slipped the rod back in his pocket. With the air of a man who had just succeeded at an impossible task, he walked out and closed the door behind him.

'But . . .' cried Nish, horrified.

'It wasn't them,' said Luxor. The fringed spot reappeared. Prominences arced from it and it grew until it covered the visible hemisphere of the miasmin. 'Whoever it was, he was just testing our defences. But now he's threatened and may hit back.'

The sphere shrank further, but the fringed spot stayed the same size until it covered the entire surface.

'Vithis has finally broken,' said Tirior. 'Let him go. Run for our strongest adepts, Luxor. I'll hold the miasmin until you get back, but . . .'

'What is it?'

'Whoever is attacking us, they've drawn the field so low that I don't think we can defend ourselves.'

'We'll have to rely on charged devices,' said Luxor.

They exchanged glances. 'And we both know how that's going to end.'

Luxor ran out, shortly to return with six Aachim, four women and two men. They assembled in a circle around the miasmin and it grew a little.

Without warning the earth rumbled and went on rumbling. Masonry ground together and a crack began to snake across the open floor outside. Nish stood by the glass for a while, staring down at the Hornrace, which looked as though it was boiling.

Vithis's door banged shut. Tirior and Luxor still had their arms in the air but the miasmin had shrunk almost to nothing.

'We can't hold it,' gasped Tirior. 'Sound the alarm!'

Someone lifted the glass bell jar, the miasmin was directed beneath and the bell jar clamped to its base.

'The tower is empty, apart from those keeping Vithis's watch,' said Luxor.

'Tell them to come down. It isn't safe.'

'They're under his direct orders.'

'Then send someone to find the lunatic!' said Tirior. 'I've had enough. I won't see one more Aachim die in pursuit of this folly. If you'd supported me against him at the beginning –'

'Not *now*!' snapped Luxor.

'Should I run outside?' called Nish, looking anxiously at the roof.

'The Span was built to resist the strongest earth tremblers,' said Tirior.

'But this isn't an earth trembler,' said Luxor. 'It's an attack directed at the Span itself.'

A grinding scream, so loud that it cobwebbed the glass of Vithis's room, rose up the register. Concentric fractures formed in the ceilings outside, rapidly grew larger; then, with a roar even more deafening, the centre of the ceiling collapsed. Nish caught a momentary glimpse of something massive hurtling down and smashing through the slit above the Hornrace, before boiling dust blotted out the scene.

Pieces of stone crashed against the glass wall, which starred in dozens of places but did not break. The floor went up and down, throwing Nish off his feet. The miasmin shrank to a glowing point and vanished. Dust poured in under the door.

Nish lay on the floor, his sleeve over his eyes and nose, expecting the roof to fall on him, or the whole of the Span to collapse into the Hornrace, but after a minute or two the crashing and grinding ceased. Outside, the dust clouds slowly began to settle.

Tirior sat up, her hair grey with dust. She shoved the door open, having to push against heaped rubble.

The Span still stood, though the needle-shaped watch-tower that had once reared above it had fallen right through the building into the Hornrace, leaving a ragged hole where the slot had been. They crept across the gritty floor, which was littered with crumbled and shattered stone. Cracks radiated out from the hole.

'Come this way,' said Tirior.

Nish looked over the edge. The debris had formed a dam in the Hornrace, out of which the twisted spire from the top of the tower extended like a dead flower in a vase. Above, the roughly circular holes went up at least a dozen floors.

'I always knew it was a folly,' said Tirior, and led the way outside.

Nish followed. The episode also reminded him of the way Nennifer had been destroyed. And if the amplimet *had* woken again, what had it done to Tiaan and Malien?

SIXTY-FIVE

Malien was at the controller, Tiaan beside her with her chart
as they cruised low across the emptiness. The Dry Sea
unrolled before them, a featureless, lifeless land two thousand
spans below the level of the Sea of Thurkad. Its bed was covered
in an icing of crusted salt tens of spans in thickness, formed
when the Sea of Perion dried up. The heat was unrelenting in
daytime, despite the lateness of the season. No cloud marred
the deep purple of the sky, darker than any sky Tiaan had
seen before. Even the air was thicker down here. Each breath
felt measurably heavier and the tang of salt dust was always in
her nostrils.

Tiaan took a sip from her water bottle and settled back
with her chart, glad to be away from Flydd and the field controller. Though she understood why he wanted it, it represented
another escalation of a war that was already out of control. On
the positive side, it was going to take at least two weeks to make
a rough map of the fields and nodes of the Dry Sea. She was
looking forward to the solitude.

Malien glanced back at the chart and set the lodestone in its
brass bowl. 'Is this heading all right?'

'A little further east of north. I thought we might fly across
the length of the Dry Sea in the direction of Taranta.'

Malien squinted into the white glare ahead, made the necessary adjustment to her course and closed her eyes. 'We'll have to make some slit goggles. I'd forgotten how bad the reflection off the salt was.'

After an hour or two Tiaan said, 'Malien?'

'Yes, Tiaan?'

'Has something happened between you and Flydd? You don't speak up in his councils anymore.'

'I've begun to have reservations about what the Council is doing.'

She did not go on and Tiaan didn't feel any need to question her. She simply gave silent thanks that she wasn't the only one.

They worked in a companionable silence for the remainder of the day. As dusk approached, Malien looked for a place to camp. The seabed below them was featureless, apart from a ridge of broken salt in the distance. She set the thapter down on the crusted surface, which revealed not the slightest sign of life. A breeze blew strongly from the west and it was no longer warm.

'It looks as if it could get cold here at night,' said Tiaan, pulling on a coat.

'It does. Let's have a look behind the salt ridge. It'll break the wind.'

She hovered across and they found a sheltered spot between iron-stained bergs of salt, their orange and yellow layers fretted by the wind into bizarre shapes. Tiaan hauled lumps of salt and hacked them into shape with a hatchet to make rude seats and a table.

'We should fly east tomorrow and fill the racks with wood,' said Malien. 'We'll need it.'

'Have you been out here before?'

Malien seemed to find that amusing. 'I've walked across the Dry Sea and back again, and survived it. Not many can say that.'

Tiaan couldn't believe she'd asked such a stupid question. 'Of course! You were in the *Tale of the Mirror*. After all the time I've known you it still doesn't seem real, to be sitting here with you knowing that two hundred years ago you lived through a Great Tale.'

Malien sat on one of the seats and began peeling fruit and cutting it into a bowl. 'It hardly seems real to me, after all this time. If only I'd known . . .'

'What?'

'No matter. The past creates the future, Tiaan. Every little thing we do shapes the way the future evolves, so I'm partly responsible for the way the world is now. We all are, those who took part in that tale and allowed the Forbidding to be broken.'

'As am I for the things I've done,' said Tiaan, slicing bread and cheese and laying them on a cloth. 'But if we did nothing, surely we'd also be to blame for the state of the world.' She filled a pot with water. 'There. It's ready.'

Malien placed her hands around the pot, closed her eyes and gave a little quiver. The air shimmered around her fingers. Steam rose from the pot, which began to bubble.

'I'll never get used to seeing you do that,' said Tiaan, taking a good handful of dried chard from a packet and stirring it in.

'I'd prefer not to do it at all. I hate using the Art for trivial purposes.'

'We'll get some wood tomorrow. A nice crackling fire will be cheery. Tea?'

'Thank you.'

After dinner they settled back with another mug of chard each and their coats wrapped around them. It was already chilly and the temperature was falling by the minute.

'I've also got reservations. I'm worried about what they'll do with my map once it's complete,' said Tiaan.

'If the field controller can be made to work, it may swing the balance,' said Malien, 'and then it'll be tempting to wipe the enemy out.'

'I hate the way people talk about them as though they're vicious brutes,' said Tiaan. 'I've known lyrinx who were every bit as decent and honourable as the best of us.'

'To survive such a war, each side must make their enemies into monsters.'

'And if the war is won and the lyrinx eliminated, what then?'

'If we have to commit atrocities to win, it's almost as bad as losing. And how will the world be shaped afterwards?'

'At least there won't be any need for scrutators, telling everyone how to live their lives.' Tiaan tossed the dregs of her chard onto the salt and stared moodily at the stain.

'Those in power can always find excuses to retain it. Your mapping may give Flydd and Yggur the secret that mancers have been looking for since the Art was first discovered – the power to shape the world.' Malien prised off a chunk of salt with her knife and began to pick the crystals apart. She tasted one and made a face. 'If such power is used by the best of leaders, for the best of motives and the benefit of all, it could transform Santhenar.'

'I don't see why the world has to be reshaped,' said Tiaan. 'Besides, even the best of people can be wrong-sighted, and in time there'll be as many evil leaders as saintly ones. As many fools as there are wise folk; as many stupid, greedy and grasping ones as there are altruistic.'

Malien began arranging her crystals in a circular wall, saying nothing.

'Once that secret is uncovered,' Tiaan went on, 'greedy men will fight to get it for themselves. There'll be another war, as far removed from what we've suffered as our war of clankers, constructs and flesh-formed creatures is from the petty wars of two hundred years ago. Whole forests have been consumed in the furnaces of our manufactories, a thousand rivers poisoned, and a million people have died brutal deaths. We've abandoned our culture and given up our freedom to try and win this war. What will we sacrifice next?'

'Something to think about,' said Malien, 'before you hand over your completed node maps.'

'But what am I to do about it?' said Tiaan.

It was a long time before Malien answered. 'I don't know.'

The days passed quickly, even though the work had taken longer than expected. Now the mapping was complete but for a diagonal strip beginning east of the Foshorn and running north-east across the sea in the direction of Tar Gaarn and Havissard. They heard occasional news of the war via the farspeaker. The enemy were closing in on Ashmode but battle, if there was going to be any, was some time off. Malien tried to reply at the appointed times but the slave farspeaker did not seem to be sending.

They'd just begun the final strip, and were flying past an isolated pinnacle north-east of the Foshorn, when Malien said, 'What's that, there on top of the peak?'

Tiaan stood up to see. 'It looks like a tower.'

'I wasn't aware that anything had ever been built out here.' Malien turned the thapter towards it.

There were hundreds of peaks and pinnacles in the Dry Sea, remnants of ancient volcanoes. This one was small, not more than a hundred and fifty spans high. The sides were precipitous, which was unusual, and an arrangement of winches big enough to lift the largest construct projected over the cliff on the western side.

On the flat top of the peak was as strange a structure as Tiaan had ever seen. A series of nine red spheres, the largest more than twenty spans across, were set on a black spire like marshmallows on a skewer. The largest sphere enveloped the base of the tower; the smallest enclosed the top, some hundred and fifty spans above the ground. Five constructs stood at the base of the western cliffs, on the salt. As the thapter approached, a number of Aachim ran out of the spire and stood staring up at them.

'I presume this isn't the work of *your* people?' Tiaan said.

'They're constructs, not thapters. It's Vithis's doing.'

'What for?'

'I have no idea.'

'Could it be a weapon directed against humanity?'

'Why would he build one out here?'

'To take advantage of a particular node?'

Tiaan mapped the node, which had an unusual field, made notes on the tower and its occupants, and they continued on their path.

Two days later they were completing the last segment of their diagonal, one that Tiaan had left until the way back because of its complexity. The thapter was passing back and forth over an area south-east of the peak of Katazza, which featured in several Great Tales. Here black rock had been thrust up along fissures and torn apart along enormous faults and fractures. The country was so rugged that it would have been difficult to walk across. Steam wisped from a myriad of cracks and vents coated with red and yellow salts, while here and there along a crested ridge the black rock oozed molten orange lava. The nodes were complex in this area, which extended in a band from the northern end of the Dry Sea towards the southern, before curving around towards the Hornrace.

'We'll have to go lower,' said Tiaan. 'I can't tell what's going on from up here.'

As Malien was flying along the molten centre of the ridge, the thapter jerked and the whine of the mechanism broke into a series of buzzes.

'Tiaan? Is there something strange about the field here?'

'There are lots of fields and the nodes are long and thin, not round. They run along the ridges and the field weakens rapidly to either side.' Tiaan took a closer look. 'That's strange. The field keeps changing from up to down; I suppose that's why we're jerking so much. Try going a little to the left of the ridge.'

Malien turned left and the jerking stopped. 'Can you still map if I follow this heading?'

'More or less.'

Twice more they had the same problem, when they passed over long faults in the rock that had shifted the mid-sea ridge to left or right. As Malien corrected yet again, Tiaan put a hand on her arm and pointed down.

'Hey, that looks like a wrecked construct.'

'What would a construct be doing way out here?' said Malien as she turned the machine and headed lower. The mechanism began to stutter and she directed it away until it resumed its normal note.

Tiaan lost sight of the wreckage in the jumble of black basalt. 'This country is too broken to hover across. Malien, what if it's a *thapter* that crashed?'

'It must be – it was broken in half, as if it had fallen a long way. And it's not one of ours, so it must be from Stassor.'

Malien went lower and turned back towards the place where they'd seen the wreckage. A construct came into view. 'Is that it?'

A shiver worked its way up the marrow of Tiaan's backbone. 'It can't be. The front is smashed in but it's all in one piece.'

'Two crashed thapters?' said Malien. 'What's going on?'

'I suppose the second came looking for the first and met the same fate – they weren't experienced enough to cope with these fields. Look, there's the first. Set down. There may be someone still alive.'

'The impact has torn it apart,' said Malien, circling about ten spans up. 'No one could have survived that.'

'Sometimes miracles happen.'

Malien settled the thapter down with some difficulty, for the basalt was scored, twisted and wrenched into stacks, blades and sheer-sided ravines. There wasn't a piece of flat ground big enough to spread a tablecloth.

The jagged rocks proved troublesome to walk on, too. Malien reached the wreckage before Tiaan, who had to go the last twenty spans on hands and knees. Her back began to ache where it had been broken.

Malien looked in through the torn metal, which had a blue tinge. 'There's no one inside.'

Tiaan went round the other side and stumbled over a body before she realised what it was. It was the colour of dark tea, the flesh desiccated to strands of muscle covered by a few scraps of flaky skin. The clothes were gone, apart from the faded shreds of seams. 'Malien, could you come here?'

Malien examined the remains. 'A natural mummy. It's so dry here that nothing rots, and the salt would help to cure it. He was a tall man, though you wouldn't know it, the way the drying flesh has pulled his backbone into a curve. He was definitely Aachim – see the extra-long fingers?' She took up a scrap of cloth, inspected it and let it flutter away.

'He must have been dead a long time,' said Tiaan.

'Months would be enough to cure a dead man, out here.'

They found another body not far away, a woman whose skull was crushed. 'Thrown out by the impact,' said Tiaan.

'One of the lucky ones. She would have died instantly.'

Others had been less fortunate. They came on a cluster of bodies twisted into positions that indicated painful, lingering deaths. Tiaan couldn't bear to examine them.

'Let's go to the other machine,' said Malien, the shadows growing under her eyes.

The second construct was only a hundred paces away, but it was easier to fly there than pick their way across the jagged ground. It was also made of blue-black metal and was full of bodies as mummified as the others, though a faint death smell lingered inside. The bodies were still clothed.

'That's ... not how your people dress,' said Tiaan. 'Malien, these people are from Aachan.'

Malien appeared to be looking right through her. 'That's right.'

'Does this mean that Vithis has thapters too? He's certainly kept the secret well . . .' Again that shiver along Tiaan's spine.

'Vithis has no thapters, Tiaan. They're constructs. Come on.'

'Where are we going?'

'Up. There may be more. Can you fly the thapter?'

'Is something the matter?'

Malien was too preoccupied to answer. Tiaan's knees were shaking as she gripped the controller and took the thapter straight up. She couldn't see anything but black rock and salt.

'Higher,' said Malien in a strained voice.

The sun reflected off something a good distance from the first two machines. Tiaan circled, scouring the rock. The wreckage was hard to pick out at first but once she'd found it, she soon saw more, and more. There were dozens of wrecked constructs down there, or pieces of constructs. Then, as the sheer scale of the site became evident, she amended that to hundreds. The sun still beat down on her but all the warmth had gone out of the day. She *knew* who they were.

'It's Vithis's people,' said Tiaan. 'Inthis First Clan. They weren't lost in the void after all.'

'Not all of them,' said Malien. 'The gate must have whiplashed across the Dry Sea as it opened, scattering them here.'

They counted hundreds of constructs, strewn over an area a couple of leagues wide and about ten long. Most were wrecked, though a few machines bore only superficial damage. Then, in the middle of the area, they saw a round structure built from the metal skins of dozens of constructs.

Tiaan set the thapter down beside it. They did not get out at once. 'Some of them survived,' she said in a flat voice.

'For quite some time,' said Malien.

'I wonder why they didn't go for help?'

'Even if they'd repaired one construct, this country is too rugged to hover across. And without knowing where to go, or how to find water on the way, anyone who left here on foot would have died of thirst.'

'But there's so many of them,' said Tiaan. 'There would have been thousands. Surely they could have found a way to send for help?'

'Maybe they didn't know what world they were on. Before the Forbidding cut off communication between the worlds, this was the beautiful Sea of Perion. They must have thought they'd been cast onto a desert world in the middle of the void.' Malien rubbed her eyes. 'We'd better go and see.'

They got out. The structure, built from the metal of as many as thirty constructs, was large enough to have accommodated some hundreds of people. The surrounding rocks had been smoothed, and paths constructed out of fragments so cunningly fitted together that they locked tight.

Tiaan walked around the building, marvelling at their ingenuity in creating so much with so little. The paths extended off in several directions to other, smaller structures, some of construct metal, others out of stone. The stonework was superb.

'How did they live so long, without water?' she said.

'Each construct carries enough drinking water for several weeks. If most of the Aachim were killed in the crashes, the water would have lasted the survivors for months. And after that, there's water in the Dry Sea, if you have the wits to look for it.'

647

'Only salt water, and you'd have to dig through spans of salt to find it.'

'Yes, but all it takes to turn salt water to fresh is sunlight or heat, and there's plenty of both here. The problem wasn't water, but food. Had everyone survived, the food would have been exhausted in a month or two. Since most were killed, it may have lasted a year, or more.'

'It's nearly a year and three-quarters since the gate was opened.' Tiaan put her head inside one of the stone structures, then sprang out again. 'It's a graveyard.'

'A mausoleum.' Malien went to the entrance and stood for a minute, head bowed. 'While any of First Clan had strength in their bodies, they would have honoured their dead according to longstanding custom.'

'They mustn't have found the first two constructs.'

'I'd say not.'

They turned back to the metal building and Malien went inside.

'I'll wait out here,' said Tiaan.

'No, come in.'

'I feel so guilty,' Tiaan whispered.

'Tiaan, you must not. You offered them the chance for survival and they took it willingly, knowing the risk. They'd been thinking about escaping through a gate for years.'

'But . . . I made it wrongly. It was my fault.'

'Why do you say that?'

'Vithis told me so.'

'Vithis sought to blame you for his own failing. I checked your port-all and it was correctly made.'

'But Vithis said that left-hand and right-hand were different from their world to ours.'

'They are, and it was known to the ancients, for I checked the records after you left Tirthrax. The failing was not in your port-all, but in the way they matched their end of the gate to yours. Vithis must have tried to correct it after the gate opened but by then it was too late. It lashed the opening gate across known space, and unknown, before finally locking in place at Tirthrax.

That's why Inthis were lost, not through any failing of yours.'

'I still feel responsible,' said Tiaan.

'And no doubt, deep in his heart, so does Vithis. But it was an accident, Tiaan. They took the risk and lost.'

The curving chambers of the building were decorated with such treasures as the Aachim had brought with them. Tiaan marvelled at small tapestries woven from threads of silk and gold, wire sculptures of astonishing complexity, subtle rugs and beautifully decorated pots and implements. Furniture had been made from native stone and salvaged metal. Everything was beautiful and harmonious, though the designs and proportions, even after her time in Tirthrax, struck Tiaan oddly.

They entered room after room. All were empty. 'This building must have housed many people,' said Tiaan. 'But –'

'As they died, the bodies would have been placed in the mausoleums which they'd already built. All except the last.'

They climbed a set of metal stairs, their feet echoing hollowly. At the top they entered an attic room with open windows looking to the east and west. Though a breeze blew through, it was hot. Malien turned the corner, stopped, then bowed her head.

Seven children lay on bedding on the floor as though asleep, though Tiaan knew that they were dead. Five were girls; two were boys. The oldest looked about thirteen, the youngest five.

'They've not been dead long,' said Tiaan.

'No!' Malien whispered. 'They met their ends in the last week.'

'They're thin, but not starved. How did they live so long?'

'We particularly cherish our children, Tiaan, for we Aachim, though long-lived, are not fecund like old humans. The adults would have gone without to feed the young ones, in the hope that, somehow, they might be rescued.'

'And in the end?'

'When the last adult was dying and all hope lost, the children would have been given a draught from which they would never wake.'

'How horrible.' Tiaan glanced at the faces, brushing away

tears. 'They were still alive when we began to survey the sea. If we'd come this way first, instead of leaving it until last, we could have saved them.'

'If only we had,' said Malien.

'It's a wonder they didn't try to smooth a path to the salt. It's only thirty or forty leagues away. Once they got a construct onto smooth salt they could have crossed the sea in a few days.'

'But if you go the wrong way, this broken country runs for hundreds of leagues. Their explorers may have thought the whole world was like this. In any case, to smooth a hover path across this country would have taken hundreds of Aachim years. They didn't have the people or the food. Once they crashed here they were doomed, and they must soon have realised it.'

An unpleasant duty was preying on Tiaan's mind. 'We should . . . we must take this news to Vithis,' said Tiaan, her heart sinking at the thought of what it would do to him.

'And Minis.'

The farspeaker, which had been silent for days, gurgled and Irisis's voice came though, shaking with tension. 'Tiaan, Malien, wherever you are, come to us on the salt below Ashmode. Hurry! The enemy –'

SIXTY-SIX

Several weeks earlier, not long after Kattiloe's thapter had been dispatched to Tiksi, Flydd and Yggur were called to the farspeaker. Irisis hurried over after them, for she'd recognised the voice.

'It's Gilhaelith,' said the operator, 'and he says he has a message for you both.'

'We're listening,' grated Yggur. 'Well, Gilhaelith?'

'You've heard, I assume?' Gilhaelith's voice was as clear as if he were in the next room.

'That the lyrinx have broken off their sieges and are racing to Ashmode? We're still waiting to hear if it's an elaborate deception.'

'It's not,' said Gilhaelith. 'They're following my orders.'

Yggur choked. *'What?'*

Flydd eased him out of the way. 'Since we no longer trust anything we hear over a farspeaker, we'll reserve our judgment on that. What have you done?'

'I've got their sacred relics,' Gilhaelith said simply. 'I ordered them to come east – all of them – with the power patterner, or I'd destroy the relics.'

Irisis tried to catch Flydd's attention. 'Ask him about Nish,' she hissed. He waved her to silence.

'What do you want?' said Yggur.

651

'Revenge,' said Gilhaelith. 'They've robbed me of everything that mattered. I'm going to do the same to them.'

'This is absurd,' said Flydd to Yggur. To Gilhaelith he said, 'Why would the lyrinx abandon everything they've fought for, these past hundred and fifty years, for a few lousy bits and pieces from the tar pits?'

'It wasn't Santhenar they were fighting for,' replied Gilhaelith. 'Or rather, Santhenar was always secondary. Their most burning desire, which was driving them long before the war, and in fact was the reason they came to Santhenar, was to find these relics. I gambled that they'd give up everything else for them and I've been proven right.'

'Now I know your mind is going,' scowled Yggur.

'You're clever men – look at the evidence. I'll leave you to work it out on the way to Ashmode.'

'What's happening there?' said Flydd.

'You'll find out in due course.' The farspeaker cut off.

'He's made a deal with the lyrinx,' said Flydd. 'I'll bet he's planning to exchange the relics for the power patterner.'

'Why does *he* want it?' said Yggur.

'I imagine we'll find out before too long.'

Irisis was walking backwards and forwards outside the conference tent. They'd gone to Hysse to meet Governor Nisbeth and Grand Commander Orgestre, who seemed to be back in favour, though Irisis couldn't understand why. Flydd, Yggur, Klarm and Troist had been inside the tent with Nisbeth and Orgestre for hours, discussing something of great moment. The guards would not allow Irisis to go near, which was vexing. It was one of the few councils she had not been admitted to, and she was now desperate to find out if they'd heard anything about Nish.

She was trying to think of a way to get inside when Flydd put his head out through the tent flap. 'Guard, would you call for –. Ah, Irisis, food and drink for six, quick as you can.'

At any other time the order would have irritated her. Now she seized the opportunity, and shortly came back with a loaded tray and baskets hanging off each arm.

'No appeasement. Ever!' snapped General Orgestre as she entered. 'Nisbeth and I are agreed on that.'

That surprised Irisis, who'd always thought of Nisbeth as soft and kindly, perhaps a little too kindly.

'Thank you, Irisis.' Flydd reached for the tray.

She sidestepped him, set down the tray and the baskets, then went around the table handing out plates, which she filled with the best available from Flydd's private stores. Irisis slid another platter into the middle, poured drinks, bowed low and retreated to the other side of the tent. There she squatted, head bowed, like the meanest of servants.

'That will be all,' said Flydd.

Irisis pretended she hadn't heard.

Yggur chuckled. 'Nice try, Irisis, but you make a poor serving maid, for all your skill at aping one. Subservience isn't in your nature.'

She stood up and went for the flap. Irisis hadn't expected it to work but was disappointed nonetheless.

'Oh, let her stay!' Troist said irritably. 'Irisis has proven herself. Now can we get on?'

Irisis took a seat at the far end of the table and a morsel of smoked fish from the central platter, and tried to look inconspicuous in case they changed their minds.

'We still have disagreement on two issues,' said Flydd. 'What to do about Gilhaelith, and how we can possibly defend ourselves against such overwhelming numbers of the enemy.'

'I've always mistrusted the scoundrel,' said Yggur. 'Gilhaelith may not be actively aiding the enemy at this moment, but he's got a long history of it.'

'His only loyalty is to himself,' said Klarm. 'And ever has been.'

'It's got to be a complex double-cross,' said Yggur. 'A way of putting us all into the enemy's hands, in repayment of a deal he's made with them.'

'Whatever he's up to, let's capitalise on the opportunity he's given us,' said Troist. 'Assuming our farspeakers can be believed.'

'What do you have in mind?' said Yggur.

No one spoke. Irisis studied the troubled faces around the table. In the past few weeks the shape of the war had changed so dramatically, and so often, that no one had come to terms with it. Not even Flydd seemed to have a plan.

'We go to the exchange under a flag of truce,' said Grand Commander Orgestre. 'We use Flydd's field controller to stop the lyrinx from flying or using the Art, then attack with our massed forces and drive them over the cliffs.'

'Where did this sudden reckless streak come from, Grand Commander?' said Flydd. 'Just last spring you were preaching withdrawal.'

'I didn't know about all your secret weapons then. They've shifted the balance our way.'

'Meaning once you got a whiff of victory you couldn't keep your snout out of the trough,' Klarm muttered.

Troist directed a furious glare at the dwarf, who met it blandly. 'I won't countenance dishonouring a truce flag, Orgestre,' said Troist. 'Besides, their troops can march from the east in the time we can reinforce my army with yours. We'll be lucky to put eighty thousand into the field, while they'll have a quarter of a million, at least.'

'Anyway, I need Tiaan's completed node map before I can use my field controller at full strength,' said Flydd.

'*If* she returns,' said Yggur. 'Which we can't rely on. We've not heard from her since she left.'

'Farspeakers aren't reliable out in the Dry Sea, and she's only been gone five days,' said Flydd. 'She'll be back when she's done.'

'That could be two more weeks,' said Yggur.

'The lyrinx infantry won't be here for three,' said Troist, 'and it'll take nearly as long to bring our scattered forces to Ashmode. Besides, the field controller isn't going to even out such long odds, *if it works*.'

'The field controller works, even without Tiaan's final map,' said Flydd. 'I've already tested it. I should be able to cut off the fields where the lyrinx are camped. They won't be able to fly.'

'They'll still be able to fight two of us at a time,' Klarm said dryly. 'And what if a vital node fails on you? They're becoming more unreliable every day.'

'With the field controller, no individual node is vital,' said Flydd. 'That's the beauty of it. So, Governor, gentlemen, the pieces are drawing together. The final confrontation is going to be held between Ashmode and the Hornrace. But what kind of confrontation will it be? Do we move our armies into place, or not?'

'If that's where the enemy are,' said Klarm, 'we have to challenge them, whatever their numbers. But we'd better camp where it suits us best and them least, Generals. And make sure we've got somewhere to retreat to.'

'If you can't put forward a simple plan, I will!' said Orgestre, whose purple cheeks were growing ever more congested. 'The Dry Sea is their worst nightmare. I say we drive them down onto it and let them die of thirst.'

'A *wet* sea is their worst nightmare,' Flydd pointed out. 'A dry one is just solid land to fight on. Anyway, considering how greatly they outnumber us, we won't be able to force them anywhere.'

'I know you have a weapon they can't resist,' said Orgestre slyly.

'Is that so, Flydd?' said Yggur. 'Why haven't I heard of this before?'

'The artificers have only just perfected it,' said Flydd, clearly annoyed that the secret had come out before he was ready to announce it.

'I don't see why you invite me to your councils if you're going to keep me in the dark.' Yggur looked angrier than Irisis had seen him in a long time.

'Secrecy is an old habit,' said Flydd.

'What's the weapon?'

'It's based on the effect Tiaan saw in Alcifer when she shouted into her farspeaker. I've found a way to make the mindshock a hundred times stronger.'

'If you can get a thousand made in the next three weeks,' said Orgestre, 'and fly them up to me at Ashmode, I'll end this war within a week.'

'Really?' said Flydd. 'I might just take you up on that, Grand Commander. Our manufactories should be able to make five hundred. They're not difficult to put together once you know how.'

Orgestre bore the smile of a man who'd gained twice what he was hoping for. 'That'll do. I'll fence the beasts around with them, you can cut off their Arts with the field controller, and then we drive the lot of them over the Grey Cliffs onto the Dry Sea.'

'I don't trust miracle weapons,' said Troist.

'It's not, General,' said Flydd. 'You did the early tests.'

Orgestre threw back his chair and thumped the table, making the plates and cups rattle. 'Enough talking! It's time to act and we've got to do it *now*. We'll not be safe while a single breeding pair of lyrinx remain alive. If they survive the cliffs, we herd them into a circle on the salt and slaughter them. We've got to kill every male, every female and every child. Exterminate the lot!'

There was a long, shocked silence. 'I'd prefer to reach some accommodation –' said Flydd.

'You've failed to come up with a plan, so listen to mine,' Orgestre ground out. 'We end the war my way *now*, or sooner or later they'll end us.'

'Nisbeth?' said Flydd. 'Does Grand Commander Orgestre have your support?'

'I don't see any other choice,' the governor said. 'If he succeeds, we've saved Borgistry. If he doesn't, how are we worse off?'

'Whatever the cost, we pay it and get on with our lives,' said Orgestre. 'It's the only way, believe me. Your votes, if you please. Right hand for their annihilation, left for our capitulation, since we don't have anything in between.'

Orgestre and Nisbeth raised their right hands at once, and Klarm shortly after. Troist put up his left hand, as did Yggur. Flydd didn't raise either.

'Well, Flydd?' said Orgestre. 'It comes down to you, as usual. What's your vote?'

'I've already come to regret using the fungus against them,' said Flydd. 'To annihilate an entire species is a terrible crime against nature, and in the future I know we'll rue it. But if we don't, the war will go on and in the end we must lose it.'

'I won't be a party to it,' said Yggur. 'I've lived long enough to know that this is the *worst* solution you could come up with. It'll lead to more war, and more killing, not less.' His frosty eyes met Flydd's across the table. 'And I won't work with you again if you support it, Flydd.'

Flydd bowed his head. 'I hear your wisdom, Yggur, and you may be right, in the long run.' He looked around the group, breathing heavily. 'But truly, for our present survival, I can see no other way.' He raised his right hand.

Yggur thrust back his seat and walked out without a word.

'Then let it be done,' said Orgestre with savage glee.

SIXTY-SEVEN

Yggur did not leave them, though he travelled with Troist's army after that as they marched for Ashmode, and refused to have anything to do with Flydd. Klarm and Flydd tried to persuade him otherwise but he wouldn't relent.

'I can see the disaster coming and I'm not going to add to it,' he said when Flydd called on him one final time. 'I can't imagine how I thought the fungus would be the answer.'

'Then what would you do differently?' Flydd said furiously.

'I don't know, but genocide is not the solution.'

'If you can't suggest an alternative, better to keep your thoughts to yourself.'

'Don't use scrutator logic on me, Flydd. The only reason the war ever came to this stage is that the Council slew all those who spoke against it.'

'What are you talking about?' said Flydd, deadly cold now.

'You're not the only one to have dug through the rubble of Nennifer, Scrutator. I went looking for the origins of this most pointless of all wars. Back in the early days, the forerunners of the Council executed all those who warned about going to war against the lyrinx. Their warnings of unending war have come true to the letter. The Council wanted war before ever the enemy did, and silenced everyone who spoke against it.'

Flydd considered that, then said, 'If you're so opposed to Orgestre's solution, what are you doing here?'

'There may yet be a chance to save you from your folly.'

Kattiloe's thapter returned from Tiksi ten days after it had left, confirming that the lyrinx had indeed abandoned the fields of war and were streaming west. Everyone knew it by then, however, for the bulk of the fliers had already reached Ashmode and were searching everywhere for Gilhaelith, as was everyone else.

An increasingly stressed and irritable Flydd had spent two and a half weeks looking for the geomancer, who hadn't gone to Ashmode at all. Gilhaelith wasn't that much of a fool. He'd headed that way after seizing the relics, but once out of sight he'd set down by the City of the Bargemen and ordered Flangers and the other soldiers out. He'd recruited new guards and servants and flown away, in darkness, to an inconspicuous ravine forty leagues away along the southern rim of the Dry Sea from Ashmode.

There he'd hidden in the Golden Terraces, an ancient village honeycombed into a layer of yellow chalk between two sets of the Grey Cliffs above the empty sea. The Golden Terraces had been abandoned when the Sea of Perion dried up two thousand years ago, and since then had only been inhabited by bats. Gilhaelith planned to hide there until the lyrinx had assembled their armies at Ashmode, and would have succeeded but for an unfortunate accident.

A metal panel at the back of his thapter, torn loose by the lyrinx that had leapt onto the racks, fell off as the thapter flew high over one of the impoverished villages not far from the Golden Terraces. It landed in a pigsty, killing the village chief's prized porker, and the chief was so incensed he insisted that his outrage be communicated to Flydd himself.

It took a week for the messenger to find someone with a far-speaker, and another day to convince him to send the message, but Irisis, who received it, understood its significance at once.

After that it was a relatively simple matter to trace Gilhaelith's possible destinations along the rim of the Dry Sea and search them one by one. If he had gone much further west he would have had to cross into Aachim lands, which were so tightly patrolled that not even a bat could have entered unnoticed.

Somehow Orgestre got wind of the discovery and insisted on coming, whereupon Yggur, whom Irisis hadn't seen for a week, decided that he had to be there as well. Flydd didn't say anything but Irisis could feel the tension between the three of them all the way.

Three weeks after Gilhaelith escaped with the relics, Flydd's thapter dropped without warning over the upper cliffs and settled onto the highest of the Golden Terraces, which was covered in powdery dust of yellow chalk.

By the time everyone got out, Gilhaelith's guards had their crossbows trained on them. 'Put your weapons on the ground, then your hands in the air,' the captain said.

Irisis laid her sword on the ground and raised her hands, scanning the guards for a short, stocky, achingly familiar figure. She didn't see Nish anywhere.

A guard collected the weapons, everyone was ordered to remove their coats, and their bodies were patted down carefully. The guard took a number of exotic items from Flydd's pockets.

'You may come in now,' the captain said.

They followed, except for Flydd, who had sat down and was taking his boot off.

'What's the matter with you?' the captain said.

'Gravel in my boot. I won't be a minute.'

They went inside, Flydd put his boot on and followed.

'Surr?' began Irisis, desperate to discover what had happened to Nish.

'Not now!' he hissed. They were led down dusty halls excavated deep into the chalk, and into a chamber lit by lamps that were just lighted wicks floating in bowls of oil. 'What game are you playing, Gilhaelith?' Flydd said as Gilhaelith turned away from his geomantic globe and came to meet them. If he was shocked at being discovered, he didn't show it.

'My own,' he replied with an almost uncanny serenity, 'and it will do you no good to threaten me. I'm beyond all threats now.'

Flydd considered that for a moment, head to one side. 'Why so?'

'As you should know by now, I'm dying. I plan to make amends with what time I have left, and you can neither bribe nor threaten me!'

Flydd regarded him sceptically. 'You can begin by handing over the relics.'

Gilhaelith smiled thinly. 'I've made sure that your Art won't avail you here. Anyway, I've won your war for you, without a life being lost, so I don't see what you're complaining about!'

'We're outnumbered three to one by a superior enemy, who are closing in on Ashmode even now. Where's the victory?'

'They'll do anything – even agree to peace – to get the relics back. I've already demonstrated that!'

'Ah, but can you hold onto them long enough to strike your bargain?' said Flydd. 'And once it's struck, what then? They'll have us at their mercy, and mercy isn't a quality associated with lyrinx!'

'Nor with the scrutators,' said Gilhaelith pointedly. 'I intend to have the lyrinx swear, on their sacred relics, to cease hostilities and not attack humanity, unless humanity strikes the first blow. Then you can negotiate for peace and I'm sure they'll agree, since they've lost everything else!'

Flydd laughed aloud. 'The damage you suffered must have been to your wits. There are few humans I'd entrust the world to on the security of an oath. As for lyrinx, none at all!'

'I've found lyrinx honour to be superior to the human kind,' said Gilhaelith. 'These relics are sacred to them.'

'Surr?' said Irisis.

Flydd trod on her toe. 'Then you'd better tell us why, Gilhaelith.'

'I intend to. Come this way.' Gilhaelith led them upstairs and along a corridor that was ankle-deep in the yellow chalk dust. He eased open a borer-riddled door into a small room cleaned of

661

dust. On the floor were three long crates. He levered the top off the first.

They crowded around, Irisis looking over the top of Flydd's head. The crate contained the perfectly preserved body of a man and a woman. Their skin was stained dark by tar but the flesh had shrunk only a little. Both wore necklaces of silver, gold and semi-precious stones. A bound book rested on its spine between them. The first few pages had been separated, revealing illuminations of great delicacy.

In the second crate were the bodies of three children, equally well preserved. At their feet were items of clothing, leather boots, three more books, and bowls, knives and other personal items.

The third crate held more books and manuscripts; a pair of unstained, woven tapestries; small carvings in wood and amber; a stringed instrument; a kind of wooden flute with nine finger-holes; scrolls covered in musical notations; painted timber panels, so tar-stained that the images were indecipherable; as well as a wooden case containing crystals of yellow brimstone, including a large, perfect one. Most items bore the marks of the tar, though the contents of the second crate were clean.

Flydd surveyed the crates again. 'I don't understand.'

'You're so used to war you can't see beyond it,' said Gilhaelith.

Irisis studied the faces in the crates. There was something about the eyes. 'Xervish –?'

Gilhaelith held up his hand and she did not go on. 'Lyrinx, it has often been remarked, are similar to us in many ways. People have noted – Tiaan for one – that some of the enemy display more humanity than humanity itself. There's good reason for it. They're just as human as we are.'

Flydd laughed in his face. 'You've been eating your poisonous caterpillars again.'

'Take another look at them, surr,' said Irisis. 'Look at the eyes. They do resemble lyrinx eyes.'

Gilhaelith shot her a keen glance. 'More than eight thousand years ago, a village was established near Snizort to harvest tar, naphtha and brimstone from the vast tar deposits there. In time the village became a town, and then a wealthy one, whose philosophers had the gold and the leisure to devote themselves to the study of arcane arts. They uncovered glimmerings of the Secret Art and were probably the first people on Santhenar to do so. In the records that have passed down through the Histories the town was named Ric Rints, but the kings' chroniclers who made those records used a different alphabet to ours and the name was written down incorrectly. The people of that town called it Lyr Rinx.

'The town grew ever wealthier from its people's restrained use of the Art, eventually attracting the attention of distant powers who saw that the Art might also be used to subdue unruly neighbours. Lyr Rinx's philosophers, or mancers as we would now call them, refused to sell their secrets or go into employment. In consequence, an edict was passed, making it a capital crime to use their Art in any way.

'The philosophers had the support of the townspeople and continued to practise their Art in secret as they sought a way to escape to a better place. However, after decades of persecution, the wrath of the great powers came down on them. Many of the philosophers were put to the sword, Lyr Rinx was razed and the fields surrounding it sowed with salt.

'But still the people would not give up their Art, for it was the keystone of their culture now, and they were close to completing the ark which would allow them to escape their persecutors. They built a floating village in the middle of the Great Seep and continued to practise their Arts for some weeks before they were discovered. Their enemies came, destroying everything, but the surviving philosophers had found the way. They used their power to tear open a hole into the void. It wasn't such a feat back then, long before the Forbidding.

'The philosophers and half the villagers fled to safety, as they thought, in the void, for its savage nature was not then known. The remainder were slain, and the living and the dead, and all their goods, were dumped into the Great Seep to disappear forever.'

Gilhaelith paused for a sip from a metal bowl. Irisis glanced at Flydd. His face was inscrutable, but she felt sure the tale was

663

true. Yggur seemed to think so too, despite his antipathy to Gilhaelith.

'But those who'd escaped into the void did not find the haven they'd expected. It was a savage place where the only rule was *eat or be eaten*. Their only hope was to transform themselves from weak humans into fierce, terrible creatures, totally dedicated to survival. And that is what those gentle philosophers did. They used the Art to flesh-form their unborn children. Such magic was possible in the void, where all things are mutable. They modelled themselves on fierce winged humanoids called thranx, but called themselves lyrinx so they would never forget where they had come from. And each succeeding generation changed themselves more, until they were more like thranx than the thranx themselves, and had lost all semblance of their former human selves.

'With their big, tough bodies, their fierce dispositions and unconquerable will to survive, not to mention their Art, the lyrinx survived and even prospered in the void. But they weren't content there, as they had been at home.

'They were never completely comfortable in those huge bodies, which didn't quite *fit*. And many were unhappy with what they had become: a savage warrior race lacking art, culture or philosophy. But they had to be warriors to survive, and in their eight thousand years in the void they eventually lost all trace of their human culture. They knew where they had come from: Lyr Rinx, on Santhenar, and that they had fled to escape persecution. They knew they had lost their souls, and longed to go home and discover who they truly were. But not even the matriarchs knew that they had once been human.

'With time, their longing became unbearable and, when the Way between the Worlds was opened, they seized the opportunity to come home. They came in peace, offering friendship, but the people of Santhenar saw them as monsters just as brutal and vicious as the thranx. The lyrinx were attacked the instant they appeared and many were slain. They tried to explain, to negotiate, but their emissaries were slaughtered. They were persecuted, hated and reviled, just as they had been in the distant past.'

'What a load of rubbish!' said Orgestre. 'You can't believe a word he's saying, Flydd.'

'But the lyrinx were survivors now,' Gilhaelith went on, unfazed. 'They took refuge in the deepest forests and the wildest mountains of Meldorin, and bided their time until they could come to terms with their new world. It wasn't easy, for their bodies were even more uncomfortable on this heavy world than they had been in the void. They stayed in hiding for more than fifty years, until they'd replaced those who'd been slain and their numbers began to increase, and then set out to take back a portion of their former world. It was only then, a hundred and fifty years ago, that the war began. It was a war for freedom, yet all the while they had one objective in mind, to go home to Lyr Rinx and discover their past.

'When they eventually tracked down the lost town to Snizort, there was not a trace of Lyr Rinx, and the peasants who now dwelt in the area, still living off the tar deposits, knew nothing of the impossibly distant past. The lyrinx set out to uncover it themselves. It proved a far greater task than they'd expected, even after they'd established their underground city at Snizort. Finally, with my help, they froze the molten tar of the Great Seep, tunnelled in and recovered these bodies and these relics.

'It turned them upside down to look upon their ancient selves, to see the relics of their proud culture – the music, the books, the art, the Histories – and compare it to what they had become. On the outside they were lyrinx; within, they longed to be human again. For a hundred and fifty years these once gentle, peace-loving philosophers had been waging war on their own kind.

'Matriarch Gyrull was transformed by the discovery, and where she led, her people followed. Flesh-forming had allowed them to survive in the void, but back on Santhenar it caused physical discomfort and mental anguish. They had gained powerful bodies, but at the expense of their spirit, their soul, their culture and their Histories.

'Gyrull realised that they looked on themselves through the wrong side of the glass. They'd seen their winged, clawed and fanged selves as the peak of perfection, and in the void they had been. Now she realised that the imperfect ones – the wingless, those lacking skin armour or the ability to skin-speak – were closest to their true selves. Before they could regain what they had lost, they would have to return to the semblance of the Sacred Ones. Their ancestors!' He indicated the people in the boxes.

'And with this realisation, last winter, came another: that they were vile cannibals who had been living on their own kind. Most gave up eating human flesh. In the battle for Borgistry, if you recall, they no longer fed on our fallen. They could not stop the war, for humanity would not rest until the lyrinx had been wiped out, but they were losing heart.'

'When did you realise all this?' said Flydd.

'I discovered part of the story before Tiaan shanghaied me to Fiz Gorgo,' said Gilhaelith, 'though it wasn't until I stole the relics, and demanded that they abandon their sieges in return for them, that I began to put the final picture together. The lyrinx would only accede to my demands if the relics mattered more than the war, and so it proved. We thought they came for conquest, but that story never fitted what I knew of them.'

'A pretty *tale*,' said General Orgestre, 'but even if it were true it doesn't change our situation. Just thirty leagues away at Ashmode are hundreds of thousands of lyrinx, each the equal of two of our finest soldiers, and more are coming all the time. We only have eighty thousand men to put against them. If they could turn themselves into humans and abandon their warlike ways, I might be prepared to listen. In the meantime, humanity stands in peril of being wiped out. We have to proceed with the plan.'

'What plan is that?' said Gilhaelith.

'Our troops are now moving, under cloaking shields, to the high ground. We will attack without warning, using Flydd's mind-shockers mounted on our thapters and air-floaters, to drive the enemy over the cliffs.'

'They can climb cliffs as easily as we walk down the garden path,' said Gilhaelith.

'Then we drive them down,' gritted Orgestre, 'and out to the Dry Sea. Once we get them there, we force them into the salt lakes to drown, or onto the salt to die of thirst. Any that try to break free, we annihilate with our massed clankers.'

'I won't allow it,' said Gilhaelith. 'And while my Art holds, you shall not have the relics.'

Flydd, who had manoeuvred himself behind Gilhaelith, withdrew a sock full of wet chalk dust from his pocket and thumped Gilhaelith over the back of the head with it.

'Your Art no longer holds. Bring the crates, troops, and let's get on with it.'

'At last he acts,' said Orgestre. 'Well done, Flydd. Now let's deal with the enemy in the only way they can understand.'

Yggur said nothing, but his eyes showed such contempt that Irisis had to look away.

As they were leaving Flydd pointed to the geomantic globe. 'Put that in its box and bring it as well. You never know when it might come in handy.'

SIXTY-EIGHT

The poorly trained guards quickly surrendered once they saw that their master had fallen. They were herded into Kimli's thapter, which had been concealed in one of the caverns. A distraught Kimli was found, reunited with her machine and told to take the soldiers to the army camp, which had been set up some leagues south of Ashmode. Yggur went with them. Daesmie and Merryl were also discovered in makeshift cells and freed. Flydd's troops loaded the crates into Kattiloe's thapter and they shot up from the terrace in clouds of yellow chalk.

'We didn't ask him about Nish,' she said miserably.

'I had more urgent business to attend to than your bloody love life,' said Flydd. 'You can ask him yourself when he comes round.'

They flew high above the cliffs towards Ashmode, but long before they reached it she saw the lyrinx camps, extending like dark ink blotches for leagues along the brink of the uppermost cliffs.

'Fly over them,' said Flydd. 'A trifle lower, Kattiloe. Let's find out exactly what we're up against.'

Kattiloe put the nose of the thapter down and headed towards the nearest of the camps, but shortly the noise of the mechanism cut out. She drew a sharp breath and her fingers danced over the controls.

'What's the matter?' said Flydd.

The thapter was falling, gathering speed, the wind whistling around it. 'I can't draw any power. The field is gone.'

Gilhaelith, who was slumped against the side wall fingering the bump on his head, gave a thin smile. 'What a pickle.'

'What's going on?' cried Flydd. 'Gilhaelith?'

'The lyrinx have walled themselves off with a dead zone. You can't approach them in any contrivance that needs power.'

'How have they done that?'

The whistling was now so loud that Irisis could hardly hear. She went up on tiptoes, looked over the side and blanched. The ground was approaching at frightening speed and, in what was obviously a game of bluff, she hoped Flydd would show sense and give in quickly.

'I should have thought that was obvious. With their power patterner, Flydd,' Gilhaelith chuckled. 'It's like your field controller, only better.'

'How did you know about it?' Flydd said.

'I tapped into Golias's globe. *You* may control the fields, if Tiaan ever comes back with her map, but *they* can control the flow of power from nodes. And they know them all. They mapped Santhenar a hundred and fifty years ago, trying to find Lyr Rinx.'

'Surr,' said Kattiloe, pulling at her blonde plaits with her free hand, 'what should I do?'

'How the hell would I know?' Flydd said savagely. He looked down at the rapidly approaching ground and cracked. 'How do we get out of this, Gilhaelith? I know you've got a way.'

'Makes no difference to me. I'm dying and you've taken away my last hope.'

'What hope? Quickly, man.'

'To exchange the relics for their power patterner, to see if I could repair the damage in my brain with it,' Gilhaelith said with provocative deliberation.

'You can use it when we get it,' Flydd said at once. 'Anything you want.'

'And I want my freedom,' said Gilhaelith. 'On your honour. As a *man*, not a scrutator, of course.'

'You have my word,' snapped Flydd.

Gilhaelith stood up, wobbly on his long shanks. 'Turn away, little Kattiloe. Make for that knobbed peak to the south, if you can.'

'Not sure that I can make it, surr,' said Kattiloe, turning the machine. 'Thapters glide like bricks.'

'Well, just do your best.'

'What if we can't reach the peak?' said Irisis.

Gilhaelith gave her a lazy smile. 'We make a hole in the ground you could fit a house in.'

Kattiloe's fingers worked furiously and the machine turned, though it still seemed to be going down much faster than across. The ground wasn't far away at all now.

The thapter hit a broad column of rising air, lurched sharply, and Kattiloe expertly used the lift to skip across to the other side. The thapter bounced as it came out again, heading directly for the knob and looking as though it was going to plunge straight into it at high speed.

The mechanism groaned, died away, grunted, then resumed its familiar whine. Kattiloe jerked the controller and the thapter shot by the side of the knob then curved away to the south.

No one spoke for a long time, although Gilhaelith was still smiling.

'Gilhaelith,' Irisis said as pleasantly as she could, 'where's Nish?'

'I left him behind when we snatched the relics,' Gilhaelith said, as if Nish were of no significance.

'What do you mean, *left him behind?*' She took him by the coat and lifted him to his toes. Gilhaelith was a good head taller, but he looked alarmed.

'Dozens of lyrinx were just seconds away and the soldiers on the ground were dead. I couldn't wait for Nish to get aboard, so I went without him.' He shrugged.

Irisis let him go, turned away, then swung back and brought a ferocious right hook out of nowhere to crash into his jaw. It drove him against the wall, and as he crumpled to the floor she said, 'If Nish is dead, so are you.'

She stumbled down the ladder, blinking tears out of her eyes, and threw herself on the floor between Merryl and one of the soldiers. Merryl gripped her shoulder.

'I think I've cracked a knuckle on the bastard,' she muttered.

Irisis was making last-minute checks of the field controller, her knuckles bound in a yellow rag, when a pair of lyrinx flew towards the command area, a blue truce flag fluttering behind them. She hastily threw a cloth over the device and went out of the tent. Flydd, Troist and Orgestre conferred, then Flydd ordered a blue flag to be raised, indicating that they would allow the parley. The lyrinx flew away, shortly returning with the flag and another lyrinx, an enormous black, golden-crested male.

He landed by the command tents and went forward to where Flydd stood with but a single attendant, as required in the truce parley. The escort waited with the flag while the black lyrinx spoke briefly with them. After a minute or two he began flashing the most violent patterns of reds and blacks Irisis had ever seen. The black lyrinx abruptly turned to the flagpole, wrenched it out of the ground and snapped it across his knee. He tore the truce flag into two, trampled it into the dust and climbed into the sky so rapidly that his escort, still holding the other flag, was left far behind.

'He didn't like your attitude?' Irisis said after they'd gone.

Yggur followed her over, with Troist.

'He demanded to know why Gilhaelith hadn't kept his word,' said Flydd, visibly shaken. 'I explained the new situation and demanded that he hand over the power patterner, sue for peace and enter into a pact of eternal friendship, after which we'd consider returning the relics. Perhaps I overplayed my hand.'

'It would appear that way,' said Yggur.

Flydd looked as if he wanted to punch Yggur in the mouth.

'He demanded that I hand over the stolen relics uncondi-tionally,' Flydd said. 'I – I went too far. I threatened to destroy them if he didn't cooperate. He pointed out that, if we did, we'd have nothing to bargain with, and they would slaughter us to the

671

last man. I suggested that he might get a surprise if he tried, and the next I knew he was gone.'

'He came to bargain in good faith,' said Yggur, 'and you showed him, yet again, that the scrutators have none.'

'Perhaps I've grown too hard, or too desperate,' said Flydd.

'Then we'd better get ready to fight,' said Troist. 'And I really hope your mind-shockers and your field controller are up to the business, Flydd, because at the moment they're the only thing between us and destruction.'

The lyrinx attacked two hours later but the defence did not go as expected. Flydd's field controller had no effect on the enemy's Arts and devices, though it had been operating perfectly that morning. While Irisis was trying to work out what the matter was, Orgestre and Troist hastily sent out four hundred clankers, each containing one of the mind-shockers tuned to a set of five specially modified master farspeakers, each with its operator, and all under the direction of Klarm. The remaining hundred mind-shockers had been kept for defence. The plan was for the clankers to encircle the enemy on three sides. The master far-speaker operator would send its signal and each mind-shocker would emit a ferocious burst of barbed mindspeech, so painful that all lyrinx nearby would be forced to flee in the only direction left to them – over the cliffs and down to the Dry Sea. There, being uncomfortable in heat and bright light, they would be at a greater disadvantage.

At least, that was the plan. Unfortunately the mind-shockers did not work either. After the first shock was sent the lyrinx fell about laughing, then formed up in their ranks and charged.

'They were working perfectly this morning!' Flydd said when the operators reported back. He wasn't so much shocked as dazed. He couldn't work out what had gone wrong. 'We tried it on three captured lyrinx and they nearly shed their skins in agony.'

'Well, it's not working here,' shrilled the operator. 'They're coming –'

They heard nothing more from her.

The master farspeaker operators tried again and again as the clankers retreated to the army, but the mind-shockers kept failing. Troist threw together a desperate defence, with eight thousand battle clankers forming a ring of armour around the foot soldiers, though such an overwhelming force of lyrinx would soon breach it. Possibly afraid that the relics would be destroyed, the enemy didn't launch an all-out attack, but they forced the army around in a sweeping curve until its only line of retreat was towards the cliffs.

Flydd and Irisis held a hurried conference to discover what had gone wrong while Troist stood by in case they made a breakthrough.

'Their power patterner must be doing it,' said Flydd, trying to get his head into the complex bowels of the field controller, though Irisis couldn't imagine what he hoped to see there.

'Surr,' said an anxious artisan, terrified that he'd do irreparable damage, 'if you could be careful –'

He whipped his head out and she leapt backwards out of the way.

'Their power patterner isn't stopping our clankers from going,' said Troist, furious that his men were dying so uselessly.

'Who knows how they can pattern power?' mused Flydd. 'What do we do now?'

'We go where they drive us,' said Troist bitterly, for the enemy were closing in all around, leaving open only a steep and rugged track that led down a gully eroded into the cliffs, all the way down to the Dry Sea. The clankers would be lucky to get down it without overturning. 'They're doing exactly what we planned on doing to them.'

'The enemy would appear to have a sense of irony,' Gilhaelith observed. 'I'm fascinated to see what you're going to do now, scrutator.'

Flydd crab-walked away and roared at the rest of the artisans, who came running. 'Irisis?' he bellowed. 'Get this wretched thing fixed or I'll have all your heads.'

The lyrinx drove them down onto the Dry Sea, where Troist set up camp and ordered his troops to prepare what defences

673

they could. Irisis was barely aware of the desperate day-long flight, or the bloody skirmishes that punctuated it. Eleven artisans and crafters had been shoehorned into a specially modified twelve-legged clanker, the only kind big enough to accommodate them and their apparatuses. They worked all day and through the night, taking the field controller apart and checking every piece. They made a number of modifications that should have improved the device if they ever got it working again, but couldn't identify any failure.

'Do you think if we asked Yggur?' Irisis said tentatively, for Flydd seethed with a cold rage that she'd only seen before on the way to Nennifer. She didn't know how to deal with it.

'I've asked!' Flydd said. 'I've begged, pleaded and even humbled myself, but he won't budge.'

'Have you . . . er, given any thought to what he said?'

'I've thought of nothing else, Crafter. I've wracked my brains for a solution that doesn't involve wiping out the enemy. My guts burn like acid, I can't sleep, I –'

He laid his head against the side of the clanker and closed his eyes for a moment. 'Anyway, that's my worry, not yours. Let's go over it one more time.'

'It's got to be their power patterner,' said Irisis blearily, much later, as the sun rose over the salt.

'Of course it is,' snapped Flydd, who'd reluctantly come to the same conclusion at the end of the sleepless night. 'I just don't see how it can be affecting our field controller. That's why we put those banks of charged crystals at the heart of it – so it wouldn't need to draw on the field at all. Otherwise any node-drainer could bring it down.'

'Maybe that's the problem,' said Irisis. 'I wonder . . .? What has the field been doing during our flight? Has anyone been watching it?'

'It's behaving oddly, Crafter,' said the youngest artisan, Nouniy, who was only seventeen and wore her blonde hair in a myriad of plaits, in imitation of famous Pilot Kattiloe. 'It's been whirling, actually.'

674

'Whirling?' said Irisis.

'That's the only way I can describe it.' Nouniy demonstrated its motion in the air with a fingertip.

'Curious,' said Irisis, touching her pliance and taking a look for herself. Pulling the rear hatch open, she knelt down and began scratching a design on the salt with the point of her knife.

'What are you doing?' said Flydd, crouching beside her with an audible click of his kneecaps.

'The cycling field must be inducing a contrary field around your sensing crystals, cancelling them out. So the rest of the field controller is working but, since you can't sense how the field is changing, you can't do anything with it. Now, if we were to just add . . .'

She sketched for five or six minutes, stood up and looked at the design from all sides, then nodded. 'That'll work. Let's get it made.' Irisis carefully carved the pattern out of the salt and crushed it under her boot, in case of spies or traitors.

An aide ran up with a folded message strip. Flydd unfolded it and handed it back to her. She bowed and withdrew.

'Better hurry,' said Flydd. 'Our entire army is on the salt. Whatever the enemy have in mind, it's not going to be long in coming. And get someone to call Tiaan again.'

Each time a thapter was heard he ran out and stared up at the sky, but Tiaan didn't appear.

After the modifications had been made, Irisis successfully tested the field controller and went looking for Flydd to tell him the good news. He was preparing a last-ditch defence. If that failed their only options were a suicidal attack on an enemy that vastly outnumbered them, or a desperate flight into the Dry Sea. And everyone knew how that would end.

Troist's twelve-legged clanker came creaking and groaning towards them, stopped, and the rear hatch was thrown open. Gilhaelith staggered out, as white as the salt beneath his feet. He threw up and wavered off towards a vacant tent.

Troist got out soon after, tally sheets under his arm, and came looking for Flydd to give his report.

675

'What's the matter with Gilhaelith?' said Flydd. 'He's usually the picture of self-control.'

'I took him up to one of the battlefronts. I thought it'd do him good to see what his meddling had caused.'

'He didn't like it?'

'It was a savage attack, and our counterattack was even more bloody. We were right in the thick of it and when it was over, the bodies – theirs and ours – were piled higher than my clanker. A lot of them were in pieces.'

'That's what war is like,' said Flydd. 'It doesn't even shock me any more.'

'It still has an impact on me,' said Troist. 'But Gilhaelith had never seen a battle before. I thought he was going to throw up all over my operator.'

'It'll do him good,' Flydd said callously.

'It's given him a lot to think about. How's it going?' said Troist, nodding towards the field controller.

'It's got to work,' said Irisis, gnawing on a leathery strip of some unidentifiable dried meat, as tasteless as anything she'd ever eaten in the manufactory.

'Only if humanity is fated to survive,' said Klarm, who'd recently came back from a spying flight in Chissmoul's thapter. He was drinking strong black ale, his third for the morning, despite the edict that only weak beer was allowed before battle. Klarm had to have his drink. 'It may be that our time is over and the lyrinx are due to inherit Santhenar.'

'I always thought, if we did lose,' said Irisis, 'it would be after some mighty siege lasting for weeks, full of incredible deeds of courage and derring-do. I didn't think they'd just drive us out onto the salt until we died of thirst.'

'There'll be an almighty battle before it comes to that. I'm not going out with a whimper.'

'Nor I,' she said fiercely.

'I'll make my last stand beside you any day,' Klarm said.

'Then bring it on,' she said savagely, flinging the dried meat away. 'With Nish gone, I don't have anything left to hope for.'

'He could have survived,' said Klarm. 'I've been to the site and found the bodies of the soldiers, but no Nish.'

'They must have taken him away to question him. And after that, to eat him.'

'The lyrinx don't eat people any more, Irisis. Gilhaelith was right about that.'

'They still kill them, though.'

Irisis stood in the shade of the canvas, watching as Flydd readied the field controller for a last desperate attempt. The struggle was going to be a long-range one, field controller against power patterner, so her work was done unless something broke or needed adjustment. The scrutator was sitting under a piece of sailcloth stretched out with ropes and propped up on poles to form an open shelter whose roof rose about four spans above the salt. He was stripped to the waist and covered in perspiration. She wished she could do the same but that wouldn't have done in an army camp. Down on the salt, autumn was like midsummer up above.

A stone's throw away, under another canvas, Klarm prepared to direct his team of operators, who were seated at a long table. Each had a farspeaker globe in front of them, tuned to the massive mind-shockers carried in the forward line of clankers. He and Flydd had concluded that the mind-shockers hadn't worked because of the failure of the field controller. Runners stood ready to carry messages back and forth between Klarm and Flydd's team at the field controller.

It squatted on five stubby legs in front of Flydd: an assortment of wires, crystals and strangely curved glass tubes protruding from the top of an open glass barrel. Its operator, Hilluly, another of those young cousins Nish had first tested at Fiz Gorgo, sat by the scrutator's side, her hands in wired gloves and a bird's nest of tangled wires and crystals on her head. She was petite, with ashy hair and Yggur's eyes. She wore a simple white gown belted tightly at a waist that could have been spanned by Klarm's hands.

A copy of Tiaan's original but incomplete node map was wrapped around the barrel of the field controller, which could be rotated back and forth. Graduated brass scales ran down the length of the barrel and around its circumference, with pointers that could be slid along to take measurements.

'What if we offered to give them the relics?' said Irisis.

'Out *here*? And give up the one small lever we have left?'

'Or threaten to destroy them?'

'I already tried that one,' Flydd said ruefully.

Ten spans away, at the far side of Flydd's shelter so the devices would not interfere with one another, Daesmie hunched over Golias's globe, relaying messages from the army detachments distributed around them to the four points of the compass, and from Chissmoul's thapter on watch high above. A runner stood by Daesmie. Because the salt was so flat, the enemy's movements could not be seen from here. If they broke, or attacked, the news would be relayed at once.

Irisis went over to read what Daesmie was writing. 'Still no change,' she said. 'None of the lyrinx armies have moved all morning.'

They're playing with us, Irisis thought. They can overrun us whenever they like. She carried the message slate to Flydd, who had a pointed ebony cane in his left hand. He scanned it, nodded and waved her away. Irisis stood well back, and the struggle began.

Flydd pointed to a purple coloured node on Tiaan's map with the tip of the cane, and said, 'Ifis 44, Nihim 5, Husp 220, Gyr 8.'

Hilluly moved her fingers inside the gloves. A green light spiralled along one of the twisted tubes; a red one slid down another like an icicle down a wire. Strange poppings came from inside the field controller. Sweat broke out on her forehead.

'They've countered your move with the power patterner, surr,' Hilluly gasped.

Flydd cursed. 'Ifis 38, Nihim 11, Husp 187, Gyr 22.' More lights and noises. Much more sweat.

'Countered at once,' panted Hilluly.

'Oh, have they?' cried the scrutator. 'Then let them try *this*!'

A third list, different names again, but the numbers were all single digits.

Hilluly was rigid, apart from her dancing fingers. A line of flies, which were everywhere down here, gathered on her wet lips. Irisis went to shoo them away but Flydd said, 'No!'

Hilluly gasped and fell forward. The flies rose and settled on the back of her gown, which was wet with perspiration.

'Now you can help her,' said Flydd.

Irisis gave the operator a cool drink. Hilluly sat up, rubbing her eyes with her gloved hands, then tore them off and examined her fingers. They were bright red. She rubbed them on her gown and said, 'Not that time either, surr.'

He rose from his seat, his every rib showing. 'Thank you, Hilluly.' Flydd went across to the farspeaker operator. 'Any movement yet?'

'No, surr,' said Daesmie. 'The enemy seem to be waiting for something to happen.'

'Keep listening. I'll be back in a minute.'

Irisis walked out with him. 'That looked like a game of Strategies.'

'It's exactly like it. I don't have a perfect understanding of the fields here, and neither do they. I have to guess where their knowledge lies, and their ignorance, and they the same about me. It seems we're evenly matched – whoever guesses or bluffs best will be the winner.'

'Or whoever lasts the longest.'

'True. They have greater endurance than we do.'

'Do you know anything about their operator?' said Irisis.

'Gilhaelith said it would be Ryll, the wingless male who made the power patterner, probably assisted by Liett. She worked with him to develop the first nylatl at Kalissin.'

'Is there any way we can target them?'

'We might if Tiaan were here. She knows them both.' Flydd glanced out at the empty sky.

'I don't think she's coming back,' Irisis said quietly.

'Neither do I.'

'It's going to be a long day.'

'I can't last all day and neither can Hilluly. She's already flagging.'

679

'We have other operators.'

'Aye, but to change from one to another in the middle of a contest rarely works. We're a team, Hilluly and I, and this extraordinary device you built.'

'Dozens of artisans worked on it, not just me.'

'And you supervised them, Crafter.'

'Let's see the device prove itself before we praise it,' Irisis said superstitiously. 'And Xervish, even if you win the game, what then?'

'We don't die immediately. More than that I can't say.'

'But you have a plan.'

'Yes. I just don't have much hope that it'll work.'

Flydd went across to Klarm. Irisis followed at a distance. She had to know what was going on.

'The enemy haven't moved,' Flydd said.

Klarm stretched and rubbed his eyes. 'How long will it be? I can't keep everyone on alert all day.'

'Tell them to put their heads down, if they want to. It'll be a while before you can use the mind-shockers, assuming we get that far,' said Flydd. 'I'll give you warning.' He swilled down a gullet full of tepid water and turned back. 'All right. Let's see what we can do now.'

The struggle went on, Flydd calling the numbers, Hilluly operating the field controller, and the flies hovering as if waiting for the inhabitants of the tent to die.

'There's movement in the south-west segment, surr,' called Operator Daesmie.

'Which way?'

'The enemy are moving away.'

'Quickly? *Fleeing*?' he said hopefully.

'No; quite slowly.'

'Oh well,' said Flydd. 'It's a point to our side, I suppose.'

'Unless it's a feint,' said Irisis.

'We'll soon know.'

It was not a feint. The enemy just seemed to be reorganising their forces. The game went on almost to dusk, by which time Hilluly was so exhausted that Irisis had to sit beside her and hold her up, and even subtly try to feed power to her, a dangerous thing to do at the best of times. Despite Flydd's earlier words, his back was as straight as ever and he seemed to be calling the numbers more confidently than before.

'Tell Klarm to get ready,' Flydd said suddenly. 'I think we're wearing them out.'

'Is that possible?' said Irisis. 'The lyrinx are tireless.'

'Physically, maybe,' he said. 'But their device must take more out of them than yours does.'

'We designed it that way.'

'They're moving,' shouted Daesmie. 'They're moving, surr!'

'Tell Klarm to do his work with the mind-shocker,' snapped Flydd. 'Yes, they're cracking. One last effort, Hilluly. Now, *now*! All the way!'

The messenger ran off.

'The enemy have broken in the southern segment,' called the farspeaker operator ten minutes later. 'You've won, surr. Well done.'

'It's just the first round,' said Flydd, 'but we'll keep the pressure up. Can you last a bit longer, Hilluly?'

'I think so,' she croaked.

'This will be easier. Holding them isn't as big a trial as breaking them in the first place.'

The struggle raged for days as Flydd and Klarm tried to drive the enemy's vastly superior forces south-west along the edge of the Dry Sea, towards the marshland and salt lakes below the Trihorn Falls, and the enemy tried to force them out into the waterless salt. After the first day, Flydd had to use a team of three operators, taking turns with them, for the work was so exhausting that none could keep it up for more than a few hours. Irisis called Tiaan over and again but heard no reply.

It was the strangest battle Irisis had ever experienced. Eighty thousand soldiers, and far more lyrinx, did little but march, sometimes towards each other and sometimes away. Flydd and his operators, and Klarm and his, sweated in their shelters, or tried to operate their devices in jouncing clankers.

'I thought the lyrinx were supposed to hate heat and bright light?' said Irisis on the second afternoon. She was practically fainting with heat exhaustion.

'They've equipped themselves with slit goggles just like ours,' said Flydd. 'As for the heat, they have adapted better than we expected.'

On the fourth day, just when they thought they had the enemy on the run, the struggle took a dramatic turn for the worse. Hilluly collapsed without warning and had to be carried out, unconscious. Her replacement lasted only a few minutes before she too slid off her chair. Flydd called for the third.

The girl sat down, trembling. Irisis gave her a hug but could see this operator would not do. Irisis exchanged glances with Flydd. His eyes were staring and she saw naked fear there. She hadn't seen that since he'd gone to meet the master flenser on the amphitheatre. As soon as Flydd caught her eye it vanished, and he was the same imperturbable scrutator she had always known, but the damage had been done. The enemy had struck back, and they were too strong.

The third operator lasted half an hour. By that time her movements were growing slower and slower. They had a little warning this time – just enough for Irisis to catch her as she fell. And not long after that, disaster struck. Klarm sat bolt upright, threw out his arms and legs and fell flat on his face. Blood poured out of his nose and mouth onto the salt. He wasn't dead but he couldn't move a finger.

Flydd looked at Irisis. He had regained control. 'Well, old friend,' he said casually, 'We're lost. I can't do any more.'

'What happens now?' She could repress her feelings too. 'Perhaps they'll make an exception and eat us.'

SIXTY-NINE

'The enemy are advancing,' Operator Daesmie said just after Irisis came back. Her face had gone white, which made the rings around her eyes stand out as purple as bruises. 'Every segment reports the same. They're coming right for us.'

'How could they attack Klarm?' said Flydd. 'I don't understand it.'

'What are you going to do?'

'Fight on, hopeless though it is without him.'

'I've sent for more field-controller operators,' said Irisis.

'It won't do any good. Hilluly and her cousins were the best. Besides, I'm being undermined and I don't know how to stop it.'

'What do you mean?'

'The power is still in the fields but now I can't get it out. It's as if someone else is attacking me from the other side.'

'Could the lyrinx have more than one power patterner?'

'I don't think so. This new attack is different. It's strong but ragged, as if whoever is using it is very powerful but not used to fighting this way.'

'Who can it be?'

Flydd made a face. 'Anabyng, their master mancer, I'd say. He'd have the power to bring Klarm down.'

'I've called for an operator to replace him too,' said Irisis.

683

'Whoever it is, he won't be strong enough.'

'It's Yggur.'

'He won't come,' said Flydd.

'He will,' said Irisis.

'How do you know?'

'Really, surr,' she grinned. 'Surely you don't expect me to reveal my wiles, even at such a time as this.'

He managed a smile, as she'd hoped. It heartened Irisis, for without Flydd the battle, the war and the world were lost. 'Not that. And what price must I pay?'

'I told him you'd save the lyrinx if we won. Somehow.'

The smile faded. 'You're assuming a lot, Crafter.'

'I'm expecting you to lose the battle, surr, so you won't have to find a solution.'

'A challenge,' said Flydd. He chuckled. 'What would I do without you, Irisis? I'll just have to prove you wrong.'

Shortly Yggur came across the salt, clad all in grey, his face carved out of granite. 'Flydd,' he said, nodding. 'You *will* hold to your word.'

Flydd stood there for a moment, in thought, then held out his hand. 'I will do everything in my power,' he said softly.

'Then let's fight the final battle,' said Yggur, and turned to Klarm's vacant seat, with the bloodstains on the salt beside it.

The runner came back with two more operators for Flydd. Irisis recognised both, though she did not know their names. Flydd sat the first girl beside him and explained what had to be done. She looked afraid. Moreover, even after three explanations she used the controller awkwardly and, as soon as power was drawn, began to cry. 'It hurts, surr. I can't do it.'

'No, you can't,' said Flydd gently. He glanced at the other, a thin, plain, stringy-haired young woman with a defiant set to her jaw. 'How about you, girl?'

'I'll do my best, surr,' she said stoutly.

'That's all I ask. What's your name?'

'Kirrily, surr.'

Kirrily did do her best, which turned out to be surprisingly good. She learned quickly and managed to last for over an hour, but after that succumbed quickly. Irisis drew off the gloves and laid her out on the ground to recover.

'The same,' said Flydd to her unspoken question. 'I was doing all right until my nemesis began to attack me at the same time. If the node map was better, or the operator stronger, I might be able to fight this new attacker as well as the lyrinx. But I can't.'

'There's fighting, surr,' called the farspeaker operator. 'The lyrinx have fallen on us in the west and the south. It's bloody.' She gave details.

'Now they're driving *us*,' said the scrutator. 'And they'll run through us in an afternoon.'

A soldier hurried in. 'The enemy is advancing this way, surr. General Troist says to pack up and get to your thapter.'

'How long do we have?'

'At the rate they're coming, they'll be here in an hour.'

'We'll keep going for a little while longer, tell him. You never know . . .' Flydd bit his lip.

The soldier saluted and ran out.

'There doesn't seem much point,' said Irisis.

'Once I pack up,' said Flydd, 'it's an admission of defeat and it'll be twice as hard to start again. Confidence is everything. I don't suppose you could operate a field controller, Irisis?'

'No.'

'I'll work without an operator for the moment. Run and see if Hilluly is any better yet. She was the best.'

After some time, Hilluly was brought back on a stretcher. She could barely sit up, but she didn't flinch from the job when Flydd asked her if she could take the gloves.

They worked for a while, whereupon Flydd turned to Irisis and shook his head. 'How long do we have?'

'Quarter of an hour, at most.'

'Then only a miracle can save us now. Tell Yggur he'd better get ready to run.'

Irisis loped across to him. Yggur was sitting at the master farspeaker, his big hands stretched over it. 'We've only got fifteen minutes, surr.'

'I'll be here until the end.'

Irisis ran back. Already she could hear the shouts of battle, the squeal of racing clankers, the cries of the dying.

'What's that?' said Irisis, cocking her head.

'I can't hear anything.'

'It sounds like a thapter.'

Flydd's face didn't change. He'd been disappointed too many times. 'Whose?'

Irisis ran outside. 'I think it's Tiaan and Malien,' she yelled.

'Signal them, quick! And tell Yggur to get his team ready, just in case I can pull something out of a very empty bag.'

'He's ready.'

The thapter was drifting around in circles, looking for the command tent. They wouldn't find it – it had been packed and loaded into a clanker long ago. All the tents were down and a line of clankers were moving out into the Dry Sea – the suicide path, as Flydd called it.

Irisis ran out into the open space, waving her arms frantically, but the thapter continued north. She stood looking after it, praying that it would come back on another sweep. The anguished cries and savage roars grew louder. There was no time to waste. Irisis ran back towards the shelter; and then she heard the thapter again.

She waved furiously and to her joy it dropped sharply, turned in her direction and came to rest just outside the shelter. Tiaan's face appeared over the side.

'Tiaan!' Irisis screamed. 'Flydd needs your map. Desperately.' She pointed to Flydd's shelter.

Tiaan seemed to hesitate for a second, then she scrambled over the side, roll of linen in hand, and ran in. Irisis wrapped the map around the barrel of the field controller, over the top of the old map.

'I've never been more glad to see anyone in my life,' said Flydd. 'Can you operate this, Tiaan?'

'Of course,' she said, putting on the gloves and helmet. 'I did the first trials, remember? Though I wouldn't be as good as a trained –'

'No time for that. He pointed with his cane to a node out in the Dry Sea, and muttered, 'Ifis 312, Nihim 99, Husp 3, Gyr 64.'

Tiaan flexed her fingers. She seemed to be taking a long time to follow him. It would not be easy to make the mental switch from flying the thapter.

Flydd glanced at Operator Daesmie, who shook her head. He pointed and rapped another series. Tiaan followed more quickly. Again the interrogative glance; again the little shake of the head.

A pair of soldiers appeared at the entrance. 'The enemy are coming on quickly, surr,' the first yelled. 'You must go now.'

'We'll just be one minute.'

Irisis could now see the army retreating towards them, only a few hundred paces away. They were still fighting, but once they broke, the enemy could cross the distance in well under a minute.

Flydd was now calling his series without a pause, his pointer flicking from one part of the map to the other so fast that Irisis could barely follow it. Sweat rolled down his bare chest. Even Tiaan was perspiring.

Irisis ran to the farspeaker operator and put an encouraging hand on her arm. 'How's it going?'

'Nothing yet,' Daesmie said, one eye on her globe and the other to the right, where the enemy were advancing. Though terrified, she held to her duty.

Irisis could feel the strain building. Her head was pounding like a racing clanker, there was a roaring in her ears and she could taste blood in her mouth. Were they all about to suffer Klarm's fate, just from being near the field controller? She squeezed her pliance in one fist and the fields flamed around her as allies and enemies drew on them for every ounce of power they could take.

The map was spinning now, the cane flicking back and forth, Flydd choking out the numbers, scarlet-faced. He looked about to have a seizure. He stood up on his toes, roared out a set and Tiaan's fingers danced.

And then Irisis felt something break with a wrench that set the fields bouncing.

'Yes!' roared Flydd, brandishing his fist at the purple sky. 'Yggur, get ready to use the mind-shocker. It'll work this time.'

'It'd better,' grunted Yggur. 'Team, *now!*'

'Have you broken the power patterner?' said Irisis to Flydd.

'No,' he said grimly, 'but I *have* broken Anabyng's attack.'

'Better get on with it,' said Irisis. 'That's the enemy just out there.'

He glanced that way and his red face paled. 'So close. All right, Tiaan, the last effort. Ryll and Liett are using the power patterner. Take advantage of any weaknesses you're aware of.'

Again the tiny hesitation before she said, 'I'll do my best.'

The struggle went on. The enemy had temporarily stalled but their numbers were overwhelming. The soldiers of the rear-guard were fighting to the death to protect them and create a chance for everyone else. But the dead were piling up and the lyrinx must break through at any moment.

'Call Troist,' she yelled at the operator. 'Tell him we're still working.'

'I have. He said his men can't hold out any longer.'

'Neither can we.' Irisis held a cool drink to Flydd's cracked lips and sponged his forehead with water. She offered a drink to Tiaan but Tiaan shook her head.

'Mind-shocker, now!' Flydd shouted to Yggur. 'Irisis, keep an eye out. Tell me if it's working.'

The air crackled as Yggur went to work, and Irisis felt a faint throb at the base of her skull, a momentary weakness in her limbs. Yggur was directing the mind-shocker so powerfully that even she could feel it.

Flydd was growing hoarse now and the cane wasn't moving as quickly as before. Irisis glanced over her shoulder and saw the enemy for the first time. Troist's line had broken.

'I can see the enemy. To the thapter, surr!'

'Wait!' said Flydd, his teeth clenched so tightly she expected them to shatter. He choked out another set of numbers.

Tiaan's fingers raced, then went still. She looked questioningly across to the scrutator, who wasn't saying anything. He was staring at the farspeaker.

'They've broken,' Operator Daesmie said, her eyes glassy. She was drenched with sweat and Irisis realised that she had neglected Daesmie, who had been working for hours without a break. 'They've broken, surr!'

Flydd lurched to his feet, looking around wildly.

'No, surr,' cried Daesmie. 'The *enemy* have broken.'

'Broken?' Flydd whispered, unable to comprehend, much less believe that they had finally done it.

Yggur was slumped in his chair, utterly drained.

'Come outside, surr,' said Irisis. She helped him out, then signalled to Malien. 'Take us up so we can see what's going on.'

Yggur looked up as Flydd staggered by. 'Well, Scrutator,' he said in a hoarse rasp, 'I've met my end of the bargain.'

'And I will honour mine,' said Flydd. 'Though I've no idea how.'

The thapter slipped into the air. The enemy line *had* broken. The clankers equipped with mind-shockers had swung around in a curving line and the lyrinx were being pushed north, further out into the Dry Sea. Malien climbed higher. It was happening on the other side as well: another curve of clankers splitting the enemy in two around the human army and driving them out into the wasteland.

Flydd shook his head. 'I never thought it was possible. Not for a second.'

'But you never gave in, either,' said Malien. 'You're quite a man, Scrutator.'

'If only you knew the despair I give way to, in the dark each night after I've gone to bed.'

'You're not alone, Xervish Flydd. You're not alone.'

SEVENTY

As soon as it became evident that they had mastery of the lyrinx, an open-air council of war was called to formally decide on the next step, the most momentous of the war. Irisis, sitting up the back with Malien and Tiaan, wasn't looking forward to the debate.

'The war will soon be over,' said Flydd. 'Our field controller now has control of most of the nodes within a forty-league semi-circle of Ashmode. We're slowly but progressively choking off their power patterner, and in a day or two it'll be useless. The enemy can no longer fly. In two more days – three at the outside – they won't be able to use any of their Arts.'

'And there's no way they can strike back?' said Nisbeth.

'They're cut off from the shore by a circle of clankers armed with mind-shockers, and they can't approach within half a league of them. They can't escape. The only question remaining is – what do we do with them?'

'We've had this argument before,' said a purple-faced General Orgestre. The golden medals danced as he shifted position and Irisis noticed that he'd added another row since Flydd and Troist's victory. Orgestre was a man who knew his priorities. 'Exterminate them! It's the only way we can ever be safe.'

'But that would be genocide,' said Gilhaelith, who still looked shaken from his day at the battlefront.

'I thought you were out for revenge?' said Flydd.

'It's not as sweet as I'd thought,' Gilhaelith muttered.

'After what they've done to our world,' said Orgestre coldly, 'a million deaths and whole nations devastated, genocide is exactly what I'm proposing.'

'They might have been human once,' said a young, yellow-haired officer up the front, 'but they forfeited their humanity when they began to flesh-form their unborn young. The lyrinx are an abomination and we cannot suffer them to live. I say we move in on them right away.'

'We're not going to make any hasty decisions,' said Flydd with a glance at Yggur, whose frosty eye was fixed on him. 'If we attack while they've still got power we could lose half our army. If we delay we can save those lives and . . . still meet our objective.'

To Irisis, he didn't sound convincing. Tiaan turned to her and Malien, saying quietly, 'This kind of talk makes me sick to my stomach. I'm going for a walk.'

'I'll come with you,' said Irisis. 'I can't bear it either.' Malien joined them.

They slipped out, crunching across the crusted salt in the moonlight. 'There has to be another way,' said Malien.

'I wish I knew one,' Tiaan replied.

'A night flight would clear your head and help you think about it.'

Beside Irisis, Tiaan stiffened.

'Vithis has to be told that his clan is no more,' said Malien.

'I – but surely I don't have to go? He . . .'

'You must, Tiaan. It's the end of his clan, and you discovered what happened to them. You have to tell him what you know. I can't do that for you. I have my own story to relate.'

'But . . . Minis will be there. How am I to face him? I don't think I can.'

'You've been running away for more than a year. If you've done him wrong – and only you and he know the truth of that – you have to face up to it.'

'I'm sure Flydd won't allow me to go.'

'He can spare you now,' said Malien. 'Nothing's going to happen until all the enemy's Arts have been stripped from them. I'll tell him I'm taking you.'

Tiaan walked away across the salt until Irisis lost sight of her in the dim light. She shifted her weight with a faint crunch.

'You think I'm pushing her too hard,' Malien said quietly.

'I can't say,' said Irisis. 'Although I couldn't bear to have it hanging over *my* head. I'd have to go at it head-on, whatever the consequences.'

Malien went in to Flydd, and came back within minutes. 'He didn't put up as much of a fight as I'd expected, even when I said I was taking you as well.'

It was a long time before Tiaan returned. 'I can see that you're right,' she said to Malien. Her face was in darkness but the tension in her voice was palpable. 'Vithis has to be faced sooner or later. And Minis. In some ways, it'd be a relief to have it over, though I don't know how I'm going to get through it.'

'I'll be standing beside you,' said Malien.

'But I can't run away and allow the lyrinx to be exterminated,' Tiaan added.

'Nice try, Tiaan, but any decision will be days yet. Besides,' Malien said slyly, 'if you were to take your node map, Orgestre wouldn't dare attack them.'

'But then the lyrinx might –'

'They won't. There's no escaping your duty, Tiaan.'

Dawn broke as they approached the Foshorn. Irisis climbed the ladder, rubbed her eyes and yawned. She'd slept most of the night and wouldn't have minded a few hours more. The rising sun lit up the towering cliffs and ramparts. Directly below, the salt lakes formed by the Trihorn Falls were still in shadow.

Tiaan, who was rigid with tension, offered her hot chard and strips of dried quince. Irisis took a handful. 'Where's the famous Foshorn, then?'

'The Trihorn Falls are straight ahead,' said Malien, who was still flying. 'The Hornrace, linking the Sea of Thurkad to the Dry Sea, lies behind them. We'll be over it in half an hour.'

'That's strange,' Malien said a few minutes later. 'I don't see much water coming over the falls.'

'I don't suppose it changes with the seasons?' said Irisis.

Malien chuckled. 'Not with an ocean behind it.' She turned to curve across the glistening lower flanks of the Trihorn. The layered rock was etched with deep slots and canyons that ran down to the salt lakes below the Trihorn, but the falls had been reduced to a few trickles.

She lifted the nose of the machine to fly up the face of the Trihorn. Irisis felt her stomach being left behind. She put down the dried quince, no longer hungry, and concentrated on not spilling her chard. Up, up and up they soared, flying faster and faster. Malien's jaw was set and she was staring fixedly ahead.

They rocketed towards the peaks and, as they reached the left-hand gap through which the falls had once flowed, Malien flattened out with a jerk of her hand, curving between the two peaks.

Irisis gagged as her stomach and intestines seemed to be pushing up into her throat. Her feet lifted off the floor and she caught desperately at the side rail.

'Sorry,' said Malien. 'I'm in a bit of a hurry –'

Below the thapter a trench, cut hundreds of spans deep and wide through solid rock, ran ahead as far as they could see.

'Was that the Hornrace?' said Irisis. It contained just a few elongated pools.

'It was.'

The thapter climbed higher. In the distance a massive, rectangular building, constructed upon a colossal arch of stone, spanned the Foshorn. Smaller cubes made a kind of pyramid at the centre of the arch.

'Where's the watch-tower?' said Tiaan.

'It's fallen,' Malien replied grimly. 'See. And not of its own accord. History repeats itself.'

Tiaan shot her a glance. Malien shook her head as if saying, *later*.

The tower's suspended arches appeared to have broken and it had speared right through the pyramidal building. The pyramid and the Span still stood, though rubble from the tower had dammed the Hornrace. The flagpole that had stood on top stuck up at an angle from the dam, still proudly flying the pennant of Inthis First Clan.

Malien circled over the arch. A ragged hole had been torn right through the vast building. Thousands of constructs were drawn up in ranks outside, not too close in case the rest collapsed. Aachim stood in groups everywhere, staring at the ruins.

Malien hovered for a while, silently taking in the scene. 'Best we go down and find Vithis,' she said at last.

'How are we going to guard the thapter?' Tiaan said in a dry croak.

'I am Matah of all my people,' said Malien with the unconscious arrogance that characterised her kind. 'And I'm bringing Vithis the most tragic news of all.'

She landed between the constructs, close by the main doors, and a small group of Aachim came to meet them. They were still covered in dust and their eyes had a faraway look.

'I am Malien,' she said. 'Matah of the Aachim of Santhenar. I must see Vithis on a matter of the utmost importance.'

'I'm sorry, Matah,' said the robed woman at their head, and they all bowed their heads respectfully. 'In the circumstances, Vithis will not see even you. I'm sure you appreciate . . .'

'It concerns the fate of his clan,' Malien said.

The Aachim stiffened and cast a glance at her fellows. 'I will take you to him at once.' She gave orders to a slender boy, who set off at a run.

They followed in more stately fashion. The Aachim said no more and Malien asked no questions of her. Inside they climbed many flights of dust-covered, gritty stairs. Irisis lost count after a while. The building was different to other Aachim structures Irisis had read about in the Histories, being extremely plain and undecorated.

The lad appeared and led them across a large open floor scattered with rubble, to a slumped figure in the centre. Vithis was sitting on the edge of the ragged hole, legs dangling down through it, staring blindly at the still waters of the Hornrace.

Tiaan hung back; then, with a visible wrench, she forced herself to come to the edge beside him.

'Matah Malien,' Vithis said dully. 'You have news of Inthis?'

He looked up at Tiaan and Irisis caught her breath, knowing the enmity between them, but Vithis's expression did not change.

Malien dusted off the floor and sat beside him, though she kept her legs clear of the hole. 'I do, but not good news. We found the wreckage of many constructs out in the Dry Sea. They were made of the blue metal which only Inthis knows the secret of working. A few of the bodies wore First Clan colours. They had survived for some time.'

'But they are all dead now?'

'Alas, all that we could find. I'm sorry.'

'They called this tower another First Clan folly.' His voice was as harsh and dry as grit grinding underfoot. 'A monument to my hubris. Not even my wretched foster-son had faith in our clan's tenacity and will to live. But I *knew* First Clan had survived and I would not abandon them, whatever it cost my own reputation.'

Vithis looked up through the hole at the sky, or perhaps the limitless void. For a moment Irisis saw the nobility in him, the dreams he'd nurtured before life had crushed them one by one.

'You did the right thing,' said Malien. 'Will you come to view the bodies, name those you know and record how they lived and died?'

'I knew every one of my people, and I will send them off with all the honour that is their due. Let us waste no time.'

On the way down Vithis opened a door and said, 'Come out, lad. You were in Tirthrax at the beginning. You might as well see the end.'

A small man came through the door, rather warily, and he was so covered in dust that at first Irisis did not recognise him. When she did, Irisis, who prided herself on her control, let out a shriek and ran.

'Nish!' She threw her arms around him, lifted him in the air and whirled him around in a circle. 'I was sure the lyrinx had eaten you. What are you doing here?' She couldn't restrain her tears, which spotted his dusty face. She kissed them away, smudging her lips and cheek.

Nish hugged her back. 'It would take a day to tell you.'

As they went out the main doors towards the thapter, Irisis, who had her arm linked through Nish's, heard a distinctive clicking sound, like a metal-shod crutch on stone. She eased him to a stop. Just ahead, Tiaan had frozen. She rotated in place like a statue on a pedestal, and could not conceal her horror.

A haggard, aged Minis emerged from the front door, moving painfully on his crutches. He saw Tiaan standing there and his face lit up. His joy brought a lump to Irisis's throat.

She glanced at Tiaan, despite herself half hoping to see it reflected there. It wasn't. Whatever Tiaan was feeling at that moment – horror at the extent of his injuries, compassion, guilt perhaps – it wasn't the naked adoration shining from Minis. She may have loved him once but it was gone forever.

Minis strained forward on his crutches as if he could compel her to love him in return, but as it became clear that she did not, would not, *could not*, the seams of his face deepened, his shoulders dropped and he sagged onto his crutches with a groan of despair.

Vithis had also turned. He looked from one to the other and his face hardened. 'What did you expect?' he said harshly. 'Come, Foster-son. I'm all you have left.'

Irisis couldn't watch any more. 'Let's go,' she whispered to Nish. 'This is none of our business.'

She led him around the other side of the thapter and they climbed in and settled companionably on the lower floor, in a shaded corner. Irisis linked her arm through his again. 'Now tell me everything. Don't leave out the tiniest detail.'

SEVENTY-ONE

'Take the controller,' Malien said, ushering Tiaan toward the thapter.

'I'm not sure I can.' Tiaan's knees were shaking.

'I think it's best. It'll give you something to do.'

'I thought you wanted me to talk to Minis?'

'You can't do that in a crowded thapter. Time enough after the dead have been dealt with.'

Vithis climbed in, followed by ten Aachim – the other clan leaders and Matah Urien – there to set down the fate of First Clan and see the dead laid to rest. Minis came last, and when no one moved to help him up the ladder, Tiaan went to do so.

'Don't take away the little self-respect he has left!' said Vithis.

She returned to the controller and fastened her straps. Minis struggled in and she could feel his feverish eyes on her. It was a relief when he went below with the others. Malien had gone down too.

'Lift off!' rasped Vithis.

She did so, as jerkily as a novice. He stood beside her, shuddering with such suppressed emotions that Tiaan began to think he would strike her down and seize the controller for himself.

They travelled in silence, for Tiaan could think of nothing to say to him, and he, it appeared, did not trust himself to speak.

An hour into the flight, Nish came up the ladder and Tiaan

had never been more glad to see him. The uncomfortable silence stretched out. Shortly they saw ahead the solitary tower, like red balls on a skewer, which the Aachim had constructed on the pinnacle in the Dry Sea.

'Nithmak Tower,' said Vithis. 'Another monument to my folly. I built it to bring First Clan home from the void. If only I had looked closer to home. All that time I wasted here, striving to beam my beacon out across the limitless void, and my people were crying out for aid just days away. Why was I so fixed on the void? Why did I not think of the Dry Sea? How could I have been so blind?'

'Is Nithmak a portal?' asked Nish.

'Not of itself, but one can readily be made there at need,' said Vithis.

'I wish I'd never made the gate at Tirthrax,' said Tiaan. 'I wish I'd never seen the amplimet, nor heard Minis's call. Nor listened to him.'

'So do I wish it,' said Vithis. 'I would shed every drop of my heart's blood to make it so. If First Clan had to disappear, why could we not have died together on our own world, with *dignity?*'

'I thought I was doing the right thing,' said Tiaan. 'Why didn't I refuse to put the port-all together?'

'Nithmak is a master zyxibule,' said Vithis. 'Nothing was done in haste this time. It was designed so carefully that a child could use it, built by masters, and checked by my own hands. It's perfect.'

She studied the structure as they went by. 'And you designed it to reach *anywhere* in the void?' she said thoughtfully.

'I wouldn't say anywhere, for the void is limitless. But anywhere my people could have ended up.'

'Could you go back to Aachan?'

'We *have* gone back,' he said grimly. 'We clan leaders have been there a dozen times, visiting all the havens and searching for survivors of any clan. We found none. Our beloved Aachan is a volcanic hell.'

Tiaan dwelt on that as they left the tower behind. And all because of choices made thousands of years ago, by Aachim desperate to have the power that mastery of an amplimet could bring.

'Whenever the way into the void has been opened, trouble has come out of it,' said Malien from the top of the ladder. 'I dread what will come through this gate if it's left for the future's fools to play with.'

'Do what you wish with it,' said Vithis. 'Destroy it! I care not. Here is the key.' From a chain around his neck he took a hexagonal rod carved from a single sapphire, whose corners were rounded from aeons of handling. He gave it to Malien.

Malien studied it for a moment, nodded and put it in her scrip. 'I will see to it.'

No one spoke for hours afterwards. Tiaan held on to her controller like a lifeline, longing for the journey to be over, though not for what lay at the end of it. In the immensity of the Dry Sea the thapter did not seem to be moving.

She flew through the night and soon after dawn began to descend. 'We saw the first construct not far ahead,' Tiaan said.

Vithis was the first to spot the wreckage. He showed no expression, apart from a hardening of the corners of his mouth.

'There's one. Go lower. I would count their number first, and make sure none have been overlooked.'

Tiaan went back and forth as he directed. As many of the Aachim as could fit came up, until the compartment was so crammed that she was hard pressed to work the levers.

Vithis's lips moved. 'Some constructs hit so hard that they were smashed to pieces, yet others are hardly damaged. Why didn't they repair one and send for help?'

'This country is so rugged that not even a construct could hover across it,' said Malien. 'You'll see what I mean when we set down.'

His mouth shut like a trap. 'I've seen enough. Go down now.'

The heat radiating from the black rocks hit them like a furnace. They visited the isolated machines, and their dead, before turning to the stone tombs. For Minis, having to pick his way on crutches across the jagged rocks must have been another kind of torture, but he neither complained nor faltered.

Vithis examined the bodies in the mausoleums, exclaiming as he recognised one, and another. 'My clan, oh my clan.'

It took all day and night, for there were many, many bodies. He checked each one, named it without hesitation; mourned over each, too. Each name seemed to take a little more from him. The lines of his face lengthened and deepened, his eyes became more sunken, his back more bent as the terrible night wore on. Tiaan had to sleep at last, but he was still going when she got up.

'Ah, Sulien,' he said, bent over the desiccated rags of a small, black-haired woman. 'You were the greatest beauty of our times. I once thought to match you with my foster-son. Would that I had.' Vithis stood up, wiped dust from his eye and shuffled to the next. 'And you, Orthis – sage, philosopher, dear friend and counsellor, how I need your wise guidance now.'

So it went on – poet, architect, Mother of the Clan, beloved niece – he mourned over every one, as the sun rose higher and sucked up the last drops of perspiration.

'You survived all this time,' he said at the last stone mausoleum. 'If only I had known to look here. Why did you not call? Did you not see my beacon?'

Vithis shuffled out like an old man. His skin had taken on a grey tinge and Minis, beside him, looked even worse. The dried paths of tears streaked his salt-crusted face.

'Is that all?' Vithis said hoarsely. 'There are many missing. Very many that I would have expected to find accompanying these.'

'There's still the building constructed from the skins of the wrecked constructs,' said Malien. 'Perhaps some you're looking for lie within.'

'Of course,' he said. 'How could I have forgotten it? Or is it that I dread what I will see inside?'

They went up the path to the metal building and began to go through each of the rooms, Vithis leading, Minis struggling along behind. Tiaan noticed that Irisis and Nish were not following and was glad. It didn't concern them.

Vithis turned into a compartment that Tiaan and Malien had

missed previously. On pallets on the floor lay an old man and an old woman, their dark robes covered in a dusting of windblown salt. They were thin to the point of emaciation and the woman's arms were folded across her breast; the man's lay by his sides. They too looked as if they were sleeping.

Vithis looked down, saying nothing. A single tear welled in his left eye. He ignored it. 'Uncle Mumis, Aunt Zefren. Why didn't I hear your cries?'

Luxor tapped Tiaan on the shoulder and jerked his head at the entrance. She went out, followed by Malien and all but Vithis and Minis.

'Clan mourning,' said Malien to the clan leader beside her. 'What comes after, Tayel?'

'I can scarcely bear to think.'

A good while later Vithis emerged, more stooped than before, and more haggard. His eyes sought Tiaan out among the gathering.

'There are more.' It was a statement.

'Upstairs.' She hesitated, unsure what he wanted, then pointed. 'You will take me there.'

Tiaan led the way. This time only Minis followed, leaving his crutches at the bottom and hauling himself up the steps. At the top, by the children's room, she stood aside to let Vithis past. The doorway was no higher than her head but he was so bowed that he passed through freely.

He walked to the centre of the room, looked at the beds, and gave forth a cry of anguish such as Tiaan had never heard from a human throat. She turned to leave him but his arm shot out and caught her hand.

'Stay! See what you've wrought by debauching my foster-son with your alien allure.' Tears coursed down his cratered cheeks. 'You seduced him with your charms and your deadly stone, and for that First Clan is no more. Ah, the children, the children!'

'Foster-father,' cried Minis. 'Have you lost your wits? We called out for help, remember, and when she answered we used her innocent infatuation –'

'Be silent!'

'You approved every action we took, Foster-father, and if the gate went wrong that was due to what you did with it after it opened.'

'It had already gone wrong. I was trying to put it right.'

'If it did go wrong,' said Malien, who had come up quietly, 'and I know it did, then you must look to your own enemies, Lord Vithis. Ask yourself who wanted to see the end of First Clan. And who seized that opportunity, when Inthis were first into the gate, to be rid of them?'

'No!' cried Vithis, putting his hands over his ears. 'I will not hear this. It is Aachim first and clan second, as it has always been. No one would attack another clan at such a desperate time. No one!'

He turned to Minis, who was leaning against the wall, panting. 'And you are just as culpable. Why could you not cleave to your own? What was so wrong with the women of First Clan that you had to call out across the void for an *old human* mate?' The very words were a curse.

'You know it wasn't like that,' began Minis. 'I was asked to join the call.'

'For help. *Not for a mate*. You could have had anyone, even beautiful Sulien who now lies out there, shrivelled like a piece of dried meat. Our clan, the greatest and oldest of all, is dying, yet you have not produced so much as a half-Inthis child. What have I done to make you hate me so?'

'I don't hate you, Foster-father. I . . .'

'Aaargh! Begone. And take *her* with you.'

Tiaan scrambled down the stairs and outside. Minis clacked after her, avoiding her eyes. A great cry of anguish came from the attic window, after which there was silence. Finally Vithis emerged. His back was no longer bent but his face was more crevassed than ever.

'All things must pass and First Clan is no more. I will send them on their longest journey, in the way that has always been foretold. Not foretold by a mooncalf with a head full of fantasies,' he spat, with a glance in Minis's direction. 'Forecast by our ancient seers. Inthis came first and we found the Well. Some say

702

it came first and First Clan was born of it. As we came, so shall we depart. No more fitting farewell can I make my people.'

He threw his arms up, clawing for the sky, and opened his mouth to speak the Great Spell.

'What are you doing?' cried Malien.

'I am summoning the Well, Matah Malien.'

Malien looked afraid. Tiaan shuddered and moved closer to her.

'The Well cannot be summoned,' said Malien. 'It just is, and presently it lies chained within Tirthrax. Even to go near it is perilous.'

'Not to me, for I am the direct heir of Inthis, founder of First Clan ten thousand years ago. I have the power and the right, for the chained Well at Tirthrax is just a shadow of what it should be.' He raised his arms again.

'Why are you doing this?' said Malien.

'The least honour I can do my people is to send them to the Well, but it is the only honour in my power.'

'Then let us take them to the Hornrace and entomb them in the time-honoured way. Here, by the great mid-sea rift, the seat of such unstable power, is neither fitting nor safe.'

'Here they fell and here they will be taken up,' said Vithis softly, but then his voice rose. 'What care I for safety? What care I if the whole of Santhenar falls into ruin? My world is gone, and my clan. I have nothing left.'

'You have Minis,' she said.

'I lost him before I lost my clan or my world. It's too late now; nothing remains of him.' He raised his voice. 'Flee now, any among you who fear death.' He fixed each one of them with his baleful glare. 'Well, Cryl-Nish Hlar?'

'I fear your kind of death, but I would honour your dead,' Nish said softly. 'I will stay.'

'There's more to you than I thought,' said Vithis. 'Not much, but something. Take your place over there.'

Vithis offered them the choice, one after another, to go or to stay. Everyone stayed. 'Then move back,' he said. 'The Well of Echoes – the *true Well* – has an appetite for the living as well as the dead.'

He reached out, clenching and unclenching his fists, and the sky changed to an ashy grey. Thunder rumbled all around them as if they were circled by storms. At least, it sounded like thunder, though it felt more like an earth trembler.

Tiaan shifted from one foot to another. They weren't far from the mid-sea rift. What might an earth trembler do here, where the very rock beneath their feet had been riven apart by forces not even a geomancer could comprehend?

'How can he summon the Well of Echoes?' Tiaan asked quietly. 'He has nothing in his hands.'

'I don't know,' said Malien, 'though there exist powers far older than the magic of crystals and devices, fields and nodes. Vithis has lived for a thousand years and is heir to Arts ten times that old, whose secrets have been passed down to none but the greatest in each generation.'

Vithis cried out a word, and a word of power it must have been, for the entire sky went black. It was an absolute darkness – no clouds showed, no moon, no stars. The ground shook so violently that loose rocks rattled like dice in a cup. Away in the distance a red glow appeared, a molten line squeezed up through the black rift.

He sang a second word. A column of yellow light seared a path down from the sky, beginning some degrees off the vertical and ending in the rocks behind the metal death-house, illuminating one of the mausoleums. The column was not solid yellow; rather it seemed to be made of a million threads of light, all different hues of yellow. And all were in motion: vibrating, revolving, shimmering.

He whispered a third word and the threads wove between one another, faster and faster, until they blended into a single bar of colour so bright that everyone had to shield their eyes. Its base drifted off the mausoleum, fingered the ground between it and the metal death-house, and began to rotate. Dust danced where it touched but the particles were instantly sucked down, apparently into the solid rock. Pieces of gravel and salt crust whirled after.

A hole appeared, a couple of spans across, though it did not actually seem to pass through the rock. It was, rather, that the hole was laid over the rock, the two existing in the same place but different dimensions.

Like Tiaan's brief glimpses into the hyperplane long ago, or the inside of the tesseract, it was all wrong. It confused the mind as well as the eye and she could only imagine what the others must be making of it. Nish, next to her, looked as if he was going to be ill.

The column of threaded light moved steadily down and as it did it thickened. The hole, which Tiaan realised was the slowly materialising Well, broadened until it was five or six spans across. Suddenly, with another rolling rumble of thunder, the column of light evaporated. They were enveloped in darkness within which the only illumination was the Well, while the stifling heat had been replaced by cold air currents coiling about them.

The walls of the Well were midnight black, threaded with shimmering yellow strands that moved when the eye attempted to focus on them. From where she was standing, Tiaan could see down a few spans, and suddenly recalled hanging off Nish's arm, half in and half out of the Well in Tirthrax. But that had been different. That had been a little, stable Well, frozen in place by powerful Arts. This was the master Well – wild and free, and only Vithis could control it.

Tiaan reached out blindly and her hand struck Nish's. It startled her. She saw the same memories in his eyes. He was shuddering with horror. She felt for him – she had some small understanding of the Well, but Nish could have none. She squeezed his hand and he gave her a weak smile.

Vithis looked around him, though Tiaan knew he was not seeing any of them. He was remembering the Histories of Inthis, the first of the clans on Aachan and always the greatest. So powerful was the moment that she could almost see the story of Clan Inthis flickering in the air in front of him.

He stood that way for a long time. No one spoke or moved. Then Vithis shook himself and held up one hand, as if to give a blessing.

'Farewell, my beloved Inthis,' he said in a majestic voice

705

drawn from somewhere deeper than the bitterness that had been his daily existence. 'We were the greatest of all clans, and it will be recognised as long as our Histories endure. But now the time of First Clan is over. Go to the soft sweet Well of Echoes, my people. Go Hulis, go Maris, go Irrien . . .'

He went through the names from memory, one by one, listing them in the order that he had found them. There were thousands of dead but not once did he hesitate. Tiaan found tears welling in her eyes yet again.

As he spoke the last name, Vithis spread his arms and the Well lifted and slid toward the mausoleum directly behind the metal death-house. Crusts of salt whirled in the air and were pulled down to nothingness. It was eerie, the way the shimmering shaft drifted through the ground with no more sound than a sigh. There was no groan or crack of shifting rocks, no wind, no clatter. It settled over, or under, or around the mausoleum, which hung there even though there now appeared to be nothing underneath it.

The Well spun like a whirlpool, brightened, and in that sudden brilliant radiance the laid-out bodies took on a fullness and a colour they'd not had since they died. They looked as if they had come alive again and were just sleeping.

The base of the mausoleum collapsed and fell into the Well. The bodies followed, one by one, and as each passed within there was a flash of yellow light and a low, reverberating *boom* that seemed to echo up and down. The last body fell, dark hair trailing. Vithis moved one hand, the Well drifted away and the mausoleum collapsed into a pile of rubble on the now solid ground.

The scene was repeated at the next mausoleum, and the one after, Vithis directing the Well until every crashed construct had been visited, every body taken. Finally he pointed it to the last and most sacred place, the building formed from the metal cladding of many constructs, that contained his uncle, aunt and the seven dead children.

The aunt and uncle passed quickly, almost gladly, into the Well, but the children hung in the air, reluctant. Their arms moved, their hair streamed out behind them and the oldest girl appeared to turn her head and look reproachfully at Tiaan. Vithis let out a desolate cry and moved one hand to still the Well, but it was surely just a trick of the light. He let the hand drop.

The children fell. Little flashes marked their passing and a brief threnody of echoes, after which the Well went dull, though it was still centred over the building. The structure of the metal death-house quivered, as if the Well's forces were trying to pull it to pieces. Vithis raised a beckoning hand and the Well moved, whirling towards him until his toes projected over the brink.

'This house shall remain, a memorial to the nobility of First Clan. A reminder of all who worked so hard to destroy us. And succeeded.' Vithis held each one of them with his gaze, but especially Tiaan and Minis. 'You and you. How will you atone, Tiaan?'

She had been waiting for this moment; dreading it. 'I cannot express how much I regret the fate of your people,' she said. 'It is a tragedy that will echo down the Histories, and I played a part in it. We all did, in some shape or another, but what amends I might make are my own affair.'

'I see,' he said grimly. 'The lives of my people have been one tragedy after another. I've lost my clan and my world, and you have nothing to atone for.'

'I didn't say that,' she began, but he waved her to silence.

'Every misery the Aachim have ever suffered originated on this wretched world,' cried Vithis. 'It was Shuthdar of Santhenar who made the Golden Flute in the first place, then broke it and brought down the Forbidding. And it was the breaking of the Forbidding that caused beloved Aachan to destroy itself in volcanic convulsions. Would that it had been Santhenar instead.'

'You misrepresent the Histories, Vithis,' Malien said coldly, 'as you always seek to blame others for your own ill-judged deeds. The lamentations of the Aachim began with the Charon coming out of the void and taking our world from us. And who allowed it? We were led by First Clan elders: Mahthis and Briorne; *your* ancestors. They were defended by a guard of First Clan, and First Clan failed their duty. First Clan surrendered our world for two people already at the end of their lives. First Clan allowed themselves to be defeated by a hundred Charon: the

Hundred as they were known ever after. In fact, as we know, the might of First Clan was defeated by a single Charon: Rulke. Only one of us struck back at him, and that was *my* ancestor and the founder of my clan: Elienor.

'That stain became etched deep into the heart of First Clan; it moulded your ancestors as it moulded you. Indeed, the bitterness of Inthis, as well as the false pride and recklessness that so marked Pitlis in ancient times, and Tensor at the time the Forbidding was broken, and which has marked you, Vithis, all the time I've known you, arose from the failure of First Clan that day. You have never come to terms with the shame. I am sorry for the passing of Clan Inthis, and for all that was fine and noble in your people, and there was much. But it is for the good of the world. All things fail and decay, sooner or later. It is fitting that Inthis passes through the Well, as you came from it in the first place. If you did.'

'You set out to destroy us!' he roared. 'From that day in Aachan, right down to this, Clan Elienor has done its best to undo us.'

'There was no Clan Elienor in ancient times, and even after Elienor founded it, my house was always the poorest, the weakest and the least in numbers. We were always looking over our shoulders.'

'Elienor wasn't weak, nor the despised *blending* Karan when she helped you to bring noble Tensor down. Nor *you*, Malien, when you helped Tiaan in Tirthrax, and ever after.'

'Then why has Inthis –'

'No more, Malien. All things must fail – it is *your* time to go to the Well.'

He did not move the Well this time. Vithis wanted to wreak revenge with his own hands. He walked forward, deliberately, took Malien about the waist and lifted her high. And, oddly, Malien did not struggle – it was almost as if she had been waiting for it. The Aachim let out cries of horror, yet no one moved to stop him.

'No,' Tiaan said to herself. Then louder, so it rang out across the jagged ground, 'No!'

708

Nish, who had been quivering beside her, threw himself at Vithis. Vithis didn't move, but he roared a word and Nish was thrown sideways, landing on broken rock at the edge of the Well. Tiaan heard ribs crack.

Vithis waggled a finger in his direction and Nish was forced slowly backward. He clasped hands around a jagged spike of basalt but the force simply broke his grip. His head went over the edge of the Well; his shoulders; his chest.

Tiaan looked from him to Malien. If she tried to save Nish, Malien would surely be lost. Tiaan couldn't see Irisis anywhere; she vaguely remembered her walking away a long time ago. What was she to do?

Malien was strong in the Art and ought to be able to defend herself, should she choose to. Nish had no chance and she saw sheer terror in his eyes. She caught hold of his belt and tried to haul him back, but the force pulling him into the Well was irresistible.

She heaved harder. It made no difference. 'Help!' she cried, but no one moved, and the Histories told her why. Sometimes, in the most desperate crises, the Aachim froze like deer staring into the eyes of the great cat about to devour them. They'd done it when the Charon had taken their world from them, and now they were doing it again.

Or did they want her and Nish, and Malien too, to die with Vithis? To make a cleansing of all those who'd played any part in the calamity, save themselves?

Now Nish's whole upper body was over the edge. Tiaan braced her heels against the rock, but the force was too much for her knees to hold against. If she didn't let go, she'd be pulled in with him. Was this an echo thrown up by the Well, an ironic reversal of the time in Tirthrax when she'd tried to throw herself down it, and Nish had struggled to save her? Was it *meant* to be?

Or was something even more sinister going on? What had Malien said earlier? *Look to your own enemies, Lord Vithis*. Were Malien and Nish, and she, taking the blame for the machinations of his clan enemies?

'Look to your own enemies, Lord Vithis!' she screamed.

'That's what Malien said and she was right. Once we're dead, and you've gone to the Well, Inthis's enemies will have achieved everything they've ever wanted. Isn't that right, clan leaders?'

Her frantic stare passed over them one by one but no one broke. No one looked guilty either. 'Vithis?' she screeched, but he didn't react. 'Malien, why don't you do something?'

Tiaan saw the look in Nish's eyes, the terror that she would let him go. He jerked over a little further. Her knees buckled and their eyes met.

'Let me go, Tiaan,' he said, somehow finding calm beyond the terror. 'You can't save me.'

How could she look into those eyes and release him to oblivion? 'I won't let you go, Nish!' She forced her knees to straighten through sheer will, but the force was pulling her fingers open.

'Save yourself. It's not worth it.'

'You *are* worth it, Nish!' She hung on.

Nish struck at her hand. 'Let me go!'

Her knees collapsed, she was dragged to the edge and they went over.

SEVENTY-TWO

Time stood still. A million yellows whirled around them and Tiaan saw echoes of the past and the present: sights and sounds, scents and tastes all mixed together. The yellows exploded, the whole world became one brilliant colour, and the next she knew, she was lying on the rocks beside the Well.

Nish had been thrown out on the other side. Vithis was wheeling around and around on one foot, the other up in the air as if trying to step over a stile. He didn't seem to know what had happened.

Malien stood across from him. Her hair was wild; she had bitten through her bottom lip and her clenched fists were jammed against her sides. She was breathing hard.

'Before the Well I must speak the unadorned truth. You were right, Vithis. Clan Elienor *has* always worked to bring Inthis down. Not to destroy you, but to humble you and strip you of your unshakeable hubris. That has been our goal since the day, all those thousands of years ago, when Elienor stood in the great hall and saw Inthis render Aachan up to Rulke without a fight.'

Vithis rotated to face her and his upraised foot slapped to the ground. Malien was doomed, and she knew it. But she kept on.

'Elienor swore an oath that day, that she would make up for the betrayal. We have renewed the oath, and followed her goal, unflinchingly since. Each time we faltered, another member of

First Clan reminded us of that fatal flaw in the character, nay, the very germ-plasm, of Inthis. There was Pitlis, who betrayed Tar Gaarn, the most beautiful of all our works, to the enemy. There was Tensor, whose folly after folly saw us lose beloved Shazmak and the Mirror of Aachan, and caused countless other tragedies. And this paltry act against Nish, who could never do you harm, shows that you, Vithis, are of the same base stock.'

Vithis took a step towards her. He flung up one hand behind him and the Well surged and flared to an incandescent brilliance, as if preparing for an entirely different class of victim.

Malien went on, unmoving, her eyes on Vithis as he came towards her. 'We set out to reduce Inthis from First Clan to last, not for ourselves but for the good of all Aachim. We continue to do so for the good of humanity. It has been a long struggle, as it must always be when the least opposes the greatest, and because we would not act contrary to our nature. We would not be corrupted by our quest.'

The instant Malien had begun to speak, Tiaan knew that there was something wrong. Oh, Elienor may well have sworn such an oath long ago, and the elders of the clan renewed it ever since. Malien may well have tried to bring Vithis down in whatever small ways she could, but the conspiracy that had destroyed First Clan was far deeper, and it hadn't come from Clan Elienor. She knew Malien well, after all the time they'd lived and worked together, and Tiaan would have sworn that there wasn't a duplicitous bone in her body.

And Yrael, the present leader of Clan Elienor, was a decent, honest man. He would have faced Vithis straight out, even if it caused him his doom, but Yrael would never have done anything underhand. And if it wasn't Elienor's leaders, it certainly wasn't the ordinary people – Aachim society simply did not work that way. So who could it be? A memory tugged at her but she could not pull it out into the light.

It had been just after the death of poor Ghaenis, Tirior's noble and handsome son, at the hands of the amplimet. He'd died the most horrible of all deaths, by anthracism, his body burning from the inside and blowing apart. After that, there had been the bitterest of fights between Tirior and Vithis, until Urien had interceded.

What had Tirior said? *You always return to the same tune, Vithis.*

And you to the same obsession that brought us ruin in the past, he had replied. Tiaan now knew that Tirior's clan, Nataz, had been obsessed with an amplimet in the distant past, and it had wrought ruin on the Aachim from which they had taken a thousand years to recover. The precise details had been lost in the deceits of time and the Histories. The deed had been covered up too well.

But that was not the memory Tiaan was searching for. It had been days later, and she had been listening to a group of Aachim argue bitterly. They were carrying her somewhere and had thought she was still unconscious. When was that? Ah! It had been after she'd collapsed from hauling constructs from Snizort to the node, using the amplimet. She struggled to recover the memories, but they were deeply submerged.

'So it was *you* made the gate go wrong!' Vithis was saying to Malien. '*You* tampered with it in Tirthrax. *You* hurled Inthis into the void to die.'

'I did not,' she said, so softly that Tiaan could barely hear her. 'I was not aware of the gate until Tiaan came to me, days later.'

Tiaan's memories were unfolding now. Tirior had taught Ghaenis how to use the amplimet. Tirior had been conspiring to get the crystal, so fatally attractive to her clan. Yes, when Tiaan ran through her earliest memories of the Aachim, long before the gate had been made, Tirior had always been there, her voice positively dripping with desire for it. And Tirior had taken Minis into Snizort, hoping he would be killed there, the last hope of Clan Inthis gone.

Vithis caught Malien, lifted her over his head and was about to hurl her bodily into the Well when Tiaan cried out, 'Clan Nataz is behind your ruin, Vithis. Tirior has been conspiring to get the amplimet for her clan since the very moment I revealed that I had it.'

'Clan Nataz?' he said, lowering Malien but not letting her go.

'Tirior taught Ghaenis how to use the amplimet,' Tiaan went on desperately. 'She took Minis into Snizort, risking the life of the last survivor of your clan, in direct defiance of your orders. Think, Vithis. *Think!*

'Which clan has been obsessed with amplimets since ancient times? Which clan covered up the disaster of the last one found on Aachan, a disaster that led inexorably to the ruin of your world?' And now Tiaan was guessing, but the train of logic was running away with her and she was sure it was right. 'And which clan leader stood beside you when the gate was opened, and was the only one who could possibly have tampered with it? It *was* tampered with, wasn't it, Malien? You told me so a long time ago, for you checked the port-all after I first left Tirthrax in the thapter, and what you found disturbed you very much.'

Vithis set Malien on her feet. 'Well?' he said.

'It was,' she said, almost inaudibly. 'Very cleverly – at the moment First Clan raced up into the gate. And then undone so that the other clans could pass through safely. It took me all night to discover what had been done.'

'And was it Nataz? Was it Tirior?'

'I couldn't tell,' said Malien.

'Where is Tirior?' said Nish.

She was nowhere to be seen. 'She's gone for the thapter,' Tiaan yelled. 'And the amplimet is inside. She's got what she wanted.'

Vithis leapt right across the Well, which flared bright as if vexed it couldn't consume him.

Before he had gone ten bounds, the thapter whined to life. 'Not just the amplimet. She's going to abandon us to the same fate as Inthis.'

Irisis bored easily and, despite the gravity with which Vithis sent his people to the Well, after interminable hours of it she'd had enough. She didn't know them, nor him, nor even Malien all that well. Nish was preoccupied with the ceremony so Irisis seized a suitable moment to slip quietly away.

She walked on the jagged basalt for a while, and climbed

a rocky spine to see how far she could see, but a dancing heat haze obscured everything in the distance. She perched behind the spine, in the shade, but the rock was too hot to sit on for long. Irisis headed back to the thapter for a drink from the water bag and discovered that, with the vents open, it was actually cooler than outside.

Not much, but at least she could sit down without roasting her backside. She found the coolest corner, settled back and, in the oppressive heat, drifted off to sleep.

The whine of the mechanism startled her awake. It was screaming, shaking the whole machine, and that wasn't right. Malien had a delicate hand on the controller and never asked more of the mechanisms than was necessary.

Tiaan used it aggressively when she had to, though that was not often, for she flew thapters with an intuitive grace. Neither would she have abused it the way it was being treated at the moment. Someone else was at the controller, someone who had no right to it.

Irisis eased her head around the corner to peer up the ladder, but couldn't see who was at the controller. But whoever was prepared to steal the thapter, out here, would hardly stop at doing her a mischief.

The mechanism roared and the thapter lifted off only to thump down again. A woman swore under her breath, and it evened the odds a fraction in Irisis's mind. She looked for a weapon but everyone had taken theirs with them and Irisis had left the camp without so much as a knife. She couldn't even see anything to throw.

She took off her boots and socks, sniffed disgustedly and laid them aside. She rose to her feet, then went back for a boot. It was better than nothing.

The thapter lifted off, screaming like a ghost in torment and shuddering so violently that Irisis had to hold on. The pilot was standing with her back to her, jerking back and forth on the controller, not understanding what she was doing. If she got the thapter up to ten spans or so, and lost control, it would be destroyed in the impact and everyone would die here.

Irisis crept up the ladder, the boot swinging in her right hand, though it was little use as a club; it didn't weigh enough. She slid her arm in, up to the elbow, settled the hard heel over her fist and kept it behind her back as she climbed one-handed.

The thapter sideslipped, steadied and began to rise, wobbling from side to side. Irisis was far enough up the ladder now to recognise the pilot, Tirior. She was a mighty mancer, second only to Vithis in power.

Irisis hesitated for a second and Tirior must have sensed that she was there, for she turned her head. Irisis went up the rest of the way in a rush as Tirior twisted her body and raised her free hand to deliver a blast that would tear Irisis apart.

She acted without thinking. There wasn't time, and physical force versus the Art normally only ended one way. Irisis swung her fist in a vicious blow to the bridge of Tirior's nose. The heel struck it full on, her nose broke and Tirior went down. Her hand slipped off the controller, the mechanism died and the thapter fell.

Irisis caught Tirior's hand, slammed it onto the flight knob of the controller and eased it up, gently. The thapter arrested, hovered, and Irisis let it down with just a minor crunching of metal, then stopped the Aachim's mouth with her knee and held her fingers until, with a bound, Vithis was perched on the hatch.

The trial took little time, since the evidence was beyond dispute. The clan leaders were unanimous in their verdict, though given that Tirior was a clan leader herself, the sentence had to be confirmed by Urien. This she did with dispatch and Tirior was sentenced to be delivered upside down to the Well by all the clan leaders, an ignominious end that would result in the demotion of Clan Nataz to Last Clan. Tirior made no defence, no statement, no plea. She simply went to the Well as if it was beneath her dignity to remark upon it.

The revelation of her betrayal had washed Vithis's despair away. First Clan hadn't fallen, it had been brought down by treachery. He stood up straight, brushed the salt dust off his garments and there was a glint in his eye that Tiaan did not like at all. It was as if he'd found new hope.

'Minis! Attend me!' he said peremptorily, after the Well had taken Tirior with a brilliant yellow flare that lit up the salt-crusted basalt for hundreds of paces around, and a positive volley of echoes.

Minis, reluctantly, levered himself to his foster-father's side and stood leaning on his crutches.

'Foster-son,' said Vithis, laying a hand on his shoulder, 'I judged you ill and I'm deeply sorry. I blamed you for failings that were due to our clan enemy. You did not let me down then and I know you won't do so now.'

'Foster-father?' said Minis.

'I despaired when I should have put my faith in you. I will do so now. Minis, Clan Inthis must be created anew and only you can do it, for as you know I am sterile. You must put aside all other objectives until you've bred me sons and daughters – especially daughters. I will chose your partners from women of other clans, who have strong Inthis blood –'

'I cannot, Foster-father,' cried Minis.

'If you lack desire,' said Vithis carefully, 'I have the remedy here.' He withdrew a capped phial from his pocket.

Minis looked as if he was going to vomit with humiliation. 'I am not . . . *incapable*, Foster-father.'

'If you were a man, you would have mated already and pro-duced the children that Inthis needs. You would have taken joy in it.'

'I –'

'No more talk, Foster-son. Take one of these today, *now*, and another every half-year. It will give you potency beyond any man alive. Women will flock to you, despite your disabilities.'

'I am not a rutting machine, Foster-father.'

'You have a duty to me and your clan. Do it, for once in your life.'

'No, Father. I will not.' Minis looked pale and terrified of the older man. Tiaan's heart went out to him.

Vithis sprang, caught Minis around the chest and thrust

a tablet into his mouth. Minis tried to spit it out. The older man held his nose until Minis had to open his mouth, then thrust it down his throat.

The crutches fell away and Minis collapsed on the ground, weeping with mortification.

'Do your duty like a man,' Vithis raged. 'If you *are* a man. I have often wondered.'

Minis found his crutches and climbed onto them as tears of helpless rage flowed down his cheeks. 'I *am* a man, Foster-father, and I will do what a real man must do.' He clacked away behind the thapter.

'You have always been a dutiful son, Minis,' said Vithis, the rage gone as quickly as it had come. 'I have every confidence in you.'

Tiaan suppressed an urge to run after the younger man, for it could do no good. In spite of her feelings about Minis, she could not bear to see him so humiliated.

'And now you, Malien,' said Vithis. 'For your clan's part –'

He broke off as Minis reappeared, carrying something in his cupped hands. Blood dripped from his knuckles. He walked up, held out his hands and pressed the red contents into Vithis's hands.

'Here, Foster-father, this is what you have always lacked. Now you may do my duty for me.'

Vithis looked into his hands and recoiled in horror. Dropping the mess onto the rock, he whispered, 'You have . . . *cut* yourself?'

'You castrated me long ago, Foster-father.'

Raising his gory hands to the sky, Vithis let out a scream of anguish that made the Well flutter. He looked into the Well, which was shivering like blades of grass in a breeze, and the Well seemed to respond. Its whirling slowed and the colours brightened.

Vithis bared his teeth in the grimmest of smiles. 'All things must pass – I can accept it now. This is the end of Inthis, first and greatest of all the clans. We came from the Well, so it is fitting that we take our departure through it.'

718

'And I will follow you,' said Minis. 'Life has nothing left for me.'

'Begone!' snarled Vithis. 'You cut your life free from First Clan; now go and live it. You are no longer Clan Inthis. You are not my foster-son and I forbid the Well to you.'

Minis gave him a blank-faced look then turned away, stumbling blindly out into the waste. He fell over repeatedly, but always pulled himself up onto his crutches, as if, after a failed life, this was the one thing he could achieve.

Vithis stepped into the Well, though it did not take him. He hung at the top of the shaft to nothingness, watching the silent watchers, and a mad, eerie smile passed across his face. 'My time is over, and I go to a better fate than anyone on Santhenar can hope for. But you – you will rue this day, Malien. All Santhenar will rue it.'

He made circular motions with his hands and snapped them down. The Well flared as bright as the sun and began to spin, pulling in loose gravel and salt dust. Vithis hung atop it a moment longer, then fell, disappearing with a purple flash and a crack that echoed up and down for minutes after.

Tiaan expected the Well to disappear, since Vithis had called it here, but it expanded right to the toes of her boots. She sprang backwards and everyone scrambled out of the way. The dark, which had come down when Vithis called the Well, suddenly lifted.

The Well began to drift away, pulling in bits of shattered rock, pieces of construct metal, shreds of cloth and every other loose object in its path. They watched it wander in the direction of the mid-sea rift.

Malien shuddered. 'No, no, no!'

'What's the matter?' said Nish, who had been holding Irisis's hand ever since she'd climbed out of the thapter. 'He's gone. It's over.'

'The Well should have collapsed as soon as it took Vithis, but ... it seems to be growing. He has set it to some dreadful purpose.'

'Can't you stop it, the way you bound the Well in Tirthrax?'

'Not this one,' said Malien. 'This is the Master Well and not I, nor all my people together, can lay a finger on it.'

'Then what are we going to do?'

'Get into the thapter! We must go, and swiftly. There are still the lyrinx to deal with, remember? The world hasn't stood still while we've been out here.'

The remaining people climbed in and Tiaan lifted off, keeping low.

'What about Minis?' said Nish. His thin figure was struggling over the rocks, away towards the distant salt.

'It would be kindest to let him go,' said Malien.

'To die?' whispered Tiaan.

'No Aachim would want to live with his burden, Tiaan. Trust me. I do know my people.'

'But to leave him out here, all alone? I just can't, Malien.'

'He won't last long, poor fellow.'

There was a long silence, interrupted only by the faint whine of the thapter.

'But you aren't going to leave him, are you?' said Tiaan.

'How can I?' said Malien. 'Go down.'

Tiaan landed the thapter beside Minis. He gave it a fleeting glance and kept walking. She scrambled down the side. 'Minis, wait.'

'Go away,' he said. 'You only remind me that I have nothing to live for.'

She ran after him and took his stained hand. 'Come back with us, Minis.'

'Do you say that because you love me, Tiaan? Or because you pity me?'

How could she answer? She had loved him once, and for that reason she still cared. But the death of little Haani had undermined her love, and his vacillation at Snizort had killed it. She could not lie to him, not even to save his life.

'Well, Tiaan?' There was a nobility in his eyes that she had never seen before.

'No, Minis. I don't love you. But I do care for you.' She was still holding his hand. The blood, already dried in the fierce heat, flaked off.

'It's not enough. If you truly care for me, let me go.'

As she released his hand, a single red flake fluttered on the breeze. 'Please come, Minis. Life –'

'I've seen enough of life,' he said over her head to Malien. 'Will you let me go, or would you take me against my will, to draw out my agony?'

'I shall not take you against your will,' Malien said softly.

He bowed to her, and then to Tiaan. 'I have to atone. My life in return for the life of little Haani.'

'It was an accident,' said Tiaan. 'And you weren't responsible.' For the first time since it had happened, nearly two years ago, she understood that. It had just been a tragic accident. No one was to blame, and her anger and bitterness afterwards had been due as much to hurt pride. Having been rejected, she'd wanted to hurt as much as she had been hurt. She too had much to atone for.

'I know that,' said Minis, 'but atoning for her death is the only worthwhile thing I can do with my life.'

'Then I won't stand in your way. Thank you, Minis. Haani would have liked you.'

'I'm sorry. So very, very sorry. I know how much you loved her.' His big eyes searched her face, perhaps, even now, hoping against hope.

She could not say it. 'I . . . I loved you too, Minis. Back then.'

'Goodbye, Tiaan.'

He turned away, moving off the black rock into a gully filled with windblown salt, and away towards the centre of the Dry Sea.

Tiaan watched him till he was just a shadow and her cheeks were crusted with salt from evaporated tears. She wiped her face. When she looked again, she could no longer see Minis through the shimmering heat haze.

'I can't help but make the comparison,' Malien said softly. 'Flydd and Minis were both unmanned, the one by the torturer's knife, the other by the impossible demands of his foster-father. Yet Flydd has risen above his maiming, while in the end, for Minis, the knife was the only way to escape.'

'No trauma can bring down the truly great in spirit,' said Tiaan.

'Nor any privilege raise up the incurably weak.'

Behind them the Well boomed. 'Come,' Malien went on.

From above they saw it intersect the mid-sea ridge, where molten rock was squeezed out along a rift ten leagues long. Great booms and crackles reached them and the Well swelled again, now resembling a tornado whirling above and through the ground. It began to track south along the ridge.

Malien set off for the Foshorn with all the speed she could manage, to take the clan leaders home and then go on to Ashmode. Tiaan said not a word during that long journey. She was thinking about wrongs that must be put right; it seemed the one worthwhile thing she could do with *her* life, for Minis, and for all that might have been. But how?

Tiaan could no longer take pleasure in wielding her Art, as once she'd done for the sheer bliss of using her abilities to the limit. Employing her Art had destroyed too much, and too many people, and the little good that had come from it seemed outweighed by the evil. She felt that she'd been used, even controlled, for most of her life.

And she began to feel increasingly alone and estranged, even from Malien, Irisis and Nish. Tiaan began to think that there was only one way out – to use her geomancy one last time to do something that no one else ever would. One question remained. Did she have the courage?

SEVENTY-THREE

They returned, having been away almost four days, to discover air-floaters in all shapes, sizes and colours moored by the camp, and a myriad of brightly coloured tents surrounded by courtiers and attendants. The dignitaries included Governor Zaeff of Roros, who had already been on her way when the battle was won. Her thapter had carried the ten most important leaders from the east. Orgestre had summoned her more than a week ago, and at the moment of victory he had called in as many of the western governors and provincial leaders as could get here.

'Orgestre has outflanked Flydd and the other moderates,' panted Fyn-Mah, who had run to meet them at the thapter. 'Come quickly, Malien. They're taking the vote now.'

'What about us?' said Tiaan.

'You won't have a vote,' Fyn-Mah said, 'but you might as well be there.'

They hurried to the meeting tent but it was too late – a white-faced Flydd was just stumbling out. 'We've lost,' he said hoarsely. 'Orgestre put his hard line to the vote and it won by thirty-two votes to three. I spoke against it for a day and a half, until I had no voice left, but it made no difference. The only votes against were mine, Yggur's and Troist's. The conclave has voted to eliminate the lyrinx!'

'Three?' said Irisis. 'Did Klarm –?'

'He wasn't well enough to get to the conclave. And that's not the worst of it. They took another vote, one I didn't even see coming. They've agreed that the Council will be disbanded immediately. The power of the scrutators, such as we were, has been smashed.'

'I suppose it had to happen,' said Malien, 'though it's a tragedy it happened now.'

'I now see that the Council was doomed, once Nennifer fell and I failed to maintain its networks of control. Klarm warned me, back then, but I couldn't do that and fight the war as well. I didn't think it would fall this quickly.'

'That victory sowed the seeds of this defeat,' said Irisis. 'You showed that the old Council was hollow, so the instant it was no longer necessary ...'

'If only it had lasted a few days longer, I could have prevented this disastrous decision. The world will come to rue it. And I made a pledge that I can't fulfil. Yggur hasn't reproached me though I'd feel better if he had.'

'You couldn't have anticipated this,' said Irisis.

'Ghorr or Fusshte would have,' said Flydd. 'They'd have arrested Orgestre on a trumped-up charge, or had him quietly slain, to make sure he couldn't have interfered. If I'd just put him out of the way for a week.'

'So you've thought of a way to save the lyrinx?' said Malien.

After a long pause he said, 'Unfortunately, I haven't.' Flydd glanced at Tiaan. 'And what the devil did you do with your map? I really can't countenance this kind of insubordination, Tiaan. Orgestre was apoplectic. I thought his head was going to explode. And he accused me of taking the wretched thing. *Me!*'

What did it matter, Tiaan thought. The lack of the map hadn't made one bit of difference.

'The enemy's defences are failing,' crowed General Orgestre at a victory dinner hosted by Governor Zaeff that night, in a vast tent flown in from Lybing. 'Their food and water are dwindling daily. All we have to do is hold them, and in a week they'll be dead, without the loss of a single man. It will be my crowning achievement.'

'If you order any more medals you'll have to pin them to your backside,' said Flydd.

Did Flydd feel he had nothing more to lose? Nish sniggered. Several others laughed. Klarm, who had been carried inside wrapped in blankets, heaved silently.

Orgestre swelled like a purple toad. 'I could have you put in irons for that, Citizen Flydd,' he said pointedly.

A murmur ran through the dignitaries, then Governor Zaeff spoke sharply to him. Irisis didn't hear what was said, though clearly he'd gone too far.

'What *is* Orgestre's achievement?' said Irisis quietly. 'Troist fought all the military battles for him, and Flydd won against their Arts. The Grand Commander has never raised a sword in combat, and now the war has been won he wants praise for being the executioner?'

'Truly the battle isn't over until the last man falls,' Orgestre was saying. 'We've risen from the ashes of our funeral pyre to overcome our enemy. Never in all the Histories has there been such a victory.'

'If it truly *is* a victory!' said Yggur, standing up and meeting everyone's eye, one by one, as if defying them to attempt anything against *him*. 'But should any lyrinx survive elsewhere on Santhenar, or in the void from whence they came, you'll create an enemy who will *never* forgive humanity, not in a thousand times a thousand years. Their vengeance will be as eternal as the stars, Grand Commander Orgestre. Your descendants will curse your name, you and all you others who've authorised this genocide, until humanity itself is no more.'

'Don't commit this dreadful atrocity. Find another way,' said Gilhaelith.

The governors were scowling now, annoyed at the dissent spoiling their celebration dinner.

'You brought them here,' said Orgestre.

'When circumstances change, an *intelligent* man changes his mind,' said Gilhaelith.

'Sit down or I'll have you in irons for dealing with the enemy.' Orgestre turned to the governors. 'We've had the debate – weary days of it. The vote has been tallied, and won. Must we go through it yet again?'

'I haven't had my say,' said Malien.

'Then please say what you've come for so we can get on with it.'

'To exterminate any race before its time is a great evil, besides what may come of it.'

'Humanity is worn out with conflict,' said Governor Zaeff, speaking for the first time, 'and so is our world. It has to end now, and here. The future must take care of itself.'

'Oh, it will,' said Malien. 'Recall, from the Histories, how the Faellem once cast their rivals on Tallallame, the Mariem, into the void to die. They thought they had eliminated them, but out of the void the Mariem returned, as Charon, and in the end it was the Faellem who lost their world, their humanity and their civilisation.'

'The irony of the Histories is indeed inexorable,' said Yggur.

'While the mighty cringe from their imagined futures,' said Orgestre, 'the common folk live in fear that the war will go on forever. We've already voted to kill the beasts. Just give me the power and I'll see it carried out to the last pregnant female and the last whining infant. Those of you who don't have the stomach may take your leave, and claim hereafter that you had no part in the business.' He glanced around, and added, 'though no doubt you'll profit from it once the war is over.'

'Before you set about your slaughter,' said Malien, coming out to the front, 'attend me a moment!' She said it so like a royal command that even Orgestre fell silent.

She told them what had happened at the Hornrace and out in the Dry Sea, of the fate of Vithis, Minis and Tirior, and about the Well of Echoes.

'What's going to happen to it?' said Gilhaelith, his eyes glowing with a geomancer's fascination for any new natural force.

'No one knows,' she said. 'It may keep growing, go quiescent, or even split into a whole swarm of little Wells.'

'How does it grow?' asked Zaeff.

'By taking power from fields and nodes.'

'Then what's to stop it growing until it's consumed them all?' said Flydd.

'Maybe nothing,' said Malien, 'though all things have a natural limit.'

'Vithis said "All Santhenar will rue this day",' Tiaan reminded them. 'What did he mean by that?'

'I don't know,' said Malien.

'You'd better keep an eye on it,' said Flydd. 'Why don't you go now? Oh, if I could have the field map before you go, Tiaan,' he said pointedly, so the whole room could hear.

'I lost it,' she said at once. 'Out in the Dry Sea.'

'*Lost it?*'

'I think Tirior must have taken it, before she was sent to the Well,' Tiaan said hastily. 'It's ironic, really, since the Well feeds on fields and nodes, that it should have consumed my map.'

Flydd eyed her sceptically. 'Well, I dare say I can get enough out of the field controller with the incomplete one.'

'If you're going to check on the Well,' said Gilhaelith quickly, 'I'd like to come too.'

Flydd followed them outside and spoke quietly with Malien for a minute or two, before going back towards the banquet tent, but then he stopped halfway. 'Incidentally, Tiaan,' he called, 'you should ask Gilhaelith to explain the art of deception.'

'What's he talking about?' Tiaan said, once Flydd had returned to the tent.

Gilhaelith chuckled. 'The best liars keep their stories simple and keep saying the same thing. At all costs, resist the urge to embroider.'

Malien and Gilhaelith headed for the thapter, the others to their tents to change their filthy clothes. When they were alone, Gilhaelith said, 'I wonder if you might use your good offices to recover my geomantic globe. Now that the war is over, Flydd has no need to hold it, and it would be a comfort to me.'

Malien considered the request, as if judging whether he was

practising the art of deception on her. 'And you could use it to repair your injuries.'

'The damage is no longer reparable. But even so, I'd like to have it by me. It was my life's work, and it's a thing of beauty that comforts me.'

'I don't see why not,' she said. Malien looked him up and down. 'You're a contradictory fellow, Gilhaelith. You brought the lyrinx here to exact revenge on them, and you've just argued for their preservation.'

'So I did,' said Gilhaelith. 'But the brutalities of war, and my own mortality, have rendered revenge meaningless.'

'You can't lie to me, you know. I read men – even geomancers – the way you read books.'

'I wouldn't try. I'd never seen war before, Malien, and I had no idea of the horror of it – bodies torn apart, heads ripped off, thousands dying in agony because some fool ordered them to fight. And to think I put it all in motion.'

'This battle was coming anyway,' said Malien. She wasn't trying to comfort him. 'But I do believe we're of a mind.'

'What I've done has made my life more meaningless than ever, and I'm beginning to see only one way out. To take my life before I lose my mind.'

'There could be another way to give your life the meaning you crave.'

'How?' he said indifferently.

'By helping to undo what you've brought about.'

'It's gone too far; there's no way to resolve it.'

'There may be. Let's get your globe. Do you know where it is?'

'In the guarded tent next to the relics from the tar pits.'

'I'll take the thapter across while we wait for the others. No one would suspect me. And, Gilhaelith, perhaps you can do something for me ...'

Tiaan was pacing across the crunchy salt on the other side of the thapter when Malien came walking towards her. 'Is something the matter, Tiaan?'

'I can't bear to think about what they're doing,' said Tiaan in a low voice. She kicked a lump of salt out of the way as if it were Orgestre's head.

'They're afraid, and they see it as a simple answer, though there are none.'

'I can think of one,' Tiaan said savagely. 'If I had the power, I'd destroy all the nodes on Santhenar.'

'That would be the death of all the Arts,' said Malien mildly. 'The good as well as the bad.'

'If the world keeps on the way it's going, building ever more powerful devices and taking more and more to operate them, the Art will be the death of Santhenar. Humanity was never meant to have such power, Malien. Look what we've done to our world during the brief course of this war, and that's nothing to what we *will* do.'

'Whether our powers are great or small, good and evil apply in the same measure. And if you succeeded, and survived it, what then?'

Tiaan hadn't thought about that. 'I suppose I'd just live a simple life without the Art, like everyone else.'

Malien sighed. 'If only it *were* that simple. Getting rid of the Art would not change the human nature that has abused it.'

'But it would limit the amount of damage that evil people could do.'

'You can't turn time back, Tiaan; neither for the world, *nor yourself*. You're what life and the Art have made of you. If you robbed yourself of that, you would be the unhappiest person in the world.'

Nish and Irisis had joined them and as soon as they were in the air, flying in darkness, Malien said casually, 'Could we fly over the lyrinx camp for a moment? I'd like to see how they're faring.'

'So would I,' said Tiaan. 'I knew some of them well. Ryll was a decent man - *male* - no, I'll call him a man. He was a better man than many humans I've known. And Liett . . .'

'Liett held me prisoner,' said Nish unexpectedly. 'After . . . er, Gilhaelith left me behind.' He glanced at the geomancer, who

729

managed to look abashed for perhaps the first time in his life. 'The other lyrinx seemed in awe of her. And when she'd finished with me, she left me in Ryll's custody. He seemed to have grown in stature since I last saw him.'

'Both Ryll and Liett have grown,' said Gilhaelith. 'They've greatly influenced the other lyrinx, and this has been recognised.'

'What do you mean?' said Tiaan.

'There's been a profound shift in their attitudes since the relics were discovered,' said Gilhaelith. 'Matriarch Gyrull forced the lyrinx to think about the future as well as the past. The lyrinx who are least flesh-formed and most human, the *reverts*, are now venerated as being closest to their ancient selves.'

'The other lyrinx must find that hard to take.'

'Many do, but most yearn for their children to be more like their ancestors. In lyrinx society, the individual must bow to the will of the whole, or even be sacrificed for the good of the whole, and most do so gladly. Once they discovered their true ancestry, most lyrinx accepted that they had to change to survive and prosper on this world. It would be a tragedy if they were to disappear.'

'There may be a way to save them,' said Tiaan. 'I er . . . neglected to mention it to Flydd and the others, but Vithis has built a portal out on a pinnacle in the Dry Sea.'

'A *portal*? Really?' Gilhaelith's eyes lit up.

'Well, it's really a device to *create* a portal,' said Malien. 'He had it made to rescue First Clan from the void. And I have the key.'

'If I could just see a working gate,' said Gilhaelith. 'If I could step across to another world, no matter how briefly, it would be the climax of my geomantic life. I would die a happy man.'

'Your mention of the fate of the Faellem gave me an idea, Malien,' said Tiaan.

'I thought it might,' said Malien.

Tiaan regarded her with a thoughtful smile. 'Shall we go down and talk to the lyrinx?'

'But we'll be branded as traitors!' said Nish. 'Flydd will be apoplectic.'

'I'll take you back if you like,' said Tiaan. 'But I simply can't stand by and see the lyrinx destroyed.'

Nish and Irisis exchanged glances. 'I've seen enough killing to last me a lifetime,' said Nish. 'But . . .'

'There'll be no going back,' said Irisis. 'What do we do, Nish?'

'Now that the war is over, and we've miraculously survived it, I just want to go home.'

'So do I,' said Irisis. 'But we can't. How would we live with ourselves?'

'You're right,' said Nish. 'Take us down, Tiaan!'

SEVENTY-FOUR

The thapter drifted low above the lyrinx prison, if prison it could be called, for it had no walls. A circle of clankers were drawn up half a league further out, and mind-shocks struck the enemy if they tried to pass beyond boundaries marked by lines carved into the salt. It was a black night and the area close to the clankers was lit, though the camp lay in almost complete darkness. Just a lantern winked here and there to show the shape of the half a million lyrinx – their great army plus all the old, the young and others who would not normally fight.

'Can we be seen from the clankers?' Tiaan said quietly.

'Surely not,' said Malien. She called down. 'Bring up the flag.'

Irisis hung a blue truce flag out on a pole, Nish directed the light from a lantern on it and shortly a lyrinx appeared in an open space in the centre of the camp, skin-changed to brilliant, luminous blue. Javelards and crossbows were trained on the thapter as they approached.

'This could go very wrong,' said Malien. 'You do realise that?'

'Minis found the courage to atone for his failings,' said Tiaan. 'How can I do less?'

She set the thapter down a little way from the blue lyrinx, who immediately changed to the black of coal. He was huge and had a golden crest, the only one Irisis had ever seen. He folded his arms and waited. A wall of lyrinx surrounded them, and their colours and patterns were threatening.

Gilhaelith lifted one leg over the side. 'Do you think showing your face is a good idea?' said Malien.

'I'm dying. What do I have to lose?'

Gilhaelith went down and planted the truce flag deep in the salt. The lyrinx made a collective ratchetting sound, perhaps representing a hiss, and surged forward as one. A female voice called a command, they stopped and the circle parted to admit five more lyrinx, two males and three females, carrying lanterns. Four lacked wings but showed blue truce colours. The fifth had thin, colourless, unarmoured skin and translucent, soaring wings. The surrounding lyrinx retreated until the circle around the thapter was about two hundred paces across.

The five joined the golden-crested male, twenty paces away from the thapter.

'The leading wingless male is Ryll,' said Tiaan. 'The colour-less female is Liett. I don't know the others.'

Irisis wondered if they could possibly be the leaders of this vast gathering. They seemed too young. Anyway, the lyrinx were led by matriarchs, so they must be here as translators.

A group of five weathered females moved across from the other side of the circle, but stopped twenty paces away, arms folded. The remaining matriarchs, Irisis assumed.

After a long interval of silence Ryll held out a hand. 'Tiaan.' He gave what passed for a smile. 'Nish; you lead a busy life. I don't know your name,' he said to Irisis, 'though I do remember you. We fought, once, on the other side of the world.'

'I haven't forgotten,' said Irisis, taking his leathery hand. 'And this is Malien, Matah of the Aachim of Santhenar.'

'Malien from the time the Forbidding was broken?' said Ryll.

'The same,' said Malien. 'You know the Histories, then?'

'We know everything we've been able to learn about humanity – our Histories that might have been.'

Malien bowed and he did too, then extended his hand. She took it.

Ryll turned to Gilhaelith. 'In the circumstances, Tetrarch, I won't shake hands with you.'

733

Gilhaelith bowed, although with his odd-shaped, elongated frame and woolly head it was not a dignified gesture. 'In the circumstances, I had not thought you would.'

'Here is Great Anabyng,' said Ryll. The black male did not offer to shake hands.

'My negotiators are Liett,' said Ryll, 'whom some of you know.' Liett shook hands with ostentatious reluctance. 'Also Daodand, H'nant and Plyyr.' Ryll indicated, in turn, the other male and the two females, one larger than him, the other smaller than Liett and also lacking skin armour. Plyyr looked almost human. The matriarchs said nothing.

Daodand carried a leather box which he opened to produce ten drinking horns, a large skin and a smaller box containing some kind of crusted delicacy. He squeezed fluid from the skin into the horns. H'nant and Plyyr passed them around, then the morsels.

Irisis surreptitiously sniffed the liquor, which was thick and had a faint citrus odour, a cross between lime and grapefruit.

'If you don't like strong drink,' said Ryll, 'take only a taste. This *hurrj* is old and very potent.'

Irisis tasted it with her tongue. It was sweet, strongly flavoured and the spirits burned her nose. She took a small sip, then one of the delicacies, which had the crumbly texture of a sweet biscuit but with a creamy tartness.

'Why have you come?' said Ryll.

'To talk about your situation,' said Malien.

'What is there to talk about?' said Liett savagely. 'Just get it over with; don't come here to gloat first.'

Ryll shook his head at her. Liett snapped her wings in his face. Great Anabyng made a peremptory noise in his throat and Liett folded her wings at once.

'Scrutator Flydd has been outvoted,' said Malien. 'The governors have decided that your people are to be expunged. We're here because we cannot agree to genocide. Yet neither do we want another war the like of which the world has suffered. Accordingly, we have a proposal.'

When she did not go on, Liett said, 'What is it?'

'Tiaan?' Malien prompted.

'Vithis the Aachim built a tower on the pinnacle of Nithmak,' said Tiaan, 'some forty leagues south-west of here.'

'We've seen this watch-tower from the air,' said Liett. 'What of it?'

'It's not a watch-tower. It was designed to create a portal, to bring Vithis's lost First Clan home from the void.'

'The decadent Aachim could not survive there,' said H'nant in a purring growl.

'Not even in their constructs?' said Malien in a frosty voice.

H'nant sneered at the very idea.

'It doesn't matter,' said Gilhaelith. 'They were found in the middle of the Dry Sea – dead! However, the portal remains.'

'Get on with it,' said Liett.

'There is a world called Tallallame,' said Tiaan. 'The third of the Three Worlds.'

'We know of it.' Ryll shifted uncomfortably, then glanced at Great Anabyng, who remained expressionless.

Irisis couldn't help wondering why neither the matriarchs nor their truly great mancer were taking part in the meeting.

'It is a paradise of forest, lake and meadow,' Tiaan went on, 'the most beautiful world that ever was, according to the Faellem. The *Tale of the Mirror* tells that Tallallame was also . . . invaded by creatures from the void when the Forbidding was broken. Thranx went there, as well as lorrsk and other savage creatures. Its native people, the Faellem, are no more. Or at least, they are civilised no more.'

'Am I to take it that you're offering us a choice?' said Ryll with a savage smile. 'To go to Tallallame and attempt to wrest it from the creatures that now possess it, or stay here and die?'

'No creature could be better fitted for Tallallame than lyrinx,' said Tiaan.

'It's a trick,' said Liett. 'They've come here to torment us – to offer us hope then snatch it away again!'

'All we want,' said Malien, 'is for the war to be over with no more killing on either side.'

'Words are always more convincing when they're backed

up by deeds,' said Ryll. 'How do you plan to demonstrate good faith?'

'I have your sacred relics in the thapter,' said Malien. 'I would give you the first crate now, and the others at the gate.'

'I didn't know that!' cried Tiaan.

Malien smiled. 'It was such a short flight that no one went down the ladder. Gilhaelith and I pulled a little trick on the guards, though we had the devil of a job getting the crates down the hatch by ourselves.'

Ryll stood up to his full height, quivering with emotion, and his skin colours flared so brightly that they lit up everything inside the circle. 'Show us the relics.'

Inside the thapter the lyrinx squeezed downstairs, in small groups, and the lids were taken off. Ryll, who came last, stared down into the crates, one after another, his skin muted now in consideration of the others. Finally he motioned for the lids to be refastened and clambered out.

'We could take the crates,' he said.

'And what better faith could we show than by bringing them here?' said Malien. 'But if we gave them to you at Nithmak it would save you carrying them forty leagues. That would save lyrinx lives, I'm sure.'

'What makes you think you can open this gate?' said Liett in a low, disturbing purr.

'Vithis gave me the key.' Malien showed them the sapphire rod.

'And how would you direct it to Tallallame?'

'I know the way of old,' said Malien.

'I don't trust them.' Liett snapped her grey teeth. 'They mean to send us back to the void!'

'Why would they bother?' Ryll said patiently.

'To salve their precious consciences. Truly these weaklings would not survive a day there. Not even an hour!'

'Not even the void would be as bad as being herded here, like beasts in our own ordure, until we die of thirst,' said Ryll, whose skin showed truce-blue again. 'We survived in the void before; if we must, we can do so again. But Tallallame, Liett!' He reached out to her. 'Just think of it! A beautiful world all for ourselves. For that, I would take the chance.'

'And I,' said H'nant.

Plyyr hesitated. 'There are places in the void of unimaginable savagery; places that are worse than dying here. I mistrust this offer. They don't want to salve their consciences; they seek the bitterest revenge they can inflict on us.'

Ryll looked to Great Anabyng as if for guidance. He glanced at the silent women, who nodded as one. 'The former matriarchs do not vote, and neither do I. Our time has passed,' Anabyng said in a deep growl. 'For myself, my beloved consort, Gyrull, is dead and I will soon join her. I would not have our bones sundered by the void. You must decide – that is why you've been appointed.'

'And swiftly,' said Ryll. 'We have little water left. Already our little children are suffering. In three days they'll start to die. In five, only the hardiest will be alive. In seven days, none of us.'

'You have been appointed leader, in defiance of all convention,' snarled Liett with another snap of her magnificent wings. 'You boasted of all the marvels you would do. *Then lead us!*'

'What convention is that?' Tiaan asked curiously.

'That we be led by a revered matriarch, not an unmated, wingless monstrosity of a *male*.'

'Matriarch Gyrull appointed me before she died,' he said mildly. 'Your own mother. You yourself told me so.'

'She was out of her mind with pain,' Liett said.

'Great Anabyng confirmed her intentions. Besides, I did not boast. Matriarch asked me what I would do if I were leader, and I told her. I had no desire to be patriarch. We've not had one in three thousand years.'

'So that's how you see yourself, you unmated male dog!' cried Liett in a passion. 'The last patriarch was a disaster; that's why we never took another. And you will be even worse.'

Ryll turned his back on her, saying to the others, 'I know Tiaan and I trust her. Malien, too, I know to be a woman of honour.'

'They're the only two in all humanity!' hissed Liett.

Ryll ignored her. 'I will go through the gate, and if it leads me asunder, even to the most desperate recesses of the void, I will

737

do all I can to lead us out again.' His eyes shone in his fervour. 'What about you, Liett?'

'I will not follow any unmated *male* unless the vote is entirely against me.'

'Since when do lyrinx vote?' said Ryll mildly. 'We do what our leaders, in their wisdom, have decided.'

'You broke the custom,' she snapped. 'I demand a vote.'

Ryll's gaze rested on each of the lyrinx, then he nodded. 'And how do you vote?'

'The past must not bind the future,' said Great Anabyng. 'I will not vote.'

The former matriarchs also declined. The other three lyrinx gave Ryll their vote. Liett did not.

'Not just *us*,' said Liett. '*All* the lyrinx must vote.' She swept around the circle of lyrinx with one arm.

'We are over half a million,' Ryll said. 'It would take days to count.'

'So be it.' Liett folded her arms across her breast.

'Do you want the small children to die, and the old folk, because of this delay?'

'In the absence of our matriarchs, I demand that convention be followed.'

'Come with me. Look at the state of the children.' Taking Liett's arm, he led her away from the other lyrinx. He had to drag her for the first three steps, whereupon she cuffed him hard over the side of the head and, mollified by the display of aggression, went willingly.

As they reached the surrounding circle, Ryll's truce-blue faded and they disappeared into the crowd. They were gone almost an hour. When they returned, Ryll said without preamble, 'We will do it.' He clasped Tiaan's hand, then each of the others'. 'But first you must break the mind-shock circle, *if you can.*'

'I can,' said Tiaan, 'since I know how it was made. How long will it take you to get to Nithmak?'

'We can run forty leagues in two days and nights,' said Daodand. 'Though, running with so little water . . .'

'The children will die of thirst,' said Tiaan.

'Most will,' said Liett. 'Unless you allow us sufficient power to fly them there.'

'We can't, Tiaan,' said Nish. 'What if they break free and begin the war over?'

'You expect us to trust you,' cried Liett, 'yet you do not trust us in return.'

'That is the privilege of the victors,' said Nish.

Malien shushed him and conferred with Tiaan for a moment, then called Irisis. 'Is there a way to cut off the field controller on one side only?'

Irisis had to think for a minute. 'You might do it this way, with the amplimet . . .'

After listening to the explanation Tiaan said, 'It won't work for long, but it should last long enough for them to break out. And once they're going full speed in the dark, the mind-shockers won't be able to encircle them again.'

'What about us?' said Irisis.

'What do you mean?'

'What if Orgestre orders the field controller directed against us?'

'They'll be far too busy trying to contain the enemy,' said Malien. 'They can't do both.'

'We wouldn't see the children die,' said Tiaan to Ryll. 'We'll allow you power for flight, but should anyone abuse this offer, I'll withdraw that power while you're flying. From all of you.'

Liett's yellow eyes glowed. 'I think that I like you after all, little human! You have my word.'

'And mine. Let it be done,' said Ryll.

'And done swiftly,' Irisis added. 'While our opponents are sleeping.'

They went up in the thapter. It was well after midnight and the night still overcast. Shortly the agreed signal was flashed vertically from the lyrinx camp. Tiaan used the amplimet to break the mind-shock circle on the western side. The lyrinx burst out and the clankers retreated in terror. Soon the fliers among the lyrinx, perhaps a tenth of their number, took to the air carrying the children.

'We're taking an almighty risk,' said Nish. 'If they break their word and the war begins again, we'll be the most reviled names in all the Histories. Our best choice will be to go straight to the Well, for there'll be no hiding on Santhenar.'

'They won't break their word,' said Tiaan, but her hand shook on the controller and the thapter dipped. She steadied it and flew west into the night.

'Tiaan,' said Gilhaelith from the base of the ladder, 'did Tirior really take your field map?'

She flushed. 'Of course not.'

'May I see it?'

'Why?'

'My globe is in error in some small respects. I'd like it to be perfect before .... you know.'

She smiled. 'I'm a geomancer too – I understand perfectly.' Withdrawing the folded map from the lining of her coat she passed it to him.

SEVENTY-FIVE

end . . .

Nish was sitting miserably on the floor of the thapter, which was lurching and bouncing all over the sky. It had been harried by two thapters since dawn, and now a third machine had joined them.

'Are you all right?' he heard Malien say to Tiaan.

'I think I can manage for a while yet.'

'Use the amplimet to keep above them.'

'I'm trying to.'

A crossbow bolt spanged off the side. Nish glanced at Irisis, who was sitting cross-legged, apparently unconcerned, making another of her pieces of jewellery. This one was a brooch in silver filigree, like two figure-eights joined at the centre. She didn't look up.

'How did we get ourselves into this mess?' said Nish. 'What if the lyrinx escape and attack our defenceless cities –?'

'Will you shut up!' she hissed. 'We made our choice, so don't start whining and wringing your hands like a third-rate Minis.' She worked for a few more minutes, then exclaimed, 'Now look what you've made me do,' and slammed the brooch down on the floor.

'I'm sorry,' Nish said at once. 'You seemed so calm.'

'Of course I'm not calm! We may have made the biggest mistake of our lives, and we're bound to pay for it. I've been regretting it since the moment I opened my mouth, but –'

741

'But what else could we have done? Come here.' She sat beside him, taking his hand. 'You're right,' Nish said. 'Let's not waste the time we have left on useless regrets. We did what was right and we'll face the consequences.'

It didn't appear as though the other thapters were trying to destroy Malien's machine, but only to force it down on the salt. Tiaan kept just ahead of them for hours as she followed a round-about course south and west, trying to draw their fire away from the lyrinx. Thus far she'd always managed to get away, through the superior range of the amplimet.

Gilhaelith was sitting up the other end, Tiaan's map spread out on the floor before him while he made minute alterations to the geomantic globe. It was like watching grass grow.

From the heights, after the sun came up, Nish had seen terrible sights. Early on, a fleet of Orgestre's constructs had torn straight through a band of running lyrinx, trampling them under the iron feet, smashing flesh and bones to jelly. There had been children among them.

Not long after that, the field had been whipped away from a group of flying lyrinx. They had done everything they could to keep aloft: their limbs went like bellows, their great wings thrashed, but without the aid of the Secret Art no effort could keep them in the air. Males, females and children all plummeted to the bed of the Dry Sea, their impacts making little purple marks that were swallowed by the white immensity of the salt. Nish had gone below after that. It had seemed better not to know, or at least not to see it. But it confirmed that he'd made the right decision.

The sound of the mechanism cut off abruptly. Nish scrambled to his feet but it started again at once as Tiaan tapped into another field.

'Is everything all right?' he said hoarsely, looking up the ladder.

'So far,' replied Malien in a strained voice.

'I just hope they know what they're doing,' said Nish to Irisis.

'They've fought this kind of battle before,' said Irisis, intent on a new brooch.

Several hours afterwards Malien called down. 'One of the thapters has turned away towards the Foshorn. I think Flydd's in it. I wonder what he's up to?'

'I'm sure we'll find out before too long,' said Irisis.

Tiaan went higher and shortly the other two craft turned back. By the time they reached Nithmak in mid-afternoon, the first of the fliers were already there. A narrow stair wound around the peak from top to bottom. Though the mighty winches were still in place, the five constructs Tiaan and Malien had seen previously were gone.

Most of the fliers were spread out around the base of the peak, or hanging from the sides, though several hundred had assembled on the flat top, Liett among them, when the thapter landed. They were assembling javelards and catapults for the inevitable attack. Tiaan remained where she was, slumped in her seat, eyes closed.

'Are you all right?' said Irisis.

'Just clearing my mind before we begin on the gate.'

'You'd better have a sleep first,' said Malien.

'There isn't time.'

'The runners won't be here for a day and a half. Remember your first gate, Tiaan. You wouldn't want anything to go wrong this time.'

When Nish rose late the following morning after the first decent sleep he'd had in weeks, Tiaan was walking around and around the tower, as if trying to find courage after the disaster of her previous gate. Everything rested on her. What if she couldn't make it work, or it went wrong again?

He was eating breakfast when he felt a shudder that made the red-topped tower sway back and forth. Rock cracked off one edge of Nithmak, taking five lyrinx with it, though three managed to flap to safety. Hundreds more flew up in a flapping of leathery wings and circled the tower.

'What was that?' said Nish, uncomfortably recalling the fall of Vithis's watch-tower.

'If it was an earth trembler, it was a mighty one,' said Malien.

'But they do have big earth tremblers around here. We'd better find out. Just in case . . .'

In case of what? Nish thought, as they headed for the thapter. It curved around Nithmak tower, rising slowly, before heading south-west. After some time, Irisis, who was peering over the side with her spyglass, sang out.

'There's smoke rising above the Hornrace. No, it's dust. It looks like a gigantic dust storm.'

'The rest of Vithis's arch must have collapsed,' said Nish from below. 'Can we take a look?'

Tiaan turned the thapter that way and climbed until it was high enough to get a good view. 'The whole of the Hornrace, leagues long, is covered by a vast line of dust,' she called down the hatch. 'It must have been the arch. It's not going to do us any harm –'

'The Trihorn Falls are flowing again,' cried Irisis. 'Oh, just look at that! Have you ever seen anything like it?'

Irisis was not given to hyperbole. Nish came scrambling up the ladder and pulled himself up onto the side next to her. Gilhaelith followed, though he was tall enough to see over. Vast arching streams of water were pouring out from the thunder-head of dust enveloping the Trihorn Falls.

'There's more water coming over than there was when I first saw them,' said Tiaan. 'Much more.'

By the time they were above the falls, the dust had begun to settle. The deluge had doubled and tripled by then. A torrent was pouring through the Hornrace, unimaginably greater than before.

'What's happened?' said Nish, whose heart was hammering. 'That's more than the blockage in the Hornrace breaking open.'

As the dust was blown away into the Sea of Thurkad, the scale of the cataclysm became evident. 'A great slab has cracked off the end of the Foshorn,' said Irisis.

'There must be ten times the flow there was before,' said Nish.

'More like a hundred,' said Tiaan. 'Just look at it.'

The flood was massive, awesome, prodigious; there were not words to describe it. And then it exploded in size again. 'The other side of the Hornrace is collapsing as well,' said Irisis. 'Nish, look!' She was on her knees, shaking his arm. 'Oh, this is unbelievable. Half of one of the Trihorns is falling down. Now the other one is going as well. They're being washed away.'

Those mighty peaks, that had split the flow of the Hornrace for thousands of years, were undermined in less than an hour. Peaks almost a thousand spans high tilted, toppled, rolled over and over and broke into pieces the size of hills before thundering to the bed of the Dry Sea, or into the salt lakes which were already overflowing. They could hear the roaring from on high, and even see the ground shake. Fissures zigzagged out across the salt for leagues.

The flow doubled and redoubled, until even from their height the noise was deafening. No one said a word. Even Gilhaelith was awed by the power of nature, so much greater than his greatest geomancy.

'It's not going to stop, is it?' shouted Nish.

'Not until it fills the Dry Sea –' Irisis stopped with her mouth open. 'They must have used the field controller to explode the node under the Foshorn.'

'Neither Flydd nor Yggur would have done this, even if Orgestre put a sword to their necks,' said Irisis.

'No geomancer has the power to do what's been done here,' said Gilhaelith.

'Then who has?'

'Earth tremblers happen for their own reasons.'

He didn't sound convinced and neither was Nish, who wasn't a believer in coincidences.

'It's the end of the Dry Sea. It's going to be the Sea of Perion again,' said Tiaan.

'And that too was foretold,' said Malien.

'How long will it take to fill?' said Irisis.

'Weeks, I should think,' said Tiaan in a wisp of a voice. 'But as soon as the water is two spans deep in this corner of the sea, all the lyrinx will drown, and Ryll will think I planned it all along. He'll think it's humanity's perfect revenge – to offer them hope, then snatch it away at the last minute. There's no death the lyrinx fear more than drowning!'

'Liett will certainly think that,' said Irisis.

'What are we going to do?' cried Tiaan, looking around wildly.

'Don't panic. There's time yet,' said Malien.

'How much?' she wailed.

'It will depend on which point of the sea is lowest, and whether they have to cross it to get to Nithmak.'

'We'd better warn them,' said Tiaan, turning out towards the lyrinx. 'Perhaps they can run a bit faster.'

The thapter raced from one end of the running horde, now stretched out over fifteen leagues of salt, to the other, though it seemed clear from their pace that the lyrinx knew what had happened. By the time they'd done that, the water was threading the bed of the Dry Sea and Tiaan was in a panic. Tiaan hurtled back to Nithmak, setting down right at the base of the tower in the middle of the afternoon, and running to the doors. They were still locked.

'I wish I'd gone in before,' she said. Tiaan threw herself back in and drove the thapter straight at the doors.

'Stop! You don't know how strongly it's built,' yelled Malien.

It was too late. The front of the thapter struck the doors with a crash that threw them all forward. The front crumpled and Malien cried out in dismay. The metal doors had buckled but still held. Tiaan pushed again and the doors tore from their hinges.

Everyone scrambled out, and Malien inspected the damage, shaking her head. 'We may come to regret that.'

Tiaan wasn't listening. She ran past and up the winding stairs into darkness. Everything had been built of basalt as black as the void itself, and there were no windows here. Irisis and Gilhaelith followed at a less precipitous pace.

Nish looked across the foyer after them. 'I think Tiaan has taken leave of her senses.'

Malien came around the side. 'She's been troubled for a long time, and Minis's sacrifice shook her.'

'She's always been a little . . . obsessive.'

He went out, inspecting the defences with a professional eye.

Nithmak Tower occupied the centre of the flat-topped peak, leaving a rim of bare rock all around. The top of the peak was only a few hundred spans across, and thousands of fliers stood in a ring around the edges, watching silently. Nish shivered. At least they'd keep the thapters away.

He did a rough calculation. At a pinch the top might accommodate a hundred thousand lyrinx, crammed close together, but four or five times that number had to pass through the gate, if they survived the journey.

Nithmak could not be attacked from below but was vulnerable to attack from air-floaters and thapters. 'I wonder why Vithis chose this place?' he said to Irisis. 'There are dozens of larger peaks in this part of the sea.'

'Something special about its node, you can be certain.'

'We'd better prepare to defend.' Nish scanned the salt with Irisis's spyglass. 'The lyrinx are awfully spread out.'

'And the water is coming in quickly. The salt lakes below the Trihorn are already overflowing.'

'It'll take days to get to the other end of the sea,' said Nish, 'so it'll be quite a while before the level starts to rise.'

'The Dry Sea isn't like a bathtub, Nish,' said Malien, joining them. 'The water's coming in faster than it can flow away. For all we know, the level could rise to the top of this peak before it even reaches the far end of the Dry Sea, three hundred leagues away. The flow could wash Nithmak away, as it collapsed the Trihorn.'

Nish began to say something, but then shook his head and hunched down, staring at the ground. He was also starting to feel panicky. The ribs he'd cracked when Vithis had tried to drag him into the Well ached and he stood up again, rubbing his side.

Malien laid a hand on his shoulder. 'But not, I think, in the next day and night. We have time yet.'

'Will it be enough?' Nish focussed his spyglass upon the straggling line of lyrinx, and the squadrons of clankers that continued to harry them, where the country permitted it. The fleetest of foot were not far from the base of Nithmak now.

'For many, though not the stragglers. Let's go up to Tiaan.'

It proved a long climb up steep and narrow stairs. 'I don't see how we're going to get half a million lyrinx up here,' panted Nish as he rested halfway up.

'The gate doesn't have to open here,' said Malien.

Tiaan was sitting on a glass chair in a room near the top of the tower. Unlike the lower sections, its walls were spiralling strips of black metal, like the metal of which constructs were made, whose spaces had been filled in with glass. The floor was made of metal crescents cunningly locked together. A table of woven wire supported a black metal cube. Tiaan's head rested on her hands and she was staring intently at the cube.

'Is that *it*?' said Nish. 'Or is it a last joke by Vithis?'

Tiaan turned her head and stared right through him, as if she didn't recognise him. Nish's scalp prickled.

'Vithis was not a joking man,' said Malien.

'There's something inside,' said Tiaan, clutching the amplimet in both hands. 'I can see its aura, but I don't know how to open the cube.'

'There's not much time,' said Gilhaelith, peering out through the thick glass.

Nish went over beside him. The air was heavy with flying lyrinx. 'Is that an air-floater, way up high?'

'If it is, it's bigger than the air-dreadnoughts that attacked Fiz Gorgo. I wonder what it's up to? Orgestre could finish this by dropping boulders on us.'

'Boulders,' sniffed Nish.

Crash! The tower gave a gentle shudder.

'Sometimes the simplest attacks are the most effective. That didn't miss by much.'

'Is there anything we can do?'

'Go up in the thapter,' said Tiaan. 'Keep them away. I can't think.'

'Come on, Nish,' said Malien. 'We've got work to do.'

'The box doesn't open,' said Tiaan, as Nish and Malien clattered down the stairs. 'Why?'

'Perhaps it's locked,' said Irisis.

748

'Of course it is. Vithis said so. And he gave Malien the key, that sapphire rod.' Tiaan ran to the top of the stairs, shouting, 'Malien. The key!'

Nish came running up with it. 'Thank you,' Tiaan said absently, already turning away. Then she swung back. 'Nish?'

'Yes?'

She put out her arms. 'Good luck.'

SEVENTY-SIX

They stopped halfway for a breather and Nish looked down through a slit in the stone. Lyrinx now clustered on every surface, wings folded. Others clung to the sides of the pinnacle and thousands more wheeled in the air. Far below, the water was flooding towards the lyrinx stragglers, still fifteen leagues away on the salt. Other lake lobes pressed towards the middle of the line, forcing the fleeing lyrinx further out into the Dry Sea. Water was pooling there in places, too.

As Nish and Malien ran through the broken door, their way was blocked by half a dozen lyrinx, Liett at their head. Her claws were fully extended.

'I knew it was a lie,' she spat. 'Well, you won't live to enjoy your revenge.'

'The flood is not our doing,' said Malien, putting her hands up.

'You'll die for it just the same,' said Liett.

She sprang and, before Malien could do anything to defend herself, the claws went around her throat. Nish went for his sword, knowing it was hopeless, but it was knocked out of his hand.

'This serves you not at all, Liett,' Malien managed to croak.

She looked up and Liett followed her gaze. Another rock fell, smashing into the edge of the peak and spraying splinters of stone everywhere.

'Those air-dreadnoughts rise higher than you can fly, Liett. One such missile, perfectly aimed, can destroy the tower and the port-all that creates the gate. And then we'll all *drown*. You, me and all of your kind. But we can save you.'

At the word *drown*, Liett's crest, the only part of her skin that had colour, shimmered with emerald green. She shuddered, then let Malien go. 'After all that's been done to us, I can't bear to put my trust in humankind.'

'I'm not humankind, Liett, I'm Aachim. *My* people have never waged war on lyrinx, and my record is inscribed in the pages of the Histories for all to read. Besides, it's not necessary to trust, merely to gamble. Lyrinx are not averse to a wager, I'm told.'

It seemed to hit the right chord. 'Everything in life is a gamble,' said Liett, letting her go. 'All right – go up in your flier. Already the water laps around my people's ankles – I can sense their cries from here.'

Three air-dreadnoughts now wheeled high above the tower. 'They're armed with javelards,' said Nish.

'So are we,' said Malien. 'Get to your post.'

As soon as he was in the shooter's position, Malien took the thapter straight up, relying on the lyrinx to get out of her path. The air-dreadnoughts were large, Nish saw, but had only a small crew, sacrificing everything to carry the greatest weight of stones and still rise beyond range of the lyrinx, whose claws could destroy an airbag in seconds.

Further off, two thapters cruised in circles, guarding the air-dreadnoughts. They turned towards him. Five against one – odds even Malien would be hard pressed to even.

'I'll go directly behind that one,' she shouted over the wind, pointing at the nearest air-dreadnought.

Nish raised a hand, not sure he understood her strategy, but she was looking forward, intent on her course. His eyes were already watering. He wished he'd thought to bring goggles.

The thapter shot sideways. Had someone fired on them? Nish couldn't tell. Malien whipped around in a circle and behind the air-dreadnought hovering over the tower. It dropped three rocks, one after another, as he fired his javelard at the rotors. He only had to hit one to disable the craft and felt sure he would, having done it before. Unfortunately the air-dreadnought rose suddenly as the weight was released, and his spear passed harmlessly below its keel.

Nish cursed and wound his cranks furiously. It took so long to reload. His eyes followed the rocks towards the tower. They seemed to be heading directly for it. He held his breath. One puff of dust rose beside the tower, and two more down the slope of the peak. Hitting the target must be harder than it looked.

The air-dreadnought moved off, though it was as slow as a tortoise compared to the thapter in Malien's nimble hands. Nish took careful aim at the port rotor and pulled the lever. At this distance he couldn't miss, and didn't. The rotor shattered to splinters, some of which flew into the starboard rotor, destroying it as well. The pilot pulled the floater-gas release rope and the air-dreadnought dropped sharply away to the south.

Malien shot away, carving a wavy trail across the sky to avoid one of the thapters. Judging by the reckless skill with which it was being flown, Chissmoul was at the controller.

Nish felt a surge of pride at the prowess of his young pupil, until he realised that she was now an enemy trying to bring him down. He mechanically loaded another spear as he searched the sky.

The other air-dreadnoughts were hovering some distance away, waiting to see what happened. The thapters approached, one on either side, and Kattiloe was the other pilot. Nish had chosen them both, supervised their training and helped them through dozens of crises. He liked Kattiloe and Chissmoul. Moreover, for the past hundred and fifty years, women of child-bearing age had been protected at all costs, for the survival of humanity. In a battle with another thapter, there was little to do but attack the pilot, but Nish wasn't sure he could fire his javelard at a woman. Shooting Chissmoul or Kattiloe was unthinkable. He wondered if they felt the same. Probably not – men weren't precious, especially not traitors like him. They would follow Orgestre's orders and do their duty.

The thapter lurched, tilted sideways, dropped sharply then stopped in mid-air as if it had landed on a mattress.

'What the blazes is that?' Malien yelled.

Had something gone wrong with the field? Were they going to fall to their doom as the lyrinx had earlier? Bile froze in his throat. Malien was looking out to the left. He followed her out-flung arm.

A dark mass like a whirling funnel, or a tornado, had just slipped over the horizon. The funnel was black at the bottom, paling upwards to grey with flecks of yellow, and it was moving steadily across the bed of the sea in their direction.

'It's the Well, grown monstrously large,' he said. 'It looks as if it's coming out of the ground, growing above it as well as below.'

Malien could not have heard him over the wind. 'It's the Well,' she called.

'What's it going to do?'

'I don't want to know.'

In the tower, an hour or two had gone by but Tiaan still hadn't worked out how to open the box. The sapphire rod was useless. It may well have been a key but there was no lock to put it in. Frustrated, she banged the box with her fist.

'Perhaps it's not meant to be opened,' said Gilhaelith. 'Can you use it without doing so?'

'I can't tell. I don't understand anything, Gilhaelith. If this is the port-all, it's completely different to the one I used at Tirth-rax. That one filled a room and had hundreds of parts, but there doesn't seem to be anything to this one. The box weighs nothing. It's as if it's empty.'

'Keep trying,' said Gilhaelith. 'Irisis, what's going on outside?'

Irisis tucked her spyglass under her arm. 'I can see the end of the lyrinx column.'

'That's something. Go down and find out how close the leaders are, before it gets dark.' Gilhaelith turned to Tiaan. 'What if you were to touch the sapphire to the box?'

'I've already tried.' Tiaan showed him what she had done, touching the smooth stone to the faces, the edges and the corners.

753

Nothing happened. The box was so perfectly built that there was not a seam visible. It looked as if it had been made in one piece.

Gilhaelith wandered over to the window and cried, 'Oh, it's beautiful; just beautiful.'

Tiaan put the sapphire down on the box and ran across.

'It's the Well,' said Gilhaelith. 'It's coming right at us, like a geomancer's dream.'

'You don't have the kind of dreams I do,' Tiaan muttered. 'Vithis said that all Santhenar would rue the day. Do you think he's sent it at us?'

'Not after he's dead.'

'It's a bit of a coincidence that it's coming straight for us, then.'

'The node might be attracting it.'

'What will the node do to it?'

'Who knows? Make it stronger, probably.'

'And if the Well meets the gate?'

He looked at her, opened his mouth, closed it again.

'Gilhaelith?'

'I wouldn't like to imagine the consequences.'

'Keep an eye on it.' Tiaan didn't know why she'd said that. Nothing could influence the path of the Well now. If it came, it came. Was it possible Vithis had set it to consume everything on Santhenar?

She raced back to the box, to discover that it had opened like a black flower, the front face drawing seamlessly inside. How had that happened? All she'd done was lay the sapphire down on top.

She looked in, but it was so black that she couldn't see the sides. Tiaan rotated the box towards the light and her head spun, just like the time at Snizort when she'd looked into the tesseract and the incomprehensible fourth dimension had exploded all around her. Was this box another tesseract – a cube in four dimensions?

Taking the amplimet in hand, she tried to create a mental map of the inside. It should have been as simple as imagining the walls of a black cube, but it wasn't. The walls kept shifting when she concentrated on them.

'Just one at a time,' said Gilhaelith, putting a hand on her hand.

Did he have any idea what she was trying to do? Tiaan supposed that he must. She fixed the left wall in her mind and attempted to attach the others to it, which was easier, though the walls still seemed to move around.

'Now what?' she said, looking up to him for advice.

'Perhaps it's all in the mind,' he said absently. 'I'm going below.'

'Whose mind? Vithis's? Yours? *Mine*?'

He was gone. Tiaan imagined passing through the rear wall of the cube and found herself in another space exactly like the original one: a cube attached to a cube, though she could not visualise how it connected to the first. She fitted it to her mental map anyhow and went through the right-side wall to another cube, which led back to the first. She recognised it because one wall was open and she could see her face staring in. The thought made Tiaan so dizzy that she fell off her chair.

Had Vithis been lying when he gave Malien the key? She didn't think so, but how could she tell? He'd deceived and manipulated her from the beginning.

Maybe the gate *was* all in the mind, and the way would only become clear if she could imagine the unimaginable – the hypercube the way it really existed.

Tiaan recreated her mental image, passing through the black walls into cubes which only led to more cubes, and more that lay back to back with each other or with the first, the one that lay open in the upper room in Nithmak. She looked out but this time did not see the room at all. Tiaan saw only stars and constellations entirely foreign to her. She tried to go further but could not get through.

She backtracked and went at what she thought was the opening again, but this time looked out on nothing but green: a dense, verdant, dripping forest. She couldn't reach it either.

Tiaan retreated, knowing she was getting further away from

what she was looking for. She dismissed the images from her mind, whereupon the hypercube flashed into view of its own volition. It only lasted a second but that was enough. It was there! She had seen it, perfect and complete.

Tiaan tried not to dwell on it, for the four-dimensional image was impossible to think about logically and she might lose it. And yet, her visual mind had done it, and now she saw a box that she had never seen before. Its walls were thinner than the others and Tiaan could make out shapes and lights through them.

She went closer. One wall showed a double sun and a field of stars sprinkled across black silk. Another, a roiling miasma like the solidification, in jelly, of a multicoloured field. A third was a pattern of dots, extending regularly in all directions. A fourth she could not make out at all until she went up close, when she realised that it was a fanged, horned and whip-carrying monster the like of which must strike terror into even the fierce heart of a lyrinx. Was she looking into the void? The fifth was equally obscure, until it resolved into an eye staring back at her. Tiaan jumped and the eye disappeared. It was her own. The sixth wall led back to the box she had just come from.

She withdrew, knowing that a long time had passed. It had grown dark while she'd been working and the moon was shining in through the glass. The tesseract was empty. She'd been looking for a device like the port-all she'd assembled at Tirthrax, but there wasn't one. And yet, there had been that aura.

What if the box itself was the device? It hardly seemed possible; how could an empty box open a gate? But on the other hand, there could be anything in compartments which were there one time she looked and not the next.

Could the port-all be *all* in the mind, something she must also visualise? Perhaps that was the answer. It wasn't hard to recall her earlier port-all to view, for she'd often done so, trying to analyse why it had gone so wrong at Tirthrax. In her spare moments she'd tinkered with her mental image of the device, using her new-found geomantic knowledge to make it perfect.

She recovered the image of that port-all, mentally dusted it off and placed it in the tesseract. Nothing happened, of course, for there was nothing to power it.

Tiaan inserted her best image of the amplimet in the centre, just as she had placed the real amplimet into the port-all in Tirthrax that fateful day nearly two years ago. There was no resistance this time, which made her feel that she was on the right path. Or so far off that . . .

No, don't think negative thoughts. It seemed as though the port-all ought to be ready. She began to operate it as she had the original. A whip crack shook the building and cries rang out from below.

Tiaan ran to the glass. Lyrinx were running everywhere, though she could not tell from what, or to what. Not the gate, at least, for Tiaan had not set any destination.

Nor could she. She had no idea where Tallallame might be, or how to look for it. That was Malien's job but Malien had gone in the thapter many hours ago, and might not come back. So what was going on down below?

She hurried down the stairs. It took precious minutes and left her knees weak. In the open area at the bottom she walked into an opaque sphere filling most of the space between the bottom step and the wrecked doors. Was it the port-all? She edged around the side of the sphere and looked out. There were lyrinx everywhere and not all of them had wings. The fleetest of the runners had made it in under two days.

'Ryll?' she called hopefully. He might not have survived. And if he had survived, he could still be leagues away.

Her call was taken up in deeper, raspier lyrinx tones. *Ryll, Ryll, Ryll* . . .

The crowd parted and he pushed through, his heavy jaw set, eyes staring. 'Is *this* the gate?' His hand motion was dismissive.

'Yes, but I don't know how to find Tallallame.'

'Then *why* did you call us here? The water rises towards the base of the peak. We're clinging to it like moths, Tiaan, and there's no room left!' His great chest rose and fell like a bellows, his skin flickered with barely suppressed panic colours. 'In half a day – no, sooner – we'll be lost. Rather would we have died of

757

thirst in the Dry Sea than be drowned in the Sea of Perion.'

'Malien knows where Tallallame is. Have you seen her?'

He pointed to the sky. 'She's guarding the tower, circling higher than the other thapters can fly.'

If Tiaan didn't make the gate soon, the rapidly approaching Well would consume all the nodes as it came. It stood out against the night, its black-and-gold-threaded funnel reaching up to the sky.

'Call her down!' cried Tiaan.

Ryll rapped out a few words in his own tongue and a lyrinx leapt into the air. Tiaan watched it in the moonlight until it converged upon the thapter, which lurched and headed down as erratically as an autumn leaf falling. The other two thapters pursued it until a cloud of lyrinx swarmed up at them, firing crossbows. The thapters turned away towards the Hornrace and the lyrinx escorted Malien down.

'Malien!' yelled Tiaan as it settled on a hastily evacuated space. 'I've made the gate but I don't know the way to Tallallame.'

They diverted around the opaque globe. Malien gave it a curious glance. By the top, her lips had gone grey and she was cold and sweaty. 'That's not a climb I care to do again. Show me the port-all.'

'It – there *is* no physical port-all. It's a *mental* construct, Malien. I imagined the tesseract,' so easy to say, so difficult to do, 'put my image of the port-all inside it, inserted the image of the amplimet and it created the cloudy sphere you saw below.'

Malien looked uncomfortable. 'I don't know that I can work the way you do, Tiaan.' She sat on the floor, legs crossed, eyes closed, concentrating hard. 'Give me your hand.'

Tiaan sat beside her and extended her hand. Malien's was unexpectedly hard. Nothing happened for so long that Tiaan found her mind wandering, projecting the rise of the waters and the terror of the lyrinx as it climbed up their chests. It was the curse of her visual memory that she could still see the faces of the two lyrinx who had drowned, pursuing her from Kalissin ages ago. The naked fear in their eyes would never leave her.

She wrenched her mind back to the gate and saw clouds, though they seemed to have more colour than any clouds she'd seen on Santhenar. The image shifted, the view looked straight up and she saw a green sky. Another shift; she was looking at trees from above. Giant trees and blue hills.

A swooping drop that left her stomach hanging over one of the branches, and they were at ground level. Blue grass waved in the breeze and there were flowering shrubs covered in red berries. Someone was whispering to her in a foreign language.

'Tiaan!' Malien was shaking her. 'It's Tallallame. Fix the gate in place and open it.'

Tiaan found it hard to let go of the vision, but did as she was told, remembering how she'd done it before in Tirthrax. And then a great roar echoed up from below, as from a hundred thousand throats.

Malien helped Tiaan to her feet, for she had no strength in her bones. 'The gate is open. Let's go down.'

Tiaan began to follow her, then looked back at the box. 'But the port-all . . .'

'It will stay open until you close it, or until the field is no longer sufficient to power it.'

At the bottom Tiaan smelled a sweet fragrance, as strong as citrus blossom. A gentle, humid breeze was flowing through the gate from Tallallame. The lyrinx waited outside, craning their necks to stare into the gate. The ones behind were standing up on their clawed toes, for just the tiniest glimpse of their new world.

'I thought you would be gone already,' she said to Ryll.

'I would thank you first.' There were tears in his eyes, and Tiaan did not recall seeing that before. 'It is beautiful. The most beautiful of all worlds.' He bowed, and at his side, even more surprisingly, Liett did too.

Tiaan gave him her hand, then took Liett's. Ryll clasped Malien's hand, Nish's, and even Gilhaelith's.

'We will never forget this,' he said. 'Humanity has a side we never expected to see. Your deeds will be inscribed on the first page of our new Histories.'

'Tallallame may not be such a kind place as you think,' she said.

'I'm sure it isn't, but we're strong. We will survive, and thrive, and rediscover our humanity.'

'I don't think you ever lost it,' said Malien.

Ryll smiled at a private thought, then waved the first lyrinx towards the gate. 'Ryll!' said Tiaan.

He turned. 'Yes?'

'Your relics are still in the thapter.'

'Ah!' said Ryll. He held up his hand and the lyrinx who had been about to step through turned to one side. 'We thought . . . when you did not produce them, we thought you had left them behind. Truly, you ennoble us all.'

'Don't stop,' said Tiaan. 'Precious lives –'

'No lyrinx would choose to go through before our relics,' said Ryll.

He selected an honour guard, who carried the three crates to the gate. Ryll stood to one side, his skin colours flickering, and Liett on the other, her wings upraised. Liett spoke to the people straining towards the gate, in her own tongue. Ryll did likewise. Then the guard ran though and vanished.

After that the lyrinx went through five abreast, as fast as they could be formed into lines. No more than five could fit at once and the gate could not be widened. It had been designed for thousands, not half a million.

'This is going to take hours,' said Tiaan.

'If the field lasts,' replied Malien. 'Your people are attacking it furiously.'

They squeezed along the walls and outside, eyeing the funnel of the Well, which was larger than ever and lit up the salt, and one side of Nithmak, brighter than moonlight. 'Is it coming at us?' said Tiaan.

'It seems to be.'

'Could it be the gate attracting it?'

'I don't think so,' said Malien.

They watched it in silence. Nish came up beside them. 'How is the field going?'

'Slowly fading,' said Tiaan absently.

'And if it dies?'

'The gate will close and we'll be trapped here, as will all the lyrinx who haven't gone through,' said Malien.

'Can we do anything to maintain the field?' said Nish.

'No. The amplimet's being used for the gate,' said Malien.

'Would Flydd really do this to us?' said Nish.

'There may be no Flydd any more.'

'What?' he cried.

'He may have fallen all the way,' said Malien. 'Many mancers could operate the field controller.'

Tiaan had to put that possibility out of mind. She couldn't cope with anything else. She went to the edge of the pinnacle and perched upon a rock, looking down. The lyrinx were scrambling up the steps and the sides of the peak, hundreds every minute, but there was still a huge throng at the base. Half the visible bed of the sea was covered with water now. Irisis came and perched beside her, spyglass in hand.

'They've mostly reached the base,' Irisis said. 'Though there are still several bands of stragglers out there.'

Tiaan put out her hand. Irisis gave her the glass.

'There must be hundreds of them, running for their lives.'

'And they're all going to drown,' said Irisis.

'But . . . !'

'We can't do anything for them, Tiaan. Malien could barely keep the thapter in the air before she came down. She'd have no hope of ferrying them back now.'

Tiaan knew she couldn't do anything either, for that would require using her amplimet. It burned hot between her breasts, drawing power for the gate.

'If only we'd started sooner,' said Tiaan. 'Another hour would have made all the difference.'

Irisis shrugged. She wasn't one to waste any time on futile regrets. They watched the islands of salt shrink around the two blotches of lyrinx.

'Tiaan!' yelled Malien. 'Quickly.'

Tiaan knew what had happened before she got there. The

761

field was fading, and once it did, the gate would fade with it.

'How many are through, Ryll?'

'Nearly twenty thousand. The gate has been open for an hour.'

Tiaan calculated swiftly. 'So it would take a full day and a night for everyone to pass through.'

'Yes.'

'The way the field is failing, we have another hour at most,' said Malien. 'Better try to draw from another field.'

Tiaan attempted to, but the nearby ones were under the command of the field controller and the more distant ones were too far away for the amplimet to use.

The Nithmak field was still under her control. Perhaps it was difficult to seize it with the Well so close. Unfortunately the Nithmak node, though potent, was a small one and the gate was draining it rapidly.

She walked back and forth, muttering to herself, then came to a decision. 'Are there nodes on Tallallame?' Tiaan said to Malien.

'I have no idea.'

'I'm going through the gate.'

'Tiaan, no!'

'Why not?'

'Tallallame is a savage place and you don't know what the effect might be, on you *or* on the amplimet. Or the gate, if the device powering it passes through to the other side.'

'If I recall the Great Tales correctly, Rulke's original construct passed safely though to Aachan.'

'But it might not have. Look how the Mirror of Aachan was corrupted on its journey.'

'I've got to take the risk, otherwise most of the lyrinx are going to drown when Nithmak goes under water. Anyway, my mental image of the port-all isn't the same as a real, physical device. It probably won't be affected by the gate.'

'You don't know that.' Malien frowned. 'All right, but wait until the last moment. If you fail, you doom everyone here, for the gate won't remain open without you. Wait one hour and another twenty thousand will be saved.'

The hour seemed to fly by in minutes. The field continued to falter. 'Will you go through in the thapter?' asked Malien.

'I'll leave it for you, and enough in the field to get you away if the best happens. Or the worst.' Tiaan shrugged her little pack on her back, snuggled a water bottle by her side and touched the amplimet for comfort. 'Farewell,' she said.

'Wait,' called Irisis. 'I think I'll come with you.'

'And I,' said Nish.

'Are you sure?' said Tiaan.

'After this . . .' Nish did not need to go on. What could be left for them here, after such a betrayal? Especially if Flydd was no more.

'I'm coming too,' said Gilhaelith. 'No geomancer could be satisfied with just one world, if a second was on offer.'

The flow of lyrinx eased to allow them into the gate. Tiaan felt faint. Nish took her by one arm, Irisis the other.

'I'm all right now,' she said, but they held her anyway and it felt good to be among friends.

Tallallame was only a few steps away. Tiaan could see the grass, the trees; she could feel warm, humid air on her face, and smell spicy floral odours. The lyrinx made way for them. The passage seemed to take an eternity and, with each step, the link between her and the black box upstairs, with its port-all that was there and yet still here in her mind, grew ever more tenuous.

The cloudy exterior of the gate went milky, fading until they could see right through it.

'The gate's failing,' she said, panicky. 'This is going to break it. I'll never be able to make it from the other side. You'll all be trapped –'

'We knew that when we decided to come,' said Irisis, easing her sword in its sheath.

Gilhaelith had a crystal in his hand and it was glowing faintly. Tiaan couldn't decide if that was good or bad. She took another step, and another. Darkness exploded in her mind and then they were through and stepping *down*, unexpectedly, onto grass that was more blue than green and unusually springy to walk on.

Tiaan let out her breath. The gate was still open after all; power still passed through to the port-all. They were standing in a clearing in the middle of a forest, though it was richer and more luxuriant than the cold forests of her distant homeland. The air smelt sweet and spicy. 'What a beautiful place,' she said.

'The most beautiful world in the universe,' said Malien. 'So the Faellem used to say, before they lost it.'

The recently arrived lyrinx had adopted defensive positions. Some had gone up trees, others to the top of a mass of purple-brown boulders away to the left. A burly male stood by a stream and scooped water with one hand. He tasted it and smacked his lips.

'Any sign of a node?' asked Gilhaelith.

'I haven't looked yet.' Tiaan scanned her surroundings in the usual way, amplimet in hand. She could sense no field at all. 'Nothing!'

'There's no saying that fields on Tallallame would be the same as ours.' Gilhaelith had his crystal out again, holding it high. It was still glowing.

'Is that coming through the gate?' asked Irisis.

'I don't think so. Let's go over by that rock.'

They followed him around the other side. 'Its glow seems a little brighter,' Gilhaelith said, 'though it could be that it's gloomier under the trees.'

'Too gloomy,' said Tiaan. 'This place might be a paradise but it's a –' She screamed and hurled herself backwards, landing in the leaves.

Irisis's sword flashed and something went flying through the air. The leaves rustled. 'Back to the clearing, quickly.'

SEVENTY-SEVEN

'What was it?' said Nish, helping Tiaan up.

'It was like a snake with legs,' said Irisis, 'and it nearly had you. It was so quick. I just cut a bit off the tail.'

'You saved my life,' said Tiaan.

'Well, at least a nasty bite on the ankle.'

In the open space, Tiaan dusted herself off, felt at her throat and said, 'The amplimet's gone.'

Nish and Irisis ran back, swords drawn. 'Here it is,' said Nish, reaching to pick it up. 'The chain must have broken when you fell.'

As his fingertip touched the crystal there came a brilliant flash of light and he was thrown backwards into the bushes.

'Nish!' Irisis ran after him.

'It's all right,' he said. 'I haven't broken anything.' He got up, holding his sore ribs.

'Come on. There's bound to be more than one of those little beasts.'

Tiaan bent over the amplimet. 'It's glowing brightly now, as if there's a powerful node nearby, but I can't sense any field at all.' She touched it gingerly. It flashed again, but did not sting her. 'It feels different.'

'It may well be,' said Gilhaelith. 'Objects carried between the worlds are often changed.'

She held it out at arm's length. 'Corrupted?'

'Not necessarily. The Mirror of Aachan took on the taint of its owner, and Shuthdar was an evil man. Once corrupted, such an artefact is impossible to cleanse, and only the strongest can control it.'

'Well, at least the gate is still working.' Lyrinx were coming through faster than ever, now running full-tilt. They'd already worn a path out of the gate.

'What say we climb that hill?' said Gilhaelith. 'I'd like to see a little of this world, if I'm to spend a day on it.' He added under his breath, 'Or a lifetime.'

They headed up an incline along a trail made by soft-footed animals that wound up the hill. Near the top they emerged from the towering trees into a clearing that capped the hill, and its neighbour. The spongy grass was long and blue-green.

They followed the ridgeline up onto the next hill, which was higher, and the one after that, which was also bare and looked over the surrounding countryside. The forest of giant trees extended in every direction. On the other side of the ridge they looked into a steep valley with a winding river; the sun, orange rather than yellow, reflected off the water.

Tiaan gazed at the scene and sighed. 'It's just lovely. I wish I could live here.'

Gilhaelith was staring into the distance, shading his eyes with his hand. Winged creatures wheeled above the river, further along. 'The lyrinx haven't wasted –'

Irisis pulled him down. 'Those aren't lyrinx! Look at the length of the necks, and the reptilian head.'

'They're hunting.' Nish crouched down in the grass, squinting at the creatures.

'They'll be hunting us if we don't find some cover,' said Irisis. 'Let's go back.'

'They've turned our way.' Nish started to run along the edge of the hill.

'Come back,' she yelled. 'Down into the forest.'

'I don't suppose anyone has a crossbow?' said Tiaan.

'Of course not!' Irisis snapped, angry with herself for not bringing a useful weapon. 'Get down. Crawl through the grass.'

They had not gone far before the winged creatures soared overhead, blotting out the sun with their membranous wings and emitting raucous cries. 'If we stand together,' said Gilhaelith, 'and put our swords up, we might have a chance.'

'I doubt it,' said Tiaan. 'There are half a dozen of them and they're as big as lyrinx.'

They did so anyway. The flying creatures came to ground not far away, staring at them and showing no fear. 'They're not afraid of humans,' said Gilhaelith, 'and that's a bad sign.'

'Masterly understatement,' said Irisis. 'Get ready.'

'For what?' said Nish, looking for a stick, a stone or anything he could throw to keep them away.

The creatures began to move inwards, until a hideous growl erupted from below, though to Tiaan's ears it was the sound of massed throats pretending to be savage beasts. A band of lyrinx came storming out of the shrubbery, wings spread, mouths agape. The racket was incredible.

The flying creatures whirled; then, as one, they kicked themselves into the air and flapped away.

'Thank you,' said Tiaan as the lyrinx made a protective circle around them.

'We will escort you back to the gate,' said the leader, a stocky female with miniature crests running down the front of her breastplates. 'This is no world for helpless humans.'

They reached it an hour later, suitably chastened. The lyrinx were coming through as fast as before. The amplimet was still glowing but Tiaan had no idea why. 'It seems to have picked up some kind of a charge,' she said.

'That's not unknown in the Histories of mancery,' said Gilhaelith. 'Some of the very first magical devices, as the Art was then called, were crystals or glasses that had become naturally charged in a field. The first mancers were just people who could make use of that power.'

'Will the charge remain if we go back through the gate?' Tiaan asked.

'It may last for a while, unless the return passage changes the amplimet again.'

'How long?'

'An hour, a day, a month? How would I know? This is surely the first time an amplimet has been taken through a portal. But sooner or later the charge will fail and then, most likely, the amplimet will be useless.'

'You mean . . .?'

'It may no longer draw power at all.'

'I don't care,' Tiaan said, 'as long as it lasts until we complete our work here.'

Ryll was still standing by the gate when they reappeared, and the gate continued to work. Nish and Irisis went out, but Tiaan remained beside Ryll. 'How many are there to go?' she asked.

'Less than forty thousand,' said Ryll. 'There were more but the . . . the waters took them. Three hundred and seven thousand have passed through, plus more than a hundred thousand children, carried.'

'So many? The gate has only been open a few hours.'

'It was before dawn when you left. Now it's morning of the next day, our last on Santhenar. If the gate lasts, in two hours we'll all be through.'

'Time passes differently in the Three Worlds,' said Gilhaelith.

They went out into the light. An easterly sun was slanting low across what had been the Dry Sea. There was no salt to be seen, just water all the way to the horizon.

'The Sea of Perion rises swiftly.' Malien detached herself from the crowd that covered every available surface on top of the pinnacle. 'Already it's over fifty spans deep.'

'And still forty thousand lyrinx to go,' said Tiaan. 'They must be clinging to every part of the peak!'

'Like bees to a honeycomb.'

'What happened to the Well?'

Malien gestured over her shoulder. It was just behind them, looming above the tower like the black eye of a cyclone. They moved around to that side of the peak. The funnel of the Well went down through the water, all the way to the bottom of the sea, and probably below that.

Apart from a few wheeling lyrinx the sky was empty, not a thapter or air-dreadnought to be seen. 'Has Orgestre given up?'

'I doubt it. Flying lyrinx have kept the thapters away.'

The Well was less than a league away now, and tracking directly towards them. Irisis studied it with her spyglass.

'I can see a clanker in there,' Irisis burst out. 'Carried up as if it were made of paper. And all sorts of other things. Trees. Bodies.' She shivered. 'What power the Well must have.'

'I wonder if it could be a kind of anti-node?' said Tiaan. 'Instead of giving out power, it grows by sucking the power from other nodes, leaving a trail of dead ones behind.'

'I don't know,' said Malien. 'I've never encountered an unshackled Well before.'

'How are we doing?' said Irisis.

'We need another hour or so.'

'The Well will be here in minutes,' said Tiaan. 'Do you think there's anything we can do to turn it aside?'

'It has the power of a hundred nodes,' said Gilhaelith. 'It's irresistible.'

'But if it's being directed . . .'

Gilhaelith cried out. 'I've got an idea. Nish, Irisis, could you give me a hand with the geomantic globe?'

They carried it in its box to the edge of the pinnacle, facing the Well. Gilhaelith unpacked it, set it up on its stand and slid the brass pointers around on their circular tracks, making sure that they moved freely.

'I've been tinkering with my globe since the escape,' he said to Tiaan. 'Gyrull concealed some vital details from me, but I've added them from your maps and I believe the globe is perfect now. Let's see what we can see.'

He began scrying with it, clamping small chips of crystal in the pointers and setting the globe spinning slowly beneath them. Tiny reddish pinpricks appeared under the glass surface, but that wasn't what Gilhaelith was looking for. He tried another five or six crystals, which he took from a small padded box, then borrowed Tiaan's amplimet and Irisis's pliance. They did not work either.

'It's no use,' said Gilhaelith. 'If someone *is* directing the Well, they're too cleverly hidden for me. We can't do anything to turn it away.'

'We'd better warn the lyrinx,' said Tiaan. 'And then, I suppose we'd better go. If we can . . .' It didn't seem right to fly away in the thapter and leave the rest of the lyrinx to their fate.

'And take the black box too,' Malien said suddenly.

'Why?'

'It would . . . not be good for it to be sucked into the Well.'

'But if we take it, won't that close the gate immediately?'

'It will remain open until you close it, Tiaan, because you're holding it in your mind.'

'Can I leave the gate open after we go?'

'No!' said Malien sharply. 'As soon as we're in the air you must close it, or else the Well might pass through the gate.'

'To Tallallame?'

'It might go anywhere in the void. It might annihilate itself, the gate and half of Santhenar. Anything might happen. The void might be disrupted . . . It is . . . the Well must *not* pass through the gate. Though it came from Aachan in the beginning, this Well is now a creature of Santhenar, and Santhenar must deal with it.'

Malien went looking for Ryll and Liett. Tiaan headed up to retrieve the black box. It proved surprisingly light, as if it was, after all, no more than an empty box. When she reached the bottom, panting and weak in the knees, Malien was talking to Ryll. Liett was pacing back and forth, casting anxious glances at the Well and stormy ones at Ryll, which he was steadfastly ignoring.

'As soon as the Well touches the side of Nithmak,' Malien was saying, 'we must close the gate. We can't risk the Well passing through.'

'Indeed not,' said Ryll. 'And then you must get in your thapter and fly to safety, knowing that you could have done no more.'

Liett beckoned furiously to him. Ryll gave an almost imperceptible shake of the head, whereupon she drove her fist into the nearest wall and stormed away, shaking her wings.

'I think Liett wants to talk to you,' Tiaan said uncomfortably. 'Is something wrong?'

'Just a disagreement about when I'm to go,' said Ryll. 'She wants me to leave now, but I can't abandon my people to die.'

'Are there many left?'

'More than twenty thousand of us,' said Ryll. 'Too many. But we knew the risk.'

Of us, Ryll had said. But if he was staying to the last, he wouldn't get through at all. He would drown here with the stragglers. Liett came storming back and took him by the arm, trying to pull him towards the gate. Ryll set his feet and did not move.

'Will you not go, Ryll?' said Tiaan.

'Not while any of my people still cling to the side of this peak.'

'You'll drown.'

A shudder passed over him and his skin colours writhed in iridescent shades of purple and grey. 'So will they, and without ever a sight of Tallallame. At least I've had that. Go, Liett.'

'Not without you.' She folded her arms across her chest.

'I order you to go through the gate,' he thundered. 'As patriarch of all the lyrinx.'

'I am the daughter of a matriarch,' Liett flashed. 'I take orders from *no* base-born unmated, wingless male.'

Ryll was so furious that his skin flashed all the colours of the spectrum, but Liett simply set her jaw and cracked her wings in his face, as she'd done so often.

The funnel of the Well now loomed so huge that it covered a quarter of the sky, and so black that the world seemed to have slipped into twilight. Tiaan ran to the edge of the pinnacle. The water was more than a third of the way up the sides of the peak, and huge, driven waves lashed up another twenty or thirty spans, washing the scrambling lyrinx away like ants off an anthill.

As the base of the funnel approached, even larger waves formed and moved ponderously out in all directions. The flow of lyrinx up the sides and into the gate slowed to a trickle. The flat area at the top of Nithmak was almost empty now.

The Well swept towards them, depressing the surface of the sea like water going down a prodigious plughole, then drew back. As it did the sea was pulled up with it, and the biggest wave Tiaan had ever seen surged out from the base of the Well; a monster at least fifty spans high. It was nowhere near as high as the pinnacle but the surge would drive the water up and up.

'It's going to overtop the pinnacle!' Tiaan yelled. 'To the thapter, everyone.'

Malien caught her wrist. 'It's too late. If it breaks over the peak, we're done.'

They watched the wave swell and grow, driving inexorably towards them, its foaming top rising higher and higher until it looked as though it would wash everything away, including the tower. Ryll ran out to the edge, shouting to the climbers to hurry.

He was too late. The wave struck well below the crest but burst in an explosion of foaming brown water that climbed the sides until it lapped the top of Nithmak and swirled across, knee-deep. It rose no further but, as it passed, Tiaan saw lyrinx thrashing in terror on the foam. One by one, they sank. When she looked over, the sides of the pinnacle had been swept clean.

Ryll stood on the brink, staring down into the churning water. His skin had turned completely grey. The Well surged again and another wave began to form, as big as the last, if not bigger.

'It's time,' said Malien. 'If there's enough left in the field to lift us.'

As they ran to the thapter, the last surviving lyrinx were passing through the gate. All but one. Ryll was still gazing at the water.

'Ryll, you must come!' screamed Liett. 'You *are* the last.'

'The last.' He teetered on the brink and it looked as though he was going to jump, to join all those thousands who had suffered the most terrible death of all.

Tiaan walked backwards to the thapter, ignoring Nish and Irisis, who were screaming at her. She felt for the ladder and began to climb.

Liett ran out to Ryll. 'Come on!' she screamed in his face.

The thapter came to life, whining gently. The wave was swelling, growing enormously, and it would sweep the top of Nithmak clean. Tiaan found herself caught around the waist and lifted bodily.

It was Irisis and she carried Tiaan all the way. Tiaan hung onto the hatch as the thapter lifted, shuddering violently.

'Who am I to go,' said Ryll to Liett, 'when so many more worthy have lost their lives to the waters? You should have been matriarch, Liett. I resign. I am not legitimate. I am unmated male.'

As he raised one foot to step over the side, Liett swung her fist in a roundhouse blow to the chin that knocked Ryll unconscious onto his back.

'On Tallallame I *will* be matriarch,' she said imperiously. 'And I choose you, weak and worthless though you are. You are now Hy-Ryll, *mated* male.'

Irisis chuckled. Tiaan had to resist the urge to clap.

Seizing Ryll under the arms, Liett dragged him across the rocks and into the gate. 'Farewell,' she said, and passed beyond.

The Well swelled again. Malien pushed the controller and the thapter moved sluggishly off the far side of the peak. 'Close the gate, Tiaan.'

Tiaan brought up her mental image of the tesseract, withdrew the port-all, took out the image of the amplimet and closed the box. The gate vanished as the Well roared up and over the peak and the sea followed it. When they looked back there was nothing but the boiling sea and the funnel hanging there, and the red spheres bobbing in the foam. The tower had gone.

'Where are we going?' said Malien.

'Where *can* we go?' said Nish, wanting to run to the ends of the earth.

'To Ashmode,' said Gilhaelith. 'That's where everyone else has gone. It's as good a place as any to watch the Sea of Perion fill again.'

'Well,' said Irisis, 'I'm not running away. I'm proud of what we've done. Let's go and face up to it.'

Seventy-eight

Nish looked over the side, dreading the coming confrontation. He couldn't be as sanguine as Irisis, nor as philosophical. Even if Flydd accepted that theirs had been the best solution, his opponents would not forgive it. And Flydd's opponents now greatly outnumbered his friends, assuming he'd survived at all. Gilhaelith, Irisis, Tiaan and he, Nish, could well be executed for treason, though Malien would undoubtedly be spared.

Ashmode, from above, was a beautiful, spacious town built entirely of the local blue-white marble. Its streets were broad and lined with palms or enormous twisting fig trees whose canopies shaded the width of the street. Its fields, orchards and vineyards, grown on the fertile, moist slopes below the cliffs, made a ribbon of green from the air, marking the boundary between the brown drylands of Carendor and the glittering whiteness of the Dry Sea. Soon they would disappear under the rising sea.

It was a lovely sunny day as they passed across the town square looking for a place to set down. It was warm, with just the gentlest breeze. A perfect autumn day to be tried for treason.

'There seem to be an awful lot of people down there,' said Tiaan.

'The war's over, remember?' said Irisis. 'The celebrations will go on until the drink runs out.'

'I hope it hasn't run out yet,' said Nish.

'They won't be giving it to condemned prisoners,' said Irisis. 'Sorry,' she muttered as Nish blanched. 'At times like this, I find it helps to joke.'

'I don't.'

The crowd moved back to form a staring circle as the thapter came in.

'There's Flydd,' said Tiaan. 'He's alive, at least. And Troist. And they don't look happy,' she added in a low voice.

Scrutator Flydd was standing at the front, with Troist. Nish didn't know whether to be relieved or not. The knot in his stomach tightened. Yggur and a pale-faced Klarm stood some distance away. Both had their arms folded against their chests.

Tiaan climbed down onto the paving stones. The others followed, standing on either side of her. There was an awkward silence.

'You bloody fools!' the scrutator said furiously. 'What gives you the right to overturn decisions voted on by the mighty after days of considered debate? You ought to be fried in your own tallow, and had it been up to General Orgestre you would have been. It's lucky he's not here or I wouldn't be able to restrain him.'

'Where is Orgestre?' said Nish in a small voice.

Flydd's eyes fixed on him and Nish squirmed. 'He had an apoplexy when he heard that you'd freed the lyrinx. It burst the vessels in his brain. He'll never walk or talk again.'

'A medal-winning performance at last,' said Irisis, almost inaudibly.

Nish wanted to laugh but he couldn't.

'Troist has taken Orgestre's position, for the moment,' Flydd went on. 'Troist?'

Nish met Troist's eyes, remembering that the general was, nominally at least, still his commanding officer.

'I'm bitterly disappointed in you, Nish,' said Troist. 'I thought I knew you. Do you realise that I could have you whipped and executed for treason?'

'Yes, surr,' said Nish.

'You'll have to stand in line to flog the little sod,' said Flydd. 'He was my man before he was yours. What the blazes were you thinking, Nish?'

'We did what we thought was right,' said Tiaan softly.

Flydd's head whipped around. 'Oh, did you? Since when are you running the world?'

'Since the scrutators failed at it,' said Gilhaelith over her shoulder.

'I thought you were dying?' Flydd said sourly.

'I'm taking it slowly, just to annoy you.'

'You've succeeded. I –'

'If you're going to execute them,' Klarm interjected, 'can you bloody well get on with it. The war's over and I need a drink.'

'I'm with you, Klarm,' said Yggur. 'We've got what we wanted. Let's go and burst a barrel or two.'

Klarm could scarcely contain his astonishment. 'You're agreeing with *me*?'

'Don't let it go to your head. I'm not planning to make a habit of it.' Yggur grinned and extended his hand.

Klarm let out a great roar that made heads turn curiously on the other side of the square, and he jerked Yggur's hand up and down in both of his. 'It'll be a pleasure drinking with you, surr.'

Flydd couldn't maintain his furious face any longer. He chuckled. 'Damn the pair of you – you've cut my feet out from under me. Well, my friends, I can't condone the way you went about it, but it was the best solution in the end. We've got our world back, the lyrinx have their own, and our future Histories aren't stained by genocide. Let's celebrate.'

Nish fell in beside Flydd as they walked. 'What did you mean, surr, when you said that General Troist was commander "for the moment"?'

'You might have expected that the governors would be grateful for what we've done.'

'Of course they're grateful –'

'There's a whole world up for the taking, Nish, and they've already got both feet in the trough. Why do you think they came here so hastily?'

776

'But you saved humanity, surr!'

'We saved the world, Nish, but we couldn't hold it, and they didn't take kindly to Tiaan's . . . er, creative solution. They accused Yggur and me of being behind it. I've been forced to give up every office I hold. If I hadn't, my head would have been on the block.'

How could this be? Flydd had worked his whole life for humanity. 'I'm sorry, surr,' whispered Nish.

'Ah well, it's done,' said Flydd. 'I'm an old man. Too old for this, so not another word of regret, eh? Anyway, the future of the world, and who's going to be running it, is being decided right now on the other side of town. And it won't be any of us.'

Tiaan moved the thapter to a little park not far from the square and left it in the shade of an ancient and gnarled fig, so it would be cool inside when they returned.

Despite the attitude of the governors, the common folk knew who'd saved them, and everyone wanted to shake their hands. It took Tiaan more than an hour to get back to her friends in the square, where they too were surrounded by laughing, cheering and crying well-wishers. It almost made up for the past two years.

Troist gave his last order as a general, that everyone was to be fed from the army's stores, and the town brought out long-hoarded delicacies from its larders. Tables and trestles were set up, and when the meal was ready the entire town took their seats in the square. It was no feast, but the fare was better than most people had tasted in long years. The mayor fetched barrels from his cellar and ladled wine into jugs.

After the speeches were over, and congratulations and gifts had been accepted from the notables of Ashmode, the companions sat down together for the last time before they went their separate ways. They were twelve now: Yggur opposite Irisis, Flydd opposite Nish, Gilhaelith opposite Tiaan, Merryl opposite Troist, Malien opposite Flangers – who'd walked for a week to rejoin the army after Gilhaelith abandoned him in Tacnah – and Fyn-Mah facing Klarm. Flydd set Golias's globe on the table in front of them, covered with a cloth. Perhaps he was afraid of losing it as well.

The jugs of wine were distributed. Yggur and Klarm splashed it into the mugs and Yggur rose, raising his drink high. 'To peace,' he said.

They stood up and everyone in the square did the same. 'To peace!' they roared.

'To a future without the lyrinx,' said Yggur. Another roar.

'Or scrutators!'

The roar dwarfed the others, though Flydd only pretended to drink this time. In the end, he was only a man, and after giving his all for the world, the world had cut him down.

When the toasts were done, Flydd downed half his mug and gagged. 'Ah, that's like chewing on an anteater's tail. I knew I should have sat at the mayor's table, rather than down here with the rabble.' He shrugged, sank the rest and poured himself another. He looked along the table. 'You've been a great company, and I'll cherish our comradeship to the end of my days. But it seems to be drawing to a close. What are your plans, my friends? Irisis?'

Tiaan saw that Nish was gazing at Irisis with a hungry look in his eye, but Irisis was looking anywhere but at him.

'I never thought I'd survive the war – in fact I was sure I wouldn't. But now it's over, I'm going to be a jeweller, of course. It's what I've dreamed about since I was a little girl . . .' She looked up at the sky, around the table and down again.

'And . . .?' said Flydd, grinning broadly. The whole table was smiling, apart from Nish, who had an anguished look on his face.

He has no idea, Tiaan thought. Irisis was right; Nish really is the thickest man on Santhenar. Please put him out of his misery.

'I never dared to love openly, but now I can. Nish is going to be my man, of course.' Irisis pulled him to her and kissed him on the mouth in front of everyone, and Nish could not restrain his tears this time.

'What about you, surr?' Irisis said after a decent interval of congratulations, and more toasts with the truly awful wine.

'I'll write the Histories of the war. I want to make sure *my* version is recorded . . . you know how it is.' Flydd glanced at Fyn-Mah and smiled. 'And then, I think, an honourable retirement. Perhaps a cottage and a garden full of flowers.'

Nish had recovered sufficiently to choke into his wine cup. 'Retirement and flowers? *You?*'

Flydd scowled down his battered nose. 'And why not?' he snapped, before turning to Tiaan. 'What will you do now, Artisan?'

'I'm going home to Tiksi,' she said. 'To find my mother.'

'And then?'

'I don't know.' Tiaan looked slantwise across the table at Nish, who was staring into Irisis's eyes again. She looked away. 'I'll find work somewhere. I don't suppose the manufactory will need artisans any more, but someone will.'

'What then?' Flydd persisted.

She hesitated. 'I'd like to find a mate, and have children. I never had a proper family, but in spite of Marnie I –'

'Marnie?' said Merryl, staring at her. He half-rose from his seat. 'Marnie who?'

'Marnie Liise-Mar,' said Tiaan. She pushed back her chair, and her scalp felt as if it had been rubbed with a chunk of ice.

'Tiaan?' he whispered, as if he had never heard the name before. 'Your name is Liise-Mar?'

'Yes. Marnie is my mother.'

'Why did I not know?' Merryl cried. 'My daughter – my precious, precious daughter.'

As she stared at his familiar yet entirely new face, a single tear ran down her cheek. 'Father?'

He walked around the table towards her. She ran and threw herself into his arms, sobbing for sheer joy.

'All my life I've been searching for you, Merryl, *Father*. I've never forgiven Marnie for sending you off to the front-lines to die.'

'I forgave her many years ago. It was a man's duty to serve and I didn't go unwillingly. I often think of her . . .'

'But you can't go back to her after what she did to you?' she cried.

'I don't expect anything of her, after all this time,' he said.

779

'Marnie was young and foolish, and so was I, but I do want to see her again. She was so slim, so beautiful. Rather like you, Tiaan.'

'She's fat!' said Tiaan. 'Fat but still beautiful.'

'And I'm aged beyond my years and lack a hand. And my only skill is to speak a language that no one on Santhenar uses. Tell me about her.'

'I'm the oldest of fifteen children, all with different fathers. All my brothers and sisters are living, the last I heard. All clever and hardworking, too.'

'Marnie was a very clever woman,' he said. 'She just chose not to use it the way other people wanted her to.'

'Father,' said Tiaan, and the word sounded strange in her ears. 'What is your name? I tried to find you in the Tiksi blood-line register but I couldn't read the writing.'

'I'm Amante Merrelyn, though I've not used my name in twenty years.'

'Merrelyn,' said Xervish Flydd. 'I thought you looked familiar.'

'Amante,' she said, rolling the name around on her tongue. 'Amante.'

'It's too grand for the man I am now. Merryl fits me much better.'

'How come you didn't know my name?' said Tiaan.

'You hadn't been named when I was sent to the war. I thought about my daughter all the time, and it was hard, without a name.'

'I never liked using her name. For twenty years I've just been Tiaan.'

'I knew your parents, Merryl,' said Flydd.

'They both had a gift for languages,' said Merryl. 'More than a gift – a talent bolstered by the Art. They travelled the world with kings and governors, and even scrutators.'

'They were among the greatest translators of the age,' said Flydd. 'A tragedy that they were lost so young.'

'It was, but at least they passed their talent to me.'

'Perhaps that's why you're the only person ever to master the lyrinx tongue.'

'It's not much use to me now,' said Merryl.

'You never know,' said Flydd. 'By the time you've written down all you know about the lyrinx and the war, for the Histories, you'll be an old man . . .' He looked up at the sky. 'What's that? Irisis, you've got the best eyes here.'

She stood up, shading her eyes with her left hand. 'It looks like an air-dreadnought, though with three airbags instead of five. A big flat one, and two smaller ones underneath.'

A cloud passed in front of the sun and the breeze bit into Tiaan's bare arms, reminding her that winter, even this far north, was not far away.

'I wonder who it could be?' said Nish.

'More governors coming to carve up the world, now we've won it for them,' said Flydd, again with that hint of bitterness. 'The news went out by farspeaker as soon as the lyrinx began to go through the gate. They'll be going to the conclave on the other side of town.' He filled his mug again and they took up their cutlery.

But Flydd was wrong. The air-dreadnought came up slowly and began to circle the square. Tiaan laid down her fork. The craft was huge, nearly twice the size of the air-dreadnoughts that had attacked Fiz Gorgo. Its airbags came to triple points at the front and were painted vermilion with threatening jags of black. The suspended vessel had triple rotors at its broad, rectangular stern, each more than two spans across.

'What a racket,' said Nish, putting his hands over his ears as it turned ponderously into the wind. The rotors made a squealing clatter that grated on the nerves.

'There's no badge or insignia,' said Flydd, putting down his mug. 'But it came from the north-east.'

Soldiers lined the sides, dressed in the same red with black jags. It was not a uniform that anyone recognised. Red helms covered their heads, the nosepieces extending down to their upper lips.

The air-dreadnought settled in an empty space on the far side of the square, its triple keels crunching on the gravel. The rotors squealed into silence. A board was lowered, like the gangplank of a ship. Everyone was staring now.

A file of soldiers marched down and stood to one side. Each was armed with a crossbow of extravagant design, and a long sword. Another file took their position on the other side.

Tiaan rose to her feet, trying to see. The plank was empty. No, someone now appeared at the top. A man, though not a tall one. He too was masked and clad in red, with a red cape. A golden chain was suspended from the back of his neck, the ends passing over his shoulders. On either end, at breast height, dangled a bag of black silk or velvet.

The man paused at the base of the plank, nodded to the guards and turned across the square. They fell in behind him.

Xervish Flydd dropped his knife. Irisis had gone white. Nish's hair was standing on end. He looked as if he had just seen the dead rise. He ran out into the open.

'Father?'

The man turned towards him and the sun flashed off the platinum mask that covered two-thirds of his face. He had only one arm.

'I thought you were dead, Father,' Nish said. 'And eaten.'

'I dare say you hoped I was,' said Jal-Nish Hlar.

Xervish Flydd lurched around the left-hand end of the table, trying to look self-possessed but not quite pulling it off. 'Quite a plan, Jal-Nish. Even I was fooled.'

Jal-Nish stopped twenty paces away. 'Not the most difficult of tasks, Xervish.'

'Only my friends call me Xervish.'

'You've told me that before.'

'And I dare say those are the tears of the node that exploded at Snizort. The lyrinx didn't have them at all.'

Jal-Nish touched the black bags, which were giving off a humming sound, and it rose in pitch. 'Do you hear the song of the tears? I don't bother with the paltry fields – I carry the power of a node with me wherever I go.'

'It was you who brought down Vithis's watch-tower,' said Nish.

'I needed to test the power of the tears,' said his father, as if no other explanation was necessary. But then he added, the visible part of his jaw tightening, 'The Aachim had no right to come here.'

'And you who flooded the Dry Sea.'

'To drown the enemy. Would that I had made up for your negligence sooner, Flydd. You trapped the enemy and failed to crush them.'

'And you directed the Well at us,' said Nish.

Jal-Nish waved a careless hand, as if none of these staggering achievements were of significance to a man who had mastered the tears.

'How did you get away?' said Nish. 'I saw your boot at Gumby Marth, with just a gnawed shinbone sticking out of it.'

'One shin looks much like another after the lyrinx have been at it,' Jal-Nish said. 'You always were slapdash, Cryl-Nish. I didn't think you'd look too closely.'

'And then you ran like a cur from the battlefield,' said Nish, 'leaving your brave men to their doom.'

Jal-Nish's head jerked up, but he recovered almost at once. 'When the battle is lost, a prudent man withdraws. And it was lost because of you.'

'Me?' cried Nish, balling up his fists.

'I knew the lyrinx were stone-formed into the pinnacles,' said Jal-Nish. 'I was waiting for them, but your clumsy flight woke them before I was ready.'

'You – you dare blame *me* –' Nish was so incoherent with rage that he couldn't get the words out.

'What a practised liar you are, Jal-Nish,' said Flydd. 'Had I realised it when you were a lowly perquisitor, I would have made sure you rose no higher.'

Jal-Nish didn't bother to argue, though his eye shone like a viper's.

'Still, I'm glad you've come,' Flydd went on. 'The tears will come in handy in the reconstruction.'

'Oh, indeed. I've already begun to make plans for that.'

Another chill prickled the top of Tiaan's head.

'You won't be involved in it, Jal-Nish,' said Flydd. 'The old Council is no more.'

'I thoroughly approve. It outlived its purpose long ago.'

'And the governors are even now meeting to carve the world up between them.'

'The world doesn't need governors either.'

'If you would hand over the tears, Jal-Nish,' said Flydd.

Jal-Nish pulled one black bag away and a gasp rippled around the square. On the end of the chain was a roiling, silvery black ball, like boiling quicksilver. He plunged his hand into it.

Flydd choked, clutched at his throat and fell down. His heels drummed on the ground for a minute, then Jal-Nish withdrew his hand. It came out slowly, as if the tears were reluctant to let go their hold, and wisps of silvery vapour clung to it. His skin was white and flaky, the nails as vermilion as his cape.

Jal-Nish smiled. 'It would be so easy, *Xervish*, but I don't plan to make it easy for any of you. You betrayed me, though I can forgive that – I'm a most forgiving man. But you also betrayed our world and that I can *never* forgive.'

'We saved it,' said Yggur, pushing back his chair and coming forward, 'and that's something the scrutators never looked like doing. It was the enemy, after all, who kept them in power.'

'Yggur,' said Jal-Nish, turning in his direction. 'A failure from the past presumes to lecture the future.'

'You might find me a more difficult failure to deal with,' said Yggur with a glance at Flydd, who still lay on the gravel.

'I doubt that.' Jal-Nish plunged his hand into the ball again and within a minute Yggur was stretched on the ground beside Flydd.

Jal-Nish looked around, his eye met Tiaan's, and she felt a sick numbness creep over her. 'Artisan Tiaan – I'll deal with you later. I've a special torment reserved for you.' His eyes flicked to Irisis and his stare became so cold that ice formed in Tiaan's belly. 'And as for you, Irisis Stirm,' he hissed, 'you're the one I came all this way for. In my two years of agony, yours is the one face that has kept me going. Guards – secure them.'

Tiaan could hardly stand up. It was the end of the world. Her stomach felt as if it was going to drop out of her belly. She looked around for help but everyone seemed as stunned as she was, and

Jal-Nish's troops were already moving in. No one had brought weapons to the luncheon anyway.

She could see everyone but Klarm, who'd been at the end of the table. But even if he'd run for the army, they wouldn't get here in time. The camp was half a league out of town.

Yggur or Flydd, she could not tell which, began to moan, and then a curious thing happened. A fracas broke out across the square and the moment Jal-Nish turned that way the crowd, which had been hanging back, flowed around the table like a multicoloured tide.

A hand caught her by the shoulder – Nish. 'This way, Tiaan.'

She eased further into the crowd with him, trying not to be noticed. Gilhaelith was just ahead, bent low. Merryl and Irisis were by him, Malien too.

'Malien thinks you might be able to do something in the thapter, Tiaan,' said Nish. 'You've still got the amplimet, haven't you?'

'Yes,' she said, putting her hand to her chest. 'But Flydd . . .'

'Jal-Nish is too strong,' said Malien. 'There's nothing we can do here.'

She began to slide through the crowd and they followed in her wake. They hadn't gone far when Jal-Nish let out a cry of fury, which was followed by a low-pitched humming, like the song of the tears only more intense.

The sound beamed into the crowd like a sonic finger and everyone in its path fell down, moaning and holding their hands over their ears. Another hum; collapsing townsfolk cut a second long embayment in the crowd, leaving Nish exposed at the very end. He was still on his feet but didn't seem able to move.

'Run!' he mouthed as Jal-Nish's soldiers pounded towards him.

Irisis, ten paces away, turned to run back but Gilhaelith jerked her away.

'He's caught and you can't do anything for him. You can't fight the tears.'

Irisis was in agony, her eyes staring from a stark white face, but she allowed Gilhaelith to take her arm. Tiaan looked back through a gap in the crowd. The soldiers held Nish and as soon as they hauled him out of the way Jal-Nish would be free to use his sound beam again.

'Where's the thapter, Tiaan?' said Gilhaelith in a low voice.

'Down there in the little park.'

'Come on.' He ran and Malien did too.

Irisis was just standing there, staring at Nish, who was being dragged off. Another sonic blast roared through the crowd, dying out not far to Tiaan's right.

Irisis took a deep breath and turned Tiaan's way, her eyes bright with anguish. 'Farewell, Tiaan.' She held out her arms.

'You're not coming?'

'I can't leave him!'

'But Jal-Nish will crucify you!'

'I'll find a way round him,' Irisis said lightly. 'You know what I'm like with men.'

Not this one! Black icicles formed in Tiaan's chest. 'I'll never see you again. I know it.'

'Of course you will. We'll be drinking together in Tiksi before the new year.' Irisis hugged Tiaan, then quickly stepped back. 'Farewell, Tiaan. It . . . knowing you has been the great privilege of my life.' She wiped her eye, then pretended that it was just a speck of dust. 'Go quickly, and do what you can for us.'

Tiaan went, Merryl at her side, slipping through the crowd, which opened before her and closed up tightly behind. She could not look back.

Before they reached the street corner and turned towards the little park, an officer shouted, 'There they are!'

She darted a glance over her shoulder. Red-coated soldiers were forcing their way after them. Merryl took her wrist and ran. Malien and Gilhaelith were almost out of sight.

Tiaan was not used to running. She'd spent most of her time in the thapter, these past two years. There was a burning pain in her side, and the soldiers were less than a hundred paces behind. One had gone to his knees, pointing his crossbow. Merryl jerked Tiaan around the corner as he fired.

In the park, Gilhaelith was climbing into the thapter. Malien must have been inside, for it began to move. Tiaan was fading badly now. She could hardly run and her backbone was a mass of pain where it had been broken long ago. The thapter raced towards them as a soldier turned the corner, levelling his crossbow.

As he fired, Malien whipped the thapter between them and the soldier, so that the bolt slammed into the side. They scrambled in and the machine was up and away, climbing fast.

Then not so fast. Then, not fast at all.

'What is it?' whispered Tiaan.

'I don't know,' said Malien. 'It's as if the air has turned to porridge and the thapter can scarcely force its way through it. Or . . .'

'Or as if he's holding us back with the tears. I'm doing everything I can but it's not working. He's too strong.'

Tiaan closed her eyes. Clutching the amplimet, she tried to sense the ebb and flow of the field, to see if there was anything linking them to Jal-Nish, but she sensed nothing.

'What if I put the amplimet in its socket,' Tiaan said suddenly, 'together with your crystal? And we try to fly the thapter together?'

'It's a big gamble,' said Malien. 'It could make things worse.'

'It's only a gamble when you've got something to lose.'

As she was inserting the amplimet, the thapter lurched and stopped in mid-air, then began to creep backwards as if Jal-Nish were reeling them in. Tiaan put her hand on the controller and Malien her longer one over it, and both tried to draw power simultaneously.

The mechanism screamed as though trying to thrash itself to pieces. The thapter lurched backwards.

'Stop!' gasped Malien. 'We're pulling in opposite directions. Take your hand off. Let me control the thapter, Tiaan. Just try to deliver the extra force I need.'

Tiaan took her hand off and the strain eased, but the thapter gave another backwards jerk, and another, and the further it went the tighter the grip of the tears became.

'Follow the way I use power,' Malien added, 'rather than trying to do it your own way. Ready?'

'Yes. I think so.' Tiaan drew power as gently as she could. A grinding sound issued from downstairs.

'Gently,' said Malien. 'Close your eyes and just sense the flow, and go with it rather than trying to drive everything before you.'

This time, after some effort, Tiaan was able to follow the way Malien worked, though it was already giving her a headache.

'More,' said Malien. 'But just a *little* more.'

Tiaan gave her more. The thapter stopped its fitful backwards jerking, floated at the point of balance for a moment, then slowly began to climb.

'A trifle more,' said Malien. 'He'll double the effort when he realises what we're doing.'

The pull on them increased. Tiaan drew more power. The pull increased again. 'This isn't going to work,' she said. 'We're giving him time to match us.'

'I can't do any more. I'm at my limit.'

'Just keep doing what you're doing. Leave the rest to me.'

Malien gave her a doubtful glance.

'Trust me,' said Tiaan. 'We've got nothing to lose.'

She tuned her mind to the stored power in the crystal, which had been there since their trip through the gate to Tallallame, and took as much as her mind could bear.

The mechanism screamed, she felt a tearing sensation like glued paper being ripped apart and the thapter shot up into the sky, faster than it had ever gone. She kept the power flowing until, with a wrench that she felt inside her skull, the pull of the tears ceased completely.

Gilhaelith cried out and crushed his knotted fists to his temples. Tiaan had forgotten he was there.

'What's the matter?' said Malien.

'The recurrence of an old pain I can do nothing about,' said Gilhaelith. 'I'll have to lie down. Could you give me a hand, Merryl?'

Merryl helped him down the ladder.

'You had a plan?' said Tiaan, removing the amplimet so Malien could take over again. She could use it, but preferred not to unless she had no choice.

'I wondered if it might be possible to draw so much power from the node at Ashmode that it failed. It would send out a sensory reverberation that might –'

'I don't think there's any way to draw such power without killing ourselves in the process,' said Tiaan. 'I've already thought about it. And there's no saying it would work anyway.'

'Then there's nothing we can do for Flydd or Yggur, or any of them,' Malien said heavily.

SEVENTY-NINE

'It's as if we've escaped under false pretences,' said Tiaan wretchedly.

'I know,' said Malien, 'though we would have wanted *them* to escape, even if we could not. Let's not lose hope – we may yet find a way to do something.'

'Then we'd better think quickly. Jal-Nish didn't seem like a man who would gloat over-long.'

Malien turned to pass around Ashmode in a great circle, keeping to a safe distance. She described three more circles, but Tiaan couldn't think of any way of attacking Jal-Nish. Her mind was like a blank room with the roiling quicksilver tears in the centre, their power overwhelming all other Arts. Then, as Malien turned again, Tiaan saw, out over the sea, the Well looming in the distance, as black as a thunderhead. The Well and the amplimet had once been linked, she recalled.

'Malien,' Tiaan said, 'do you know anything about the link between the Well and the amplimet? They seemed to communicate in Tirthrax, remember?'

'I could hardly forget it,' said Malien.

'Why would it do that? If the amplimet draws from nodes, and the Well is a kind of anti-node, wouldn't it be a threat?'

'I dare say. Perhaps the amplimet wanted to take advantage of the chaos a freed Well would create.'

'What if we were to throw the amplimet into the Well? Could that destroy them both?'

'No. The amplimet would be destroyed by heat at the bottom of the Well first.'

'Oh!' said Tiaan. Something else occurred to her. 'The Well grows by sucking power out of nodes, and it's a kind of anti-node. So why don't node and anti-node come together and annihilate one another?'

'That's a question I've often wondered about. I think the core of the Well must contain a barrier to stop them getting too close.'

'And there's no way to overcome it?'

'None,' said Malien, 'except a gate –'

Tiaan started. 'What is it?' said Malien.

'I've had an idea. Well, it was your idea really. A way we might be able to save everyone.'

'I think I know what it is,' said Malien with a faint smile. 'I'll set a course for the Well then, shall I?'

Malien's suggestion about setting off a sensory vibration through the ethyr had given Tiaan the clue. Jal-Nish had previously used the tears to direct the Well. If they could eliminate it, the subsequent vibrations might be reflected back through the tears to him. She couldn't guess what the effect would be, but it might give their friends a chance.

She went halfway down the ladder to check on Gilhaelith, who was asleep on the floor. Merryl was watching over him from the bench. 'Is he all right?' she said. 'Father?'

'He's better than he was,' said Merryl. 'Do what you have to do, Tiaan.'

She went back up again. 'Malien?'

'Yes?'

'Can you set the thapter to fly by itself for a minute? I may need Gilhaelith's geomantic globe. It shows things that my field map doesn't.'

They carried its box up, put it in the rear right corner and closed the hatch. Malien took the controller again. Tiaan opened the box and lifted it off the geomantic globe. It was revolving on its mist cushion in the green-tinged nickel bowl. She stood for a moment, admiring its perfection. 'He's done a beautiful job. Gilhaelith has captured every nuance of the fields, every peculiarity of the nodes.'

'He's a brilliant man,' said Malien.

Tiaan tried to concentrate on what she had to do once they got inside the Well. She planned to create another gate with the black tesseract, though not between worlds. This would be just a simple portal between the node and the Well. She began to rehearse the process in her mind. There would be no time to think about it once they got there; she had to get it right first time.

'What will the Aachim do now?' she asked absently as she worked.

'Life will go on as before, in isolation, until eventually my people die out.'

'But surely not?' said Tiaan.

'They're cowards who fear to live in the real world. Back in Aachan, they even went into slavery rather than fighting for freedom, and lied about it afterwards.'

'What about the ones who came from Aachan?'

'They plan to make a home in Faranda,' said Malien, 'in the mountains and the lands east of them. Luxor spoke to Flydd about it when Flydd went to the Hornrace, not long before it collapsed. Eastern Faranda is empty now, but with the Sea of Perion restored the rains will come again. They'll make it blossom, in time.'

'I hope so,' said Tiaan, though all she could think about was Minis walking out onto the salt. His body would lie fifty spans below the water by now. Poor, sad, weak Minis. He'd redeemed himself in the only way he could. 'The Aachim do deserve to find peace at last, and a land to call their own.'

Before Tiaan had the procedure complete in her mind, the Well rose up before them. It had changed direction again and was drifting parallel to the southern shore of the Sea of Perion, a few leagues out, moving in the general direction of the Hornrace. 'It's bigger yet, and higher,' she went on. 'Do you think we can reach the top?'

'I don't know.' Malien frowned, then tilted the battered front of the thapter up until it began to climb.

Tiaan was painstakingly trying to think through all the consequences of what they were going to do. 'If we do destroy the Well, could that drive the amplimet to the third stage – full awakening?'

'No,' said Malien firmly.

'Why not?'

'Full awakening can only come once the amplimet is at the second stage. Flydd drove it back to the first stage of awakening after Nennifer, and we later made sure of it.'

Gilhaelith stirred in his painful slumber, muttered under his breath and went silent again. When Tiaan looked down he was fast asleep. 'That's all right then,' she said.

They continued climbing. Tiaan had a nagging feeling that she'd neglected to take account of an important detail. She went through her procedure again from the beginning, just to make sure. She found nothing wrong, but the worry remained.

'I'm ready,' she said.

'You'll be looking for the black box,' said Malien. 'It's in there.' She indicated a compartment with her foot.

Tiaan got it out and opened it with Vithis's sapphire key. Recalling the true shape of the tesseract, she placed her mental model of the port-all inside and set it to open a gate from the core of the Well to the centre of the node it was presently drawing from. She checked the node on Gilhaelith's globe to make sure she had it right. 'That's it.' She began to close the box.

'It has to be open,' said Malien as they tracked along the edge of the whirling funnel.

'Why?'

'The gate will take the easiest path. If the box is closed, the gate may open via another world or another dimension. You don't want that, for the same reason as we didn't want the Well to go through the gate. Get ready. The thapter won't go any higher, probably because of the damage some nitwit did, crashing it through the door of Nithmak.'

'I'm sorry.' Tiaan felt a fool.

'So you should be,' said Malien. 'But it is a problem. Since we can't fly high enough to go over the top, we'll have to pass through the funnel wall of the Well.'

'Is that possible?'

Malien considered, head to one side. 'That's a good question.'

Into the Well, Tiaan thought with a shiver. 'Can we get out again?'

'An even better question.'

Without warning, Malien turned the thapter sharply and plunged into the maelstrom. Tiaan clutched at the side rail. Everything went black and yellow, the thapter turned upside down, righted itself without any effort from Malien and they were through the inner wall. Tiaan was looking down at the bed of the sea as if the water did not exist, and even *through* the bed into darkness. In the abyssal depths something red gleamed – a moving node, perhaps, tracking through the solid earth below the Well.

'Ready?' said Malien. 'Be quick. I don't like being here at all.'

'Is this like going to the Well without really going?' Tiaan said perceptively.

'In a way, though if we get it wrong we *will* be going to the Well, and more spectacularly than anyone has ever gone before.'

Tiaan took a deep breath, lifted the black box in both hands, held it open and tossed it over the side.

'Now what do we do?' she said, watching it fall, the door flapping.

'We make sure we're not still here when that gets to the bottom and the core of the Well materialises in the centre of the node,' said Malien.

She hurled the controller over and flew at the wall. The thapter struck the whirling funnel at an angle and bounced off. She tried again. The same thing happened. Malien bit her lip.

The black box was already out of sight. Tiaan's fingernails dug into her palms. She wiped sweat from her eyes.

Malien turned towards the centre of the Well, which was leagues across, curved back and hurled the thapter forwards as fast as it would go. It stuck the funnel hard, shuddered so violently that Tiaan's bones felt like they were rattling, and passed into the maelstrom. Unfortunately it did not make it through to the outer side, but was whipped around in a circle, inside the roiling wall. Malien threw the thapter at the outer barrier, again and again, but could only strike it at a low angle, and the thapter kept bouncing off.

'I can't get through,' she gasped.

'Instead of crashing, what if you force?' said Tiaan.

Malien tried that, creeping to the outside edge, putting the thapter's battered front against it and pushing hard. The fabric of the funnel bulged out, out, out, finally enclosing them in a bubble that tore off and was fired away like a speck of mud from a wheel.

Tiaan looked back. 'Don't look back,' said Malien.

Tiaan ducked her head as a glow lit up the sky, brighter than a hundred suns. It became ever brighter, and the shock began to reverberate back and forth inside her head, building up and up and up until, finally, she had to let go.

'Tiaan!' Malien was shaking her. 'Wake up.'

'Don't think I can,' Tiaan said groggily.

Malien shook her harder. 'You have to. We forgot one vital thing.'

'Wassat?' Tiaan slurred.

'When the node and anti-node annihilated each other, it disrupted all the fields for leagues around. It's destroyed my crystal, I can't draw any power and we're falling.'

'So what can I do?' Tiaan was too dazed to be worried.

'Use the amplimet, if *it* works. Failing that, draw on its stored power to get us to the ground.'

Tiaan stood up shakily.

'We're falling fast,' Malien said urgently.

Tiaan's thoughts flowed as sluggishly as molasses. She staggered and had to hang onto the side rail.

Malien snatched the amplimet from around Tiaan's neck, tore out her shattered crystal and put Tiaan's in its socket. She brought Tiaan's hand down on the controller.

'Now, Tiaan!'

They were plunging to the ground like a meteor. 'Thirty seconds,' said Malien.

Tiaan's head hurt, and she could hardly remember what to do to make the thapter go. 'The amplimet won't obey me. It won't draw power from *any* field. It must have lost the ability, going through the gate.'

'Twenty seconds,' said Malien. 'Use its stored power.'

Tiaan struggled but her mind remained blank.

'Ten seconds!' Malien slapped her hard across the cheek. 'Wake up.'

Tiaan found just enough in her to pull the machine out, a bare few hundred spans above a line of arid hills. It jerked forwards, then sideways, bucking and shuddering like a buffalo in a pen. A long way behind them the steaming waters were already rushing in to reclaim the space that the Well had occupied.

Tiaan rode the careering thapter for as long as she could, which wasn't even a minute. She could barely stand up. 'I think –' It lurched wildly. 'Help me, Malien.'

Malien placed her hand on Tiaan's, on the controller, but the thapter shot left, twisted right then spun in a circle. 'Oh, the amplimet's all wrong now!' she cried.

Tiaan's bones felt plastic and her head was flashing from hot to cold in sickening waves. She couldn't hold it up. She leaned it against the cold wall, which felt a little better.

'Do you think we've made any difference?' she said directly. 'To Jal-Nish, I mean?'

'I – I don't think so, Tiaan.'

'How can you be sure?'

'I can't. I just have a bad feeling, and I've learned to trust my feelings over the centuries.'

'What if we were to sneak back to Ashmode? Could we mount an attack on Jal-Nish? Or his air-floater?'

'Not a chance,' said Malien, squeezing Tiaan's hand. The mechanism was hardly making any sound, now, and the thapter was slowing rapidly.

'Why not?'

796

'There's not enough power stored in the amplimet to take us there. It's practically drained, and the fields here may be disrupted for weeks. There's power in them but I can't get to it.'

It didn't seem right for the great adventure to end this way. 'Where are we, anyway?' said Tiaan.

'Somewhere south of the Trihorn Falls, as they once were. Those are the Jelbohn Hills on the southern horizon.'

Tiaan stood up to look over the brown, featureless land. 'How far is it to Ashmode?' Once she would have known it instantly, but her mind couldn't recall the map.

'About eighty leagues. When we came out of the Well it hurled us away at colossal speed. We're the best part of twenty days' march away, in this trackless country.'

'What are we going to do?'

'I'll head for the coast of the Sea of Thurkad. See it, across to our right?' The mechanism sputtered and Malien put the nose down. 'I can't risk flying, in case we lose power suddenly. Once we do, this thapter will only be good for cutlery.'

'Or ploughshares,' said Tiaan. There was a gentle tap on the hatch. She pulled back the bolt with her toe.

'I'll hover it along the coast as long as the power lasts,' said Malien. 'When we get to a decent town you can take ship wherever you want to go. At least we're not short of coin.'

Merryl lifted the hatch and put his head up, flashing Tiaan that heart-warming smile. 'Did I hear some kind of a bang a while back?'

'You could say that,' said Tiaan. 'We destroyed the Well, hoping it would disable Jal-Nish, too. Unfortunately it's disrupted the fields and we can't get back to Ashmode.'

'Yggur and Flydd are resourceful,' said Merryl. 'I'm sure they'll come up with something.'

Tiaan could not be so sanguine, though she appreciated him putting the best face on it. Not even two decades of slavery had been able to curb Merryl's optimistic outlook.

The thapter skimmed up a gentle rise covered in short grass with a hint of green, unusual in this brown land, and sighed to a stop on the crest. Tiaan looked down a long slope, also sward-covered, to a rocky creek littered with boulders.

'That's it,' said Malien. 'The amplimet is finished, and so is the thapter.'

'But . . .' said Tiaan.

'There probably isn't a hedron within a hundred leagues that could replace the amplimet. It's over, Tiaan. The thapter has no power. It's useless metal. From here, we have to walk.'

Tiaan climbed down the side, took off her boots and socks and walked around the thapter, taking pleasure in the springy grass under her soles. The great adventure is over, she thought, and I'm tainted. A criminal. I'll never fly a thapter again. She put one hand on the black flank of the machine and felt a tear well in her eye.

Merryl clambered down, rubbing his back. 'I think I'll walk down to the creek. I've spent too much of my life cooped up in caves and thapters.'

'You'll have all the walking you can take before we get home,' said Tiaan.

'I can't wait.' He grinned and set off, arms swinging. Tiaan watched him halfway down the hill, infected by his cheer.

Malien had just stepped off the ladder when there came a cry of terror from the thapter.

'No!' Gilhaelith cried. 'No!'

Tiaan began scrambling up as Gilhaelith appeared at the top. He was shuddering, wild-eyed, and his woolly hair was sticking out in all directions.

'The amplimet!' he said hoarsely. 'Where is it?'

'It's still in its socket,' said Tiaan calmly, thinking he must have had a nightmare. 'It's all right. It's drained of all power.'

'Get it out! Quick!' His head disappeared, then he heaved himself up onto the side, the geomantic globe in his arms, and slid down onto the grass.

'What's the matter?' said Malien.

He ran about ten strides, put down the globe and knelt beside it. 'I've just realised something that I should have understood a long time ago. Tiaan, do you remember when you flew over Alcifer a month or more back, and something very strange happened?'

'Someone – Ryll I suppose – tried to bring us down with the power patterner,' said Tiaan. It had been a week after they'd dropped the spores into the bellows. 'And then, for an instant, time itself seemed to freeze.'

'I did that, by accident,' said Gilhaelith. 'I was using my globe at the one place in Alcifer where power was still sleeping since the days of Rulke. But something else happened at that moment. As time froze, I was looking up through the dimensions and I saw the amplimet light up like a searchlight.'

'What?' said Malien, staring at him. 'Do you mean it *woke*?'

'It must have been driven to the second stage of awakening,' Gilhaelith said grimly.

'And it's been quietly biding its time ever since. And now the destruction of the Well could have tipped it over the edge to the third stage – *full awakening*.'

'What does full awakening mean?' said Tiaan, looking from one to the other.

'You don't want to know,' said Malien.

'But surely it can't do anything here, with the local nodes disrupted and its stored power drained?'

'In full awakening, it can take power from *anywhere*. Tiaan, grab the amplimet and chuck it down to me.'

Tiaan went up the side. 'What are you going to do with it?'

'Just do it!' Malien shouted, her jaw muscles spasming.

As Tiaan went up, Gilhaelith began moving the pointers furiously on his globe. She withdrew the amplimet, extremely gingerly. It didn't feel any different; indeed, the light passing down the centre was dull red and beating sluggishly. Nonetheless, just holding the crystal sent a shiver up her back. She'd seen what it could do, too many times.

She tossed it to Malien but Gilhaelith shot up like an unleashed spring and plucked it out of the air high above her head.

'What are you doing?' she said.

799

'Destroying it isn't the way.' Gilhaelith sat it on the ground between the geomantic globe and himself, and resumed his rapid but controlled movements.

'It's the *only* way . . .' said Malien, but did not attempt to take it off him. 'Tiaan?' She walked away across the hill.

Tiaan followed. 'What's he doing, Malien?'

'I would have thrown the amplimet into the red-hot compartment underneath the thapter and let the heat destroy it,' she said. 'Assuming it didn't anthracise me first. But Gilhaelith is a truly great geomancer; perhaps his way is less risky.'

'Perhaps,' said Tiaan, admiring the way he worked. The geomantic globe was the most perfect device she'd ever seen. The nodes had lit up all across it, and threads of light were inching out from a number of the brightest. She went back and walked around it, keeping at a distance. There were seven bright nodes. One represented the node at Alcifer, another Tirthrax, and a third one was near Nennifer. The others were spread across the world at places she'd never been.

'They're the controlling nodes,' said Gilhaelith, carefully adjusting his pointers.

And perhaps the ones to be controlled, she thought suddenly. *Or used to take control of all of them.*

Gilhaelith looked around, gave a great sigh, as if of bliss, and began to work faster. All his long adult life, more than a hundred and fifty years, he had worked to discover the secret of the great forces that moved and shaped the world. His great project, he'd called it in Nyriandiol. After coming back from Alcifer he'd claimed to have given up the search, but clearly he hadn't. That must be what he was doing now. He wasn't trying to curb the amplimet at all.

Tiaan could scarcely believe it. Was Gilhaelith prepared to risk everything to satisfy his own lust for knowledge, at such a desperate moment? Truly, she reflected, humanity doesn't deserve the Art. We simply can't be trusted to use it wisely.

And then Tiaan came to a far less pleasant realisation. The geomantic globe was *too* perfect a model of Santhenar. *As the small is to the great* was one of the key principles of the Art.

The Principle of Similarity was another. What if the amplimet took control of the globe? It would provide the perfect conduit to control all the nodes in the world.

'Gilhaelith?' she called.

He shuttled his hands back and forth, then came halfway to his feet, knees bent, plucking at the back of his head as if trying to pull out an errant hair. What was the matter with him? Gilhaelith gave a great shudder and sat down again, his long, gawky legs crossed. He resumed his work, more mechanically now, as if his joints had gone stiff.

'Gilhaelith?' she said sharply.

He turned his head jerkily, stared at her with glittering eyes and turned back to the globe. The controlling nodes began to pulse slowly, in unison with the pulsing of the amplimet. The threads of light were still slowly extending from them. And when all the controlling nodes were linked? What then?

Tiaan's heart gave a painful lurch as she realised what was happening. 'Malien,' she shrieked. 'The amplimet is taking control of him.'

Again Gilhaelith turned, more stiffly than before, but this time she saw terror in his semi-crystalline eyes. His mouth came open. 'Help me,' he said in a brittle croak.

If she tried, the amplimet would seize her as well, and Malien wouldn't be able to do anything about it. And then it would take over the world. Tiaan knew she lacked the strength to fight the amplimet, and didn't see how she could destroy it. It would kill her first. But if she did nothing, Gilhaelith would die an excruciating death.

He forced back with all his strength, reversing the crystallisation agonisingly, but the amplimet's power was relentless. 'Tiaan,' he gasped, 'for the friendship that was once between us, *help me.*'

EIGHTY

Malien came running up, then stopped beside Tiaan, staring at the geomancer. She shook her head and drew Tiaan aside. 'There's nothing we can do to save him unless you're game to snatch up the amplimet and toss it into the red-hot compartment. I'm not.'

Tiaan was remembering Ghaenis's hideous death by anthracism. 'Attacking the amplimet would be suicide.'

'I know.' Malien squatted down and put her head in her hands. 'I should do it anyway, for the good of the world, but . . .'

'I'm not brave enough either,' said Tiaan after a long pause, for an idea was slowly coming into focus. 'But I wonder if there's another way.'

'What other way?'

'Help me!' Gilhaelith reached out to Tiaan. The crystallisation had run up his fingers, across his hands and was now extending up his arms. His feet and lower legs had gone too, and his eyes had the most peculiar, faceted glitter.

'I can't,' she said, turning away. She couldn't bear to watch what was happening to him, and do nothing.

'Which way, Tiaan?' said Malien.

'I've been thinking about this for a long time,' she said quietly. 'How no one can be trusted with the power to control the nodes. Especially not Jal-Nish.'

'There's nothing can be done to stop him,' said Malien.

'I think there might be.'

'Oh?' Malien said with a sharp intake of breath.

Tiaan's eyes were drawn back to Gilhaelith, whose brittle hands were still moving over the globe, though very slowly and mechanically now. The threads of light would soon link all the controlling nodes. Four of them were connected already, and fainter threads had begun to extend from them to other, less powerful nodes. 'I think I know how to close down all the nodes for good, and Jal-Nish's tears with them.'

Malien's head jerked around. 'We talked about that once before, Tiaan.'

It would spell the end of the Secret Art, at least the way humanity had been using it since the great Nunar codified the laws of mancing. There would be no more thapters, air-floaters, constructs or farspeakers. No field-powered Arts or devices of any kind, save those that had been laboriously charged up in the ways known to the ancients. And maybe not them either.

'You're . . . not going to do anything, are you?' croaked Gilhaelith.

'I'm sorry, Gilhaelith,' Tiaan said, and she was, for she did care for him. Tears pricked at the insides of her eyelids, as if crystals were forming there in mimicry of his transformation. She had to let him die. If she saved him, her friends would all be slain. 'I can't.'

He began to curse her, bitterly and unrelentingly, in a voice that sounded like someone walking over broken glass. Then Gilhaelith broke off in mid-word, his face twisted in agony.

'It did this to me,' he whispered. 'It planned it all long ago, and I was too stupid to see it.'

'What did?' she said.

'Way back in Snizort, when I was trapped in the tar, I heard a whisper in my head telling me to create a phantom crystal and use it to save myself. I did so, but its fragments have been there ever since and no matter what I did I couldn't get rid of them – it wouldn't let them go. They just lay there, burning me whenever I used power, and doing more damage. But as soon as

I brought the globe down here, the fragments came together in my mind and they were just like a model of the amplimet, linking it to the real one. I couldn't resist it. I tried, Tiaan, I really did, but it was too strong.'

He was cut off by another agonised spasm. The crystallisation must be reaching his vital organs. And, from the corner of her inner eye, Tiaan could see filaments beginning to extend out of the geomantic globe, into the ethyr. The amplimet was using the globe to mimic the real nodes and the links between them. Once it had done that, it would be too late to stop it.

And she *had* to stop it, but if she just smashed the amplimet, or hurled it into the red-hot compartment, she would have lost the opportunity to do anything for her friends, *or* to stop Jal-Nish. Tiaan was determined to do both, even at the cost of all the nodes. Gilhaelith's folly only reinforced her determination that such unfettered power could not be allowed to exist.

Her plan was desperately dangerous. In all likelihood, she would die even more horribly than Gilhaelith.

Just do it! She dived, snatched the amplimet from between Gilhaelith's feet and held it high. It was pulsing even more slowly now, and the blood-red light glowed right through her hand, picking out the pale and fragile bones.

'Don't take the risk, Tiaan!' shouted Malien. 'Throw it into the heat under the thapter.'

If she tried that now, she would die. Tiaan stepped back a couple of paces and fixed on the geomantic globe, seeing its perfection in her mind and forming the sequence of links between its controlling nodes into a vast mental network. Now for the most desperate step of all – she had to act as if she were supporting the amplimet, doing what it wanted. To oppose it would be to suffer instant anthracism.

She drew power. Though there had been none just minutes ago, it was effortless now. Tiaan directed it into the controlling nodes, as if to reinforce what the amplimet had been doing. She sent power around and around that network, amplifying it at every turn, and pumping more and more power in. The nodes glowed brighter and brighter until she could no longer look at them. They were pulsing in time with the beat of the amplimet, and now the whole geomantic globe began to throb. Threads of mist rose from its northern pole.

This was it, the point of no turning back. If she succeeded, and survived, the aftermath would rob her of all that made her special – indeed, unique. Her inner talents, that had sustained her all her life, would be useless. Could she bear that?

Tiaan hesitated. In the background she could hear the crackling as crystallisation proceeded up Gilhaelith's thighs and in across his shoulders. To the left she could see Malien's frozen face. Malien could lose her great Arts too. All the world might. Was it worth it?

Tiaan didn't know. She couldn't think.

'Use the globe, Tiaan.' Gilhaelith's voice was a screeching crackle. 'You can reverse the crystallisation.'

But she didn't know how. The controlling nodes were linked on the globe now. Soon the controlling nodes of Santhenar would also be linked to it, an endless source of power for good or evil. What would Gilhaelith do with it, if she saved him? What would Jal-Nish do, if she didn't stop him? What would the amplimet do if it gained what it had been searching for so long?

'We can fight it,' crackled Gilhaelith. 'We're stronger.'

'It means more war,' said Tiaan. 'More destruction, death and ruin. I won't have it.'

'Noooo . . .' Gilhaelith said, in a hissing whisper that faded to nothing, for his lungs had crystallised and he could no longer breathe.

'Don't, Tiaan,' said Malien. 'You'll only make things worse.'

'How can they be worse!' Tiaan cried, and as Malien tried to stop her, she sent an overwhelming surge of power into the controlling nodes, which emitted a burst of light so bright that it burned her skin. Gilhaelith jerked spastically and the crystallisation slowly proceeded up his torso to his throat.

Suddenly it grew dark and cold, as if something had blocked out the sun. All around her the loops and whorls of the field flared to visibility and the sky was lit up by vast green and yellow auroras. The ground shook so hard that the thapter toppled onto its side, exposing the still-glowing cavity beneath. Tiaan might have tossed the amplimet into it, but that was even more dangerous now.

Malien threw herself at Tiaan and tried to tear the crystal out of her hand. Fighting her off, Tiaan staggered around to the other side of the geomantic globe. Gilhaelith laboriously extended a crystalline arm towards her but it was easy to evade his reach.

Tiaan knocked over the green nickel bowl and the globe rolled out, still spinning on its freezing mist on the short grass. She saw the horror in his eyes and averted her own. It had to be done.

The globe was icy and its cold burned her from here. She pumped more power into the controlling nodes, as much as she could draw. She could feel the amplimet's triumph as she slipped it into her pocket.

Tiaan picked up the globe and lifted it above her head. It was incredibly heavy. She staggered under its weight.

'Noooooo!' Gilhaelith's wail seemed to have been formed outside his throat, and then the disembodied voice began to curse her again.

Tiaan held the globe up for a moment, feeling her knees wobble, and hurled it down the hill. It resisted as if it didn't want to leave her, then nearly took her with it, for her hands had stuck to the thick, frigid glass. Tiaan overbalanced and the globe pulled free, tearing skin off her fingers and palms. It landed a few spans away, unharmed on the springy grass, and began to roll down the slope.

The sky blackened to the colour of midnight, the hillside lit only by the shimmering auroras and the fading glow from the underside of the thapter. Rays extended out from the controlling nodes in all directions. One struck through her pocket, charring the cloth, and the amplimet fell out. She scooped it up in her bleeding hand as the fields went wild. The ground shook harder; the auroras flared so brilliantly that for a moment it became as bright as day.

The geomantic globe gathered speed down the long slope.

Tiaan watched it go. The task was nearly done. She felt very weak now. If she could just hold out another minute.

And then, and it was like a fist closing around her heart, Merryl appeared from behind one of the boulders down at the creek, right in the path of the globe. She wanted to scream at him to run, but her tongue felt as though it had frozen to the roof of her mouth.

He saw it coming. He didn't run or panic, but calmly walked the other way. Then Malien threw herself at Tiaan and tried to tear the amplimet out of her hand. Tiaan fought off the old woman, pushed her down and stumbled away. She couldn't see Merryl now. Dare she attempt it, with him so close? She had to – it was all, or *nothing*.

Gilhaelith's eyes lit up as they crystallised last of all and behind the facets she saw bliss, ecstasy. There was no time to wonder about it, though for a moment she wavered. She could feel his joy; could even share in it, for they were not so different, after all. Could she put out the light in those faceted eyes?

She had to. The geomantic globe hurtled up a small bank and bounced high in the air, heading towards the largest boulder in the creek bed. All of a sudden the amplimet lit up so brightly that it burned her fingers. It fell onto the grass, which began to smoke.

It *knew*!

Her brain began to heat up from the inside and a hot shaft of fire shot down her spine. As the globe fell towards the boulder, Tiaan scooped up the crystal in the nickel bowl and staggered towards the thapter. At the moment the globe impacted and smashed to smithereens, the amplimet glowed like a miniature sun.

The metal bowl was burning her but she couldn't give in now. She held on, smoke rising from her fingers, just long enough to toss the amplimet into the cavity under the thapter. Tiaan threw herself out of the way, rolling down the hill. Rays streaked across the sky. The boulder exploded, the auroras went wild and the ground shook again. The mechanism of the thapter screamed as if power had been poured directly into it, then faded to nothing.

The fire in her head and down her spine ebbed away, leaving a dull, burning ache. The glow of the amplimet simply went out. The auroras danced for a moment, but disappeared as the sun shone again. There was complete and utter silence.

Tiaan felt a terrible wrench as the amplimet died, and then the most agonising sense of withdrawal and loss. It was gone, and soon her inner abilities would be lost forever.

She rolled over and lifted her head with an effort, to stare down the hill. It was covered in wreaths of smoke and pieces of shattered rock and glass, but to her joy she saw Merryl running up, a long way to the left. The relief was so great that she allowed her head to flop back to the ground. Had she done what she'd intended, or not? All that power, forced around and around the links and amplified at every node, had to go somewhere.

Nothing happened. Malien stood about ten paces away, staring into the distance. Merryl had slowed to a trot.

An incandescent jet shot into the air from beyond a range of hills, followed by a billowing cloud of dust and smoke. The ground gave a gentle quiver, then another. The first node had exploded. The thunder took longer to arrive. And then, distantly, the other nodes began to go off, one by one. As each did, the force would spread to the others, and it would not stop until every node in the world was gone.

'It's done,' she said. The explosions would not create more tears, for the force was not contained but spread from one node to another. 'No one has proven worthy of such power, so no one may have it.'

Malien stormed across and stood directly above her. 'Do you realise what you've done?' she raged. 'How dare you take it upon yourself to play God!'

'I know what I've lost, and every day of my life I'll rue it. But what choice did I have?'

'You might have put your trust in humanity,' said Malien.

'They're not worthy of it.'

'Not even me?'

808

Tiaan had no answer. 'Well, it's done.'

'And never to be undone,' said Malien. 'You're a fool, Tiaan, and well may you rue it. Evil comes from the hearts of men and women, not the power of the fields.'

'Such power allowed them to do far greater evil.'

'And greater good, too. The balance is maintained in the end.'

Was it? Tiaan no longer felt confident about anything. What if she had been terribly wrong? 'Well, at least I've ended Jal-Nish's brief reign, and saved our friends. What can he do to them now?'

Tiaan was squeezing her bloody, singed, throbbing palms together when something crackled behind them. She turned wearily. Gilhaelith, crystallised even to his frizzy hair, seemed to be smiling. At least she'd done one thing right. In a glorious irony, as the amplimet took over his damaged faculties, Gilhaelith had finally *understood*. The great game was over – he'd fulfilled his life's purpose and died in an ecstasy of bliss. His life had been pure numbers, and in the end he'd discovered that they were beautiful numbers.

Farewell, Gilhaelith, she thought. I'm glad for you.

She watched Merryl coming up the hill, just walking, now that he could see she was unhurt. Another thing she'd done right.

'I suppose we'd better head for home,' said Tiaan. 'It's going to be a long, long march. Will you – will you walk with me a little of the way, Malien?'

'My way and yours are sundered, Tiaan,' Malien snapped, and stalked off down the hill. But after thirty or forty paces she slowed, stopped, and turned around, staring at Tiaan; then she came trudging back.

'We've been great friends and companions, this past year and three-quarters, and I would not have us part in such a way.' Malien held out her hand, took one look at Tiaan's bloody palms and opened her arms instead. 'It falls to few people to change the world, but you're one of them. And who am I to say that you haven't done the right thing? Farewell, Tiaan. The times have certainly been eventful since we met. I'm glad we did.'

Tiaan embraced her. 'And so am I. Thank you, Malien. You've done so much for me. Are you sure we can't walk a little way together?'

Malien shook her head. 'You're heading south to the sea, while I'm going back to Ashmode to find Clan Elienor's soldiers. But you'll have Merryl with you – the best of company.'

He joined them and Malien shook his hand. 'If we never meet again, live well. Farewell, Tiaan. Farewell, Merryl.'

'Farewell,' they echoed, 'wherever you roam.'

They gathered their gear from the thapter and Tiaan turned towards the south and the Sea of Thurkad, with her father. She regretted, for a moment, that she would probably not see Nish or Irisis, nor any of the others, again. But all things must pass, and that phase of her life was over.

Malien watched her go, collected her possessions, then began her own weary journey east to Ashmode. She felt closer to Clan Elienor now than she did to her own people, who had exiled her from Stassor. Clan Elienor would not go to Faranda with the rest of the Aachan Aachim, for they were exiles too. She planned to offer them a home at Shazmak, in the mountains behind Bannador, across the Sea of Thurkad in Meldorin. It would take a lot of work to restore Shazmak to the grandeur and the glory it had possessed in ancient times, especially without the Art to assist them, but her people had never been afraid of hard work.

And besides, her beloved son Rael had died at Shazmak and she'd not been back since the time of the Forbidding. It would be like going home.

What would have happened, she wondered, had the crystal succeeded in gaining control of the nodes of Santhenar? Would it have turned the world into a volcanic hell like Aachan? Or used it to extend its reach to other worlds, and perhaps, after infinite time, even to the stars themselves? No one would ever know. Only one person had ever achieved the mastery of geomancy to have a hope of understanding the amplimet's purpose, and he was no more.

Well, it was over. Malien shrugged her bag over her shoulder, adjusted her hat and set out in the direction of Ashmode. She felt as though a great weight had left her shoulders. Perhaps Tiaan had done the right thing after all.

As Tiaan trudged up the road beside Merryl, she wondered where it had all gone wrong. How could her youthful dreams have all come to nothing? Had she made the wrong choices, or was she incapable of the right ones? Or had it just been luck, or fate? Had her life, in a sense, been doomed from the beginning?

Would it have been better if she'd never lived at all? Would her ghosts, especially Minis, haunt her forever? She felt very low. She'd made bad choices for good reasons, Tiaan knew, and she couldn't forgive herself for what had come from them. She'd tried to do what was good and right and decent, and over and again it had gone terribly wrong. Yet Irisis, who seldom agonised over her choices, had ended up ennobling herself.

Perhaps it's because, in the end, I'm always thinking of myself, Tiaan thought. I could never be as selfless as Irisis, who gives simply because that is her nature, with no expectation of return. I've become afraid to give, and afraid to share myself.

'What am I going to do, Merryl?' she cried. 'I've failed at everything I've done, and now I've got nothing left.'

'But you found me and saved me,' he said gently. 'I'll always love you, and even when we're apart we'll always have each other.'

She didn't answer straight away, just plodded on, head down, watching the dust rise with every step.

'Thank you,' she said. 'Sometimes I become so obsessed by what I've lost, and how I've failed, that I can't see what I've gained. What are *you* going to do now?'

'I'm going home to Tiksi, to find Marnie.'

'After what she did to you?' Tiaan said, a little sharply, before she remembered that she was talking to her father. 'Sorry.'

'In my years as a slave I learned to forgive all sorts of things. It was the one part of my life I had control over. I've even forgiven the lyrinx who enslaved me and ate my hand, and I'm all the better for it. Hate is corrosive, Tiaan. It's far better to forgive, once you can, and get on with life and living.'

'I've always found it hard to forgive my enemies,' said Tiaan. 'But surely you can't believe that you and Marnie could ever live together? She's my mother and I love her, but she's the most thoughtless, vain and selfish woman who ever lived.'

'I don't expect it to go well,' he said mildly. 'I learned long ago that *expecting* things out of life is the road to misery. But I can still *hope* for it.'

'Why would you want to?'

'She was my first and only love and, after I got over my fury, the thought of her sustained me through all the years of slavery. As well as the thought of you, Tiaan – the beautiful child we made together.' He kicked a pebble off the path, watching thoughtfully as it rustled through the dry grass. 'And then, look at Marnie's children – all living, healthy, clever and hardworking, so there must be more to her than you think. And maybe, just maybe, after the hard times she's endured since the breeding factory was destroyed, she's changed.'

'Maybe,' Tiaan said dubiously. 'But I think you'll have rather a lot of forgiving to do.'

'I'm prepared to forgive her every day of my life. So, shall we go looking for Marnie?'

'Yes,' said Tiaan. 'Let's put the past behind us.' Her eyes were shining. She lifted her chin and looked east and south, to where Tiksi lay beyond sea and plains and mountains. It would be a long and perilous journey but every step would be a step closer to home. 'A new start.'

'For all of us,' he said, taking her hand. 'And for you most of all, my precious daughter.'

EIGHTY-ONE

Nish was tied up by two burly guards and thrust to the ground beside Flydd and Yggur. He watched the thapter hurtling away from Ashmode, and Jal-Nish working the tears to try to bring it back. The song of the tears rose to a shriek but after a struggle of some minutes the thapter broke free. 'That's not going to put Father in a better frame of mind,' he said to himself.

'Masterly understatement, as usual,' said Irisis behind him.

Nish's heart froze solid. The troops had her as well. As he turned, they forced Irisis to her knees then stepped back with the other guards, hands on their sword hilts. No soldier of Jal-Nish would dare to fail in watchfulness.

'What are you doing here?' he cried. 'I thought you were gone; *safe.*'

'More fool you,' she said blithely, 'if you thought I was going to abandon my best friend in all the world.'

Nish tore at his hair. 'Father will kill you. He'll rend you limb from limb.'

'I don't abandon my friends,' said Irisis. '*Ever.* Besides,' she said in a low voice, 'Tiaan has a plan and I've got every confidence in her.'

Nish had felt the same way until he saw Irisis. Now he knew that Tiaan's plan, whatever it was, couldn't work. A numb terror spread through him. This was the end. He was going to lose her.

She'd always said she wouldn't live to old age and he'd always scoffed. Why hadn't he protected her?

'I *hope* it works. I'm afraid, Nish.' Suddenly she wasn't bold, reckless Irisis any more, the stalwart who had survived a thousand crises barely ruffled. She was just a frightened young woman whom he loved with all his heart, and that made it so very much worse.

'So am I.'

Jal-Nish paid them no attention. He seemed to be suffering aftersickness from his struggle to bring the thapter back, for he was bent right over, arm hanging. Unfortunately it didn't give them a chance to escape. His red-coated soldiers had secured the remainder of Troist's officers and, backed by the manifest power of the tears, no one had dared resist them. At least, not after the initial demonstration, which had left three officers crisped and belching black smoke in the centre of the square.

'I wonder what Tiaan has in mind?' said Irisis.

'I don't know, but I'm sure Yggur or Flydd do.' They were still lying on the ground, though both were alive and conscious. Nish could see one of Flydd's eyes staring across the square. Had Jal-Nish paralysed him, or was Flydd just waiting his chance?

'How are you . . . surr?' Nish said quietly.

'It's not one of the greatest days of my life,' Flydd said, speaking with an effort. He groaned. 'I can't think how I allowed this to happen.'

'What do you mean?'

'I knew what a sneaking, treacherous dog your father was. I should have gone over the Gumby Marth battlefield with a pair of tweezers. As if he'd allow himself to be eaten by the enemy.'

'As if the lyrinx would eat him,' said Yggur, sitting up. 'His flesh would be as poisonous as a toad's.'

'I was so pleased to hear of his passing,' said Flydd, now moving an arm experimentally, 'that I failed to make sure that he had. And now we suffer for it.'

'Tiaan has got something in mind,' said Nish. 'She got away with Malien, Gilhaelith and Merryl.'

'I saw the end of her struggle with Jal-Nish,' said Flydd.

814

'She's gone towards the Well,' said Irisis.

'Irisis!' choked Flydd, rolling over and staring in her direction. 'They got you too?'

'I couldn't go without Nish or you, surr.'

'Bloody fool! I'd abandon you quickly enough, if the need required it.'

'I know you would, surr,' she said softly. 'But at heart you're a wicked and corrupt scrutator, whose whole purpose in life is to use others. I, on the other hand, am an innocent artisan from an obscure manufactory, and I cannot abandon a friend who was once my lover.'

Flydd managed a chuckle. 'A long time ago.'

'Even so.'

'Well, don't expect any gratitude,' he said gruffly. 'I think less of you for it.'

'I know you do. It changes nothing.'

He pushed himself to a sitting position. 'Do you have any idea what Tiaan has in mind?'

'No,' said Nish.

Quite some time after that, there came a brilliant flash from the direction of the Hornrace. Jal-Nish snapped upright onto his toes, and his arm reached up to the sky, the red-tipped fingers clawed. His mouth opened in a silent cry, then he fell to his knees again, gasping. Green scum foamed through the mouth hole of the mask.

'That was our chance,' said Flydd. 'Unfortunately I can't do anything with it. The tears haven't released me.' He glanced at Nish. 'I wasn't joking about the cottage and the flowers, lad. Even gnarled old scrutators dream of retiring one day.'

'It has less to recommend it than you might imagine,' said Yggur dryly.

'Oh well,' said Flydd. 'It's not going to happen now.'

'No, but let's defy him to the end. If we can't defeat him, at least we can show him up by the manner of our deaths.'

Jal-Nish slowly began to recover. He wiped his chin and pushed himself to his feet. His hand moved towards the tears but stopped before it reached them. Flydd spoke out of the corner of his mouth to Yggur. Nish didn't catch what was said. Yggur took a long time to answer.

He broke off. Jal-Nish had recovered and was heading their way, supported by his guards. 'Gather them up for the trial,' he said, his voice slightly slurred.

The guards dragged Yggur and Flydd to their feet. Others seized Nish and Irisis. Troist, Fyn-Mah and Flangers were led from another direction, along with the surviving army officers.

They were hauled into the centre of the square, each with a guard at their back, and there they stood for an hour or more, unmoving, while Jal-Nish vented his rage at them. Nish began to feel faint. He swayed on his feet and the guard smacked him in the ear.

'Don't move!'

A distant flash illuminated part of the sky. Shortly Nish saw another, and a third. The earth shivered beneath him and some time after that he heard a rumble in the western distance. Even the guards looked that way.

'Tiaan's done it this time,' said Flydd in the common speech of the south-east, which these guards would probably not know. 'Get ready to run.'

There were further flashes, more ground shakes. Another rumble sounded, closer, then another, closer still. Jal-Nish was trying vainly to see what was happening. He clutched at the tears, suddenly uncertain of his power.

'The tears won't do you any good, *Scrutator*,' Flydd sneered. 'Tiaan's succeeded this time.'

'At what?' Jal-Nish said furiously. There was a brittle edge to his voice.

'Over the past year she's mapped all the nodes, and the links between them,' said Yggur, speaking slowly and precisely. 'She's found a way to destroy them all –'

A flash that lit up the sky was followed within seconds by a far louder boom.

'– including the tears around your neck, Jal-Nish.'

With a great shudder, Jal-Nish tore the chain and the tears from his neck and made to hurl them into the crowd. The

816

humming of the tears became a shrill wailing. But then, with an effort of will, he held them back.

'I've nothing to fear from death. I look forward to it.' Jal-Nish put the chain around his neck again, though as the tears touched his chest he was overcome by a shudder of horror. The song of the tears died away to nothing.

They all stared at him, expecting to die in a monstrous conflagration. More roars and booms were heard, some only leagues away, others just a tickle of the air or a shudder through the ground. Finally, red roiling clouds erupted into the sky less than a league away along the cliffs, the whole square rocked, and there was silence.

Someone screamed in the crowd. It was Pilot Chissmoul, her face a mask of anguish as she realised that she'd never operate a thapter again.

Absolute silence. The song of the tears returned, a high-pitched, edgy sound, more potent than before. The first one to move was Jal-Nish. He put his hand into one of the tears, gave a visible wrench and the gravel danced a few paces away until it glowed white hot and sagged into a solid, molten mass.

Turning to the dumbstruck pair, Yggur and Flydd, he roared with laughter. 'Oh, this is wonderful, *glorious!* The tears are a wild force, quite separate from nodes and fields. Tiaan has delivered Santhenar freely into my hands. I expected the fight of my life. Instead, I've won with no more than a whimper.'

'What is it?' cried Nish. 'What's gone wrong?'

Jal-Nish came right up to him. 'I'll tell you, idiot son.' Pulling off the platinum mask he thrust his ravaged and pustulent face right in Nish's.

Nish drew back in horror. He could not help it.

'You show your true feelings toward your father, boy.'

'What's happened?' cried Nish. 'Tell me.'

'Tiaan has destroyed all the nodes, and all the fields with them,' Irisis said limply. 'But when the tears were distilled from the Snizort node, it must have torn them free of the system of nodes and links. All power that relies on fields is gone, perhaps forever, but Jal-Nish has lost none of his.'

'And now I'm going to crush the lot of you,' said Jal-Nish, 'beginning with you, Xervish Flydd. Take him over there. I'm not going to draw this out – I've a world to set in order.'

Four guards seized Flydd, but before they could haul him away he managed to turn towards Yggur and gave an almost imperceptible nod.

'Get ready,' Yggur muttered to Nish and Irisis. 'Klarm's about to attack.'

Nish looked over his shoulder. His guards were a few paces away now. 'Klarm's going to do something,' he said softly. 'Get ready to run.'

'What's he going to do?' said Irisis.

'I don't know.'

Nish met Yggur's eye. Yggur flexed his fingers. 'If any one of us falls behind,' he said quietly, 'we must be abandoned for the good of the struggle. It's going to be a long one.'

'I know the rules of war,' said Nish. 'Where do we run?'

'To Jal-Nish's air-dreadnought. I have a concealed crystal, though it won't drive such a big air-floater far. Let's hope it's far enough.'

Flydd had been hauled over next to the molten patch of gravel, which was still glowing. He spat on it as he went past and a small puff of steam rose there.

'Xervish Flydd,' said Jal-Nish, 'you are hereby –'

'Before you do the business, Jal-Nish,' Flydd said with studied casualness, 'could you answer one question for me?'

'Be damned!' said Jal-Nish. 'I'll give you no satisfaction whatsoever.'

Flydd shrugged. 'Oh well. I didn't think it could be you. You don't have that kind of power.' He wasn't looking at Jal-Nish, but in the direction of the cloth-covered banquet table they'd sat at earlier. Nish casually glanced that way but couldn't see anything.

'What are you talking about?' said Jal-Nish.

'I didn't think you could possibly be the Numinator – you don't have the *nobility* either.'

'Numinator? What the devil are you talking about?'

'Nothing,' said Flydd. 'It doesn't matter at all.'

Nish caught Yggur's eye. Jal-Nish doesn't know that there's a higher power than the scrutators, Nish thought. One tiny advantage for us. Perhaps.

'Enough of your pathetic mind games,' said Jal-Nish. 'I –'

Again he broke off. Out of the corner of his eye Nish saw Klarm slide out from under the tablecloth, stand up and bowl something towards them, underarm. Nish couldn't tell what it was at first, but as it sped across the ground he realised that it was Golias's globe. What did he hope to achieve? The globe had a self-powered crystal at its core, but that was all.

Jal-Nish watched it all the way. Nish exchanged glances with Irisis. He expected Golias's globe to explode, but it simply rolled up to Jal-Nish, who stopped it with his foot and stood looking down at it.

'Is this the best your half-sized ally can do?' Jal-Nish sneered. He thrust one hand into the tears. 'There's no harm in the globe. It's not been booby-trapped in any way.'

No, Klarm wouldn't be that crude. He would use its true nature, but how? The farspeaker was just eight concentric glass spheres filled with quicksilver, and the crystal at the centre. The self-powered crystal.

Jal-Nish was about to kick the globe out of the way when Yggur moved his bound hands in a particular way. The globe instantly glowed hot, then its layers split from the inside to the outside and a cone of boiling quicksilver burst out.

It caught Jal-Nish across the exposed cheek and the platinum mask. He reeled back, screaming and tearing at the mask. The soldiers holding Flydd also went down, letting out anguished squeals, for boiling quicksilver was hotter than molten lead. Flydd had known to turn his head away in time, but drops of quicksilver burned smoking holes through his coat. Three of the troops by Nish and Yggur also fell, struck down by crossbow fire.

'Run!' Klarm roared. The table was thrown over and his three soldiers fired from behind it. Klarm pointed a glassy rod and the remaining soldiers went down like a series of coloured dolls.

Jal-Nish had the platinum mask off and was clawing at the

festering hideousness that it concealed, making a keening noise like an injured beast as he tried to rend out the embedded, burning globules. Bloody, smoking welts were rising across his mouth and cheeks, and the area that had been beneath the overheated mask looked red-raw.

Flydd hacked through his bonds with a shard of glass and tried to get to the tears, but Jal-Nish's scrabbling fingers reached them first, throwing up a clear barrier around himself. He crouched on the ground inside it, squealing in agony, but he still had his hand in the tears.

'Come on!' shouted Flydd. 'We can't do anything here.' He began to lurch in the direction of the air-dreadnought, his cloak trailing fumes.

Klarm appeared beside Yggur, slashing his bonds, then those of the other prisoners. Yggur took off like a hare for the air-dreadnought, his long legs flashing. Troist and Fyn-Mah ran too. Flangers was running towards the crowd. Irisis and Nish followed.

As they were three-quarters of the way to the craft, one of the guards rose shakily to his knees and sent his sword spinning through the air. The back of the blade struck Nish behind the knees and he went down. He tried to get up but his whole leg had gone numb.

Flydd, Yggur, Fyn-Mah and Troist were climbing into the air-dreadnought. Klarm wasn't far behind, not looking back. Flangers was running around the edge of the crowd, carrying a silent Chissmoul. Irisis glanced over her shoulder, saw Nish on the ground and skidded to a stop.

'No, Irisis,' he screamed. 'Go, go!'

She came running back and helped him up. 'Put your arm across my shoulder.'

'I can't walk,' Nish said. His father was already on his feet. Two more of the guards were up now, and staggering towards them. 'Run, Irisis. He won't hurt me, but he'll flay you alive.'

'I'm not leaving you,' she said stubbornly. 'We can still get there.'

'Please, Irisis,' he begged. The soldiers were recovering, starting to trot.

'No, Nish.' She picked him up in her arms and headed for the air-dreadnought as fast as she could go.

Nish looked back. It would be a near thing. The soldiers were recovering rapidly, running now. He looked for help at the air-dreadnought, but Klarm had just cast his useless crystal on the ground and the others weren't armed. Jal-Nish's guards had cut down Klarm's soldiers, and now the air-dreadnought began to lift at the stern.

'Put me down, Irisis. Please.'

She glanced over her shoulder and tried to run harder, but before they were even close to the air-dreadnought, the guards had their swords at Irisis's throat.

She clung to Nish's neck for a moment. 'I'm sorry,' she said.

'Ah, Irisis,' he wept. 'Why did you come back? He hates you more than anyone.'

'Because you're my dearest friend, Nish,' she said simply, 'and I love you as I've never loved anyone before. I couldn't leave you, even at the cost of my life.'

The air-dreadnought rose into the air, turned away and disappeared over the trees.

The guards tied Nish and Irisis's hands and dragged them back to the middle of the square, where Jal-Nish still swayed inside his protective barrier. He had forced the mask back on over his swollen, raw cheeks. Blood formed congealed drops on his chin. Quicksilver had puddled at his feet and its vapour drifted around the inside of the barrier. He pried his eye open and fixed on Irisis.

'Put her there,' he slurred through lips that were bursting apart.

Jal-Nish pointed to the glassy patch on the ground, no longer molten but still hot. They stood her on it.

'Irisis Stirm,' said Jal-Nish, allowing the barrier to fade away. 'Two years I've waited for this day.'

'I'll bet you have – I know your kind all too well,' she said with an arrogant lift of her chin.

'And I know yours. The world was a better place when women knew their place in it. Cryl-Nish's mother taught me that lesson.

821

She only wanted me for what I had, and once I became this maimed monster, in the service of my world, she cast me out.'

'You were a monster long before Ryll put his claws in you,' said Irisis.

'And you were a liar, a cheat and a fraud, as the record of your trial at the manufactory shows only too well. For fifteen years you've been an artisan under false pretences, an offence punishable by death.'

'I recovered my powers long ago. Besides, the war is over, Jal-Nish. It doesn't matter any more.'

'The war is only just beginning, and the first stage is to rid the world of those who betrayed it: you and Tiaan most of all. You destroyed my life, though that matters not. You conspired to save the debauched, depraved, flesh-forming lyrinx, the greatest abominations this world has ever seen. You cozened and coddled and yes, maybe even mated with them –'

'You're sick, Jal-Nish. You're mad.'

'You set the lyrinx free!' he screamed. 'You gave them a world of their own, and one day *they'll be back*. For that alone you must die. Beg and grovel all you like –'

Smoke was rising from Irisis's boots but she did not flinch. 'Then die I will,' she said calmly, 'but it won't make a jot of difference.'

'Oh, I think it will,' he hissed.

'I go to my death knowing that I've fought for what was right and good,' she said. 'Whereas you, Jal-Nish, if you live to be a hundred, will always know that you gambled with the lives of your soldiers, lost, then ran like a cur from the battlefield. That's the kind of man you are, and the Histories will tell of it long after my name is forgotten.'

How Irisis had grown from the petty, mean-spirited woman Nish had once known. She was entirely selfless and noble now, and it threw Jal-Nish's character into sharp relief.

He knew it, too. He could not meet her eyes for the moment, but then he said, 'The means is justification enough. I've won the world, and he who owns the world writes the Histories.'

'May you have joy of your victory, you craven dog! I'd sooner die than live in a world of your shaping.'

'And die you will. The greatest pleasure of victory is revenge, and mine will be unending. Guards!'

The guards dragged Irisis to her knees. Her yellow hair hung over her face, but she tossed her head and looked Jal-Nish in the eye, defiant to the last. To Nish she was the most beautiful sight in the world.

'You'll never break me,' she said, 'though you torture me for a thousand years.'

'There's more than one way to break a person,' Jal-Nish said, testing the blade of a soldier's outstretched sword with his thumb. 'I have no need to torture you. Guards, let it be done.'

Nish broke free of his guards. 'Father, no,' he screamed. 'Please, no!'

'Nothing you say can change her fate,' said Jal-Nish, with a look so hideous that it made Nish's flesh creep.

'No. Take me instead.' He threw out his arms in entreaty, weeping so hard that he could barely see.

'You?' said Jal-Nish. 'But you are my beloved son.'

'That's not what you said when you condemned me to death at Snizort.'

'I was wrong about you, my son. Since then, you have proven yourself. I am well pleased with you, Cryl-Nish, for without you I would not have *her*.'

'Then grant me one small favour. Please, Father. Give her life into my custody.'

'A favour?' Jal-Nish pretended to consider it. 'And what will you give me in return?'

'Anything, Father. Just name it.'

'Then serve me, Cryl-Nish. I could force you, with the compulsion I laid on you at Gumby Marth, but I'd rather you aided me willingly. Be my son and heir as you have never been. Stand at my right hand and help me tame this unruly world!'

Out of the corner of his eye Nish saw the nose of the air-dreadnought peeping from behind the trees. Flydd and Yggur must have armed themselves. If they'd found enough power to overcome his greatly weakened father, it might be all right after all.

Nish felt a glimmer of hope. 'Yes, Father. I will serve you.'

'Splendid. And in return, I give her life into your custody.'

'Thank you,' said Nish, surprised that it had been so easy. 'What would you have me do with Irisis?'

'Guard,' said Jal-Nish, inclining his head towards Nish.

The guard handed Nish his sword.

'I don't understand,' said Nish, clenching the hilt so tightly that his arm shook.

'Take her head from her shoulders, Nish, if you truly would serve me.'

'But . . .' Nish looked from Jal-Nish to Irisis, then back to Jal-Nish. 'You promised to save her life.'

'I did not; only to give it into your custody. And so I shall, for you to give me what you promised in return. Anything I want, I believe you said. I want her head.'

'And if I do not?'

'The guard does it for you. You have rather a dilemma, Cryl-Nish.'

Nish felt as if his eyes were boiling out of his face. Then he snapped and leapt at his father, swinging the sword in a wild arc.

'You made the wrong decision, Son,' said Jal-Nish, placing his hand into the left-most tear, and Nish's blade glanced harmlessly off the renewed shield. Jal-Nish raised his hand and one of the bags of the air-dreadnought burst with a boom. It turned sharply and wobbled across the sky, out of sight.

All hope was lost. Irisis, his beautiful Irisis, was on her knees, her slender neck laid bare. She gazed lovingly up at him and, strangely, Irisis was smiling.

'I always knew it would come to this,' she whispered. 'Farewell, Nish. You've been the best friend any woman could hope for.'

This was what Minis had been talking about, long ago in his construct, when he'd foreseen the death of one of Nish's friends. Nish ran at the guard but he was always going to be too late. The man swung his sword high and, even as Nish wailed, 'No!' he brought it down. The blade was keen and it made barely a sound, doing the business.

Too late. It was done. There was nothing anyone could do for Irisis now. Nish fell to his knees and screamed until blood ran from his mouth.

'Take Cryl-Nish Hlar to the deepest cell in Santhenar and lock him in,' said Jal-Nish. 'After you have served your term – ten years, my son – I will make the offer again. Be my right hand and I will set you free. Refuse and you'll get another ten.'

'I will never serve you,' Nish said numbly. 'Never!' he roared at the empty sky.

'We'll see,' Jal-Nish said indifferently.

Nish's rage built up until he felt that his head would explode. He fought it down, forcing himself to become as hard and cold as his father, for that was the only way he could survive. And then he saw a way – the only way to bring something good out of this most evil of all days. He ran halfway across the square and threw out his arms to the silent gathering.

'The greatest hero of the war has sacrificed herself that I should live. Without Irisis Stirm, none of us would be here today!' Nish could feel his tears welling and fought them all the way. No time for mourning now. He must get it out before the guards took him. 'Irisis is the one person who never compromised, no matter who she faced. There has to be a purpose behind her sacrifice, and I will make it my own. I will survive whatever this monster does to me. I will endure, and you must endure with me, for the coming years are going to be the cruellest in all memory.'

His voice shook, but firmed as the guards came at him. 'Let the name Irisis become a rallying cry for the resistance. Let the resistance grow until not even the tears can stand against it. And on that day we will tear down this evil tyrant –'

'Knock him down!' snarled Jal-Nish, and one of the guards clubbed Nish to the ground.

'Take him to the cells. Let him begin his ten years without delay.'

Two soldiers dragged Nish off.

'When he comes out, he'll only have one ambition left – to serve.' Turning to the shocked and silent crowd, Jal-Nish said softly to the soldiers, 'The world *will* be mine, and there is nothing anyone can do to prevent it. Prepare for the *aftermath*.'

THE END
OF THE WELL OF ECHOES

Nish's tale continues in
THE SONG OF THE TEARS

GLOSSARY

NAMES (MAIN CHARACTERS IN ITALICS)

Aachim: The human species native to Aachan, once conquered and enslaved by a small force of invading Charon (the Hundred). The Aachim are great artisans and engineers, but melancholy or prone to hubris and arrogance. In ancient times, many were brought to Santhenar by Rulke in the fruitless hunt for the Golden Flute. The Aachim flourished on Santhenar but were later betrayed by Rulke and ruined in the Clysm. They then withdrew from the world to their hidden mountain cities. The ones remaining on Aachan gained their freedom after the Forbidding was broken, when the surviving Charon went back to the void. Two hundred years later, volcanic activity on Aachan had become so violent that it threatened to destroy all life on the planet. The Aachim sought for a way of escape and one of them, Minis, managed to contact Tiaan on Santhenar, because of her amplimet. The Aachim showed her how to open a gate between Aachan and Santhenar. She thought she was saving her beloved, Minis, and a small number of Aachim, but when they came through, they were a hundred and fifty thousand, a host ready for war, in eleven thousand mighty constructs.

Chissmoul: An instinctive thapter pilot, shy but known for her reckless verve at the controller of her machine.

Cryl-Nish Hlar: A former scribe, prober in secret and reluctant artificer, generally known as Nish. Nish has grown greatly since the tale began and is now the trusted confidant of Xervish Flydd.

Daesmie: A farspeaker operator.

Eiryn Muss: Halfwit; an air-moss grower and harmless pervert, he turned out to be the scrutator's prober (spy) in the manufactory. He vanished, subsequently turned up when Flydd went to the west, but was sent out from Fiz Gorgo on a spying mission and did not return.

Elienor (Clan): Elienor was a great Aachim heroine of ancient times, who almost defeated Rulke when the Hundred invaded Aachan. She was the founder of Clan Elienor, the least of the Aachim clans, who, since coming to Aachan with Vithis, have been ostracised for allowing Tiaan to escape with a construct.

Faellem: A long-lived human species who have passed out of the Histories, though some may still dwell in isolated parts of Santhenar.

Flangers: A soldier and hero in past battles against the lyrinx, he is stricken by guilt for his part in shooting down a Council chapter, and desperate to atone.

Fusshte: A treacherous member of the Council of Scrutators, second to Ghorr.

Fyn-Mah: Former querist (chief of the municipal intelligence bureau) at Tiksi and a loyal supporter of Xervish Flydd, she nurtures a secret passion for him.

Ghorr: Chief Scrutator of the Council of Scrutators, and Flydd's enemy.

Gilhaelith: An eccentric, amoral geomancer and mathemancer who dwelt at Nyriandiol. Because of his dismal early years he is obsessed with controlling everyone and everything in his life. When unable to do this the stress causes him to have panic attacks. His overriding goal is to understand the nature of the physical world, so as to control it too. He was captured by the lyrinx so he could aid their excavations in the tar pits at Snizort, and subsequently taken to their underground city of Oellyll, beneath Alcifer, from which he has since been rescued (against his will by Tiaan) and taken to Fiz Gorgo. There Yggur, mistrusting him, cast him into prison and Gilhaelith's geomantic attempts to escape led the scrutators to Fiz Gorgo.

Gyrull: Matriarch of the lyrinx city at Snizort. A powerful, farsighted mancer, profoundly intelligent.

Haani: Tiaan's adopted sister, accidentally killed by the Aachim in Tirthrax.

Halie: A scrutator on the Council and a former supporter of Flydd.

Inouye: The pilot of Jal-Nish's air-floater, stolen by Fyn-Mah and now used by Flydd. Inouye is a sad little creature, terrified that her children and her man have been executed because she was forced to ally with Flydd.

Inthis: Vithis's clan of Aachim, since time immemorial first of the eleven clans (First Clan). All Clan Inthis, apart from Vithis and Minis, were lost when the portal between Aachan and Tirthrax was opened, to Vithis's unending grief.

Irisis Stirm: *Crafter, originally in charge of the controller artisans at the manufactory; niece of Barkus; one-time lover of Xervish Flydd, now a friend and comrade-in-arms.*

Jal-Nish Hlar: *Acting Scrutator; Nish's father. He suffered massive injuries from a lyrinx attack and begged to be allowed to die, but Nish and Irisis saved his life. Now, hideously maimed, he has a bitter loathing for them both, and an unquenchable desire to be the greatest scrutator of all. He stole the tears formed by the destruction of the Snizort node but was subsequently eaten by the lyrinx at the battle of Gumby Marth.*

Joeyn (Joe): An old miner, Tiaan's friend, who died in a roof fall.

Kattiloe: A young thapter pilot.

Kimli: A young thapter pilot

Klarm: Scrutator for Borgistry. A handsome and cheerful man, despite his dwarfish stature.

Liett: *Gyrull's daughter, and a lyrinx with unarmoured skin and no chameleon ability; a talented flesh-former and brilliant flier who yearns to lead her people, even though she is regarded as incomplete. She has a turbulent relationship with Ryll.*

Liliwen: Daughter of Troist and Yara, twin of Meriwen.

Luxor: A conciliatory Aachim clan leader.

Lyrinx: Massive winged humanoids who escaped from the void to Santhenar after the Forbidding was broken. Highly intelligent, many of them are able to use the Secret Art, most commonly for keeping their heavy bodies in flight. They have armoured skin and a chameleon-like ability to change their colours and patterns, often used for communication (skin-speech). Some lyrinx are also flesh-formers; they can change small organisms into desired forms using the Art. In the void they used a similar ability to pattern their unborn young so as to survive in that harsh environment. As a consequence, they are not entirely comfortable in their powerful but much changed bodies. The lyrinx were forced to abandon their culture and heritage in the void. Their lives are entirely martial, and now some of them are beginning to regret their loss and wonder what to do about it once they've won the war.

Malien: *A venerable but ostracised Aachim living in Tirthrax. A heroine from the time of the Mirror (also known as the Matah). She helped Tiaan make the thapter, or flying construct, subsequently took her to Stassor and then on to Fiz Gorgo.*

Meriwen: Daughter of Troist and Yara, twin of Liliwen.

Merryl: A slave who taught human languages to the lyrinx in Snizort; also known as Tutor. He was kind to Tiaan.

Minis: *A young Aachim man of high status; foster-son of Vithis; Tiaan's dream lover who was forced to spurn her when the Aachim came through the gate to Tirthrax. He feels guilty about his treatment of her, yearns for her, but is totally in thrall to Vithis. Minis is so weak and vacillating that he couldn't even choose to save Tiaan from Vithis. He was maimed during her escape in a construct.*

Mira: Yara's sister who dwells at Morgadis, embittered after the loss of her husband and her three sons in the war. She communicates with a coalition of like-minded people by skeet. Nish fled her home in fear for his life after a liaison which ended with an unfortunate misunderstanding.

M'lainte: Flydd's mechanician, the genius who built the first air-floater.

Myllii: Ullii's long-lost twin brother for whom she had been searching all her life. He was accidentally slain by Nish.

Nish: *Cryl-Nish's nickname.*

Numinator, the: A mysterious figure mentioned by Flydd when in his cups, said to secretly control the Council of Scrutators.

Nylatl: A malicious creature created by Ryll and Liett's flesh-forming. It killed Haani's aunts and attacked Tiaan. Nish destroyed it after it attacked him and Ullii near Tirthrax.

Orgestre: General Orgestre is Grand Commander of the Army of Greater Borgistry.

Rulke: The greatest of all the Charon, he created the first construct. He was killed at the time the Forbidding was broken.

Ryll: *An ostracised wingless lyrinx who captured Tiaan and subsequently used her in flesh-forming. He was an honourable lyrinx and after Tiaan saved his life he allowed her to escape from Kalissin. He later captured her again when she came to Snizort looking for Gilhaelith, and used her in the patterners. After the destruction of Snizort, Ryll went to*

Oellyll, where he was put to work to create a flisnadr, or power patterner.

Seeker: Ullii. Also, one who can sense the use of the Secret Art or people who have that talent, or even enchanted objects.

Tiaan Liise-Mar: *A young artisan; a visual thinker and talented controller-maker. With the amplimet, she picked up Minis's cry for help, fell in love with him and carried the amplimet all the way to Tirthrax, where she used it in opening a gate to Aachan, to save Minis and his people. She subsequently helped Malien make a thapter in Tirthrax, departed in it, attacked the Aachim camp and later crashed near Nyriandiol when the amplimet refused to do what she wanted. Her back was broken in the crash. She was taken back to Nyriandiol by Gilhaelith, who began to teach her geomancy. When he was kidnapped by Gyrull and taken to Snizort, she followed in the thapter but was captured and put to use in the patterners, to pattern torgnadrs or node-drainers. This was only partly successful, because of her broken back, so the lyrinx flesh-formed it to repair her spine. After Snizort was abandoned, Merryl helped Tiaan to escape the patterners. She was subsequently captured by the Aachim, escaped back to Tirthrax, and travelled with Malien to Fiz Gorgo, 'rescuing' Gilhaelith on the way.*

Tirior: A manipulative Aachim clan leader.

Troist: An ambitious junior officer in the army destroyed by the lyrinx at Nilkerrand. He formed a smaller army out of the survivors. Troist became a general much loved by his troops. Nish rescued his daughters Liliwen and Meriwen from ruffians, and again when they were lost in an underground labyrinth.

Ullii: *A hypersensitive seeker, used by Scrutator Flydd to track Tiaan and the amplimet. She accompanied Nish to Tirthrax in the balloon and found Tiaan, but Malien intervened. Her talent failed her for a while, but subsequently she was used by Jal-Nish at the manufactory, before being rescued by Flydd and taken to Nennifer, then west to help in the war at Snizort. She escaped from Snizort with Flydd and Nish, where they discovered that she had become pregnant to Nish in the balloon. Ullii had just found her long-lost brother, Myllii, whom the scrutators had used to find her, when he was accidentally killed by Nish. Ullii lost her baby and, consumed by a lust for revenge on Nish, was captured by Ghorr and used to hunt down Flydd and his allies, which she eventually did.*

Vithis: *Minis's foster-father; an Aachim from Aachan and the head of Inthis First Clan, who led the Aachim to Santhenar. When all First*

Clan (except Minis) were lost in the gate, he became angry and bitter. He forced Minis to repudiate Tiaan. He subsequently led the Aachim across Santhenar but did not hold to his original purpose, to seize land, instead pursuing Tiaan and her thapter across the continent of Lauralin. After Minis was maimed, Vithis retreated to the Foshorn, seized land there and closed the borders.

Xervish Flydd: The scrutator (spymaster and master inquisitor) for Einunar. He was commander-in-chief of all the scrutators' forces at Snizort, charged with defeating the lyrinx army there. Secretly, he was also required to sneak into Snizort and destroy the lyrinx's node-drainer. He, Irisis and Ullii succeeded but the device he'd been given was faulty, destroying both node-drainer and node in a catastrophic explosion. The field vanished, of course, rendering both the army's clankers and the Aachim's constructs useless, and the soldiers defenceless against the attacking lyrinx. Flydd was blamed for the subsequent defeat, stripped of his position and condemned to die as a slave hauling constructs out of the mire. He escaped with Nish and after many adventures eventually ended up at Fiz Gorgo. He is determined to overthrow the corrupt scrutators, knowing that they can never win the war.

Yara: A brilliant advocate, wife to Troist.

Yggur: A great long-lived mancer of ancient times, subsequently found to be still living at Fiz Gorgo. After Flydd's company seeks refuge there, he comes to aid them in their quest to overthrow the scrutators, though he and Flydd will ever be rivals.

MAJOR ARTEFACTS, FORCES AND POWERFUL NATURAL PLACES

Alcifer: The long-abandoned city of Rulke the Charon, in Meldorin. The entire city was believed to have been a magical construct and it still has an aura of barely leashed power.

Amplimet: A rare hedron which, even in its natural state, can draw power from the force (the *field*) surrounding and permeating a node. Occasionally can be very powerful. Inexplicably, Tiaan's amplimet shows signs of a crystal instinct or purpose, for in Tirthrax it communicated with the node and woke the trapped Well of Echoes. It also communicated with nodes elsewhere, denied Tiaan control when she wanted to take the thapter to places it did not want to go, and drew threads of force throughout Snizort, including to the node and to Gilhaelith.

Anthracism: Human internal combustion due to a mancer or an artisan drawing more power than the body can handle. Invariably fatal (gruesomely).

Booreah Ngurle (the Burning Mountain): A large, double-cratered volcano in northern Worm Wood with a blue crater lake. It has a strange and powerful double node. Gilhaelith's home, Nyriandiol, is built on the inner rim of the crater.

Clanker: An armoured mechanical war cart with six, eight, ten or (rarely) twelve legs and an articulated body, driven by the Secret Art via a *controller* mechanism which is used by a trained operator. Armed with a rock-throwing catapult and a javelard (heavy spear-thrower) which are fired by a shooter riding on top. Clankers are made under supervision of a mechanician, artisan and weapons artificer. Emergency power is stored in a pair of heavy spinning fly-wheels, in case the field is interrupted.

Construct: A vehicle powered by the Secret Art, based on some of the secrets of Rulke's legendary vehicle. Unlike Rulke's, those made by the Aachim cannot fly, but only hover, and therefore cannot cross obstacles like deep, wide ditches, cliffs, very steep slopes or rugged terrain (but see *Thapter*).

Controller: A mind-linked mechanical system of many flexible arms which draws power through a *hedron* and feeds it to the drive mechanisms of a *clanker*. A controller is attuned to a particular hedron, and the operator must be trained to use each controller, which takes time. Operators suffer withdrawal if removed from their machines for long periods, and inconsolable grief if their machines are destroyed, although this may be alleviated if the controller survives and can be installed in another clanker.

Crystal fever: An hallucinatory madness suffered by artisans and clanker operators, brought on by overuse of a *hedron*. Few recover from it. Mancers can suffer from related ailments.

Field: The diffuse (or weak) force surrounding and permeating (and presumably generated by) a *node*. It is the source of a mancer's power. Various strong forces are also known to exist, though no one knows how to tap them safely (see *Power*). Non-nodal stress-fields also exist, though on Santhenar these are weak and little used.

Flesh-forming: A branch of the Secret Art that only lyrinx can use. Developed to adapt themselves to the ever-mutable void where they came from, it now involves the slow transformation of a living creature, tailoring it to suit some particular purpose. It is painful for both creature and lyrinx, and can only be employed on small creatures, though the lyrinx seek to change that.

Gate: A portal between one place (or one world) and another, connected by a trans-dimensional 'wormhole'.

Geomancy: The most difficult and powerful of all the Secret Arts. An adept is able to draw upon the forces that move and shape the world. A most dangerous Art for the user.

Hedron: A natural or shaped crystal, formed deep in the earth from fluids circulating through a natural *node*. Trained artisans can tune a hedron to draw power from the field surrounding a node, via the ethyr. Rutilated quartz, that is, quartz crystal containing dark needles of rutile, is commonly used. The artisan must first 'wake' the crystal using his or her *pliance*. Too far from a node, a hedron is unable to draw power and becomes useless. If a hedron is not used for long periods it may have to be rewoken by an artisan, though this can be hazardous.

Mathemancy: An Art developed by Gilhaelith, though since that time it has been discovered independently by other mancers, notably Bilfis.

Nennifer: The great bastion of the Council of Scrutators, on the escarpment over Kalithras, the Desolation Sink. Nennifer is home to countless mancers, artisans and artificers, all furiously working to design new kinds of Art-powered devices to aid the war against the lyrinx.

Nodes: Rare places in the world where the Secret Art works better. Once identified, a *hedron* (or a mancer) can sometimes draw *power* from the node's *field* through the ethyr, though the amount diminishes with distance, not always regularly. A *clanker* operator must be alert for the loss and ready to draw on another node, if available. The field can be drained, in which case the node may not be usable for years, or even for centuries. Mancers have long sought the secret of drawing on the far greater power of a node itself (see *Power*, Nunar's *General Theory of Power*) but so far it has eluded them (or maybe those that succeeded did not live to tell about it).

There are also anti-nodes where the Art does not work at all, or is dangerously disrupted. Nodes and anti-nodes are frequently (though not always) associated with natural features or forces such as mountains, faults and hot spots.

Nyriandiol: Gilhaelith's home, fortress and laboratory on top of Booreah Ngurle; the entire building is a geomantic artefact designed to protect him, ensure his control and enhance his work.

Oellyll: A lyrinx city in Meldorin.

Patterner: A semi-organic device developed by the lyrinx to pattern *torgnadrs* and other artefacts used with their Art. The patterner essentially copies a particular human's talent into the growing torgnadr, greatly enhancing the talent and allowing it to be controlled by a lyrinx skilled in the Art.

Pliance: Device that enables an artisan to see the *field* and tune a *controller* to it.

Port-all: Tiaan's name for the device she makes in Tirthrax to open the gate.

Power: A mancer, Nunar, codified the laws of mancing, noting how limited it was, mainly because of lack of power. She recognised that mancing was held back because power came from diffuse and poorly understood sources. It all went through the mancer first, causing aftersickness that grew greater the more powerful it was. Eventually power, or aftersickness, would kill the mancer using it.

The traditional way around this was to charge up an artefact (such as a mirror or ring) with power over a long time, and to simply trigger it when needed. This had some advantages, though objects could be hard to control or could become corrupted, and once discharged were essentially useless. Yet some of the ancients had used devices that held a charge, or perhaps replenished themselves. No one knew how, but it had to be so, else how could they maintain their power for hundreds if not thousands of years (for example, the Mirror of Aachan), or use quite prodigious amounts of power without becoming exhausted (Rulke's legendary construct)?

Nunar assembled a team of mancers utterly devoted to her project (no mean feat) and she set out to answer these questions. Mancing was traditionally secretive – people tried (and often wasted their lives in dead ends) and usually failed alone. Only the desperate state of the war could have made them work together, sharing their discoveries, until the genius of Nunar put together the *Special Theory of Power* that described where the diffuse force came from and how a mancer actually tapped it, drawing not through the earthly elements but through the ultradimensional ethyr.

The ultimate goals of theoretical mancers are the *General Theory of Power*, which deals with how nodes work and how they might be tapped safely, and ultimately, the *Unified Power Theory*, which reconciles all fields, weak and strong, in terms of a single force.

Secret Art: The use of magical or sorcerous powers (mancing).

Snizort: A place in Taltid with a potent and concentrated node, near the famous tar pits and seeps. The lyrinx took Gilhaelith there to help them find the remains of a village lost in the Great Seep thousands of years ago. When he did so, they excavated a tunnel into the seep by freezing the tar, and took out a number of crystals, other artefacts and long-dead human bodies. After the node exploded, the tar caught fire and Snizort had to be abandoned.

Strong Forces: Forces which are speculated to exist, though no mancer has yet survived to prove their existence.

Thapter: Tiaan's name for the flying *construct* she and Malien created in Tirthrax.

Torgnadr: A device patterned by the lyrinx to drain a *field* dry, or to channel power from the field for their own purposes. Torgnadrs are extremely difficult to *pattern* and most attempts fail, though some result in weak devices such as phynadrs which can draw small amounts of power for a particular purpose. Tiaan was used, with her amplimet, to pattern particularly strong torgnadrs, though the patterning was not entirely successful. Related devices include zygnadrs (sentinels), and the flisnadr (power patterner).

Well of Echoes, the: An Aachim concept to do with the reverberation of time, memory and the Histories. Sometimes a place of death and rebirth (to the same cycling fate). Also a sense of being trapped in history, of being helpless to change collective fate (of a family, clan or species). Its origin is sometimes thought to be a sacred well on Aachan, sometimes on Santhenar. The term has become part of Aachim folklore. 'I have looked in the Well of Echoes.' 'I heard it at the Well.' 'I will go to the Well.' Possibly also a source; a great *node*.

The Well is symbolised by the three-dimensional symbol of infinity, the universe and nothingness. A Well of Echoes, trapped in Tirthrax, is held there only by the most powerful magic.

DATES AND MEASUREMENTS

The Santhenar year has 396 days.

A span is roughly six feet or slightly less than two metres.

A league is about three miles or five kilometres.